THE NEW COLLECTED SHORT STORIES

JEFFREY ARCHER, whose novels and short stories include *Kane and Abel*, *A Prisoner of Birth* and *Cat O' Nine Tales*, has topped the bestseller lists around the world, with sales of over 270 million copies.

He is the only author ever to have been a number one bestseller in fiction (eighteen times), short stories (four times) and non-fiction (*The Prison Diaries*).

The author is married to Dame Mary Archer, and they have two sons and one grandson.

www.jeffreyarcher.com

Facebook.com/JeffreyArcherAuthor

@Jeffrey_Archer

JEFFREY ARCHER

THE NEW COLLECTED SHORT STORIES

TO CUT A LONG STORY SHORT

CAT O' NINE TALES

AND THEREBY HANGS A TALE

PAN BOOKS

To Cut a Long Story Short first published 2000 by HarperCollins*Publishers*
First published by Pan Books 2010
Cat O' Nine Tales first published 2007 by Macmillan
First published by Pan Books 2007
And Thereby Hangs a Tale first published 2010 by Macmillan
First published by Pan Books 2010

This collected volume first published 2011 by Pan Books

This edition published 2014 by Pan Books
an imprint of Pan Macmillan, a division of Macmillan Publishers Limited
Pan Macmillan, 20 New Wharf Road, London N1 9RR
Basingstoke and Oxford
Associated companies throughout the world
www.panmacmillan.com

ISBN 978-0-330-45445-2

1 3 5 7 9 8 6 4 2

A CIP catalogue record for this book is available from the British Library.

Typeset by SetSystems Ltd, Saffron Walden, Essex
Printed and bound by CPI Group (UK) Ltd, Croydon, CR0 4YY

CONTENTS

TO CUT A LONG STORY SHORT

CAT O' NINE TALES

AND THEREBY HANGS A TALE

* Based on true incidents

TO CUT A LONG STORY SHORT

STEPHAN, ALISON AND DAVID

PREFACE

Before you begin this volume of fourteen short stories, as in the past I would like to acknowledge that several of them are based on true incidents. On the contents page you will find these indicated by an asterisk (*).

In my travels around the globe, always searching for some vignette which might have a life of its own, I came across 'Death Speaks', and was so moved by it that I have placed the story at the beginning of the book.

It was originally translated from the Arabic, and despite extensive research, the author remains 'Anon', though the tale appeared in Somerset Maugham's play *Sheppey*, and later as a preface to John O'Hara's *Appointment in Samarra*.

I have rarely come across a better example of the simple art of storytelling. A gift that truly lacks any prejudice, it is bestowed without regard to birth, upbringing or education. You only have to consider the contrasting upbringings of Joseph Conrad and Walter Scott, of John Buchan and O. Henry, of H. H. Munro and Hans Christian Andersen, to prove my point.

In this, my fourth volume of stories, I have attempted two very short examples of the genre: 'The Letter' and 'Love at First Sight'.

But first, 'Death Speaks':

DEATH SPEAKS

THERE WAS a merchant in Bagdad who sent his servant to market to buy provisions and in a little while the servant came back, white and trembling, and said, Master, just now when I was in the market-place I was jostled by a woman in the crowd and when I turned I saw it was death that jostled me. She looked at me and made a threatening gesture; now, lend me your horse, and I will ride away from this city and avoid my fate. I will go to Samarra and there death will not find me. The merchant lent him his horse, and the servant mounted it, and he dug his spurs in its flanks and as fast as the horse could gallop he went. Then the merchant went down to the market-place and he saw me standing in the crowd and he came to me and said, Why did you make a threatening gesture to my servant when you saw him this morning? That was not a threatening gesture, I said, it was only a start of surprise. I was astonished to see him in Bagdad, for I had an appointment with him tonight in Samarra.

THE EXPERT WITNESS★

'DAMN GOOD DRIVE,' said Toby, as he watched his opponent's ball sail through the air. 'Must be every inch of 230, perhaps even 250 yards,' he added, as he held up his hand to his forehead to shield his eyes from the sun, and continued to watch the ball bouncing down the middle of the fairway.

'Thank you,' said Harry.

'What did you have for breakfast this morning, Harry?' Toby asked when the ball finally came to a halt.

'A row with my wife,' came back his opponent's immediate reply. 'She wanted me to go shopping with her this morning.'

'I'd be tempted to get married if I thought it would improve my golf that much,' said Toby as he addressed his ball. 'Damn,' he added a moment later, as he watched his feeble effort squirt towards the heavy rough no more than a hundred yards from where he stood.

Toby's game did not improve on the back nine, and when they headed for the clubhouse just before lunch, he warned his opponent, 'I shall have to take my revenge in court next week.'

'I do hope not,' said Harry, with a laugh.

'Why's that?' asked Toby as they entered the clubhouse.

'Because I'm appearing as an expert witness on your side,' Harry replied as they sat down for lunch.

'Funny,' Toby said. 'I could have sworn you were against me.'

Sir Toby Gray QC and Professor Harry Bamford were not always on the same side when they met up in court.

—◦—

'All manner of persons who have anything to do before My Lords the Queen's Justices draw near and give your attendance.' The Leeds Crown Court was now sitting. Mr Justice Fenton presided.

Sir Toby eyed the elderly judge. A decent and fair man, he considered, though his summings-up could be a trifle long-winded. Mr Justice Fenton nodded down from the bench.

Sir Toby rose from his place to open the defence case. 'May it please Your Lordship, members of the jury, I am aware of the great responsibility that rests on my shoulders. To defend a man charged with murder can never be easy. It is made even more difficult when the victim is his wife, to whom he had been happily married for over twenty years. This the Crown has accepted, indeed formally admitted.

'My task is not made any easier, m'lud,' continued Sir Toby, 'when all the circumstantial evidence, so adroitly presented by my learned friend Mr Rodgers in his opening speech yesterday, would on the face of it make the defendant appear guilty. However,' said Sir Toby, grasping the tapes of his black silk gown and turning to face the jury, 'I intend to call a witness whose reputation is beyond reproach. I am confident that he will leave you, members of the jury, with little choice but to return a verdict of not guilty. I call Professor Harold Bamford.'

A smartly dressed man, wearing a blue double-breasted suit, white shirt and a Yorkshire County Cricket Club tie, entered the courtroom and took his place in the witness box. He was presented with a copy of the New Testament, and read the oath with a confidence that would have left no member of the jury in any doubt that this wasn't his first appearance at a murder trial.

Sir Toby adjusted his gown as he stared across the courtroom at his golfing partner.

'Professor Bamford,' he said, as if he had never set eyes on the man before, 'in order to establish your expertise, it will be necessary to ask you some preliminary questions that may well embarrass you. But it is of overriding importance that I am able to show the jury the relevance of your qualifications as they affect this particular case.'

Harry nodded sternly.

'You were, Professor Bamford, educated at Leeds Grammar School,' said Sir Toby, glancing at the all-Yorkshire jury, 'from where you won an open scholarship to Magdalen College, Oxford, to read Law.'

Harry nodded again, and said, 'That is correct,' as Toby glanced back down at his brief – an unnecessary gesture, as he had often been over this routine with Harry before.

'But you did not take up that offer,' continued Sir Toby, 'preferring to spend your undergraduate days here in Leeds. Is that also correct?'

'Yes,' said Harry. This time the jury nodded along with him. Nothing more loyal or more proud than a Yorkshireman when it comes to things Yorkshire, thought Sir Toby with satisfaction.

'When you graduated from Leeds University, can you confirm for the record that you were awarded a first-class honours degree?'

'I was.'

'And were you then offered a place at Harvard University to study for a masters degree and thereafter for a doctorate?'

Harry bowed slightly and confirmed that he was. He wanted to say, 'Get on with it, Toby,' but he knew his old sparring partner was going to milk the next few moments for all they were worth.

'And for your Ph.D. thesis, did you choose the subject of handguns in relation to murder cases?'

'That is correct, Sir Toby.'

'Is it also true,' continued the distinguished QC, 'that when your thesis was presented to the examining board, it created such interest that it was published by the Harvard University Press, and is now prescribed reading for anyone specialising in forensic science?'

'It's kind of you to say so,' said Harry, giving Toby the cue for his next line.

'But *I* didn't say so,' said Sir Toby, rising to his full height and staring at the jury. 'Those were the words of none other than Judge Daniel Webster, a member of the Supreme Court of the United States. But allow me to move on. After leaving Harvard and returning to England, would it be accurate to say that Oxford University tried to tempt you once again, by offering you the first Chair of Forensic Science, but that you spurned them a second time, preferring to return to your alma mater, first as a senior lecturer, and later as a professor? Am I right, Professor Bamford?'

'You are, Sir Toby,' said Harry.

'A post you have held for the past eleven years, despite the fact that several universities around the world have made you lucrative offers to leave your beloved Yorkshire and join them?'

At this point Mr Justice Fenton, who had also heard it all before, peered down and said, 'I think I can say, Sir Toby, that you have established the fact that your witness is a pre-eminent expert in his chosen field. I wonder if we could now move on and deal with the case in hand.'

'I am only too happy to do so, m'lud, especially after your generous words. It won't be necessary to heap any more

accolades on the good professor's shoulders.' Sir Toby would
have loved to have told the judge that he had actually come to
the end of his preliminary comments moments before he had
been interrupted.

'I will therefore, with your permission, m'lud, move on to
the case before us, now that you feel I have established the
credentials of this particular witness.' He turned back to face
the professor, with whom he exchanged a knowing wink.

'Earlier in the case,' continued Sir Toby, 'my learned friend
Mr Rodgers set out in detail the case for the prosecution, leaving no doubt that it rested on a single piece of evidence: namely,
the smoking gun that never smoked' – an expression Harry had
heard his old friend use many times in the past, and was in no
doubt he would use on many more occasions in the future.

'I refer to the gun, covered in the defendant's fingerprints,
that was discovered near the body of his unfortunate wife, Mrs
Valerie Richards. The prosecution went on to claim that after
killing his wife, the defendant panicked and ran out of the
house, leaving the firearm in the middle of the room.' Sir Toby
swung round to face the jury. 'On this one, flimsy, piece of
evidence – and flimsy I shall prove it to be – you, the jury, are
being asked to convict a man for murder and place him behind
bars for the rest of his life.' He paused to allow the jury to take
in the significance of his words.

'So, now I return to you, Professor Bamford, and ask you
as a pre-eminent expert in your field – to use m'lud's description of your status – a series of questions.' Harry realised the
preamble was finally over, and that he would now be expected
to live up to his reputation.

'Let me start by asking you, Professor, is it your experience
that after a murderer has shot his victim, he or she is likely to
leave the murder weapon at the scene of the crime?'

'No, Sir Toby, it is most unusual,' replied Harry. 'In nine

cases out of ten where a handgun is involved, the weapon is never recovered, because the murderer makes sure that he or she disposes of the evidence.'

'Quite so,' said Sir Toby. 'And in the one case out of ten where the gun is recovered, is it common to find fingerprints all over the murder weapon?'

'Almost unknown,' replied Harry. 'Unless the murderer is a complete fool, or is actually caught in the act.'

'The defendant may be many things,' said Sir Toby, 'but he is clearly not a fool. Like you, he was educated at Leeds Grammar School; and he was arrested not at the scene of the crime, but in the home of a friend on the other side of the city.' Sir Toby omitted to add, as prosecuting counsel had pointed out several times in his opening statement, that the defendant was discovered in bed with his mistress, who turned out to be the only alibi he had.

'Now, I'd like to turn to the gun itself, Professor. A Smith and Wesson K4217 B.'

'It was actually a K4127 B,' said Harry, correcting his old friend.

'I bow to your superior knowledge,' said Sir Toby, pleased with the effect his little mistake had made on the jury. 'Now, returning to the handgun. The Home Office laboratory found the murder victim's fingerprints on the weapon?'

'They did, Sir Toby.'

'And, as an expert, does this lead you to form any conclusions?'

'Yes, it does. Mrs Richards's prints were most prominent on the trigger and the butt of the gun, which causes me to believe that she was the last person to handle the weapon. Indeed, the physical evidence suggests that it was she who squeezed the trigger.'

'I see,' said Sir Toby. 'But couldn't the gun have been

placed in the hand of Mrs Richards by her murderer, in order to mislead the police?'

'I would be willing to go along with that theory if the police had not also found Mr Richards's prints on the trigger.'

'I'm not sure I fully understand what you're getting at, Professor,' said Sir Toby, fully understanding.

'In almost every case I have been involved in, the first thing a murderer does is to remove his own fingerprints from the murder weapon before he considers placing it in the hand of the victim.'

'I take your point. But correct me if I am wrong,' said Sir Toby. 'The gun was not found in the hand of the victim, but nine feet away from her body, which is where the prosecution claims it was dropped when the defendant fled in panic from his marital home. So, let me ask you, Professor Bamford: if someone committing suicide held a gun to their temple and pulled the trigger, where would you expect the gun to end up?'

'Anywhere between six and ten feet from the body,' Harry replied. 'It's a common mistake – often made in poorly researched films and television programmes – for victims to be shown still holding onto the gun after they have shot themselves. Whereas what actually happens in the case of suicide is that the force of the gun's recoil jerks it from the victim's grip, propelling it several feet from the body. In thirty years of dealing with suicides involving guns, I have never once known a weapon to remain in the hand of the victim.'

'So, in your opinion as an expert, Professor, Mrs Richards's fingerprints and the position of the weapon would be more consistent with suicide than with murder.'

'That is correct, Sir Toby.'

'One final question, Professor,' said the defence QC, tugging his lapels. 'When you have given evidence for the defence in cases such as this in the past, what percentage of juries have returned a not guilty verdict?'

'Mathematics was never my strong subject, Sir Toby, but twenty-one cases out of twenty-four ended in acquittal.'

Sir Toby turned slowly to face the jury. 'Twenty-one cases out of twenty-four,' he said, 'ended in acquittal after you were called as an expert witness. I think that's around 85 per cent, m'lud. No more questions.'

Toby caught up with Harry on the courtroom steps. He slapped his old friend on the back. 'You played another blinder, Harry. I'm not surprised the Crown caved in after you'd given your evidence – I've never seen you in better form. Got to rush, I've a case starting at the Bailey tomorrow, so I'll see you at the first hole, ten o'clock on Saturday. That is, if Valerie will allow it.'

'You'll be seeing me long before then,' murmured the Professor, as Sir Toby jumped into a taxi.

◂◦▸

Sir Toby glanced through his notes as he waited for the first witness. The case had begun badly. The prosecution had been able to present a stack of evidence against his client that he was in no position to refute. He wasn't looking forward to the cross-examination of a string of witnesses who would undoubtedly corroborate that evidence.

The judge on this occasion, Mr Justice Fairborough, nodded towards prosecuting counsel. 'Call your first witness, Mr Lennox.'

Mr Desmond Lennox QC rose slowly from his place. 'I am obliged, m'lud. I call Professor Harold Bamford.'

A surprised Sir Toby looked up from his notes to see his old friend heading confidently towards the witness box. The London jury looked quizzically at the man from Leeds.

Sir Toby had to admit that Mr Lennox established his

expert witness's credentials rather well – without once referring to Leeds. Mr Lennox then proceeded to take Harry through a series of questions, which ended up making his client sound like a cross between Jack the Ripper and Dr Crippen.

Mr Lennox finally said, 'No more questions, m'lud,' and sat down with a smug expression on his face.

Mr Justice Fairborough looked down at Sir Toby and asked, 'Do you have any questions for this witness?'

'I most certainly do, m'lud,' said Toby, rising from his place. 'Professor Bamford,' he said, as if it were their first encounter, 'before I come to the case in hand, I think it would be fair to say that my learned friend Mr Lennox made great play of establishing your credentials as an expert witness. You will have to forgive me if I revisit that subject, and clear up one or two small details that puzzled me.'

'Certainly, Sir Toby,' said Harry.

'This first degree you took at . . . er, yes, at Leeds University. What subject was it that you studied?'

'Geography,' said Harry.

'How interesting. I wouldn't have thought that was an obvious preparation for someone who would go on to become an expert in handguns. However,' he continued, 'allow me to move on to your Ph.D., which was awarded by an American university. Can I ask if that degree is recognised by English universities?'

'No, Sir Toby, but . . .'

'Please confine yourself to answering the questions, Professor Bamford. For example, does Oxford or Cambridge University recognise your Ph.D.?'

'No, Sir Toby.'

'I see. And, as Mr Lennox was at pains to point out, this whole case may well rest on your credentials as an expert witness.'

Mr Justice Fairborough looked down at the defence counsel and frowned. 'It will be up to the jury to make that decision, based on the facts presented to them, Sir Toby.'

'I agree m'lud. I just wished to establish how much credence the members of the jury should place in the opinions of the Crown's expert witness.'

The judge frowned again.

'But if you feel I have made that point, m'lud, I will move on,' said Sir Toby, turning back to face his old friend.

'You told the jury, Professor Bamford – as an expert – that in this particular case the victim couldn't have committed suicide, because the gun was found in his hand.'

'That is correct, Sir Toby. It's a common mistake – often made in poorly researched films and television programmes – for victims to be shown still holding onto the gun after they have shot themselves.'

'Yes, yes, Professor Bamford. We have already been entertained by your great knowledge of television soap operas, when my learned friend was examining you. At least we've found something you're an expert in. But I should like to return to the real world. Can I be clear about one thing, Professor Bamford: you are not suggesting even for a moment, I hope, that your evidence proves that the defendant placed the gun in her husband's hand. If that were so, you wouldn't be an expert, Professor Bamford, but a clairvoyant.'

'I made no such assumption, Sir Toby.'

'I'm grateful to have your support in that. But tell me, Professor Bamford: in your experience, have you ever come across a case in which the murderer placed the gun in the victim's hand, in order to try to suggest that the cause of death was suicide?'

Harry hesitated for a moment.

'Take your time, Professor Bamford. The rest of a woman's life may depend on your reply.'

'I have come across such cases in the past' – he hesitated again – 'on three occasions.'

'On three occasions?' repeated Sir Toby, trying to look surprised, despite the fact that he himself had appeared in all three cases.

'Yes, Sir Toby,' said Harry.

'And, in these three cases, did the jury return a verdict of not guilty?'

'No,' said Harry quietly.

'No?' repeated Sir Toby, facing the jury. 'In how many of the cases did the jury find the defendant not guilty?'

'In two of the cases.'

'And what happened in the third?' asked Sir Toby.

'The man was convicted of murder.'

'And sentenced . . . ?' asked Sir Toby.

'To life imprisonment.'

'I think I'd like to know a little bit more about that case, Professor Bamford.'

'Is this leading anywhere, Sir Toby?' asked Mr Justice Fairborough, staring down at the defence counsel.

'I suspect we are about to find out, m'lud,' said Sir Toby, turning back to the jury, whose eyes were now fixed on the expert witness. 'Professor Bamford, do let the court know the details of that particular case.'

'In that case, the Queen against Reynolds,' said Harry, 'Mr Reynolds served eleven years of his sentence before fresh evidence was produced to show that he couldn't have committed the crime. He was later pardoned.'

'I hope you'll forgive my next question, Professor Bamford, but a woman's reputation, not to mention her freedom, is at stake in this courtroom.' He paused, looked gravely at his old friend and said, 'Did you appear on behalf of the prosecution in that particular case?'

'I did, Sir Toby.'

'As an expert witness for the Crown?'

Harry nodded. 'Yes, Sir Toby.'

'And an innocent man was convicted for a crime that he did not commit, and ended up serving eleven years in prison?'

Harry nodded again. 'Yes, Sir Toby.'

'No "buts" in that particular case?' asked Sir Toby. He waited for a reply, but Harry didn't speak. He knew he no longer had any credibility as an expert witness in this particular case.

'One final question, Professor Bamford: in the other two cases, to be fair, did the juries' verdicts support your interpretation of the evidence?'

'They did, Sir Toby.'

'You will recall, Professor Bamford, that the Crown made great play of the fact that in the past your evidence has been crucial in cases such as these, in fact – to quote Mr Lennox verbatim – "the decisive factor in proving the Crown's case". However, we now learn that in the three cases in which a gun was found in the victim's hand, you have a 33 per cent failure rate as an expert witness.'

Harry didn't comment, as Sir Toby knew he wouldn't.

'And as a result, an innocent man spent eleven years in jail.' Sir Toby switched his attention to the jury and said quietly, 'Professor Bamford, let us hope that an innocent woman isn't about to spend the rest of her life in jail because of the opinion of an "expert witness" who manages to get it wrong 33 per cent of the time.'

Mr Lennox rose to his feet to protest at the treatment the witness was being made to endure, and Mr Justice Fairborough wagged an admonishing finger. 'That was an improper comment, Sir Toby,' he warned.

But Sir Toby's eyes remained on the jury, who no longer hung on the expert witness's every word, but were now whispering among themselves.

Sir Toby slowly resumed his seat. 'No more questions, m'lud.'

––<o>––

'Damn good shot,' said Toby, as Harry's ball disappeared into the cup on the eighteenth hole. 'Lunch on me again, I fear. You know, I haven't beaten you for weeks, Harry.'

'Oh, I don't know about that, Toby,' said his golfing partner, as they headed back to the clubhouse. 'How would you describe what you did to me in court on Thursday?'

'Yes, I must apologise for that, old chap,' said Toby. 'Nothing personal, as you well know. Mind you, it was damn stupid of Lennox to select you as his expert witness in the first place.'

'I agree,' said Harry. 'I did warn them that no one knew me better than you, but Lennox wasn't interested in what happened on the North-Eastern Circuit.'

'I wouldn't have minded so much,' said Toby, as he took his place for lunch, 'if it hadn't been for the fact . . .'

'Hadn't been for the fact . . . ?' Harry repeated.

'That in both cases, the one in Leeds and the one at the Bailey, any jury should have been able to see that my clients were as guilty as sin.'

THE ENDGAME

CORNELIUS BARRINGTON hesitated before he made his next move. He continued to study the board with great interest. The game had been going on for over two hours, and Cornelius was confident that he was only seven moves away from checkmate. He suspected that his opponent was also aware of the fact.

Cornelius looked up and smiled across at Frank Vintcent, who was not only his oldest friend but had over the years, as the family solicitor, proved to be his wisest adviser. The two men had many things in common: their age, both over sixty; their background, both middle-class sons of professionals; they had been educated at the same school and at the same university. But there the similarities ended. For Cornelius was by nature an entrepreneur, a risk-taker, who had made his fortune mining in South Africa and Brazil. Frank was a solicitor by profession, cautious, slow to decision, fascinated by detail.

Cornelius and Frank also differed in their physical appearance. Cornelius was tall, heavily built, with a head of silver hair many men half his age would have envied. Frank was slight, of medium stature, and apart from a semicircle of grey tufts, was almost completely bald.

Cornelius had been widowed after four decades of happy married life. Frank was a confirmed bachelor.

Among the things that had kept them close friends was their enduring love of chess. Frank joined Cornelius at The Willows for a game every Thursday evening, and the result usually remained in the balance, often ending in stalemate.

The evening always began with a light supper, but only one glass of wine each would be poured – the two men took their chess seriously – and after the game was over they would return to the drawing room to enjoy a glass of brandy and a cigar; but tonight Cornelius was about to shatter that routine.

'Congratulations,' said Frank, looking up from the board. 'I think you've got me beaten this time. I'm fairly sure there's no escape.' He smiled, placed the red king flat on the board, rose from his place and shook hands with his closest friend.

'Let's go through to the drawing room and have a brandy and a cigar,' suggested Cornelius, as if it were a novel idea.

'Thank you,' said Frank as they left the study and strolled towards the drawing room. As Cornelius passed the portrait of his son Daniel, his heart missed a beat – something that hadn't changed for the past twenty-three years. If his only child had lived, he would never have sold the company.

As they entered the spacious drawing room the two men were greeted by a cheerful fire blazing in the grate, which had been laid by Cornelius's housekeeper Pauline only moments after she had finished clearing up their supper. Pauline also believed in the virtues of routine, but her life too was about to be shattered.

'I should have trapped you several moves earlier,' said Cornelius, 'but I was taken by surprise when you captured my queen's knight. I should have seen that coming,' he added, as he strolled over to the sideboard. Two large cognacs and two Monte Cristo cigars had been laid out on a silver tray. Cornelius picked up the cigar-clipper and passed it across to his friend, then struck a match, leaned over and watched Frank puff away until he was convinced his cigar was alight. He then completed the same routine himself before sinking into his favourite seat by the fire.

Frank raised his glass. 'Well played, Cornelius,' he said, offering a slight bow, although his host would have been the first to acknowledge that over the years his guest was probably just ahead on points.

Cornelius allowed Frank to take a few more puffs before shattering his evening. Why hurry? After all, he had been preparing for this moment for several weeks, and was unwilling to share the secret with his oldest friend until everything was in place.

They both remained silent for some time, relaxed in each other's company. Finally Cornelius placed his brandy on a side table and said, 'Frank, we have been friends for over fifty years. Equally importantly, as my legal adviser you have proved to be a shrewd advocate. In fact, since the untimely death of Millicent there has been no one I rely on more.'

Frank continued to puff away at his cigar without interrupting his friend. From the expression on his face, he was aware that the compliment was nothing more than an opening gambit. He suspected he would have to wait some time before Cornelius revealed his next move.

'When I first set up the company some thirty years ago, it was you who was responsible for executing the original deeds; and I don't believe I've signed a legal document since that day which has not crossed your desk – something that was unquestionably a major factor in my success.'

'It's generous of you to say so,' said Frank, before taking another sip of brandy, 'but the truth is that it was always your originality and enterprise that made it possible for the company to go from strength to strength – gifts that the gods decided not to bestow on me, leaving me with little choice but to be a mere functionary.'

'You have always underestimated your contribution to the

company's success, Frank, but I am in no doubt of the role you played over the years.'

'Where is this all leading?' asked Frank with a smile.

'Patience, my friend,' said Cornelius. 'I still have a few moves to make before I reveal the stratagem I have in mind.' He leaned back and took another long puff of his cigar. 'As you know, when I sold the company some four years ago, it had been my intention to slow down for the first time in years. I had promised to take Millie on an extended holiday to India and the Far East – ' he paused ' – but that was not to be.'

Frank nodded his head in understanding.

'Her death served to remind me that I am also mortal, and may myself not have much longer to live.'

'No, no, my friend,' protested Frank. 'You still have a good many years to go yet.'

'You may be right,' said Cornelius, 'although funnily enough it was you who made me start to think seriously about the future . . .'

'Me?' said Frank, looking puzzled.

'Yes. Don't you remember some weeks ago, sitting in that chair and advising me that the time had come for me to consider rewriting my will?'

'Yes, I do,' said Frank, 'but that was only because in your present will virtually everything is left to Millie.'

'I'm aware of that,' said Cornelius, 'but it nevertheless served to concentrate the mind. You see, I still rise at six o'clock every morning, but as I no longer have an office to go to, I spend many self-indulgent hours considering how to distribute my wealth now that Millie can no longer be the main beneficiary.'

Cornelius took another long puff of his cigar before continuing. 'For the past month I have been considering those around me – my relatives, friends, acquaintances and employees – and I began to think about the way they have always treated me, which caused me to wonder which of them would show the same amount of devotion, attention and loyalty if I were not worth millions, but was in fact a penniless old man.'

'I have a feeling I'm in check,' said Frank, with a laugh.

'No, no, my dear friend,' said Cornelius. 'You are absolved from any such doubts. Otherwise I would not be sharing these confidences with you.'

'But are such thoughts not a little unfair on your immediate family, not to mention . . .'

'You may be right, but I don't wish to leave that to chance. I have therefore decided to find out the truth for myself, as I consider mere speculation to be unsatisfactory.' Once again, Cornelius paused to take a puff of his cigar before continuing. 'So indulge me for a moment while I tell you what I have in mind, for I confess that without your cooperation it will be impossible for me to carry out my little subterfuge. But first allow me to refill your glass.' Cornelius rose from his chair, picked up his friend's empty goblet and walked to the sideboard.

'As I was saying,' continued Cornelius, passing the refilled glass back to Frank, 'I have recently been wondering how those around me would behave if I were penniless, and I have come to the conclusion that there is only one way to find out.'

Frank took a long gulp before enquiring, 'What do you have in mind? A fake suicide perhaps?'

'Not quite as dramatic as that,' replied Cornelius. 'But almost, because – ' he paused again ' – I intend to declare myself bankrupt.' He stared through the haze of smoke, hoping to observe his friend's immediate reaction. But, as so often in the past, the old solicitor remained inscrutable, not least because, although his friend had just made a bold move, he knew the game was far from over.

He pushed a pawn tentatively forward. 'How do you intend to go about that?' he asked.

'Tomorrow morning,' replied Cornelius, 'I want you to write to the five people who have the greatest claim on my estate: my brother Hugh, his wife Elizabeth, their son Timothy, my sister Margaret, and finally my housekeeper Pauline.'

'And what will be the import of this letter?' asked Frank, trying not to sound too incredulous.

'You will explain to all of them that, due to an unwise investment I made soon after my wife's death, I now find myself in debt. In fact, without their help I may well be facing bankruptcy.'

'But . . .' protested Frank.

Cornelius raised a hand. 'Hear me out,' he pleaded, 'because your role in this real-life game could prove crucial. Once you have convinced them that they can no longer expect anything from me, I intend to put the second phase of my plan into operation, which should prove conclusively whether they really care for me, or simply for the prospect of my wealth.'

'I can't wait to learn what you have in mind,' said Frank.

Cornelius swirled the brandy round in his glass while he collected his thoughts.

'As you are well aware, each of the five people I have named has at some time in the past asked me for a loan. I have never required anything in writing, as I have always considered the repayment of these debts to be a matter of trust. These loans range from £100,000 to my brother Hugh to purchase the lease for his shop – which I understand is doing quite well – to my housekeeper Pauline, who borrowed £500 for a deposit on a secondhand car. Even young Timothy needed £1,000 to pay off his university loan, and as he seems to be progressing well in his chosen profession, it should not be too much to ask him – like all of the others – to repay his debt.'

'And the second test?' enquired Frank.

'Since Millie's death, each of them has performed some

little service for me, which they have always insisted they
enjoyed carrying out, rather than it being a chore. I'm about
to find out if they are willing to do the same for a penniless
old man.'

'But how will you know . . .' began Frank.

'I think that will become obvious as the weeks go by. And
in any case, there is a third test, which I believe will settle the
matter.'

Frank stared across at his friend. 'Is there any point in
trying to talk you out of this crazy idea?' he asked.

'No, there is not,' replied Cornelius without hesitation. 'I
am resolved in this matter, although I accept that I cannot
make the first move, let alone bring it to a conclusion, without
your cooperation.'

'If it is truly what you want me to do, Cornelius, then I
shall carry out your instructions to the letter, as I have always
done in the past. But on this occasion there must be one
proviso.'

'And what might that be?' asked Cornelius.

'I shall not charge a fee for this commission, so that I will
be able to attest to anyone who should ask that I have not
benefited from your shenanigans.'

'But . . .'

'No "buts", old friend. I made a handsome profit from my
original shareholding when you sold the company. You must
consider this a small attempt to say thank you.'

Cornelius smiled. 'It is I who should be grateful, and
indeed I am, as always, conscious of your valued assistance
over the years. You are truly a good friend, and I swear I
would leave my entire estate to you if you weren't a bachelor,
and if I didn't know it wouldn't change your way of life one
iota.'

'No, thank you,' said Frank with a chuckle. 'If you did that,
I would only have to carry out exactly the same test with a

different set of characters.' He paused. 'So, what is your first move?'

Cornelius rose from his chair. 'Tomorrow you will send out five letters informing those concerned that a bankruptcy notice has been served on me, and that I require any outstanding loans to be repaid in full, and as quickly as possible.'

Frank had already begun making notes on a little pad he always carried with him. Twenty minutes later, when he had written down Cornelius's final instruction, he placed the pad back in an inside pocket, drained his glass and stubbed out his cigar.

When Cornelius rose to accompany him to the front door, Frank asked, 'But what is to be the third of your tests, the one you're convinced will prove so conclusive?'

The old solicitor listened carefully as Cornelius outlined an idea of such ingenuity that he departed feeling all the victims would be left with little choice but to reveal their true colours.

-<o>-

The first person to call Cornelius on Saturday morning was his brother Hugh. It must have been only moments after he had opened Frank's letter. Cornelius had the distinct feeling that someone else was listening in on the conversation.

'I've just received a letter from your solicitor,' said Hugh, 'and I simply can't believe it. Please tell me there's been some dreadful mistake.'

'I'm afraid there has been no mistake,' Cornelius replied. 'I only wish I could tell you otherwise.'

'But how could you, who are normally so shrewd, have allowed such a thing to happen?'

'Put it down to old age,' Cornelius replied. 'A few weeks after Millie died I was talked into investing a large sum of money in a company that specialised in supplying mining equipment to the Russians. All of us have read about the endless supply of oil there, if only one could get at it, so I was confident my investment would show a handsome return. Last Friday I was informed by the company secretary that they had filed a 217 order, as they were no longer solvent.'

'But surely you didn't invest everything you had in the one company?' said Hugh, sounding even more incredulous.

'Not originally, of course,' said Cornelius, 'but I fear I got sucked in whenever they needed a further injection of cash. Towards the end I had to go on investing more, as it seemed to me the only way I would have any chance of getting back my original investment.'

'But doesn't the company have any assets you can lay your hands on? What about all the mining equipment?'

'It's all rusting away somewhere in central Russia, and so far we haven't seen a thimbleful of oil.'

'Why didn't you get out when your losses were still manageable?' asked Hugh.

'Pride, I suppose. Unwilling to admit I'd backed a loser, always believing my money would be safe in the long run.'

'But they must be offering some recompense,' said Hugh desperately.

'Not a penny,' replied Cornelius. 'I can't even afford to fly over and spend a few days in Russia to find out what the true position is.'

'How much time have they given you?'

'A bankruptcy notice has already been served on me, so my very survival depends on how much I can raise in the short term.' Cornelius paused. 'I'm sorry to remind you of this, Hugh, but you will recall that some time ago I loaned you £100,000. So I was rather hoping . . .'

'But you know that every penny of that money has been sunk into the shop, and with High Street sales at an all-time low, I don't think I could lay my hands on more than a few thousand at the moment.'

Cornelius thought he heard someone whispering the words 'And no more' in the background.

'Yes, I can see the predicament you're in,' said Cornelius. 'But anything you can do to help would be appreciated. When you've settled on a sum – ' he paused again ' – and naturally you'll have to discuss with Elizabeth just how much you can spare – perhaps you could send a cheque direct to Frank Vintcent's office. He's handling the whole messy business.'

'The lawyers always seem to end up getting their cut, whether you win or lose.'

'To be fair,' said Cornelius, 'Frank has waived his fee on this occasion. And while you're on the phone, Hugh, the people you're sending to refit the kitchen were due to start later this week. It's even more important now that they complete the job as quickly as possible, because I'm putting the house on the market and a new kitchen will help me get a better price. I'm sure you understand.'

'I'll see what I can do to help,' said Hugh, 'but I may have to move that particular team onto another assignment. We've got a bit of a backlog at the moment.'

'Oh? I thought you said money was a little tight right now,' Cornelius said, stifling a chuckle.

'It is,' said Hugh, a little too quickly. 'What I meant to say was that we're all having to work overtime just to keep our heads above water.'

'I think I understand,' said Cornelius. 'Still, I'm sure you'll do everything you can to help, now you're fully aware of my situation.' He put the phone down and smiled.

The next victim to contact him didn't bother to phone, but arrived at the front door a few minutes later, and wouldn't take her finger off the buzzer until the door had been opened.

'Where's Pauline?' was Margaret's first question when her brother opened the door. Cornelius stared down at his sister, who had put on a little too much make-up that morning.

'I'm afraid she's had to go,' said Cornelius as he bent down to kiss his sister on the cheek. 'The petitioner in bankruptcy takes a rather dim view of people who can't afford to pay their creditors, but still manage to retain a personal entourage. It was considerate of you to pop round so quickly in my hour of need, Margaret, but if you were hoping for a cup of tea, I'm afraid you'll have to make it yourself.'

'I didn't come round for a cup of tea, as I suspect you know only too well, Cornelius. What I want to know is how you managed to fritter away your entire fortune.' Before her brother could deliver some well-rehearsed lines from his script, she added, 'You'll have to sell the house, of course. I've always said that since Millie's death it's far too large for you. You can always take a bachelor flat in the village.'

'Such decisions are no longer in my hands,' said Cornelius, trying to sound helpless.

'What are you talking about?' demanded Margaret, rounding on him.

'Just that the house and its contents have already been seized by the petitioners in bankruptcy. If I'm to avoid going bankrupt, we must hope that the house sells for a far higher price than the estate agents are predicting.'

'Are you telling me there's absolutely nothing left?'

'Less than nothing would be more accurate,' said Cornelius, sighing. 'And once they've evicted me from The Willows, I'll have nowhere to go.' He tried to sound plaintive. 'So I was rather hoping that you would allow me to take up the kind offer you made at Millie's funeral and come and live with you.'

His sister turned away, so that Cornelius was unable to see the expression on her face.

'That wouldn't be convenient at the present time,' she said without explanation. 'And in any case, Hugh and Elizabeth have far more spare rooms in their house than I do.'

'Quite so,' said Cornelius. He coughed. 'And the small loan

I advanced you last year, Margaret – I'm sorry to raise the subject, but . . .'

'What little money I have is carefully invested, and my brokers tell me that this is not a time to sell.'

'But the allowance I've provided every month for the past twenty years – surely you have a little salted away?'

'I'm afraid not,' Margaret replied. 'You must understand that being your sister has meant I am expected to maintain a certain standard of living, and now that I can no longer rely on my monthly allowance, I shall have to be even more careful with my meagre income.'

'Of course you will, my dear,' said Cornelius. 'But any little contribution would help, if you felt able . . .'

'I must be off,' said Margaret, looking at her watch. 'You've already made me late for the hairdresser.'

'Just one more little request before you go, my dear,' said Cornelius. 'In the past you've always been kind enough to give me a lift into town whenever . . .'

'I've always said, Cornelius, that you should have learned to drive years ago. If you had, you wouldn't expect everyone to be at your beck and call night and day. I'll see what I can do,' she added as he opened the door for her.

'Funny, I don't recall you ever saying that. But then, perhaps my memory is going as well,' he said as he followed his sister out onto the drive. He smiled. 'New car, Margaret?' he enquired innocently.

'Yes,' his sister replied tartly as he opened the door for her. Cornelius thought he detected a slight colouring in her cheeks. He chuckled to himself as she drove off. He was learning more about his family by the minute.

Cornelius strolled back into the house, and returned to his study. He closed the door, picked up the phone on his desk and dialled Frank's office.

'Vintcent, Ellwood and Halfon,' said a prim voice.

'I'd like to speak to Mr Vintcent.'

'Who shall I say is calling?'

'Cornelius Barrington.'

'I'll have to see if he's free, Mr Barrington.'

Very good, thought Cornelius. Frank must have convinced even his receptionist that the rumours were true, because in the past her response had always been, 'I'll put you straight through, sir.'

'Good morning, Cornelius,' said Frank. 'I've just put the phone down on your brother Hugh. That's the second time he's called this morning.'

'What did he want?' asked Cornelius.

'To have the full implications explained to him, and also his immediate obligations.'

'Good,' said Cornelius. 'So can I hope to receive a cheque for £100,000 in the near future?'

'I doubt it,' said Frank. 'From the tone of his voice I don't think that's what he had in mind, but I'll let you know just as soon as I've heard back from him.'

'I shall look forward to that, Frank.'

'I do believe you're enjoying yourself, Cornelius.'

'You bet I am,' he replied. 'I only wish Millie was here to share the fun with me.'

'You know what she would have said, don't you?'

'No, but I have a feeling you're about to tell me.'

'You're a wicked old man.'

'And, as always, she would have been right,' Cornelius confessed with a laugh. 'Goodbye, Frank.' As he replaced the receiver there was a knock at the door.

'Come in,' said Cornelius, puzzled as to who it could possibly be. The door opened and his housekeeper entered, carrying a tray with a cup of tea and a plate of shortbread biscuits. She was, as always, neat and trim, not a hair out of place, and showed no sign of embarrassment. She can't have received Frank's letter yet, was Cornelius's first thought.

'Pauline,' he said as she placed the tray on his desk, 'did you receive a letter from my solicitor this morning?'

'Yes, I did, sir,' Pauline replied, 'and of course I shall sell the car immediately, and repay your £500.' She paused before looking straight at him. 'But I was just wondering, sir . . .'

'Yes, Pauline?'

'Would it be possible for me to work it off in lieu? You see, I need a car to pick up my girls from school.'

For the first time since he had embarked on the enterprise, Cornelius felt guilty. But he knew that if he agreed to Pauline's request, someone would find out, and the whole enterprise would be endangered.

'I'm so sorry, Pauline, but I've been left with no choice.'

'That's exactly what the solicitor explained in his letter,' Pauline said, fiddling with a piece of paper in the pocket of her pinafore. 'Mind you, I never did go much on lawyers.'

This statement made Cornelius feel even more guilty, because he didn't know a more trustworthy person than Frank Vintcent.

'I'd better leave you now, sir, but I'll pop back this evening just to make sure things don't get too untidy. Would it be possible, sir . . . ?'

'Possible . . . ?' said Cornelius.

'Could you give me a reference? I mean, you see, it's not that easy for someone of my age to find a job.'

'I'll give you a reference that would get you a position at Buckingham Palace,' said Cornelius. He immediately sat down at his desk and wrote a glowing homily on the service Pauline Croft had given for over two decades. He read it through, then handed it across to her. 'Thank you, Pauline,' he said, 'for all you have done in the past for Daniel, Millie and, most of all, myself.'

'My pleasure, sir,' said Pauline.

Once she had closed the door behind her, Cornelius could only wonder if water wasn't sometimes thicker than blood.

He sat back down at his desk and began writing some notes to remind him what had taken place that morning. When he had finished he went through to the kitchen to make himself some lunch, and found a salad had been laid out for him.

After lunch, Cornelius took a bus into town – a novel experience. It was some time before he located a bus stop, and then he discovered that the conductor didn't have change for a twenty-pound note. His first call after he had been dropped off in the town centre was to the local estate agent, who didn't seem that surprised to see him. Cornelius was delighted to find how quickly the rumour of his financial demise must be spreading.

'I'll have someone call round to The Willows in the morning, Mr Barrington,' said the young man, rising from behind his desk, 'so we can measure up and take some photographs. May we also have your permission to place a sign in the garden?'

'Please do,' said Cornelius without hesitation, and barely stopped himself from adding, the bigger the better.

After he'd left the estate agent, Cornelius walked a few yards down the street and called into the local removal firm. He asked another young man if he could make an appointment for them to take away the entire contents of the house.

'Where's it all to go, sir?'

'To Botts' Storeroom in the High Street,' Cornelius informed him.

'That will be no problem, sir,' said the young assistant, picking up a pad from his desk. Once Cornelius had completed the forms in triplicate, the assistant said, 'Sign there, sir,' pointing to the bottom of the form. Then, looking a little nervous, he added, 'We'll need a deposit of £100.'

'Of course,' said Cornelius, taking out his chequebook.

'I'm afraid it will have to be cash, sir,' the young man said in a confidential tone.

Cornelius smiled. No one had refused a cheque from him for over thirty years. 'I'll call back tomorrow,' he said.

On the way back to the bus stop Cornelius stared through the window of his brother's hardware store, and noted that the staff didn't seem all that busy. On arriving back at The Willows, he returned to his study and made some more notes on what had taken place that afternoon.

As he climbed the stairs to go to bed that night, he reflected that it must have been the first afternoon in years that no one had called him to ask how he was. He slept soundly that night.

◄◦►

When Cornelius came downstairs the following morning, he picked up his post from the mat and made his way to the kitchen. Over a bowl of cornflakes he checked through the letters. He had once been told that if it was known you were likely to go bankrupt, a stream of brown envelopes would begin to drop through the letterbox, as shopkeepers and small businessmen tried to get in before anyone else could be declared a preferred creditor.

There were no brown envelopes in the post that morning, because Cornelius had made certain every bill had been covered before he began his journey down this particular road.

Other than circulars and free offers, there was just one white envelope with a London postmark. It turned out to be a handwritten letter from his nephew Timothy, saying how sorry he was to learn of his uncle's problems, and that although he didn't get back to Chudley much nowadays, he would make every effort to travel up to Shropshire at the weekend and call in to see him.

Although the message was brief, Cornelius silently noted that Timothy was the first member of the family to show any sympathy for his predicament.

When he heard the doorbell ring, he placed the letter on the kitchen table and walked out into the hall. He opened the front door to be greeted by Elizabeth, his brother's wife. Her face was white, lined and drained, and Cornelius doubted if she had slept a great deal the previous night.

The moment Elizabeth had stepped into the house she began to pace around from room to room, almost as though she were checking to see that everything was still in place, as if she couldn't accept the words she had read in the solicitor's letter.

Any lingering doubts must have been dispelled when, a few minutes later, the local estate agent appeared on the doorstep, tape measure in hand, with a photographer by his side.

'If Hugh was able to return even part of the hundred thousand I loaned him, that would be most helpful,' Cornelius remarked to his sister-in-law as he followed her through the house.

It was some time before she spoke, despite the fact that she had had all night to consider her response.

'It's not quite that easy,' she eventually replied. 'You see, the loan was made to the company, and the shares are distributed among several people.'

Cornelius knew all three of the several people. 'Then perhaps the time has come for you and Hugh to sell off some of your shares.'

'And allow some stranger to take over the company, after all the work we've put into it over the years? No, we can't afford to let that happen. In any case, Hugh asked Mr Vintcent what the legal position was, and he confirmed that there was no obligation on our part to sell any of our shares.'

'Have you considered that perhaps you have a moral obligation?' asked Cornelius, turning to face his sister-in-law.

'Cornelius,' she said, avoiding his stare, 'it has been your irresponsibility, not ours, that has been the cause of your downfall. Surely you wouldn't expect your brother to sacrifice everything he's worked for over the years, simply to place my family in the same perilous position in which you now find yourself?'

Cornelius realised why Elizabeth hadn't slept the previous night. She was not only acting as spokeswoman for Hugh, but was obviously making the decisions as well. Cornelius had always considered her to be the stronger-willed of the two, and he doubted if he would come face to face with his brother before an agreement had been reached.

'But if there's any other way we might help . . .' Elizabeth added in a more gentle tone, as her hand rested on an ornate gold-leafed table in the drawing room.

'Well, now you mention it,' replied Cornelius, 'I'm putting the house on the market in a couple of weeks' time, and will be looking for . . .'

'That soon?' said Elizabeth. 'And what's going to happen to all the furniture?'

'It will all have to be sold to help cover the debts. But, as I said . . .'

'Hugh has always liked this table.'

'Louis XIV,' said Cornelius casually.

'I wonder what it's worth,' Elizabeth mused, trying to make it sound as if it were of little consequence.

'I have no idea,' said Cornelius. 'If I remember correctly, I paid around £60,000 for it – but that was over ten years ago.'

'And the chess set?' Elizabeth asked, picking up one of the pieces.

'It's a worthless copy,' Cornelius replied. 'You could pick up a set just like it in any Arab bazaar for a couple of hundred pounds.'

'Oh, I always thought . . .' Elizabeth hesitated before replacing the piece on the wrong square. 'Well, I must be off,' she said, sounding as if her task had been completed. 'We must try not to forget that I still have a business to run.'

Cornelius accompanied her as she began striding back down the long corridor in the direction of the front door. She walked straight by the portrait of her nephew Daniel. In the past she had always stopped to remark on how much she missed him.

'I was wondering . . .' began Cornelius as they walked out into the hall.

'Yes?' said Elizabeth.

'Well, as I have to be out of here in a couple of weeks, I hoped it might be possible to move in with you. That is, until I find somewhere I can afford.'

'If only you'd asked a week ago,' said Elizabeth, without missing a beat. 'But unfortunately we've just agreed to take in my mother, and the only other room is Timothy's, and he comes home most weekends.'

'Is that so?' said Cornelius.

'And the grandfather clock?' asked Elizabeth, who still appeared to be on a shopping expedition.

'Victorian – I purchased it from the Earl of Bute's estate.'

'No, I meant how much is it worth?'

'Whatever someone is willing to pay for it,' Cornelius replied as they reached the front door.

'Don't forget to let me know, Cornelius, if there's anything I can do to help.'

'How kind of you, Elizabeth,' he said, opening the door to find the estate agent hammering a stake into the ground with a sign on it declaring FOR SALE. Cornelius smiled, because it was the only thing that morning that had stopped Elizabeth in her tracks.

—◦—

Frank Vintcent arrived on the Thursday evening, carrying a bottle of cognac and two pizzas.

'If I'd realised that losing Pauline was to be part of the deal, I would never have agreed to go along with your plan in the first place,' Frank said as he nibbled at his microwaved pizza. 'How do you manage without her?'

'Rather badly,' Cornelius admitted, 'although she still drops in for an hour or two every evening. Otherwise this place would look like a pigsty. Come to think of it, how do *you* cope?'

'As a bachelor,' Frank replied, 'you learn the art of survival from an early age. Now, let's stop this small-talk and get on with the game.'

'Which game?' enquired Cornelius with a chuckle.

'Chess,' replied Frank. 'I've had enough of the other game for one week.'

'Then we'd better go through to the library.'

Frank was surprised by Cornelius's opening moves, as he had never known his old friend to be so daring. Neither of them spoke again for over an hour, most of which Frank spent trying to defend his queen.

'This might well be the last game we play with this set,' said Cornelius wistfully.

'No, don't worry yourself about that,' said Frank. 'They always allow you to keep a few personal items.'

'Not when they're worth a quarter of a million pounds,' replied Cornelius.

'I had no idea,' said Frank, looking up.

'Because you're not the sort of man who has ever been interested in worldly goods. It's a sixteenth-century Persian masterpiece, and it's bound to cause considerable interest when it comes under the hammer.'

'But surely you've found out all you need to know by now,' said Frank. 'Why carry on with the exercise when you could lose so much that's dear to you?'

'Because I still have to discover the truth.'

Frank sighed, stared down at the board and moved his queen's knight. 'Checkmate,' he said. 'It serves you right for not concentrating.'

—◆—

Cornelius spent most of Friday morning in a private meeting with the managing director of Botts and Company, the local fine art and furniture auctioneers.

Mr Botts had already agreed that the sale could take place in a fortnight's time. He had often repeated that he would have preferred a longer period to prepare the catalogue and send out an extensive mailing for such a fine collection, but at least he showed some sympathy for the position Mr Barrington found himself in. Over the years, Lloyd's of London, death duties and impending bankruptcy had proved the auctioneer's best friends.

'We will need to have everything in our storeroom as soon as possible,' said Mr Botts, 'so there's enough time to prepare a catalogue, while still allowing the customers to view on three consecutive days before the sale takes place.'

Cornelius nodded his agreement.

The auctioneer also recommended that a full page be taken in the *Chudley Advertiser* the following Wednesday, giving details of what was coming under the hammer, so they could reach those people they failed to contact by post.

Cornelius left Mr Botts a few minutes before midday, and on his way back to the bus stop dropped into the removal company. He handed over £100 in fives and tens, leaving the impression that it had taken him a few days to raise the cash.

While waiting for the bus, he couldn't help noticing how few people bothered to say good morning, or even acknowledge him. Certainly no one crossed the road to pass the time of day.

◄○►

Twenty men in three vans spent the next day loading and unloading as they travelled back and forth between The Willows and the auctioneers' storeroom in the High Street. It was not until the early evening that the last stick of furniture had been removed from the house.

As he walked through the empty rooms, Cornelius was surprised to find himself thinking that, with one or two exceptions, he wasn't going to miss many of his worldly possessions. He retired to the bedroom – the only room in the house that was still furnished – and continued to read the novel Elizabeth had recommended before his downfall.

The following morning he only had one call, from his nephew Timothy, to say he was up for the weekend, and wondered if Uncle Cornelius could find time to see him.

'Time is the one thing I still have plenty of,' replied Cornelius.

'Then why don't I drop round this afternoon?' said Timothy. 'Shall we say four o'clock?'

◄○►

'I'm sorry I can't offer you a cup of tea,' said Cornelius, 'but I finished the last packet this morning, and as I'm probably leaving the house next week . . .'

'It's not important,' said Timothy, who was unable to mask

48

his distress at finding the house stripped of his uncle's possessions.

'Let's go up to the bedroom. It's the only room that still has any furniture in it – and most of that will be gone by next week.'

'I had no idea they'd taken everything away. Even the picture of Daniel,' Timothy said as he passed an oblong patch of a lighter shade of cream than the rest of the wall.

'And my chess set,' sighed Cornelius. 'But I can't complain. I've had a good life.' He began to climb the stairs to the bedroom.

Cornelius sat in the only chair while Timothy perched on the end of the bed. The old man studied his nephew more closely. He had grown into a fine young man. An open face, with clear brown eyes that served to reveal, to anyone who didn't already know, that he had been adopted. He must have been twenty-seven or twenty-eight – about the same age Daniel would have been if he were still alive. Cornelius had always had a soft spot for his nephew, and had imagined that his affection was reciprocated. He wondered if he was about to be disillusioned once again.

Timothy appeared nervous, shuffling uneasily from foot to foot as he perched on the end of the bed. 'Uncle Cornelius,' he began, his head slighdy bowed, 'as you know, I have received a letter from Mr Vintcent, so I thought I ought to come to see you and explain that I simply don't have £1,000 to my name, and therefore I'm unable to repay my debt at present.'

Cornelius was disappointed. He had hoped that just one of the family . . .

'However,' the young man continued, removing a long, thin envelope from an inside pocket of his jacket, 'on my twenty-first birthday my father presented me with shares of 1 per cent of the company, which I think must be worth at least £1,000, so I wondered if you would consider taking them in exchange for my debt – that is, until I can afford to buy them back.'

Cornelius felt guilty for having doubted his nephew even for a moment. He wanted to apologise, but knew he couldn't if the house of cards was to remain in place for a few more days. He took the widow's mite and thanked Timothy.

'I am aware just how much of a sacrifice this must be for you,' said Cornelius, 'remembering how many times you have told me in the past of your ambition to take over the company when your father eventually retires, and your dreams of expanding into areas he has refused even to contemplate.'

'I don't think he'll ever retire,' said Timothy, with a sigh. 'But I was hoping that after all the experience I've gained working in London he might take me seriously as a candidate for manager when Mr Leonard retires at the end of the year.'

'I fear your chances won't be advanced when he learns that you've handed over 1 per cent of the company to your bankrupt uncle.'

'My problems can hardly be compared with the ones you are facing, Uncle. I'm only sorry I can't hand over the cash right now. Before I leave, is there anything else I can do for you?'

'Yes, there is, Timothy,' said Cornelius, returning to the script. 'Your mother recommended a novel, which I've been enjoying, but my old eyes seem to tire earlier and earlier, and I wondered if you'd be kind enough to read a few pages to me. I've marked the place I've reached.'

'I can remember you reading to me when I was a child,' said Timothy. '*Just William* and *Swallows and Amazons*,' he added as he took the proffered book.

Timothy must have read about twenty pages when he suddenly stopped and looked up.

'There's a bus ticket at page 450. Shall I leave it there, Uncle?'

'Yes, please do,' said Cornelius. 'I put it there to remind

me of something.' He paused. 'Forgive me, but I'm feeling a little tired.'

Timothy rose and said, 'I'll come back soon and finish off the last few pages.'

'No need to bother yourself, I'll be able to manage that.'

'Oh, I think I'd better, Uncle, otherwise I'll never find out which one of them becomes Prime Minister.'

◄◦►

The second batch of letters, which Frank Vintcent sent out on the following Friday, caused another flurry of phone calls.

'I'm not sure I fully understand what it means,' said Margaret, in her first communication with her brother since calling round to see him a fortnight before.

'It means exactly what it says, my dear,' said Cornelius calmly. 'All my worldly goods are to come under the hammer, but I am allowing those I consider near and dear to me to select one item that, for sentimental or personal reasons, they would like to see remain in the family. They will then be able to bid for them at the auction next Friday.'

'But we could all be outbid and end up with nothing,' said Margaret.

'No, my dear,' said Cornelius, trying not to sound exasperated. 'The *public* auction will be held in the afternoon. The selected pieces will be auctioned separately in the morning, with only the family and close friends present. The instructions couldn't be clearer.'

'And are we able to see the pieces before the auction takes place?'

'Yes, Margaret,' said her brother, as if addressing a backward child. 'As Mr Vintcent stated clearly in his letter, "Viewing Tuesday, Wednesday, Thursday, 10 a.m. to 4 p.m., before the sale on Friday at eleven o'clock".'

'But we can only select one piece?'

51

'Yes,' repeated Cornelius, 'that is all the petitioner in bankruptcy would allow. But you'll be pleased to know that the portrait of Daniel, which you have commented on so many times in the past, will be among the lots available for your consideration.'

'Yes, I do like it,' said Margaret. She hesitated for a moment. 'But will the Turner also be up for sale?'

'It certainly will,' said Cornelius. 'I'm being forced to sell everything.'

'Have you any idea what Hugh and Elizabeth are after?'

'No, I haven't, but if you want to find out, why don't you ask them?' he replied mischievously, aware that they scarcely exchanged a word from one year's end to the next.

The second call came only moments after he had put the phone down on his sister.

'At last,' said a peremptory voice, as if it were somehow Cornelius's fault that others might also wish to speak to him.

'Good morning, Elizabeth,' said Cornelius, immediately recognising the voice. 'How nice to hear from you.'

'It's about the letter I received this morning.'

'Yes, I thought it might be,' said Cornelius.

'It's just, well, I wanted to confirm the value of the table – the Louis XIV piece – and, while I'm on the line, the grand-father clock that used to belong to the Earl of Bute.'

'If you go to the auction house, Elizabeth, they will give you a catalogue, which tells you the high and low estimate for every item in the sale.'

'I see,' said Elizabeth. She remained silent for some time. 'I don't suppose you know if Margaret will be bidding for either of those pieces?'

'I have no idea,' replied Cornelius. 'But it was Margaret who was blocking the line when you were trying to get through, and she asked me a similar question, so I suggest you give her a call.' Another long silence. 'By the way, Elizabeth, you do realise that you can only bid for one item?'

'Yes, it says as much in the letter,' replied his sister-in-law tartly.

'I only ask because I always thought Hugh was interested in the chess set.'

'Oh no, I don't think so,' said Elizabeth. Cornelius wasn't in any doubt who would be doing the bidding on behalf of that family on Friday morning.

'Well, good luck,' said Cornelius. 'And don't forget the 15 per cent commission,' he added as he put the phone down.

—<o>—

Timothy wrote the following day to say he was hoping to attend the auction, as he wanted to pick up a little memento of The Willows and his uncle and aunt.

Pauline, however, told Cornelius as she tidied up the bedroom that she had no intention of going to the auction.

'Why not?' he asked.

'Because I'd be sure to make a fool of myself and bid for something I couldn't afford.'

'Very wise,' said Cornelius. 'I've fallen into that trap once or twice myself. But did you have your eye on anything in particular?'

'Yes, I did, but my savings would never stretch to it.'

'Oh, you can never be sure with auctions,' said Cornelius. 'If no one else joins in the bidding, sometimes you can make a killing.'

'Well, I'll think about it, now I've got a new job.'

'I'm so pleased to hear that,' said Cornelius, who was genuinely disappointed to learn her news.

—<o>—

Neither Cornelius nor Frank was able to concentrate on their weekly chess match that Thursday evening, and after half an hour they abandoned the game and settled on a draw.

'I must confess that I can't wait for things to return to normal,' said Frank as his host poured him a glass of cooking sherry.

'Oh, I don't know. I find the situation has its compensations.'

'Like what for example?' said Frank, who frowned after his first sip.

'Well, for a start, I'm looking forward to tomorrow's auction.'

'But that could still go badly wrong,' said Frank.

'What can possibly go wrong?' asked Cornelius.

'Well, for a start, have you considered . . . ?' But he didn't bother to complete the sentence, because his friend wasn't listening.

◄○►

Cornelius was the first to arrive at the auction house the following morning. The room was laid out with 120 chairs in neat rows of twelve, ready for the anticipated packed house that afternoon, but Cornelius thought the real drama would unfold in the morning, when only six people would be in attendance.

The next person to appear, fifteen minutes before the auction was due to begin, was Cornelius's solicitor Frank Vintcent. Observing his client deep in conversation with Mr Botts, who would be conducting the auction, he took a seat towards the back of the room on the right-hand side.

Cornelius's sister Margaret was the next to make an appearance, and she was not as considerate. She charged straight up to Mr Botts and asked in a shrill voice, 'Can I sit anywhere I like?'

'Yes, madam, you most certainly can,' said Mr Botts. Margaret immediately commandeered the centre seat in the front row, directly below the auctioneer's podium.

Cornelius gave his sister a nod before walking down the aisle and taking a chair three rows in front of Frank.

Hugh and Elizabeth were the next to arrive. They stood at the back for some time while they considered the layout of the room. Eventually they strolled up the aisle and occupied two seats in the eighth row, which afforded them a perfect sightline to the podium, while at the same time being able to keep an eye on Margaret. Opening move to Elizabeth, thought Cornelius, who was quietly enjoying himself.

As the hour hand of the clock on the wall behind the auctioneer's rostrum ticked inexorably towards eleven, Cornelius was disappointed that neither Pauline nor Timothy made an appearance.

Just as the auctioneer began to climb the steps to the podium, the door at the back of the room eased open and Pauline's head peered round. The rest of her body remained hidden behind the door until her eyes settled on Cornelius, who smiled encouragingly. She stepped inside and closed the door, but showed no interest in taking a seat, retreating into a corner instead.

The auctioneer beamed down at the handpicked invitees as the clock struck eleven.

'Ladies and gentlemen,' he began, 'I've been in the business for over thirty years, but this is the first time I've conducted a private sale, so this is a most unusual auction even for me. I'd better go over the ground rules, so that no one can be in any doubt should a dispute arise later.

'All of you present have some special association, whether as family or friends, with Mr Cornelius Barrington, whose personal effects are coming under the hammer. Each of you has been invited to select one item from the inventory, for which you will be allowed to bid. Should you be successful you may not bid for any other lot, but if you fail on the item of your first choice, you may join in the bidding for any other lot. I hope that is clear,' he said, as the door was flung open and Timothy rushed in.

'So sorry,' he said a little breathlessly, 'but my train was held up.' He quickly took a seat in the back row. Cornelius smiled – every one of his pawns was now in place.

'As there are only five of you eligible to bid,' continued Mr Botts as if there had been no interruption, 'only five items will come under the hammer. But the law states that if anyone has previously left a written bid, that bid must be recognised as part of the auction. I shall make things as easy to follow as possible by saying if I have a bid at the table, from which you should assume it is a bid left at our office by a member of the public. I think it would be only fair to point out,' he added, 'that I have outside bids on four of the five items.

'Having explained the ground rules, I will with your permission begin the auction.' He glanced towards the back of the room at Cornelius, who nodded his assent.

'The first lot I am able to offer is a long-case clock, dated 1892, which was purchased by Mr Barrington from the estate of the late Earl of Bute.

'I shall open the bidding for this lot at £3,000. Do I see £3,500?' Mr Botts asked, raising an eyebrow. Elizabeth looked a little shocked, as three thousand was just below the low estimate and the figure she and Hugh had agreed on that morning.

'Is anyone interested in this lot?' asked Mr Botts, looking directly at Elizabeth, but she remained apparently mesmerised. 'I shall ask once again if anyone wishes to bid £3,500 for this magnificent long-case clock. Fair warning. I see no bids, so I shall have to withdraw this item and place it in the afternoon sale.'

Elizabeth still seemed to be in a state of shock. She immediately turned to her husband and began a whispered conversation with him. Mr Botts looked a little disappointed, but moved quickly on to the second lot.

'The next lot is a charming watercolour of the Thames by William Turner of Oxford. Can I open the bidding at £2,000?'

Margaret waved her catalogue furiously.

'Thank you, madam,' said the auctioneer, beaming down at her. 'I have an outside bid of £3,000. Will anyone offer me £4,000?'

'Yes!' shouted Margaret, as if the room were so crowded that she needed to make herself heard above the din.

'I have a bid of five thousand at the table – will you bid six, madam?' he asked, returning his attention to the lady in the front row.

'I will,' said Margaret equally firmly.

'Are there any other bids?' demanded the auctioneer, glancing around the room – a sure sign that the bids at the table had dried up. 'Then I'm going to let this picture go for £6,000 to the lady in the front row.'

'Seven,' said a voice behind her. Margaret looked round to see that her sister-in-law had joined in the bidding.

'Eight thousand!' shouted Margaret.

'Nine,' said Elizabeth without hesitation.

'Ten thousand!' bellowed Margaret.

Suddenly there was silence. Cornelius glanced across the room to see a smile of satisfaction cross Elizabeth's face, having left her sister-in-law with a bill for £10,000.

Cornelius wanted to burst out laughing. The auction was turning out to be even more entertaining than he could have hoped.

'There being no more bids, this delightful water-colour is sold to Miss Barrington for £10,000,' said Mr Botts as he brought the hammer down with a thump. He smiled down at Margaret, as if she had made a wise investment.

'The next lot,' he continued, 'is a portrait simply entitled *Daniel*, by an unknown artist. It is a well-executed work, and I was hoping to open the bidding at £100. Do I see a bid of one hundred?'

To Cornelius's disappointment, no one in the room seemed to be showing any interest in this lot.

'I am willing to consider a bid of £50 to get things started,' said Mr Botts, 'but I am unable to go any lower. Will anyone bid me £50?'

Cornelius glanced around the room, trying to work out from the expressions on their faces who had selected this item, and why they no longer wished to bid when the price was so reasonable.

'Then I fear I will have to withdraw this lot as well.'

'Does that mean I've got it?' asked a voice from the back. Everyone looked round.

'If you are willing to bid £50, madam,' said Mr Botts, adjusting his spectacles, 'the picture is yours.'

'Yes please,' said Pauline. Mr Botts smiled in her direction as he brought down the hammer. 'Sold to the lady at the back of the room,' he declared, 'for £50.'

'Now I move on to lot number four, a chess set of unknown provenance. What shall I say for this item? Can I start someone off with £100? Thank you, sir.'

Cornelius looked round to see who was bidding. 'I have two hundred at the table. Can I say three hundred?'

Timothy nodded.

'I have a bid at the table of three fifty. Can I say four hundred?'

This time Timothy looked crestfallen, and Cornelius assumed the sum was beyond his limit. 'Then I am going to have to withdraw this piece also and place it in this afternoon's sale.' The auctioneer stared at Timothy, but he didn't even blink. 'The item is withdrawn.'

'And finally I turn to lot number five. A magnificent Louis XIV table, circa 1712, in almost mint condition. Its provenance can be traced back to its original owner, and it has been in the possession of Mr Barrington for the past eleven years. The full details are in your catalogue. I must warn you that there has been a lot of interest in this item, and I shall open the bidding at £50,000.'

Elizabeth immediately raised her catalogue above her head.

'Thank you, madam. I have a bid at the table of sixty thousand. Do I see seventy?' he asked, his eyes fixed on Elizabeth.

Her catalogue shot up again.

'Thank you, madam. I have a bid at the table of eighty thousand. Do I see ninety?' This time Elizabeth seemed to hesitate before raising her catalogue slowly.

'I have a bid at the table of one hundred thousand. Do I see a hundred and ten?'

Everyone in the room was now looking towards Elizabeth, except Hugh, who, head down, was staring at the floor. He obviously wasn't going to have any influence on the bidding. 'If there are no further bids, I shall have to withdraw this lot and place it in the afternoon sale. Fair warning,' declared Mr Botts. As he raised his hammer, Elizabeth's catalogue suddenly shot up.

'One hundred and ten thousand. Thank you, madam. Are there any more bids? Then I shall let this fine piece go for £110,000.' He brought down his hammer and smiled at Elizabeth. 'Congratulations, madam, it is indeed a magnificent example of the period.' She smiled weakly back, a look of uncertainty on her face.

Cornelius turned round and winked at Frank, who

remained impassively in his seat. He then rose from his place and made his way to the podium to thank Mr Botts for a job well done. As he turned to leave, he smiled at Margaret and Elizabeth, but neither acknowledged him, as they both seemed to be preoccupied. Hugh, head in hands, continued to stare down at the floor.

As Cornelius walked towards the back of the hall, he could see no sign of Timothy, and assumed that his nephew must have had to return to London. Cornelius was disappointed, as he had hoped the lad might join him for a pub lunch. After such a successful morning he felt a little celebrating was in order.

He had already decided that he wasn't going to attend the afternoon sale, as he had no desire to witness his worldly goods coming under the hammer, even though he wouldn't have room for most of them once he moved into a smaller house. Mr Botts had promised to call him the moment the sale was over and report how much the auction had raised.

Having enjoyed the best meal since Pauline had left him, Cornelius began his journey back from the pub to The Willows. He knew exactly what time the bus would appear to take him home, and arrived at the bus stop with a couple of minutes to spare. He now took it for granted that people would avoid his company.

Cornelius unlocked the front door as the clock on the nearby church struck three. He was looking forward to the inevitable fall-out when it sank in to Margaret and Elizabeth how much they had really bid. He grinned as he headed towards his study and glanced at his watch, wondering when he might expect a call from Mr Botts. The phone began to ring just as he entered the room. He chuckled to himself. It was too early for Mr Botts, so it had to be Elizabeth or Margaret, who would need to see him urgently. He picked up the phone to hear Frank's voice on the other end of the line.

'Did you remember to withdraw the chess set from the afternoon sale?' Frank asked, without bothering with any formalities.

'What are you talking about?' said Cornelius.

'Your beloved chess set. Have you forgotten that as it failed to sell this morning, it will automatically come up in the afternoon sale? Unless of course you've already given orders to withdraw it, or tipped off Mr Botts about its true value.'

'Oh my God,' said Cornelius. He dropped the phone and ran back out of the door, so he didn't hear Frank say, 'I'm sure a telephone call to Mr Botts's assistant is all that will be needed.'

Cornelius checked his watch as he ran down the path. It was ten past three, so the auction would have only just begun. Running towards the bus stop, he tried to recall what lot number the chess set was. All he could remember was that there were 153 lots in the sale.

Standing at the bus stop, hopping impatiently from foot to foot, he scanned the road in the hope of hailing a passing taxi, when to his relief he saw a bus heading towards him. Although his eyes never left the driver, that didn't make him go any faster.

When it eventually drew up beside him and the doors opened, Cornelius leapt on and took his place on the front seat. He wanted to tell the driver to take him straight to Botts and Co. in the High Street, and to hell with the fare, but he doubted if the other passengers would have fallen in with his plan.

He stared at his watch – 3.17 p.m. – and tried to remember how long it had taken Mr Botts that morning to dispose of each lot. About a minute, a minute and a half perhaps, he concluded. The bus came to a halt at every stop on its short journey into town, and Cornelius spent as much time following the progress of the minute hand on his watch as he did the journey. The driver finally reached the High Street at 3.31 p.m.

Even the door seemed to open slowly. Cornelius leapt out onto the pavement, and despite not having run for years, sprinted for the second time that day. He covered the two hundred yards to the auction house in less than record pace, but still arrived exhausted. He charged into the auction room as Mr Botts declared, 'Lot number 32, a long-case clock originally purchased from the estate of . . .'

Cornelius's eyes swept the room, coming to rest on an auctioneer's clerk who was standing in the corner with her catalogue open, entering the hammer price after each lot had been sold. He walked over to her just as a woman he thought he recognised slipped quickly past him and out of the door.

'Has the chess set come up yet?' asked a still-out-of-breath Cornelius.

'Let me just check, sir,' the clerk replied, flicking back through her catalogue. 'Yes, here it is, lot 27.'

'How much did it fetch?' asked Cornelius.

'£450, sir,' she replied.

—◁o▷—

Mr Botts called Cornelius later that evening to inform him that the afternoon sale had raised £902,800 – far more than he had estimated.

'Do you by any chance know who bought the chess set?' was Cornelius's only question.

'No,' replied Mr Botts. 'All I can tell you is that it was purchased on behalf of a client. The buyer paid in cash and took the item away.'

As he climbed the stairs to go to bed, Cornelius had to admit that everything had gone to plan except for the disastrous loss of the chess set, for which he realised he had only himself to blame. What made it worse was that he knew Frank would never refer to the incident again.

—◦—

Cornelius was in the bathroom when the phone rang at 7.30 the following morning. Obviously someone had been lying awake wondering what was the earliest moment they could possibly disturb him.

'Is that you, Cornelius?'

'Yes,' he replied, yawning noisily. 'Who's this?' he added, knowing only too well.

'It's Elizabeth. I'm sorry to call you so early, but I need to see you urgently.'

'Of course, my dear,' Cornelius replied, 'why don't you join me for tea this afternoon?'

'Oh no, it can't wait until then. I have to see you this morning. Could I come round at nine?'

'I'm sorry, Elizabeth, but I already have an appointment at nine.' He paused. 'But I could fit you in at ten for half an hour, then I won't be late for my meeting with Mr Botts at eleven.'

'I could give you a lift into town if that would help,' suggested Elizabeth.

'That's extremely kind of you, my dear,' said Cornelius, 'but I've got used to taking the bus, and in any case I wouldn't want to impose on you. Look forward to seeing you at ten.' He put the phone down.

Cornelius was still in the bath when the phone rang a second time. He wallowed in the warm water until the ringing had ceased. He knew it was Margaret, and he was sure she would call back within minutes.

He hadn't finished drying himself before the phone rang again. He walked slowly to the bedroom, picked up the receiver by his bed and said, 'Good morning Margaret.'

'Good morning, Cornelius,' she said, sounding surprised. Recovering quickly, she added, 'I need to see you urgently.'

'Oh? What's the problem?' asked Cornelius, well aware exactly what the problem was.

'I can't possibly discuss such a delicate matter over the phone, but I could be with you by ten.'

'I'm afraid I've already agreed to see Elizabeth at ten. It seems that she also has an urgent matter she needs to discuss with me. Why don't you come round at eleven?'

'Perhaps it would be better if I came over immediately,' said Margaret, sounding flustered.

'No, I'm afraid eleven is the earliest I can fit you in, my dear. So it's eleven or afternoon tea. Which would suit you best?'

'Eleven,' said Margaret without hesitation.

'I thought it might,' said Cornelius. 'I'll look forward to seeing you then,' he added before replacing the receiver.

When Cornelius had finished dressing, he went down to the kitchen for breakfast. A bowl of cornflakes, a copy of the local paper and an unstamped envelope were awaiting him, although there was no sign of Pauline.

He poured himself a cup of tea, tore open the envelope and extracted a cheque made out to him for £500. He sighed. Pauline must have sold her car.

He began to turn the pages of the Saturday supplement, stopping when he reached 'Houses for Sale'. When the phone rang for the third time that morning, he had no idea who it might be.

'Good morning, Mr Barrington,' said a cheerful voice. 'It's Bruce from the estate agents. I thought I'd give you a call to let you know we've had an offer for The Willows that is in excess of the asking price.'

'Well done,' said Cornelius.

'Thank you, sir,' said the agent, with more respect in his

voice than Cornelius had heard from anyone for weeks, 'but I think we should hold on for a little longer. I'm confident I can squeeze some more out of them. If I do, my advice would be to accept the offer and ask for a 10 per cent deposit.'

'That sounds like good advice to me,' said Cornelius. 'And once they've signed the contract, I'll need you to find me a new house.'

'What sort of thing are you looking for, Mr Barrington?'

'I want something about half the size of The Willows, with perhaps a couple of acres, and I'd like to remain in the immediate area.'

'That shouldn't be too hard, sir. We have one or two excellent houses on our books at the moment, so I'm sure we'll be able to accommodate you.'

'Thank you,' said Cornelius, delighted to have spoken to someone who had begun the day well.

He was chuckling over an item on the front page of the local paper when the doorbell rang. He checked his watch. It was still a few minutes to ten, so it couldn't be Elizabeth. When he opened the front door he was greeted by a man in a green uniform, holding a clipboard in one hand and a parcel in the other.

'Sign here,' was all the courier said, handing over a biro.

Cornelius scrawled his signature across the bottom of the form. He would have asked who had sent the parcel if he had not been distracted by a car coming up the drive.

'Thank you,' he said. He left the package in the hall and walked down the steps to welcome Elizabeth.

When the car drew up outside the front door, Cornelius was surprised to find Hugh seated in the passenger seat.

'It was kind of you to see us at such short notice,' said Elizabeth, who looked as if she had spent another sleepless night.

'Good morning, Hugh,' said Cornelius, who suspected his

brother had been kept awake all night. 'Please come through to the kitchen – I'm afraid it's the only room in the house that's warm.'

As he led them down the long corridor, Elizabeth stopped in front of the portrait of Daniel. 'I'm so glad to see it back in its rightful place,' she said. Hugh nodded his agreement.

Cornelius stared at the portrait, which he hadn't seen since the auction. 'Yes, back in its rightful place,' he said, before taking them through to the kitchen. 'Now, what brings you both to The Willows on a Saturday morning?' he asked as he filled the kettle.

'It's about the Louis XIV table,' said Elizabeth diffidently.

'Yes, I shall miss it,' said Cornelius. 'But it was a fine gesture on your part, Hugh,' he added.

'A fine gesture . . .' repeated Hugh.

'Yes. I assumed it was your way of returning my hundred thousand,' said Cornelius. Turning to Elizabeth, he said, 'How I misjudged you, Elizabeth. I suspect it was your idea all along.'

Elizabeth and Hugh just stared at each other, then both began speaking at once.

'But we didn't . . .' said Hugh.

'We were rather hoping . . .' said Elizabeth. Then they both fell silent.

'Tell him the truth,' said Hugh firmly.

'Oh?' said Cornelius. 'Have I misunderstood what took place at the auction yesterday morning?'

'Yes, I'm afraid you have,' said Elizabeth, any remaining colour draining from her cheeks. 'You see, the truth of the matter is that the whole thing got out of control, and I carried on bidding for longer than I should have done.' She paused. 'I'd never been to an auction before, and when I failed to get the grandfather clock, and then saw Margaret pick up the Turner so cheaply, I'm afraid I made a bit of a fool of myself.'

'Well, you can always put it back up for sale,' said Cornelius with mock sadness. 'It's a fine piece, and sure to retain its value.'

'We've already looked into that,' said Elizabeth. 'But Mr Botts says there won't be another furniture auction for at least three months, and the terms of the sale were clearly printed in the catalogue: settlement within seven days.'

'But I'm sure that if you were to leave the piece with him . . .'

'Yes, he suggested that,' said Hugh. 'But we didn't realise that the auctioneers add 15 per cent to the sale price, so the real bill is for £126,500. And what's worse, if we put it up for sale again they also retain 15 per cent of the price that's bid, so we would end up losing over thirty thousand.'

'Yes, that's the way auctioneers make their money,' said Cornelius with a sigh.

'But we don't have thirty thousand, let alone 126,500,' cried Elizabeth.

Cornelius slowly poured himself another cup of tea, pretending to be deep in thought. 'Umm,' he finally offered. 'What puzzles me is how you think I could help, bearing in mind my current financial predicament.'

'We thought that as the auction had raised nearly a million pounds . . .' began Elizabeth.

'Far higher than was estimated,' chipped in Hugh.

'We hoped you might tell Mr Botts you'd decided to keep the piece; and of course we would confirm that that was acceptable to us.'

'I'm sure you would,' said Cornelius, 'but that still doesn't solve the problem of owing the auctioneer £16,500, and a possible further loss if it fails to reach £110,000 in three months' time.'

Neither Elizabeth nor Hugh spoke.

'Do you have anything you could sell to help raise the money?' Cornelius eventually asked.

'Only our house, and that already has a large mortgage on it,' said Elizabeth.

'But what about your shares in the company? If you sold them, I'm sure they would more than cover the cost.'

'But who would want to buy them,' asked Hugh, 'when we're only just breaking even?'

'I would,' said Cornelius.

Both of them looked surprised. 'And in exchange for your shares,' Cornelius continued, 'I would release you from your debt to me, and also settle any embarrassment with Mr Botts.'

Elizabeth began to protest, but Hugh asked, 'Is there any alternative?'

'Not that I can think of,' said Cornelius.

'Then I don't see that we're left with much choice,' said Hugh, turning to his wife.

'But what about all those years we've put into the company?' wailed Elizabeth.

'The shop hasn't been showing a worthwhile profit for some time, Elizabeth, and you know it. If we don't accept Cornelius's offer, we could be paying off the debt for the rest of our lives.'

Elizabeth remained unusually silent.

'Well, that seems to be settled,' said Cornelius. 'Why don't you just pop round and have a word with my solicitor? He'll see that everything is in order.'

'And will you sort out Mr Botts?' asked Elizabeth.

'The moment you've signed over the shares, I'll deal with the problem of Mr Botts. I'm confident we can have everything settled by the end of the week.'

Hugh bowed his head.

'And I think it might be wise,' continued Cornelius – they both looked up and stared apprehensively at him – 'if Hugh were to remain on the board of the company as Chairman, with the appropriate remuneration.'

'Thank you,' said Hugh, shaking hands with his brother. 'That's generous of you in the circumstances.' As they returned down the corridor Cornelius stared at the portrait of his son once again.

'Have you managed to find somewhere to live?' asked Elizabeth.

'It looks as if that won't be a problem after all, thank you, Elizabeth. I've had an offer for The Willows far in excess of the price I'd anticipated, and what with the windfall from the auction, I'll be able to pay off all my creditors, leaving me with a comfortable sum over.'

'Then why do you need our shares?' asked Elizabeth, swinging back to face him.

'For the same reason you wanted my Louis XIV table, my dear,' said Cornelius as he opened the front door to show them out. 'Goodbye Hugh,' he added as Elizabeth got into the car.

Cornelius would have returned to the house, but he spotted Margaret coming up the drive in her new car, so he stood and waited for her. When she brought the little Audi to a halt, Cornelius opened the car door to allow her to step out.

'Good morning, Margaret,' he said as he accompanied her up the steps and into the house. 'How nice to see you back at The Willows. I can't remember when you were last here.'

'I've made a dreadful mistake,' his sister admitted, long before they had reached the kitchen.

Cornelius refilled the kettle and waited for her to tell him something he already knew.

'I won't beat about the bush, Cornelius. You see, I had no idea there were two Turners.'

'Oh, yes,' said Cornelius matter-of-factly. 'Joseph Mallord William Turner, arguably the finest painter ever to hail from these shores, and William Turner of Oxford, no relation, and although painting at roughly the same period, certainly not in the same league as the master.'

'But I didn't realise that . . .' Margaret repeated. 'So I ended up paying far too much for the wrong Turner – not helped by my sister-in-law's antics,' she added.

'Yes, I was fascinated to read in the morning paper that you've got yourself into the *Guinness Book of Records* for having paid a record price for the artist.'

'A record I could have done without,' said Margaret. 'I was rather hoping you might feel able to have a word with Mr Botts, and . . .'

'And what . . . ?' asked Cornelius innocently, as he poured his sister a cup of tea.

'Explain to him that it was all a terrible mistake.'

'I'm afraid that won't be possible, my dear. You see, once the hammer has come down, the sale is completed. That's the law of the land.'

'Perhaps you could help me out by paying for the picture,' Margaret suggested. 'After all, the papers are saying you made nearly a million pounds from the auction alone.'

'But I have so many other commitments to consider,' said Cornelius with a sigh. 'Don't forget that once The Willows is sold, I will have to find somewhere else to live.'

'But you could always come and stay with me . . .'

'That's the second such offer I've had this morning,' said Cornelius, 'and as I explained to Elizabeth, after being turned down by both of you earlier, I have had to make alternative arrangements.'

'Then I'm ruined,' said Margaret dramatically, 'because I don't have £10,000, not to mention the 15 per cent. Something else I didn't know about. You see, I'd hoped to make a small profit by putting the painting back up for sale at Christie's.'

The truth at last, thought Cornelius. Or perhaps half the truth.

'Cornelius, you've always been the clever one in the family,'

Margaret said, with tears welling up in her eyes. 'Surely you can think of a way out of this dilemma.'

Cornelius paced around the kitchen as if in deep thought, his sister watching his every step. Eventually he came to a halt in front of her. 'I do believe I may have a solution.'

'What is it?' cried Margaret. 'I'll agree to anything.'

'Anything?'

'Anything,' she repeated.

'Good, then I'll tell you what I'll do,' said Cornelius. 'I'll pay for the picture in exchange for your new car.'

Margaret remained speechless for some time. 'But the car cost me £12,000,' she said finally.

'Possibly, but you wouldn't get more than eight thousand for it second-hand.'

'But then how would I get around?'

'Try the bus,' said Cornelius. 'I can recommend it. Once you've mastered the timetable it changes your whole life.' He glanced at his watch. 'In fact, you could start right now; there's one due in about ten minutes.'

'But . . .' said Margaret as Cornelius stretched out his open hand. Then, letting out a long sigh, she opened her handbag and passed the car keys over to her brother.

'Thank you,' said Cornelius. 'Now I mustn't hold you up any longer, or you'll miss the bus, and there won't be another one along for thirty minutes.' He led his sister out of the kitchen and down the corridor. He smiled as he opened the door for her.

'And don't forget to pick up the picture from Mr Botts, my dear,' he said. 'It will look wonderful over the fireplace in your drawing room, and will bring back so many happy memories of our times together.'

Margaret didn't comment as she turned to walk off down the long drive.

Cornelius closed the door and was about to go to his study and call Frank to brief him on what had taken place that morning when he thought he heard a noise coming from the kitchen. He changed direction and headed back down the corridor. He walked into the kitchen, went over to the sink, bent down and kissed Pauline on the cheek.

'Good morning, Pauline,' he said.

'What's that for?' she asked, her hands immersed in soapy water.

'For bringing my son back home.'

'It's only on loan. If you don't behave yourself, it goes straight back to my place.'

Cornelius smiled. 'That reminds me – I'd like to take you up on your original offer.'

'What are you talking about, Mr Barrington?'

'You told me that you'd rather work off the debt than have to sell your car.' He removed her cheque from an inside pocket. 'I know just how many hours you've worked here over the past month,' he said, tearing the cheque in half, 'so let's call it quits.'

'That's very kind of you, Mr Barrington, but I only wish you'd told me that before I sold the car.'

'That's not a problem, Pauline, because I find myself the proud owner of a new car.'

'But how?' asked Pauline as she began to dry her hands.

'It was an unexpected gift from my sister,' Cornelius said, without further explanation.

'But you don't drive, Mr Barrington.'

'I know. So I'll tell you what I'll do,' said Cornelius. 'I'll swap it for the picture of Daniel.'

'But that's not a fair exchange, Mr Barrington. I only paid £50 for the picture, and the car must be worth far more.'

'Then you'll also have to agree to drive me into town from time to time.'

'Does that mean I've got my old job back?'

'Yes – if you're willing to give up your new one.'

'I don't have a new one,' said Pauline with a sigh. 'They found someone a lot younger than me the day before I was due to begin.'

Cornelius threw his arms around her.

'And we'll have less of that for a start, Mr Barrington.'

Cornelius took a pace back. 'Of course you can have your old job back, and with a rise in salary.'

'Whatever you consider is appropriate, Mr Barrington. After all, the labourer is worthy of his hire.'

Cornelius somehow stopped himself from laughing.

'Does this mean all the furniture will be coming back to The Willows?'

'No, Pauline. This house has been far too large for me since Millie's death. I should have realised that some time ago. I'm going to move out and look for something smaller.'

'I could have told you to do that years ago,' Pauline said. She hesitated. 'But will that nice Mr Vintcent still be coming to supper on Thursday evenings?'

'Until one of us dies, that's for sure,' said Cornelius with a chuckle.

'Well, I can't stand around all day chattering, Mr Barrington. After all, a woman's work is never done.'

'Quite so,' said Cornelius, and quickly left the kitchen. He walked back through the hall, picked up the package, and took it through to his study.

He had removed only the outer layer of wrapping paper when the phone rang. He put the package to one side and picked up the receiver to hear Timothy's voice.

'It was good of you to come to the auction, Timothy. I appreciated that.'

'I'm only sorry that my funds didn't stretch to buying you the chess set, Uncle Cornelius.'

'If only your mother and aunt had shown the same restraint . . .'

'I'm not sure I understand, Uncle.'

'It's not important,' said Cornelius. 'So, what can I do for you, young man?'

'You've obviously forgotten that I said I'd come over and read the rest of that story to you – unless of course you've already finished it.'

'No, I'd quite forgotten about it, what with the drama of the last few days. Why don't you come round tomorrow evening, then we can have supper as well. And before you groan, the good news is that Pauline is back.'

'That's excellent news, Uncle Cornelius. I'll see you around eight tomorrow.'

'I look forward to it,' said Cornelius. He replaced the receiver and returned to the half-opened package. Even before he had removed the final layer of paper, he knew exactly what was inside. His heart began beating faster. He finally raised the lid of the heavy wooden box and stared down at the thirty-two exquisite ivory pieces. There was a note inside: 'A small appreciation for all your kindness over the years. Hugh.'

Then he recalled the face of the woman who had slipped past him at the auction house. Of course, it had been his brother's secretary. The second time he had misjudged someone.

'What an irony,' he said out loud. 'If Hugh had put the set up for sale at Sotheby's, he could have held on to the Louis XIV table and had the same amount left over. Still, as Pauline would have said, it's the thought that counts.'

He was writing a thank-you note to his brother when the phone rang again. It was Frank, reliable as ever, reporting in on his meeting with Hugh.

'Your brother has signed all the necessary documents, and the shares have been transferred as requested.'

'That was quick work,' said Cornelius.

'The moment you gave me instructions last week, I had all the legal papers drawn up. You're still the most impatient client I have. Shall I bring the share certificates round on Thursday evening?'

'No,' said Cornelius. 'I'll drop in this afternoon and pick them up. That is, assuming Pauline is free to drive me into town.'

'Am I missing something?' asked Frank, sounding a little bewildered.

'Don't worry, Frank. I'll bring you up to date when I see you on Thursday evening.'

—◁○▷—

Timothy arrived at The Willows a few minutes after eight the following evening. Pauline immediately put him to work peeling potatoes.

'How are your mother and father?' asked Cornelius, probing to discover how much the boy knew.

'They seem fine, thank you Uncle. By the way, my father's offered me the job of shop manager. I begin on the first of next month.'

'Congratulations,' said Cornelius. 'I'm delighted. When did he make the offer?'

'Some time last week,' replied Timothy.

'Which day?'

'Is it important?' asked Timothy.

'I think it might be,' replied Cornelius, without explanation.

The young man remained silent for some time, before he finally said, 'Yes, it was Saturday evening, after I'd seen you.' He paused. 'I'm not sure Mum's all that happy about it. I meant to write and let you know, but as I was coming back for the auction, I thought I'd tell you in person. But then I didn't get a chance to speak to you.'

'So he offered you the job before the auction took place?'

'Oh yes,' said Timothy. 'Nearly a week before.' Once again, the young man looked quizzically at his uncle, but still no explanation was forthcoming.

Pauline placed a plate of roast beef in front of each of them as Timothy began to reveal his plans for the company's future.

'Mind you, although Dad will remain as Chairman,' he said, 'he's promised not to interfere too much. I was wondering, Uncle Cornelius, now that you own 1 per cent of the company, whether you would be willing to join the board?'

Cornelius looked first surprised, then delighted, then doubtful.

'I could do with your experience,' added Timothy, 'if I'm to go ahead with my expansion plans.'

'I'm not sure your father would consider it a good idea to have me on the board,' said Cornelius, with a wry smile.

'I can't think why not,' said Timothy. 'After all, it was his idea in the first place.'

Cornelius remained silent for some time. He hadn't expected to go on learning more about the players after the game was officially over.

'I think the time has come for us to go upstairs and find out if it's Simon Kerslake or Raymond Gould who becomes Prime Minister,' he eventually said.

Timothy waited until his uncle had poured himself a large brandy and lit a cigar – his first for a month – before he started to read.

He became so engrossed in the story that he didn't look up again until he had turned the last page, where he found an envelope sellotaped to the inside of the book's cover. It was addressed to 'Mr Timothy Barrington'.

'What's this?' he asked.

Cornelius would have told him, but he had fallen asleep.

—◦—

The doorbell rang at eight, as it did every Thursday evening. When Pauline opened the door, Frank handed her a large bunch of flowers.

'Oh, Mr Barrington will appreciate those,' she said. 'I'll put them in the library.'

'They're not for Mr Barrington,' said Frank, with a wink.

'I'm sure I don't know what's come over you two gentlemen,' Pauline said, scurrying away to the kitchen.

As Frank dug into a second bowl of Irish stew, Cornelius warned him that it could be their last meal together at The Willows.

'Does that mean you've sold the house?' Frank asked, looking up.

'Yes. We exchanged contracts this afternoon, but on the condition that I move out immediately. After such a generous offer, I'm in no position to argue.'

'And how's the search for a new place coming along?'

'I think I've found the ideal house, and once the surveyors have given the all clear, I'll be putting an offer in. I'll need you to push the paperwork through as quickly as possible so that I'm not homeless for too long.'

'I certainly will,' said Frank, 'but in the meantime, you'd better come and camp out with me. I'm all too aware what the alternatives are.'

'The local pub, Elizabeth or Margaret,' said Cornelius, with a grin. He raised his glass. 'Thank you for the offer. I accept.'

'But there's one condition,' said Frank.

'And what might that be?' asked Cornelius.

'That Pauline comes as part of the package, because I have no intention of spending all my spare time tidying up after you.'

'What do you think about that, Pauline?' asked Cornelius as she began to clear away the plates.

'I'm willing to keep house for both of you gentlemen, but only for one month. Otherwise you'd never move out, Mr Barrington.'

'I'll make sure there are no hold-ups with the legal work, I promise,' said Frank.

Cornelius leant across to him conspiratorially. 'She hates lawyers, you know, but I do think she's got a soft spot for you.'

'That may well be the case, Mr Barrington, but it won't stop me leaving after a month, if you haven't moved into your new house.'

'I think you'd better put down that deposit fairly quickly,' said Frank. 'Good houses come on the market all the time, good housekeepers rarely.'

'Isn't it time you two gentlemen got on with your game?'

'Agreed,' said Cornelius. 'But first, a toast.'

'Who to?' asked Frank.

'Young Timothy,' said Cornelius, raising his glass, 'who will start as Managing Director of Barrington's, Chudley, on the first of the month.'

'To Timothy,' said Frank, raising his glass.

'You know he's asked me to join the board,' said Cornelius.

'You'll enjoy that, and he'll benefit from your experience. But it still doesn't explain why you gave him all your shares in the company, despite him failing to secure the chess set for you.'

'That's precisely why I was willing to let him take control of the company. Timothy, unlike his mother and father, didn't allow his heart to rule his head.'

Frank nodded his approval as Cornelius drained the last drop of wine from the one glass they allowed themselves before a game.

'Now, I feel I ought to warn you,' said Cornelius as he rose from his place, 'that the only reason you have won the last three encounters in a row is simply because I have had other things on my mind. Now that those matters have been resolved, your run of luck is about to come to an end.'

'We shall see,' said Frank, as they marched down the long corridor together. The two men stopped for a moment to admire the portrait of Daniel.

'How did you get that back?' asked Frank.

'I had to strike a mean bargain with Pauline, but we both ended up with what we wanted.'

'But how . . . ?' began Frank.

'It's a long story,' Cornelius replied, 'and I'll tell you the details over a brandy after I've won the game.'

Cornelius opened the library door and allowed his friend to enter ahead of him, so that he could observe his reaction. When the inscrutable lawyer saw the chess set laid out before him, he made no comment, but simply walked across to the far side of the table, took his usual place and said, 'Your move first, if I remember correctly.'

'You're right,' said Cornelius, trying to hide his irritation. He pushed his queen's pawn to Q4.

'Back to an orthodox opening gambit. I see I shall have to concentrate tonight.'

They had been playing for about an hour, no word having passed between them, when Cornelius could bear it no longer. 'Are you not in the least bit curious to discover how I came back into possession of the chess set?' he asked.

'No,' said Frank, his eyes remaining fixed on the board. 'Not in the least bit.'

'But why not, you old dullard?'

'Because I already know,' Frank said as he moved his queen's bishop across the board.

'How can you possibly know?' demanded Cornelius, who responded by moving a knight back to defend his king.

Frank smiled. 'You forget that Hugh is also my client,' he said, moving his king's rook two squares to the right.

Cornelius smiled. 'And to think he need never have sacrificed his shares, if he had only known the true value of the chess set.' He returned his queen to its home square.

'But he did know its true value,' said Frank, as he considered his opponent's last move.

'How could he possibly have found out, when you and I were the only people who knew?'

'Because I told him,' said Frank matter-of-factly.

'But why would you do that?' asked Cornelius, staring across at his oldest friend.

'Because it was the only way I could find out if Hugh and Elizabeth were working together.'

'So why didn't he bid for the set in the morning auction?'

'Precisely because he didn't want Elizabeth to know what he was up to. Once he discovered that Timothy was also hoping to purchase the set in order to give it back to you, he remained silent.'

'But he could have kept bidding once Timothy had fallen out.'

'No, he couldn't. He had agreed to bid for the Louis XIV table, if you recall, and that was the last item to come under the hammer.'

'But Elizabeth failed to get the long-case clock, so she could have bid for it.'

'Elizabeth is not my client,' said Frank, as he moved his queen across the board. 'So she never discovered the chess set's true value. She believed what you had told her – that at best it was worth a few hundred pounds – which is why Hugh instructed his secretary to bid for the set in the afternoon.'

'Sometimes you can miss the most obvious things, even when they are staring you right in the face,' said Cornelius, pushing his rook five squares forward.

'I concur with that judgement,' said Frank, moving his queen across to take Cornelius's rook. He looked up at his opponent and said, 'I think you'll find that's checkmate.'

THE LETTER

ALL THE GUESTS were seated around the breakfast table when Muriel Arbuthnot strode into the room, clutching the morning post. She extracted a long white envelope from the pile and handed it over to her oldest chum.

A puzzled look came over Anna Clairmont's face. Who could possibly know that she was spending the weekend with the Arbuthnots? Then she saw the familiar handwriting, and had to smile at his ingenuity. She hoped her husband Robert, who was seated at the far end of the table, hadn't noticed, and was relieved to see that he remained engrossed in his copy of *The Times*.

Anna was trying to wedge her thumb into the corner of the envelope while keeping a wary eye on Robert, when suddenly he glanced across at her and smiled. She returned the smile, dropped the envelope in her lap, picked up her fork and jabbed it into a lukewarm mushroom.

She made no attempt to retrieve the letter until her husband had disappeared back behind his paper. Once he had turned to the business section, she placed the envelope on her right-hand side, picked up the butter knife and slipped it into the thumbed corner. Slowly, she began to slit open the envelope. Having completed the task, she returned the knife to its place by the side of the butter dish.

Before making her next move, she once again glanced across in the direction of her husband, to check that he was still hidden behind his newspaper. He was.

She held down the envelope with her left hand, while carefully extracting the letter with her right. She then placed the envelope in the bag by her side.

She looked down at the familiar Basildon Bond cream notepaper, folded in three. One more casual glance in Robert's direction; as he remained out of sight, she unfolded the two-page letter.

No date, no address, the first page, as always, written on continuation paper.

'*My darling Titania*'. The first night of the *Dream* at Stratford, followed by the first night they had slept together. Two firsts on the same night, he had remarked. '*I am sitting in my bedroom, our bedroom, penning these thoughts only moments after you have left me. This is a third attempt, as I can't find the right words to let you know how I really feel.*'

Anna smiled. For a man who had made his fortune with words, that must have been quite difficult for him to admit.

'*Last night you were everything a man could ask from a lover. You were exciting, tender, provocative, teasing, and, for an exquisite moment, a rampant whore.*

'*It's been over a year since we met at the Selwyns' dinner party in Norfolk, and, as I have often told you, I wanted you to come back home with me that evening. I lay awake all night imagining you lying next to the prune.*' Anna glanced across the table to see that Robert had reached the back page of his paper.

'*And then there was that chance meeting at Glyndebourne – but it was still to be another eleven days before you were unfaithful for the first time, and then not until the prune was away in Brussels. That night went far too quickly for me.*

'I can't imagine what the prune would have made of it, if he had seen you in your maid's outfit. He'd have probably assumed that you always tidied up the drawing room in Lonsdale Avenue in a white see-through blouse, no bra, a skin-tight black leather skirt with a zip up the front, fishnet stockings and stiletto heels, not forgetting the shocking-pink lipstick.'

Anna looked up again and wondered if she was blushing. If he had really enjoyed himself that much, she would have to go on another shopping trip in Soho as soon as she got back to town. She continued to read the letter.

'My darling, there is no aspect of our lovemaking that I don't relish, but I confess that what turns me on the most is the places you choose when you can only take an hour off work during your lunch break. I can recall every one of them. On the back seat of my Mercedes in that NCP carpark in Mayfair; the service lift in Harrods; the loo at the Caprice. But most exciting of all was that little box in the dress circle at Covent Garden during a performance of Tristan and Isolde. *Once before the first interval and then again during the final act – well, it is a long opera.'*

Anna giggled and quickly placed the letter back into her lap as Robert peered round the side of his newspaper.

'What made you laugh, my dear?' he asked.

'The picture of James Bond landing on the Dome,' she said. Robert looked puzzled. 'On the front of your paper.'

'Ah, yes,' said Robert, glancing at the front page, but he didn't smile as he returned to the business section.

Anna retrieved the letter.

'What maddens me most about your spending the weekend with Muriel and Reggie Arbuthnot is the thought of you being in the same bed as the prune. I've tried to convince myself that as the Arbuthnots are related to the Royal family, they've probably given you separate bedrooms.'

Anna nodded, wishing she could tell him he had guessed correctly.

'*And does he really snore like the* QE II *coming into Southampton harbour? I can see him now, sitting on the far side of the breakfast table. Harris tweed jacket, grey trousers, checked shirt, wearing an MCC tie, as thought to be fashionable by* Hare and Hound *circa 1966.*'

This time Anna did burst out laughing, and was only rescued by Reggie Arbuthnot rising from his end of the table to enquire, 'Anyone care to make up a four for tennis? The weather forecast is predicting that the rain will stop long before the morning's out.'

'I'll be happy to join you,' said Anna, secreting the letter back under the table.

'How about you, Robert?' Reggie asked.

Anna watched as her husband folded up *The Times*, placed it on the table in front of him and shook his head.

Oh my God, thought Anna. He *is* wearing a tweed jacket and an MCC tie.

'I'd love to,' said Robert, 'but I'm afraid I have to make several phone calls.'

'On a Saturday morning?' said Muriel, who was standing at the laden sideboard, filling her plate for a second time.

'Afraid so,' replied Robert. 'You see, criminals don't work a five-day, forty-hour week, so they don't expect their lawyers to do so either.' Anna didn't laugh. After all, she had heard him make the same observation every Saturday for the past seven years.

Robert rose from the table, glanced towards his wife and said, 'If you need me, my dear, I'll be in my bedroom.'

Anna nodded and waited for him to leave the room.

She was about to return to her letter when she noticed that Robert had left his glasses on the table. She would take them through to him as soon as she had finished breakfast. She placed the letter on the table in front of her and turned to the second page:

'*Let me tell you what I have planned for our anniversary weekend while the prune is away at his conference in Leeds. I've booked us back into the Lygon Arms, so we'll be in the same room in which we spent our first night together. This time I've got tickets for* All's Well. *But I plan a change of atmosphere once we have returned from Stratford to the privacy of our room in Broadway.*

'*I want to be tied up to a four-poster bed, with you standing over me in a police sergeant's uniform: truncheon, whistle, handcuffs, wearing a tight black outfit with silver buttons down the front, which you will undo slowly to reveal a black bra. And, my darling, you're not to release me until I have made you scream at the top of your voice, the way you did in that underground carpark in Mayfair.*

'*Until then,*

'*Your loving Oberon.*'

Anna raised her head and smiled, wondering where she could get her hands on a police sergeant's uniform. She was about to turn back to the front page and read the letter again when she noticed the P.S.

'*P.S. I wonder what the prune is up to right now.*'

Anna looked up to see that Robert's glasses were no longer on the table.

'What scoundrel could write such an outrageous letter to a married woman?' demanded Robert as he adjusted his glasses.

Anna turned, horrified to see her husband standing behind her and staring down at the letter, beads of sweat appearing on his forehead.

'Don't ask me,' said Anna coolly, as Muriel appeared by her side, tennis racket in hand. Anna folded her letter, passed it over to her oldest friend, winked and said, 'Fascinating, my dear, but for your sake I do hope Reggie never finds out.'

CRIME PAYS*

KENNY MERCHANT – that wasn't his real name, but then, little was real about Kenny – had selected Harrods on a quiet Monday morning as the venue for the first part of the operation.

Kenny was dressed in a pinstriped suit, white shirt and Guards tie. Few of the shop's customers would have realised it was a Guards tie, but he was confident that the assistant he had selected to serve him would recognise the crimson and dark-blue stripes immediately.

The door was held open for him by a commissionaire who had served in the Coldstream Guards, and who on spotting the tie immediately saluted him. The same commissionaire had not saluted him on any of his several visits during the previous week, but to be fair, Kenny had been dressed then in a shiny, well-worn suit, open-necked shirt and dark glasses. But last week had only been for reconnaissance; today he planned to be arrested.

Although Harrods has over a hundred thousand customers a week, the quietest period is always between ten and eleven on a Monday morning. Kenny knew every detail about the great store, in the way a football fan knows all the statistics of his favourite team.

He knew where all the CCTV cameras were placed, and

could recognise any of the security guards at thirty paces. He even knew the name of the assistant who would be serving him that morning, although Mr Parker had no idea that he had been selected as a tiny cog in Kenny's well-oiled machine.

When Kenny appeared at the jewellery department that morning, Mr Parker was briefing a young assistant on the changes he required to the shelf display.

'Good morning, sir,' he said, turning to face his first customer of the day. 'How can I help you?'

'I was looking for a pair of cufflinks,' Kenny said, in the clipped tones he hoped made him sound like a Guards officer.

'Yes, of course sir,' said Mr Parker.

It amused Kenny to see the deferential treatment he received as a result of the Guards tie, which he had been able to purchase in the men's department the previous day for an outlay of £23.

'Any particular style?' asked the sales assistant.

'I'd prefer silver.'

'Of course, sir,' said Mr Parker, who proceeded to place on the counter several boxes of silver cufflinks.

Kenny already knew the pair he wanted, as he had picked them out the previous Saturday afternoon. 'What about those?' he asked, pointing to the top shelf. As the sales assistant turned away, Kenny checked the TV surveillance camera and took a pace to his right, to be sure that they could see him more clearly. While Mr Parker reached up to remove the cufflinks, Kenny slid the chosen pair off the counter and slipped them into his jacket pocket before the assistant turned back round.

Out of the corner of his eye, Kenny saw a security guard moving swiftly towards him, while at the same time speaking into his walkie-talkie.

'Excuse me, sir,' said the guard, touching his elbow. 'I wonder if you would be kind enough to accompany me.'

'What's this all about?' demanded Kenny, trying to sound annoyed, as a second security guard appeared on his other side.

'Perhaps it might be wise if you were to accompany us, so that we can discuss the matter privately,' suggested the second guard, holding onto his arm a little more firmly.

'I've never been so insulted in my life,' said Kenny, now speaking at the top of his voice. He took the cufflinks out of his pocket, replaced them on the counter and added, 'I had every intention of paying for them.'

The guard picked up the box. To his surprise the irate customer then accompanied him to the interview room without uttering another word.

On entering the little green-walled room, Kenny was asked to take a seat on the far side of a desk. One guard returned to his duties on the ground floor while the other remained by the door. Kenny knew that on an average day, forty-two people were arrested for shoplifting at Harrods, and over 90 per cent of them were prosecuted.

A few moments later, the door opened and a tall, thin man with a weary look on his face entered the room. He took a seat on the other side of the desk and glanced across at Kenny before pulling open a drawer and removing a green form.

'Name?' he said.

'Kenny Merchant,' Kenny replied without hesitation.

'Address?'

'42 St Luke's Road, Putney.'

'Occupation?'

'Unemployed.'

Kenny spent several more minutes accurately answering the tall man's enquiries. When the inquisitor reached his final question, he spent a moment studying the silver cufflinks before filling in the bottom line. Value: £90. Kenny knew all too well the significance of that particular sum.

The form was then swivelled round for Kenny to sign, which to the inquisitor's surprise he did with a flourish.

The guard then accompanied Kenny to an adjoining room, where he was kept waiting for almost an hour. The guard was surprised that Kenny didn't ask what would happen next. All the others did. But then, Kenny knew exactly what was going to happen next, despite the fact that he had never been charged with shoplifting before.

About an hour later the police arrived and he was driven, along with five others, to Horseferry Road Magistrates' Court. There followed another long wait before he came up in front of the magistrate. The charge was read out to him and he pleaded guilty. As the value of the cufflinks was under £100, Kenny knew he would receive a fine rather than a custodial sentence, and he waited patiently for the magistrate to ask the same question he had when Kenny had sat at the back of the court and listened to several cases the previous week.

'Is there anything else you would like me to take into consideration before I pass sentence?'

'Yes, sir,' said Kenny. 'I stole a watch from Selfridges last week. It's been on my conscience ever since, and I would like to return it.' He beamed up at the magistrate.

The magistrate nodded and, looking down at the defendant's address on the form in front of him, ordered that a constable should accompany Mr Merchant to his home and retrieve the stolen merchandise. For a moment the magistrate almost looked as if he was going to praise the convicted criminal for his act of good citizenship, but like Mr Parker, the guard and the inquisitor, he didn't realise he was simply another cog in a bigger wheel.

Kenny was driven to his home in Putney by a young constable, who told him that he'd only been on the job for a few weeks. Then you're in for a bit of a shock, thought Kenny as he unlocked the front door of his home and invited the officer in.

'Oh my God,' said the young man the moment he stepped into the sitting room. He turned, ran back out of the flat and immediately called his station sergeant on the car radio. Within minutes, two patrol cars were parked outside Kenny's home in St Luke's Road. Chief Inspector Travis marched through the open door to find Kenny sitting in the hall, holding up the stolen watch.

'To hell with the watch,' said the Chief Inspector. 'What about this lot?' he said, his arms sweeping around the sitting room.

'It's all mine,' said Kenny. 'The only thing I admit to stealing, and am now returning, is one watch. Timex Masterpiece, value £44, taken from Selfridges.'

'What's your game, laddie?' asked Travis.

'I have no idea what you mean,' said Kenny innocently.

'You know exactly what I mean,' said the Chief Inspector. 'This place is full of expensive jewellery, paintings, *objets d'art* and antique furniture' – around £300,000-worth, Kenny would have liked to have told him – 'and I don't believe any of it belongs to you.'

'Then you'll have to prove it, Chief Inspector, because should you fail to do so, the law assumes that it belongs to me. And that being the case, I will be able to dispose of it as I wish.' The Chief Inspector frowned, informed Kenny of his rights and arrested him for theft.

When Kenny next appeared in court, it was at the Old Bailey, in front of a judge. Kenny was dressed appropriately for the occasion in a pinstriped suit, white shirt and Guards tie. He stood in the dock charged with the theft of goods to the value of £24,000.

The police had made a complete inventory of everything

they found in the flat, and spent the next six months trying to trace the owners of the treasure trove. But despite advertising in all the recognised journals, and even showing the stolen goods extensively on television's *Crimewatch*, as well as putting them on display for the public to view, over 80 per cent of the items remained unclaimed.

Chief Inspector Travis tried to bargain with Kenny, saying he would recommend a lenient sentence if he would cooperate and reveal who the property belonged to.

'It all belongs to me,' repeated Kenny.

'If that's going to be your game, don't expect any help from us,' said the Chief Inspector.

Kenny hadn't expected any help from Travis in the first place. It had never been part of his original plan.

Kenny had always believed that if you penny-pinch when it comes to selecting a lawyer, you could well end up paying dearly for it. So when he stood in the dock he was represented by a leading firm of solicitors and a silky barrister called Arden Duveen, QC, who wanted £10,000 on his brief.

Kenny pleaded guilty to the indictment, aware that when the police gave evidence they would be unable to mention any of the goods that had remained unclaimed, and which the law therefore assumed belonged to him. In fact, the police had already reluctantly returned the property that they were unable to prove had been stolen, and Kenny had quickly passed it on to a dealer for a third of its value, compared with the tenth he had been offered by a fence six months before.

Mr Duveen, QC, defending, pointed out to the judge that not only was it his client's first offence, but that he had invited the police to accompany him to his home, well aware that they would discover the stolen goods and that he would be arrested. Could there be better proof of a repentant and remorseful man, he asked.

Mr Duveen went on to point out to the court that Mr Merchant had served nine years in the armed services, and had been honourably discharged following active service in the Gulf, but that since leaving the army he seemed unable to settle down to civilian life. Mr Duveen did not claim this as an excuse for his client's behaviour, but he wished the court to know that Mr Merchant had vowed never to commit such a crime again, and therefore pleaded with the judge to impose a lenient sentence.

Kenny stood in the dock, his head bowed.

The judge lectured him for some time on how evil his crime had been, but added that he had taken into consideration all the mitigating circumstances surrounding this case, and had settled on a prison sentence of two years.

Kenny thanked him, and assured him that he would not be bothering him again. He knew that the next crime he had planned could not end up with a prison sentence.

Chief Inspector Travis watched as Kenny was taken down, then, turning to the prosecuting counsel, asked, 'How much do you imagine that bloody man has made by keeping to the letter of the law?'

'About a hundred thousand would be my bet,' replied the Crown's silk.

'More than I'd be able to put by in a lifetime,' the Chief Inspector commented, before uttering a string of words that no one present felt able to repeat to their wives over dinner that evening.

Prosecuting counsel was not far out. Kenny had deposited a cheque at the Hongkong and Shanghai Bank earlier that week for £86,000.

What the Chief Inspector couldn't know was that Kenny had completed only half of his plan, and that now the seed money was in place, he was ready to prepare for an early retirement. Before he was taken away to prison, he made one further request of his solicitor.

◄o►

While Kenny was holed up in Ford Open Prison he used his time well. He spent every spare moment going over various Acts of Parliament that were currently being debated in the House of Commons. He quickly dismissed several Green Papers, White Papers and Bills on health, education and the social services, before he came across the Data Protection Bill, each clause of which he set about studying as assiduously as any Member of the House of Commons at the report stage of the Bill. He followed each new amendment that was placed before the House, and each new clause as it was passed. Once the Act had become law in 1992, he sought a further interview with his solicitor.

The solicitor listened carefully to Kenny's questions and, finding himself out of his depth, admitted he would have to seek counsel's opinion. 'I will get in touch with Mr Duveen immediately,' he said.

While Kenny waited for his QC's judgement, he asked to be supplied with copies of every business magazine published in the United Kingdom.

The solicitor tried not to look puzzled by this request, as he had done when he had been asked to supply every Act of Parliament currently being debated in the House of Commons. During the next few weeks, bundles and bundles of magazines arrived at the prison, and Kenny spent all his spare time cutting out any advertisements that appeared in three magazines or more.

A year to the day after Kenny had been sentenced, he was released on parole following his exemplary behaviour. When he walked out of Ford Open Prison, having served only half his term, the one thing he took with him was a large brown envelope containing three thousand advertisements and the written opinion of leading counsel on clause 9, paragraph 6, subsection (a) of the Data Protection Act 1992.

A week later, Kenny took a flight to Hong Kong.

◄○►

The Hong Kong police reported back to Chief Inspector Travis that Mr Merchant had booked into a small hotel, and spent his days visiting local printers, seeking quotes for the publication of a magazine entitled *Business Enterprise UK*, and the retail price of headed notepaper and envelopes. The magazine, they quickly discovered, would contain a few articles on finance and shares, but the bulk of its pages would be taken up with small advertisements.

The Hong Kong police confessed themselves puzzled when they discovered how many copies of the magazine Kenny had ordered to be printed.

'How many?' asked Chief Inspector Travis.

'Ninety-nine.'

'Ninety-nine? There has to be a reason,' was Travis's immediate response.

He was even more puzzled when he discovered that there was already a magazine called *Business Enterprise*, and that it published 10,000 copies a month.

The Hong Kong police later reported that Kenny had ordered 2,500 sheets of headed paper, and 2,500 brown envelopes.

'So what's he up to?' demanded Travis.

No one in Hong Kong or London could come up with a convincing suggestion.

Three weeks later, the Hong Kong police reported that Mr Merchant had been seen at a local post office, despatching 2,400 letters to addresses all over the United Kingdom.

The following week, Kenny flew back to Heathrow.

◄○►

Although Travis kept Kenny under surveillance, the young constable was unable to report anything untoward, other than that the local postman had told him Mr Merchant was receiving around twenty-five letters a day, and that like clockwork he would drop into Lloyd's Bank in the King's Road around noon and deposit several cheques for amounts ranging from two hundred to two thousand pounds. The constable didn't report that Kenny gave him a wave every morning just before entering the bank.

After six months the letters slowed to a trickle, and Kenny's visits to the bank almost came to a halt.

The only new piece of information the Constable was able to pass on to Chief Inspector Travis was that Mr Merchant had moved from his small flat in St Luke's Road, Putney, to an imposing four-storey mansion in Chester Square, SW1.

Just as Travis turned his attention to more pressing cases, Kenny flew off to Hong Kong again. 'Almost a year to the day,' was the Chief Inspector's only comment.

The Hong Kong police reported back to the Chief Inspector that Kenny was following roughly the same routine as he had the previous year, the only difference being that this time he had booked himself into a suite at the Mandarin. He had selected the same printer, who confirmed that his client had made another order for *Business Enterprise UK*. The second issue had some new articles, but would contain only 1,971 advertisements.

'How many copies is he having published this time?' asked the Chief Inspector.

'The same as before,' came back the reply. 'Ninety-nine. But he's only ordered two thousand sheets of headed paper and two thousand envelopes.'

'What is he up to?' repeated the Chief Inspector. He received no reply.

Once the magazine had rolled off the presses, Kenny

returned to the post office and sent out 1,971 letters, before taking a flight back to London, care of British Airways, first class.

Travis knew Kenny must be breaking the law somehow, but he had neither the staff nor the resources to follow it up. And Kenny might have continued to milk this particular cow indefinitely had a complaint from a leading company on the stock exchange not landed on the Chief Inspector's desk.

A Mr Cox, the company's financial director, reported that he had received an invoice for £500 for an advertisement his firm had never placed.

The Chief Inspector visited Mr Cox in his City office. After a long discussion, Cox agreed to assist the police by pressing charges.

The Crown took the best part of six months to prepare its case before sending it to the CPS for consideration. They took almost as long before deciding to prosecute, but once they had, the Chief Inspector drove straight to Chester Square and personally arrested Kenny on a charge of fraud.

Mr Duveen appeared in court the following morning, insisting that his client was a model citizen. The judge granted Kenny bail, but demanded that he lodge his passport with the court.

'That's fine by me,' Kenny told his solicitor. 'I won't be needing it for a couple of months.'

◄○►

The trial opened at the Old Bailey six weeks later, and once again Kenny was represented by Mr Duveen. While Kenny stood to attention in the dock, the clerk of the court read out seven charges of fraud. On each charge he pleaded not guilty. Prosecuting counsel made his opening statement, but the jury, as in so many financial trials, didn't look as if they were following his detailed submissions.

Kenny accepted that twelve good men and women true would decide whether they believed him or Mr Cox, as there wasn't much hope that they would understand the niceties of the 1992 Data Protection Act.

When Mr Cox read out the oath on the third day, Kenny felt he was the sort of man you could trust with your last penny. In fact, he thought he might even invest a few thousand in his company.

Mr Matthew Jarvis, QC, counsel for the Crown, took Mr Cox through a series of gentle questions designed to show him to be a man of such probity that he felt it was nothing less than his public duty to ensure that the evil fraud perpetrated by the defendant was stamped out once and for all.

Mr Duveen rose to cross-examine him.

'Let me begin, Mr Cox, by asking you if you ever saw the advertisement in question.'

Mr Cox stared down at him in righteous indignation.

'Yes, of course I did,' he replied.

'Was it of a quality that in normal circumstances would have been acceptable to your company?'

'Yes, but . . .'

'No "buts", Mr Cox. It either was, or it was not, of a quality acceptable to your company.'

'It was,' replied Mr Cox, through pursed lips.

'Did your company end up paying for the advertisement?'

'Certainly not,' said Mr Cox. 'A member of my staff queried the invoice, and immediately brought it to my attention.'

'How commendable,' said Duveen. 'And did that same member of staff spot the wording concerning payment of the invoice?'

'No, it was I who spotted that,' said Mr Cox, looking towards the jury with a smile of satisfaction.

'Most impressive, Mr Cox. And can you still recall the exact wording on the invoice?'

'Yes, I think so,' said Mr Cox. He hesitated, but only for a moment. '"If you are dissatisfied with the product, there is no obligation to pay this invoice."'

'"No obligation to pay this invoice,"' repeated Duveen.

'Yes,' Mr Cox replied. 'That's what it stated.'

'So you didn't pay the bill?'

'No, I did not.'

'Allow me to sum up your position, Mr Cox. You received a free advertisement in my client's magazine, of a quality that would have been acceptable to your company had it been in any other periodical. Is that correct?'

'Yes, but . . .' began Mr Cox.

'No more questions, m'lud.'

Duveen had avoided mentioning those clients who *had* paid for their advertisements, as none of them was willing to appear in court for fear of the adverse publicity that would follow. Kenny felt his QC had destroyed the prosecution's star witness, but Duveen warned him that Jarvis would try to do the same to him the moment he stepped into the witness box.

The judge suggested a break for lunch. Kenny didn't eat – he just perused the Data Protection Act once again.

When the court resumed after lunch, Mr Duveen informed the judge that he would be calling only the defendant.

Kenny entered the witness box dressed in a dark-blue suit, white shirt and Guards tie.

Mr Duveen spent some considerable time allowing Kenny to take him through his army career and the service he had given to his country in the Gulf, without touching on the service he had more recently given at Her Majesty's pleasure. He then proceeded to guide Kenny through the evidence in brief. By the time Duveen had resumed his place, the jury were in no doubt that they were dealing with a businessman of unimpeachable rectitude.

Mr Matthew Jarvis QC rose slowly from his place, and

made great play of rearranging his papers before asking his first question.

'Mr Merchant, allow me to begin by asking you about the periodical in question, *Business Enterprise UK*. Why did you select that particular name for your magazine?'

'It represents everything I believe in.'

'Yes, I'm sure it does, Mr Merchant, but isn't the truth that you were trying to mislead potential advertisers into confusing your publication with *Business Enterprise*, a magazine of many years' standing and an impeccable reputation. Isn't that what you were really up to?'

'No more than *Woman* does with *Woman's Own*, or *House and Garden* with *Homes and Gardens*,' Kenny retorted.

'But all the magazines you have just mentioned sell many thousands of copies. How many copies of *Business Enterprise UK* did you publish?'

'Ninety-nine,' replied Kenny.

'Only ninety-nine? Then it was hardly likely to top the bestsellers' list, was it? Please enlighten the court as to why you settled on that particular figure.'

'Because it is fewer than a hundred, and the Data Protection Act 1992 defines a publication as consisting of at least one hundred copies. Clause 2, subsection 11.'

'That may well be the case, Mr Merchant, which is all the more reason,' suggested Mr Jarvis, 'that to expect clients to pay £500 for an unsolicited advertisement in your magazine was outrageous.'

'Outrageous, perhaps, but not a crime,' said Kenny, with a disarming smile.

'Allow me to move on, Mr Merchant. Perhaps you could explain to the court on what you based your decision, when it came to charging each company.'

'I found out how much their accounts departments were

authorised to spend without having to refer to higher authority.'

'And what deception did you perpetrate to discover that piece of information?'

'I called the accounts department and asked to speak to the billing clerk.'

A ripple of laughter ran through the courtroom. The judge cleared his throat theatrically and demanded the court come to order.

'And on that alone you based your decision on how much to charge?'

'Not entirely. You see, I did have a rate card. Prices varied between £2,000 for a full-colour page and £200 for a quarter-page, black and white. I think you'll find we're fairly competitive – if anything, slightly below the national average.'

'Certainly you were below the national average for the number of copies produced,' snapped Mr Jarvis.

'I've known worse.'

'Perhaps you can give the court an example,' said Mr Jarvis, confident that he had trapped the defendant.

'The Conservative Party.'

'I'm not following you, Mr Merchant.'

'They hold a dinner once a year at Grosvenor House. They sell around five hundred programmes and charge £5,000 for a full-page advertisement in colour.'

'But at least they allow potential advertisers every opportunity to refuse to pay such a rate.'

'So do I,' retorted Kenny.

'So, you do not accept that it is against the law to send invoices to companies who were never shown the product in the first place?'

'That may well be the law in the United Kingdom,' said Kenny, 'even in Europe. But it does not apply if the magazine is produced in Hong Kong, a British colony, and the invoices are despatched from that country.'

Mr Jarvis began sifting through his papers.

'I think you'll find it's amendment 9, clause 4, as amended in the Lords at report stage,' said Kenny.

'But that is not what their Lordships intended when they drafted that particular amendment,' said Jarvis, moments after he had located the relevant clause.

'I am not a mind-reader, Mr Jarvis,' said Kenny, 'so I cannot be sure what their Lordships intended. I am only interested in keeping to the letter of the law.'

'But you broke the law by receiving money in England and not declaring it to the Inland Revenue.'

'That is not the case, Mr Jarvis. *Business Enterprise UK* is a subsidiary of the main company, which is registered in Hong Kong. In the case of a British colony, the Act allows subsidiaries to receive the income in the country of distribution.'

'But you made no attempt to distribute the magazine, Mr Merchant.'

'A copy of *Business Enterprise UK* was placed in the British Library and several other leading institutions, as stipulated in clause 19 of the Act.'

'That may be true, but there is no escaping the fact, Mr Merchant, that you were demanding money under false pretences.'

'Not if you state clearly on the invoice that if the client is dissatisfied with the product, they are not required to make any payment.'

'But the wording on the invoice is so small that you would need a magnifying glass to see it.'

'Consult the Act, Mr Jarvis, as I did. I could not find anything to indicate what size the lettering should be.'

'And the colour?'

'The colour?' asked Kenny, feigning surprise.

'Yes, Mr Merchant, the colour. Your invoices were printed on dark-grey paper, while the lettering was light grey.'

'Those are the company colours, Mr Jarvis, as anyone would know who had looked at the cover of the magazine. And there is nothing in the Act to suggest what colour should be used when sending out invoices.'

'Ah,' said prosecuting counsel, 'but there is a clause in the Act stating in unambiguous terms that the wording should be placed in a prominent position. Clause 3, paragraph 14.'

'That is correct, Mr Jarvis.'

'And do you feel that the back of the paper could be described as a prominent position?'

'I certainly do,' said Kenny. 'After all, there wasn't anything else on the back of the page. I do also try to keep to the spirit of the law.'

'Then so will I,' snapped Jarvis. 'Because once a company has paid for an advertisement in *Business Enterprise UK*, is it not also correct that that company must be supplied with a copy of the magazine?'

'Only if requested – clause 42, paragraph 9.'

'And how many companies requested a copy of *Business Enterprise UK*?'

'Last year it was 107. This year it dropped to ninety-one.'

'And did they all receive copies?'

'No. Unfortunately, in some cases they didn't last year, but this year I was able to fulfil every order.'

'So you broke the law on that occasion?'

'Yes, but only because I was unable to print a hundred copies of the magazine, as I explained earlier.'

Mr Jarvis paused to allow the judge to complete a note. 'I think you'll find it's clause 84, paragraph 6, m'lud.'

The judge nodded.

'Finally, Mr Merchant, let me turn to something you lamentably failed to tell your defence counsel when he was questioning you.'

Kenny gripped the side of the witness box.

'Last year you sent out 2,400 invoices. How many companies sent back payments?'

'Around 45 per cent.'

'How many, Mr Merchant?'

'1,130,' admitted Kenny.

'And this year, you sent out only 1,900 invoices. May I ask why five hundred companies were reprieved?'

'I decided not to invoice those firms that had declared poor annual results and had failed to offer their shareholders a dividend.'

'Most commendable, I'm sure. But how many still paid the full amount?'

'1,090,' said Kenny.

Mr Jarvis stared at the jury for some time before asking, 'And how much profit did you make during your first year?'

The courtroom was as silent as it had been at any point during the eight-day trial as Kenny considered his reply. '£1,412,000,' he eventually replied.

'And this year?' asked Mr Jarvis quietly.

'It fell a little, which I blame on the recession.'

'How much?' demanded Mr Jarvis.

'A little over £1,200,000.'

'No more questions, m'lud.'

Both leading counsels made robust final statements, but Kenny sensed that the jury would wait to hear the judge's summing-up on the following day before they came to their verdict.

Mr Justice Thornton took a considerable time to sum the case up. He pointed out to the jury that it was his responsibility to explain to them the law as it applied in this particular case.

'And we are certainly dealing with a man who has studied the letter of the law. And that is his privilege, because it is parliamentarians who make the law, and it is not for the courts to try and work out what was in their minds at the time.

'To that end I must tell you that Mr Merchant is charged on seven counts, and on six of them I must advise you to return a verdict of "not guilty", because I direct you that Mr Merchant has not broken the law.

'On the seventh charge – that of failing to supply copies of his magazine, *Business Enterprise UK*, to those customers who had paid for an advertisement and then requested a copy – he admitted that, in a few cases, he failed so to do. Members of the jury, you may feel that he certainly broke the law on that occasion, even though he rectified the position a year later – and then I suspect only because the number of requests had fallen below one hundred copies. Members of the jury will possibly recall that particular clause of the Data Protection Act, and its significance.' Twelve blank expressions didn't suggest that they had much idea what he was talking about.

The judge ended with the words, 'I hope you will not take your final decision lightly, as there are several parties beyond this courtroom who will be awaiting your verdict.'

The defendant had to agree with that sentiment as he watched the jury file out of the courtroom, accompanied by the ushers. He was taken back down to his cell, where he declined lunch, and spent over an hour lying on a bunk before he was asked to return to the dock and learn his fate.

Once Kenny had climbed the stairs and was back in the dock, he only had to wait a few minutes before the jury filed back into their places.

The judge took his seat, looked down towards the clerk of the court and nodded. The clerk then turned his attention to the foreman of the jury and read out each of the seven charges.

On the first six counts of fraud and deception, the foreman followed the instructions of the judge and delivered verdicts of 'not guilty'.

The clerk then read out the seventh charge: failure to supply a copy of the magazine to those companies who, having paid for an advertisement in the said magazine and requested a copy of the said magazine, failed to receive one. 'How do you find the defendant on this charge – guilty or not guilty?' asked the clerk.

'Guilty,' said the foreman, and resumed his seat.

The judge turned his attention to Kenny, who was standing to attention in the dock.

'Like you, Mr Merchant,' he began, 'I have spent a considerable time studying the Data Protection Act 1992, and in particular the penalties for failing to adhere to clause 84, paragraph 1. I have decided that I am left with no choice but to inflict on you the maximum penalty the law allows in this particular case.' He stared down at Kenny, looking as if he was about to pronounce the death sentence.

'You will be fined £1,000.'

Mr Duveen did not rise to seek leave for appeal or time to pay, because it was exactly the verdict Kenny had predicted before the trial opened. He had made only one error during the past two years, and he was happy to pay for it. Kenny left the dock, wrote out a cheque for the amount demanded and passed it across to the clerk of the court.

Having thanked his legal team, he checked his watch and quickly left the courtroom. The Chief Inspector was waiting for him in the corridor.

'So that should finally put paid to your little business enterprise,' said Travis, running alongside him.

'I can't imagine why,' said Kenny, as he continued jogging down the corridor.

'Because Parliament will now have to change the law,' said

the Chief Inspector, 'and this time it will undoubtedly tie up all your little loopholes.'

'Not in the near future would be my bet, Chief Inspector,' Kenny said as he left the building and began jogging down the courtroom steps. 'As Parliament is about to rise for the summer recess, I can't see them finding time for new amendments to the Data Protection Act much before February or March of next year.'

'But if you try to repeat the exercise, I'll arrest you the moment you get off the plane,' Travis said as Kenny came to a halt on the pavement.

'I don't think so, Chief Inspector.'

'Why not?'

'I can't imagine the CPS will be willing to go through another expensive trial, if all they're likely to end up with is a fine of £1,000. Think about it, Chief Inspector.'

'Well, I'll get you the following year,' said Travis.

'I doubt it. You see, by then Hong Kong will no longer be a Crown Colony, and I will have moved on,' said Kenny as he climbed into a taxi.

'Moved on?' said the Chief Inspector, looking puzzled.

Kenny pulled the taxi window down, smiled at Travis and said, 'If you've nothing better to do with your time, Chief Inspector, I recommend that you study the new Financial Provisions Act. You wouldn't believe how many loopholes there are in it. Goodbye, Chief Inspector.'

'Where to, guv?' asked the taxi driver.

'Heathrow. But could we stop at Harrods on the way? There's a pair of cufflinks I want to pick up.'

CHALK AND CHEESE

'SUCH A TALENTED CHILD,' said Robin's mother, as she poured her sister another cup of tea. 'The headmaster said on speech day that the school hadn't produced a finer artist in living memory.'

'You must be so proud of him,' said Miriam, before sipping her tea.

'Yes, I confess I am,' admitted Mrs Summers, almost purring. 'Of course, although everyone knew he would win the Founder's Prize, even his art master was surprised when he was offered a place at the Slade before he had sat his entrance exam. It's only sad that his father didn't live long enough to enjoy his triumph.'

'And how's John getting on?' enquired Miriam, as she selected a jam tart.

Mrs Summers sighed as she considered her older son. 'John will finish his Business Management course at Manchester some time in the summer, but he doesn't seem able to make up his mind what he wants to do.' She paused as she dropped another lump of sugar in her tea. 'Heaven knows what will become of him. He talks about going into business.'

'He always worked so hard at school,' said Miriam.

'Yes, but he never quite managed to come top of anything, and he certainly didn't leave with any prizes. Did I tell you that Robin has been offered the chance of a one-man show in October? It's only a local gallery, of course, but as he pointed out, every artist has to start somewhere.'

◄○►

John Summers travelled back to Peterborough to attend his brother's first one-man show. His mother would never have forgiven him had he failed to put in an appearance. He had just learned the result of his Business Management examinations. He had been awarded a 2.1 degree, which wasn't bad considering he had been Vice President of the student union, with a President who had rarely made an appearance once he'd been elected. He wouldn't tell Mother about his degree, as it was Robin's special day.

After years of being told by his mother what a brilliant artist his brother was, John had come to assume it would not be long before the rest of the world acknowledged the fact. He often reflected about how different the two of them were; but then, did people know how many brothers Picasso had? No doubt one of them went into business.

It took John some time to find the little back street where the gallery was located, but when he did he was pleased to discover it packed with friends and wellwishers. Robin was standing next to his mother, who was suggesting the words 'magnificent', 'outstanding', 'truly talented' and even 'genius' to a reporter from the *Peterborough Echo*.

'Oh, look, John has arrived,' she said, leaving her little coterie for a moment to acknowledge her other son.

John kissed her on the cheek and said, 'Robin couldn't have a better send-off to his career.'

'Yes, I'm bound to agree with you,' his mother concurred. 'And I'm sure it won't be long before you can bask in his glory. You'll be able to tell everyone that you're Robin Summers's elder brother.'

Mrs Summers left John to have another photograph taken with Robin, which gave him the opportunity to stroll around the room and study his brother's canvases. They consisted mainly of the portfolio he had put together during his last year at school. John, who readily confessed his ignorance when it came to art, felt it must be his own inadequacy that caused him not to appreciate his brother's obvious talent, and he felt guilty that they weren't the kind of pictures he would want to see hanging in his home. He stopped in front of a portrait of his mother, which had a red dot next to it to indicate that it had been sold. He smiled, confident that he knew who had bought it.

'Don't you think it captures the very essence of her soul?' said a voice from behind him.

'It certainly does,' said John, as he swung round to face his brother. 'Well done. I'm proud of you.'

'One of the things I most admire about you,' said Robin, 'is that you have never envied my talent.'

'Certainly not,' said John. 'I delight in it.'

'Then let's hope that some of my success rubs off on you, in whatever profession you should decide to follow.'

'Let's hope so,' said John, not sure what else he could say.

Robin leaned forward and lowered his voice. 'I don't suppose you could lend me a pound? I'll pay it back, of course.'

'Of course.'

John smiled – at least some things never changed. It had begun years earlier, with sixpence in the playground, and had ended up with a ten-shilling note on Speech Day. Now he needed a pound. Of only one thing could John be certain: Robin would never return a penny. Not that John begrudged his younger brother the money. After all, it wouldn't be long before their roles would surely be reversed. John removed his wallet, which contained two pound-notes and his train ticket back to Manchester. He extracted one of the notes and handed it over to Robin.

John was going to ask him a question about another picture – an oil called *Barabbas in Hell* – but his brother had already turned on his heel and rejoined his mother and the adoring entourage.

◄○►

When John left Manchester University he was immediately offered a job as a trainee with Reynolds and Company, by which time Robin had taken up residence in Chelsea. He had moved into a set of rooms which his mother described to Miriam as small, but certainly in the most fashionable part of town. She didn't add that he was having to share them with five other students.

'And John?' enquired Miriam.

'He's joined a company in Birmingham that makes wheels; or at least I think that's what they do,' she said.

John settled into digs on the outskirts of Solihull, in a very unfashionable part of town. They were conveniently situated, close to a factory that expected him to clock in by eight o'clock from Monday to Saturday while he was still a trainee.

John didn't bore his mother with the details of what Reynolds and Company did, as manufacturing wheels for the nearby Longbridge car plant didn't have quite the same cachet as being an *avant garde* artist residing in bohemian Chelsea.

Although John saw little of his brother during Robin's days at the Slade, he always travelled down to London to view the end-of-term shows.

In their freshman year, students were invited to exhibit two of their works, and John admitted – only to himself – that when it came to his brother's efforts, he didn't care for either of them. But then, he accepted that he had no real knowledge of art. When the critics seemed to agree with John's judgement, their mother explained it away as Robin being ahead of his time, and assured him that it wouldn't be long before the rest of the world came to the same conclusion. She also pointed out that both pictures had been sold on the opening day, and suggested that they had been snapped up by a well-known collector who knew a rising talent when he saw one.

John didn't get the chance to engage in a long conversation with his brother, as he seemed preoccupied with his own set, but he did return to Birmingham that night with £2 less in his wallet than he'd arrived with.

At the end of his second year, Robin showed two new pictures at the end-of-term show – *Knife and Fork in Space* and *Death Pangs*. John stood a few paces away from the canvases, relieved to find from the expressions on the faces of those who stopped to study his brother's work that they were left equally puzzled, not least by the sight of two red dots that had been there since the opening day.

He found his mother seated in a corner of the room, explaining to Miriam why Robin hadn't won the second-year prize. Although her enthusiasm for Robin's work had not dimmed, John felt she looked frailer than when he had last seen her.

'How are you getting on, John?' asked Miriam when she looked up to see her nephew standing there.

'I've been made a trainee manager, Aunt Miriam,' he replied, as Robin came across to join them.

'Why don't you join us for dinner?' suggested Robin. 'It will give you a chance to meet some of my friends.' John was touched by the invitation, until the bill for all seven of them was placed in front of him.

'It won't be long before I can afford to take you to the Ritz,' Robin declared after a sixth bottle of wine had been consumed.

Sitting in a third-class compartment on the journey back to Birmingham New Street, John was thankful that he had purchased a return ticket, because after he had loaned his brother £5 his wallet was empty.

John didn't return to London again until Robin's graduation. His mother had written insisting that he attend, as all the prizewinners would be announced, and she had heard a rumour that Robin would be among them.

When John arrived at the exhibition it was already in full swing. He walked slowly round the hall, stopping to admire some of the canvases. He spent a considerable time studying Robin's latest efforts. There was no plaque to suggest that he had won any of the star prizes – in fact he wasn't even 'specially commended'. But, perhaps more importantly, on this occasion there were no red dots. It served to remind John that his mother's monthly allowance was no longer keeping up with inflation.

'The judges have their favourites,' his mother explained, as she sat alone in a corner looking even frailer than she had when he last saw her. John nodded, feeling that this was not the time to let her know that the company had given him another promotion.

'Turner never won any prizes when he was a student,' was his mother's only other comment on the subject.

'So what does Robin plan to do next?' asked John.

'He's moving into a studio flat in Pimlico, so he can remain with his set – most essential when you're still making your name.' John didn't need to ask who would be paying the rent while Robin was 'still making his name'.

When Robin invited John to join them for dinner, he made some excuse about having to get back to Birmingham. The hangers-on looked disappointed, until John extracted a £10 note from his wallet.

Once Robin had left college, the two brothers rarely met.

—◦—

It was some five years later, when John had been invited to address a CBI conference in London on the problems facing the car industry, that he decided to make a surprise visit to his brother and invite him out to dinner.

When the conference closed, John took a taxi over to Pimlico, suddenly feeling uneasy about the fact that he had not warned Robin he might drop by.

As he climbed the stairs to the top floor, he began to feel even more apprehensive. He pressed the bell, and when the door was eventually opened it was a few moments before he realised that the man standing in front of him was his brother. He could not believe the transformation after only five years.

Robin's hair had turned grey. There were bags under his eyes, his skin was puffy and blotched, and he must have put on at least three stone.

John,' he said. 'What a surprise. I had no idea you were in town. Do come in.'

What hit John as he entered the flat was the smell. At first he wondered if it could be paint, but as he looked around he noticed that the half-finished canvases were outnumbered by the empty wine bottles.

'Are you preparing for an exhibition?' asked John as he stared down at one of the unfinished works.

'No, nothing like that at the moment,' said Robin. 'Lots of interest, of course, but nothing definite. You know what London dealers are like.'

'To be honest, I don't,' said John.

'Well, you have to be either fashionable or newsworthy before they'll consider offering you wall space. Did you know that Van Gogh never sold a picture in his lifetime?'

Over dinner in a nearby restaurant John learned a little more about the vagaries of the art world, and what some of the critics thought of Robin's work. He was pleased to discover that his brother had not lost any of his self-confidence, or his belief that it was only a matter of time before he would be recognised.

Robin's monologue continued throughout the entire meal, and it wasn't until they were back at his flat that John had a chance to mention that he had fallen in love with a girl named Susan, and was about to get married. Robin certainly hadn't enquired about his progress at Reynolds and Co., where he was now the deputy managing director.

Before John left for the station, he settled Robin's bills for several unpaid meals and also slipped his brother a cheque for £100, which neither of them bothered to suggest was a loan. Robin's parting words as John stepped into the taxi were, 'I've just submitted two paintings for the Summer Exhibition at the Royal Academy, which I'm confident will be accepted by the hanging committee, in which case you must come up for the opening day.'

At Euston, John popped into Menzies to buy an evening paper, and noticed on the top of the remainders pile a book entitled *An Introduction to the World of Art from Fra Angelico to Picasso*. As the train pulled out of the station he opened the first page, and by the time he had reached Caravaggio it was pulling into New Street, Birmingham.

He heard a tap at the window and saw Susan smiling up at him.

'That must have been some book,' she said, as they walked down the platform arm in arm.

'It certainly was. I only hope I can get my hands on Volume II.'

—◦—

The two brothers were brought together twice during the following year. The first was a sad occasion, when they attended their mother's funeral. After the service was over, they returned to Miriam's home for tea, where Robin informed his brother that the Academy had accepted both his entries for the Summer Exhibition.

Three months later John travelled to London to attend the opening day. By the time he entered the hallowed portals of the Royal Academy for the first time, he had read a dozen art books, ranging from the early Renaissance to Pop. He had visited every gallery in Birmingham, and couldn't wait to explore the galleries in the back streets of Mayfair.

As he strolled around the spacious rooms of the Academy, John decided the time had come for him to invest in his first picture. Listen to the experts, but in the end trust your eye, Godfrey Barker had written in the *Telegraph*. His eye told him Bernard Dunstan, while the experts were suggesting William Russell Flint. The eyes won, because Dunstan cost £75, while the cheapest Russell Flint was £600.

John strode from room to room searching for the two oils by his brother, but without the aid of the Academy's little blue book he would never have found them. They had been hung in the middle gallery in the top row, nearly touching the ceiling. He noticed that neither of them had been sold.

After he had been round the exhibition twice and settled on the Dunstan, he went over to the sales counter and wrote out a deposit for the purchases he wanted. He checked his watch: it was a few minutes before twelve, the hour at which he had agreed to meet his brother.

Robin kept him waiting for forty minutes, and then, without the suggestion of an apology, guided him around the exhibition for a third time. He dismissed both Dunstan and Russell Flint as society painters, without giving a hint of who he did consider talented.

Robin couldn't hide his disappointment when they came across his pictures in the middle gallery. 'What chance do I have of selling either of them while they're hidden up there?' he said in disgust. John tried to look sympathetic.

Over a late lunch, John took Robin through the implications of their mother's will, as the family solicitors had failed to elicit any response to their several letters addressed to Mr Robin Summers.

'On principle, I never open anything in a brown envelope,' explained Robin.

Well, at least that couldn't be the reason Robin had failed to turn up to his wedding, John thought. Once again, he returned to the details of his mother's will.

'The bequests are fairly straightforward,' he said. 'She's left everything to you, with the exception of one picture.'

'Which one?' Robin immediately asked.

'The one you did of her when you were still at school.'

'It's one of the best things I've ever done,' said Robin. 'It must be worth at least £50, and I've always assumed that she would leave it to me.'

John wrote out a cheque for the sum of £50. When he returned to Birmingham that night, he didn't let Susan know how much he had paid for the two pictures. He placed the Dunstan of *Venice* in the drawing room above the fireplace, and the one of his mother in his study.

◄○►

When their first child was born, John suggested that Robin might be one of the godparents.

'Why?' asked Susan. 'He didn't even bother to come to our wedding.'

John could not disagree with his wife's reasoning, and although Robin was invited to the christening he neither responded nor turned up, despite the invitation being sent in a white envelope.

◄○►

It must have been about two years later that John received an invitation from the Crewe Gallery in Cork Street to Robin's long-awaited one-man show. It actually turned out to be a two-man show, and John certainly would have snapped up one of the works by the other artist, if he hadn't felt it would offend his brother.

He did in fact settle on an oil he wanted, made a note of its number, and the following morning asked his secretary to call the gallery and reserve it in her name.

'I'm afraid the Peter Blake you were after was sold on the opening night,' she informed him.

He frowned. 'Could you ask them how many of Robin Summers's pictures have sold?'

The secretary repeated the question, and cupping her hand over the mouthpiece, told him, 'Two.'

John frowned for a second time.

The following week, John had to return to London to represent his company at the Motor Show at Earls Court. He decided to drop into the Crewe Gallery to see how his brother was selling. No change. Only two red dots on the wall, while Peter Blake was almost sold out.

John left the gallery disappointed on two counts, and headed back towards Piccadilly. He almost walked straight past her, but as soon as he noticed the delicate colour of her cheeks and her graceful figure it was love at first sight. He stood staring at her, afraid she might turn out to be too expensive.

He stepped into the gallery to take a closer look. She was tiny, delicate and exquisite.

'How much?' he asked softly, staring at the woman seated behind the glass table.

'The Vuillard?' she enquired.

John nodded.

'£1,200.'

As if in a daydream, he removed his chequebook and wrote out a sum that he knew would empty his account.

The Vuillard was placed opposite the Dunstan, and thus began a love affair with several painted ladies from all over the world, although John never admitted to his wife how much these framed mistresses were costing him.

◄◦►

Despite the occasional picture to be found hanging in obscure corners of the Summer Exhibition, Robin didn't have another one-man show for several years. When it comes to artists whose canvases remain unsold, dealers are unsympathetic to the suggestion that they could represent a sound investment because they might be recognised after they are dead – mainly because by that time the gallery owners will also be dead.

When the invitation for Robin's next one-man show finally appeared, John knew he had little choice but to attend the opening.

John had recently been involved in a management buy-out of Reynolds and Company. With car sales increasing every year during the seventies, so did the necessity to put wheels on them, which allowed him to indulge in his new hobby as an amateur art collector. He had recently added Bonnard, Dufy, Camoin and Luce to his collection, still listening to the advice of experts, but in the end trusting his eye.

John stepped out of the train at Euston and gave the cabby at the front of the queue the address he needed to be dropped at. The cabby scratched his head for a moment before setting off in the direction of the East End.

When John stepped into the gallery, Robin rushed across to greet him with the words, 'And here is someone who has never doubted my true worth.' John smiled at his brother, who offered him a glass of white wine.

John glanced around the little gallery, to observe knots of people who seemed more interested in gulping down mediocre wine than in taking any interest in mediocre pictures. When would his brother learn that the last thing you need at an opening are other unknown artists accompanied by their hangers-on?

Robin took him by the arm and guided him from group to group, introducing him to people who couldn't have afforded to buy one of the frames, let alone one of the canvases.

The longer the evening dragged on, the more sorry John began to feel for his brother, and on this occasion he happily fell into the dinner trap. He ended up entertaining twelve of Robin's companions, including the owner of the gallery, who John feared wouldn't be getting much more out of the evening than a three-course meal.

'Oh, no,' he tried to assure John. 'We've already sold a couple of pictures, and a lot of people have shown interest. The truth is that the critics have never fully understood Robin's work, as I'm sure no one is more aware than you.'

John looked on sadly as his brother's friends added such comments as 'never been properly recognised', 'unappreciated talent', and 'should have been elected to the RA years ago'. At this suggestion Robin rose unsteadily to his feet and declared, 'Never! I shall be like Henry Moore and David Hockney. When the invitation comes, I shall turn them down.' More cheering, followed by even more drinking of John's wine.

When the clock chimed eleven, John made some excuse about an early-morning meeting. He offered his apologies, settled the bill and left for the Savoy. In the back seat of the taxi, he finally accepted something he had long suspected: his brother simply didn't have any talent.

‹o›

It was to be some years before John heard from Robin again. It seemed that there were no London galleries who were willing to display his work, so he felt it was nothing less than his duty to leave for the South of France and join up with a group of friends who were equally talented and equally misunderstood.

'It will give me a new lease of life,' he explained in a rare letter to his brother, 'a chance to fulfil my true potential, which has been held up for far too long by the pygmies of the London art establishment. And I wondered if you could possibly . . .'

John transferred £5,000 to an account in Vence, to allow Robin to disappear to warmer climes.

◄○►

The takeover bid for Reynolds and Co. came out of the blue, although John had always accepted that they were an obvious target for any Japanese car company trying to gain a foothold in Europe. But even he was surprised when their biggest rivals in Germany put in a counter-bid.

He watched as the value of his shares climbed each day, and not until Honda finally outbid Mercedes did he accept that he would have to make a decision. He opted to cash in his shares and leave the company. He told Susan that he wanted to take a trip around the world, visiting only those cities that boasted great art galleries. First stop the Louvre, followed by the Prado, then the Uffizi, the Hermitage in St Petersburg, and finally on to New York, leaving the Japanese to put wheels on cars.

John wasn't surprised to receive a letter from Robin with a French postmark, congratulating him on his good fortune and wishing him every success in his retirement, while pointing out that he himself had been left with no choice but to battle on until the critics finally came to their senses.

John transferred another £10,000 to the account in Vence.

◄○►

John had his first heart attack in New York while admiring a Bellini at the Frick.

He told Susan that night as she sat by his bedside that he was thankful they had already visited the Metropolitan and the Whitney.

The second heart attack came soon after they had arrived back in Warwickshire. Susan felt obliged to write to Robin in the South of France and warn him that the doctors' prognosis was not encouraging.

Robin didn't reply. His brother died three weeks later.

<o>

The funeral was well attended by John's friends and colleagues, but few of them recognised the heavily built man who demanded to be seated in the front row. Susan and the children knew exactly why he had turned up, and it wasn't to pay his respects.

'He promised I would be taken care of in his will,' Robin told the grieving widow only moments after they had left the graveside. He later sought out the two boys in order to deliver the same message, though he had had little contact with them during the past thirty years. 'You see,' he explained, 'your dad was one of the few people who understood my true worth.'

Over tea back at the house, while others consoled the widow, Robin strolled from room to room, studying the pictures his brother had collected over the years. 'A shrewd investment,' he assured the local vicar, 'even if they do lack originality or passion.' The vicar nodded politely.

When Robin was introduced to the family solicitor, he immediately asked, 'When are you expecting to announce the details of the will?'

'I have not yet discussed with Mrs Summers the arrangements for when the will should be read. However, I anticipate it being towards the end of next week.'

Robin booked himself into the local pub, and rang the solicitor's office every morning until he confirmed that he would be divulging the contents of the will at three o'clock on the following Thursday.

Robin appeared at the solicitor's offices a few minutes before three that afternoon, the first time he had been early for an appointment in years. Susan arrived shortly afterwards, accompanied by the boys, and they took their seats on the other side of the room without acknowledging him.

Although the bulk of John Summers's estate had been left to his wife and the two boys, he had made a special bequest to his brother Robin.

'*During my lifetime I was fortunate enough to put together a collection of paintings, some of which are now of considerable value. At the last count, there were eighty-one in all. My wife Susan may select twenty of her choice, my two boys Nick and Chris may then also select twenty each, while my younger brother Robin is to be given the remaining twenty-one, which should allow him to live in a style worthy of his talent.*'

Robin beamed with satisfaction. His brother had gone to his deathbed never doubting his true worth.

When the solicitor had completed the reading of the will, Susan rose from her place and walked across the room to speak to Robin.

'We will choose the pictures we wish to keep in the family, and having done so, I will have the remaining twenty-one sent over to you at the Bell and Duck.'

She turned and left before Robin had a chance to reply. Silly woman, he thought. So unlike his brother – she wouldn't recognise real talent if it were standing in front of her.

Over dinner at the Bell and Duck that evening, Robin began to make plans as to how he would spend his new-found wealth. By the time he had consumed the hostelry's finest bottle of claret, he had made the decision that he would limit himself to placing one picture with Sotheby's and one with Christie's every six months, which would allow him to live in a style worthy of his talent, to quote his brother's exact words.

He retired to bed around eleven, and fell asleep thinking about Bonnard, Vuillard, Dufy, Camoin and Luce, and what twenty-one such masterpieces might be worth.

He was still sound asleep at ten o'clock the following morning, when there was a knock on the door.

'Who is it?' he mumbled irritably from under the blanket.

'George, the hall porter, sir. There's a van outside. The driver says he can't release the goods until you've signed for them.'

'Don't let him go!' shouted Robin. He leapt out of bed for the first time in years, threw on his old shirt, trousers and shoes, and bolted down the stairs and out into the courtyard.

A man in blue overalls, clipboard in hand, was leaning against a large van.

Robin marched towards him. 'Are you the gentleman who's expecting a delivery of twenty-one paintings?' the van driver asked.

'That's me,' said Robin. 'Where do I sign?'

'Right there,' said the van driver, placing his thumb below the word 'Signature'.

Robin scribbled his name quickly across the form and then followed the driver to the back of the van. He unlocked the doors and pulled them open.

Robin was speechless.

He stared at a portrait of his mother, that was stacked on top of twenty other pictures by Robin Summers, painted *circa* 1951 to 1999.

A CHANGE OF HEART*

THERE IS A MAN from Cape Town who travels to the black township of Crossroads every day. He spends the morning teaching English at one of the local schools, the afternoon coaching rugby or cricket according to the season, and his evenings roaming the streets trying to convince the young that they shouldn't form gangs or commit crimes, and that they should have nothing to do with drugs. He is known as the Crossroads Convert.

No one is born with prejudice in their hearts, although some people are introduced to it at an early age. This was certainly true of Stoffel van den Berg. Stoffel was born in Cape Town, and never once in his life travelled abroad. His ancestors had emigrated from Holland in the eighteenth century, and Stoffel grew up accustomed to having black servants who were there to carry out his slightest whim.

If the boys – none of the servants appeared to be graced with a name, whatever their age – didn't obey Stoffel's orders, they were soundly beaten or simply not fed. If they carried out a job well, they weren't thanked, and were certainly never praised. Why bother to thank someone who has only been put on earth to serve you?

When Stoffel attended his first primary school in the Cape this unthinking prejudice was simply reinforced, with classrooms full of white children being taught only by white teachers. The few blacks he ever came across at school were cleaning lavatories that they would never be allowed to use themselves.

During his school days Stoffel proved to be above average in the classroom, excelling in maths, but in a class of his own on the playing field.

By the time Stoffel was in his final year of school, this six-foot-two-inch, fair-haired Boer was playing fly half for the 1st XV in the winter and opening the batting for the 1st XI during the summer. There was already talk of him playing either rugby or cricket for the Springboks even before he had applied for a place at any university. Several college scouts visited the school in his final year to offer him scholarships, and on the advice of his headmaster, supported by his father, he settled on Stellenbosch.

Stoffel's unerring progress continued from the moment he arrived on the campus. In his freshman year he was selected to open the batting for the university eleven when one of the regular openers was injured. He didn't miss a match for the rest of the season. Two years later, he captained an undefeated varsity side, and went on to score a century for Western Province against Natal.

On leaving university, Stoffel was recruited by Barclays Bank to join their public relations department, although it was made clear to him at the interview that his first priority was to ensure that Barclays won the Inter-Bank Cricket Cup.

He had been with the bank for only a few weeks when the Springbok selectors wrote to inform him that he was being considered for the South African cricket squad which was preparing for the forthcoming tour by England. The bank was delighted, and told him he could take as much time off as he needed to prepare for the national side. He dreamed of scoring a century at Newlands, and perhaps one day even at Lord's.

He followed with interest the Ashes series that was taking place in England. He had only read about players like Underwood and Snow, but their reputations did not worry him. Stoffel intended to despatch their bowling to every boundary in the country.

The South African papers were also following the Ashes series with keen interest, because they wanted to keep their readers informed of the strengths and weaknesses of the opposition their team would be facing in a few weeks' time. Then, overnight, these stories were transferred from the back pages to the front, when England selected an all-rounder who played for Worcester called Basil D'Oliveira. Mr D'Oliveira, as the press called him, made the front pages because he was what the South Africans classified as 'Cape Coloured'. Because he had not been allowed to play first-class cricket in his native South Africa, he had emigrated to England.

The press in both countries began to speculate on the South African government's attitude should D'Oliveira be selected by the MCC as a member of the touring side to visit South Africa.

'If the English were stupid enough to select him,' Stoffel told his friends at the bank, 'the tour would have to be cancelled.' After all, he couldn't be expected to play against a coloured man.

The South Africans' best hope was that Mr D'Oliveira would fail in the final Test at The Oval, and would not be considered for the coming tour, and thus the problem would simply go away.

D'Oliveira duly obliged in the first innings, scoring only eleven runs and taking no Australian wickets. But in the second innings he played a major role in winning the match and squaring the series, scoring a chanceless 158. Even so, he was controversially left out of the touring team for South Africa. But when another player pulled out because of injury, he was selected as his replacement.

The South African government immediately made their position clear: only white players would be welcome in their land. Robust diplomatic exchanges took place over the following weeks, but as the MCC refused to remove D'Oliveira from the party the tour had to be cancelled. It was not until after Nelson Mandela became President in 1994 that an official English team once again set foot in South Africa.

Stoffel was shattered by the decision, and although he played regularly for Western Province and ensured that Barclays retained the Inter-Bank Cup, he doubted if he would ever be awarded a Test cap.

But, despite his disappointment, Stoffel remained in no doubt that the government had made the right decision. After all, why should the English imagine they could dictate who should visit South Africa?

It was while he was playing against Transvaal that he met Inga. Not only was she the most beautiful creature he had ever set eyes on, but she also fully agreed with his sound views on the superiority of the white race. They were married a year later.

When sanctions began to be imposed on South Africa by country after country, Stoffel continued to back the government, proclaiming that the decadent Western politicians had all become liberal weaklings. Why didn't they come to South Africa and see the country for themselves, he would demand of anyone who visited the Cape. That way they would soon discover that he didn't beat his servants, and that the blacks received a fair wage, as recommended by the government. What more could they hope for? In fact, he could never understand why the government didn't hang Mandela and his terrorist cronies for treason.

Piet and Marike nodded their agreement whenever their father expressed these views. He explained to them over breakfast again and again that you couldn't treat people who had recently fallen out of trees as equals. After all, it wasn't how God had planned things.

—<o>—

When Stoffel stopped playing cricket in his late thirties, he took over as head of the bank's public relations department, and was invited to join the board. The family moved into a large house a few miles down the Cape, overlooking the Atlantic.

While the rest of the world continued to enforce sanctions, Stoffel only became more convinced that South Africa was the one place on earth that had got things right. He regularly expressed these views, both in public and in private.

'You should stand for Parliament,' a friend told him. 'The country needs men who believe in the South African way of life, and aren't willing to give in to a bunch of ignorant foreigners, most of whom have never even visited the country.'

To begin with, Stoffel didn't take such suggestions seriously. But then the National Party's Chairman flew to Cape Town especially to see him.

'The Political Committee were hoping you would allow your name to go forward as a prospective candidate at the next general election,' he told Stoffel.

Stoffel promised he would consider the idea, but explained that he would need to speak to his wife and fellow board members at the bank before he could come to a decision. To his surprise, they all encouraged him to take up the offer. 'After all, you are a national figure, universally popular, and no one can be in any doubt about your attitude to apartheid.' A week later, Stoffel phoned the National Party Chairman to say that he would be honoured to stand as a candidate.

When he was selected to fight the safe seat of Noordhoek, he ended his speech to the adoption committee with the words, 'I'll go to my grave knowing apartheid must be right, for blacks as well as for whites.' He received a standing ovation.

◄○►

That all changed on 18 August 1989.

Stoffel left the bank a few minutes early that evening, because he was due to address a meeting at his local town hall. The election was now only weeks away, and the opinion polls were indicating that he was certain to become the Member for the Noordhoek constituency.

As he stepped out of the lift he bumped into Martinus de Jong, the bank's General Manager. 'Another half-day, Stoffel?' he asked with a grin.

'Hardly. I'm off to address a meeting in the constituency, Martinus.'

'Quite right, old fellow,' de Jong replied. 'And don't leave them in any doubt that no one can afford to waste their vote this time – that is, if they don't want this country to end up being run by the blacks. By the way,' he added, 'we don't need assisted places for blacks at universities either. If we allow a bunch of students in England to dictate the bank's policy, we'll end up with some black wanting my job.'

'Yes, I read the memo from London. They're acting like a herd of ostriches. Must dash, Martinus, or I'll be late for my meeting.'

'Yes, sorry to have held you up, old fellow.'

Stoffel checked his watch and ran down the ramp to the cárpark. When he joined the traffic in Rhodes Street, it quickly became clear that he had not managed to avoid the bumper-to-bumper exodus of people heading out of town for the weekend.

Once he had passed the city limits, he moved quickly into top gear. It was only fifteen miles to Noordhoek, although the terrain was steep and the road winding. But as Stoffel knew every inch of the journey, he was usually parked outside his front door in under half an hour.

He glanced at the clock on the dashboard. With luck, he would still be home with enough time to shower and change before he had to head off for the meeting.

As he swung south onto the road which would take him up into the hills, Stoffel pressed his foot down hard on the accelerator, nipping in and out to overtake slow-moving lorries and cars that weren't as familiar with the road as he was. He scowled as he shot past a black driver who was struggling up the hill in a clapped-out old van that shouldn't have been allowed on the road.

Stoffel accelerated round the next bend to see a lorry ahead of him. He knew there was a long, straight section of road before he would encounter another bend, so he had easily enough time to overtake. He put his foot down and pulled out to overtake, surprised to discover how fast the lorry was travelling.

When he was about a hundred yards from the next bend, a car appeared around the corner. Stoffel had to make an instant decision. Should he slam his foot on the brake, or on the accelerator? He pressed his foot hard down until the accelerator was touching the floor, assuming the other fellow would surely brake. He eased ahead of the lorry, and the moment he had overtaken it, he swung in as quickly as he could, but still he couldn't avoid clipping the mudguard of the oncoming car. For an instant he saw the terrified eyes of the other driver, who had slammed on his brakes, but the steep gradient didn't help him. Stoffel's car rammed into the safety barrier before bouncing back onto the other side of the road, eventually coming to a halt in a clump of trees.

That was the last thing he remembered, before he regained consciousness five weeks later.

◄○►

Stoffel looked up to find Inga standing at his bedside. When she saw his eyes open, she grasped his hand and then rushed out of the room to call for a doctor.

The next time he woke they were both standing by his bedside, but it was another week before the surgeon was able to tell him what had happened following the crash.

Stoffel listened in horrified silence when he learned that the other driver had died of head injuries soon after arriving at the hospital.

'You're lucky to be alive,' was all Inga said.

'You certainly are,' said the surgeon, 'because only moments after the other driver died, your heart also stopped beating. It was just your luck that a suitable donor was in the next operating theatre.'

'Not the driver of the other car?' said Stoffel.

The surgeon nodded.

'But . . . wasn't he black?' asked Stoffel in disbelief.

'Yes, he was,' confirmed the surgeon. 'And it may come as a surprise to you, Mr van den Berg, that your body doesn't realise that. Just be thankful that his wife agreed to the transplant. If I recall her words' – he paused – 'she said, "I can't see the point in both of them dying." Thanks to her, we were able to save your life, Mr van den Berg.' He hesitated and pursed his lips, then said quietly, 'But I'm sorry to have to tell you that your other internal injuries were so severe that despite the success of the heart transplant, the prognosis is not at all good.'

Stoffel didn't speak for some time, but eventually asked, 'How long do I have?'

'Three, possibly four years,' replied the surgeon. 'But only if you take it easy.'

Stoffel fell into a deep sleep.

—◄◦►—

It was another six weeks before Stoffel left the hospital, and even then Inga insisted on a long period of convalescence. Several friends came to visit him at home, including Martinus de Jong, who assured him that his job at the bank would be waiting for him just as soon as he had fully recovered.

'I shall not be returning to the bank,' Stoffel said quietly. 'You will be receiving my resignation in the next few days.'

'But why?' asked de Jong. 'I can assure you . . .' Stoffel waved his hand. 'It's kind of you, Martinus, but I have other plans.'

—◄◦►—

The moment the doctor said Stoffel could leave the house, he asked Inga to drive him to Crossroads, so he could visit the widow of the man he had killed.

The tall, fair-haired white couple walked among the shacks of Crossroads, watched by sullen, resigned eyes. When they reached the little hovel where they had been told the driver's wife lived, they stopped.

Stoffel would have knocked on the door if there had been one. He peered through the gap and into the darkness to see a young woman with a baby in her arms, cowering in the far corner.

'My name is Stoffel van den Berg,' he told her. 'I have come to say how sorry I am to have been the cause of your husband's death.'

'Thank you, master,' she replied. 'No need to visit me.'

As there wasn't anything to sit on, Stoffel lowered himself to the ground and crossed his legs.

'I also wanted to thank you for giving me the chance to live.'

'Thank you, master.'

'Is there anything I can do for you?' He paused. 'Perhaps you and your child would like to come and live with us?'

'No, thank you, master.'

'Is there nothing I can do?' asked Stoffel helplessly.

'Nothing, thank you, master.'

Stoffel rose from his place, aware that his presence seemed to disturb her. He and Inga walked back through the township in silence, and did not speak again until they had reached their car.

'I've been so blind,' he said as Inga drove him home.

'Not just you,' his wife admitted, tears welling up in her eyes. 'But what can we do about it?'

'I know what I must do.'

Inga listened as her husband described how he intended to spend the rest of his life.

◄○►

The next morning Stoffel called in at the bank, and with the help of Martinus de Jong worked out how much he could afford to spend over the next three years.

'Have you told Inga that you want to cash in your life insurance?'

'It was her idea,' said Stoffel.

'How do you intend to spend the money?'

'I'll start by buying some second-hand books, old rugby balls and cricket bats.'

'We could help by doubling the amount you have to spend,' suggested the General Manager.

'How?' asked Stoffel.

'By using the surplus we have in the sports fund.'

'But that's restricted to whites.'

'And you're white,' said the General Manager.

Martinus was silent for some time before he added, 'Don't imagine that you're the only person whose eyes have been opened by this tragedy. And you are far better placed to . . .' he hesitated.

'To . . . ?' repeated Stoffel.

'Make others, more prejudiced than yourself, aware of their past mistakes.'

That afternoon Stoffel returned to Crossroads. He walked around the township for several hours before he settled on a piece of land surrounded by tin shacks and tents.

Although it wasn't flat, or the perfect shape or size, he began to pace out a pitch, while hundreds of young children stood staring at him.

The following day some of those children helped him paint the touchlines and put out the corner flags.

◄○►

For four years, one month and eleven days, Stoffel van den Berg travelled to Crossroads every morning, where he would teach English to the children in what passed for a school.

In the afternoons, he taught the same children the skills of rugby or cricket, according to the season. In the evenings, he would roam the streets trying to persuade teenagers that they shouldn't form gangs, commit crime or have anything to do with drugs.

Stoffel van den Berg died on 24 March 1994, only days before Nelson Mandela was elected as President. Like Basil D'Oliveira, he had played a small part in defeating apartheid.

The funeral of the Crossroads Convert was attended by over two thousand mourners who had travelled from all over the country to pay their respects.

The journalists were unable to agree whether there had been more blacks or more whites in the congregation.

TOO MANY COINCIDENCES*

WHENEVER RUTH looked back on the past three years – and she often did – she came to the conclusion that Max must have planned everything right down to the last detail – yes, even before they'd met.

They first bumped into each other by accident – or that's what Ruth assumed at the time – and to be fair to Max it wasn't the two of them, but their boats, that had bumped into each other.

Sea Urchin was easing its way into the adjoining mooring in the half-light of the evening when the two bows touched. Both skippers quickly checked to see if there had been any damage to their boat, but as both had large inflatable buoys slung over their sides, neither had come to any harm. The owner of *The Scottish Belle* gave a mock salute and disappeared below deck.

Max poured himself a gin and tonic, picked up a paperback that he had meant to finish the previous summer, and settled down in the bow. He began to thumb through the pages, trying to recall the exact place he had reached, when the skipper of *The Scottish Belle* reappeared on the deck.

The older man gave the same mock salute, so Max lowered his book and said, 'Good evening. Sorry about the bump.'

'No harm done,' the skipper replied, raising his glass of whisky.

Max rose from his place and, walking across to the side of the boat, thrust out a hand and said, 'My name's Max Bennett.'

'Angus Henderson,' the older man replied, with a slight Edinburgh burr.

'You live in these parts, Angus?' asked Max casually.

'No,' replied Angus. 'My wife and I live on Jersey, but our twin boys are at school here on the south coast, so we sail across at the end of every term and take them back for their holidays. And you? Do you live in Brighton?'

'No, London, but I come down whenever I can find the time to do a spot of sailing, which I fear isn't often enough – as you've already discovered,' he added with a chuckle, as a woman appeared from below the deck of *The Scottish Belle*.

Angus turned and smiled. 'Ruth, this is Max Bennett. We literally bumped into each other.'

Max smiled across at a woman who could have passed as Henderson's daughter, as she was at least twenty years younger than her husband. Although not beautiful, she was striking, and from her trim, athletic build she looked as if she might work out every day. She gave Max a shy smile.

'Why don't you join us for a drink?' suggested Angus.

'Thank you,' said Max, and clambered across onto the larger boat. He leaned forward and shook Ruth's hand. 'How nice to meet you, Mrs Henderson.'

'Ruth, please. Do you live in Brighton?' she asked.

'No,' said Max. 'I was just telling your husband that I only come down for the odd weekend to do a little sailing. And what do you do on Jersey?' he asked, turning his attention back to Angus. 'You certainly weren't born there.'

'No, we moved there from Edinburgh after I retired seven years ago. I used to manage a small broking business. All I do nowadays is keep an eye on one or two of my family properties to make sure they're showing a worthwhile return, sail a little and play the occasional round of golf. And you?' he enquired.

'Not unlike you, but with a difference.'

'Oh? What's that?' asked Ruth.

'I also look after property, but it belongs to other people. I'm a junior partner with a West End estate agent.'

'How are property prices in London at the moment?' asked Angus after another gulp of whisky.

'It's been a bad couple of years for most agents – no one wants to sell, and only foreigners can afford to buy. And anybody whose lease comes up for renewal demands that their rent should be lowered, while others are simply defaulting.'

Angus laughed. 'Perhaps you should move to Jersey. At least that way you would avoid . . .'

'We ought to think about getting changed, if we're not going to be late for the boys' concert,' interrupted Ruth.

Henderson checked his watch. 'Sorry, Max,' he said. 'Nice to talk to you, but Ruth's right. Perhaps we'll bump into each other again.'

'Let's hope so,' replied Max. He smiled, placed his glass on a nearby table and clambered back onto his own boat as the Hendersons disappeared below deck.

Once again, Max picked up his much-thumbed novel, and although he finally found the right place, he discovered he couldn't concentrate on the words. Thirty minutes later the Hendersons reappeared, suitably dressed for a concert. Max gave them a casual wave as they stepped onto the quay and into a waiting taxi.

–<o>–

When Ruth appeared on the deck the following morning, clutching a cup of tea, she was disappointed to find that *Sea*

Urchin was no longer moored next to them. She was about to disappear back below deck when she thought she recognised a familiar boat entering the harbour.

She didn't move as she watched the sail become larger and larger, hoping that Max would moor in the same spot as he had the previous evening. He waved when he saw her standing on the deck. She pretended not to notice.

Once he'd fixed the moorings, he called across, 'So, where's Angus?'

'Gone to pick up the boys and take them off to a rugby match. I'm not expecting him back until this evening,' she added unnecessarily.

Max tied a bowline to the jetty, looked up and said, 'Then why don't you join me for lunch, Ruth? I know a little Italian restaurant that the tourists haven't come across yet.'

Ruth pretended to be considering his offer, and eventually said, 'Yes, why not?'

'Shall we meet up in half an hour?' Max suggested.

'Suits me,' replied Ruth.

Ruth's half-hour turned out to be nearer fifty minutes, so Max returned to his paperback, but once again made little progress.

When Ruth did eventually reappear, she had changed into a black leather mini-skirt, a white blouse and black stockings, and had put on a little too much make-up, even for Brighton.

Max looked down at her legs. Not bad for thirty-eight, he thought, even if the skirt was a little too tight and certainly too short.

'You look great,' he said, trying to sound convincing. 'Shall we go?'

Ruth joined him on the quay, and they strolled towards the town, chatting inconsequentially until he turned down a side street, coming to a halt in front of a restaurant called Venitici. When he opened the door to let her in, Ruth couldn't hide her disappointment at discovering how crowded the room was. 'We'll never get a table,' she said.

'Oh, I wouldn't be so sure of that,' said Max, as the maître d' headed towards them.

'Your usual table, Mr Bennett?'

'Thank you, Valerio,' he said, as they were guided to a quiet table in the corner of the room.

Once they were seated, Max asked, 'What would you like to drink, Ruth? A glass of champagne?'

'That would be nice,' she said, as if it were an everyday experience for her. In fact she rarely had a glass of champagne before lunch, as it would never have crossed Angus's mind to indulge in such extravagance, except perhaps on her birthday.

Max opened the menu. 'The food here is always excellent, especially the gnocchi, which Valerio's wife makes. Simply melts in your mouth.'

'Sounds great,' said Ruth, not bothering to open her menu.

'And a mixed salad on the side, perhaps?'

'Couldn't be better.'

Max closed his menu and looked across the table. 'The boys can't be yours,' he said. 'Not if they're at boarding school.'

'Why not?' asked Ruth coyly.

'Why . . . because of Angus's age. I suppose I just assumed they must be his by a previous marriage.'

'No,' said Ruth, laughing. 'Angus didn't marry until he was in his forties, and I was very flattered when he asked me to be his wife.'

Max made no comment.

'And you?' asked Ruth, as a waiter offered her a choice of four different types of bread.

'Been married four times,' Max said.

Ruth looked shocked, until he burst out laughing.

'In truth, never,' he said quietly. 'I suppose I just haven't bumped into the right girl.'

'But you're still young enough to have any woman you like,' said Ruth.

'I'm older than you,' said Max gallantly.

'It's different for a man,' said Ruth wistfully.

The maître d' reappeared by their side, a little pad in his hand.

'Two gnocchi and a bottle of your Barolo,' said Max, handing back the menu. 'And a side salad large enough for both of us: asparagus, avocado, lettuce heart – you know what I like.'

'Of course, Mr Bennett,' replied Valerio.

Max turned his attention back to his guest. 'Doesn't someone of your age find Jersey a little dull?' he asked as he leaned across the table and pushed back a strand of blonde hair that had fallen across her forehead.

Ruth smiled shyly. 'It has its advantages,' she replied a little unconvincingly.

'Like what?' pressed Max.

'Tax at 20 per cent.'

'That sounds like a good reason for Angus being on Jersey – but not you. In any case, I'd still rather be in England and pay 40 per cent.'

'Now that he's retired and living on a fixed income, it suits us. If we'd stayed in Edinburgh, we couldn't have maintained the same standard of living.'

'So, Brighton's as good as it gets,' said Max, with a grin.

The maître d' reappeared carrying two plates of gnocchi, which he placed in front of them, while another waiter deposited a large side salad in the centre of the table.

'I'm not complaining,' said Ruth, as she sipped her champagne. 'Angus has always been very considerate. I want for nothing.'

'Nothing?' Max repeated, as a hand disappeared under the table and rested on her knee.

Ruth knew that she should have removed it immediately, but she didn't.

When Max eventually took his hand away and began to concentrate on the gnocchi, Ruth tried to act as if nothing had happened.

'Anything worth seeing in the West End?' she asked casually. 'I'm told *An Inspector Calls* is good.'

'It certainly is,' replied Max. 'I went to the opening night.'

'Oh, when was that?' asked Ruth innocently.

'About five years ago,' Max replied.

Ruth laughed. 'So, now that you know just how out of date I am, you can tell me what I should be seeing.'

'There's a new Tom Stoppard opening next month.' He paused. 'If you were able to escape for a couple of days, we could go and see it together.'

'It's not that easy, Max. Angus expects me to stay with him on Jersey. We don't come to the mainland all that often.'

Max stared down at her empty plate. 'It looks as if the gnocchi lived up to my claims.'

Ruth nodded her agreement.

'You should try the *crème brulée*, also made by the patron's wife.'

'Certainly not. This trip already means I'm going to be out of the gym for at least three days, so I'll settle for a coffee,' said Ruth, as another glass of champagne was placed by her side. She frowned.

'Just pretend it's your birthday,' Max said, as the hand disappeared back under the table – this time resting a few inches higher up her thigh.

Looking back, that was the moment when she should have got up and walked out.

'So, how long have you been an estate agent?' she asked instead, still trying to pretend nothing was happening.

'Since I left school. I started at the bottom of the firm, making the tea, and last year I became a partner.'

'Congratulations. Where is your office?'

'Right in the centre of Mayfair. Why don't you drop in some time? Perhaps when you're next in London.'

'I don't get to London all that often,' Ruth said.

When Max spotted a waiter heading towards their table, he removed the hand from her leg. Once the waiter had placed two cappuccinos in front of them, Max smiled up at him and said, 'And perhaps I could have the bill.'

'Are you in a hurry?' Ruth asked.

'Yes,' he replied. 'I've just remembered that I have a bottle of vintage brandy hidden away on board *Sea Urchin*, and this might be the ideal occasion to open it.' He leaned across the table and took her hand. 'You know, I've been saving this particular bottle for something or someone special.'

'I don't think that would be wise.'

'Do you always do everything that is wise?' asked Max, not letting go of her hand.

'It's just that I really ought to be getting back to *The Scottish Belle*.'

'So you can hang around for three hours, waiting for Angus to return?'

'No. It's just that. . .'

'You're afraid I might try to seduce you.'

'Is that what you had in mind?' asked Ruth, releasing his hand.

'Yes, but not before we sample the brandy,' said Max, as he was passed the bill. He flicked over the little white slip, pulled out his wallet and placed four £10 notes on the silver tray.

Angus had once told her that anyone who pays cash in a restaurant either doesn't need a credit card or earns too little to qualify for one.

Max rose from his place, thanked the head waiter a little too ostentatiously, and slipped him a £5 note when the door was held open for them. They didn't speak as they crossed the road on the way back to the quay. Ruth thought she saw someone jumping off *Sea Urchin*, but when she looked again there was no one in sight. When they reached the boat, Ruth had planned to say goodbye, but she found herself following Max on board and down to the cabin below.

'I hadn't expected it to be so small,' she said, when she reached the bottom step. She turned a complete circle and ended up in Max's arms. She gently pushed him away.

'It's ideal for a bachelor,' was his only comment, as he poured two large brandies. He passed over one of the goblets to Ruth, placing his other arm around her waist. He pulled her gently towards him, allowing their bodies to touch. He leaned forward and kissed her on the lips, before releasing her to take a sip of brandy.

He watched as she raised the glass to her lips, and then once again took her in his arms. This time when they kissed, their lips parted, and she made little effort to stop him undoing the top button of her blouse.

Every time she tried to resist he would break off, waiting for her to take another sip before returning to his task. It took several more sips before he managed to remove the white blouse and locate the zip on the tight-fitting mini-skirt, but by then she was no longer even pretending to try to stop him.

'You're only the second man I've ever made love to,' she said quietly as she lay on the floor afterwards.

'You were a virgin when you met Angus?' said Max in disbelief.

'He wouldn't have married me if I hadn't been,' she replied quite simply.

'And there's been no one else during the past twenty years?' he said as he poured himself another brandy.

'No,' she replied, 'although I have a feeling that Gerald Prescott, the boys' housemaster at their old prep school, fancies me. But he's never got beyond a peck on the cheek, and staring at me with forlorn eyes.'

'But do you fancy him?'

'Yes, I do actually. He's rather nice,' Ruth admitted for the first time in her life. 'But he's not the sort of man who would make the first move.'

'More fool him,' said Max, taking her into his arms again.

Ruth glanced at her watch. 'Oh my God, is that really the time? Angus could be back at any moment.'

'Don't panic, my darling,' said Max. 'We still have enough time for another brandy, and perhaps even another orgasm – whichever you fancy most.'

'Both, but I don't want to risk him finding us together.'

'Then we'll have to save it for another time,' said Max, putting the cork firmly back in the bottle.

'Or for the next girl,' said Ruth, as she began pulling her tights on.

Max picked up a biro from the side table and wrote on the label of the bottle, 'To be drunk only when I'm with Ruth'.

'Will I see you again?' she asked.

'That will be up to you, my darling,' replied Max, before kissing her again. When he released her, she turned and climbed up the steps and onto the deck, quickly disappearing out of sight.

Once she was back on *The Scottish Belle*, she tried to erase the memory of the last two hours, but when Angus reappeared later that evening with the boys, she realised that forgetting Max wasn't going to be quite that easy.

When she emerged on the deck the following morning, *Sea Urchin* was nowhere to be seen.

'Were you looking for anything in particular?' Angus asked when he joined her.

She turned and smiled at him. 'No. It's just that I can't wait to get back to Jersey,' she replied.

—◆◦▶—

It must have been about a month later that she picked up the phone and found Max on the other end of the line. She felt the same breathless feeling she had experienced the first time they had made love.

'I'm coming over to Jersey tomorrow, to look at a piece of property for a client. Any chance of seeing you?'

'Why don't you join us for dinner?' Ruth heard herself saying.

'Why don't you join me at my hotel?' he replied. 'And don't let's bother with dinner.'

'No, I think it might be wiser if you came over for dinner. On Jersey, even the letterboxes chatter.'

'If that's the only way I'm going to be able to see you, then I'll settle for dinner.'

'Eight o'clock?'

'Eight o'clock will be just fine,' he said, and put the phone down.

When Ruth heard the phone click she realised that she hadn't given him their address, and she couldn't phone him back, because she didn't know his number.

When she warned Angus that they would have a guest for dinner the next night, he seemed pleased. 'Couldn't be better timing,' he said. 'There's something I need Max to advise me on.'

Ruth spent the following morning shopping in St Helier, selecting only the finest cuts of meat, the freshest vegetables, and a bottle of claret that she knew Angus would have considered highly extravagant.

She spent the afternoon in the kitchen, explaining to the cook exactly how she wanted the meal prepared, and even

longer that evening in the bedroom, choosing and then rejecting what she might wear that night. She was still naked when
the doorbell rang a few minutes after eight.

Ruth opened the bedroom door and listened from the top
of the stairs as her husband welcomed Max. How old Angus
sounded, she thought, as she listened to the two men chatting.
She still hadn't discovered what he wanted to speak to Max
about, as she didn't wish to appear too interested.

She returned to the bedroom and settled on a dress that a
friend had once described as seductive. 'Then it will be wasted
on this island,' she remembered replying.

The two men rose from their places when Ruth walked
into the drawing room, and Max stepped forward and kissed
her on both cheeks in the same way Gerald Prescott always
did.

'I've been telling Max about our cottage in the Ardennes,'
said Angus, even before they had sat down again, 'and our
plans to sell it, now that the twins will be going away to
university.'

How typical of Angus, thought Ruth. Get the business out
of the way before you even offer your guest a drink. She went
over to the sideboard and poured Max a gin and tonic without
thinking what she was doing.

'I've asked Max if he would be kind enough to visit the
cottage, value it, and advise when would be the best time to
put it on the market.'

'That sounds sensible enough,' said Ruth. She avoided
looking directly at Max, for fear that Angus might realise how
she felt about their guest.

'I could travel on to France tomorrow,' said Max, 'if you'd
like me to. I've nothing else planned for the weekend,' he
added. 'I could report back to you on Monday.'

'That sounds good to me,' Angus responded. He paused

and sipped the malt whisky his wife had handed him. 'I was thinking, my dear, it might expedite matters if you went along as well.'

'No, I'm sure Max can handle . . .'

'Oh no,' said Angus. 'It was he who suggested the idea. After all, you could show him round the place, and he wouldn't have to keep calling back if he had any queries.'

'Well, I'm rather busy at the moment, what with . . .'

'The bridge society, the health club and . . . No, I think they'll all somehow manage to survive without you for a few days,' said Angus with a smile.

Ruth hated being made to sound so provincial in front of Max. 'All right,' she said. 'If you think it will help, I'll accompany Max to the Ardennes.' This time she did look up at him.

The Chinese would have been impressed by the inscrutability of Max's expression.

◄◦►

The trip to the Ardennes took them three days and, more memorably, three nights. By the time they returned to Jersey, Ruth just hoped it wasn't too obvious that they were lovers.

After Max had presented Angus with a detailed report and valuation, the old man accepted his advice that the property should be placed on the market a few weeks before the beginning of the summer season. The two men shook hands on the deal, and Max said he would be in touch the moment anyone showed some interest.

Ruth drove him to the airport, and her final words before he disappeared through Customs were, 'Could you make it a little less than a month before I hear from you again?'

Max rang the following day to inform Angus that he had placed the property in the hands of two reputable agencies in Paris whom his company had dealt with for many years. 'Before you ask,' he added, 'I'm splitting my fee, so there will be no extra charge.'

'A man after my own heart,' said Angus. He put the phone down before Ruth had a chance to have a word with Max.

Over the next few days, Ruth always picked up the phone before Angus could get to it, but Max didn't call again that week. When he eventually phoned on the following Monday, Angus was sitting in the same room.

'I can't wait to tear your clothes off again, my darling,' were Max's opening words.

She replied, 'I'm pleased to hear that, Max, but I'll pass you straight over to Angus, so you can tell him the news.' As she handed the phone across to her husband, she only hoped that Max did have some news to pass on.

'So, what's this news you've got for me?' asked Angus.

'We've had an offer of 900,000 francs for the property,' said Max, 'which is almost £100,000. But I'm not going to settle yet, as two other parties have also asked to view it. The French agents are recommending that we accept anything over a million francs.'

'If that's also your advice, I'm happy to go along with it,' said Angus. 'And if you close the deal, Max, I'll fly over and sign the contract. I've been promising Ruth a trip to London for some time.'

'Good. It would be nice to see you both again,' said Max, before ringing off.

He phoned again at the end of the week, and although Ruth managed a whole sentence before Angus appeared at her side, she didn't have time to respond to his sentiments.

'£107,600?' said Angus. 'That's far better than I'd expected. Well done, Max. Why don't you draw up the contracts, and the moment you've got the deposit in the bank, I'll fly over.' Angus put the phone down and, turning to Ruth, said, 'Well, it looks as if it might not be too long before we make that promised trip to London.'

—◦—

After checking into a small hotel in Marble Arch, Ruth and Angus joined Max at a restaurant in South Audley Street that Angus had never heard of. And when he saw the prices on the menu, he knew he wouldn't have selected it if he had. But the staff were very attentive, and seemed to know Max well.

Ruth found the dinner frustrating, because all Angus wanted to talk about was the deal, and once Max had satisfied him on that front, he went on to discuss his other properties in Scotland.

'They seem to be showing a poor return on capital investment,' Angus said. 'Perhaps you could check them out, and advise me on what I should do?'

'I'd be delighted,' said Max, as Ruth looked up from her *foie gras* and stared at her husband. 'Are you feeling all right, my dear?' she asked. 'You've turned quite white.'

'I've got a pain down my right side,' complained Angus. 'It's been a long day, and I'm not used to these swanky restaurants. I'm sure it's nothing a good night's sleep won't sort out.'

'That may be the case, but I still think we should go straight back to the hotel,' Ruth said, sounding concerned.

'Yes, I agree with Ruth,' chipped in Max. 'I'll settle the bill and ask the doorman to find us a taxi.'

Angus rose unsteadily to his feet and walked slowly across the restaurant, leaning heavily on Ruth's arm. When Max joined them in the street a few moments later, Ruth and the doorman were helping Angus into a taxi.

'Good night, Angus,' said Max. 'I hope you're feeling better in the morning. Don't hesitate to call me if I can be of any assistance.' He smiled and closed the taxi door.

By the time Ruth had managed to get her husband into bed, he didn't look any better. Although she knew he wouldn't approve of the extra expense, she called for the hotel doctor.

The doctor arrived within the hour, and after a full examination he surprised Ruth by asking for the details of what Angus had eaten for dinner. She tried to recollect the courses he had chosen, but all she could remember was that he had fallen in with Max's suggestions. The doctor advised that Mr Henderson should be visited by a specialist first thing in the morning.

'Poppycock,' said Angus weakly. 'There's nothing wrong with me that our local GP won't sort out just as soon as we're back on Jersey. We'll get the first flight home.'

Ruth agreed with the doctor, but knew there was no point in arguing with her husband. When he eventually fell asleep, she went downstairs to phone Max and warn him that they would be returning to Jersey in the morning. He sounded concerned, and repeated his offer to do anything he could to help.

When they boarded the aircraft the following morning and the chief steward saw the state Angus was in, it took all Ruth's powers of persuasion to convince him to allow her husband to remain on the flight. 'I must get him back to his own doctor as quickly as possible,' she pleaded. The steward reluctantly acquiesced.

Ruth had already phoned ahead to arrange for a car to meet them – something else Angus would not have approved of. But by the time the plane landed, Angus was no longer in any state to offer an opinion.

As soon as Ruth had got him back to the house and into his own bed, she immediately called their GP. Dr Sinclair carried out the same examination as the London doctor had put him through, and he too asked what Angus had eaten the night before. He came to the same conclusion: Angus must see a specialist immediately.

An ambulance came to pick him up later that afternoon and take him to the Cottage Hospital. When the specialist had completed his examination, he asked Ruth to join him in his room. 'I'm afraid the news is not good, Mrs Henderson,' he told her. 'Your husband has suffered a heart attack, possibly aggravated by a long day and something he ate that didn't agree with him. In the circumstances, I think it might be wise to bring the children back from school.'

Ruth returned home later that night, not knowing who she could turn to. The phone rang, and when she picked it up she recognised the voice immediately.

'Max,' she blurted out, 'I'm so glad you called. The specialist says Angus hasn't long to live, and that I ought to bring the boys back home.' She paused. 'I don't think I'm up to telling them what's happened. You see, they adore their father.'

'Leave it to me,' said Max quietly. 'I'll ring the headmaster, go down and pick them up tomorrow morning, and fly over to Jersey with them.'

'That's so kind of you, Max.'

'It's the least I could do in the circumstances,' said Max. 'Now try and get some rest. You sound exhausted. I'll call back as soon as I know which flight we're on.'

Ruth returned to the hospital and spent most of the night sitting by her husband's bedside. The only other visitor, who Angus insisted on seeing, was the family solicitor. Ruth arranged for Mr Craddock to come the following morning, while she was at the airport picking up Max and the twins.

Max strode out of the customs hall, the two boys walking on either side of him. Ruth was relieved to find that they were far calmer than she was. Max drove the three of them to the hospital. She was disappointed that Max planned to return to

England on the afternoon flight, but as he explained, he felt this was a time for her to be with her family.

◄◦►

Angus died peacefully in the St Helier Cottage Hospital the following Friday. Ruth and the twins were at his bedside.

Max flew over for the funeral, and the next day accompanied the twins back to school. When Ruth waved them goodbye she wondered if she would ever hear from Max again.

He phoned the next morning to ask how she was.

'Lonely, and feeling a little guilty that I miss you more than I should.' She paused. 'When are you next planning to come to Jersey?'

'Not for some time. Try not to forget that it was you who warned me that even the letterboxes chatter on Jersey.'

'But what shall I do? The boys are away at school, and you're stuck in London.'

'Why don't you join me in town? It will be a lot easier to lose ourselves over here, and frankly no one will recognise you in London.'

'Perhaps you're right. Let me think about it, and then I'll call you.'

Ruth flew into Heathrow a week later, and Max was at the airport to greet her. She was touched by how thoughtful and gentle he was, never once complaining about her long silences, or the fact that she didn't want to make love.

When he drove her back to the airport on Monday morning, she clung on to him.

'You know,' she said, 'I didn't even get to see your flat or your office.'

'I think it was sensible that you booked into a hotel this time. You can always see my office next time you come over.'

She smiled for the first time since the funeral. When they parted at the airport, he took her in his arms and said, 'I know it's early days, my darling, but I want you to know how much I love you and hope that at some time in the future you might feel me worthy of taking Angus's place.'

She returned to St Helier that evening continually repeating his words, as if they were the lyrics of a song she could not get out of her mind.

◄○►

It must have been about a week later that she received a phone call from Mr Craddock, the family solicitor, who suggested that she drop into his office and discuss the implications of her late husband's will. She made an appointment to see him the following morning.

Ruth had assumed that as she and Angus had always led a comfortable life, her standard of living would continue much as before. After all, Angus was not the sort of man who would leave his affairs unresolved. She recalled how insistent he had been that Mr Craddock should visit him at the hospital.

Ruth had never shown any interest in Angus's business affairs. Although he was always careful with his money, if she had ever wanted something, he had never refused her. In any case, Max had just deposited a cheque for over £100,000 in Angus's account, so she set off for the solicitor's office the following morning confident that her late husband would have left quite enough for her to live on.

She arrived a few minutes early. Despite this, the receptionist accompanied her straight through to the senior partner's room. When she walked in, she found three men seated around the boardroom table. They immediately rose from their places, and Mr Craddock introduced them as partners of the firm. Ruth assumed they must have come to pay their respects, but they resumed their seats and continued to study the thick files placed in front of them. For the first time, Ruth became anxious. Surely Angus's estate was in order?

The senior partner took his seat at the top of the table, untied a bundle of documents and extracted a thick parchment, then looked up at his late client's wife.

'Firstly, may I express on behalf of the firm the sadness we all felt when we learned of Mr Henderson's death,' he began.

'Thank you,' said Ruth, bowing her head.

'We asked you to come here this morning so that we could advise you of the details of your late husband's will. Afterwards, we shall be happy to answer any questions you might have.'

Ruth went cold, and began trembling. Why hadn't Angus warned her that there were likely to be problems?

The solicitor read through the preamble, finally coming to the bequests.

'I leave all my worldly goods to my wife Ruth, with the exception of the following bequests:

'a) £200 each to both of my sons Nicholas and Ben, which I would like them to spend on something in my memory.

'b) £500 to the Scottish Royal Academy, to be used for the purchase of a picture of their choice, which must be by a Scottish artist.

'c) £1,000 to George Watson College, my old school, and a further £2,000 to Edinburgh University.'

The solicitor continued with a list of smaller bequests, ending with a gift of £100 to the Cottage Hospital which had taken such good care of Angus during the last few days of his life.

The senior partner looked up at Ruth and asked, 'Do you have any questions, Mrs Henderson, which we might advise you on? Or will you be happy for us to administer your affairs in the same way as we did your late husband's?'

'To be honest, Mr Craddock, Angus never discussed his affairs with me, so I'm not sure what all this means. As long as there's enough for the boys and myself to go on living in the way we did when he was alive, I'm happy for you to continue to administer our affairs.'

The partner seated on Mr Craddock's right said, 'I had the privilege of advising Mr Henderson since he first arrived on the island some seven years ago, Mrs Henderson, and would be happy to answer any questions you may have.'

'That's extremely kind of you,' said Ruth, 'but I have no idea what questions to ask, other than perhaps to know roughly how much my husband was worth.'

'That is not quite so easy to answer,' Mr Craddock said, 'because he left so little in cash. However, it has been my responsibility to calculate a figure for probate,' he added, opening one of the files in front of him. 'My initial judgement, which is perhaps on the conservative side, would suggest a sum of somewhere between eighteen and twenty million.'

'Francs?' said Ruth in a whisper.

'No, pounds, madam,' said Mr Craddock matter-of-factly.

—◦—

After some considerable thought, Ruth decided that she would not let anyone know of her good fortune, including the children. When she flew into London the following weekend, she told Max that Angus's solicitors had briefed her on the contents of Angus's will and the value of his estate.

'Any surprises?' Max asked.

'No, not really. He left the boys a couple of hundred pounds each, and with the £100,000 you managed to raise on the sale of our house in the Ardennes, there should be just about enough to keep the wolves from the door, as long as I'm not too extravagant. So I fear you'll have to go on working if you still want me to be your wife.'

'Even more. I would have hated the idea of living off Angus's money. In fact, I've got some good news for you. The firm has asked me to look into the possibility of opening a branch in St Helier early in the new year. I've told them that I'll only consider the offer on one condition.'

'And what's that?' asked Ruth.

'That one of the locals agrees to be my wife.'

Ruth took him in her arms, never more confident that she had found the right man to spend the rest of her life with.

—◦—

Max and Ruth were married at the Chelsea register office three months later, with only the twins as witnesses, and even they had been reluctant to attend. 'He'll never take the place of our father,' Ben had told his mother with considerable feeling. Nicholas had nodded his agreement.

'Don't worry,' said Max, as they drove to the airport. 'Only time will sort out that problem.'

As they flew out of Heathrow to begin their honeymoon, Ruth mentioned that she had been a little disappointed that none of Max's friends had attended the ceremony.

'We don't need to attract unpleasant comments so soon after Angus's death,' he told her. 'It might be wise to let a little time go by before I launch you on London society.' He smiled and took her hand. Ruth accepted his assurance, and put aside any anxieties she might have had.

The plane touched down at Venice airport three hours later, and they were whisked away on a motorboat to a hotel overlooking St Mark's Square. Everything seemed so well organised, and Ruth was surprised at how willing her new husband was to spend hours in the fashion shops helping her select numerous outfits. He even chose a dress for her that she considered far too expensive. For a whole week of lazing about on gondolas, he never once left her side for a moment.

On the Friday, Max hired a car and drove his bride south to Florence, where they strolled back and forth over the bridges together, visiting the Uffizi, the Pitti Palace and the Accademia. In the evenings they ate too much pasta and joined in the dancing in the market square, often returning to their hotel just as the sun was rising. They reluctantly flew on to Rome for the third week, where the hotel bedroom, the Coliseum, the opera house and the Vatican occupied most of their spare moments. The three weeks passed so quickly that Ruth couldn't recall the individual days.

She wrote to the boys every evening before going to bed, describing what a wonderful holiday she was having, always emphasising how kind Max was. She so much wanted them to accept him, but feared that might take more than time.

When she and Max returned to St Helier, he continued to be considerate and attentive. The only disappointment for Ruth was that he didn't have much success in finding premises for the new branch of his company. He would disappear at around ten every morning, but seemed to spend more time at the golf club than he did in town. 'Networking,' he would explain, 'because that's what will matter once the branch is open.'

'When do you think that will be?' Ruth asked.

'Not too much longer now,' he assured her. 'You have to remember that the most important thing in my business is to open in the right location. It's much better to wait for a prime site than to settle for second best.'

But as the weeks passed, Ruth became anxious that Max didn't seem to be getting any nearer to finding that prime site. Whenever she raised the subject he accused her of nagging, which meant that she didn't feel able to bring it up again for at least another month.

When they had been married for six months, she suggested that they might take a weekend off and visit London. 'It would give me a chance to meet some of your friends and catch up with the theatre, and you could report back to your company.'

Each time, Max found some new excuse for not falling in with her plans. But he did agree that they should return to Venice to celebrate their first wedding anniversary.

◄○►

Ruth hoped the two-week break would revive the memories of their previous visit, and might even inspire Max, when he returned to Jersey, to finally settle on some premises. As it was, the anniversary couldn't have been in greater contrast to the honeymoon they had shared the year before.

It was raining as the plane touched down at Venice airport, and they stood shivering in a long queue as they waited for a taxi. When they arrived at the hotel, Ruth discovered that Max thought she had organised the booking. He lost his temper with the innocent manager, and stormed out of the building. After they had trudged around in the rain with their luggage for over an hour, they ended up in a backstreet hotel that could only supply a small room with single beds, above the bar.

Over drinks that evening, Max confessed that he had left his credit cards in Jersey, so he hoped Ruth wouldn't mind covering the bills until they got home. She seemed to have been covering most of the bills lately anyway, but decided now was not the time to raise the subject.

In Florence, Ruth hesitantly mentioned over breakfast that she hoped he would have more luck in finding premises for his company once they returned to Jersey, and enquired innocently if the firm was becoming at all anxious about his lack of progress.

Max immediately flew into a rage and walked out of the breakfast room, telling her to stop nagging him all the time. She didn't see him for the rest of the day.

In Rome it continued to rain, and Max didn't help matters

by regularly going off without warning, sometimes arriving back at the hotel long after she had gone to bed.

Ruth was relieved when the plane took off for Jersey. Once they were back in St Helier she made every effort not to nag, and to try to be supportive and understanding about Max's lack of progress. But however hard she tried, her efforts were met either with long sullen silences or bouts of temper.

As the months passed, they seemed to grow further and further apart, and Ruth no longer bothered to ask how the search for premises was going. She had long ago assumed that the whole idea had been abandoned, and could only wonder if Max had ever been given such an assignment in the first place.

It was over breakfast one morning that Max suddenly announced that the firm had decided against opening a branch in St Helier, and had written to tell him that if he wanted to remain as a partner, he would have to return to London and resume his old position.

'And if you refuse?' asked Ruth. 'Is there an alternative?'

'They've made it all too clear that they would expect me to hand in my resignation.'

'I'd be quite happy to move to London,' Ruth suggested, hoping that might solve their problems.

'No, I don't think that would help,' said Max, who had obviously already decided what the solution was. 'I think it would be better if I spent the week in London, and then flew back to be with you at weekends.'

Ruth did not think that was a good idea, but she knew that any protest would be pointless.

Max flew to London the following day.

—◇—

Ruth couldn't remember the last time they had made love, and when Max didn't return to Jersey for their second wedding anniversary she accepted an invitation to join Gerald Prescott for dinner.

The twins' old housemaster was, as always, kind and considerate, and when they were alone he did no more than kiss Ruth on the cheek. She decided to tell him about the problems she was having with Max, and he listened attentively, occasionally nodding his understanding. As Ruth looked across the table at her old friend, she felt the sad first thoughts of divorce. She dismissed them quickly from her mind.

When Max returned home the following weekend, Ruth decided to make a special effort. She spent the morning shopping in the market, selecting fresh ingredients for his favourite dish, coq au vin, and picking out a vintage claret to complement it. She wore the dress he had chosen for her in Venice, and drove to the airport to meet him off the plane. He didn't arrive on his usual flight, but strolled through the barrier two hours later, explaining that he had been held up at Heathrow. He didn't apologise for the hours she had spent pacing around the airport lounge, and when they eventually arrived back home and sat down for dinner, he made no comment on the meal, the wine or her dress.

When Ruth had finished clearing away after dinner, she hurried up to the bedroom to find he was pretending to be fast asleep.

Max spent most of Saturday at the golf club, and on Sunday he took the afternoon flight back to London. His last words before departing for the airport were that he couldn't be sure when he would be returning.

Second thoughts of divorce.

—◇—

As the weeks passed, with only the occasional phone call from London and the odd snatched weekend together, Ruth started seeing more and more of Gerald. Although he never attempted to do anything more than kiss her on the cheek at the beginning and end of their clandestine meetings, and certainly never placed a hand on her thigh, it was she who finally decided 'the time had come' to seduce him.

'Will you marry me?' she asked, as she watched him getting dressed at six the next morning.

'But you're already married,' Gerald gently reminded her.

'You know perfectly well that it's a sham, and has been for months. I was swept off my feet by Max's charm, and behaved like a schoolgirl. Heaven knows I'd read enough novels about marrying on the rebound.'

'I'd marry you tomorrow, old girl, given half the chance,' Gerald said, smiling. 'You know I've adored you from the first day we met.'

'Although you're not down on one knee, Gerald, I shall consider that an acceptance,' said Ruth, laughing. She paused and looked at her lover, standing in the half-light. 'When I next see Max I'll ask him for a divorce,' she added quietly.

Gerald took off his clothes and climbed back into bed.

◄○►

It was to be another month before Max returned to the island, and although he took the late flight, Ruth was waiting for him when he walked in the front door. When he leaned down to kiss her on the cheek, she turned away.

'I want a divorce,' she said matter-of-factly.

Max followed her into the drawing room without saying a word. He slumped down into a chair and remained silent for some time. Ruth sat patiently waiting for his response.

'Is there another man?' he eventually asked.

'Yes,' she replied.

'Do I know him?'

'Yes.'

'Gerald?' he asked, looking up at her.

'Yes.'

Once again Max fell into a morose silence.

'I'll be only too happy to make it easy for you,' said Ruth. 'You can sue me for divorce on the grounds of my adultery with Gerald, and I won't put up a fight.'

She was surprised by Max's response. 'I'd like a little time to think about it,' he said. 'Perhaps it would be sensible for us not to do anything until the boys come home at Christmas.'

Ruth reluctantly agreed, but was puzzled, because she couldn't remember when he had last mentioned the boys in her presence.

Max spent the night in the spare room, and flew back to London the following morning, accompanied by two packed suitcases.

He didn't return to Jersey for several weeks, during which time Ruth and Gerald began to plan their future together.

—◇—

When the twins returned from university for the Christmas holidays, they sounded neither surprised nor disappointed that their mother would be getting a divorce.

Max made no attempt to join the family for the festive season, but flew over to Jersey the day after the boys had returned to university. He took a taxi straight to the house, but stayed for only an hour.

'I am willing to agree to a divorce,' he told Ruth, 'and I intend to start proceedings just as soon as I return to London.'

Ruth simply nodded her agreement.

'If you want things to go through quickly and smoothly, I suggest you appoint a London solicitor. That way I won't have to keep flying back and forth to Jersey, which will only hold things up.'

Ruth put up no objection to the idea, as she had reached

the stage where she didn't want to place any obstacles in Max's way.

A few days after Max had returned to the mainland, Ruth was served with divorce papers from a London law firm she had never heard of. She instructed Angus's old solicitors in Chancery Lane to handle the proceedings, explaining over the phone to a junior partner that she wanted to get it over with as quickly as possible.

'Are you hoping for a maintenance settlement of any kind?' the solicitor asked.

'No,' said Ruth, trying not to laugh. 'I don't want anything other than for the whole matter to be settled quickly, on the grounds of my adultery.'

'If those are your instructions, madam, I'll draw up the necessary papers and have them ready for you to sign within the next few days.'

When the decree nisi was served, Gerald suggested they celebrate by taking a holiday. Ruth agreed to the idea, just as long as they didn't have to go anywhere near Italy.

'Let's sail around the Greek islands,' said Gerald. 'That way there will be less chance of bumping into any of my pupils, not to mention their parents.' They flew to Athens the next day.

When they sailed into the harbour at Skyros, Ruth said, 'I'd never thought I would spend my third wedding anniversary with another man.'

Gerald took her in his arms. 'Try to forget Max,' he said. 'He's history.'

'Well, nearly,' Ruth said. 'I was rather hoping that the divorce would have been absolute before we left Jersey.'

'Have you any idea what's caused the hold-up?' Gerald asked.

'Heaven knows,' Ruth replied, 'but whatever it is, Max will

have his reasons.' She paused. 'You know, I never did get to see his office in Mayfair, or meet any of his colleagues or friends. It's almost as if it was all a figment of my imagination.'

'Or his,' said Gerald, putting an arm around her waist. 'But don't let's waste any more time talking about Max. Let's think about Greeks, and bacchanalian orgies.'

'Is that what you teach those innocent little children in their formative years?'

'No, it's what they teach me,' Gerald replied.

For the next three weeks the two of them sailed around the Greek islands, eating too much moussaka, drinking too much wine, and hoping that too much sex would keep their weight down. By the end of their holiday Gerald was a little too red, and Ruth was dreading being reintroduced to her bathroom scales. The holiday could not have been more fun; not only because Gerald was such a good sailor, but because, as Ruth discovered, even during a storm he could make her laugh.

Once they were back on Jersey, Gerald drove Ruth to the house. When she opened the front door she was greeted by a pile of letters. She sighed. They could all wait until tomorrow, she decided.

Ruth spent a restless night tossing and turning. After snatching a few hours' sleep, she decided that she might as well get up and make herself a cup of tea. She began to thumb through the post, only stopping when she came to a long buff envelope marked 'Urgent' and bearing a London postmark.

She tore it open and extracted a document that brought a smile to her face: 'A decree absolute has been granted between the aforesaid parties: Max Donald Bennett and Ruth Ethel Bennett.'

'That settles that once and for all,' she said out loud, and immediately phoned Gerald to tell him the good news.

'Disappointing,' he said.

'Disappointing?' she repeated.

'Yes, my darling. You have no idea how much my street cred has risen since the boys at school discovered I've been on holiday with a married woman.'

Ruth laughed. 'Behave yourself, Gerald, and try to get used to the idea of being a respectable married man.'

'Can't wait,' he said. 'But must dash. It's one thing to be living in sin; it's quite another to be late for morning prayers.'

Ruth went up to the bathroom and stood gingerly on the scales. She groaned when she saw where the little indicator finally stopped. She decided she would have to spend at least an hour in the gym that morning. The phone rang just as she was stepping into the bath. She got back out and grabbed a towel, thinking it must be Gerald again.

'Good morning, Mrs Bennett,' said a rather formal voice. How she hated even the sound of that name.

'Good morning,' she replied.

'It's Mr Craddock, madam. I've been trying to get in touch with you for the past three weeks.'

'Oh, I'm so sorry,' said Ruth, 'but I only returned from a holiday in Greece last night.'

'Yes, I see. Well, perhaps we could meet as soon as it's convenient?' he said, showing no interest in her holiday.

'Yes, of course, Mr Craddock. I could pop into your office around twelve, if that would suit you.'

'Any time you decide will suit us, Mrs Bennett,' said the formal voice.

Ruth worked hard in the gym that morning, determined to lose the surplus pounds she had put on in Greece – respectable married woman or not, she still wanted to be slim. By the time she'd come off the running machine, the gym clock was chiming twelve. Despite hurrying through to the locker room and showering and changing as quickly as possible, she was still thirty-five minutes late for Mr Craddock.

Once again the receptionist ushered her through to the senior partner's office, without her having to see the inside of a waiting room. As she entered, she found Mr Craddock pacing around the room.

'I'm sorry to have kept you,' she said, feeling a little guilty, as two of the partners rose from their places at the boardroom table.

This time Mr Craddock did not suggest a cup of tea, but simply ushered her into a chair at the other end of the table. Once she was seated, he resumed his place, glanced down at a pile of papers lying in front of him and extracted a single sheet.

'Mrs Bennett, we have received a summons from your husband's solicitors demanding a full settlement following your divorce.'

'But we never discussed a settlement at any time,' said Ruth in disbelief. 'It was never part of the deal.'

'That may well be the case,' said the senior partner, looking down at the papers. 'But unfortunately, you agreed to the divorce being granted on the grounds of your adultery with a Mr Gerald' – he checked the name – 'Prescott, at a time when your husband was working in London.'

'That's true, but we only agreed to that in order to speed matters up. You see, we both wanted the divorce to go through as quickly as possible.'

'I'm sure that was the case, Mrs Bennett.'

She would always hate that name.

'However, by agreeing to Mr Bennett's terms, he became the innocent party in this action.'

'But that is no longer relevant,' said Ruth, 'because this morning I received confirmation from my London solicitors that I have been granted a decree absolute.'

The partner seated on Mr Craddock's right turned and looked directly at her.

'May I be permitted to ask if it was at Mr Bennett's suggestion that you instructed a solicitor from the mainland to handle your divorce proceedings?'

Ah, so that's what's behind all this, thought Ruth. They're just annoyed that I didn't consult them. 'Yes,' she replied firmly. 'It was simply a matter of convenience, as Max was living in London at the time, and didn't want to have to keep flying back and forth to the island.'

'It certainly turned out to be most convenient for Mr Bennett,' said the senior partner. 'Did your husband ever discuss a financial settlement with you?'

'Never,' said Ruth even more firmly. 'He had no idea what I was worth.'

'I have a feeling,' continued the partner seated on Mr Craddock's left, 'that Mr Bennett knew only too well how much you were worth.'

'But that's not possible,' insisted Ruth. 'You see, I never once discussed my finances with him.'

'Nevertheless, he has presented a claim against you, and seems to have made a remarkably accurate assessment of the value of your late husband's estate.'

'Then you must refuse to pay a penny, because it was never part of our agreement.'

'I accept that what you are telling us is correct, Mrs Bennett. But I fear that as you were the guilty party, we have no defence to offer.'

'How can that be possible?' demanded Ruth.

'The law of divorce on Jersey is unequivocal on the subject,' said Mr Craddock. 'As we would have been happy to advise you, had you consulted us.'

'What law?' asked Ruth, ignoring the barbed comment.

'Under the law of Jersey, once it has been accepted that one of the parties is innocent in divorce proceedings, that person – whatever their sex – is automatically entitled to one third of the other's estate.'

Ruth began trembling. 'Are there no exceptions?' she asked quietly.

'Yes,' replied Mr Craddock.

Ruth looked up hopefully.

'If you have been married for less than three years, the law does not apply. You were, however, Mrs Bennett, married for three years and eight days.' He paused, readjusted his spectacles and added, 'I have a feeling that Mr Bennett was not only aware of exactly how much you were worth, but also knew the laws of divorce as they apply on Jersey.'

Three months later, after both sides of solicitors had agreed on the value of Ruth Ethel Bennett's estate, Max Donald Bennett received a cheque for £6,270,000 in full and final settlement.

Whenever Ruth looked back on the past three years – and she often did – she came to the conclusion that Max must have planned everything right down to the last detail. Yes, even before they had bumped into each other.

LOVE AT FIRST SIGHT*

ANDREW WAS running late, and would have grabbed a taxi if it hadn't been the rush hour. He entered the crowded Metro and dodged in and out of the hordes of commuters as they headed down the escalator on their way home.

Andrew wasn't on his way home. After only four stops he would re-emerge from the bowels of the earth to keep an appointment with Ely Bloom, the Chief Executive of Chase Manhattan in Paris. Although Andrew had never met Bloom, like all his colleagues at the bank, he was well aware of his reputation. He didn't 'take a meeting' with anyone unless there was a good reason.

Andrew had spent the forty-eight hours since Bloom's secretary had called to make the appointment trying to work out what that good reason could possibly be. A simple switch from Crédit Suisse to Chase seemed the obvious answer – but it was unlikely to be that simple if Bloom was involved. Was he about to make Andrew an offer he couldn't refuse? Would he expect him to return to New York after he had spent less than two years in Paris? So many questions floated through his mind. He knew he should stop speculating, as they would all be answered at six o'clock. He would have run down the escalator, but it was too crowded.

Andrew knew he had a few chips stacked on his side of the

table – he had headed up the foreign exchange desk at Crédit Suisse for almost two years, and it was common knowledge that he was outperforming all of his rivals. The French bankers had simply shrugged their shoulders when they were told of Andrew's success, while his American rivals just tried to persuade him to leave his present position and join them. Whatever Bloom might offer him, Andrew was confident Crédit Suisse would match it. Whenever he had received other approaches during the past twelve months he had dismissed them with the same polite, boyish grin – but he knew that this time would be different. Bloom wasn't a man who could be bought off with a polite, boyish grin.

Andrew didn't want to move banks, as he was well satisfied with the package Crédit Suisse had given him – and at his age, what young man wouldn't enjoy working in Paris? However, it was that time of the year when annual bonuses were being considered, so he was happy to be seen 'taking a meeting' with Ely Bloom in the American Bar at the Georges V. It would be only a matter of hours before someone reported the sighting to his superiors.

When Andrew stepped onto the platform of the Metro, it was so crowded that he wondered if he would be able to get on the first train that pulled into the station. He checked his watch: 5.37. He should still be well in time for the meeting, but as he had no intention of being late for Mr Bloom, he began to slip through any tiny opening or gap that appeared until he found himself at the front of the mêlée, well placed to climb on board the next train. Even if he didn't reach an agreement with Mr Bloom, the man was going to be an important figure in the banking world for years to come, so there was no point in turning up late and making a bad impression.

Andrew waited impatiently for the next train to emerge

from the tunnel. He stared across the track at the opposite platform, and tried to concentrate on what questions Bloom might ask.

What is your present salary?

Can you break your contract?

Are you on a bonus scheme?

Are you willing to return to New York?

The southbound platform was just as crowded as the one he was standing on, and Andrew's concentration was broken when his eyes settled on a young woman who was glancing at her watch. Perhaps she also had an appointment she couldn't afford to be late for.

When she raised her head, he immediately forgot Ely Bloom. He just stared into those deep brown eyes. She remained unaware of her admirer. She must have been about five foot eight, with the most perfect oval face, olive skin that would never require make-up, and a mop of curly black hair that no hairdresser could possibly have permed. I'm on the wrong side of the track, he told himself, and it's too late to do anything about it.

She wore a beige-coloured raincoat, the tied belt leaving no question as to how slim and graceful her figure was, and her legs – or as much as he could see of them – completed a perfect package. Better than any Mr Bloom could offer.

She checked her watch again and then looked up, suddenly aware that he was staring at her.

He smiled. She blushed and lowered her head just as two trains glided into the station from opposite ends of the platform. Everyone standing behind Andrew pushed forward to claim a place on the waiting train.

When it pulled out of the station, Andrew was the only person left on the platform. He stared across at the train on the other side, and watched it slowly accelerate out of the station. When it had disappeared into the tunnel, Andrew smiled again. Only one person remained on the opposite platform, and this time she returned his smile.

You may ask how I know this story to be true. The answer is simple. I was told it at Andrew and Claire's tenth wedding anniversary earlier this year.

BOTH SIDES AGAINST
THE MIDDLE★

'THERE'S ONE PROBLEM I haven't touched on,' said Billy Gibson. 'But first, let me refill your glass.'

For the past hour the two men had sat quietly in the corner of the King William Arms discussing the problems of running a police station on the border of Northern Ireland and Eire. Billy Gibson was retiring after thirty years in the force, the past six of them as Chief of Police. His successor, Jim Hogan, had been brought in from Belfast, and the talk was that if he made a good fist of it, his next stop would be as Chief Constable.

Billy took a long draught, and settled back before he began his story.

'No one can be quite sure of the truth about the house that straddles the border, but, as with all good Irish stories, there are always several half-truths circulating at any one time. I need to tell you a little of the house's history before I come to the problem I'm having with its present owners. To do that I must mention, if only in passing, one Patrick O'Dowd, who worked in the planning department of Belfast City Council.'

'A nest of vipers at the best of times,' chipped in the new Chief.

'And those were not the best of times,' said the retiring

Chief, before taking another sip of Guinness. His thirst quenched, he continued his story.

'No one has ever understood why O'Dowd granted planning permission for a house to be built on the border in the first place. It was not until it had been completed that someone in the rates department in Dublin got hold of an Ordnance Survey map, and pointed out to the authorities in Belfast that the border ran right through the middle of the sitting room. Old lags in the village say the local builder misread the plans, but others assure me that he knew exactly what he was doing.

'At the time, no one cared too much, because the man the house was built for – Bertie O'Flynn, a widower – was a godfearing man who attended Mass at St Mary's in the South, and sipped his Guinness at the Volunteer in the North. I think it's also worth mentioning,' said the Chief, 'that Bertie had no politics.

'Dublin and Belfast managed to reach a rare compromise, and agreed that as the house's front door was in the North, Bertie should pay his taxes to the Crown, but as his kitchen and half-acre of garden were in the South, he should pay his rates to the local council on the other side of the border. For years this agreement caused no difficulties, until dear old Bertie departed this life and left the house to his son, Eamonn. To cut a long story short, Eamonn was, is, and always will be a bad lot.

'The boy had been sent to school in the North, although he attended church in the South, and he showed little interest in either. In fact, by the age of eleven, the only thing he didn't know about smuggling was how to spell it. By the time he turned thirteen, he was buying cartons of cigarettes in the North, and trading them for crates of Guinness in the South. At the age of fifteen, he was earning more money than his headmaster, and when he left school he was already running a flourishing business, importing spirits and wine from the South while exporting cannabis and condoms from the North.

'Whenever his probation officer knocked on the front door in the North, he retreated to his kitchen in the South. If the local Garda was seen walking up the garden path, Eamonn disappeared into the dining room, and stayed there until they got bored and drove away. Bertie, who always ended up having to answer the door, got heartily sick of it, which I suspect in the end was the reason he gave up the ghost.

'Now, when I took up my appointment as Chief of Police six years ago, I decided to make it my personal ambition to put Eamonn O'Flynn behind bars. But what with the problems I've had to handle on the border and normal policing duties, the truth is I never got round to it. I'd even started to turn a blind eye, until O'Flynn met Maggie Crann, a well-known prostitute from the South, who was looking to expand her trade in the North. A house with four upstairs bedrooms, two on either side of the border, seemed to be the answer to her prayers – even if from time to time one of her half-naked customers had to be moved from one side of the house to the other rather quickly, to avoid being arrested.

'When the Troubles escalated, my opposite number south of the border and I agreed to treat the house as a "no go" area – that was, until Eamonn opened a casino in the South in a new conservatory which was never to grow a flower – planning permission agreed by Dublin – with the cashier's office situated in a newly constructed garage that could take a fleet of buses, but has not yet housed a vehicle of any description – planning permission agreed by Belfast.'

'Why didn't you oppose planning permission?' asked Hogan.

'We did, but it quickly became clear that Maggie had customers in both departments.' Billy sighed. 'But the final blow came when the farmland surrounding the house came up for sale. No one else got a look-in, and O'Flynn ended up with sixty-five acres, in which he could post lookouts. That gives him more than enough time to move any incriminating evidence from one side of the house to the other, long before we can reach the front door.'

The glasses were empty. 'My round,' said the younger man. He went up to the bar and ordered two more pints.

When he returned, he asked his next question even before he had placed the glasses on the table.

'Why haven't you applied for a search warrant? With the number of laws he must be breaking, surely you could have closed the place down years ago?'

'Agreed,' said the Chief, 'but whenever I apply for a warrant, he's the first person to hear about it. By the time we arrive, all we find is a happily married couple living alone in a peaceful farmhouse.'

'But what about your opposite number in the South? It must be in his interests to work with you and . . .'

'You'd think so, wouldn't you? But there have been five of them in the past seven years, and what with not wishing to harm their promotion prospects, their desire for an easy life, or straightforward bribery, not one of them has been willing to cooperate. The current Garda Chief is only months away from retirement, and won't do anything that might harm his pension. No,' continued Billy, 'whichever way you look at it, I've failed. And I can tell you, unlike my opposite number, if I could sort out Eamonn O'Flynn once and for all, I would even be willing to forgo my pension.'

'Well, you still have another six weeks, and after all you've told me, I'd be relieved if O'Flynn was off the patch before I took over. So let's see if I can come up with a solution that will solve both our problems.'

'I'd agree to anything, short of murdering the man – and don't think that hasn't crossed my mind.'

Jim Hogan laughed, looked at his watch and said, 'I must be getting back to Belfast.'

The old Chief nodded, downed his last drop of Guinness and accompanied his colleague to the carpark at the back of the pub. Hogan didn't speak again until he was seated behind the wheel of his car. He turned on the engine and wound the window down.

'Are you going to have a farewell party?'

'Yes,' said the Chief. 'On the Saturday before I retire. Why do you ask?'

'Because I always think a farewell party is an occasion to let bygones be bygones,' said Jim, without explanation.

The Chief looked puzzled as Jim drove out of the carpark, turned right, and headed north towards Belfast.

‒◄o►‒

Eamonn O'Flynn was somewhat surprised to receive the invitation, as he hadn't expected to feature on the Chief of Police's guest list.

Maggie studied the embossed card inviting them to Chief Gibson's farewell party at the Queen's Arms in Ballyroney.

'Are you going to accept?' she asked.

'Why would I want to do that,' responded Eamonn, 'when the bastard has spent the past six years trying to put me behind bars?'

'Perhaps it's his way of burying the hatchet,' suggested Maggie.

'Yes, right in the middle of my back, would be my bet. In any case, surely you wouldn't want to be seen dead with that lot.'

'Now, there's where you're wrong for once,' said Maggie.

'Why's that?'

'Because it would amuse me to see the faces of the wives of those councillors, not to mention the police officers, I've shared a bed with.'

'But it could turn out to be a trap.'

'I can't imagine how,' said Maggie, 'when we know for certain that them in the South won't give us any trouble, and anyone who could in the North is sure to be at the party.'

'That wouldn't stop them raiding our place while we're off the premises.'

'What a disappointment that will be for them,' said Maggie, 'when they discover the staff have been given the night off, and it's nothing more than the home of two decent, law-abiding citizens.'

Eamonn remained sceptical, and it wasn't until Maggie arrived back from Dublin with a new dress she wanted everyone to see her in that he finally surrendered and agreed to accompany her to the party. 'But we won't stay for more than an hour, and that's my final word on the subject,' he warned her.

─◦─

When they left the house on the night of the party, Eamonn checked that every window was locked and every door was bolted before he set the alarm. He then drove slowly around the perimeter of his land, warning all the guards to be especially careful and to call him on his mobile if they spotted anything suspicious – and he meant anything.

Maggie, who was checking her hair in the car mirror, told him that if he took much longer there wouldn't be any party left to go to.

When they walked into the ballroom of the Queen's Arms

half an hour later, Billy Gibson seemed genuinely pleased to see them, which only made Eamonn feel even more suspicious.

'I don't think you've met my successor,' said the Chief, before introducing Eamonn and Maggie to Jim Hogan. 'But I'm sure you know of his reputation.'

Eamonn knew of his reputation only too well, and wanted to return home immediately, but someone pressed a pint of Guinness into his hand, and a young constable asked Maggie for a dance.

While she was dancing, Eamonn looked around the room to see if there was anyone he knew. Far too many, he concluded, and couldn't wait for an hour to pass so he could go home. But then his eyes rested on Mick Burke, a local pickpocket who was serving behind the bar. Eamonn was surprised that, with Mick's record, they had let him past the front door. But at least he had found someone he could have a quiet chat to.

When the band stopped playing, Maggie joined the queue for food and filled a plate with salmon and new potatoes. She took the offering across to Eamonn, who for a few minutes looked almost as if he was enjoying himself. After a second helping he started swapping stories with one or two members of the Garda, who appeared to be hanging on his every word.

But the moment Eamonn heard eleven chime on the ballroom clock, he suddenly wanted to escape. 'Even Cinderella didn't leave the ball before twelve,' Maggie told him. 'And in any case, it would be rude to leave just as the Chief's about to deliver his farewell speech.'

The toastmaster banged his gavel and called for order. A warm round of applause greeted Billy Gibson as he stepped forward to take his place in front of the microphone. He rested his speech on the lectern and smiled down at the assembled gathering.

'My friends,' he began, ' – not to mention one or two sparring partners.' He raised his glass in the direction of Eamonn, delighted to see he was still among them. 'It is with a heavy heart that I appear before you tonight, aware of how much I am indebted to all of you.' He paused. 'And I mean *all* of you.' Cheers and catcalls followed these remarks, and Maggie was delighted to see that Eamonn was joining in the laughter.

'Now, I well remember when I first joined the force. That was when things were really tough.' More cheers followed, and louder catcalls from the young. The noise died down eventually when the Chief resumed his speech, no one wishing to deny him the opportunity of reminiscing at his own farewell party.

Eamonn was still sober enough to notice the young constable entering the room, an anxious look on his face. He made his way quickly towards the stage, and although he evidently didn't feel able to interrupt Billy's speech, he carried out Mr Hogan's instructions and placed a note in the middle of the lectern.

Eamonn began to fumble for his mobile, but he couldn't find it in any of his pockets. He could have sworn he'd had it with him when he arrived.

'When I hand in my badge at midnight . . .' Billy said, glancing down at his speech to see the note in front of him. He paused and adjusted his glasses, as if trying to take in the significance of the message, then frowned and looked back up at his guests. 'I must apologise, my friends, but it seems that there's been an incident on the border that requires my personal attention. I have no choice but to leave immediately, and ask that all ranking officers join me outside. I hope our guests will continue to enjoy the party, and be assured we'll return just as soon as we've sorted the little problem out.'

Only one person reached the front door before the Chief, and he was driving out of the carpark before even Maggie realised he'd left the room. However, the Chief, siren blaring, still managed to overtake Eamonn some two miles from the border.

'Shall I have him stopped for speeding?' asked the Chief's driver.

'No, I don't think so,' said Billy Gibson. 'What's the point of this whole performance if the principal actor is unable to make an entrance?'

When Eamonn brought his car to a halt at the edge of his property a few minutes later, he found it encircled by thick blue-and-white tape proclaiming 'DANGER. DO NOT ENTER.'

He jumped out of his car and ran over to the Chief, who was receiving a briefing from a group of officers.

'What the hell is going on?' demanded Eamonn.

'Ah, Eamonn, I'm so glad you were able to make it. I was just about to call you, in case you were still at the party. It seems that about an hour ago an IRA patrol was spotted on your land.'

'Actually, that hasn't been confirmed,' said a young officer, who was listening intently to someone on a hand-phone. 'There's conflicting intelligence coming out of Ballyroney suggesting that they may have been loyalist paramilitaries.'

'Well, whoever they are, my first interest must be the protection of lives and property, and to that end I've sent in the bomb squad to make sure it will be safe for you and Maggie to return to your home.'

'That's bollocks, Billy Gibson, and you know it,' said Eamonn. 'I'm ordering you off my land before I instruct my men to forcibly remove you.'

'Well, it's not quite as easy as that,' said the Chief. 'You see, I've just had a message from the bomb squad that they've already broken into your house. You'll be relieved to know they found no one on the premises, but they were most concerned to come across an unidentifiable package in the conservatory, and a similar one in the garage.'

'But they're nothing more than . . .'

'Nothing more than what?' asked the Chief innocently.

'How did your people manage to get past my guards?' demanded Eamonn. 'They had orders to throw you off if you put so much as a toe on my land.'

'Now there's the thing, Eamonn. They must have wandered off your property for a moment without realising it, and because of the imminent danger to their lives I felt it necessary to take them all into custody. For their own protection, you understand.'

'I'll bet you don't even have a search warrant to enter my property.'

'I don't need one,' said the Chief, 'if I'm of the opinion that someone's life is in danger.'

'Well, now you know that no one's life is in danger, and never was in the first place, you can get off my property and back to your party.'

'There's my next problem, Eamonn. You see, we've just had another call, this time from an anonymous informant, to warn us that he has placed a bomb in the garage and another in the conservatory, and that they'll be detonated just before midnight. The moment I was informed of this threat, I realised that it was my duty to check the safety manual to find out what the correct procedure is in circumstances such as these.' The Chief removed a thick green booklet from an inside pocket, as if it were always with him.

'You're bluffing,' said O'Flynn. 'You don't have the authority to . . .'

'Ah, here's what I was after,' said the Chief, after he had flicked over a few pages. Eamonn looked down to see a paragraph underlined in red ink.

'Let me read you the exact words, Eamonn, so that you'll

fully comprehend the terrible dilemma I'm facing. *"If an officer above the rank of Major or Chief Inspector believes that the lives of civilians may be at risk at the scene of a suspected terrorist attack, and he has a qualified member of the bomb squad present, he must first clear the area of all civilians and, having achieved this, if he deems it appropriate, carry out an isolated explosion."* Couldn't be clearer,' said the Chief. 'Now, are you able to let me know what's in those boxes, Eamonn? If not, I must assume the worst, and proceed according to the book.'

'If you harm my property in any way, Billy Gibson, let me warn you that I'll sue you for every penny you're worth.'

'You're worrying unnecessarily, Eamonn. Let me reassure you that there's page after page in the manual concerning compensation for innocent victims. We would naturally feel it our obligation to rebuild your lovely home, brick by brick, recreating a conservatory Maggie would be proud of and a garage large enough to house all your cars. However, if we were to spend that amount of taxpayers' money, we would have to ensure that the house was built on one side of the border or the other, so that an unhappy incident such as this one could never happen again.'

'You'll never get away with it,' said Eamonn, as a heavily-built man appeared by the Chief's side, carrying a plunger.

'You'll remember Mr Hogan, of course. I introduced you at my farewell party.'

'You put a finger on that plunger, Hogan, and I'll have you facing inquiries for the rest of your working life. And you'll be able to forget any ideas of becoming Chief Constable.'

'Mr O'Flynn makes a fair point, Jim,' said the Chief, checking his watch, 'and I certainly wouldn't want to be responsible for harming your career in any way. But I see that you don't take over command for another seven minutes, so it will be my sad duty to carry out this onerous responsibility.'

As the Chief bent down to place his hand on the plunger, Eamonn leapt at his throat. It took three officers to restrain him, while he shouted obscenities at the top of his voice.

The Chief sighed, checked his watch, gripped the handle of the plunger and pressed down slowly.

The explosion could be heard for miles around as the roof of the garage – or was it the conservatory? – flew high into the air. Within moments the buildings were razed to the ground, leaving nothing in their place but smoke, dust and a pile of rubble.

When the noise had finally died away, the chimes of St Mary's could be heard striking twelve in the distance. The former Chief of Police considered it the end of a perfect day.

'You know, Eamonn,' he said, 'I do believe that was worth sacrificing my pension for.'

A WEEKEND TO REMEMBER*

I FIRST MET Susie six years ago, and when she called to ask if I would like to join her for a drink, she can't have been surprised that my immediate response was a little frosty. After all, my memory of our last meeting wasn't altogether a happy one.

I had been invited to the Keswicks for dinner, and like all good hostesses, Kathy Keswick considered it nothing less than her duty to pair off any surviving bachelor over the age of thirty with one of her more eligible girlfriends.

With this in mind, I was disappointed to find that she had placed me next to Mrs Ruby Collier, the wife of a Conservative Member of Parliament who was seated on the left of my hostess at the other end of the table. Only moments after I had introduced myself she said, 'You've probably read about my husband in the press.' She then proceeded to tell me that none of her friends could understand why her husband wasn't in the Cabinet. I felt unable to offer an opinion on the subject, because until that moment I had never heard of him.

The name-card on the other side of me read 'Susie', and the lady in question had the sort of looks that made you wish you were sitting opposite her at a table set for two. Even after a sideways glance at that long fair hair, blue eyes, captivating smile and slim figure, I would not have been surprised to discover that she was a model. An illusion she was happy to dispel within minutes.

I introduced myself by explaining that I had been at Cambridge with our host. 'And how do you know the Keswicks?' I enquired.

'I was in the same office as Kathy when we both worked for *Vogue* in New York.'

I remember feeling disappointed that she lived overseas. For how long, I wondered. 'Where do you work now?'

'I'm still in New York,' she replied. 'I've just been made the commissioning editor for *Art Quarterly*.'

'I renewed my subscription only last week,' I told her, rather pleased with myself. She smiled, evidently surprised that I'd even heard of the publication.

'How long are you in London for?' I asked, glancing at her left hand to check that she wore neither an engagement nor a wedding ring.

'Only a few days. I flew over for my parents' wedding anniversary last week, and I was hoping to catch the Lucian Freud exhibition at the Tate before I go back to New York. And what do you do?' she asked.

'I own a small hotel in Jermyn Street,' I told her.

I would happily have spent the rest of the evening chatting to Susie, and not just because of my passion for art, but my mother had taught me from an early age that however much you like the person on one side of you, you must be equally attentive to the one sitting on the other side.

I turned back to Mrs Collier, who pounced on me with the words, 'Have you read the speech my husband made in the Commons yesterday?'

I confessed that I hadn't, which turned out to be a mistake, because she then delivered the entire offering verbatim.

Once she had completed her monologue on the subject of the Draft Civic Amenities (Landfill) Act, I could see why her husband wasn't in the Cabinet. In fact, I made a mental note to avoid him when we retired to the drawing room for coffee.

'I much look forward to making your husband's acquaintance after dinner,' I told her, before turning my attention back to Susie, only to find that she was staring at someone on the other side of the table. I glanced across to see that the man in question was deep in conversation with Mary Ellen Yarc, an American woman who was seated next to him, and seemed unaware of the attention he was receiving.

I remembered that his name was Richard something, and that he had come with the girl seated at the other end of the table. She too, I noticed, was looking in Richard's direction. I had to confess that he had the sort of chiselled features and thick wavy hair that make it unnecessary to have a degree in quantum physics.

'So, what's big in New York at the moment?' I asked, trying to recapture Susie's attention.

She turned back to me and smiled. 'We're going to have a new Mayor at any moment now,' she informed me, 'and it could even be a Republican for a change. Frankly, I'd vote for anyone who can do something about the crime figures. One of them, I can't remember his name, keeps talking about zero tolerance. Whoever he is, he'd get my vote.'

Although Susie's conversation remained lively and informative, her attention frequently strayed back to the other side of the table. I would have assumed she and Richard were lovers, if he had given her as much as a glance.

Over pudding, Mrs Collier took a hatchet to the Cabinet, giving reasons why every one of them should be replaced – I didn't need to ask by whom. By the time she'd reached the Minister of Agriculture, I felt I'd done my duty, and glanced back to find Susie pretending to be preoccupied by her summer pudding, while actually still taking far more interest in Richard.

Suddenly he looked in her direction. Without warning, Susie grabbed my hand and began talking intently about an Eric Rohmer film she had recently seen in Nice.

Few men object to a woman grabbing their hand, particularly when that woman is graced with Susie's looks, but preferably not while she is gazing at another man.

The moment Richard resumed his conversation with our hostess, Susie immediately released my hand and dug a fork into her summer pudding.

I was grateful to be spared a third round with Mrs Collier, as Kathy rose from her place and suggested that we all go through to the drawing room. I fear this meant I had to miss out on the details of the Private Member's Bill Mrs Collier's husband was preparing to present to the House the following week.

Over coffee I was introduced to Richard, who turned out to be a banker from New York. He continued to ignore Susie – or perhaps, inexplicably, he simply wasn't aware of her presence. The girl whose name I didn't know came across to join us, and murmured in his ear, 'We shouldn't leave it too late, darling. Don't forget we're booked on the early flight to Paris.'

'I hadn't forgotten, Rachel,' he replied, 'but I'd prefer not to be the first to leave.' Someone else who had been brought up by a fastidious mother.

I felt someone touch my arm, and swung round to find Mrs Collier beaming up at me.

'This is my husband Reginald. I told him how keen you were to learn more about his Private Member's Bill.'

It must have been about ten minutes later, although it felt more like a month, that Kathy came to my rescue. 'Tony, I wonder if you'd be kind enough to give Susie a lift home. It's pouring with rain, and finding a taxi at this time of night won't be easy.'

'I'd be delighted,' I replied. 'I must thank you for including me in such charming company. It's all been quite fascinating,' I said, smiling down at Mrs Collier.

The Member's wife beamed back. My mother would have been proud of me.

In the car on the way back to her flat, Susie asked me if I had seen the Freud exhibition. 'Yes,' I said. 'I thought it was spectacular, and I'm planning to see it again before it closes.'

'I was thinking of popping in tomorrow morning,' she said, touching my hand. 'Why don't you join me?' I happily agreed, and when I dropped her off in Pimlico she gave me the sort of hug that suggests 'I would like to get to know you better.' Now, I am not an expert on many things, but I consider myself to be a world authority when it comes to hugs, as I have experienced every one – from a squeeze to a bearhug. I can interpret any message from 'I can't wait to get your clothes off' to 'Get lost.'

I arrived at the Tate early the following morning, anticipating that there would be a long queue for the exhibition, and giving myself time to pick up the tickets before Susie arrived. I had been waiting on the steps for only a few minutes when she appeared. She was wearing a short yellow dress that emphasised her slim figure, and as she climbed the steps I noticed men glance across to follow her progress. The moment she saw me, she began to run up the steps, and she greeted me with a long hug. An 'I feel I know you better already' hug.

I enjoyed the exhibition even more the second time, not least because of Susie's knowledge of Lucian Freud's work, as she took me through the different phases of his career. When we reached the last picture in the show, *Fat Women Looking Out of the Window*, I remarked a little feebly, 'Well, one thing's for certain, you'll never end up looking like that.'

'Oh, I wouldn't be so sure,' she said. 'But if I did, I'd never let you find out.' She took my hand. 'Do you have time for lunch?'

'Of course, but I haven't booked anywhere.'

'I have,' said Susie with a smile. 'The Tate has a super restaurant, and I booked a table for two, just in case . . .' She smiled again.

I don't recall much about lunch, except that when the bill came we were the last two left in the restaurant.

'If you could do anything in the world right now,' I said – a chat-up line I've used many times in the past – 'what would it be?'

Susie remained silent for some time before replying, 'Take the shuttle to Paris, spend the weekend with you and visit the Picasso exhibition "His Early Days", which is on at the Musée d'Orsay right now. How about you?'

'Take the shuttle to Paris, spend the weekend with you, and visit the Picasso exhibition "His Early Days", which . . .'

She burst out laughing, took my hand and said, 'Let's do it!'

I arrived at Waterloo some twenty minutes before the train was due to depart. I had already booked a suite in my favourite hotel, and a table at a restaurant that prides itself on not being in the tourist guides. I bought two first-class tickets and stood under the clock, as we'd agreed. Susie was only a couple of minutes late, and gave me a hug that was a definite step towards 'I can't wait to get your clothes off.'

She held my hand as we sped through the English country-side. Once we were in France – it always makes me angry that the trains speed up on the French side – I leaned over and kissed her for the first time.

She chatted about her work in New York, the exhibitions that were a 'must', and gave me a taste of what I might expect when we visited the Picasso exhibition. 'The pencil portrait of his father sitting in a chair, which he drew when he was only sixteen, was the harbinger of all that was to come.' She continued to talk about Picasso and his work with a passion one could never gain from merely reading a book on the subject. When the train pulled into the Gare du Nord, I grabbed both our cases and jumped off to make sure we would be among the first in the taxi queue.

Susie spent most of the journey to the hotel staring out of the taxi's window, like a schoolgirl on her first visit abroad. I remember thinking how strange this was for someone who had so obviously travelled extensively.

When the taxi swung into the entrance of the Hôtel du Coeur, I told her it was the sort of place I would love to own – comfortable but unpretentious, and offering a level of service Anglo-Saxons are rarely able to match. 'And the owner, Albert, is a gem.'

'I can't wait to meet him,' she said, as the taxi came to a halt outside the front door.

Albert was standing on the steps waiting to greet us. I knew he would be, as I would have been if he had accompanied a beautiful woman to London for the weekend.

'We have reserved your usual room, Mr Romanelli,' he said, looking as if he wanted to wink at me.

Susie stepped forward and, looking directly at Albert, said, 'And where will my room be?'

Without blinking, he smiled at her and said, 'There is an adjoining room that I'm sure you will find convenient, madame.'

'That's very thoughtful of you, Albert,' she said, 'but I would prefer to have a room on another floor.'

This time Albert was taken by surprise, although he quickly recovered, called for the reservations book and studied the entries for a few moments before saying, 'I see we have a room available overlooking the park, on the floor below Mr Romanelli's room.' He clicked his fingers and handed the two keys to a bellboy who was hovering nearby.

'Room 574 for madame, and the Napoleon suite for monsieur.'

The bellboy held the lift open for us, and once we were inside he pressed buttons 5 and 6. When the doors opened on the fifth floor, Susie said with a smile, 'Shall we meet in the foyer just before eight?'

I nodded, as my mother had never told me what to do in these circumstances.

Once I'd unpacked, I took a shower and slumped onto the redundant double bed. I flicked on the television and settled for a black-and-white French movie. I became so engrossed in the plot that I still wasn't dressed at ten to eight, when I was about to discover who had drowned the woman in the bath.

I cursed, quickly threw on some clothes, not even checking my appearance in the mirror, and rushed out of the door still wondering who the murderer could possibly be. I jumped into the lift and cursed again when the doors opened at the ground floor, because there was Susie standing in the foyer waiting for me.

I had to admit that in that long black dress, with an elegant slit down the side which allowed you a glimpse of thigh with every step she took, I was almost willing to forgive her.

In the taxi on the way to the restaurant she was at pains to tell me how pleasant her room was and how attentive the staff had been.

Over dinner – I must confess the meal was sensational – she chatted about her work in New York, and mused over whether she would ever return to London. I tried to sound interested.

After I had settled the bill, she took my arm and suggested

that as it was such a pleasant evening and she had eaten far too much, perhaps we should walk back to the hotel. She squeezed my hand, and I began to wonder if perhaps . . .

She didn't let go of my hand all the way back to the hotel. When we entered the lobby, the bellboy ran over to the lift and held the doors open for us.

'Which floor, please?' he asked.

'Fifth,' said Susie firmly.

'Sixth,' I said reluctantly.

Susie turned and kissed me on the cheek just as the doors slid open. 'It's been a memorable day,' she said, and slipped away.

For me too, I wanted to say, but remained silent. Back in my room I lay awake, trying to fathom it out. I realised I must be a pawn in a far bigger game; but would it be a bishop or a knight that finally removed me from the board?

I don't recall how long it was before I fell asleep, but when I woke at a few minutes before six, I jumped out of bed and was pleased to see that *Le Figaro* had already been pushed under the door. I devoured it from the first page to the last, learning all about the latest French scandals – none of them sexual, I might add – and then cast it aside to take a shower.

I strolled downstairs around eight to find Susie seated in the corner of the breakfast room, sipping an orange juice. She was dressed to kill, and although I obviously wasn't the chosen victim, I was even more determined than before to find out who was.

I slipped into the seat opposite her, and as neither of us spoke, the other guests must have assumed we had been married for years.

'I hope you slept well,' I offered finally.

'Yes, thank you, Tony,' she replied. 'And you?' she asked innocently.

I could think of a hundred responses I would have liked to make, but I knew that if I did, I would then never find out the truth.

'What time would you like to visit the exhibition?' I asked.

'Ten o'clock,' she said firmly, and then added, 'if that suits you.'

'Suits me fine,' I replied, glancing at my watch. 'I'll book a taxi for around 9.30.'

'I'll meet you in the foyer,' she said, making us sound more like a married couple by the minute.

After breakfast, I returned to my room, began to pack and phoned down to Albert to say I didn't think we'd be staying another night.

'I am sorry to hear that, monsieur,' he replied. 'I can only hope that it wasn't . . .'

'No, Albert, it was no fault of yours, that I can assure you. If ever I discover who is to blame, I'll let you know. By the way, I'll need a taxi around 9.30, to take us to the Musée d'Orsay.'

'Of course, Tony.'

I will not bore you with the mundane conversation that took place in the taxi between the hotel and the museum, because it would take a writer of far greater abilities than I possess to hold your attention. However, it would be less than gracious of me not to admit that the Picasso drawings were well worth the trip. And I should add that Susie's running commentary caused a small crowd to hang around in our wake.

'The pencil,' she said, 'is the cruellest of the artist's tools, because it leaves nothing to chance.' She stopped in front of the drawing Picasso had made of his father sitting in a chair. I was spellbound, and unable to move on for some time.

'What is so remarkable about this picture,' said Susie, 'is that Picasso drew it at the age of sixteen; so it was already clear that he would be bored by conventional subjects long before he'd left art school. When his father first saw it – and he was an artist himself – he . . .' Susie failed to finish the sentence. Instead, she suddenly grabbed my hand and, looking into my eyes, said, 'It's such fun being with you, Tony.' She leaned forward as if she were going to kiss me.

I was about to say, 'What the hell are you up to?' when I saw him out of the corner of my eye.

'Check,' I said.

'What do you mean, "Check"?' she asked.

'The knight has advanced across the board – or, to be more accurate, the Channel – and I have a feeling he's about to be brought into play.'

'What are you talking about, Tony?'

'I think you know very well what I'm talking about,' I replied.

'What a coincidence,' a voice said from behind her.

Susie swung round and put on a convincing display of surprise when she saw Richard standing there.

'What a coincidence,' I repeated.

'Isn't it a wonderful exhibition?' said Susie, ignoring my sarcasm.

'It certainly is,' said Rachel, who had obviously not been informed that she, like me, was only a pawn in this particular game, and was about to be taken by the queen.

'Well, now that we've all met up again, why don't we have lunch?' suggested Richard.

'I'm afraid we've already made other plans,' said Susie, taking my hand.

'Oh, nothing that can't be rearranged, my darling,' I said, hoping to be allowed to remain on the board for a little longer.

'But we'll never be able to find a table in a half-decent restaurant at such short notice,' Susie insisted.

'That shouldn't prove a problem,' I assured her with a smile. 'I know a little bistro where we will be welcome.'

Susie scowled as I moved out of check, and refused to talk to me as we all left the museum and walked along the left bank of the Seine together. I began chatting to Rachel. After all, I thought, we pawns must stick together.

Jacques threw his arms up in Gallic despair when he saw me standing in the doorway.

'How many, Monsieur Tony?' he asked, a sigh of resignation in his voice.

'Four,' I told him with a smile.

It turned out to be the only meal that weekend that I actually enjoyed. I spent most of the time talking to Rachel, a nice enough girl, but frankly not in Susie's league. She had no idea what was happening on the other side of the board, where the black queen was about to remove her white knight. It was a pleasure to watch the lady in full flow.

While Rachel was chatting away to me, I made every effort to listen in on the conversation that was taking place on the other side of the table, but I was only able to catch the occasional snippet.

'When are you expecting to be back in New York . . .'

'Yes, I planned this trip to Paris weeks ago . . .'

'Oh, you'll be in Geneva on your own . . .'

'Yes, I did enjoy the Keswicks' party . . .'

'I met Tony in Paris. Yes, just another coincidence, I hardly know him . . .'

True enough, I thought. In fact, I enjoyed her performance so much that I didn't even resent ending up with the bill.

After we had said our goodbyes, Susie and I strolled back along the Seine together, but not hand in hand. I waited until I was certain Richard and Rachel were well out of sight before I stopped and confronted her. To do her justice, she looked suitably guilty as she waited to be chastised.

'I asked you yesterday, also after lunch, "If you could do

anything in the world right now, what would it be?" What would your reply be this time?'

Susie looked unsure of herself for the first time that weekend.

'Be assured,' I added as I looked into those blue eyes, 'nothing you can say will surprise or offend me.'

'I would like to return to the hotel, pack my bags and leave for the airport.'

'So be it,' I said, and stepped into the road to hail a taxi.

Susie didn't speak on the journey back to the hotel, and as soon as we arrived, she disappeared upstairs while I settled the bill and asked if my bags, already packed, could be brought down.

Even then, I have to admit that when she stepped out of the lift and smiled at me, I almost wished my name was Richard.

To Susie's surprise, I accompanied her to Charles de Gaulle, explaining that I would be returning to London on the first available flight. We said goodbye below the departure board with a hug – a sort of 'Perhaps we'll meet again, but then perhaps we won't' hug.

I waved goodbye and began walking away, but couldn't resist turning to see which airline counter Susie was heading for.

She joined the queue for the Swissair check-in desk. I smiled, and headed for the British Airways counter.

◄○►

Six years have passed since that weekend in Paris, and I didn't come across Susie once during that time, although her name did occasionally pop up in dinner-party conversations.

I discovered that she had become the editor of *Art Nouveau*, and had married an Englishman called Ian, who was in sports promotion. On the rebound, someone said, after an affair with an American banker.

Two years later I heard that she'd given birth to a son, followed by a daughter, but no one seemed to know their names. And finally, about a year ago, I read of her divorce in one of the gossip columns.

And then, without warning, Susie suddenly rang and suggested we might meet for a drink. When she chose the venue, I knew that she hadn't lost her nerve. I heard myself saying yes, and wondered if I'd recognise her.

As I watched her walking up the steps of the Tate, I realised that the only thing I had forgotten was just how beautiful she was. If anything, she was even more captivating than before.

We had been in the gallery for only a few minutes before I was reminded what a pleasure it was to listen to her talk about her chosen subject. I had never really come to terms with Damien Hirst, having only recently accepted that Warhol and Lichtenstein were more than just draughtsmen, but I certainly left the exhibition with a new respect for his work.

I suppose I shouldn't have been surprised that Susie had booked a table for lunch in the Tate restaurant, or that she never once referred to our weekend in Paris until, over coffee, she asked, 'If you could do anything in the world right now, what would it be?'

'Spend the weekend in Paris with you,' I said, laughing.

'Then let's do it,' she said. 'There's a Hockney exhibition at the Pompidou Centre that has had glowing reviews, and I know a comfortable but unpretentious little hotel that I haven't visited in years, not to mention a restaurant that prides itself on not being in any of the tourist guides.'

—◦—

I have always considered it ignoble for any man to discuss a lady as if she were simply a conquest or a trophy, but I must confess that, as I watched Susie disappear through the departure gate to catch her flight back to New York on the following Monday morning, it had been well worth the years of waiting.

She has never contacted me since.

SOMETHING FOR
NOTHING*

JAKE BEGAN to dial the number slowly, as he had done almost every evening at six o'clock since the day his father had passed away. For the next fifteen minutes he settled back to listen to what his mother had been up to that day.

She led such a sober, orderly life that she rarely had anything of interest to tell him. Least of all on a Saturday. She had coffee every morning with her oldest friend, Molly Schultz, and on some days that would last until lunchtime. On Mondays, Wednesdays and Fridays she played bridge with the Zaccharis who lived across the street. On Tuesdays and Thursdays she visited her sister Nancy, which at least gave her something to grumble about when he rang on those evenings.

On Saturdays, she rested from her rigorous week. Her only strenuous activity being to purchase the bulky Sunday edition of the *Times* just after lunch – a strange New York tradition, which at least gave her the chance to inform her son which stories he should check up on the following day.

For Jake, every evening the conversation would consist of a few appropriate questions, depending on the day. Monday, Wednesday, Friday: How did the bridge go? How much did you win/lose? Tuesday, Thursday: How is Aunt Nancy? Really? That bad? Saturday: Anything interesting in the *Times* that I should look out for tomorrow?

Observant readers will be aware that there are seven days in any given week, and will want to know what Jake's mother did on a Sunday. On Sunday, she always joined his family for lunch, so there was no need for him to call her that evening.

Jake dialled the last digit of his mother's number and waited for her to pick up the phone. He had already prepared himself to be told what he should look out for in tomorrow's *New York Times*. It usually took two or three rings before she answered the phone, the amount of time required for her to walk from her chair by the window to the phone on the other side of the room. When the phone rang four, five, six, seven times, Jake began to wonder if she might be out. But that wasn't possible. She was never out after six o'clock, winter or summer. She kept to a routine that was so regular it would have brought a smile to the lips of a Marine drill sergeant.

Finally, he heard a click. He was just about to say, 'Hi, Mom, it's Jake,' when he heard a voice that was certainly not his mother's, and was already in mid-conversation. Thinking he had a crossed line, he was about to put the phone down when the voice said, 'There'll be $100,000 in it for you. All you have to do is turn up and collect it. It's in an envelope for you at Billy's.'

'So where's Billy's?' asked a new voice.

'On the corner of Oak Street and Randall. They'll be expecting you around seven.'

Jake tried not to breathe in or out as he wrote down 'Oak and Randall' on the pad by the phone.

'How will they know the envelope is for me?' asked the second voice.

'You just ask for a copy of the *New York Times* and hand over a $100 bill. He'll give you a quarter change, as if you'd handed him a dollar. That way, if there's anyone else in the shop, they won't be suspicious. Don't open the envelope until you're in a safe place – there are a lot of people in New York who'd like to get their hands on $100,000. And whatever you do, don't ever contact me again. If you do, it won't be a pay-off you'll get next time.'

The line went dead.

Jake hung up, having completely forgotten that he was meant to be ringing his mother.

He sat down and considered what to do next – if anything. His wife Ellen had taken the kids to a movie, as she did most Saturday evenings, and they weren't expected back until around nine. His dinner was in the microwave, with a note to tell him how many minutes it would take to cook. He always added one minute.

Jake found himself flicking through the telephone directory. He turned over the pages until he reached B: Bi . . . , Bil . . . , Billy's. And there it was, at 1127 Oak Street. He closed the directory and walked through to his den, where he searched the bookshelf behind his desk for a street atlas of New York. He found it wedged in between *The Memoirs of Elisabeth Schwarzkopf* and *How to Lose Twenty Pounds When You're Over Forty*.

He turned to the index in the back and quickly found the entry for Oak Street. He checked the grid reference and placed his finger on the correct square. He calculated that, were he to go, it would take him about half an hour to get over to the West Side. He checked his watch. It was 6.14. What was he thinking of? He had no intention of going anywhere. To start with, he didn't have $100.

Jake took out his wallet from the inside pocket of his jacket, and counted slowly: $37. He walked through to the kitchen to check Ellen's petty-cash box. It was locked, and he couldn't remember where she hid the key. He took a screwdriver from the drawer beside the stove and forced the box open: another $22. He paced around the kitchen, trying to think. Next he went to the bedroom and checked the pockets of all his jackets and trousers. Another $1.75 in loose change. He left the bedroom and moved on to his daughter's room. Hesther's Snoopy moneybox was on her dressing table. He picked it up and walked over to the bed. He turned the box upside down and shook all the coins out onto the quilt: another $6.75.

He sat on the end of the bed, desperately trying to concentrate, then recalled the $50 bill he always kept folded in his driving licence for emergencies. He added up all his gatherings: they came to $117.50.

Jake checked his watch. It was 6.23. He would just go and have a look. No more, he told himself.

He took his old overcoat from the hall cupboard and slipped out of the apartment, checking as he left that all three locks on the front door were securely bolted. He pressed the elevator button, but there was no sound. Out of order again, Jake thought, and began to jog down the stairs. Across the street was a bar he often dropped into when Ellen took the children to the movies.

The barman smiled as he walked in. 'The usual, Jake?' he asked, somewhat surprised to see him wearing a heavy overcoat when he only had to cross the road from his apartment.

'No thanks,' said Jake, trying to sound casual. 'I just wondered if you had a $100 bill.'

'Not sure if I do,' the barman replied. He rummaged around in a stack of notes, then turned to Jake and said, 'You're in luck. Just the one.'

Jake handed over the fifty, a twenty, two tens and ten ones, and received a $100 bill in exchange. Folding the note carefully in four, he slipped it into his wallet, which he returned to the inside pocket of his jacket. He then left the bar and walked out onto the street.

He ambled slowly west for two blocks until he came to a bus stop. Perhaps he would be too late, and the problem would take care of itself, he thought. A bus drew into the kerb. Jake climbed the steps, paid his fare and took a seat near the back, still uncertain what he planned to do once he reached the West Side.

He was so deep in thought that he missed his stop and had to walk almost half a mile back to Oak Street. He checked the numbers. It would be another three or four blocks before Oak Street crossed with Randall.

As he got nearer, he found his pace slowing with every step. But suddenly, there it was on the next corner, halfway up a lamppost: a white-and-green sign that read 'Randall Street'.

He quickly checked all four corners of the street, then looked at his watch again. It was 6.49.

As he stared across from the opposite side of the street, one or two people went in and out of Billy's. The light started flashing 'Walk', and he found himself being carried across with the other pedestrians.

He checked his watch yet again: 6.51. He paused at the doorway of Billy's. Behind the counter was a man stacking some newspapers. He wore a black T-shirt and jeans, and must have been around forty, a shade under six foot, with shoulders that could only have been built by spending several hours a week in the gym.

A customer brushed past Jake and asked for a packet of Marlboros. While the man behind the counter was handing him his change, Jake stepped inside and pretended to take an interest in the magazine rack.

As the customer turned to leave, Jake slipped his hand into the inside pocket of his jacket, took out his wallet and touched the edge of the $100 bill. Once the Marlboro man had left the shop, Jake put his wallet back into his pocket, leaving the bill in the palm of his hand.

The man behind the counter stood waiting impassively as Jake slowly unfolded the bill.

'The *Times*,' Jake heard himself saying, as he placed the $100 bill on the counter.

The man in the black T-shirt glanced at the money and checked his watch. He seemed to hesitate for a moment before reaching under the counter. Jake tensed at the movement, until he saw a long, thick, white envelope emerge. The man proceeded to slip it into the heavy folds of the newspaper's business section, then handed the paper over to Jake, his face remaining impassive. He took the $100 bill, rang up seventy-five cents on the cash register, and gave Jake a quarter change. Jake turned and walked quickly out of the shop, nearly knocking over a small man who looked as nervous as Jake felt.

Jake began to run down Oak Street, frequently glancing over his shoulder to see if anyone was following him. Checking again, he spotted a Yellow Cab heading towards him, and quickly hailed it.

'The East Side,' he said, jumping in.

As the driver eased back into the traffic, Jake slid the envelope out from the bulky newspaper and transferred it to an inside pocket. He could hear his heart thumping. For the next fifteen minutes he spent most of the time looking anxiously out of the cab's rear window.

When he spotted a subway entrance coming up on the right, he told the driver to pull into the kerb. He handed over $10 and, not waiting for his change, jumped out of the taxi and dashed down the subway steps, emerging a few moments later on the other side of the road. He then hailed another taxi going in the opposite direction. This time he gave the driver his home address. He congratulated himself on his little subterfuge, which he'd seen carried out by Gene Hackman in the Movie of the Week.

Nervously, Jake touched his inside pocket to be sure the envelope was still in place. Confident that no one was following him, he no longer bothered to look out of the cab's rear window. He was tempted to check inside the envelope, but there would be time enough for that once he was back in the safety of his apartment. He checked his watch: 7.21. Ellen and the children wouldn't be home for at least another half-hour.

'You can drop me about fifty yards on the left,' Jake told the driver, happy to be back on familiar territory. He cast one final glance through the back window as the taxi drew into the kerb outside his block. There was no other traffic close by. He paid the driver with the dimes and quarters he had shaken out of his daughter's Snoopy moneybox, then jumped out and walked as casually as he could into the building.

Once he was inside, he rushed across the hall and thumped the elevator button with the palm of his hand. It still wasn't working. He cursed, and started to run up the seven flights of stairs to his apartment, going slower and slower with each floor, until he finally came to a halt. Breathless, he unbolted the three locks, almost fell inside, and slammed the door quickly behind him. He rested against the wall while he got his breath back.

He was pulling the envelope out of his inside pocket when the phone rang. His first thought was that they had traced him somehow and wanted their money back. He stared at the phone for a moment, then nervously picked up the receiver.

'Hello, Jake, is that you?'

Then he remembered. 'Yes, Mom.'

'You didn't call at six,' she said.

'I'm sorry, Mom. I did, but . . .' He decided against telling her why he didn't try a second time.

'I've been calling you for the past hour. Have you been out or something?'

'Only to the bar across the road. I sometimes go there for a drink when Ellen takes the kids to the movies.'

He placed the envelope next to the phone, desperate to be rid of her, but aware that he would have to go through the usual Saturday routine.

'Anything interesting in the *Times*, Mom?' he heard himself saying, rather too quickly.

'Not much,' she replied. 'Hillary looks certain to win the Democratic nomination for Senate, but I'm still going to vote for Giuliani.'

'Always have done, always will,' said Jake, mouthing his mother's oft-repeated comment on the Mayor. He picked up the envelope and squeezed it, to see what $100,000 felt like.

'Anything else, Mom?' he said, trying to move her on.

'There's a piece in the style section about widows at seventy rediscovering their sex drive. As soon as their husbands are safely in their graves it seems they're popping HRT and getting back into the old routine. One of them's quoted as saying, "I'm not so much trying to make up for lost time, as to catch up with him."'

As he listened, Jake began to ease open a corner of the envelope.

'I'd try it myself,' his mother was saying, 'but I can't afford the facelift that seems to be an essential part of the deal.'

'Mom, I think I can hear Ellen and the kids at the door, so I'd better say goodbye. Look forward to seeing you at lunch tomorrow.'

'But I haven't told you about a fascinating piece in the business section.'

'I'm still listening,' said Jake distractedly, slowly beginning to ease the envelope open.

'It's a story about a new scam that's being carried out in Manhattan. I don't know what they'll think of next.'

The envelope was half-open.

'It seems that a gang has found a way of tapping into your phone while you're dialling another number . . .'

Another inch and Jake would be able to tip the contents of the envelope out onto the table.

'So when you dial, you think you've got a crossed line.'

Jake took his finger out of the envelope and began to listen more carefully.

'Then they set you up by making you believe you're overhearing a real conversation.'

Sweat began to appear on Jake's forehead, as he stared down at the almost-opened envelope.

'They make you think that if you travel to the other side of the city and hand over a $100 bill, you'll get an envelope containing $100,000 in exchange for it.'

Jake felt sick as he thought of how readily he had parted with his $100, and how easily he had fallen for it.

'They're using tobacconists and newsagents to carry out the scam,' continued his mother.

'So what's in the envelope?'

'Now that's where they're really clever,' said his mother. 'They put in a small booklet that gives advice on how you can make $100,000. And it's not even illegal, because the price on the cover is $100. You've got to hand it to them.'

I already have, Mom, Jake wanted to say, but he just slammed the phone down and stared at the envelope.

The front doorbell began to ring. Ellen and the kids must be back from the movie, and she'd probably forgotten her key again.

The bell rang a second time.

'OK, I'm coming, I'm coming!' shouted Jake. He seized the envelope, determined not to leave any trace of its embarrassing existence. As the bell rang a third time he ran into the kitchen, opened the incinerator and threw the envelope down the chute.

The bell continued to ring. This time the caller must have left a finger on the button.

Jake ran to the door. He pulled it open to find three massive men standing in the hallway. The one wearing a black T-shirt leapt in and put a knife to his throat, while the other two each grabbed an arm. The door slammed shut behind them.

'Where is it?' T-shirt shouted, holding the knife against Jake's throat.

'Where's what?' gasped Jake. 'I don't know what you're talking about.'

'Don't play games with us,' shouted the second man. 'We want our $100,000 back.'

'But there was no money in the envelope, only a book. I threw it down the incinerator chute. Listen, you can hear it for yourself.'

The man in the black T-shirt cocked his head, while the other two fell silent. There was a crunching sound coming from the kitchen.

'OK, then you'll have to go the same way,' said the man holding the knife. He nodded, and his two accomplices picked up Jake like a sack of potatoes and carried him through to the kitchen.

Just as Jake's head was about to disappear down the incinerator chute, the phone and the front doorbell began ringing at the same time . . .

OTHER BLIGHTERS'
EFFORTS

IT ALL BEGAN innocently enough, when Henry Pascoe, the First Secretary at the British High Commission on Aranga, took a call from Bill Paterson, the manager of Barclays Bank. It was late on a Friday afternoon, and Henry rather hoped that Bill was calling to suggest a round of golf on Saturday morning, or perhaps with an invitation to join him and his wife Sue for lunch on Sunday. But the moment he heard the voice on the other end of the line, he knew the call was of an official nature.

'When you come to check the High Commission's account on Monday, you'll find you've been credited with a larger sum than usual.'

'Any particular reason?' responded Henry, in his most formal tone.

'Quite simple really, old chap,' replied the bank manager. 'The exchange rate moved in your favour overnight. Always does when there's a rumour of a coup,' he added matter-of-factly. 'Feel free to call me on Monday if you have any queries.'

Henry wondered about asking Bill if he felt like a round of golf tomorrow, but thought better of it.

It was Henry's first experience of a rumoured coup, and the exchange rate wasn't the only thing to have a bad weekend. On Friday night the head of state, General Olangi, appeared on television in full-dress uniform to warn the good citizens of

Aranga that, due to some unrest among a small group of dissidents in the army, it had proved necessary to impose a curfew on the island which he hoped would not last for more than a few days.

On Saturday morning Henry tuned in to the BBC World Service to find out what was really going on on Aranga. The BBC's correspondent, Roger Parnell, was always better informed than the local television and radio stations, which were simply bleating out a warning to the island's citizens every few minutes that they should not stray onto the streets during the day, because if they did, they would be arrested. And if they were foolish enough to do so at night, they would be shot.

That put a stop to any golf on Saturday, or lunch with Bill and Sue on Sunday. Henry spent a quiet weekend reading, bringing himself up to date with unanswered letters from England, clearing the fridge of any surplus food, and finally cleaning those parts of his bachelor apartment that his daily always seemed to miss.

On Monday morning, the head of state still appeared to be safely in his palace. The BBC reported that several young officers had been arrested, and that one or two of them were rumoured to have been executed. General Olangi reappeared on television to announce that the curfew had been lifted.

When Henry arrived at his office later that day, he found that Shirley, his secretary – who had experienced several coups – had already opened his mail and left it on his desk for him to consider. There was one pile marked 'Urgent, Action Required', a second, larger pile marked 'For Your Consideration', and a third, by far the largest, marked 'See and Bin'.

The itinerary for the imminent visit of the Under-Secretary of State for Foreign Affairs from the UK had been placed on top of the 'Urgent, Action Required' pile, although the Minister was only dropping in on St George's, the capital of Aranga, because it was a convenient refuelling stop on his way back to London following a trip to Jakarta. Few people bothered to visit the tiny protectorate of Aranga unless they were on their way to or from somewhere else.

This particular Minister, Mr Will Whiting, known at the Foreign Office as 'Witless Will', was, *The Times* assured its readers, to be replaced in the next reshuffle by someone who could do joined-up writing. However, thought Henry, as Whiting was staying at the High Commissioner's residence overnight, this would be his one opportunity to get a decision out of the Minister on the swimming pool project. Henry was keen to start work on the new pool that was so badly needed by the local children. He had pointed out in a lengthy memo to the Foreign Office that they had been promised the go-ahead when Princess Margaret had visited the island four years earlier and laid the foundation stone, but feared that the project would remain in the Foreign Office's 'pending' file unless he kept continually badgering them about it.

In the second pile of letters was the promised bank statement from Bill Paterson, which confirmed that the High Commission's external account was 1,123 kora better off than expected because of the coup that had never taken place that weekend. Henry took little interest in the financial affairs of the protectorate, but as First Secretary it was his duty to countersign every cheque on behalf of Her Majesty's Government.

There was only one other letter of any significance in the 'For Your Consideration' pile: an invitation to give a speech replying on behalf of the guests at the annual Rotary Club dinner in November. Every year a senior member of the High Commission staff was expected to carry out this task. It seemed that it was Henry's turn. He groaned, but placed a tick on the top right corner of the letter.

There were the usual letters in the 'See and Bin' pile –

people sending out unnecessary free offers, circulars and invitations to functions no one ever attended. He didn't even bother to flick through them, but turned his attention back to the 'Urgent' pile, and began to check the Minister's programme.

August 27th

3.30 p.m.: Will Whiting, Under-Secretary of State at the Foreign Office, to be met at the airport by the High Commissioner, Sir David Fleming, and the First Secretary, Mr Henry Pascoe.

4.30 p.m.: Tea at the High Commission with the High Commissioner and Lady Fleming.

6.00 p.m.: Visit to the Queen Elizabeth College, where the Minister will present the prizes to leaving sixth-formers (speech enclosed).

7.00 p.m.: Cocktail party at the High Commission. Around one hundred guests expected (names attached).

8.00 p.m.: Dinner with General Olangi at the Victoria Barracks (speech enclosed).

Henry looked up as his secretary entered the room.

'Shirley, when am I going to be able to show the Minister the site for the new swimming pool?' he asked. 'There's no sign of it on his itinerary.'

'I've managed to fit in a fifteen-minute visit tomorrow morning, when the Minister will be on his way back to the airport.'

'Fifteen minutes to discuss something which will affect the lives of ten thousand children,' said Henry, looking back down at the Minister's schedule. He turned the page.

August 28th

8.00 a.m.: Breakfast at the Residence with the High Commissioner and leading local business representatives (speech enclosed)

9.00 a.m.: Depart for airport.

10.30 a.m.: British Airways Flight 0177 to London Heathrow.

'It's not even on his official schedule,' grumbled Henry, looking back up at his secretary.

'I know,' said Shirley, 'but the High Commissioner felt that as the Minister had such a short stopover, he should concentrate on the most important priorities.'

'Like tea with the High Commissioner's wife,' snorted Henry. 'Just be sure that he sits down to breakfast on time, and that the paragraph I dictated to you on Friday about the future of the swimming pool is included in his speech.' Henry rose from his desk. 'I've been through the letters and marked them up. I'm just going to pop into town and see what state the swimming pool project is in.'

'By the way,' said Shirley, 'Roger Parnell, the BBC's correspondent, has just called wanting to know if the Minister will be making any official statement while he's visiting Aranga.'

'Phone back and tell him yes, then fax him the Minister's breakfast speech, highlighting the paragraph on the swimming pool.'

Henry left the office and jumped into his little Austin Mini. The sun was beating down on its roof. Even with both windows open, he was covered in sweat after driving only a few hundred yards from his office. Some of the locals waved at him when they recognised the Mini and the diplomat from England who seemed genuinely to care about their well-being.

He parked the car on the far side of the cathedral, which would have been described as a parish church in England, and walked the three hundred yards to the site designated for the swimming pool. He cursed, as he always did whenever he saw the patch of barren wasteland. The children of Aranga had so few sporting facilities: a brick-hard football pitch, which was transformed into a cricket square on May 1st every year; a town hall which doubled as a basketball court when the local council wasn't in session; and a tennis court and golf course at the Britannia Club, which the locals were not invited to join, and where the children were never allowed past the front gate – unless it was to sweep the drive. In the Victoria Barracks, less than half a mile away, the army had a gymnasium and half a dozen squash courts, but only officers and their guests were allowed to use them.

Henry decided there and then to make it his mission to see that the swimming pool was completed before the Foreign Office posted him to another country. He would use his speech to the Rotary Club to galvanise the members into action. He must convince them to select the swimming pool project as their Charity of the Year, and would press Bill Paterson into becoming Chairman of the Appeal. After all, as manager of the bank and secretary of the Rotary Club, he was the obvious candidate.

But first there was the Minister's visit. Henry began to consider the points he would raise with him, remembering that he had only fifteen minutes in which to convince the damn man to press the Foreign Office for more funding.

He turned to leave, and spotted a small boy standing on the edge of the site, trying to read the words chiselled on the foundation stone: 'St George's Swimming Pool. This foundation stone was laid by HRH Princess Margaret, September 12th, 1987.'

'Is this a swimming pool?' the little boy asked innocently.

Henry repeated those words to himself as he walked back to his car, and made up his mind to include them in his speech to the Rotary Club. He checked his watch, and decided he still had time to drop into the Britannia Club, in the hope that Bill Paterson might be having lunch there. When he walked into the clubhouse, he spotted Bill, seated on his usual stool at the bar, reading an out-of-date copy of the *Financial Times*.

Bill looked up as Henry approached the bar, 'I thought you had a visiting Minister to take care of today?'

'His plane doesn't land until 3.30,' Henry said. 'I dropped by because I wanted to have a word with you.'

'Need some advice on how you should spend the surplus you made on the exchange rate last Friday?'

'No. I'll have to have a little more than that if I'm ever going to get this swimming pool project off the ground – or rather, into it.'

Henry left the club twenty minutes later, having extracted a promise from Bill that he would chair the Appeal Committee, open an account at the bank and ask head office in London if they would make the first donation.

On his way to the airport in the High Commissioner's Rolls-Royce, Henry told Sir David the latest news about the swimming pool project. The High Commissioner smiled and said, 'Well done, Henry. Now we must hope that you're as successful with the Minister as you obviously have been with Bill Paterson.'

The two men were standing on the runway of St George's airport, six feet of red carpet in place, when the Boeing 727 touched down. As it was rare for more than one plane a day to land at St George's, and there was only one runway, 'International Airport' was, in Henry's opinion, a little bit of a misnomer.

The Minister turned out to be a rather jolly fellow, insisting that everyone should call him Will. He assured Sir David that he had been looking forward with keen anticipation to his visit to St Edward's.

'St George's, Minister,' the High Commissioner whispered in his ear.

'Yes, of course, St George's,' replied Will, without even blushing.

Once they had arrived at the High Commission, Henry left the Minister to have tea with Sir David and his wife, and returned to his office. After even such a short journey, he was convinced that Witless Will was unlikely to carry much clout back in Whitehall; but that wouldn't stop him pressing ahead with his case. At least the Minister had read the briefing notes, because he told them how much he was looking forward to seeing the new swimming pool.

'Not yet started,' Henry had reminded him.

'Funny,' said the Minister. 'I thought I read somewhere that Princess Margaret had already opened it.'

'No, she only laid the foundation stone, Minister. But perhaps all that will change once the project receives your blessing.'

'I'll do what I can,' promised Will. 'But you know we've been told to make even more cutbacks in overseas funding.' A sure sign that an election was approaching, thought Henry.

At the cocktail party that evening, Henry was able to say no more than 'Good evening, Minister,' as the High Commissioner was determined that Will would be introduced to every one of the assembled guests in under sixty minutes. When the two of them departed to have dinner with General Olangi, Henry went back to his office to check over the speech the Minister would be delivering at breakfast the following morning. He was pleased to see that the paragraph he had written on the swimming pool project remained in the final draft, so at least it would be on the record. He checked the seating plan, making sure that he had been placed next to the editor of the *St George's Echo*. That way he could be certain that the paper's next edition would lead on the British government's support for the swimming pool appeal.

Henry rose early the following morning, and was among

the first to arrive at the High Commissioner's Residence. He took the opportunity to brief as many of the assembled local businessmen as possible on the importance of the swimming pool project in the eyes of the British government, pointing out that Barclays Bank had agreed to open the fund with a substantial donation.

The Minister arrived for breakfast a few minutes late. 'A call from London,' he explained, so they didn't sit down to eat until 8.15. Henry took his place next to the editor of the local paper and waited impatiently for the Minister to make his speech.

Will rose at 8.47. He spent the first five minutes talking about bananas, and finally went on to say: 'Let me assure you that Her Majesty's Government have not forgotten the swimming pool project that was inaugurated by Princess Margaret, and we hope to be able to make an announcement on its progress in the near future. I was delighted to learn from Sir David,' he looked across at Bill Paterson, who was seated opposite him, 'that the Rotary Club have taken on the project as their Charity of the Year, and several prominent local businessmen have already generously agreed to support the cause.' This was followed by a round of applause, instigated by Henry.

Once the Minister had resumed his seat, Henry handed the editor of the local paper an envelope which contained a thousand-word article, along with several pictures of the site. Henry felt confident that it would form the centre-page spread in next week's *St George's Echo*.

Henry checked his watch as the Minister sat down: 8.56. It was going to be close. When Will disappeared up to his room, Henry began pacing up and down the hallway, checking his watch as each minute passed.

The Minister stepped into the waiting Rolls at 9.24 and, turning to Henry, said, 'I fear I'm going to have to forgo the pleasure of seeing the swimming pool site. However,' he promised, 'I'll be sure to read your report on the plane, and will brief the Foreign Secretary the moment I get back to London.'

As the car sped past a barren plot of land on the way to the airport, Henry pointed out the site to the Minister. Will glanced out of the window and said, 'Admirable, worthwhile, important,' but never once did he commit himself to spending one penny of government money.

'I'll do my damnedest to convince the mandarins at the Treasury,' were his final words as he boarded the plane.

Henry didn't need to be told that Will's 'damnedest' was unlikely to convince even the most junior civil servant at the Treasury.

A week later, Henry received a fax from the Foreign Office giving details of the changes the Prime Minister had made in his latest reshuffle. Will Whiting had been sacked, to be replaced by someone Henry had never heard of.

-<o>-

Henry was going over his speech to the Rotary Club when the phone rang. It was Bill Paterson.

'Henry, there are rumours of another coup brewing, so I was thinking of waiting until Friday before changing the High Commission's pounds into kora.'

'Happy to take your advice, Bill – the money market is beyond me. By the way, I'm looking forward to this evening, when we finally get a chance to launch the Appeal.'

Henry's speech was well received by the Rotarians, but when he discovered the size of the donations some of the members had in mind, he feared it could still be years before the project was completed. He couldn't help remembering that there were only another eighteen months before his next posting was due.

It was in the car on the way home that he recalled Bill's

words at the Britannia Club. An idea began to form in his mind.

Henry had never taken the slightest interest in the quarterly payments that the British government made to the tiny island of Aranga. The Foreign Office allocated £5 million a year from its contingency fund, made up of four payments of £1.25 million, which was automatically converted into the local currency of kora at the current exchange rate. Once Henry had been informed of the rate by Bill Paterson, the Chief Administrator at the High Commission dealt with all the Commission's payments over the next three months. That was about to change.

Henry lay awake that night, all too aware that he lacked the training and expertise to carry out such a daring project, and that he must pick up the knowledge he required without anyone else becoming aware of what he was up to.

By the time he rose the following morning, a plan was beginning to form in his mind. He started by spending the weekend at the local library, studying old copies of the *Financial Times*, noting in particular what caused fluctuating exchange rates and whether they followed any pattern.

Over the next three months, at the golf club, cocktail parties in the Britannia Club, and whenever he was with Bill, he gathered more and more information, until finally he was confident that he was ready to make his first move.

When Bill rang on the Monday morning to say that there would be a small surplus of 22,107 kora on the current account because of the rumours of another coup, Henry gave orders to place the money in the Swimming Pool Account.

'But I usually switch it into the Contingency Fund,' said Bill.

'There's been a new directive from the Foreign Office – K14792,' said Henry. 'It says that surpluses can now be used on local projects, if they've been approved by the Minister.'

'But that Minister was sacked,' the bank manager reminded the First Secretary.

'That may well be the case, but I've been instructed by my masters that the order still applies.' Directive K14792 did in fact exist, Henry had discovered, although he doubted that when the Foreign Office issued it they had had swimming pools in mind.

'Fine by me,' said Bill. 'Who am I to argue with a Foreign Office directive, especially when all I have to do is move money from one High Commission account to another within the bank?'

The Chief Administrator didn't comment on any missing money during the following week, as he had received the same number of kora he had originally expected. Henry assumed he'd got away with it.

As there wasn't another payment due for three months, Henry had ample time to refine his plan. During the next quarter, a few of the local businessmen came up with their donations, but Henry quickly realised that even with this influx of cash, they could only just about afford to start digging. He would have to deliver something a great deal more substantial if he hoped to end up with more than a hole in the ground.

Then an idea came to him in the middle of the night. But for Henry's personal coup to be effective, he would need to get his timing spot on.

When Roger Parnell, the BBC's correspondent, made his weekly call to enquire if there was anything he should be covering other than the swimming pool appeal, Henry asked if he could have a word with him off the record.

'Of course,' said the correspondent. 'What do you want to discuss?'

'HMG is a little worried that no one has seen General Olangi for several days, and there are rumours that his recent medical check-up has found him to be HIV positive.'

'Good God,' said the BBC man. 'Have you got any proof?'

'Can't say I have,' admitted Henry, 'although I did overhear his personal doctor being a little indiscreet with the High Commissioner. Other than that, nothing.'

'Good God,' the BBC man repeated.

'This is, of course, strictly off the record. If it were traced back to me, we would never be able to speak again.'

'I never disclose my sources,' the correspondent assured him indignantly.

The report that came out on the World Service that evening was vague, and hedged with 'ifs' and 'buts'. However, the next day, when Henry visited the golf course, the Britannia Club and the bank, he found the word 'AIDS' on everyone's lips. Even the High Commissioner asked him if he had heard the rumour.

'Yes, but I don't believe it,' said Henry, without blushing.

The kora dropped 4 per cent the following day, and General Olangi had to appear on television to assure his people that the rumours were false, and were being spread by his enemies. All his appearance on television did was to inform anyone who hadn't already heard them about the rumours, and as the General seemed to have lost some weight, the kora dropped another 2 per cent.

'You did rather well this month,' Bill told Henry on Monday. 'After that false alarm about Olangi's HIV problem, I was able to switch 118,000 kora into the Swimming Pool Account, which means my committee can go ahead and instruct the architects to draw up some more detailed plans.'

'Well done,' said Henry, passing the praise on to Bill for his personal coup. He put the phone down aware that he couldn't risk repeating the same stunt again.

Despite the architects' plans being drawn up and a model of the pool placed in the High Commissioner's office for all to see, another three months went by with only a trickle of small donations coming in from local businessmen.

Henry wouldn't normally have seen the fax, but he was in the High Commissioner's office, going over a speech Sir David was due to make to the Banana Growers' Annual Convention, when it was placed on the desk by the High Commissioner's secretary.

The High Commissioner frowned and pushed the speech to one side. 'It hasn't been a good year for bananas,' he grunted. The frown remained in place as he read the fax. He passed it across to his First Secretary.

'To all Embassies and High Commissions: The government will be suspending Britain's membership of the Exchange Rate Mechanism. Expect an official announcement later today.'

'If that's the way of things, I can't see the Chancellor lasting the day,' commented Sir David. 'However, the Foreign Secretary will remain in place, so it's not our problem.' He looked up at Henry. 'Still, perhaps it would be wise if we were not to mention the subject for at least a couple of hours.'

Henry nodded his agreement and left the High Commissioner to continue working on his speech.

The moment he had closed the door of the High Commissioner's office, he ran along the corridor for the first time in two years. As soon as he was back at his desk, he dialled a number he didn't need to look up.

'Bill Paterson speaking.'

'Bill, how much have we got in the Contingency Fund?' he asked, trying to sound casual.

'Give me a second and I'll let you know. Would you like me to call you back?'

'No, I'll hold on,' said Henry. He watched the second hand of the clock on his desk sweep nearly a full circle before the bank manager spoke again.

'A little over £1 million,' said Bill. 'Why did you want to know?'

'I've just been instructed by the Foreign Office to switch

all available monies into German marks, Swiss francs and American dollars immediately.'

'You'd be charged a hefty fee for that,' said the bank manager, suddenly sounding rather formal. 'And if the exchange rate were to go against you . . .'

'I'm aware of the implications,' said Henry, 'but the telegram from London doesn't leave me with any choice.'

'Fair enough,' said Bill. 'Has this been approved by the High Commissioner?'

'I've just left his office,' said Henry.

'Then I'd better get on with it, hadn't I?'

Henry sat sweating in his air-conditioned office for twenty minutes until Bill called back.

'We've converted the full amount into Swiss francs, German marks and American dollars, as instructed. I'll send you the details in the morning.'

'And no copies, please,' said Henry. 'The High Commissioner isn't keen that this should be seen by any of his staff.'

'I quite understand, old boy,' said Bill.

The Chancellor of the Exchequer announced the suspension of Britain's membership of the Exchange Rate Mechanism from the steps of the Treasury in Whitehall at 7.30 p.m., by which time all the banks in St George's had closed for the day.

Henry contacted Bill the moment the markets opened the following morning, and instructed him to convert the francs, marks and dollars back into sterling as quickly as possible, and let him know the outcome.

It was to be another twenty minutes of sweating before Bill called back.

'You made a profit of £64,312. If every Embassy around the world has carried out the same exercise, the government will be able to cut taxes long before the next election.'

'Quite right,' said Henry. 'By the way, could you convert

the surplus into kora, and place it in the Swimming Pool Account? And Bill, I assured the High Commissioner the matter would never be referred to again.'

'You have my word on it,' replied the bank manager.

—◦—

Henry informed the editor of the *St George's Echo* that contributions to the swimming pool fund were still pouring in, thanks to the generosity of local businessmen and many private individuals. In truth the outside donations made up only about half of what had been raised to date.

Within a month of Henry's second coup, a contractor had been selected from a shortlist of three, and lorries, bulldozers and diggers rolled onto the site. Henry paid a visit every day so that he could keep an eye on progress. But it wasn't long before Bill was reminding him that unless more funds were forthcoming, they wouldn't be able to consider his plan for a high diving board and changing rooms for up to a hundred children.

The *St George's Echo* continually reminded their readers of the appeal, but after a year, just about everyone who could afford to give anything had already done so. The trickle of donations had dried up almost entirely, and the income raised from bring-and-buy sales, raffles and coffee mornings was becoming negligible.

Henry began to fear that he would be sent to his next posting long before the project was completed, and that once he left the island Bill and his committee would lose interest and the job might never be finished.

Henry and Bill visited the site the following day, and stared down into a fifty-by-twenty-metre hole in the ground, surrounded by heavy equipment that had been idle for days and would soon have to be transferred to another site.

'It will take a miracle to raise enough funds to finish the

project, unless the government finally keeps its promise,' the First Secretary remarked.

'And we haven't been helped by the kora remaining so stable for the past six months,' added Bill.

Henry began to despair.

━◦━

At the morning briefing with the High Commissioner the following Monday, Sir David told Henry that he had some good news.

'Don't tell me. HMG has finally kept its promise, and . . .'

'No, nothing as startling as that,' said Sir David, laughing. 'But you are on the list for promotion next year, and will probably be given a High Commission of your own.' He paused. 'One or two good appointments are coming up, I'm told, so keep your fingers crossed. And by the way, when Carol and I go back to England for our annual leave tomorrow, try to keep Aranga off the front pages – that is, if you want to get Bermuda rather than the Ascension Islands.'

Henry returned to his office and began to go through the morning post with his secretary. In the 'Urgent, Action Required' pile was an invitation to accompany General Olangi back to his place of birth. This was an annual ritual the President carried out to demonstrate to his people that he hadn't forgotten his roots. The High Commissioner would usually have accompanied him, but as he would be back in England at the time, the First Secretary was expected to represent him. Henry wondered if Sir David had organised it that way.

From the 'For Your Consideration' pile, Henry had to decide between accompanying a group of businessmen on a banana fact-finding tour around the island, or addressing St George's Political Society on the future of the euro. He placed a tick on the businessmen's letter and wrote a note suggesting to the Political Society that the Controller was better placed than he to talk about the euro.

He then moved on to the 'See and Bin' pile. A letter from Mrs Davidson, donating twenty-five kora to the swimming pool fund; an invitation to the church bazaar on Friday; and a reminder that it was Bill's fiftieth birthday on Saturday.

'Anything else?' asked Henry.

'Just a note from the High Commissioner's office with a suggestion for your trek up into the hills with the President: take a case of fresh water, some anti-malaria pills and a mobile phone. Otherwise you could become dehydrated, break out in a fever and be out of contact all at the same time.'

Henry laughed. 'Yes, yes and yes,' he said, as the phone on his desk rang.

It was Bill, who warned him that the bank could no longer honour cheques drawn on the Swimming Pool Account, as there hadn't been any substantial deposits for over a month.

'I don't need reminding,' said Henry, staring down at Mrs Davidson's cheque for twenty-five kora.

'I'm afraid the contractors have left the site, as we're unable to cover their next stage payment. What's more, your quarterly payment of £1.25 million won't be yielding any surplus while the President looks so healthy.'

'Happy fiftieth on Saturday, Bill,' said Henry.

'Don't remind me,' the bank manager replied. 'But now you mention it, I hope you'll be able to join Sue and me for a little celebration that evening.'

'I'll be there,' said Henry. 'Nothing will stop me.'

—◦—

That evening, Henry began taking his malaria tablets each night before going to bed. On Thursday, he picked up a crate of fresh water from the local supermarket. On Friday morning his secretary handed him a mobile phone just before he was due to leave. She even checked that he knew how to operate it.

At nine o'clock, Henry left his office and drove his Mini to the Victoria Barracks, having promised that he'd check in with his secretary the moment they arrived at General Olangi's village. He parked his car in the compound, and was escorted to a waiting Mercedes near the back of the motorcade that was flying the Union Jack. At 9.30, the President emerged from the palace and walked over to the open-topped Rolls-Royce at the front of the motorcade. Henry couldn't help thinking that he had never seen the General looking healthier.

An honour guard sprang to attention and presented arms as the motorcade swept out of the compound. As they drove slowly through St George's, the streets were lined with children waving flags, who had been given the day off school so they could cheer their leader as he set off on the long journey to his birthplace.

Henry settled back for the five-hour drive up into the hills, dozing off from time to time, but was rudely woken whenever they passed through a village, where the ritual cheering children would be paraded to greet their President.

At midday, the motorcade came to a halt in a small village high in the hills where the locals had prepared lunch for their honoured guest. An hour later they moved on. Henry feared that the tribesmen had probably sacrificed the best part of their winter stores to fill the stomachs of the scores of soldiers and officials who were accompanying the President on his pilgrimage.

When the motorcade set off again, Henry fell into a deep sleep and began dreaming about Bermuda, where, he was confident, there would be no need to build a swimming pool.

He woke with a start. He thought he'd heard a shot. Had it taken place in his dream? He looked up to see his driver jumping out of the car and fleeing into the dense jungle.

Henry calmly opened the back door, stepped out of the limousine, and, seeing a commotion taking place in front of him, decided to go and investigate. He had walked only a few paces when he came across the massive figure of the President, lying motionless at the side of the road in a pool of blood, surrounded by soldiers. They suddenly turned and, seeing the High Commissioner's representative, raised their rifles.

'Shoulder arms!' said a sharp voice. 'Try to remember that we are not savages.' A smartly dressed army captain stepped forward and saluted. 'I am sorry for any inconvenience you have suffered, First Secretary,' he said, in a clipped Sandhurst voice, 'but be assured that we wish you no harm.'

Henry didn't comment, but continued to stare down at the dead President.

'As you can see, Mr Pascoe, the late President has met with a tragic accident,' continued the captain. 'We will remain with him until he has been buried with full honours in the village where he was born. I'm sure that is what he would have wished.'

Henry looked down at the prostrate body, and doubted it.

'May I suggest, Mr Pascoe, that you return to the capital immediately and inform your masters of what has happened.'

Henry remained silent.

'You may also wish to tell them that the new President is Colonel Narango.'

Henry still didn't voice an opinion. He realised that his first duty was to get a message through to the Foreign Office as quickly as possible. He nodded in the direction of the captain and began walking slowly back to his driverless car.

He slipped in behind the wheel, relieved to see that the keys had been left in the ignition. He switched on the engine, turned the car around and began the long journey back down the winding track to the capital. It would be nightfall before he reached St George's.

After he had covered a couple of miles and was certain that no one was following him, he brought the car to a halt by the side of the road, took out his mobile phone and dialled his office number.

His secretary picked up the phone.

'It's Henry.'

'Oh, I'm so glad you phoned,' Shirley said. 'So much has happened this afternoon. But first, Mrs Davidson has just called to say that it looks as if the church bazaar might raise as much as two hundred kora, and would it be possible for you to drop in on your way back so they can present you with the cheque? And by the way,' Shirley added before Henry could speak, 'we've all heard the news.'

'Yes, that's what I was calling about,' said Henry. 'We must contact the Foreign Office immediately.'

'I already have,' said Shirley.

'What did you tell them?'

'That you were with the President, carrying out official duties, and would be in touch with them just as soon as you returned, High Commissioner.'

'High Commissioner?' said Henry.

'Yes, it's official. I assumed that's what you were calling about. Your new appointment. Congratulations.'

'Thank you,' said Henry casually, not even asking where he'd been appointed to. 'Any other news?'

'No, not much else happening this end. It's a typically quiet Friday afternoon. In fact, I was wondering if I could go home a little early this evening. You see, I promised to drop in and help Sue Paterson prepare for her husband's fiftieth.'

'Yes, why not,' said Henry, trying to remain calm. 'And do let Mrs Davidson know that I'll make every effort to call in at the bazaar. Two hundred kora should make all the difference.'

'By the way,' Shirley asked, 'how's the President getting on?'

'He's just about to take part in an earth-moving ceremony,' said Henry, 'so I'd better leave you.'

Henry touched the red button, then immediately dialled another number.

'Bill Paterson speaking.'

'Bill, it's Henry. Have you exchanged our quarterly cheque yet?'

'Yes, I did it about an hour ago. I got the best rate I could, but I'm afraid the kora always strengthens whenever the President makes his official trip back to his place of birth.'

Henry avoided adding 'And death', simply saying, 'I want the entire amount converted back into sterling.'

'I must advise you against that,' said Bill. 'The kora has strengthened further in the last hour. And in any case, such an action would have to be sanctioned by the High Commissioner.'

'The High Commissioner is in Dorset on his annual leave. In his absence, I am the senior diplomat in charge of the mission.'

'That may well be the case,' said Bill, 'but I would still have to make a full report for the High Commissioner's consideration on his return.'

'I would expect nothing less of you, Bill,' said Henry.

'Are you sure you know what you're doing, Henry?'

'I know exactly what I'm doing,' came back the immediate reply. 'And while you're at it, I also require that the kora we are holding in the Contingency Fund be converted into sterling.'

'I'm not sure . . .' began Bill.

'Mr Paterson, I don't have to remind you that there are several other banks in St George's, who for years have made it clear how much they would like to have the British government's account.'

'I shall carry out your orders to the letter, First Secretary,' replied the bank manager, 'but I wish it to be placed on the record that it is against my better judgement.'

'Be that as it may, I wish this transaction to be carried out before the close of business today,' said Henry. 'Do I make myself clear?'

'You most certainly do,' said Bill.

It took Henry another four hours to reach the capital. As all the streets in St George's were empty, he assumed that the news of the President's death must have been announced, and that a curfew was in force. He was stopped at several check-points – grateful to have the Union Jack flying from his bonnet – and ordered to proceed to his home immediately. Still, it meant he wouldn't have to drop into Mrs Davidson's bazaar and pick up the cheque for two hundred kora.

The moment Henry arrived back home he switched on the television, to see President Narango, in full-dress uniform, addressing his people.

'Be assured, my friends,' he was saying, 'you have nothing to fear. It is my intention to lift the curfew as soon as possible. But until then, please do not stray out onto the streets, as the army has been given orders to shoot on sight.'

Henry opened a tin of baked beans and remained indoors for the entire weekend. He was sorry to miss Bill's fiftieth, but he felt on balance it was probably for the best.

–◦–

HRH Princess Anne opened St George's new swimming pool on her way back from the Commonwealth Games in Kuala Lumpur. In her speech from the poolside, she said how impressed she was by the high diving board and the modern changing facilities.

She went on to single out the work of the Rotary Club and to congratulate them on the leadership they had shown throughout the campaign, in particular the chairman, Mr Bill

Paterson, who had received an OBE for his services in the Queen's Birthday Honours.

Sadly, Henry Pascoe was not present at the ceremony, as he had recently taken up his post as High Commissioner to the Ascensions – a group of islands which isn't on the way to anywhere.

THE RECLINING WOMAN *

'YOU MAY WONDER why this sculpture is numbered "13",' said the curator, a smile of satisfaction appearing on his face. I was standing at the back of the group, and assumed we were about to be given a lecture on artists' proofs.

'Henry Moore,' the curator continued, in a voice that made it clear he believed he was addressing an ignorant bunch of tourists who might muddle up Cubism with sugar lumps, and who obviously had nothing better to do on a bank holiday Monday than visit a National Trust house, 'would normally produce his works in editions of twelve. To be fair to the great man, he died before approval was given for the only casting of a thirteenth example of one of his masterpieces.'

I stared across at the vast bronze of a nude woman that dominated the entrance of Huxley Hall. The magnificent, curvaceous figure, with the trademark hole in the middle of her stomach, head resting in a cupped hand, stared out imperiously at a million visitors a year. She was, to quote the handbook, classic Henry Moore, 1952.

I continued to admire the inscrutable lady, wanting to lean across and touch her – always a sign that the artist has achieved what he set out to do.

'Huxley Hall,' the curator droned on, 'has been administered by the National Trust for the past twenty years. This sculpture, *The Reclining Woman*, is considered by scholars to be among the finest examples of Moore's work, executed when he was at the height of his powers. The sixth edition of the sculpture was purchased by the fifth Duke – a Yorkshireman, like Moore – for the princely sum of £1,000. When the Hall was passed on to the sixth Duke, he discovered that he was unable to insure the masterpiece, because he simply couldn't afford the premium.

'The seventh Duke went one better – he couldn't even afford the upkeep of the Hall, or the land that surrounded it. Shortly before his demise, he avoided leaving the eighth Duke with the burden of death duties by handing over the Hall, its contents and its thousand-acre grounds to the National Trust. The French have never understood that if you wish to kill off the aristocracy, death duties are far more effective than revolutions.' The curator laughed at his little *bon mot*, and one or two at the front of the crowd politely joined in.

'Now, to return to the mystery of the edition of thirteen,' continued the curator, resting a hand on *The Reclining Woman*'s ample bottom. 'To do this, I must first explain one of the problems the National Trust faces whenever it takes over someone else's home. The Trust is a registered charity. It currently owns and administers over 250 historic buildings and gardens in the British Isles, as well as more than 600,000 acres of countryside and 575 miles of coastline. Each piece of property must meet the Trust's criterion of being "of historic interest or natural beauty". In taking over the responsibility for maintaining the properties, we also have to insure and protect their fabric and contents without bankrupting the Trust. In the case of Huxley Hall, we have installed the most advanced security system available, backed up by guards who work around the clock. Even so, it is impossible to protect all our many treasures for twenty-four hours a day, every day of the year.

'When something is reported missing, we naturally inform the police immediately. Nine times out of ten the missing item is returned to us within days.' The curator paused, confident that someone would ask why.

'Why?' asked an American woman, dressed in tartan Bermuda shorts and standing at the front of our group.

'A good question, madam,' said the curator condescendingly. 'It's simply because most petty criminals find it almost impossible to dispose of such valuable booty, unless it has been stolen to order.'

'Stolen to order?' queried the same American woman, bang on cue.

'Yes, madam,' said the curator, only too happy to explain. 'You see, there are gangs of criminals operating around the globe who steal masterpieces for clients who are happy that no one else should ever see them, as long as they can enjoy them in private.'

'That must come expensive,' suggested the American woman.

'I understand that the current rate is around a fifth of the work's market value,' confirmed the curator. This seemed to finally silence her.

'But that doesn't explain why so many treasures are returned so quickly,' said a voice from the middle of the crowd.

'I was about to come to that,' said the curator, a little sharply. 'If an artwork has not been stolen to order, even the most inexperienced fence will avoid it.'

He quickly added, 'Because . . .' before the American woman could demand 'Why?'

'. . . all the leading auctioneers, dealers and galleries will have a full description of the missing piece on their desks within hours of its being stolen. This leaves the thief in possession of something no one is willing to handle, because if it were to come onto the market the police would swoop within hours. Many of our stolen masterpieces are actually returned within a few days, or dumped in a place where they are certain to be found. The Dulwich Art Gallery alone has experienced this on no fewer than three separate occasions in the past ten years, and, surprisingly, very few of the treasures are returned damaged.'

This time, several 'Whys?' emanated from the little gathering.

'It appears,' said the curator, responding to the cries, 'that the public may be inclined to forgive a daring theft, but what they will not forgive is damage being caused to a national treasure. I might add that the likelihood of a criminal being charged if the stolen goods are returned undamaged is also much reduced.

'But, to continue my little tale of the edition of thirteen,' he went on. 'On September 6th 1997, the day of Diana, Princess of Wales's funeral, just at the moment the coffin was entering Westminster Abbey, a van drove up and parked outside the main entrance of Huxley Hall. Six men dressed in National Trust overalls emerged and told the guard on duty that they had orders to remove *The Reclining Woman* and transport her to London for a Henry Moore exhibition that would shortly be taking place in Hyde Park.

'The guard had been informed that because of the funeral, the pick-up had been postponed until the following week. But as the paperwork all seemed to be in order, and as he wanted to hurry back to his television, he allowed the six men to remove the sculpture.

'Huxley Hall was closed for the two days after the funeral, so no one gave the incident a thought until a second van appeared the following Tuesday with the same instructions to remove *The Reclining Woman* and transport her to the Moore exhibition in Hyde Park. Once again, the paperwork was in order, and for some time the guards assumed it was simply a clerical error. One phone call to the organisers of the Hyde Park exhibition disabused them of this idea. It became clear that the masterpiece had been stolen by a gang of professional criminals. Scotland Yard was immediately informed.

'The Yard,' continued the curator, 'has an entire department devoted to the theft of works of art, with the details of many thousands of pieces listed on computer. Within moments of being notified of a crime, they are able to alert all the leading auctioneers and art dealers in the country.'

The curator paused, and placed his hand back on the lady's bronze bottom. 'Quite a large piece to transport and deliver, you might think, even though the roads were unusually empty on the day of the theft, and the public's attention was engaged elsewhere.

'For weeks, nothing was reported of *The Reclining Woman*, and Scotland Yard began to fear that they were dealing with a successful "stolen to order" theft. But some months later, when a petty thief called Sam Jackson was picked up trying to remove a small oil of the second Duchess from the Royal Robing Room, the police obtained their first lead. When the suspect was taken back to the local station to be questioned, he offered the arresting officer a deal.

'"And what could *you* possibly have to offer, Jackson?" the Sergeant asked incredulously.

'"I'll take you to *The Reclining Woman*," said Jackson, "if in return you only charge me with breaking and entering" – for which he knew he had a chance of getting off with a suspended sentence.

'"If we recover *The Reclining Woman*," the Sergeant told him, "you've got yourself a deal." As the portrait of the second Duchess was a poor copy that would only have fetched a few hundred pounds at a boot sale, the deal was struck. Jackson was bundled into the back of a car, and guided three police officers across the Yorkshire border and on into Lancashire, where they drove deeper and deeper into the countryside until they came to a deserted farmhouse. From there, Jackson led the police on foot across several fields and into a valley, where they found an outbuilding hidden behind a copse of trees. The police forced the lock and pulled open the door, to discover they were in an abandoned foundry. Several scraps of lead piping were lying on the floor, probably stolen from the roofs of churches and old houses in the vicinity.

'The police searched the building, but couldn't find any trace of *The Reclining Woman*. They were just about to charge Jackson with wasting police time when they saw him standing in front of a large lump of bronze.

'"I didn't say you'd get it back in its original condition," said Jackson. "I only promised to take you to it."'

The curator waited for the slower ones to join in the 'ums' and 'ahs', or simply to nod their understanding.

'Disposing of the masterpiece had obviously proved difficult, and as the criminals had no wish to be apprehended in possession of stolen goods to the value of over a million pounds, they had simply melted down *The Reclining Woman*. Jackson denied knowing who was responsible, but he did admit that someone had tried to sell him the lump of bronze for £1,000 – ironically, the exact sum the fifth Duke had paid for the original masterpiece.

'A few weeks later, a large lump of bronze was returned to the National Trust. To our dismay, the insurance company refused to pay a penny in compensation, claiming that the stolen bronze had been returned. The Trust's lawyers studied the policy carefully, and discovered that we were entitled to claim for the cost of restoring damaged items to their original state. The insurance company gave in, and agreed to pay for any restoration charges.

'Our next approach was to the Henry Moore Foundation,

asking if they could help in any way. They studied the large lump of bronze for several days, and after weighing and chemically testing it, they agreed with the police laboratory that it could well be the metal which was cast into the original sculpture bought by the fifth Duke.

'After much deliberation, the Foundation agreed to make an unprecedented exception to Henry Moore's usual practice, and to cast a thirteenth edition of *The Reclining Woman*, provided the Trust was willing to cover the foundry's costs. We naturally agreed to this request, and ended up with a bill for a few thousand pounds, which was covered by our insurance policy.

'However, the Foundation did make two provisos before agreeing to create this unique thirteenth edition. Firstly, they insisted that we never allow the statue to be put up for sale, publicly or privately. And secondly, if the stolen sixth edition were ever to reappear anywhere in the world, we would immediately return the thirteenth edition to the Foundation so that it could be melted down.

'The Trust agreed to abide by these terms, which is why you are able to enjoy the masterpiece you see before you today.'

A ripple of applause broke out, and the curator gave a slight bow.

-◁◦▷-

I was reminded of this story a few years later, when I attended a sale of modern art at Sotheby Parke-Bernet in New York, where the third edition of *The Reclining Woman* came under the hammer and was sold for $1,600,000.

I am assured that Scotland Yard has closed the file on the missing sixth edition of *The Reclining Woman* by Henry Moore, as they consider the crime solved. However, the Chief Inspector who had been in charge of the case did admit to me that if an enterprising criminal were able to convince a foundry to cast another edition of *The Reclining Woman*, and to mark it '6/12', he could then dispose of it to a 'stolen to order' customer for around a quarter of a million pounds. In fact, no one can be absolutely sure how many sixth editions of *The Reclining Woman* are now in private hands.

THE GRASS IS ALWAYS GREENER...

BILL WOKE with a start. It was always the same following a long sleep-in over the weekend. Once the sun had risen on Monday morning they would expect him to move on. He had slept under the archway of Critchley's Bank for more years than most of the staff had worked in the building.

Bill would turn up every evening at around seven o'clock to claim his spot. Not that anyone else would have dared to occupy his pitch after all these years. Over the past decade he had seen them come and go, some with hearts of gold, some silver and some bronze. Most of the bronze ones were only interested in the other kind of gold. He had sussed out which was which, and not just by the way they treated him.

He glanced up at the clock above the door: ten to six. Young Kevin would appear through that door at any moment and ask if he would be kind enough to move on. Good lad, Kevin – often slipped him a bob or two, which must have been a sacrifice, what with another baby on the way. He certainly wouldn't have been treated with the same consideration by most of the posher ones who came in later.

Bill allowed himself a moment to dream. He would have liked to have Kevin's job, dressed in that heavy, warm coat and peaked hat. He would still have been on the street, but with a real job and regular pay. Some people had all the luck. All

Kevin had to do was say, 'Good morning, sir. Hope you had a pleasant weekend.' Didn't even have to hold the door open since they'd made it automatic.

But Bill wasn't complaining. It hadn't been too bad a weekend. It didn't rain, and nowadays the police never tried to move him on – not since he'd spotted that IRA man parking his van outside the bank all those years ago. That was his army training.

He'd managed to get hold of a copy of Friday's *Financial Times* and Saturday's *Daily Mail*. The *Financial Times* reminded him that he should have invested in Internet companies and kept out of clothes manufacturers, because their stocks were dropping rapidly following the slowdown in High Street sales. He was probably the only person attached to the bank who read the *Financial Times* from cover to cover, and certainly the only one who then used it as a blanket.

He'd picked up the *Mail* from the bin at the back of the building – amazing what some of those yuppies dropped in that bin. He'd had everything from a Rolex watch to a packet of condoms. Not that he had any use for either. There were quite enough clocks in the City without needing another one, and as for the condoms – not much point in those since he'd left the army. He had sold the watch and given the condoms to Vince, who worked the Bank of America pitch. Vince was always bragging about his latest conquests, which seemed a little unlikely given his circumstances. Bill had decided to call his bluff and give him the condoms as a Christmas present.

The lights were being switched on all over the building, and when Bill glanced through the plate-glass window he spotted Kevin putting on his coat. Time to gather up his belongings and move on: he didn't want to get Kevin into any trouble, on account of the fact he hoped the lad would soon be getting the promotion he deserved.

Bill rolled up his sleeping bag – a present from the

Chairman, who hadn't waited until Christmas to give it to him. No, that wasn't Sir William's style. A born gentleman, with an eye for the ladies – and who could blame him? Bill had seen one or two of them go up in the lift late at night, and he doubted if they were seeking advice on their PEPs. Perhaps he should have given *him* the packet of condoms.

He folded up his two blankets – one he'd bought with some of the money from the watch sale, the other he'd inherited when Irish died. He missed Irish. Half a loaf of bread from the back of the City Club, after he'd advised the manager to get out of clothes manufacturers and into the Internet, but he'd just laughed. He shoved his few possessions into his QC's bag – another dustbin job, this time from the back of the Old Bailey.

Finally, like all good City men, he must check his cash position – always important to be liquid when there are more sellers than buyers. He fumbled around in his pocket, the one without a hole, and pulled out a pound, two 10p pieces and a penny. Thanks to government taxes, he wouldn't be able to afford any fags today, let alone his usual pint. Unless of course Maisie was behind the bar at The Reaper. He would have liked to reap her, he thought, even though he was old enough to be her father.

Clocks all over the city were beginning to chime six. He tied up the laces of his Reebok trainers – another yuppie reject: the yuppies all wore Nikes now. One last glance as Kevin stepped out onto the pavement. By the time Bill returned at seven that evening – more reliable than any security guard – Kevin would be back home in Peckham with his pregnant wife Lucy. Lucky man.

Kevin watched as Bill shuffled away, disappearing among the early-morning workers. He was good like that, Bill. He would never embarrass Kevin, or want to be the cause of him losing his job. Then he spotted the penny underneath the arch.

He picked it up and smiled. He would replace it with a pound coin that evening. After all, wasn't that what banks were meant to do with your money?

Kevin returned to the front door just as the cleaners were leaving. They arrived at three in the morning, and had to be off the premises by six. After four years he knew all of their names, and they always gave him a smile.

Kevin had to be out on the pavement by six o'clock on the dot, shoes polished, clean white shirt, the bank's crested tie and the regulation brass-buttoned long blue coat – heavy in winter, light in summer. Banks are sticklers for rules and regulations. He was expected to salute all board members as they entered the building, but he had added one or two others he'd heard might soon be joining the board.

Between six and seven the yuppies would arrive with, 'Hi, Kev. Bet I make a million today.' From seven to eight, at a slightly slower pace, came the middle management, already having lost their edge after dealing with the problems of young children, school fees, new car or new wife: 'Good morning,' not bothering to make eye contact. From eight to nine, the dignified pace of senior management, having parked their cars in reserved spaces in the carpark. Although they went to football matches on a Saturday like the rest of us, thought Kevin, they had seats in the directors' box. Most of them realised by now that they weren't going to make the board, and had settled for an easier life. Among the last to arrive would be the bank's Chief Executive, Phillip Alexander, sitting in the back of a chauffeur-driven Jaguar, reading the *Financial Times*. Kevin was expected to run out onto the pavement and open the car door for Mr Alexander, who would then march straight past him without so much as a glance, let alone a thank-you.

Finally, Sir William Selwyn, the bank's Chairman, would be dropped off in his Rolls-Royce, having been driven up from somewhere in Surrey. Sir William always found time to have a word with him. 'Good morning, Kevin. How's the wife?'

'Well, thank you, sir.'

'Let me know when the baby's due.'

Kevin grinned as the yuppies began to appear, the automatic door sliding open as they dashed through. No more having to pull open heavy doors since they'd installed that contraption. He was surprised they bothered to keep him on the payroll – at least, that was the opinion of Mike Haskins, his immediate superior.

Kevin glanced around at Haskins, who was standing behind the reception desk. Lucky Mike. Inside in the warmth, regular cups of tea, the odd perk, not to mention a rise in salary. That was the job Kevin was after, the next step up the bank's ladder. He'd earned it. And he already had ideas for making reception run more efficiently. He turned back the moment Haskins looked up, reminding himself that his boss only had five months, two weeks and four days to go before he was due to retire. Then Kevin would take over his job – as long as they didn't bypass him and offer the position to Haskins's son.

Ronnie Haskins had been appearing at the bank pretty regularly since he'd lost his job at the brewery. He made himself useful, carrying parcels, delivering letters, hailing taxis and even getting sandwiches from the local Pret A Manger for those who wouldn't or couldn't risk leaving their desks.

Kevin wasn't stupid – he knew exactly what Haskins's game was. He intended to make sure Ronnie got the job that was Kevin's by right, while Kevin remained out on the pavement. It wasn't fair. He had served the bank conscientiously, never once missing a day's work, standing out there in all weathers.

'Good morning, Kevin,' said Chris Parnell, almost running past him. He had an anxious look on his face. He should have my problems, thought Kevin, glancing round to see Haskins stirring his first cup of tea of the morning.

'That's Chris Parnell,' Haskins told Ronnie, before sipping his tea. 'Late again – he'll blame it on British Rail, always does. I should have been given his job years ago, and I would have been, if like him I'd been a Sergeant in the Pay Corps, and not a Corporal in the Greenjackets. But management didn't seem to appreciate what I had to offer.'

Ronnie made no comment, but then, he had heard his father express this opinion every workday morning for the past six weeks.

'I once invited him to my regimental reunion, but he said he was too busy. Bloody snob. Watch him, though, because he'll have a say in who gets my job.'

'Good morning, Mr Parker,' said Haskins, handing the next arrival a copy of the *Guardian*.

'Tells you a lot about a man, what paper he reads,' Haskins said to Ronnie as Roger Parker disappeared into the lift. 'Now, you take young Kevin out there. He reads the *Sun*, and that's all you need to know about him. Which is another reason I wouldn't be surprised if he doesn't get the promotion he's after.' He winked at his son. 'I, on the other hand, read the *Express* – always have done, always will do.'

'Good morning, Mr Tudor-Jones,' said Haskins, as he passed a copy of the *Telegraph* to the bank's Chief Administrator. He didn't speak again until the lift doors had closed.

'Important time for Mr Tudor-Jones,' Haskins informed his son. 'If he doesn't get promoted to the board this year, my bet is he'll be marking time until he retires. I sometimes look at these jokers and think I could do their jobs. After all, it wasn't my fault my old man was a brickie, and I didn't get the chance to go to the local grammar school. Otherwise I might have ended up on the sixth or seventh floor, with a desk of my own and a secretary.'

'Good morning, Mr Alexander,' said Haskins as the bank's

Chief Executive walked past him without acknowledging his salutation.

'Don't have to hand him a paper. Miss Franklyn, his secretary, picks the lot up for him long before he arrives. Now he wants to be Chairman. If he gets the job, there'll be a lot of changes round here, that's for sure.' He looked across at his son. 'You been booking in all those names, the way I taught you?'

'Sure have, Dad. Mr Parnell, 7.47; Mr Parker, 8.09; Mr Tudor-Jones, 8.11; Mr Alexander, 8.23.'

'Well done, son. You're learning fast.' He poured himself another cup of tea, and took a sip. Too hot, so he went on talking. 'Our next job is to deal with the mail – which, like Mr Parnell, is late. So, I suggest . . .' Haskins quickly hid his cup of tea below the counter and ran across the foyer. He jabbed the 'up' button, and prayed that one of the lifts would return to the ground floor before the Chairman entered the building. The doors slid open with seconds to spare.

'Good morning, Sir William. I hope you had a pleasant weekend.'

'Yes, thank you, Haskins,' said the Chairman, as the doors closed. Haskins blocked the way so that no one could join Sir William in the lift, and he would have an uninterrupted journey to the fourteenth floor.

Haskins ambled back to the reception desk to find his son sorting out the morning mail. 'The Chairman once told me that the lift takes thirty-eight seconds to reach the top floor, and he'd worked out that he'd spend a week of his life in there, so he always read the *Times* leader on the way up and the notes for his next meeting on the way down. If he spends a week trapped in there, I reckon I must spend half my life,' he added, as he picked up his tea and took a sip. It was cold. 'Once you've sorted out the post, you can take it up to Mr

Parnell. It's his job to distribute it, not mine. He's got a cushy enough number as it is, so there's no reason why I should do his work for him.'

Ronnie picked up the basket full of mail and headed for the lift. He stepped out on the second floor, walked over to Mr Parnell's desk and placed the basket in front of him.

Chris Parnell looked up, and watched as the lad disappeared back out of the door. He stared at the pile of letters. As always, no attempt had been made to sort them out. He must have a word with Haskins. It wasn't as if the man was run off his feet, and now he wanted his boy to take his place. Not if *he* had anything to do with it.

Didn't Haskins understand that his job carried real responsibility? He had to make sure the office ticked like a Swiss clock. Letters on the correct desks before nine, check for any absentees by ten, deal with any machinery breakdowns within moments of being notified of them, arrange and organise all staff meetings, by which time the second post would have arrived. Frankly, the whole place would come to a halt if he ever took a day off. You only had to look at the mess he always came back to whenever he returned from his summer holiday.

He stared at the letter on the top of the pile. It was addressed to 'Mr Roger Parker'. 'Rog', to him. He should have been given Rog's job as Head of Personnel years ago – he could have done it in his sleep, as his wife Janice never stopped reminding him: 'He's no more than a jumped-up office clerk. Just because he was at the same school as the Chief Cashier.' It wasn't fair.

Janice had wanted to invite Roger and his wife round to dinner, but Chris had been against the idea from the start.

'Why not?' she had demanded. 'After all, you both support Chelsea. Is it because you're afraid he'll turn you down, the stuck-up snob?'

To be fair to Janice, it had crossed Chris's mind to invite Roger out for a drink, but not to dinner at their home in Romford. He couldn't explain to her that when Roger went to Stamford Bridge he didn't sit at the Shed end with the lads, but in the members' seats.

Once the letters had been sorted out, Chris placed them in different trays according to their departments. His two assistants could cover the first ten floors, but he would never allow them anywhere near the top four. Only *he* got into the Chairman and Chief Executive's offices.

Janice never stopped reminding him to keep his eyes open whenever he was on the executive floors. 'You can never tell what opportunities might arise, what openings could present themselves.' He laughed to himself, thinking about Gloria in Filing, and the openings she offered. The things that girl could do behind a filing cabinet. That was one thing he didn't need his wife to find out about.

He picked up the trays for the top four floors, and headed towards the lift. When he reached the eleventh floor, he gave a gentle knock on the door before entering Roger's office. The Head of Personnel glanced up from a letter he'd been reading, a preoccupied look on his face.

'Good result for Chelsea on Saturday, Rog, even if it was only against West Ham,' Chris said as he placed a pile of letters in his superior's in-tray. He didn't get any response, so he left hurriedly.

Roger looked up as Chris scurried away. He felt guilty that he hadn't chatted to him about the Chelsea match, but he didn't want to explain why he had missed a home game for the first time that season. He should be so lucky as only to have Chelsea on his mind.

He turned his attention back to the letter he had been reading. It was a bill for £1,600, the first month's fee for his mother's nursing home.

Roger had reluctantly accepted that she was no longer well enough to remain with them in Croydon, but he hadn't been expecting a bill that would work out at almost £20,000 a year. Of course he hoped she'd be around for another twenty years, but with Adam and Sarah still at school, and Hazel not wanting to go back to work, he needed a further rise in salary, at a time when all the talk was of cutbacks and redundancies.

It had been a disastrous weekend. On Saturday he had begun to read the McKinsey report, outlining what the bank would have to do if it was to continue as a leading financial institution into the twenty-first century.

The report had suggested that at least seventy employees would have to participate in a downsizing programme – a euphemism for 'You're sacked.' And who would be given the unenviable task of explaining to those seventy individuals the precise meaning of the word 'downsizing'? The last time Roger had had to sack someone, he hadn't slept for days. He had felt so depressed by the time he put the report down that he just couldn't face the Chelsea match.

He realised he would have to make an appointment to see Godfrey Tudor-Jones, the bank's Chief Administrator, although he knew that Tudor-Jones would brush him off with, 'Not my department, old boy, people problems. And you're the Head of Personnel, Roger, so I guess it's up to you.' It wasn't as if he'd been able to strike up a personal relationship with the man, which he could now fall back on. He had tried hard enough over the years, but the Chief Administrator had made it all too clear that he didn't mix business with pleasure – unless, of course, you were a board member.

'Why don't you invite him to a home game at Chelsea?' suggested Hazel. 'After all, you paid enough for those two season tickets.'

'I don't think he's into football,' Roger had told her. 'More a rugby man, would be my guess.'

'Then invite him to your club for dinner.'

He didn't bother to explain to Hazel that Godfrey was a member of the Carlton Club, and he didn't imagine he would feel at ease at a meeting of the Fabian Society.

The final blow had come on Saturday evening, when the headmaster of Adam's school had phoned to say he needed to see him urgently, about a matter that couldn't be discussed over the phone. He had driven there on the Sunday morning, apprehensive about what it could possibly be that couldn't be discussed over the phone. He knew that Adam needed to buckle down and work a lot harder if he was to have a chance of being offered a place at any university, but the headmaster told him that his son had been caught smoking marijuana, and that the school rules on that particular subject couldn't be clearer – immediate expulsion and a full report to the local police the following day. When he heard the news, Roger felt as if he were back in his own headmaster's study.

Father and son had hardly exchanged a word on the journey home. When Hazel had been told why Adam had come back in the middle of term she had broken down in tears, and proved inconsolable. She feared it would all come out in the *Croydon Advertiser*, and they would have to move. Roger certainly couldn't afford a move at the moment, but he didn't think this was the right time to explain to Hazel the meaning of negative equity.

On the train up to London that morning, Roger couldn't help thinking that none of this would have arisen if he had landed the Chief Administrator's job. For months there had been talk of Godfrey joining the board, and when he eventually did, Roger would be the obvious candidate to take his place. But he needed the extra cash right now, what with his mother in a nursing home and having to find a sixth-form college that would take Adam. He and Hazel would have to forget celebrating their twentieth wedding anniversary in Venice.

As he sat at his desk, he thought about the consequences of his colleagues finding out about Adam. He wouldn't lose his job, of course, but he needn't bother concerning himself with any further promotion. He could hear the snide whispers in the washroom that were meant to be overheard.

'Well, he's always been a bit of a lefty, you know. So, frankly, are you surprised?' He would have liked to explain to them that just because you read the *Guardian*, it doesn't automatically follow that you go on Ban the Bomb marches, experiment with free love and smoke marijuana at weekends.

He returned to the first page of the McKinsey report, and realised he would have to make an early appointment to see the Chief Administrator. He knew it would be no more than going through the motions, but at least he would have done his duty by his colleagues.

He dialled an internal number, and Godfrey Tudor-Jones's secretary picked up the phone.

'The Chief Administrator's office,' said Pamela, sounding as if she had a cold.

'It's Roger. I need to see Godfrey fairly urgently. It's about the McKinsey report.'

'He has appointments most of the day,' said Pamela, 'but I could fit you in at 4.15 for fifteen minutes.'

'Then I'll be with you at 4.15.'

Pamela replaced the phone and made a note in her boss's diary.

'Who was that?' asked Godfrey.

'Roger Parker. He says he has a problem and needs to see you urgently. I fitted him in at 4.15.'

He doesn't know what a problem is, thought Godfrey, continuing to sift through his letters to see if any had 'Confidential' written on them. None had, so he crossed the room and handed them all back to Pamela.

She took them without a word passing between them.

Nothing had been the same since that weekend in Manchester. He should never have broken the golden rule about sleeping with your secretary. If it hadn't rained for three days, or if he'd been able to get a ticket for the United match, or if her skirt hadn't been quite so short, it might never have happened. If, if, if. And it wasn't as if the earth had moved, or he'd had it more than once. What a wonderful start to the week to be told she was pregnant.

As if he didn't have enough problems at the moment, the bank was having a poor year, so his bonus was likely to be about half what he'd budgeted for. Worse, he had already spent the money long before it had been credited to his account.

He looked up at Pamela. All she'd said after her initial outburst was that she hadn't made up her mind whether or not to have the baby. That was all he needed right now, what with two sons at Tonbridge and a daughter who couldn't make up her mind if she wanted a piano or a pony, and didn't understand why she couldn't have both, not to mention a wife who had become a shopaholic. He couldn't remember when his bank balance had last been in credit. He looked up at Pamela again, as she left his office. A private abortion wouldn't come cheap either, but it would be a damn sight cheaper than the alternative.

It would all have been so different if he had taken over as Chief Executive. He'd been on the shortlist, and at least three members of the board had made it clear that they supported his application. But the board in its wisdom had offered the position to an outsider. He had reached the last three, and for the first time he understood what it must feel like to win an Olympic silver medal when you're the clear favourite. Damn it, he was just as well qualified for the job as Phillip Alexander, and he had the added advantage of having worked for the bank for the past twelve years. There had been hints of a place on the board as compensation, but that would bite the dust the moment they found out about Pamela.

And what was the first recommendation Alexander had put before the board? That the bank should invest heavily in Russia, with the cataclysmic result that seventy people would now be losing their jobs and everyone's bonus was having to be readjusted. What made it worse was that Alexander was now trying to shift the blame for his decision onto the Chairman.

Once again, Godfrey's thoughts returned to Pamela. Perhaps he should take her out to lunch and try to convince her that an abortion would be the wisest course of action. He was about to pick up the phone and suggest the idea to her when it rang.

It was Pamela. 'Miss Franklyn just called. Could you pop up and see Mr Alexander in his office?' This was a ploy Alexander used regularly, to ensure you never forgot his position. Half the time, whatever needed to be discussed could easily have been dealt with over the phone. The man had a bloody power-complex.

On the way up to Alexander's office, Godfrey remembered that his wife had wanted to invite him to dinner, so she could meet the man who had robbed her of a new car.

'He won't want to come,' Godfrey had tried to explain. 'You see, he's a very private person.'

'No harm in asking,' she had insisted. But Godfrey had turned out to be right: *Phillip Alexander thanks Mrs Tudor-Jones for her kind invitation to dinner, but regrets that due to . . .*

Godfrey tried to concentrate on why Alexander wanted to see him. He couldn't possibly know about Pamela – not that it was any of his business in the first place. Especially if the rumours about his own sexual preferences were to be believed. Had he been made aware that Godfrey was well in excess of the bank's overdraft limit? Or was he going to try to drag him onside over the Russian fiasco? Godfrey could feel the palms of his hands sweating as he knocked on the door.

'Come in,' said a deep voice.

Godfrey entered to be greeted by the Chief Executive's secretary, Miss Franklyn, who had joined him from Morgans. She didn't speak, just nodded in the direction of her boss's office.

He knocked for a second time, and when he heard 'Come,' he entered the Chief Executive's office. Alexander looked up from his desk.

'Have you read the McKinsey report?' he asked. No 'Good morning, Godfrey.' No 'Did you have a pleasant weekend?' Just 'Have you read the McKinsey report?'

'Yes, I have,' replied Godfrey, who hadn't done much more than speed-read through it, checking the paragraph headings and then studying in more detail the sections that would directly affect him. On top of everything else, he didn't need to be one of those who were about to be made redundant.

'The bottom line is that we can make savings of three million a year. It will mean having to sack up to seventy of the staff, and halving most of the bonuses. I need you to give me a written assessment on how we go about it, which departments can afford to shed staff, and which personnel we would risk losing if we halved their bonuses. Can you have that ready for me in time for tomorrow's board meeting?'

The bastard's about to pass the buck again, thought Godfrey. And he doesn't seem to care if he passes it up or down, as long as he survives. Wants to present the board with a *fait accompli*, on the back of my recommendations. No way.

'Have you got anything on at the moment that might be described as priority?'

'No, nothing that can't wait,' Godfrey replied. He didn't think he'd mention his problem with Pamela, or the fact that his wife would be livid if he failed to turn up for the school play that evening, in which their younger son was playing an angel. Frankly, it wouldn't have mattered if he were playing Jesus. Godfrey would still have to be up all night preparing his report for the board.

'Good. I suggest we meet up again at ten o'clock tomorrow morning, so you can brief me on how we should go about implementing the report.' Alexander lowered his head and returned his attention to the papers on his desk – a sign that the meeting was over.

Phillip Alexander looked up once he heard the door close. Lucky man, he thought, not to have any real problems. He was up to his eyes in them. The most important thing now was to make sure he continued to distance himself from the Chairman's disastrous decision to invest so heavily in Russia. He had backed the move at a board meeting the previous year, and the Chairman had made sure that his support had been minuted. But the moment he found out what was happening over at the Bank of America and Barclays, he had put an immediate stop on the bank's second instalment – as he continually reminded the board.

Since that day Phillip had flooded the building with memos, warning every department to be sure it covered its own positions, and urging them all to retrieve whatever money they could. He kept the memos flowing on a daily basis, with the result that by now almost everyone, including several members of the board, was convinced that he had been sceptical about the decision from the outset.

The spin he'd put on events to one or two board members who were not that close to Sir William was that he hadn't felt he could go against the Chairman's wishes when he'd only been in the Chief Executive's job for a few weeks, and that had been his reason for not opposing Sir William's recommendation for a £500 million loan to the Nordsky Bank in

St Petersburg. The situation could still be turned to his advantage, because if the Chairman was forced to resign, the board might feel an internal appointment would be the best course of action, given the circumstances. After all, when they had appointed Phillip as Chief Executive, the Deputy Chairman, Maurice Kington, had made it clear that he doubted if Sir William would serve his full term – and that was before the Russian débâcle. About a month later, Kington had resigned; it was well known in the City that he only resigned when he could see trouble on the horizon, as he had no intention of giving up any of his thirty or so other directorships.

When the *Financial Times* published an unfavourable article about Sir William, it covered itself by opening with the words: *'No one will deny that Sir William Selwyn's record as Chairman of Critchley's Bank has been steady, even at times impressive. But recently there have been some unfortunate errors, which appear to have emanated from the Chairman's office.'* Alexander had briefed the journalist with chapter and verse of those 'unfortunate errors'.

Some members of the board were now whispering 'Sooner rather than later.' But Alexander still had one or two problems of his own to sort out.

Another call last week, and demands for a further payment. The damn man seemed to know just how much he could ask for each time. Heaven knows, public opinion was no longer so hostile towards homosexuals. But with a rent boy it was still different – somehow the press could make it sound far worse than a heterosexual man paying a prostitute. And how the hell was he to know the boy was under age at the time? In any case, the law had changed since then – not that the tabloids would allow that to influence them.

And then there was the problem of who should become Deputy Chairman now that Maurice Kington had resigned. Securing the right replacement would be crucial for him, because that person would be presiding when the board came to appoint the next Chairman. Phillip had already made a pact with Michael Butterfield, who he knew would support his cause, and had begun dropping hints in the ears of other board members about Butterfield's qualifications for the job: 'We need someone who voted against the Russian loan . . . Someone who wasn't appointed by Sir William . . . Someone with an independent mind . . . Someone who . . .'

He knew the message was getting through, because one or two directors had already dropped into his office and suggested that Butterfield was the obvious candidate for the job. Phillip was happy to fall in with their sage opinion.

And now it had all come to a head, because a decision would have to be made at tomorrow's board meeting. If Butterfield was appointed Deputy Chairman, everything else would fall neatly into place.

The phone on his desk rang. He picked it up and shouted, 'I said no calls, Alison.'

'It's Julian Burr again, Mr Alexander.'

'Put him through,' said Alexander quietly.

'Good morning, Phil. Just thought I'd call in and wish you all the best for tomorrow's board meeting.'

'How the hell did you know about that?'

'Oh, Phil, surely you must realise that not everyone at the bank is heterosexual.' The voice paused. 'And one of them in particular doesn't love you any more.'

'What do you want, Julian?'

'For you to be Chairman, of course.'

'What do you want?' repeated Alexander, his voice rising with every word.

'I thought a little break in the sun while you're moving up a floor. Nice, Monte Carlo, perhaps a week or two in St Tropez.'

'And how much do you imagine that would cost?' Alexander asked.

'Oh, I would have thought ten thousand would comfortably cover my expenses.'

'Far too comfortably,' said Alexander.

'I don't think so,' said Julian. 'Try not to forget that I know exactly how much you're worth, and that's without the rise in salary you can expect once you become Chairman. Let's face it, Phil, it's far less than the *News of the World* would be willing to offer me for an exclusive. I can see the headline now: "Rent Boy's Night with Chairman of Family Bank".'

'That's criminal,' said Alexander.

'No. As I was under age at the time, I think you'll find it's you who's the criminal.'

'You can go too far, you know,' said Alexander.

'Not while you have ambitions to go even further,' said Julian, with a laugh.

'I'll need a few days.'

'I can't wait that long – I want to catch the early flight to Nice tomorrow. Be sure that the money has been transferred to my account before you go into the board meeting at eleven, there's a good chap. Don't forget it was you who taught me about electronic transfers.'

The phone went dead, then rang again immediately.

'Who is it this time?' snapped Alexander.

'The Chairman's on line two.'

'Put him through.'

'Phillip, I need the latest figures on the Russian loans, along with your assessment of the McKinsey report.'

'I'll have an update on the Russian position on your desk within the hour. As for the McKinsey report, I'm broadly in agreement with its recommendations, but I've asked Godfrey Tudor-Jones to let me have a written opinion on how we should go about implementing it. I intend to present his report at tomorrow's board meeting. I hope that's satisfactory, Chairman?'

'I doubt it. I have a feeling that by tomorrow it will be too late,' the Chairman said without explanation, before replacing the phone.

Sir William knew it didn't help that the latest Russian losses had exceeded £500 million. And now the McKinsey report had arrived on every director's desk, recommending that seventy jobs, perhaps even more, should be shed in order to make a saving of around £3 million a year. When would management consultants begin to understand that human beings were involved, not just numbers on a balance sheet – among them seventy loyal members of staff, some of whom had served the bank for more than twenty years?

There wasn't a mention of the Russian loan in the McKinsey report, because it wasn't part of their brief; but the timing couldn't have been worse. And in banking, timing is everything.

Phillip Alexander's words to the board were indelibly fixed in Sir William's memory: 'We mustn't allow our rivals to take advantage of such a one-off windfall. If Critchley's is to remain a player on the international stage, we have to move quickly while there's still a profit to be made.' The short-term gains could be enormous, Alexander had assured the board – whereas in truth the opposite had turned out to be the case. And within moments of things falling apart, the little shit had begun digging himself out of the Russian hole, while dropping his Chairman right into it. He'd been on holiday at the time, and Alexander had phoned him at his hotel in Marrakech to tell him that he had everything under control, and there was no need for him to rush home. When he did eventually return, he found that Alexander had already filled in the hole, leaving him at the bottom of it.

After reading the article in the *Financial Times*, Sir William knew his days as Chairman were numbered. The resignation of Maurice Kington had been the final blow, from which he knew he couldn't hope to recover. He had tried to talk him out of it, but there was only one person's future Kington was ever interested in.

The Chairman stared down at his handwritten letter of resignation, a copy of which would be sent to every member of the board that evening.

His loyal secretary Claire had reminded him that he was fifty-seven, and had often talked of retiring at sixty to make way for a younger man. It was ironic when he considered who that younger man might be.

True, he was fifty-seven. But the last Chairman hadn't retired until he was seventy, and that was what the board and the shareholders would remember. It would be forgotten that he had taken over an ailing bank from an ailing Chairman, and increased its profits year on year for the past decade. Even if you included the Russian disaster, they were still well ahead of the game.

Those hints from the Prime Minister that he was being considered for a peerage would quickly be forgotten. The dozen or so directorships that are nothing more than routine for the retiring Chairman of a major bank would suddenly evaporate, along with the invitations to Buck House, the Guildhall and the centre court at Wimbledon – the one official outing his wife always enjoyed.

He had told Katherine over dinner the night before that he was going to resign. She had put down her knife and fork, folded her napkin and said, 'Thank God for that. Now it won't be necessary to go on with this sham of a marriage any longer. I shall wait for a decent interval, of course, before I file for divorce.' She had risen from her place and left the room without uttering another word.

Until then, he'd had no idea that Katherine felt so strongly. He'd assumed she was aware that there had been other women, although none of his affairs had been all that serious. He thought they had reached an understanding, an accommodation. After all, so many married couples of their age did. After dinner he had travelled up to London and spent the night at his club.

He unscrewed the top of his fountain pen and signed the twelve letters. He had left them on his desk all day, in the hope that before the close of business some miracle would occur which would make it possible for him to shred them. But in truth he knew that was never likely.

When he finally took the letters through to his secretary, she had already typed the recipients' names on the twelve envelopes. He smiled at Claire, the best secretary he'd ever had.

'Goodbye, Claire,' he said, giving her a kiss on the cheek.

'Goodbye, Sir William,' she replied, biting her lip.

He returned to his office, picked up his empty briefcase and a copy of *The Times*. Tomorrow he would be the lead story in the Business Section – he wasn't quite well enough known to make the front page. He looked around the Chairman's office once again before leaving it for the last time. He closed the door quietly behind him and walked slowly down the corridor to the lift. He pressed the button and waited. The doors opened and he stepped inside, grateful that the lift was empty, and that it didn't stop on its journey to the ground floor.

He walked out into the foyer and glanced towards the reception desk. Haskins would have gone home long ago. As the plate-glass door slid open he thought about Kevin sitting at home in Peckham with his pregnant wife. He would have liked to have wished him luck for the job on the reception desk. At least that wouldn't be affected by the McKinsey report.

As he stepped out onto the pavement, something caught his eye. He turned to see an old tramp settling down for the night in the far corner underneath the arch.

Bill touched his forehead in a mock salute. 'Good evening, Chairman,' he said with a grin.

'Good evening, Bill,' Sir William replied, smiling back at him.

If only they could change places, Sir William thought, as he turned and walked towards his waiting car.

CAT O'NINE
TALES

For Elizabeth

Foreword

While I was incarcerated for two years, in five different prisons, I picked up several stories that were not appropriate to include in the day-to-day journals of a prison diary. These tales are marked in the contents with an asterisk.

Although all nine stories have been embellished, each is rooted in fact. In all but one, the prisoner concerned has asked me not to reveal his real name.

The other three stories included in this volume are also true, but I came across them after being released from prison: in Athens – 'A Greek Tragedy', in London – 'The Wisdom of Solomon', and in Rome my favourite – 'In the Eye of the Beholder'.

The Man Who Robbed His Own Post Office

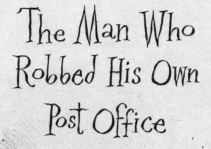

The Beginning

MR JUSTICE GRAY STARED down at the two defendants in the dock. Chris and Sue Haskins had pleaded guilty to the theft of £250,000, being the property of the Post Office, and to falsifying four passports.

Mr and Mrs Haskins looked about the same age, which was hardly surprising as they had been at school together some forty years before. You could have passed them in the street without giving either of them a second look. Chris was about five foot nine, his dark wavy hair turning grey, and he was at least a stone overweight. He stood upright in the dock, and although his suit was well worn, his shirt was clean and his striped tie suggested that he was a member of a club. His black shoes looked as if they had been spit-and-polished every morning. His wife Sue stood by his side. Her neat floral dress and sensible shoes hinted at an organized and tidy woman, but then they were both wearing the clothes that they would normally have worn to church. After all, they considered the law to be nothing less than an extension of the Almighty.

Mr Justice Gray turned his attention to Mr and Mrs Haskins's barrister, a young man who had been selected on the grounds of cost, rather than experience.

'No doubt you wish to suggest there are mitigating circumstances in this case, Mr Rodgers,' prompted the judge helpfully.

'Yes, m'lord,' admitted the newly qualified barrister as

he rose from his place. He would like to have told his lordship that this was only his second case, but he felt his lordship would be unlikely to consider that a mitigating circumstance.

Mr Justice Gray settled back as he prepared to listen to how poor Mr Haskins had been thrashed by a ruthless step-father, night after night, and Mrs Haskins had been raped by an evil uncle at an impressionable age, but no; Mr Rodgers assured the court that the Haskins came from happy, well-balanced backgrounds and had in fact been at school together. Their only child, Tracey, a graduate of Bristol University, was now working as an estate agent in Ashford. A model family.

Mr Rodgers glanced down at his brief before going on to explain how the Haskins had ended up in the dock that morning. Mr Justice Gray became more and more intrigued by their tale, and by the time the barrister had resumed his place the judge felt he needed a little more time to consider the length of the sentence. He ordered the two defendants to appear before him the following Monday at ten o'clock in the forenoon, by which time he would have come to a decision.

Mr Rodgers rose a second time.

'You were no doubt hoping that I would grant your clients bail, Mr Rodgers?' enquired the judge, raising an eyebrow, and before the surprised young barrister could respond Mr Justice Gray said, 'Granted.'

Jasper Gray told his wife about the plight of Mr and Mrs Haskins over lunch on Sunday. Long before the judge had devoured his rack of lamb, Vanessa Gray had offered her opinion.

'Sentence them both to an hour of community service, and then issue a court order instructing the Post Office to return their original investment in full,' she declared, revealing a common sense not always bestowed on the male of the species. To do him justice, the judge agreed with his spouse, although he told her that he would never get away with it.

'Why not?' she asked.

'Because of the four passports.'

Mr Justice Gray was not surprised to find Mr and Mrs Haskins standing dutifully in the dock at ten o'clock the following morning. After all, they were not criminals.

The judge raised his head, stared down at them and tried to look grave. 'You have both pleaded guilty to the crimes of theft from a post office and of falsifying four passports.' He didn't bother to add any adjectives such as evil, heinous or even disgraceful, as he didn't consider them appropriate on this occasion. 'You have therefore left me with no choice,' he continued, 'but to send you both to prison.' The judge turned his attention to Chris Haskins. 'You were obviously the instigator of this crime, and with that in mind, I sentence you to three years' imprisonment.' Chris Haskins was unable to hide his surprise: his barrister had warned him to expect at least five years. Chris had to stop himself from saying, thank you, my lord.

The judge then looked across at Mrs Haskins. 'I accept that your part in this conspiracy was possibly no more than an act of loyalty to your husband. However, you are well aware of the difference between right and wrong, and therefore I shall send you to prison for one year.'

'My lord,' protested Chris Haskins.

Mr Justice Gray frowned for the first time. He was not in the habit of being interrupted while passing sentence. 'Mr Haskins, if it is your intention to appeal against my judgement—'

'Certainly not, my lord,' said Chris Haskins, interrupting the judge for a second time. 'I was just wondering if you would allow me to serve my wife's sentence.'

Mr Justice Gray was so taken aback by the request that he couldn't think of a suitable reply to a question he had never been asked before. He banged his hammer, stood up and quickly left the courtroom. An usher hurriedly shouted, 'All rise.'

Chris and Sue first met in the playground of their local primary school in Cleethorpes, a seaside town on the east coast of England. Chris was standing in a queue waiting for his third of a pint of milk – government regulation for all schoolchildren under the age of sixteen. Sue was the milk monitor. Her job was to make sure everyone received their correct allocation. As she handed over the little bottle to Chris, neither of them gave the other a second look. Sue was in the class above Chris, so they rarely came across each other during the day, except when Chris was standing in the milk queue. At the end of the year Sue passed her eleven-plus and took up a place at the local grammar school. Chris was appointed the new milk monitor. The following September he also passed his eleven-plus, and joined Sue at Cleethorpes Grammar.

They remained oblivious to each other throughout their school days until Sue became head girl. After that, Chris couldn't help but notice her because at the end of morning assembly she would read out the school notices for the day. Bossy was the adjective most often trotted out by the lads whenever Sue's name came up in conversation (strange how women in positions of authority so often acquire the sobriquet *bossy*, while a man holding the same rank is somehow invested with qualities of leadership).

When Sue left at the end of the year Chris once again forgot all about her. He did not follow in her illustrious footsteps and become head boy, although he had a success-ful – by his standards – if somewhat uneventful year. He played for the school's second eleven cricket team, came fifth in the cross-country match against Grimsby Grammar, and did well enough in his final exams for them to be unworthy of mention either way.

No sooner had Chris left school than he received a letter from the Ministry of Defence, instructing him to report to his local recruiting office to sign up for a spell of National Service – a two-year compulsory period for all boys at the age of eighteen, when they had to serve in the armed forces. Chris's only choice in the matter was between the Army, the Royal Navy or the Royal Air Force.

He selected the RAF, and even spent a fleeting moment wondering what it might be like to be a jet pilot. Once Chris had passed his medical and filled in all the necessary forms at the local recruiting office, the duty sergeant handed him a rail pass to somewhere called Mablethorpe; he was to report to the guardhouse by eight o'clock on the first of the month.

Chris spent the next twelve weeks being put through basic training, along with a hundred and twenty other raw recruits. He quickly discovered that only one applicant in a thousand was selected to be a pilot. Chris was not one in a thousand. At the end of the twelve weeks he was given the choice of working in the canteen, the officers' mess, the quartermaster's stores or flight operations. He opted for flight operations, and was allocated a job in the stores.

It was when he reported for duty the following Monday that he once again met up with Sue, or to be more accurate Corporal Sue Smart. She was inevitably standing at the head of the line; this time giving out job instructions. Chris didn't immediately recognize her, dressed in her smart blue uniform with her hair almost hidden under a cap. In any case, he was admiring her shapely legs when she said, 'Haskins, report to the quartermaster's stores.' Chris raised his head. It was that voice he could never forget.

'Sue?' he ventured tentatively. Corporal Smart looked up from her clipboard and glared at the recruit who dared to address her by her first name. She recognized the face, but couldn't place him.

'Chris Haskins,' he volunteered.

'Ah, yes, Haskins,' she said, and hesitated before adding, 'report to Sergeant Travis in the stores, and he'll brief you on your duties.'

'Yes, Corp,' Chris replied and quickly disappeared off in the direction of the quartermaster's stores. As he walked away, Chris didn't notice that Sue was taking a second look.

Chris didn't come across Corporal Smart again until his first weekend leave. He spotted her sitting at the other end of a railway carriage on the journey back to Cleethorpes. He made no attempt to join her, even pretending not to see her. However, he did find himself looking up from time to time, admiring her slim figure – he didn't remember her being as pretty as that.

When the train pulled into Cleethorpes station, Chris spotted his mother chatting to another woman. He knew immediately who she must be – the same red hair, the same trim figure, the same . . .

'Hello, Chris,' Mrs Smart greeted him as he joined his mother on the platform. 'Was Sue on the train with you?'

'I didn't notice,' said Chris, as Sue walked up to join them.

'I expect you see a lot of each other now you're based at the same camp,' suggested Chris's mother.

'No, not really,' said Sue, trying to sound disinterested.

'Well, we'd better be off,' said Mrs Haskins. 'I have to give Chris and his dad dinner before they go off to watch the football,' she explained.

'Do you remember him?' asked Mrs Smart as Chris and his mother walked along the platform towards the exit.

'Snotty Haskins?' Sue hesitated. 'Can't say I do.'

'Oh, you like him that much, do you?' said Sue's mother with a smile.

✸ ✸ ✸

When Chris boarded the train that Sunday evening, Sue was already sitting in her place at the end of the carriage. Chris was about to walk straight past her and find a seat in the next carriage, when he heard her say, 'Hi, Chris, did you have a nice weekend?'

'Not bad, Corp,' said Chris, stopping to look down at her. 'Grimsby beat Lincoln three–one, and I'd forgotten how good the fish and chips are in Cleethorpes compared to camp.'

Sue smiled. 'Why don't you join me?' she said, patting the seat beside her. 'And I think it will be all right to call me Sue when we're not in barracks.'

On the journey back to Mablethorpe, Sue did most of the talking, partly because Chris was so smitten with her – could this be the same skinny little girl who had handed out the milk each morning? – and partly because he realized the bubble would burst the moment they set foot back in camp. Non-commissioned officers just don't fraternize with the ranks.

The two of them parted at the camp gates and went their separate ways. Chris walked back to the barracks, while Sue headed off for the NCO quarters. When Chris strolled into his Nissen hut to join his fellow conscripts, one of them was bragging about the WRAF he'd had it off with. He even went into graphic detail, describing what RAF knickers look like. 'A dark shade of blue held up by thick elastic,' he assured the mesmerized onlookers. Chris lay on his bed and stopped listening to the unlikely tale, as his thoughts returned to Sue. He wondered how long it would be before he saw her again.

Not as long as he feared because when Chris went to the canteen for lunch the following day he spotted Sue sitting in the corner with a group of girls from the ops room. He wanted to stroll across to her table and, like David Niven, casually ask her out on a date. There was a Doris Day film showing at the Odeon that he thought she might enjoy, but he'd sooner have walked across a minefield than interrupt her while his mates were watching.

Chris selected his lunch from the counter – a bowl of vegetable soup, sausage and chips, and custard pie. He carried his tray across to a table on the other side of the room and joined a group of his fellow conscripts. He was tucking into the custard pie, while discussing Grimsby's chances against Blackpool, when he felt a hand touch his shoulder. He looked round to see Sue smiling down at him. Everyone else at the table stopped talking. Chris turned a bright shade of red.

'Doing anything on Saturday night?' Sue asked. The red deepened to crimson as he shook his head. 'I was thinking of going to see *Calamity Jane*.' She paused. 'Care to join me?' Chris nodded. 'Why don't we meet outside the camp gates at six?' Another nod. Sue smiled. 'See you then.' Chris turned back to find his friends staring at him in awe.

Chris didn't remember much about the film because he spent most of his time trying to summon up enough courage to put his arm round Sue's shoulder. He didn't even manage it when Howard Keel kissed Doris Day. However, after they left the cinema and walked back towards the waiting bus, Sue took his hand.

'What are you going to do once you've finished your National Service?' Sue asked as the last bus took them back to camp.

'Join my dad on the buses, I suppose,' said Chris. 'How about you?'

'Once I've served three years, I have to decide if I want to become an officer, and make the RAF my career.'

'I hope you come back and work in Cleethorpes,' Chris blurted out.

Chris and Sue Haskins were married a year later in St Aidan's parish church.

After the wedding, the bride and groom set off for Newhaven in a hired car, intending to spend their honeymoon on the south coast of Portugal. After only a few days on the Algarve, they ran out of money. Chris drove them back to Cleethorpes, but vowed that they would return to Albufeira just as soon as he could afford it.

Chris and Sue began married life by renting three rooms on the ground floor of a semi-detached in Jubilee Road. The two milk monitors were unable to hide their contentment from anyone who came into contact with them.

Chris joined his father on the buses and became a conductor with the Green Line Municipal Coach Company, while Sue was employed as a trainee with a local insurance company. A year later Sue gave birth to Tracey and left her job to bring up their daughter. This spurred Chris on to work even harder and seek promotion. With the occasional prod from Sue, Chris began to study for the company's promotion exam. Four years later Chris was appointed an inspector. All boded well in the Haskins household.

When Tracey informed her father that she wanted a pony for Christmas, he had to point out that they didn't have enough room. Chris compromised, and on Tracey's seventh birthday presented her with a Labrador puppy, which they christened Corp. The Haskins family wanted for nothing,

and that might have been the end of this tale if Chris hadn't got the sack. It happened thus.

The Green Line Municipal Coach Company was taken over by the Hull Carriage Bus Company. With the merger of the two firms, job losses became inevitable, and Chris was among those offered a redundancy package. The only alternative the new management came up with was the reinstatement of Chris as a conductor. Chris turned his nose up at the offer. He felt confident of finding another job, and therefore accepted the settlement.

It wasn't long before the redundancy money ran out, and despite Ted Heath's promise of a brave new world, Chris quickly discovered that alternative employment wasn't that easy to find in Cleethorpes. Sue never once complained and, now that Tracey was going to school, took on a part-time job at Parsons', a local fish-and-chip shop. Not only did this bring in a weekly wage, supplemented by the occasional tip, but it also allowed Chris to enjoy a large plate of cod and chips every lunchtime.

Chris continued to try and find a job. He visited the employment exchange every morning, except on Friday, when he stood in a long line, waiting to collect his meagre unemployment benefit. After twelve months of failed interviews, and sorry-you-don't-seem-to-have-the-necessary-qualifications, Chris became anxious enough to seriously consider returning to his old job as a bus conductor. Sue assured him that it wouldn't be long before he was once again promoted to inspector.

Meanwhile, Sue took on more responsibility at the fish-and-chip shop and a year later was made assistant manager. Once again, this tale might have reached its natural conclusion, except this time it was Sue who was given her notice.

She warned Chris over a fish supper that Mr and Mrs Parsons were considering early retirement and planning to put the shop up for sale.

'How much are they expecting it to fetch?'

'I heard Mr Parsons mention the figure of five thousand pounds.'

'Then let's hope the new owners know a good thing when they see it,' said Chris, forking another chip.

'The new owners are far more likely to come with their own staff. Don't forget what happened to you when the bus company was taken over.'

Chris thought about it.

At eight thirty the following morning, Sue left the house to take Tracey to school, before going on to work. Once the two of them had departed, Chris and Corp set out for their morning constitutional. The dog was puzzled when his master didn't head for the beach, where he could enjoy his usual frolic in the waves, but instead marched off in the opposite direction, towards the centre of the town. Corp loyally bounded after him, and ended up being tied to a railing outside the Midland Bank in the High Street.

The manager of the bank could not hide his surprise

when Mr Haskins requested an interview to discuss a business venture. He quickly checked Mr and Mrs Haskins' joint bank account, to find that they were seventeen pounds and twelve shillings in credit. He was pleased to note that they had never run up an overdraft, despite Mr Haskins being out of work for over a year.

The manager listened sympathetically to his client's proposal, but sadly shook his head even before Chris had come to the end of his well-rehearsed presentation.

'The bank couldn't consider such a risk,' the manager explained, 'at least not while you have so little security to offer as collateral. You don't even own your own home,' the banker pointed out. Chris thanked him, shook him by the hand and left undaunted.

He crossed the High Street, tied Corp to another railing and entered Martins Bank. Chris had to wait for quite some time before the manager was able to see him. He was greeted with the same response, but at least on this occasion the manager recommended that Chris should approach Britannia Finance, who, he explained, were a new company specializing in start-up loans for small businesses. Chris thanked him, left the bank, untied Corp and jogged back to Jubilee Road, arriving only moments before Sue returned home with his lunch: cod and chips.

After lunch, Chris left the house and headed for the nearest phone box. He put four pennies in the box and pressed button A. The conversation lasted for less than a minute. He then returned home, but didn't tell Sue who he had an appointment with the following day.

The next day Chris waited for Sue to take Tracey off to school before he slipped back upstairs to their bedroom. He took off his jeans and sweater, and replaced them with the suit he'd worn at his wedding, a cream shirt he only put on for church on Sundays, and a tie his mother-in-law had given him for Christmas, which he thought he'd never wear. He then shone his shoes until even his old drill sergeant would have agreed that they passed muster. He checked himself in the mirror, hoping he looked like the potential manager of a new business venture. He left the dog in the back garden, and headed into town.

Chris was fifteen minutes early for his meeting with a Mr Tremaine, the loans manager with Britannia Finance Company. He was asked to take a seat in the waiting room. Chris picked up a copy of the *Financial Times* for the first time in his life. He couldn't find the sports pages. Fifteen minutes later a secretary ushered him through to Mr Tremaine's office.

The loans executive listened with sympathy to Chris's ambitious proposal, and then enquired, just as the two bank managers had, 'What security do you have to offer?'

'Nothing,' replied Chris without guile, 'other than the fact that my wife and I will work all the hours we're awake, and she already knows the business backwards.' Chris waited to hear the many reasons why Britannia couldn't consider his request.

Instead Mr Tremaine asked, 'As your wife would constitute half of our investment, what does she think about this whole enterprise?'

'I haven't even discussed it with her yet,' Chris blurted out.

'Then I suggest you do so,' said Mr Tremaine, 'and fairly quickly, because before we would consider investing in Mr and Mrs Haskins, we will need to meet Mrs Haskins in order to find out if she's half as good as you claim.'

Chris broke the news to his wife over supper that evening. Sue was speechless. A problem Chris had not come up against all that often in the past.

Once Mr Tremaine had met Mrs Haskins, it was only a matter of filling in countless forms before Britannia Finance advanced them a loan of £5,000. A month later Mr and Mrs Haskins moved from their three rooms in Jubilee Road to a fish-and-chip shop on Beach Street.

The Middle

Chris and Sue spent their first Sunday scraping the name *PARSONS* off the front of the shop, and painting in *HASKINS: under new management*. Sue quickly set about teaching Chris how to prepare the right ingredients to make the finest batter. If it was that easy, she kept reminding him, there wouldn't be a queue outside one chippy while a rival a few yards up the road remained empty. It was some weeks before Chris could guarantee his chips were always crisp and not hard or, worse, soggy. While he became the front-of-house manager, wrapping up the fish and dispensing the salt and vinegar, Sue took her place behind the till and collected the takings. In the evening, Sue always brought the books up to date, but she didn't go upstairs to join Chris in their little self-contained flat until the shop was spotless and you could see your face in the counter-top.

Sue was always the last to finish, but then Chris was the first to rise in the morning. He would be up by four o'clock, pull on an old tracksuit and head off for the docks with Corp.

He returned a couple of hours later, having selected the finest cod, hake, skate and plaice, moments after the trawlers had docked with their morning catch.

Although Cleethorpes has several fish-and-chip shops, it was not long before a queue began to form outside Haskins, sometimes even before Sue had turned the closed sign round to allow the first customer to enter the shop. The queue never slackened between the hours of eleven a.m. and three p.m., or from five to nine in the evening, when the sign would finally be turned back round – but not until the last customer had been served.

At the end of their first year the Haskins declared a profit of just over £900. As the queues lengthened, the debt to Britannia Finance diminished, so they were able to return the loan in full, with interest, eight months before the five-year agreement ended.

During the next decade, the Haskins' reputation grew on land, as well as sea, which resulted in Chris being invited to join the Cleethorpes Rotary Club, and Sue becoming deputy chairman of the Mothers' Union.

On their twentieth wedding anniversary Sue and Chris returned to Portugal for a second honeymoon. They stayed in a four-star hotel for a fortnight and this time they didn't have to come home early. Mr and Mrs Haskins returned to Albufeira every summer for the next ten years. Creatures of habit, the Haskins.

Tracey left Cleethorpes Grammar School to attend Bristol University, where she studied business management. The only sadness in the Haskins' life was when Corp died. But then he was fourteen years old.

***

Chris was enjoying a drink with some fellow Rotarians when Dave Quenton, the manager of the town's most prestigious post office, told him that he was moving to the Lake District and planning to sell his interest in the business.

This time Chris did discuss his latest proposal with his wife. Sue was once again taken by surprise and, when she recovered, needed several questions answered before she agreed to pay a return visit to Britannia Finance.

'How much do you have on deposit with the Midland Bank?' asked Mr Tremaine, recently promoted to loans manager.

Sue checked her ledger. 'Thirty-seven thousand, four hundred and eight pounds,' she replied.

'And what value have you put on the fish-and-chip shop?' was his next question.

'We will be considering offers over one hundred thousand,' said Sue confidently.

'And how much has the post office been valued at, remembering that it's in such a prime location?'

'Mr Quenton says that the Post Office is looking for two hundred and seventy thousand, but he assures me they would settle for a quarter of a million, if they can find a suitable applicant.'

'So you're likely to be a little over one hundred thousand short of your target,' said the analyst, not having to refer to a ledger. He paused. 'What was the post office's turnover last year?'

'Two hundred and thirty thousand pounds,' replied Sue.
'Profit?'

Once again, Sue needed to check her figures. 'Twenty-six thousand, four hundred, but that doesn't include the added bonus of spacious living accommodation, with rates and taxes covered in the annual return.' She paused. 'And this time we would own the property.'

'If all those figures can be confirmed by our accountants,' said Mr Tremaine, 'and you are able to sell the fish-and-chip shop for around a hundred thousand, it certainly appears to be a sound investment. But . . .' The two would-be clients looked apprehensive. 'And there always is a but, when it comes to lending money. The loan would, of course, be subject to the post office maintaining its category A status. Property in that area is currently trading at around twenty thousand, so the real value of the post office is as a business, and only then if, I repeat, if, it continues to have category A status.'

'But it's been a category A post office for the past thirty years,' said Chris. 'Why should that change in the future?'

'If I could predict the future, Mr Haskins,' replied the analyst, 'I would never make a bad investment, but as I can't I have to take the occasional risk. Britannia invests in people, and on that front you have nothing to prove.' He smiled. 'We would, as with our first investment, expect any loan to be repaid in quarterly instalments, over a period of five years, and on this occasion, as such a large sum is involved, we would want to take a charge over the property.'

'At what percentage?' demanded Chris.

'Eight and a half per cent, with added penalties should increments not be paid on time.'

'We'll need to consider your offer carefully,' said Sue, 'and we'll let you know once we've made our decision.'

Mr Tremaine stifled a smile.

✳ ✳ ✳

'What was all that about category A status?' asked Sue as they walked quickly back towards the seafront, still hoping to open the shop in time for their first customer.

'Category A is where all the profits are,' said Chris. 'Savings accounts, pensions, postal orders, vehicle road tax and even premium bonds all guarantee you a handsome profit. Without them, you have to rely on TV licences, stamps, electricity bills, and perhaps a little extra income if they allow you to run a shop on the side. If that was all Mr Quenton had to offer, we'd be better off continuing to run the fish-and-chip shop.'

'And is there any risk of us losing our category A status?' asked Sue.

'None whatsoever,' said Chris, 'or that's what the area manager assured me, and he's a fellow member of Rotary. He told me that the matter has never even come up for discussion at headquarters, and you can be pretty confident that Britannia will also have checked that out long before they would be willing to part with a hundred thousand.'

'So you still think we should go ahead?'

'With a few refinements to their terms,' said Chris.

'Like what?'

'Well, to start with, I've no doubt that Mr Tremaine will come down to eight per cent, now that the High Street banks have also begun investing in business ventures, and don't forget, this time he will have a charge over the property.'

The Haskins sold their fish-and-chip shop for £112,000 and were able to add a further £38,000 from their credit account. Britannia topped it up with a loan of £100,000 at 8 per cent. A cheque for £250,000 was sent to Post Office headquarters in London.

'Time to celebrate,' declared Chris.

THE NEW COLLECTED SHORT STORIES

'What do you have in mind?' asked Sue. 'Because we can't afford to spend any more money.'

'Let's drive down to Ashford and spend the weekend with our daughter –' he paused – 'and on the way back . . .'

'And on the way back?' repeated Sue.

'Let's drop into Battersea Dogs' Home.'

A month later, Mr and Mrs Haskins and Stamps, another Labrador, this time black, moved from their fish-and-chip shop on Beach Street to a category A post office in Victoria Crescent.

Chris and Sue quickly returned to working hours that they hadn't experienced since they first opened the fish-and-chip shop. For the next five years they cut down on any little extras, and even went without holidays, although they often thought about another trip to Portugal, but that had to be put on hold until they completed their quarterly payments to Britannia. Chris continued to carry out his Rotary Club duties, while Sue became chairman of the Cleethorpes branch of the Mothers' Union. Tracey was promoted to sites manager, and Stamps ate more food than the three of them put together.

In their fourth year, Mr and Mrs Haskins won the 'Area Post Office of the Year' award, and nine months later paid off the final instalment to Britannia.

The board of Britannia invited Chris and Sue to join them for lunch at the Royal Hotel to celebrate the fact that they now owned the post office without a penny of debt to their name.

'We still have to earn back our original investment,' Chris reminded them. 'A mere matter of two hundred and fifty thousand pounds.'

'If you keep going at your present rate,' suggested the chairman of Britannia, 'it should only take you another five years to achieve and then you could be sitting on a business worth over a million.'

'Does that mean I'm a millionaire?' asked Chris.

'No, it does not,' butted in Sue. 'Our current account is showing a credit of a little over ten thousand pounds. You're a ten thousandaire.'

The chairman laughed, and invited the board to raise their glasses to Chris and Sue Haskins.

'My spies tell me, Chris,' added the chairman, 'that you are likely to be the next president of our local Rotary.'

'Many a slip,' said Chris as he lowered his glass, 'and certainly not before Sue takes her place on the area committee of the Mothers' Union. Don't be surprised if she ends up as national chairman,' he added, with considerable pride.

'So what do you plan to do next?' asked the chairman.

'Take a month's holiday in Portugal,' said Chris without hesitation. 'After five years of having to make do with the beach at Cleethorpes and a plate of fish and chips, I think we've earned it.'

That also would have made a satisfactory conclusion to this tale, had officialdom not stepped in once again; this time with a letter addressed to Mr and Mrs Hoskins from the finance director of the Post Office. They found it waiting for them on the mat when they returned from Albufeira.

Post Office Headquarters,
148 Old Street, London EC1V 9HQ

Dear Mr and Mrs Hoskins,
The Post Office is in the process of re-evaluating its

*property portfolio, and to that end, will be making some
changes to the status of some of its older establishments.*

*I therefore have to inform you that the board has
come to the reluctant conclusion that we will no longer
require two category A status facilities in the Cleethorpes
area. While the new High Street branch will continue
as a category A post office, Victoria Crescent will be
downgraded to category B. In order that you can make
the necessary adjustments, we do not propose to bring in
these changes until the New Year.*

*We look forward to continuing our relationship with
you.*

Yours sincerely,

Finance Director

'Does that mean what I think it means?' said Sue after
she had read the letter a second time.

'In simple terms, love,' said Chris, 'we can never hope
to earn back our original investment of two hundred and fifty
thousand, even if we go on working for the rest of our lives.'

'Then we'll have to put the post office up for sale.'

'But who will want to buy it at that price,' asked
Chris, 'once they discover that the business no longer has
category A status?'

'The man from Britannia assured us that once we'd paid
off the debt it would be worth a million.'

'Only while the business has a turnover of five hundred
thousand and generates a profit of around eighty thousand
a year,' said Chris.

'We should take legal advice.'

Chris reluctantly agreed, although he wasn't in much doubt what his solicitor's opinion would be. The law, their advocate dutifully advised them, was not on their side, and therefore he wouldn't recommend them to sue the Post Office, as he couldn't guarantee the outcome. 'You might well win a moral victory,' he said, 'but that won't assist your bank balance.'

The next decision Chris and Sue made was to put the post office on the market as they wanted to find out if anyone would show an interest. Once again Chris's judgement turned out to be correct: only three couples even bothered to look over the property, and none of them returned for a second viewing once they discovered it was no longer category A status.

'My bet,' said Sue, 'is that those officials back at headquarters knew only too well they were going to change our status long before they pocketed our money, but it suited them not to tell us.'

'You may well be right,' said Chris, 'but you can be sure of one thing – they won't have put anything in writing at the time, so we would never be able to prove it.'

'And neither did we.'

'What are you getting at, love?'

'How much have they stolen from us?' demanded Sue.

'Well, if by that you mean our original investment—'

'Our life savings, every penny we've earned over the past thirty years, not to mention our pension.'

Chris paused and raised his head, while he made some calculations. 'Not including any profit we might have hoped for, once we'd seen our capital returned—'

'Yes, only what they've stolen from us,' Sue repeated.

'A little over two hundred and fifty thousand, if you don't include interest,' said Chris.

'And we have no hope of seeing a penny of that original investment back, even if we were to work for the rest of our lives?'

'That's about the sum of it, love.'

'Then it's my intention to retire on January the first.'

'And what are you expecting to live off for the rest of your life?' asked Chris.

'Our original investment.'

'And how do you intend to go about that?'

'By taking advantage of our spotless reputation.'

The End

Chris and Sue rose early the following morning: after all, they had a lot of work to do during the next three months if they hoped to accumulate enough capital to retire by 1 January. Sue warned Chris that meticulous preparation would be needed if her plan was to succeed. He didn't disagree. They both knew that they couldn't risk pressing the button until the second Friday in November, when they would have a six-week window of opportunity – Chris's expression – before 'those people back in London' worked out what they were really up to. But that didn't mean there wasn't a lot of preliminary work to be done in the meantime. To start with, they needed to plan their getaway, even before they set about retrieving any stolen money.

Neither considered what they were about to embark on as theft.

Sue unfolded a map of Europe and spread it across the post office counter. They discussed the different alternatives for several days and finally settled on Portugal, which they both considered would be ideal for early retirement. On their many visits to the Algarve they had always returned to Albufeira, the town where they had spent their shortened honeymoon, and revisited on their tenth, twentieth, and many more wedding anniversaries. They had even promised themselves that was where they would retire if they won the lottery.

The next day Sue purchased a tape of *Portuguese for Beginners* which they played before breakfast every morning, and then spent an hour in the evening, testing out their new skills. They were pleased to discover that over the years they had both picked up more of the language than they realized. Although not fluent, they were certainly not beginners. The two of them quickly moved on to the advanced tapes.

'We won't be able to use our own passports,' Chris pointed out to his wife while shaving one morning. 'We'll have to consider a change of identity, otherwise the authorities would be on to us in no time.'

'I've already thought about that,' said Sue, 'and we should take advantage of working in our own post office.'

Chris stopped shaving, and turned to listen to his wife.

'Don't forget, we already supply all the necessary forms for customers who want to obtain passports.'

Chris didn't interrupt as Sue went over how she planned to make sure that they could safely leave the country under assumed names.

Chris chuckled. 'Perhaps I'll grow a beard,' he said, putting his razor down.

Over the years, Chris and Sue had made friends with several customers who regularly shopped at the post office. The two of them wrote down on separate sheets of paper the names of all their customers who fulfilled the criteria Sue was looking for. They ended up with a list of two dozen candidates: thirteen women and eleven men. From that moment on, whenever one of the unsuspecting regulars entered the shop, Sue or Chris would strike up a conversation that had only one purpose.

'Going away for Christmas this year, are we, Mrs Brewer?'

'No, Mrs Haskins, my son and his wife will be joining us on Christmas Eve so that we can get to know our new granddaughter.'

'How nice for you, Mrs Brewer,' replied Sue. 'Chris and I are thinking of spending Christmas in the States.'

'How exciting,' said Mrs Brewer. 'I've never even been abroad,' she admitted, 'let alone America.'

Mrs Brewer had reached the second round, but would not be questioned again until her next visit.

By the end of September, seven other names had joined Mrs Brewer on the shortlist – four women and three men, all between the ages of fifty-one and fifty-seven, who had only one thing in common: they had never travelled abroad.

The next problem the Haskins faced was filling in an application for a birth certificate. This required far more detailed questioning, and both Sue and Chris quickly backed off whenever one of the shortlisted candidates showed the slightest sign of suspicion. By the beginning of October they were down to the names of four customers who had unwittingly supplied their date of birth, place of birth, mother's maiden name and father's first name.

The Haskins' next visit was to Boots the chemist in St Peter's Avenue, where they took turns to sit in a little cubicle and have several strips of photographs taken at £2.50 a time. Sue then set about completing the necessary application forms for a passport, on behalf of four of her unsuspecting customers. She filled in all the relevant details, while enclosing photographs of herself and Chris, along with a postal order for £42. As the postmaster, Chris was only too happy to pen his real signature on the bottom of each form Sue filled in.

The four application forms were posted to the passport office at Petty France in London on the Monday, Thursday, Friday and Saturday of the last week in October.

On Wednesday, 11 November the first passport arrived back at Victoria Crescent, addressed to Mr Reg Appleyard. Two days later, a second appeared, for Mrs Audrey

Ramsbottom. The following day Mrs Betty Brewer's turned up, and finally, a week later, Mr Stan Gerrard's.

Sue had already pointed out to Chris that they would have to leave the country using one set of passports, which they would then need to discard, before they switched to the second pair, but not until they had found somewhere to live in Albufeira.

Chris and Sue continued to practise their Portuguese whenever they were alone in the shop, while informing any regulars that they would be away over the Christmas period as they were planning a trip to America. The inquisitive were rewarded with such details as a week in San Francisco, followed by a few days in Seattle.

By the second week in November, everything was in place to press the button for Operation Money Back Guaranteed.

·····≫≫≫✵≪≪·····

At nine o'clock on Friday morning Sue made her weekly phone call to headquarters. She entered her personal code before being transferred to forward finance. The only difference this time was that she could hear her heart beating. Sue repeated her code before informing the credit officer how much cash she would require for the following week – an amount large enough to allow her to cover withdrawals for any post office savings accounts, pensions and cashed postal orders. Although an accountant from headquarters always checked the books at the end of every month, considerable leeway was allowed in the run-up to Christmas. A demanding audit was then carried out in January to make sure the books balanced, but neither Chris nor Sue had any intention of being around in January. For the past six years

Sue's books had always balanced, and she was considered by headquarters to be a model manager.

Sue had to check the records to remind herself of the amount she had requested in the same week of the previous year – £40,000, which had turned out to be £800 more than she needed. This year she asked for £60,000, and waited for some comment from the credit officer, but the voice from headquarters sounded neither surprised nor concerned. The full amount was delivered by a security van the following Monday.

During the week Chris and Sue fulfilled all their customers' obligations; after all, it had never been their intention to short-change any of their regulars, but they still found themselves with a surplus of £21,000 at the end of week one. They left the cash – used notes only – locked up in the safe, just in case some fastidious official from headquarters decided to carry out a spot-check.

Once Sue had closed the front door at six o'clock and pulled down the blinds, the two of them would only converse in Portuguese, while they spent the rest of the evening filling in postal orders, rubbing out scratch cards and entering lottery numbers, often falling asleep as they worked.

Every morning Chris would rise early and climb into his ageing Rover, with Stamps as his only companion. He travelled north, east, south and west – Monday Lincoln, Tuesday Louth, Wednesday Skegness, Thursday Hull and Friday Immingham, where he would cash several postal orders, and also collect his winnings on the scratch cards and lottery tickets, enabling him to supplement their newly acquired savings with an extra few hundred pounds each day.

On the last Friday in November, week two, Sue applied

for £70,000 from head office, so that by the following Saturday they were able to add a further £32,000 to their invisible earnings.

On the first Friday in December, Sue raised the stakes to £80,000, and was surprised to discover that there were still no questions back at headquarters: after all, hadn't Sue Haskins been manager of the year, with a special commendation from the board? A security van dutifully delivered the full amount in cash early on the Monday morning.

Another week of increased profits allowed Sue Haskins to add a further £39,000 to the pot without any of the other players round the table demanding to see her hand. They were now showing a surplus of well over £100,000, which was stacked up in neat little piles of used notes, resting on top of the four passports buried at the bottom of the safe.

Chris hardly slept at night as he continued to sign countless postal orders, rub out piles of scratch cards and, before going to bed, fill in numerous lottery tickets with endless combinations. By day he visited every post office within a fifty-mile radius, gathering his spoils, but, despite his dedication, by the second week in December Mr and Mrs Haskins had only collected just over half the amount required to retrieve the £250,000 they had originally invested.

Sue warned Chris that they would have to take an even bigger risk if they still hoped to acquire the full amount by Christmas Eve.

On the second Friday in December, week four, Sue called the issuing manager at headquarters, and made a request for £115,000.

'You're having a busy Christmas,' suggested a voice on the other end of the line. First sign of any suspicion, thought Sue, but she had her script well prepared.

'Run off my feet,' Sue told him, 'but don't forget, more people retire to Cleethorpes than any other seaside town in Britain.'

'You learn something new every day,' came back the voice on the other end of the line, before adding, 'Don't worry, the cash will be with you on Monday. Keep up the good work.'

'I will,' promised Sue, and, emboldened by the exchange, requested £140,000 for the final week before Christmas, aware that any sum above £150,000 was always referred back to head office in London.

When Sue pulled down the blinds at six o'clock on Christmas Eve, both of them were exhausted.

Sue was the first to recover. 'We haven't a moment to waste,' she reminded her husband as she walked across to the bulging safe. She entered the code, pulled open the door and withdrew everything from their current account. She then placed the money on the counter in neat bundles – fifties, twenties, tens and fives – before they set about counting their spoils.

Chris checked the final figure and confirmed that they were £267,300 in credit. They put £17,300 back in the safe, and locked the door. After all, they had never intended to make a profit – that would be stealing. Sue began to put elastic bands around each thousand, while Chris transferred the two hundred and fifty bundles carefully into an old RAF duffel bag. By eight o'clock they were ready to leave. Chris set the alarm, slipped quietly out of the back door and placed the duffel bag in the boot of their Rover, on top of four other cases his wife had packed earlier that morning. Sue joined him in the front of the car, as Chris turned on the ignition.

'We've forgotten something,' said Sue as she pulled the door closed.

'Stamps,' they said in unison. Chris turned off the ignition, got out of the car and returned to the post office. He re-entered the code, switched off the alarm and opened the back door in search of Stamps. He found him fast asleep in the kitchen, reluctant to be enticed out of his warm basket and into the back seat of the car. Didn't they realize it was Christmas Eve?

Chris reset the alarm and locked the door for a second time.

At eight nineteen p.m. Mr and Mrs Haskins set out on the journey for Ashford in Kent. Sue worked out that they had four clear days before anyone would be aware of their absence. Christmas Day, Boxing Day, Sunday, Monday (a bank holiday), back in theory on Tuesday morning, by which time they would be viewing properties in the Algarve.

The two of them hardly spoke a word on the long journey to Kent, not even in Portuguese. Sue couldn't believe they'd gone through with it, and Chris was even more surprised that they'd got away with it.

'We haven't yet,' Sue reminded him, 'not until we drive into Albufeira, and don't forget, Mr Appleyard, we no longer have the same names.'

'Living in sin after all these years are we, Mrs Brewer?'

Chris brought the car to a halt outside their daughter's home just after midnight. Tracey opened the front door to greet her mother, while Chris removed one of the suitcases and the duffel bag from the boot. Tracey had never seen her parents looking so exhausted, and felt they had aged since she'd last seen them in the summer. Perhaps it was just the long journey. Tracey took them through to the kitchen, sat them both down and made them a cup of tea. They hardly spoke, and when Tracey eventually bundled them off to bed, her father wouldn't allow her to carry the old duffel bag up to the guest bedroom.

Sue woke every time she heard a car come to a halt in the street outside, wondering if it was marked with the bold fluorescent lettering POLICE. Chris waited for the front-door bell to ring before someone came bounding up the stairs to drag the duffel bag from under the bed, arrest them and escort them both to the nearest police station.

After a sleepless night they joined Tracey in the kitchen for breakfast.

'Happy Christmas,' said Tracey, before kissing them both on the cheek. Neither of them responded. Had they forgotten it was Christmas Day? They both looked embarrassed as they stared at the two wrapped boxes that their daughter had placed on the table. They hadn't remembered to buy Tracey a Christmas present and resorted to giving her cash, something they hadn't done since she was a teenager. Tracey hoped that it was nothing more than the Christmas rush, and excitement at the thought of their visit to the States, which had caused such uncharacteristic behaviour.

Boxing Day turned out to be a little better. Sue and Chris appeared more relaxed, although they often lapsed into long silences. After lunch Tracy suggested that they take Stamps for a run across the Downs and get some fresh air. During the long walk one of them would begin a sentence and then fall silent. A few minutes later the other would finish it.

By Sunday morning Tracey felt that they both looked a lot better, even chatting away about their trip to America.

But two things puzzled her. When she saw her parents coming down the stairs carrying the duffel bag with Stamps in their wake, she could have sworn they were speaking Portuguese. And why bother to take Stamps to America, when she had already offered to take care of the dog while they were away?

The next surprise came when they set off for Heathrow after breakfast. When her father packed the duffel bag and their suitcase into the boot of the car, she was surprised to see three large bags already in the boot. Why bother with so much luggage when they were only going away for a fortnight?

Tracey stood on the pavement and waved goodbye, as her parents' car trundled off down the road. When the old Rover reached the end of the street it swung right, instead of left, which took them in the opposite direction to Heathrow. Something was wrong. Tracey dismissed the mistake, aware that they could correct their error long before they reached the motorway.

Once Chris and Sue had joined the motorway, they followed the signs for Dover. The two of them became more and more nervous as each minute passed, aware that there was now no turning back. Only Stamps seemed to be enjoying the adventure as he stared out of the back window wagging his tail.

Once again, Mr Appleyard and Mrs Brewer went over their plan. When they reached the docks, Sue would jump out of the car and join the queue of foot passengers waiting to board, while Chris drove the Rover up the car ramp and on to the ferry. They agreed not to meet again until the boat had docked in Calais and Chris had driven on to the dockside.

Sue stood at the bottom of the gangway and waited nervously at the back of the queue as she watched their Rover edge towards the entrance of the hold. Her heart raced when she saw a customs officer double-check Chris's passport, and invite him to step out of the car and stand to one side. She had to stop herself from running across so she could overhear their conversation – she couldn't risk it now they were no longer married.

'Good morning, Mr Appleyard,' said the customs officer, and then added after looking in the back of the car, 'were you hoping to take the dog abroad with you?'

'Oh yes,' replied Chris. 'We never travel anywhere without Stamps.'

The customs official studied Mr Appleyard's passport more carefully. 'But you don't have the necessary documents to take a dog abroad with you.'

Chris felt beads of sweat running down his forehead. Stamps's papers were still attached to the passport of Mr Haskins, which he had left in the safe back at Cleethorpes.

'Oh hell,' said Chris. 'I must have left them at home.'

'Bad luck, sir. I hope you don't have far to travel because there isn't another ferry until this time tomorrow.'

Chris glanced helplessly across at his wife, before climbing back into the car. He looked down at Stamps, who was sleeping soundly on the back seat, oblivious to the problem he was causing. Chris swung the car round and joined an overwrought Sue, who was waiting impatiently to find out why he hadn't been allowed to board. Once Chris had explained the problem, all she said was, 'We can't risk returning to Cleethorpes.'

'I agree,' said Chris, 'we'll have to go back to Ashford, and hope we can find a vet that's open on a bank holiday.'

'That wasn't part of our plan,' said Sue.

'I know,' said Chris, 'but I'm not willing to leave Stamps behind.' Sue nodded in agreement.

Chris swung the Rover onto the main road, and began the journey back to Ashford. Mr and Mrs Haskins arrived just in time to join their daughter for lunch. Tracey was delighted that her parents were able to spend a couple more days with her, but she still couldn't understand why they weren't willing to leave Stamps with her; after all, it wasn't as if they were going away for the rest of their lives.

Chris and Sue spent another uncommunicative day and a further sleepless night in Ashford. A duffel bag containing a quarter of a million pounds was tucked under the bed.

On Monday a local vet kindly agreed to give Stamps all the necessary injections. He then attached a certificate to Mr Appleyard's passport, but not in time for them to catch the last ferry.

The Haskins didn't sleep a wink on the Monday night, and by the time the street lights went out the following morning, they both knew they could no longer go through with it. They lay awake, preparing a new plan – in English.

Chris and Sue finally left their daughter after breakfast the following morning. They drove to the end of the road and this time, to Tracey's relief, turned left, not right, and headed back in the direction of Cleethorpes. By the time they'd swept past the Heathrow exit, their revised plan was in place.

'The moment we arrive home,' said Sue, 'we'll put all the money back in the safe.'

'How will we explain having that amount of cash, when the Post Office accountant carries out his annual audit next month?' asked Chris.

'By the time they get around to checking what's left in the safe, as long as we don't apply for any more money, we should have been able to dispose of most of the cash simply by carrying out our regular transactions.'

'What about the postal orders that we've already cashed?'

'There's still enough cash left in the safe to cover them,' Sue reminded her husband.

'But the scratch cards and the lottery tickets?'

'We'll have to make up the difference from our own money – that way they'll end up none the wiser.'

'I agree,' said Chris, sounding relieved for the first time in days, and then he remembered the passports.

'We'll destroy them,' said Sue, 'as soon as we get home.'

By the time the Haskins had crossed the Lincolnshire border, they had made up their minds to continue running the post office, despite its diminished status. Sue had already come up with several ideas for extra items they could sell over the counter, while making the best of what was left of their franchise.

A smile settled on Sue's lips when Chris finally turned into Victoria Crescent, a smile that was quickly removed when she saw the flashing blue lights. When the old Rover came to a halt, a dozen policemen surrounded the car.

'Oh shit,' said Sue. Extreme language for the chairman of the Mothers' Union, thought Chris, but on balance, he had to agree with her.

Mr and Mrs Haskins were arrested on the evening of 29 December. They were driven to Cleethorpes police station and placed in separate interview rooms. There was no need for the local police to conduct a good cop, bad cop routine, as both of them confessed immediately. They spent the night in separate cells, and the following morning they were charged with the theft of £250,000, being the property of the Post Office, and obtaining, by deception, four passports.

They pleaded guilty to both charges.

Sue Haskins was released from Moreton Hall after serving four months of her sentence. Chris joined her a year later.

While he was in prison Chris worked on another plan. However, when he was released Britannia Finance didn't feel able to back him. To be fair, Mr Tremaine had retired.

Mr and Mrs Haskins sold their property on Victoria Crescent for £100,000. A week later they climbed into their ancient Rover and drove off to Dover, where they boarded the ferry after presenting the correct passports. Once they had found a suitable location on the seafront in Albufeira, they opened a fish-and-chip shop. Haskins' hasn't caught on with the locals yet, but with a hundred thousand Brits visiting the Algarve every year, there's proved to be no shortage of customers.

I was among those who risked a small investment in the new enterprise, and I am happy to report that I have recouped every penny with interest. Funny old world. But then as Mr Justice Gray observed, Mr and Mrs Haskins were not criminals.

Only one footnote. Stamps died while Sue and Chris were in prison.

Maestro

THE ITALIANS ARE THE ONLY RACE I know who have the ability to serve without appearing subservient. The French will happily spill sauce all over your favourite tie, with no hint of an apology, at the same time cursing you in their native tongue. The Chinese don't speak to you at all, and the Greeks think nothing of leaving you alone for an hour before they even offer you a menu. The Americans are at pains to let you know that they aren't really waiters at all, but out-of-work actors, who then proceed to recite the specials on the menu as if performing for an audition. The English are quite likely to engage you in a long conversation, leaving an impression that you ought to be having dinner with them, rather than your guest, and as for the Germans . . . well, when did you last eat at a German restaurant?

So it is left to the Italians to sweep the board and gather up the crumbs. They combine the charm of the Irish, the culinary expertise of the French and the thoroughness of the Swiss, and despite their ability to produce a bill that never seems to add up, we allow them to go on fleecing us.

This was certainly true of Mario Gambotti.

Mario came from a long line of Florentines who could not sing, paint or play football, so he happily joined his fellow exiles in London, where he began an apprenticeship in the restaurant business.

Whenever I go to his fashionable little restaurant in

Fulham for lunch, he somehow manages to hide his disapproval when I order minestrone soup, spaghetti Bolognese and a bottle of Chianti classico.

'What an excellent choice, maestro,' he declares, not bothering to scribble down my order on his pad. Please note 'maestro': not my lord, which would be sycophantic, not sir, which would be ridiculous after twenty years of friendship, but maestro, a particularly flattering sobriquet, as I have it on good authority (his wife) that he has never read one of my books.

When I was in attendance at North Sea Camp open prison, Mario wrote to the governor and suggested that he might be allowed to come down one Friday and cook lunch for me. The governor was amused by the request, and wrote a formal reply, explaining that should he grant the boon, it would not only break several penal regulations, but undoubtedly stir the tabloids into a frenzy of headlines. When the governor showed me a copy of his reply, I was surprised to see that he had signed the letter, *yours ever, Michael.*

'Are you also a customer of Mario's?' I enquired.

'No,' replied the governor, 'but he has been a customer of mine.'

Mario's can be found on the Fulham Road in Chelsea, and the restaurant's popularity is due in no small part to his wife, Teresa, who runs the kitchen. Mario always remains front of house. I regularly have lunch there on a Friday, often accompanied by my two sons and their latest girlfriends, who used to change more often than the menu.

Over the years I have become aware that many of the customers are regulars, which leaves an impression that we are all part of an exclusive club, in which it's almost impossible to book a table unless you are a member. However, the real proof of Mario's popularity is that the restaurant does not accept credit cards – cheques, cash and account-paying customers are all welcome, but **NO CREDIT CARDS** is printed in bold letters at the foot of every menu.

During the month of August the establishment is closed, in order for the Gambotti family to return to their native Florence and reunite with all the other Gambottis.

Mario is quintessentially Italian. His red Ferrari can be seen parked outside the restaurant, his yacht – my son James assures me – is moored in Monte Carlo, and his children, Tony, Maria and Roberto, are being educated at St Paul's, Cheltenham and Summer Fields respectively. After all, it is important that they mix with the sort of people they will be expected to fleece at some time in the future. And whenever I see them at the opera – Verdi and Puccini, never Wagner or Weber – they are always seated in their own box.

So, I hear you ask, how did such a shrewd and intelligent man end up serving at Her Majesty's pleasure? Was he involved in some fracas following a football match between Arsenal and Fiorentina? Did he drive over the speed limit once too often in that Ferrari of his? Perhaps he forgot to pay his poll tax? None of the above. He broke an English law with an action that in the land of his forefathers would be considered no more than an acceptable part of everyday life.

Enter Mr Dennis Cartwright, who worked for another of Her Majesty's establishments.

Mr Cartwright was an inspector with the Inland Revenue. He rarely ate out at a restaurant, and certainly not one as exclusive as Mario's. Whenever he and his wife Doris 'went Italian', it was normally Pizza Express. However, he took a great interest in Mr Gambotti, and in how he could possibly maintain such a lifestyle on the amount he was declaring to his local tax office. After all, the restaurant was showing a profit of a mere £172,000, on a turnover of just over two million. So, after tax, Mr Gambotti was only taking home – Dennis carefully checked the figures – just over £100,000. With a home in Chelsea, three children at private schools and a Ferrari to maintain, not to mention the yacht moored in Monte Carlo, and heaven knows what else in Florence, how did he manage it? Mr Cartwright, a determined man, was determined to find out.

The tax inspector checked all the figures in Mario's books, and he had to admit they balanced and, what's more,

Mr Gambotti always paid his taxes on time. However, Mr Cartwright wasn't in any doubt that Mr Gambotti had to be siphoning off large sums of cash, but how? He must have missed something. Cartwright leapt up in the middle of the night and shouted out loud, '*No credit cards.*' He woke his wife.

The next morning, Cartwright went over the books yet again; he was right. There were no credit-card entries. Although all the cheques were properly accounted for, and all the customers' accounts tallied, when you considered that there were no credit-card entries, the small amount of cash declared seemed completely out of proportion to the over-all takings.

Mr Cartwright didn't need to be told that his masters would not allow him to waste much time dining at Mario's in order to resolve the mystery of how Mr Gambotti was salting away such large sums of money. Mr Buchanan, his supervisor, reluctantly agreed to allow Dennis an advance of £200 to try to discover what was happening on the inside – every penny was to be accounted for – and he only agreed to this after Dennis had pointed out that if he was able to gather enough evidence to put Mr Gambotti behind bars, imagine just how many other restaurateurs might feel obliged to start declaring their true incomes.

Mr Cartwright was surprised that it took him a month to book a table at Mario's, and it was only after several calls, always made from home, that he finally was able to secure a reservation. He asked his wife Doris to join him, hoping it would appear less suspicious than if he was sitting on his own, compiling notes. His supervisor agreed with the ploy, but told Dennis that he would have to cover his wife's half of the bill, at his own expense.

'It never crossed my mind to do otherwise,' Dennis assured his supervisor.

During a meal of Tuscan bean soup and gnocchi – he was hoping to pay more than one visit to Mario's – Dennis kept a wary eye on his host as he circled the different tables, making small talk and attending to his customers' slightest whims. His wife couldn't help but notice that Dennis seemed distracted, but she decided not to comment, as it was a rare occurrence for her husband to invite her out for a meal, other than on her birthday.

Mr Cartwright began committing to memory that there were thirty-nine tables dotted around the restaurant (he double-checked) and roughly a hundred and twenty covers. He also observed, by taking time over his coffee, that Mario managed two sittings on several of the tables. He was

impressed by how quickly three waiters could clear a table, replace the cloth and napkins, and moments later make it appear as if no one had ever been sitting there.

When Mario presented Mr Cartwright with his bill, he paid in cash and insisted on a receipt. When they left the restaurant, Doris drove them both home, which allowed Dennis to write down all the relevant figures in his little book while they still remained fresh in his memory.

'What a lovely meal,' commented his wife on their journey back to Romford. 'I do hope that we'll be able to go there again some time.'

'We will, Doris,' he promised her, 'next week.' He paused. 'If I can get a table.'

Mr and Mrs Cartwright visited the restaurant again three weeks later, this time for dinner. Dennis was impressed that Mario not only remembered his name, but even seated him at the same table. On this occasion, Mr Cartwright observed that Mario was able to fit in a pre-theatre booking – almost full; an evening sitting – packed out; and a post-theatre sitting – half full; while last orders were not taken until eleven o'clock.

Mr Cartwright estimated that nearly three hundred and fifty customers passed through the restaurant during the evening, and if you added that to the lunchtime clientele, the total came to just over five hundred a day. He also calculated that around half of them were paying cash, but he still had no way of proving it.

Dennis's dinner bill came to £75 (it's fascinating how restaurants appear to charge more in the evening than they do for lunch, even when they serve exactly the same food). Mr Cartwright estimated that each customer was being charged between £25 and £40, and that was probably on the conservative side. So in any given week, Mario had to be serving at least three thousand customers, returning him an income of around £90,000 a week, which was in excess of four million pounds a year, even if you discounted the month of August.

When Mr Cartwright returned to his office the following morning, he once again went over the restaurant's books. Mr Gambotti was declaring a turnover of £2,120,000, and showing, after outgoings, a profit of £172,000. So what was happening to the other two million?

Mr Cartwright remained baffled. He took the ledgers home in the evening, and continued to study the figures long into the night.

'Eureka,' he declared just before putting on his pyjamas. One of the outgoings didn't add up. The following morning he made an appointment to see his supervisor. 'I'll need to get my hands on the details of these particular weekly numbers,' Dennis told Mr Buchanan, as he placed a forefinger on one of the items listed under outgoings, 'and more important,' he added, 'without Mr Gambotti realizing what I'm up to.' Mr Buchanan sanctioned a request for him to be out of the office, as long as it didn't require any further visits to Mario's.

Mr Cartwright spent most of the weekend refining his plan, aware that just the slightest hint of what he was up to would allow Mr Gambotti enough time to cover his tracks.

On Monday Mr Cartwright rose early and drove to Fulham, not bothering to check in at the office. He parked his Skoda down a side street that allowed him a clear view of the entrance to Mario's restaurant. He removed a notebook from an inside pocket and began to write down the names of every tradesman who visited the premises that morning.

The first van to arrive and park on the double yellow line outside the restaurant's front door was a well-known purveyor of vegetables, followed a few minutes later by a master butcher. Next to unload her wares was a fashionable florist, followed by a wine merchant, a fishmonger and finally the one vehicle Mr Cartwright had been waiting for – a laundry van. Once the driver had unloaded three large crates, dumped them inside the restaurant and come back out, lugging three more crates, he drove away. Mr Cartwright didn't need to follow the van as the company's name, address and telephone number were emblazoned across both sides of the vehicle.

Mr Cartwright returned to the office, and was seated behind his desk just before midday. He reported immediately to his supervisor, and sought his authority to make a spot-check on the company concerned. Mr Buchanan again sanctioned his request, but on this occasion recommended caution. He advised Cartwright to carry out a

routine enquiry, so that the company concerned would not work out what he was really looking for. 'It may take a little longer,' Buchanan added, 'but it will give us a far better chance of success in the long run. I'll drop them a line today, and then you can fix up a meeting, at their convenience.'

Dennis went along with his supervisor's suggestion, which meant that he didn't turn up at the offices of the Marco Polo laundry company for another three weeks. On arrival at the laundry, by appointment, he made it clear to the manager that his visit was nothing more than a routine check, and he wasn't expecting to find any irregularities.

Dennis spent the rest of the day checking through every one of their customers' accounts, only stopping to make detailed notes whenever he came across an entry for Mario's restaurant. By midday he had gathered all the evidence he needed, but he didn't leave Marco Polo's offices until five, so that no one would become suspicious. When Dennis departed for the day, he assured the manager that he was well satisfied with their bookkeeping, and there would be no follow-up. What he didn't tell him was that one of their most important customers would be followed up.

Mr Cartwright was seated at his desk by eight o'clock the following morning, making sure his report was completed before his boss appeared.

When Mr Buchanan walked in at five to nine, Dennis leapt up from behind his desk, a look of triumph on his face. He was just about to pass on his news, when the supervisor placed a finger to his lips and indicated that he should follow him through to his office. Once the door was closed, Dennis placed the report on the table and took his boss through the details of his enquiries. He waited patiently while Mr Buchanan studied the documents and considered their implications. He finally looked up, to indicate that Dennis could now speak.

'This shows,' Dennis began, 'that every day for the past twelve months Mr Gambotti has sent out two hundred tablecloths and over five hundred napkins to the Marco Polo laundry. If you then look at this particular entry,' he added, pointing to an open ledger on the other side of the desk, 'you will observe that Gambotti is only declaring a hundred and twenty bookings a day, for around three hundred customers.' Dennis paused before delivering his accountant's coup de grâce. 'Why would you need a further three thousand table-cloths and forty-five thousand napkins to be laundered every year, unless you had another forty-five thousand customers?' he asked. He paused once again. 'Because he's laundering money,' said Dennis, clearly pleased with his little pun.

'Well done, Dennis,' said the head of department. 'Prepare a full report and I'll see that it ends up on the desk of our fraud department.'

Try as he might, Mario could not explain away 3,000 tablecloths and 45,000 napkins to Mr Gerald Henderson, his cynical solicitor. The lawyer only had one piece of advice for his client, 'Plead guilty, and I'll see if I can make a deal.'

The Inland Revenue successfully claimed back two million pounds in taxes from Mario's restaurant, and the judge sent Mario Gambotti to prison for six months. He ended up only having to serve a four-week sentence – three months off for good behaviour and, as it was his first offence, he was put on a tag for two months.

Mr Henderson, an astute lawyer, even managed to get the trial set in the court calendar for the last week in July.

He explained to the presiding judge that it was the only time Mr Gambotti's eminent QC would be available to appear before his lordship. The date of 30 July was agreed by all parties.

After a week spent in Belmarsh high-security prison in south London, Mario was transferred to North Sea Camp open prison in Lincolnshire, where he completed his sentence. Mario's lawyer had selected the prison on the grounds that he was unlikely to meet up with many of his old customers deep in the fens of Lincolnshire.

Meanwhile, the rest of the Gambotti family flew off to Florence for the month of August, not able fully to explain to the grandmothers why Mario couldn't be with them on this occasion.

Mario was released from North Sea Camp at nine o'clock on Monday, 1 September.

As he walked out of the front gate, he found Tony seated behind the wheel of his Ferrari, waiting to pick his father up. Three hours later Mario was standing at the front door of his restaurant to greet the first customer. Several regulars commented on the fact that he appeared to have lost a few pounds while he'd been away on holiday, while others remarked on how tanned and fit he looked.

Six months after Mario had been released, a newly promoted deputy supervisor decided to carry out another spot-check on Marco Polo's laundry. This time Dennis turned up unannounced. He ran a practised eye over the books, to find that Mario's was now sending only 120 tablecloths to the laundry each day, along with 300 napkins, despite the fact that the restaurant appeared to be just as popular. How was he managing to get away with it this time?

The following morning Dennis parked his Skoda down a side street off the Fulham Road once again, allowing him an uninterrupted view of Mario's front door. He felt confident that Mr Gambotti must now be using more than one laundry service, but to his disappointment the only van to appear and deposit and collect any laundry that day was Marco Polo's.

Mr Cartwright drove back to Romford at eight that evening, completely baffled. Had he hung around until just after midnight, Dennis would have seen several waiters leaving the restaurant, carrying bulging sports bags with squash racquets poking out of the top. Do you know any Italian waiters who play squash?

Mario's staff were delighted that their wives could earn some extra cash by taking in a little laundry each day, especially as Mr Gambotti had supplied each of them with a brand-new washing machine.

I booked a table for lunch at Mario's on the Friday after I had been released from prison. He was standing on the doorstep, waiting to greet me, and I was immediately ushered through to my usual table in the corner of the room by the window, as if I had never been away.

Mario didn't bother to offer me a menu because his wife appeared out of the kitchen carrying a large plate of spaghetti, which she placed on the table in front of me. Mario's son Tony followed close behind with a steaming bowl of Bolognese sauce, and his daughter Maria with a large chunk of Parmesan cheese and a grater.

'A bottle of Chianti classico?' suggested Mario, as he removed the cork. 'On the house,' he insisted.

'Thank you, Mario,' I said, and whispered, 'by the way, the governor of North Sea Camp asked me to pass on his best wishes.'

'Poor Michael,' Mario sighed, 'what a sad existence. Can you begin to imagine a lifetime spent eating toad-in-the-hole, followed by semolina pudding?' He smiled as he poured me a glass of wine. 'Still, maestro, you must have felt quite at home.'

Don't Drink The Water

'IF YOU WANT TO murder someone,' said Karl, 'don't do it in England.'

'Why not?' I asked innocently.

'The odds are against you getting away with it,' my fellow inmate warned me, as we continued to walk round the exercise yard. 'You've got a much better chance in Russia.'

'I'll try to remember that,' I assured him.

'Mind you,' added Karl, 'I knew a countryman of yours who did get away with murder, but at some cost.'

It was Association, that welcome 45-minute break when you're released from your cell. You can either spend your time on the ground floor, which is about the size of a basketball court, sitting around chatting, playing table tennis or watching television, or you can go out into the fresh air and stroll around the perimeter of the yard – about the size of a football pitch. Despite being surrounded by a twenty-foot-high concrete wall topped with razor wire, and with only the sky to look up at, this was, for me, the highlight of the day.

While I was incarcerated at Belmarsh, a category A high-security prison in south-east London, I was locked in my cell for twenty-three hours a day (think about it). You are let out only to go to the canteen to pick up your lunch (five minutes), which you then eat in your cell. Five hours later you collect your supper (five more minutes), when they also hand you tomorrow's breakfast in a plastic bag so that they don't have to let you out again before lunch the following day. The only other blessed release is Association, and even that can be cancelled if the prison is short-staffed (which happens about twice a week).

I always used the 45-minute escape to power-walk, for two reasons: one, I needed the exercise because on the outside I attend a local gym five days a week, and, two, not many prisoners bothered to try and keep up with me. Karl was the exception.

Karl was a Russian by birth who hailed from that beautiful city of St Petersburg. He was a contract killer who had just begun a 22-year sentence for disposing of a fellow countryman who was proving tiresome to one of the Mafia gangs back home. He cut his victims up into small pieces, and put what was left of them into an incinerator. Incidentally, his fee – should you want someone disposed of – was five thousand pounds.

Karl was a bear of a man, six foot two and built like a weightlifter. He was covered in tattoos and never stopped talking. On balance, I didn't consider it wise to interrupt his flow. Like so many prisoners, Karl didn't talk about his own crime, and the golden rule – should you ever end up inside – is never ask what a prisoner is in for, unless they raise the subject. However, Karl did tell me a tale about an Englishman he'd come across in St Petersburg, which he claimed to have witnessed in the days when he'd been a driver for a government minister.

Although Karl and I were resident on different blocks, we met up regularly for Association. But it still took several perambulations of the yard before I squeezed out of him the story of Richard Barnsley.

✲ ✲ ✲

DON'T DRINK THE WATER. Richard Barnsley stared at the little plastic card that had been placed on the washbasin in his bathroom. Not the kind of warning you expect to find when you're staying in a five-star hotel, unless, of course, you're in St Petersburg. By the side of the notice stood two bottles of Evian water. When Dick strolled back into his spacious bedroom, he found two more bottles had been placed on each side of the double bed, and another two on a table by the window. The management weren't taking any chances.

Dick had flown into St Petersburg to close a deal with the Russians. His company had been selected to build a pipeline that would stretch from the Urals to the Red Sea, a project that several other, more established, companies had tendered for. Dick's firm had been awarded the contract, against considerable odds, but those odds had shortened once he guaranteed Anatol Chenkov, the Minister for Energy and close personal friend of the President, two million dollars a year for the rest of his life – the only currencies the Russians trade in are dollars and death – especially when the money is going to be deposited in a numbered account.

Before Dick had started up his own company, Barnsley Construction, he had learnt his trade working in Nigeria for Bechtel, in Brazil for McAlpine and in Saudi Arabia for Hanover, so along the way he had picked up a trick or two about bribery. Most international companies treat the practice simply as another form of tax, and make the necessary provision for it whenever they present their tender. The secret is always to know how much to offer the minister, and how little to dispose of among his acolytes.

Anatol Chenkov, a Putin appointee, was a tough negotiator, but then under a former regime he had been a major in the KGB. However, when it came to setting up a bank account in Switzerland, the minister was clearly a novice. Dick took full advantage of this; after all, Chenkov had never travelled beyond the Russian border before he was appointed to the Politburo. Dick flew him to Geneva for the weekend, while he was on an official visit to London for trade talks. He opened a numbered account for him with Picket & Co, and deposited $100,000 – seed money – but more than Chenkov had been paid in his lifetime. This sweetener was to ensure that the umbilical cord would last for the necessary nine months until the contract was signed; a contract that would allow Dick to retire – on far more than two million a year.

Dick returned to the hotel that morning after his final meeting with the minister, having seen him every day for the past week, sometimes publicly, more often privately. It was no different when Chenkov visited London. Neither man trusted the other, but then Dick never felt at ease with anyone who was willing to take a bribe because there was always someone else happy to offer him another percentage point. However, Dick felt more confident this time, as both of them seemed to have signed up for the same retirement policy.

Dick also helped to cement the relationship with a few added extras that Chenkov quickly became accustomed to. A Rolls-Royce would always pick him up at Heathrow and drive him to the Savoy Hotel. On arrival, he would be shown to his usual riverside suite, and women appeared every evening as regularly as the morning papers. He preferred two of both, one broadsheet, one tabloid.

When Dick checked out of the St Petersburg hotel half

an hour later, the minister's BMW was parked outside the front door waiting to take him to the airport. As he climbed into the back seat, he was surprised to find Chenkov waiting for him. They had parted after their morning meeting just an hour before.

'Is there a problem, Anatol?' he asked anxiously.

'On the contrary,' said Chenkov. 'I have just had a call from the Kremlin which I didn't feel we should discuss over the phone, or even in my office. The President will be visiting St Petersburg on the sixteenth of May and has made it clear that he wishes to preside over the signing ceremony.'

'But that gives us less than three weeks to complete the contract,' said Dick.

'You assured me at our meeting this morning,' Chenkov reminded him, 'that there were only a few *is* to dot and *ts* to cross – an expression I'd not come across before – before you'd be able to finalize the contract.' The minister paused and lit his first cigar of the day before adding, 'With that in mind, my dear friend, I look forward to seeing you back in St Petersburg in three weeks' time.' Chenkov's statement sounded casual, whereas, in truth, it had taken almost three years for the two men to reach this stage, and now it would only be another three weeks before the deal was finally sealed.

Dick didn't respond as he was already thinking about what needed to be done the moment his plane touched down at Heathrow.

'What's the first thing you'll do after the deal has been signed?' asked Chenkov, breaking into his thoughts.

'Put in a tender for the sanitation contract in this city, because whoever gets it would surely make an even larger fortune.'

The minister looked round sharply. 'Never raise that subject in public,' he said gravely. 'It's a very sensitive issue.'

Dick remained silent.

'And take my advice, don't drink the water. Last year we lost countless numbers of our citizens who contracted . . .' the minister hesitated, unwilling to add credence to a story that had been splashed across the front pages of every Western paper.

'How many is countless?' enquired Dick.

'None,' replied the minister. 'Or at least that's the official statistic released by the Ministry of Tourism,' he added as the car came to a halt on a double red line outside the entrance of Pulkovo II airport. He leant forward. 'Karl, take Mr Barnsley's bags to check-in, while I wait here.'

Dick leant across and shook hands with the minister for the second time that morning. 'Thank you, Anatol, for everything,' he said. 'See you in three weeks' time.'

'Long life and happiness, my friend,' said Chenkov as Dick stepped out of the car.

Dick checked in at the departure desk an hour before boarding was scheduled for his flight to London.

'This is the last call for Flight 902 to London Heathrow,' came crackling over the tannoy.

'Is there another flight going to London right now?' asked Dick.

'Yes,' replied the man behind the check-in desk. 'Flight 902 has been delayed, but they're just about to close the gate.'

'Can you get me on it?' asked Dick, as he slid a thousand-rouble note across the counter.

✵ ✵ ✵

Dick's plane touched down at Heathrow three and a half hours later. Once he'd retrieved his case from the carousel, he pushed his trolley through the Nothing to Declare channel and emerged into the arrivals hall.

Stan, his driver, was already waiting among a group of chauffeurs, most of whom were holding up name cards. As soon as Stan spotted his boss, he walked quickly across and relieved him of his suitcase and overnight bag.

'Home or the office?' Stan asked as they walked towards the short-stay carpark.

Dick checked his watch: just after four. 'Home,' he said. 'I'll work in the back of the car.'

Once Dick's Jaguar had emerged from the carpark to begin the journey to Virginia Water, Dick immediately called his office.

'Richard Barnsley's office,' said a voice.

'Hi, Jill, it's me. I managed to catch an earlier flight, and I'm on my way home. Is there anything I should be worrying about?'

'No, everything's running smoothly this end,' Jill replied. 'We're all just waiting to find out how things went in St Petersburg.'

'Couldn't have gone better. The minister wants me back on May sixteenth to sign the contract.'

'But that's less than three weeks away.'

'Which means we'll all have to get a move on. So set up a board meeting for early next week, and then make an appointment for me to see Sam Cohen first thing tomorrow morning. I can't afford any slip-ups at this stage.'

'Can I come to St Petersburg with you?'

'Not this time, Jill, but once the contract has been signed

block out ten days in the diary. Then I'll take you somewhere a little warmer than St Petersburg.'

Dick sat silently in the back of the car, going over everything that needed to be covered before he returned to St Petersburg. By the time Stan drove through the wrought-iron gates and came to a halt outside the neo-Georgian mansion, Dick knew what had to be done. He jumped out of the car and ran into the house. He left Stan to unload the bags, and his housekeeper to unpack them. Dick was surprised not to find his wife standing on the top step, waiting to greet him, but then he remembered that he'd caught an earlier flight, and Maureen wouldn't be expecting him back for at least another couple of hours.

Dick ran upstairs to his bedroom, and quickly stripped off his clothes, dropping them in a pile on the floor. He went into the bathroom and turned on the shower, allowing the warm jets of water to slowly remove the grime of St Petersburg and Aeroflot.

After he'd put on some casual clothes, Dick checked his appearance in the mirror. At fifty-three, his hair was turning prematurely grey, and although he tried to hold his stomach in, he knew he ought to lose a few pounds, just a couple of notches on his belt – once the deal was signed and he had a little more time, he promised himself.

He left the bedroom and went down to the kitchen. He asked the cook to prepare him a salad, and then strolled into the drawing room, picked up *The Times*, and glanced at the headlines. A new leader of the Tory Party, a new leader of the Liberal Democrats, and now Gordon Brown had been elected leader of the Labour Party. None of the major political parties would be fighting the next election under the same leader.

Dick looked up when the phone began to ring. He walked across to his wife's writing desk and picked up the receiver, to hear Jill's voice on the other end of the line.

'The board meeting is fixed for next Thursday at ten o'clock, and I've also arranged for you to see Sam Cohen in his office at eight tomorrow morning.' Dick removed a pen from an inside pocket of his blazer. 'I've emailed every member of the board to warn them that it's a priority,' she added.

'What time did you say my meeting was with Sam?'

'Eight o'clock at his office. He has to be in court by ten for another client.'

'Fine.' Dick opened his wife's drawer and grabbed the first piece of paper available. He wrote down, *Sam, office, 8, Thur board mtg, 10.* 'Well done, Jill,' he added. 'Better book me back into the Grand Palace Hotel, and email the minister to warn him what time I'll be arriving.'

'I already have,' Jill replied, 'and I've also booked you on a flight to St Petersburg on the Friday afternoon.'

'Well done. See you around ten tomorrow.' Dick put the phone down, and strolled through to his study, with a large smile on his face. Everything was going to plan.

When he reached his desk, Dick transferred the details of his appointments to his diary. He was just about to drop the piece of paper into a wastepaper basket when he decided just to check and see if it contained anything important. He unfolded a letter, which he began to read. His smile turned to a frown, long before he'd reached the final paragraph. He started to read the letter, marked private and personal, a second time.

Dear Mrs Barnsley,

*This is to confirm your appointment at our office on
Friday, 30 April, when we will continue our discussions
on the matter you raised with me last Tuesday.
Remembering the full implications of your decision,
I have asked my senior partner to join us on this occasion.
We both look forward to seeing you on the 30th.*

Yours sincerely,

Andrew Symonds

Dick immediately picked up the phone on his desk, and
dialled Sam Cohen's number, hoping he hadn't already left
for the day. When Sam pick up his private line, all Dick
said was, 'Have you come across a lawyer called Andrew
Symonds?'

'Only by reputation,' said Sam, 'but then I don't
specialize in divorce.'

'Divorce?' said Dick, as he heard a car coming up the
gravel driveway. He glanced out of the window to see a
Volkswagen swing round the circle and come to a halt
outside the front door. Dick watched as his wife climbed out
of her car. 'I'll see you at eight tomorrow, Sam, and the
Russian contract won't be the only thing on the agenda.'

Dick's driver dropped him outside Sam Cohen's office in
Lincoln's Inn Field a few minutes before eight the following
morning. The senior partner rose to greet his client as he
entered the room. He gestured to a comfortable chair on the
other side of the desk.

Dick had opened his briefcase even before he'd sat

down. He took out the letter and passed it across to Sam. The lawyer read it slowly, before placing it on the desk in front of him.

'I've thought about the problem overnight,' said Sam, 'and I've also had a word with Anna Rentoul, our divorce partner. She's confirmed that Symonds only handles matrimonial disputes, and with that in mind, I'm sorry to say that I'll have to ask you some fairly personal questions.'

Dick nodded without comment.

'Have you ever discussed divorce with Maureen?'

'No,' said Dick firmly. 'We've had rows from time to time, but then what couples who've been together for over twenty years haven't?'

'No more than that?'

'She once threatened to leave me, but I thought that was all in the past.' Dick paused. 'I'm only surprised that she hasn't raised the subject with me, before consulting a lawyer.'

'That's all too common,' said Sam. 'Over half the husbands who are served with a divorce petition claim they never saw it coming.'

'I certainly fall into that category,' admitted Dick. 'So what do I do next?'

'Not a lot you can do before she serves the writ, and I can't see that there's anything to be gained by raising the subject yourself. After all, nothing may come of it. However, that doesn't mean we shouldn't prepare ourselves. Now, what grounds could she have for divorce?'

'None that I can think of.'

'Are you having an affair?'

'No. Well, yes, a fling with my secretary – but it's not going anywhere. She thinks it's serious, but I plan to replace her once the pipeline contract is signed.'

'So the deal is still on course?' said Sam.

'Yes, that's originally why I needed to see you so urgently,' replied Dick. 'I have to be back in St Petersburg for May the sixteenth, when both sides will be signing the contract.' He paused. 'And it's going to be witnessed by President Putin.'

'Congratulations,' said Sam. 'How much will that be worth to you?'

'Why do you ask?'

'I'm wondering if you're not the only person who's hoping that the deal will go through.'

'Around sixty million –' Dick hesitated – 'for the company.'

'And do you still own fifty-one per cent of the shares?'

'Yes, but I could always hide—'

'Don't even think about it,' said Sam. 'You won't be able to hide anything if Symonds is on the case. He'll sniff out every last penny, like a pig hunting for truffles. And if the court were to discover that you attempted to deceive them, it would only make the judge more sympathetic to your wife.' The senior partner paused, looked directly at his client, and repeated, 'Don't even think about it.'

'So what should I do?'

'Nothing that will arouse suspicion; go about your business as usual, as if you have no idea what she's up to. Meanwhile, I'll fix a consultation with counsel, so at least we'll be better prepared than Mr Symonds will be anticipating. And one more thing,' said Sam, once again looking directly at his client, 'no more extra-marital activities until this problem has been resolved. That's an order.'

Dick kept a close eye on his wife during the next few days, but she gave no sign of there being anything untoward. If anything, she showed an unusual interest in how the trip to St Petersburg had gone, and over dinner on Thursday evening even asked if the board had come to a decision.

'They most certainly have,' Dick replied emphatically. 'Once Sam had taken the directors through each clause, gone over every detail, and answered all of their questions, they virtually rubber-stamped the contract.' Dick poured himself a second cup of coffee. He was taken by surprise by his wife's next question.

'Why don't I join you when you go to St Petersburg? We could fly out on the Friday,' she added, 'and spend the weekend visiting the Hermitage and the Summer Palace. We might even find enough time to see Catherine's amber collection – something I've always wanted to do.'

Dick didn't reply immediately, aware that this was not a casual suggestion as it had been years since Maureen had accompanied him on a business trip. Dick's first reaction was to wonder what she was up to. 'Let me think about it,' he eventually responded, leaving his coffee to go cold.

Dick rang Sam Cohen within minutes of arriving at his office and reported the conversation to his lawyer.

'Symonds must have advised her to witness the signing of the contract,' suggested Cohen.

'But why?'

'So that Maureen will be able to claim that over the years she has played a leading role in your business success, always being there to support you at those critical moments in your career . . . '

'Balls,' said Dick, 'she's never taken any interest in how I make my money, only in how she can spend it.'

' . . . and therefore she must be entitled to fifty per cent of your assets.'

'But that could amount to over thirty million pounds,' Dick protested.

'Symonds has obviously done his homework.'

'Then I'll simply tell her that she can't come on the trip. It's not appropriate.'

'Which will allow Mr Symonds to change tack. He'll then portray you as a heartless man, who, the moment you became a success, cut his client out of your life, often travelling abroad, accompanied by a secretary who—'

'OK, OK, I get the picture. So allowing her to come to St Petersburg might well prove to be the lesser of two evils.'

'On the one hand . . . ' counselled Sam.

'Bloody lawyers,' said Dick before he could finish the sentence.

'Funny how you only need us when you're in trouble,' Sam rejoined. 'So let's make sure that this time we antici- pate her next move.'

'And what's that likely to be?'

'Once she's got you to St Petersburg, she'll want to have sex.'

'We haven't had sex for years.'

'And not because I haven't wanted to, m'lord.'

'Oh, hell,' said Dick, 'I can't win.'

'You can as long as you don't follow Lady Longford's advice – when asked if she had ever considered divor- cing Lord Longford, she replied, "Divorce, never, murder, often."'

Mr and Mrs Richard Barnsley checked into the Grand Palace Hotel in St Petersburg a fortnight later. A porter placed their bags on a trolley, and then accompanied them to the Tolstoy Suite on the ninth floor.

'Must go to the loo before I burst,' said Dick as he rushed into the room ahead of his wife. While her husband disappeared into the bathroom, Maureen looked out of the window and admired the golden domes of St Nicholas's Cathedral.

Once he'd locked the door, Dick removed the DON'T DRINK THE WATER sign that was perched on the wash-basin and tucked it into the back pocket of his trousers. Next he unscrewed the tops of the two Evian bottles and poured the contents down the sink. He then refilled both bottles with tap water, before screwing the tops firmly back on and returning them to their place on the corner of the basin. He unlocked the door and strolled out of the bathroom.

Dick started to unpack his suitcase, but stopped the moment Maureen disappeared into the bathroom. First, he transferred the DON'T DRINK THE WATER sign from his back pocket into the side flap of his suitcase. He zipped up the flap, before checking around the room. There was a small bottle of Evian water on each side of the bed, and two large bottles on the table by the window. He grabbed the bottle by his wife's side of the bed and retreated into the kitchenette at the far end of the room. Dick poured the contents down the sink, and refilled the bottle with tap water. He then returned it to Maureen's side of the bed. Next, he took the two large bottles from the table by the window and repeated the process.

By the time his wife had come out of the bathroom, Dick had almost finished unpacking. While Maureen continued to unpack her suitcase, Dick strolled across to his side of the bed and dialled a number he didn't need to look up. As

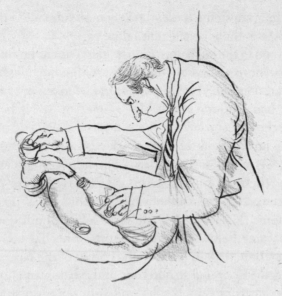

he waited for the phone to be answered, he opened the bottle of Evian water on his side of the bed, and took a gulp.

'Hi, Anatol, it's Dick Barnsley. I thought I'd let you know that we've just checked in to the Grand Palace.'

'Welcome back to St Petersburg,' said a friendly voice. 'And is your wife with you on this occasion?'

'She most certainly is,' replied Dick, 'and very much looking forward to meeting you.'

'Me too,' said the minister, 'so make sure that you have a relaxed weekend because everything is set up for Monday morning. The President is due to fly in tomorrow night so he'll be present when the contract is signed.'

'Ten o'clock at the Winter Palace?'

'Ten o'clock,' repeated Chenkov. 'I'll pick you up from your hotel at nine. It's only a thirty-minute drive, but we can't afford to be late for this one.'

'I'll be waiting for you in the lobby,' said Dick. 'See you then.' He put the phone down and turned to his wife. 'Why don't we go down to dinner, my darling? We've got a long day ahead of us tomorrow.' He adjusted his watch by three hours and added, 'So perhaps it would be wise to have an early night.'

Maureen placed a long silk nightdress on her side of the bed and smiled in agreement. As she turned to place her empty case in the wardrobe, Dick slipped an Evian bottle from the bedside table into his jacket pocket. He then accompanied his wife down to the dining room.

The head waiter guided them to a quiet table in the corner and, once they were seated, offered his two guests menus. Maureen disappeared behind the large leather cover while she considered the table d'hôte, which allowed Dick enough time to remove the bottle of Evian from his pocket, undo the cap and fill his wife's glass.

Once they had both selected their meals, Maureen went over her proposed itinerary for the next two days. 'I think we should begin with the Hermitage, first thing in the morning,' she suggested, 'take a break for lunch, and then spend the rest of the afternoon at the Summer Palace.'

'What about the amber collection?' asked Dick, as he topped up her water glass. 'I thought that was a no-miss.'

'I'd already scheduled in the amber collection and the Russian Museum for Sunday.'

'Sounds as if you have everything well organized,' said Dick, as a waiter placed a bowl of borscht in front of his wife.

Maureen spent the rest of the meal telling Dick about some of the treasures that they would see when they visited the Hermitage. By the time Dick had signed the bill, Maureen had drunk the bottle of water.

Dick slipped the empty bottle back in his pocket. Once they had returned to their room, he filled it with tap water and left it in the bathroom.

By the time Dick had undressed and climbed into bed, Maureen was still studying her guidebook.

'I feel exhausted,' Dick said. 'It must be the time change.' He turned his back on her, hoping she wouldn't work out that it was just after eight p.m. in England.

Dick woke the following morning feeling very thirsty. He looked at the empty bottle of Evian on his side of the bed and remembered just in time. He climbed out of bed, walked across to the fridge and selected a bottle of orange juice.

'Will you be going to the gym this morning?' he asked a half-awake Maureen.

'Do I have time?'

'Sure, the Hermitage doesn't open until ten, and one of the reasons I always stay here is because of the hotel's gym.'

'So what about you?'

'I still have to make some phone calls if everything is to be set up for Monday.'

Maureen slipped out of bed and disappeared into the bathroom, which allowed Dick enough time to top up her glass and replace the empty bottle of Evian on her side of the bed.

When Maureen emerged a few minutes later, she checked her watch before slipping on her gym kit. 'I should be back in about forty minutes,' she said, after tying up her trainers.

'Don't forget to take some water with you,' said Dick, handing her one of the bottles from the table by the window. 'They may not have one in the gym.'

'Thank you,' she said.

Dick wondered, from the expression on her face, if he was being just a little too solicitous.

While Maureen was in the gym, Dick took a shower. When he walked back into the bedroom, he was pleased to see that the sun was shining. He put on a blazer and slacks, but only after he'd checked that none of the bottles had been replaced by the hotel staff while he'd been in the bathroom.

Dick ordered breakfast for both of them, which arrived moments after Maureen returned from the gym, clutching the half-empty Evian bottle.

'How did your training go?' Dick asked.

'Not great,' Maureen replied. 'I felt a bit listless.'

'Probably just jetlag,' suggested Dick as he took his place on the far side of the table. He poured his wife a glass of water, and himself another orange juice. Dick opened a copy of the *Herald Tribune*, which he began to read while he waited for his wife to dress. Hillary Clinton said she wouldn't be running for president, which only convinced Dick that she would, especially as she made the announcement standing by her husband's side.

Maureen came out of the bathroom wearing a hotel dressing gown. She took the seat opposite her husband and sipped the water.

'Better take a bottle of Evian with us when we visit the Hermitage,' said Maureen. Dick looked up from behind his paper. 'The girl in the gym warned me not, under any circumstances, to drink the local water.'

'Oh yes, I should have warned you,' said Dick, as Maureen took a bottle from the table by the window and put it in her bag. 'Can't be too careful.'

Dick and Maureen strolled through the front gates of the Hermitage a few minutes before ten, to find themselves at the back of a long queue. The crocodile of visitors progressed slowly forward along an unshaded cobbled path. Maureen took several sips of water between turning the pages of the guidebook. It was ten forty before they reached the ticket booth. Once inside, Maureen continued to study her guidebook. 'Whatever we do, we must be sure to see Michelangelo's *Crouching Boy*, Raphael's *Virgin*, and Leonardo's *Madonna Benois*.'

Dick smiled his agreement, but knew he wouldn't be concerning himself with the masters.

As they climbed the wide marble staircase, they passed several magnificent statues nestled in alcoves. Dick was surprised to discover just how vast the Hermitage was. Despite visiting St Petersburg several times during the past three years, he had only ever seen the building from the outside.

'Housed on three floors, Tsar Peter's collection displays treasures in over two hundred rooms,' Maureen told him, reading from the guidebook. 'So let's get started.'

By eleven thirty they had only covered the Dutch and Italian schools on the first floor, by which time Maureen had finished the large bottle of Evian.

Dick volunteered to go and buy another bottle. He left his wife admiring Caravaggio's *The Lute Player*, while he slipped into the nearest rest room. He refilled the empty Evian bottle with tap water before rejoining his wife. If

Maureen had spent a little time studying one of the many drinks counters situated on each floor, she would have discovered that the Hermitage doesn't stock Evian, because it has an exclusive contract with Volvic.

By twelve thirty they had all but covered the sixteen rooms devoted to the Renaissance artists, and agreed it was time for lunch. They left the building and strolled back into the midday sun. The two of them walked for a while along the bank of the Moika River, stopping only to take a photograph of a bride and groom posing on the Blue Bridge in front of the Mariinsky Palace.

'A local tradition,' said Maureen, turning another page of her guidebook.

After walking another block, they came to a halt outside a small pizzeria. Its sensible square tables with neat red-and-white check tablecloths and smartly dressed waiters tempted them inside.

'I must go to the loo,' said Maureen. 'I'm feeling a little queasy. It must be the heat.' She added, 'Just order me a salad and a glass of water.'

Dick smiled, removed the Evian bottle from her bag and filled up the glass on her side of the table. When the waiter appeared, Dick ordered a salad for his wife, and ravioli plus a large diet Coke for himself. He was desperate for something to drink.

Once she'd eaten her salad, Maureen perked up a little, and even began to tell Dick what they should look out for when they visited the Summer Palace.

On the long taxi ride through the north of the city, she continued to read extracts from her guidebook. 'Peter the Great built the Summer Palace after he had visited Versailles, and on returning to Russia employed the finest landscape

gardeners and most gifted craftsmen in the land to repro-
duce the French masterpiece. He intended the finished work
to be a homage to the French, whom he greatly admired as
the leaders of style throughout Europe.'

The taxi driver interrupted her flow with a snippet of
information of his own. 'We are just passing the recently
constructed Winter Palace, which is where President Putin
stays whenever he's in St Petersburg.' The driver paused.
'And, as the national flag is flying, he must be in town.'

'He's flown down from Moscow especially to see me,'
said Dick.

The taxi driver dutifully laughed.

The taxi drove through the gates of the Summer Palace half
an hour later and the driver dropped his passengers off in a
crowded carpark, bustling with sightseers and traders, who
were standing behind their makeshift stalls plying their
cheap souvenirs.

'Let's go and see the real thing,' suggested Maureen.

'I wait for you here,' said the taxi driver. 'No extra charge.
How long?' he added.

'I should think we'd be a couple of hours,' said Dick. 'No
more.'

'I wait for you here,' he repeated.

The two of them strolled around the magnificent gardens,
and Dick could see why it was described in the guidebooks
as a 'can't afford to miss', with five stars. Maureen continued to brief him between sips of water. 'The grounds
surrounding the palace cover over a hundred acres, with
more than twenty fountains, as well as eleven other palatial
residences.' Although the sun was no longer burning down,

the sky was still clear and Maureen continued to take regular gulps of water, but however many times she offered the bottle to Dick, he always replied, 'No thanks.'

When they finally climbed the steps of the palace, they were greeted by another long queue, and Maureen admitted that she was feeling a little tired.

'Pity to have travelled this far,' said Dick, 'and not take a look inside.'

His wife reluctantly agreed.

When they reached the front of the queue, Dick purchased two entrance tickets and, for a small extra charge, selected an English-speaking guide to show them around.

'I don't feel too good,' said Maureen as they entered the Empress Catherine's bedroom. She clung onto the four-poster bed.

'You must drink lots of water on such a hot day,' suggested the tour guide helpfully. By the time they had reached Tsar Nicholas IV's study, Maureen warned her husband that she thought she was going to faint. Dick apologized to their guide, put an arm around his wife's shoulder and assisted her out of the palace on an unsteady journey back to the carpark. They found their taxi driver standing by his car waiting for them.

'We must return to the Grand Palace Hotel immediately,' said Dick, as his wife fell into the back seat of the car like a drunk who has been thrown out of a pub on a Saturday night.

On the long drive back to St Petersburg, Maureen was violently sick in the back of the taxi, but the driver didn't comment, just maintained a steady speed as he continued along the highway. Forty minutes later, he came to a halt outside the Grand Palace Hotel. Dick handed over a wodge of notes and apologized.

'Hope madam better soon,' he said.

'Yes, let's hope so,' replied Dick.

Dick helped his wife out of the back of the car, and guided her up the steps into the hotel lobby and quickly towards the lifts, not wishing to draw attention to himself. He had her safely back in their suite moments later. Maureen immediately disappeared into the bathroom, and even with the door closed Dick could hear her retching. He searched around the room. In their absence, all the bottles of Evian had been replaced. He only bothered to empty the one by Maureen's bedside, which he refilled with tap water from the kitchenette.

Maureen finally emerged from the bathroom, and collapsed onto the bed. 'I feel awful,' she said.

'Perhaps you ought to take a couple of aspirin, and try to get some sleep?'

Maureen nodded weakly. 'Could you fetch them for me? They're in my wash bag.'

'Of course, my darling.' Once he'd found the pills, he filled a glass with tap water, before returning to his wife's side. She had taken off her dress, but not her slip. Dick helped her to sit up and became aware for the first time that she was soaked in sweat. She swilled down the two aspirins with the glass of water Dick offered her. He lowered her gently down onto the pillow before drawing the curtains. He then strolled across to the bedroom door, opened it, and placed the *Do Not Disturb* sign on the door knob. The last thing he needed was for a solicitous maid to come barging in and find his wife in her present state. Once Dick was certain she was asleep, he went down to dinner.

'Will madam be joining you this evening?' enquired the head waiter, once Dick was seated.

'No, sadly not,' replied Dick, 'she has a slight migraine. Too much sun I fear, but I'm sure she'll be fine by the morning.'

'Let's hope so, sir. What can I interest you in tonight?'

Dick took his time perusing the menu, before he eventually said, 'I think I'll start with the foie gras, followed by a rump steak –' he paused – 'medium rare.'

'Excellent choice, sir.'

Dick poured himself a glass of water from the bottle on the table and quickly gulped it down, before filling his glass a second time. He didn't hurry his meal, and when he returned to his suite just after ten, he was delighted to find his wife was fast asleep. He picked up her glass, took it to the bathroom and refilled it with tap water. He then put it back on her side of the bed. Dick took his time undressing, before finally slipping under the covers to settle down next to his wife. He turned out the bedside light and slept soundly.

When Dick woke the following morning, he found that he too was covered in sweat. The sheets were also soaked, and when he turned over to look at his wife all the colour had drained from her cheeks.

Dick eased himself out of bed, slipped into the bathroom and took a long shower. Once he had dried himself, he put on one of the hotel's towelling dressing gowns and returned to the bedroom. He crept over to his wife's side of the bed and once again refilled her empty glass with tap water. She had clearly woken during the night, but not disturbed him.

He drew the curtains before checking that the *Do Not Disturb* sign was still on the door. He returned to his wife's side of the bed, pulled up a chair and began to read the *Herald Tribune*. He had reached the sports pages by the time she woke. Her words were slurred. She managed, 'I feel awful.' A long pause followed before she added, 'Don't you think I ought to see a doctor?'

'He's already been to examine you, my dear,' said Dick. 'I called for him last night. Don't you remember? He told you that you'd caught a fever, and you'll just have to sweat it out.'

'Did he leave any pills?' asked Maureen plaintively.

'No, my darling. He just said you weren't to eat anything, but to try and drink as much water as possible.' He held the glass up to her lips and she attempted to gulp some more down. She even managed, 'Thank you,' before collapsing back onto the pillow.

'Don't worry, my darling,' said Dick. 'You're going to be just fine, and I promise you I won't leave your side, even for a moment.' He leant over and kissed her on the forehead. She fell asleep again.

The only time Dick left Maureen's side that day was to assure the housekeeper that his wife did not wish to have the sheets changed, to refill the glass of water on her bedside table, and late in the afternoon to take a call from the minister.

'The President flew in yesterday,' were Chenkov's opening words. 'He's staying at the Winter Palace, where I've just left him. He wanted me to let you know how much he is looking forward to meeting you and your wife.'

'How kind of him,' said Dick, 'but I have a problem.'

'A problem?' said a man who didn't like problems, especially when the President was in town.

'It's just that Maureen seems to have caught a fever. We were out in the sun all day yesterday, and I'm not sure that she will have fully recovered in time to join us for the signing ceremony, so I may be on my own.'

'I'm sorry to hear that,' said Chenkov, 'and how are you?'

'Never felt better,' said Dick.

'That's good,' said Chenkov, sounding relieved. 'So I'll pick you up at nine o'clock, as agreed. I don't want to keep the President waiting.'

'Neither do I, Anatol,' Dick assured him. 'You'll find me standing in the lobby long before nine.'

There was a knock on the door. Dick quickly put the phone down and rushed across to open it before anyone was given a chance to barge in. A maid was standing in the corridor next to a trolley laden with sheets, towels, bars of soap, shampoo bottles and cases of Evian water.

'You want the bed turned down, sir?' she asked, giving him a smile.

'No, thank you,' said Dick. 'My wife is not feeling well.' He pointed to the *Do Not Disturb* sign.

'More water, perhaps?' she suggested, holding up a large bottle of Evian.

'No,' he repeated firmly and closed the door.

The only other call that evening came from the hotel manager. He asked politely if madam would like to see the hotel doctor.

'No, thank you,' said Dick. 'She just caught a little sun but she's on the mend, and I feel sure she will have fully recovered by the morning.'

'Just give me a call,' said the manager, 'should she change her mind. The doctor can be with you in minutes.'

'That's very considerate of you,' said Dick, 'but it won't be necessary,' he added before putting the phone down. He returned to his wife's side. Her skin was now pallid and blotchy. He leant forward until he was almost touching her lips – she was still breathing. He walked across to the fridge, opened it and took out all the unopened bottles of Evian water. He placed two of them in the bathroom, and one each side of the bed. His final action, before undressing, was to take the DON'T DRINK THE WATER sign out of his suitcase and replace it on the side of the washbasin.

Chenkov's car pulled up outside the Grand Palace Hotel a few minutes before nine the following morning. Karl jumped out to open the back door for the minister.

Chenkov walked quickly up the steps and into the hotel, expecting to find Dick waiting for him in the lobby. He looked up and down the crowded corridor, but there was no sign of his business partner. He marched across to the reception desk and asked if Mr Barnsley had left a message for him.

'No, Minister,' replied the concierge. 'Would you like me to call his room?' The minister nodded briskly. They both waited for some time, before the concierge added, 'No one is answering the phone, Minister, so perhaps Mr Barnsley is on his way down.'

Chenkov nodded again, and began pacing up and down the lobby, continually glancing towards the elevator, before checking his watch. At ten past nine, the minister became even more anxious, as he had no desire to keep the President waiting. He returned to the reception desk.

'Try again,' he demanded.

The concierge immediately dialled Mr Barnsley's room number, but could only report that there was still no reply.

'Send for the manager,' barked the minister. The concierge nodded, picked up the phone once again and dialled a single number. A few moments later, a tall, elegantly dressed man in a dark suit was standing by Chenkov's side.

'How may I assist you, Minister?' he asked.

'I need to go up to Mr Barnsley's room.'

'Of course, Minister, please follow me.'

When the three men arrived on the ninth floor, they quickly made their way to the Tolstoy Suite, where they found the *Do Not Disturb* sign hanging from the door knob. The minister banged loudly on the door, but there was no response.

'Open the door,' he demanded. The concierge obeyed without hesitation.

The minister marched into the room, followed by the

manager and the concierge. Chenkov came to an abrupt halt when he saw two motionless bodies lying in bed. The concierge didn't need to be told to call for a doctor.

Sadly, the doctor had attended three such cases in the past month, but with a difference – they had all been locals. He studied his two patients for some time before he passed a judgement.

'The Siberian disease,' he confirmed, almost in a whisper. He paused and, looking up at the minister, added, 'The lady undoubtedly died during the night, whereas the gentleman has passed away within the last hour.'

The minister made no comment.

'My initial conclusion,' continued the doctor, 'is that she probably caught the disease from drinking too much of the local water –' he paused as he looked down at Dick's lifeless body – 'while her husband must have contracted the virus from his wife, probably during the night. Not an uncommon occurrence among married couples,' he added. 'Like so many of our countrymen, he clearly wasn't aware that –' he hesitated before uttering the word in front of the minister – '*Siberius* is one of those rare diseases that is not only infectious but highly contagious.'

'But I called him last night,' protested the manager, 'and asked if he'd like to see a doctor, and he said it wasn't necessary, as his wife was on the mend and he was confident that she would be fully recovered by the morning.'

'How sad,' said the doctor, before adding, 'if only he'd said yes. It would have been too late to revive his wife, but I still might have saved him.'

It Can't Be October Already

PATRICK O'FLYNN STOOD in front of H. Samuel, the jeweller's, holding a brick in his right hand. He was staring intently at the window. He smiled, raised his arm and hurled the brick at the glass pane. The window shattered like a spider's web, but remained firmly in place. An alarm was immediately set off, which in the still of a clear, cold October night could be heard half a mile away. More important to Pat, the alarm was directly connected to the local police station.

Pat didn't move as he continued to stare at his handiwork. He only had to wait ninety seconds before he heard the sound of a siren in the distance. He bent down and retrieved the brick from the pavement, as the whining noise grew louder and louder. When the police car came to a screeching halt by the kerbside, Pat raised the brick above his head and leant back, like an Olympic javelin thrower intent on a gold medal. Two policemen leapt out of the car. The older one ignored Pat, who remained poised, arm above his head with the brick in his hand, and walked across to the window to check the damage. Although the pane was shattered, it was still firmly in place. In any case, an iron security grille had descended behind the window, something Pat knew full well would happen. But when the sergeant returned to the station, he would still have to phone the manager, get him out of bed and ask him to come down to the shop and turn off the alarm.

The sergeant turned round to find Pat still standing with the brick high above his head.

'OK, Pat, hand it over and get in,' said the sergeant, as he held open the back door of the police car.

Pat smiled, passed the brick to the fresh-faced constable and said, 'You'll need this as evidence.'

The young constable was speechless.

'Thank you, Sergeant,' said Pat as he climbed into the back of the car, and, smiling at the young constable, who took his place behind the wheel, asked, 'Have I ever told you about the time I tried to get a job on a building site in Liverpool?'

'Many times,' interjected the sergeant, as he took his place next to Pat and pulled the back door closed.

'No handcuffs?' queried Pat.

'I don't want to be handcuffed to you,' said the sergeant, 'I want to be rid of you. Why don't you just go back to Ireland?'

'An altogether inferior class of prison,' Pat explained, 'and in any case, they don't treat me with the same degree of respect as you do, Sergeant,' he added, as the car moved away from the kerb and headed back towards the police station.

'Can you tell me your name?' Pat asked, leaning forward to address the young constable.

'Constable Cooper.'

'Are you by any chance related to Chief Inspector Cooper?'

'He's my father.'

'A gentleman,' said Pat. 'We've had many a cup of tea and biscuits together. I hope he's in fine fettle.'

'He's just retired,' said Constable Cooper.

'I'm sorry to hear that,' said Pat. 'Will you tell him that Pat O'Flynn asked after him? And please send him, and your dear mother, my best wishes.'

'Stop taking the piss, Pat,' said the sergeant. 'The boy's only been out of Peel House for a few weeks,' he added, as the car came to a halt outside the police station. The sergeant climbed out of the back and held the door open for Pat.

'Thank you, Sergeant,' said Pat, as if he was addressing the doorman at the Ritz. The constable grinned as the sergeant accompanied Pat up the stairs and into the police station.

'Ah, and a very good evening to you, Mr Baker,' said Pat when he saw who it was standing behind the desk.

'Oh, Christ,' said the duty sergeant. 'It can't be October already.'

'I'm afraid so, Sergeant,' said Pat. 'I was wondering if my usual cell is available. I'll only be staying overnight, you understand.'

'I'm afraid not,' said the desk sergeant, 'it's already

occupied by a real criminal. You'll have to be satisfied with cell number two.'

'But I've always had cell number one in the past,' protested Pat.

The desk sergeant looked up and raised an eyebrow.

'No, I'm to blame,' admitted Pat. 'I should have asked my secretary to call and book in advance. Do you need to take an imprint of my credit card?'

'No, I have all your details on file,' the desk sergeant assured him.

'How about fingerprints?'

'Unless you've found a way of removing your old ones, Pat, I don't think we need another set. But I suppose you'd better sign the charge sheet.'

Pat took the proffered biro and signed on the bottom line with a flourish.

'Take him down to cell number two, Constable.'

'Thank you, Sergeant,' said Pat as he was led away. He stopped, turned around and said, 'I wonder, Sergeant, if you could give me a wake-up call around seven, a cup of tea, Earl Grey preferably, and a copy of the *Irish Times*.'

'Piss off, Pat,' said the desk sergeant, as the constable tried to stifle a laugh.

'Which reminds me,' said Pat, 'have I told you about the time I tried to get a job on a building site in Liverpool, and the foreman—'

'Get him out of my sight, Constable, if you don't want to spend the rest of the month on traffic duty.'

The constable grabbed Pat by the elbow and hurried him downstairs.

'No need to come with me,' said Pat. 'I can find my own way.' This time the constable did laugh as he placed a key in the lock of cell number two. The young policeman unlocked the cell and pulled open the heavy door, allowing Pat to stroll in.

'Thank you, Constable Cooper,' said Pat. 'I look forward to seeing you in the morning.'

'I'll be off duty,' said Constable Cooper.

'Then I'll see you this time next year,' said Pat without explanation, 'and don't forget to pass on my best wishes to your father,' he added as the four-inch-thick iron door was slammed shut.

Pat studied the cell for a few moments: a steel washbasin, a bog and a bed, one sheet, one blanket and one pillow. Pat was reassured by the fact that nothing had changed since last year. He fell on the horsehair mattress, placed his head on the rock-hard pillow and slept all night – for the first time in weeks.

Pat was woken from a deep sleep at seven the following morning, when the cell-door flap was flicked open and two black eyes stared in.

'Good morning, Pat,' said a friendly voice.

'Good morning, Wesley,' said Pat, not even opening his eyes. 'And how are you?'

'I'm well,' replied Wesley, 'but sorry to see you back.' He paused. 'I suppose it must be October.'

'It certainly is,' said Pat climbing off the bed, 'and it's important that I look my best for this morning's show trial.'

'Anything you need in particular?'

'A cup of tea would be most acceptable, but what I really require is a razor, a bar of soap, a toothbrush and some toothpaste. I don't have to remind you, Wesley, that a defendant is entitled to this simple request before he makes an appearance in court.'

'I'll see you get them,' said Wesley, 'and would you like to read my copy of the *Sun*?'

'That's kind of you, Wesley, but if the chief superintendent has finished with yesterday's *Times*, I'd prefer that.' A West Indian chuckle was followed by the closing of the shutter on the cell door.

Pat didn't have to wait long before he heard a key turn in the lock. The heavy door was pulled open to reveal the smiling face of Wesley Pickett, a tray in one hand, which he placed on the end of the bed.

'Thank you, Wesley,' said Pat as he stared down at the bowl of cornflakes, small carton of skimmed milk, two slices of burnt toast and a boiled egg. 'I do hope Molly remembered,' added Pat, 'that I like my eggs lightly boiled, for two and a half minutes.'

'Molly left last year,' said Wesley. 'I think you'll find the egg was boiled last night by the desk sergeant.'

'You can't get the staff nowadays,' said Pat. 'I blame it on the Irish, myself. They're no longer committed to domestic service,' he added as he tapped the top of his egg with a plastic spoon. 'Wesley, have I told you about the time I tried to get a labouring job on a building site in Liverpool, and the foreman, a bloody Englishman—' Pat looked up and sighed as he heard the door slam and the key turn in the lock. 'I suppose I must have told him the story before,' he muttered to himself.

After Pat had finished breakfast, he cleaned his teeth with a toothbrush and a tube of toothpaste that were even smaller than the ones they'd supplied on his only experience of an Aer Lingus flight to Dublin. Next, he turned on the hot tap in the tiny steel washbasin. The slow trickle of water took some time to turn from cold to lukewarm. He rubbed the mean piece of soap between his fingers until he'd whipped up enough cream to produce a lather, which he then smeared all over his stubbled face. Next he picked up the plastic Bic razor, and began the slow process of removing a four-day-old stubble. He finally dabbed his face with a rough green hand towel, not much larger than a flannel.

Pat sat on the end of the bed and, while he waited, read Wesley's *Sun* from cover to cover in four minutes. Only an article by their political editor Trevor Kavanagh – he must surely be an Irishman, thought Pat – was worthy of his attention. Pat's thoughts were interrupted when the heavy metal door was pulled open once again.

'Let's be 'avin you, Pat,' said Sergeant Webster. 'You're first on this morning.'

Pat accompanied the officer back up the stairs, and when he saw the desk sergeant, asked, 'Could I have my valuables back, Mr Baker? You'll find them in the safe.'

'Like what?' said the desk sergeant, looking up.

'My pearl cufflinks, the Cartier Tank watch and a silver-topped cane engraved with my family crest.'

'I flogged 'em all off last night, Pat,' said the desk sergeant.

'Probably for the best,' remarked Pat. 'I won't be needing them where I'm going,' he added, before following Sergeant Webster out of the front door and onto the pavement.

'Jump in the front,' said the sergeant, as he climbed behind the wheel of a panda car.

'But I'm entitled to two officers to escort me to court,' insisted Pat. 'It's a Home Office regulation.'

'It may well be a Home Office regulation,' the sergeant replied, 'but we're short-staffed this morning, two off sick, and one away on a training course.'

'But what if I tried to escape?'

'A blessed release,' said Sergeant Webster, as he pulled away from the kerb, 'because that would save us all a lot of trouble.'

'And what would you do if I decided to punch you?'

'I'd punch you back,' said an exasperated sergeant.

'That's not very friendly,' suggested Pat.

'Sorry, Pat,' said the sergeant. 'It's just that I promised my wife that I'd be off duty by ten this morning, so we could go shopping.' He paused. 'So she won't be best pleased with me – or you for that matter.'

'I apologize, Sergeant Webster,' said Pat. 'Next October I'll try to find out which shift you're on, so I can be sure to avoid it. Perhaps you'd pass on my apologies to Mrs Webster.'

The sergeant would have laughed, if it had been anyone else, but he knew Pat meant it.

'Any idea who I'll be up in front of this morning?' asked Pat as the car came to a halt at a set of traffic lights.

'Thursday,' said the sergeant, as the lights turned green and he pushed the gear lever back into first. 'It must be Perkins.'

'Councillor Arnold Perkins OBE, oh good,' said Pat. 'He's got a very short fuse. So if he doesn't give me a long enough sentence, I'll just have to light it,' he added as the car swung into the private carpark at the back of Marylebone Road Magistrates' Court. A court officer was heading towards the police car just as Pat stepped out.

'Good morning, Mr Adams,' said Pat.

'When I looked at the list of defendants this morning, Pat, and saw your name,' said Mr Adams, 'I assumed it must be that time of the year when you make your annual appearance. Follow me, Pat, and let's get this over with as quickly as possible.'

Pat accompanied Mr Adams through the back door of the courthouse and on down the long corridor to a holding cell.

'Thank you, Mr Adams,' said Pat as he took a seat on a thin wooden bench that was cemented to a wall along one side of the large oblong room. 'If you'd be kind enough to just leave me for a few moments,' Pat added, 'so that I can compose myself before the curtain goes up.'

Mr Adams smiled, and turned to leave.

'By the way,' said Pat, as Mr Adams touched the handle of the door, 'did I tell you about the time I tried to get a labouring job on a building site in Liverpool, but the foreman, a bloody Englishman, had the nerve to ask me—'

'Sorry, Pat, some of us have got a job to do, and in any case, you told me that story last October.' He paused. 'And, come to think of it, the October before.'

Pat sat silently on the bench and, as he had nothing else to read, considered the graffiti on the wall. *Perkins is a prat.* He felt able to agree with that sentiment. *Man U are the champions.* Someone had crossed out *Man U* and replaced it with *Chelsea*. Pat wondered if he should cross out Chelsea, and write in Cork, whom neither team had ever defeated. As there was no clock on the wall, Pat couldn't be sure how much time had passed before Mr Adams finally returned to escort him up to the courtroom. Adams was now dressed in a long black gown, looking like Pat's old headmaster.

'Follow me,' Mr Adams intoned solemnly.

Pat remained unusually silent as they proceeded down the yellow brick road, as the old lags call the last few yards before you climb the steps and enter the back door of the court. Pat ended up standing in the dock, with a bailiff by his side.

Pat stared up at the bench and looked at the three magistrates who made up this morning's panel. Something was wrong. He had been expecting to see Mr Perkins, who had been bald this time last year, almost Pickwickian. Now, suddenly, he seemed to have sprouted a head of fair hair. On his right was Councillor Steadman, a liberal, who was much too lenient for Pat's liking. On the chairman's left sat a middle-aged lady whom Pat had never seen before; her thin lips and piggy eyes gave Pat a little confidence that the liberal could be outvoted two to one, especially if he played his cards right. Miss Piggy looked as if she would have happily supported capital punishment for shoplifters.

Sergeant Webster stepped into the witness box and took the oath.

'What can you tell us about this case, Sergeant?' Mr Perkins asked, once the oath had been administered.

'May I refer to my notes, your honour?' asked Sergeant Webster, turning to face the chairman of the panel. Mr Perkins nodded, and the sergeant turned over the cover of his notepad.

'I apprehended the defendant at two o'clock this morning, after he had thrown a brick at the window of H. Samuel, the jeweller's, on Mason Street.'

'Did you see him throw the brick, Sergeant?'

'No, I did not,' admitted Webster, 'but he was standing on the pavement with the brick in his hand when I apprehended him.'

'And had he managed to gain entry?' asked Perkins.

'No, sir,' said the sergeant, 'but he was about to throw the brick again when I arrested him.'

'The same brick?'

'I think so.'

'And had he done any damage?'

'He had shattered the glass, but a security grille prevented him from removing anything.'

'How valuable were the goods in the window?' asked Mr Perkins.

'There were no goods in the window,' replied the sergeant, 'because the manager always locks them up in the safe, before going home at night.'

Mr Perkins looked puzzled and, glancing down at the charge sheet, said, 'I see you have charged O'Flynn with attempting to break and enter.'

'That is correct, sir,' said Sergeant Webster, returning his notebook to a back pocket of his trousers.

Mr Perkins turned his attention to Pat. 'I note that you have entered a plea of guilty on the charge sheet, O'Flynn.'

'Yes, m'lord.'

'Then I'll have to sentence you to three months, unless you can offer some explanation.' He paused and looked down at Pat over the top of his half-moon spectacles. 'Do you wish to make a statement?' he asked.

'Three months is not enough, m'lord.'

'I am not a lord,' said Mr Perkins firmly.

'Oh, aren't you?' said Pat. 'It's just that I thought as you were wearing a wig, which you didn't have this time last year, you must be a lord.'

'Watch your tongue,' said Mr Perkins, 'or I may have to consider putting your sentence up to six months.'

'That's more like it, m'lord,' said Pat.

'If that's more like it,' said Mr Perkins, barely able to control his temper, 'then I sentence you to six months. Take the prisoner down.'

'Thank you, m'lord,' said Pat, and added under his breath, 'see you this time next year.'

The bailiff hustled Pat out of the dock and quickly down the stairs to the basement.

'Nice one, Pat,' he said before locking him back up in a holding cell.

Pat remained in the holding cell while he waited for all the necessary forms to be filled in. Several hours passed before the cell door was finally opened and he was escorted out of the courthouse to his waiting transport; not on this occasion a panda car driven by Sergeant Webster, but a long blue-and-white van with a dozen tiny cubicles inside, known as the sweat box.

'Where are they taking me this time?' Pat asked a not very communicative officer whom he'd never seen before.

'You'll find out when you get there, Paddy,' was all he got in reply.

'Have I ever told you about the time I tried to get a job on a building site in Liverpool?'

'No,' replied the officer, 'and I don't want to 'ear—'

'—and the foreman, a bloody Englishman, had the nerve to ask me if I knew the difference between a—' Pat was shoved up the steps of the van and pushed into a little cubicle that resembled a lavatory on a plane. He fell onto the plastic seat as the door was slammed behind him.

Pat stared out of the tiny square window, and when the vehicle turned south onto Baker Street, realized it had to be Belmarsh. Pat sighed. At least they've got a half-decent library, he thought, and I may even be able to get back my old job in the kitchen.

When the Black Maria pulled up outside the prison gates, his guess was confirmed. A large green board attached to the prison gate announced BELMARSH, and some wag had replaced BEL with HELL. The van proceeded through one set of double-barred gates, and then another, before finally coming to a halt in a barren yard.

Twelve prisoners were herded out of the van and marched up the steps to an induction area, where they waited in line. Pat smiled when he reached the front of the queue and saw who was behind the desk, checking them all in.

'And how are we this fine pleasant evening, Mr Jenkins?' Pat asked.

The Senior Officer looked up from behind his desk and said, 'It can't be October already.'

'It most certainly is, Mr Jenkins,' Pat confirmed, 'and may I offer my commiserations on your recent loss.'

'My recent loss,' repeated Mr Jenkins. 'What are you talking about, Pat?'

'Those fifteen Welshmen who appeared in Dublin earlier this year, passing themselves off as a rugby team.'

'Don't push your luck, Pat.'

'Would I, Mr Jenkins, when I was hoping that you would allocate me my old cell?'

The SO ran his finger down the list of available cells. ''Fraid not, Pat,' he said with an exaggerated sigh, 'it's already double-booked. But I've got just the person for you to spend your first night with,' he added, before turning to the night officer. 'Why don't you escort O'Flynn to cell one nineteen.'

The night officer looked uncertain, but after a further look from Mr Jenkins, all he said was, 'Follow me, Pat.'

'So who has Mr Jenkins selected to be my pad mate on this occasion?' enquired Pat, as the night officer accompanied him down the long, grey-brick corridor before coming to a halt at the first set of double-barred gates. 'Is it to be Jack the Ripper, or Michael Jackson?'

'You'll find out soon enough,' responded the night officer as the second of the barred gates slid open.

'Have I ever told you,' asked Pat, as they walked out on to the ground floor of B block, 'about the time I tried to get a job on a building site in Liverpool, and the foreman, a bloody Englishman, had the nerve to ask me if I knew the difference between a joist and a girder?'

Pat waited for the officer to respond, as they came to a halt outside cell number 119. He placed a large key in the lock.

'No, Pat, you haven't,' the night officer said as he pulled open the heavy door. 'So what is the difference between a ist and a girder?' he demanded.

Pat was about to reply, but when he looked into the cell s momentarily silenced.

'Good evening, m'lord,' said Pat, for the second time that day. The night officer didn't wait for a reply. He slammed the door closed, and turned the key in the lock.

Pat spent the rest of the evening telling me, in graphic detail, all that had taken place since two o'clock that morning. When he had finally come to the end of his tale, I simply asked, 'Why October?'

'Once the clocks go back,' said Pat, 'I prefer to be inside, where I'm guaranteed three meals a day and a cell with central heating. Sleeping rough is all very well in the summer, but it's not so clever during an English winter.'

'But what would you have done if Mr Perkins had sentenced you to a year?' I asked.

'I'd have been on my best behaviour from day one,' said Pat, 'and they would have released me in six months. They have a real problem with overcrowding at the moment,' he explained.

'But if Mr Perkins had stuck to his original sentence of

just three months, you would have been released in January, mid-winter.'

'Not a hope,' said Pat. 'Just before I was due to be let out, I would have been found with a bottle of Guinness in my cell. A misdemeanour for which the governor is obliged to automatically add a further three months to your sentence, and that would have taken me comfortably through to April.'

I laughed. 'And is that how you intend to spend the rest of your life?' I asked.

'I don't think that far ahead,' admitted Pat. 'Six months is quite enough to be going on with,' he added, as he climbed on to the top bunk and switched off the light.

'Goodnight, Pat,' I said, as I rested my head on the pillow.

'Have I ever told you about the time I tried to get a job on a building site in Liverpool?' asked Pat, just as I was falling asleep.

'No, you haven't,' I replied.

'Well, the foreman, a bloody Englishman, no offence intended –' I smiled – 'had the nerve to ask me if I knew the difference between a joist and a girder.'

'And do you?' I asked.

'I most certainly do. Joyce wrote *Ulysses*, and Goethe wrote *Faust*.'

Patrick O'Flynn died of hypothermia on 23 November 2005, while sleeping under the arches on Victoria Embankment in central London.

His body was discovered by a young constable, just a hundred yards away from the Savoy Hotel.

The Red King

'THEY CHARGED ME with the wrong offence, and sentenced me for the wrong crime,' Max said as he lay in the bunk below me, rolling another cigarette.

While I was in prison, I heard this claim voiced by inmates on several occasions, but in the case of Max Glover it turned out to be true.

Max was serving a three-year sentence for obtaining money by false pretences. Not his game. Max's speciality was removing small items from large homes. He once told me, with considerable professional pride, that it could be years before an owner became aware that a family heirloom has gone missing, especially, Max added, if you take one small, but valuable, object from a cluttered room.

'Mind you,' continued Max, 'I'm not complaining, because if they had charged me with the crime I did commit, I would have ended up with a much longer sentence –' he paused – 'and nothing to look forward to once I'm released.'

Max knew he had aroused my curiosity, and as I had nowhere to go for the next three hours before the cell door would be opened for Association – that glorious forty-five minutes when prisoners are allowed out of their cell for a stroll around the yard – I picked up my pen, and said, 'OK, Max, I'm hooked. So tell me how you came to be sentenced for the wrong crime.'

Max struck a match, lit his hand-rolled cigarette and inhaled deeply before he began. In prison, every action is exaggerated, as no one is in a hurry. I lay on the bunk above and waited patiently.

'Does the Kennington Set mean anything to you?' Max began.

'No,' I replied, assuming he must be referring to a group of red-coated gentlemen on horseback, glass of port in one hand, whip in the other, surrounded by a pack of hounds with intent to spend their Saturday morning in pursuit of a furry animal with a bushy tail. I was wrong. The Kennington Set, as Max went on to explain, was in fact a chess set.

'But no ordinary chess set,' he assured me. I became more interested. The pieces were probably crafted by Lu Ping (1469–1540), a master craftsman of the Ming Dynasty (1368–1644). All thirty-two ivory pieces were exquisitely carved and then delicately painted in red and white. The details have been faithfully recorded in several historic documents, though it has never been conclusively established exactly how many sets Lu Ping was responsible for producing in his lifetime.

'Three complete sets were known to be in existence,' continued Max as smoke spiralled up from the lower bunk. 'The first is displayed in the throne room of the People's Palace in Peking; the second in the Mellon Collection in Washington, and the third at the British Museum. Many collectors scoured the great continent of China in search of the fabled fourth set, and although such efforts always ended in failure, several individual pieces appeared on the market from time to time.'

Max stubbed out the smallest cigarette butt I have ever seen. 'I was at the time,' continued Max, 'carrying out some research into the smaller objects of Kennington Hall in Yorkshire.'

'How did you manage that?' I asked.

'*Country Life* commissioned Lord Kennington to write a coffee-table book for Christmas, in which he detailed the treasures of Kennington Hall,' Max said, before rolling a second cigarette. 'Most considerate of him,' he added.

'Among the peer's ancestors was one James Kennington (1552–1618), a true adventurer, buccaneer, and loyal servant of Queen Elizabeth I. James rescued the first set in 1588, only moments before he sunk the *Isabella*. On returning to Plymouth, following a seventeen–four victory in the match against the Spanish, Captain Kennington lavished treasure plundered from the sinking ship on his monarch. Her Majesty always showed a great deal of interest in anything solid, especially if she could wear it – gold, silver, pearls or rare gems – and rewarded Captain Kennington with a knighthood. Elizabeth had no use for the chess set, so Sir James was stuck with it. Unlike Sir Francis or Sir Walter, Sir James continued to plunder the high seas. He was so successful that, a decade later, his monarch elevated him to the House of Lords, with the title the first Lord Kennington, for services rendered to the Crown.' Max paused before adding, 'The only difference between a pirate and a peer is who you divide the spoils with.'

The second Lord Kennington, like his monarch, showed no interest in chess, so the set was left to gather dust in one of the ninety-two rooms in Kennington Hall. As there were few historical incidents worthy of mention during the uneventful lives of the third, fourth, fifth or sixth Lords Kennington, we can only assume that the remarkable chess set remained in situ, its pieces never moved in anger. The seventh Lord Kennington served as a colonel in the 12th Light Dragoons at the time of Waterloo. The colonel played the occasional game of chess, so the set was dusted down and returned to the Long Gallery.

The eighth Lord Kennington was slaughtered during the Charge of the Light Brigade, the ninth in the Boer War, and the tenth at Ypres. The eleventh, a playboy, led a more peaceful life, but eventually found it necessary, for pecuniary reasons – Kennington Hall required a new roof – to open his home to the public. They turned up every weekend in countless numbers, and for a small sum were allowed to stroll around the Hall; when they ventured into the Long Gallery they came across the Chinese masterpiece on its stand, surrounded by a red rope.

With mounting debts, which the public's entrance fees could not offset, the eleventh Lord Kennington was forced to sell off several of the family heirlooms, including the Kennington Set.

Christie's placed an estimate of £100,000 on the masterpiece, but the auctioneer's hammer finally fell at £230,000.

'When you next visit Washington,' added Max between puffs, 'you can view the original Kennington Set, as it's now part of the Mellon Collection. This would have been the end of my tale,' continued Max, 'if the eleventh Lord Kennington hadn't married an American striptease artiste, who gave birth to a son. This child displayed a quality that the Kennington lineage had not troubled themselves with for several generations – brains.

'The Hon. Harry Kennington became, much to the disapproval of his father, a hedge-fund manager, and thus the natural heir to the first Lord Kennington. He was a man who took as easily to the currency market as his pirate ancestor had to the high seas. By the age of twenty-seven, Harry had plundered his first million as an asset stripper, much to his mother's amusement, who suggested that stripping was clearly a hereditary trait. By the time Harry inherited the title he was chairman of Kennington's Bank. The first thing he did with his new-found wealth was to set about restoring Kennington Hall to its former glory. He certainly did not allow members of the public to pay five pounds to park their cars on his front lawn.

'The twelfth Lord Kennington, like his father, also married a remarkable woman. Elsie Trumpshaw was the offspring of a Yorkshire cotton mill proprietor, and the product of a Cheltenham Ladies' College education. Like any self-respecting Yorkshire lass, Elsie considered the saying, *If you take care of the pennies, the pounds will take care of themselves* to be a creed, not a cliché.

'While her husband was away making money, Elsie was unquestionably the mistress of Kennington Hall. Having spent her formative years wearing her elder sister's hand-me-downs, carrying her thumbed books to school and later borrowing her lipstick, whatever the colour, Elsie was well qualified to be the guardian of a hereditary pile. With consummate skill, diligence and good housekeeping, she set about the maintenance and upkeep of the newly restored Hall. Although she had no interest in the game of chess, she was irritated by the empty display cabinet in the Long Gallery. She finally solved the problem while strolling around a local car-boot sale,' said Max, 'and at the same time changed the fortunes of so many people, myself included.' Max stubbed out his second cigarette and I was relieved that he didn't immediately roll another, as our little cell was fast coming to resemble Paddington Station in the era of the steam engine.

※ ※ ※

Elsie was trudging around a car-boot sale in Pudsey on a rainy Sunday morning – she only ever attended such events when it was raining, as that ensured fewer customers and it was therefore easier for her to strike a bargain. She was rummaging through some clothes when she came across the chessboard. The red and white squares brought back memories of a photograph she had seen in the old Christie's catalogue, dating from when the original set had been sold. Elsie bargained for some time with the man standing at the back of an ancient Jaguar, and ended up having to part with £23 for the ivory chessboard.

When Elsie returned to the Hall, she placed the newly acquired board in the empty display cabinet and was delighted to discover that it was a perfect fit. She thought nothing more of the coincidence, until her uncle Bertie advised her to have it valued – for insurance purposes, he explained.

Unconvinced, but unwilling to slight her uncle, Elsie took the board up to London on one of her monthly trips to visit her aunt Gertrude. Lady Kennington – she was always Lady Kennington in London – dropped into Sotheby's on her way to Fortnum & Mason. A young assistant in the Chinese department asked if her ladyship would be kind enough to come back later that afternoon, by which time their expert would have placed a value on the board.

Elsie returned to Sotheby's after a leisurely lunch with Aunt Gertrude. She was greeted by a Mr Sencill, the head of the Chinese department, who offered the opinion that the piece was unquestionably Ming Dynasty.

'And are you able to place a value on it –' she paused – 'for insurance purposes?'

'Two thousand, two thousand five hundred, m'lady,' said

Mr Sencill. 'Ming chessboards are fairly common,' he explained. 'It is the individual pieces that are rare, and a complete set . . .' He raised the palms of his hands and placed them together, as if praying to the unseen God of auctioneers. 'Are you perhaps considering selling the board?' he enquired.

'No,' replied Elsie firmly. 'On the contrary, I'm thinking of adding to it.'

The expert smiled. After all, Sotheby's is nothing more than a glorified pawn shop, with each generation of the aristocracy either buying or selling.

On arriving back at Kennington Hall, Elsie returned the board to its position of honour in the drawing room.

Aunt Gertrude set the ball rolling. On Christmas Day she presented her niece with a white pawn. Elsie placed the single piece on the empty board. It looked lonely.

'And now, my dear, you must see if you can complete the set in your lifetime,' the old lady challenged, unaware of the chain of events she was about to set in motion. What had begun as a whim, while attending a car-boot sale in Pudsey, turned into an obsession, as Elsie began to search the globe for the missing pieces. The first Lord Kennington would have been proud of her.

When Lady Kennington gave birth to their first son, Edward, a grateful husband presented his wife with a white queen. A magnificently sculptured ivory lady adorned in a long, intricately carved royal gown. Her Majesty stared down with disdain on the single pawn.

The next acquisition was another white pawn, acquired by Uncle Bertie from a dealer in New York. This allowed the white queen to reign over two of her subjects.

The birth of a second son, James, was rewarded with a

red bishop, resplendent in a flowing surplice and carrying a shepherd's crook. The queen and her two subjects were now able to celebrate Holy Communion, even if they had to travel to the other side of the board to do so. Soon the whole family began to join in the search for the missing pieces. A red pawn was the next acquisition, when it came under the auctioneer's hammer at Bonham's. He took up his place on the far side of the board, waiting to be taken. By now, everyone in the trade was only too aware of Lady Kennington's lifetime mission.

Next to find its place on the board was a white castle, which Aunt Gertrude left Elsie in her will.

In 1991 the twelfth Lord Kennington passed away, by which time the white set was lacking only two pawns and a knight, while the red set was short of four pawns, one rook and a king.

On 11 May 1992, a dealer in possession of three red pawns and a white knight knocked on the door of Kennington Hall. He had recently returned from a journey through the outer regions of China. A long and arduous trek, he told her ladyship. But, he assured her, he had not returned empty-handed.

Although her ladyship was in her declining years, she still held out for several days, before the dealer finally settled his bill at the Kennington Arms and left clutching a cheque for £26,000.

Despite following up rumours from Hong Kong, flying to Boston, contacting dealers as far afield as Moscow and Mexico, rumour rarely became reality in Lady Kennington's unremitting search for the last of the missing pieces.

During the next few years, Edward, the thirteenth Lord

Kennington, came across the last red pawn and a red rook in the home of a penniless peer, who had been on the same staircase as Eddie at Eton. His brother James, not to be out-done, acquired two white pawns from a dealer in Bangkok.

This left only the red king to be unearthed.

The family had for some time been paying well over the odds for any missing pieces, since every dealer across the globe was well aware that if Lady Kennington was able to complete the set it would be worth a fortune.

When Elsie entered her ninth decade, she informed her

sons that on her demise she planned to divide the estate equally between the two of them, with one proviso. She intended to bequeath the chess set to whichever one of them found the missing red king.

Elsie died at the age of eighty-three, without her king.

Edward had already acquired the title – something you can't dispose of in a will – and now, after death duties, also inherited the Hall and a further £857,000. James moved into the Cadogan Square apartment, and also received the sum of £857,000. The Kennington Set remained in its display case for all to admire, one square still unoccupied, ownership unresolved. Enter Max Glover.

Max had one undisputed gift, his ability to wield a willow. Educated at one of England's minor public schools, his talent as a stylish left-handed batsman allowed him to mix with the very people that he would later rob. After all, a chap who can score an effortless half century is obviously somebody one can trust.

Away fixtures suited Max best, as they allowed him the opportunity to meet eleven potential new victims. Kennington Village XI was no exception. By the time his lordship had joined the two teams for tea in the pavilion, Max had wormed out of the local umpire the history of the Kennington Set, including the provision in the will that whichever son came up with the missing red king would automatically inherit the complete set.

Max boldly asked his lordship, while devouring a portion of Victoria sponge, if he might be allowed to view the Kennington Set, as he was fascinated by the game of chess. Lord Kennington was only too happy to invite a man with such an effortless cover drive into his drawing room.

The moment Max spotted the empty square, a plan began to form in his mind. A few well-planted questions were indiscreetly answered by his host. Max avoided making any reference to his lordship's brother, or the clause in the will. He then spent the rest of the afternoon at square leg, refining his plan. He dropped two catches.

When the match was over, Max declined an invitation to join the rest of the team at the village pub, explaining that he had urgent business in London.

Moments after arriving back at his flat in Hammersmith, Max phoned an old lag he'd shared a pad with when he'd been locked up in a previous establishment. The former inmate assured Max that he could deliver, but it would take him about a month and 'would cost 'im'.

Max chose a Sunday afternoon to return to Kennington Hall and continue his research. He left his ancient MG – soon to become a collector's item, he tried to convince himself – in the visitors' carpark. He followed signs to the front door, where he handed over five pounds in exchange for an entrance ticket. Maintenance and running costs had once again made it necessary for the Hall to be opened to the public at weekends.

Max walked purposefully down a long corridor adorned with ancestral portraits painted by such luminaries as Romney, Gainsborough, Lely and Stubbs. Each would have fetched a fortune on the open market, but Max's eyes were set on a far smaller object, currently residing in the Long Gallery.

When Max entered the room that displayed the Kennington Set, he found the masterpiece surrounded by an attentive group of visitors who were being addressed by a tour guide. Max stood at the back of the crowd and listened to a tale he knew only too well. He waited patiently for the group to move on to the dining room and admire the family silver.

'Several pieces were captured at the time of the Armada,' the tour guide intoned as the group followed him into an adjoining room.

Max looked back down the corridor to check that the next group was not about to descend upon him. He placed a hand in his pocket and withdrew the red king. Other than the colour, the intricately carved piece was identical in every detail to the white king standing on the opposite side of the board. Max knew the counterfeit would not pass a carbon-dating test, but he was satisfied that he was in possession of a perfect copy. He left Kennington Hall a few minutes later, and drove back to London.

Max's next problem was to decide which city would have the most relaxed security to carry out his coup: London, Washington or Peking. The People's Palace in Peking won by a short head. However, when it came to considering the cost of the whole exercise, the British Museum was the only horse left in the race. But what finally tipped the balance for Max was the thought of spending the next five years locked up in a Chinese jail, an American penitentiary, or residing at an open prison in the east of England. England won in a canter.

The following morning Max visited the British Museum for the first time in his life. The lady seated behind the information desk directed him to the back of the ground floor, where the Chinese collection is housed.

Max discovered that hundreds of Chinese artefacts occupied the fifteen rooms, and it took him the best part of an hour to locate the chess set. He had considered seeking guidance from one of the uniformed guards, but as he had no desire to draw attention to himself, and also doubted that they would be able to answer his question, he thought better of it.

Max had to hang around for some time before he was left alone in the room. He could not afford a member of the public or, worse, a guard, to witness his little subterfuge. Max noted that the security guard covered four rooms every thirty minutes. He would therefore have to wait until the guard had departed for the Islam room, while at the same time being sure that no other visitors were in sight, before he could make his move.

It was another hour before Max felt confident enough to take the bastard out of his pocket and compare the piece with the legitimate king, standing proudly on its red square in the display cabinet. The two kings stared at each other, identical twins, except that one was an impostor. Max glanced around – the room was still empty. After all, it was eleven o'clock on a Tuesday morning, half term, and the sun was shining.

Max waited until the guard had moved on to Islamic artefacts before he carried out his well-rehearsed move. With the help of a Swiss Army knife, he carefully prised open the lid of the display cabinet that covered the Chinese master-piece. A raucous alarm immediately sounded, but long before the first guard appeared, Max had switched the two kings, replaced the cover of the case, opened a window and strolled casually into the next room. He was studying the costume of a samurai when two guards rushed into the adjoining room. One cursed when he spotted the open win-dow, while the other checked to see if anything was missing.

'Now, you'll want to know,' suggested Max, clearly enjoying himself, 'how I trapped both brothers into a fool's mate.' I nodded, but he didn't speak again until he'd rolled another cigarette. 'To start with,' continued Max, 'never rush a transaction when you're in possession of something *two* buyers want, and in this case, *desperately* want. My next visit –' he paused to light his cigarette – 'was to a shop in the Charing Cross Road. This had not required a great deal of research, because they advertised themselves in the *Yellow Pages* under Chess, as Marlowe's, *the people who serve the masters and advise the beginners.*'

Max stepped into the musty old shop, to be greeted by an elderly gentleman who resembled one of life's pawns: some-one who took the occasional move forward, but still looked as if he must eventually be taken – certainly not the type who reached the other side of the board to become a king. Max asked the old man about a chess set that he had spotted in the window. There then followed a series of well-rehearsed questions, which casually led to the value of a red king in the Kennington Set.

'Were such a piece ever to come onto the market,' the elderly assistant mused, 'the price could be in excess of fifty thousand pounds, as everyone knows there are two certain bidders.'

It was this piece of information that caused Max to make a few adjustments to his plan. His next problem was that he knew his bank account wouldn't stretch to a visit to New York. He ended up having to 'acquire' several small objects from large houses, which could be disposed of quickly, so he could visit the States with enough capital to put his plan into effect. Luckily it was in the middle of the cricket season.

When Max landed at JFK, he didn't bother to visit Sotheby's or Christie's, but instead instructed the yellow cab to drive him to Phillips Auctioneers on East 79th Street. He was relieved to find that, when he produced the delicate carving stolen from the British Museum, the young assistant didn't show a great deal of interest in the piece.

'Are you aware of its provenance?' asked the assistant.

'No,' replied Max, 'it's been in my family for years.'

Six weeks later a sales catalogue was published. Max was delighted to find that Lot 23 was listed as being of no known provenance, with a high value of $300. As it was not one of the items graced with a photograph, Max felt confident that few, if any, would take much interest in the red king, and it would therefore be unlikely to come to the attention of either Edward or James Kennington. That is, until he made them aware of it.

A week before the sale was due to take place, Max rang Phillips in New York. He had only one question for the young assistant, who replied that although the catalogue had been available for over a month, no one had shown any par- ticular interest in his red king. Max feigned disappointment.

The next call Max made was to Kennington Hall. He tempted his lordship with several ifs, buts and even a maybe, which elicited an invitation to join Lord Kennington for lunch at White's.

Lord Kennington explained to his guest over a bowl of brown Windsor soup that Max could not produce any papers over lunch as it was against the club rules. Max nodded, placed the Phillips catalogue under his chair, and began an elaborate tale of how by sheer accident, while viewing the figure of a mandarin on behalf of a client, he had come across the red king.

'I would have missed it myself,' said Max, 'if you hadn't acquainted me with its history.'

Lord Kennington did not bother with pudding (bread and butter), cheese (Cheddar) or biscuits (water), but suggested they took coffee in the library, where you are allowed to discuss business.

Max opened the Phillips catalogue to reveal Lot 23, along with several loose photographs he had not shown the auctioneer. When Lord Kennington saw the estimate of three hundred dollars, his next question was, 'Do you think Phillips might have told my brother about the sale?'

'There is no reason to believe so,' replied Max. 'I've been assured by one of the assistants working on the sale that the public have shown little interest in lot twenty-three.'

'But how can you be so sure of its provenance?'

'That's what I do for a living,' said Max with confidence. 'But you can always have the piece carbon-dated, and if I'm proved wrong, you won't have to pay for it.'

'Can't ask for more than that,' said Lord Kennington, 'so

I suppose I'll have to fly to America and bid for the piece myself,' he added, thumping the arm of the leather chair. A cloud of elderly dust rose into the air.

'I wonder if that would be wise, my lord,' said Max, 'after all—'

'And why not?' demanded Kennington.

'It's just that, if you were to fly to the States without explanation, it might arouse unnecessary curiosity among certain members of your family,' Max paused, 'and if you were then spotted in an auction house . . . '

'I take your point,' said Kennington, and looking across at Max added, 'so what do you advise, old boy?'

'I would be only too happy to represent your lordship's interests,' said Max.

'And what would you charge for such a service?' Lord Kennington enquired.

'One thousand pounds plus expenses,' said Max, 'against two and a half per cent of the hammer price, which I can assure you is standard practice.'

Lord Kennington removed his chequebook from an inside pocket and wrote out the figure £1,000. 'How much do you estimate the piece might fetch?' he asked casually.

Max was pleased that Lord Kennington had raised the subject of price, as it would have been his next question. 'That will depend on whether anyone else is privy to our little secret,' said Max. 'However, I would suggest that you place an upper limit of fifty thousand dollars on the piece.'

'Fifty thousand?' spluttered Kennington in disbelief.

'Hardly excessive,' suggested Max, 'remembering that a complete set could fetch more than a million –' he paused – 'or nothing, were your brother to acquire the red king.'

THE NEW COLLECTED SHORT STORIES

'I take your point,' repeated Kennington. 'But you still might be able to pick it up for a few hundred dollars.'

'Let's hope so,' said Max.

Max Glover left White's Club a few minutes after three, explaining to his host that he had another appointment that afternoon, which indeed he did.

Max checked his watch and decided he still had enough time to stroll through Green Park and not be late for his next meeting.

Max arrived in Sloane Square a few minutes before four, and took a seat on a bench opposite the statue of Sir Francis Drake. He began to rehearse his new script. When he heard the clock on a nearby tower chime four times, he leapt up and walked briskly across to Cadogan Square. He stopped at No 16, climbed the steps, and rang the doorbell.

James Kennington opened the door and greeted his guest with a smile.

'I rang earlier this morning,' explained Max. 'My name's Glover.'

James Kennington ushered him through to the drawing room and offered Max a seat by an unlit fire. The younger brother took the seat opposite him.

Although the apartment was spacious, even grand, there were one or two clear outlines on the walls to suggest where pictures had once hung. Max suspected that they were not being cleaned or reframed. Gossip columns regularly referred to the Hon. James's drinking habits and hinted at several unpaid gambling debts.

When Max came to the end of his tale, he was well prepared for the Hon. James's first question.

'How much do you imagine the piece will fetch, Mr Glover?'

'A few hundred dollars,' Max replied. 'That's assuming your brother doesn't find out about the auction.' He paused, sipped his tea, and added, 'In excess of fifty thousand, if he does.'

'But I don't have fifty thousand,' said James, something else Max was well aware of. 'And if my brother were to find out,' James continued, 'there would be nothing I could do about it. The terms of the will couldn't be clearer – whoever finds the red king inherits the set.'

'I'd be willing to put up the necessary capital to secure the piece,' said Max, not missing a beat, 'if in turn you would then agree to sell me the set.'

'And how much would you be willing to pay?' asked James.

'Half a million,' said Max.

'But Sotheby's have already valued a complete set at over a million,' protested James.

'That may well be the case,' said Max, 'but half a million is surely better than nothing, which would be the outcome if your brother were to learn of the red king's existence.'

'But you said that the red king might sell for a few hundred—'

'In which case, I would require only a thousand pounds in advance, against two and a half per cent of the hammer price,' said Max for the second time that afternoon.

'That's a risk I am quite willing to take,' said James with the smile of someone who believes he has gained the upper hand. 'If the red king should sell for less than fifty thousand,' he continued, 'I'd be able to raise the money myself. If it goes for more than fifty thousand, you can purchase the piece and I'll sell you the set for half a million.' James sipped his tea, before adding, 'I can't lose either way.'

Neither can I, thought Max, as he extracted a contract from an inside pocket. James read the document slowly. He looked up and said, 'You obviously felt confident that I would fall in with your plan, Mr Glover.'

'If you hadn't,' said Max, 'my next visit would have been to your brother, which would have left you with nothing. At least now, to quote you, you can't lose either way.'

'Presumably I will have to travel to New York,' said James.

'Not necessary,' replied Max. 'You can bid for the piece by phone, which has the added advantage that no one else will know who's on the other end of the line.'

'But how do I go about that?' asked James.

'It couldn't be easier,' Max assured him. 'The New York sale begins at two in the afternoon, which will be seven o'clock in the evening in London. The red king is lot twenty-three, so I'll arrange for Phillips to place a call through to you once they reach lot twenty-one. Just be sure you're sitting by the phone, with no one else blocking the line.'

'And you'll take over, if it goes above fifty thousand?'

'You have my word,' said Max, looking him straight in the eye.

Max flew to New York the weekend before the sale was due to take place. He booked himself into a small hotel on the East Side and settled for a room not much larger than our cell, but then he only had enough money left over to cover the endgame.

Max rose early on the Monday morning. He hadn't been able to sleep because of an orchestra of New York traffic and police sirens. He used the time to go over and over the different permutations that might occur once the sale began.

He would be on centre stage for less than two minutes and, if he failed, would be back on the next plane to Heathrow, with nothing to show for his efforts other than an overdrawn bank account.

He grabbed a bagel on the corner of Third and 66th, before walking another few blocks to Phillips. He spent the rest of the morning at a manuscript sale that was being held in the room where the Chinese auction would take place. He sat silently at the back of the room, watching how the Americans conduct an auction, so that he wouldn't be wrong-footed later that afternoon.

Max didn't eat any lunch, and not just because his meagre funds were already stretched to their limit. Instead, he used the time to make two overseas calls; the first to Lord Kennington, to confirm that he still had his authority to take the bidding for the red king up to fifty thousand dollars. Max assured him that, the moment the hammer fell, he would call to let him know what sum the piece had sold for. A few minutes later Max made a second call, this time to the Hon. James Kennington at his home in Cadogan Square. James picked up the phone after one ring, clearly relieved to hear Max's voice on the other end of the line. Max made the Hon. James Kennington exactly the same promise.

Max replaced the phone and made his way across to the bidding counter, where he gave an assistant the details of James Kennington's telephone number in London and told her of his intention to bid for Lot 23.

'Leave it to us, sir,' the assistant replied. 'I'll make sure we're in touch with him well in time.'

Max thanked the assistant, made his way back to the sale-room and took his favoured place on the end of the eighth row, just to the right of the auctioneer. He began to turn the pages of the catalogue, checking on items in which he had no interest. While he sat around, impatiently waiting for the auctioneer to invite bids for lot number one, he tried to work out who were the dealers, who the serious bidders and who the simply curious.

By the time the auctioneer climbed the steps of the rostrum at five minutes to two, the saleroom was full of expectant faces. At two o'clock the auctioneer smiled down at his clientele.

'Lot number one,' he declared, 'a delicately crafted ivory fisherman.'

The piece sold for $850, giving no hint of the drama that was about to follow.

Lot 2 reached $1,000, but it wasn't until Lot 17, the figure of a mandarin bent over a desk reading a ledger, that the $5,000 mark was achieved.

One or two dealers whose only interest was clearly in later lots began to drift into the room, while a couple of others left, having failed or succeeded in acquiring the items they'd been after. Max could hear his heart pounding, although it would still be some time before the auctioneer reached Lot 23.

He turned his attention to the row of phones on a long table by the side of the room. Only three were manned. When the auctioneer called Lot 21, an assistant started to dial. A few moments later, she cupped a hand over the mouthpiece and began to whisper. When Lot 22 was offered, she spoke briefly to her client again. Max assumed that she must be warning James Kennington that the red king would be the next item to come under the hammer.

'Lot twenty-three,' declared the auctioneer glancing down

at his notes. 'An exquisitely carved red king, provenance unknown. Do I have an opening bid of three hundred dollars?'

Max raised his catalogue.

'Five hundred?' enquired the auctioneer turning to face the assistant on the phone. She whispered into the mouthpiece and then nodded firmly. The auctioneer turned his attention back to Max, who had raised his catalogue even before a price had been suggested.

'I have a bid of a thousand dollars,' said the auctioneer, returning to face the telephone bidder. 'Two thousand,' he ventured, surprised to see the assistant nod so quickly.

'Three thousand?' he suggested as he looked back at Max. The catalogue shot up again, and several dealers at the back of the room began chatting among themselves.

'Four thousand?' enquired the auctioneer, staring in disbelief at the assistant on the phone. $5,000, $6,000, $7,000, $8,000, $9,000 and $10,000 were overtaken in less than a minute. The auctioneer tried desperately to look as if this was exactly what he had anticipated as the murmurs in the room grew louder and louder. Everyone seemed to have an opinion. One or two dealers abandoned their favoured places and quickly walked to the back of the room, hoping to find an explanation for the bidding frenzy. Some were already beginning to make assumptions, but were in no position to bid under such pressure, especially as the amounts were now going up in leaps of $5,000.

Max raised his catalogue in response to the auctioneer's enquiry, 'Forty-five thousand? Are you bidding fifty thousand?' he enquired of the lady on the telephone. Everyone in the room turned to see how she would respond. For the first time she hesitated. The auctioneer repeated,

'Fifty thousand.' She whispered the figure into the phone and, after a long pause, nodded, but not quite so enthusiastically.

When Max was offered the piece for $55,000, he also hesitated, taking his time before he finally raised his catalogue.

'Sixty thousand?' suggested the auctioneer to the assistant on the phone. Max waited nervously as she cupped her hand over the mouthpiece and repeated the figure. Beads of sweat began to appear on Max's forehead, as he wondered if James Kennington had managed to raise more than $50,000, in which case he would just about clear his expenses on the whole exercise. After what seemed like an eternity, but was, in fact, only twenty seconds, the assistant shook her head. She put the phone down.

When the auctioneer smiled in Max's direction and said, 'Sold to the gentleman on my left, for fifty-five thousand dollars,' Max felt sick, triumphant, dazed and relieved all at the same time.

Max remained in his place, as he waited for the furore to die down. After a dozen more lots had been disposed of, he slipped quietly out of the room, unaware of the suspicious stares from dealers, who wondered who he was. He strolled across the thick green carpet and stopped at the purchasing counter.

'I wish to leave a deposit on lot twenty-three.'

The clerk looked down at her list. 'A red king,' she said, and double-checked the price. 'Fifty-five thousand dollars,' she added, and looked up at Max for confirmation.

He nodded as the assistant began to fill in the little boxes on the purchasing document. A few moments later she swivelled the form round for Max to sign.

'That will be five thousand, five hundred dollars deposit,' she said, 'and the full amount must be settled within twenty-eight days.' Max nodded nonchalantly, as if this was a procedure he was well familiar with. He signed the agreement and then wrote out a cheque for $5,500, aware that it would empty his account. He pushed it across the counter. The assistant handed him back the top copy of the agreement and retained the duplicate. When she checked the signature, she hesitated. It might have been a coincidence: after all, Glover was a common enough name. She didn't want to insult a customer, but she knew she would have to report the anomaly to their compliance department, before they could consider cashing the cheque.

Max left the auction house and headed north to Park Avenue. He strode confidently into Sotheby Parke Bernet and approached the reception desk. He asked if he could have a word with the Head of the Oriental Department. He was kept waiting for only a few minutes.

On this occasion, Max didn't waste time with any preliminary questions that would have only been a smoke-screen to disguise his true intent. After all, as the sales clerk at Phillips had pointed out, he only had twenty-eight days to complete the transaction.

'Should the Kennington Chess Set come onto the market, what would you expect it to fetch?' Max asked.

The expert looked incredulous, although he had already been briefed on the sale of the red king at Phillips, and on the price the piece had fetched. 'Seven hundred and fifty thousand, possibly as much as a million,' came back the reply.

'And if I was able to deliver the Kennington Set, and you were in a position to authenticate it, what amount would Sotheby's be willing to advance against a future sale?'

'Four hundred thousand, possibly five, if the family were able to confirm that it was the Kennington Set.'

'I'll be in touch,' promised Max, all his immediate and long-term problems solved.

✻ ✢ ✻

Max checked out of his little hotel on the East Side later that evening, and took a taxi to Kennedy Airport. Once the plane had taken off, he slept soundly for the first time in days.

The 727 touched down at Heathrow just as the sun was rising over the Thames. Having nothing to declare, Max took the Heathrow Express to Paddington, and was back in his flat in time for breakfast. He began to fantasize about what it would be like to dine regularly at his favourite restaurant and always hail a taxi, rather than having to wait for the next bus.

Once he'd finished breakfast, Max put the plates in the sink and settled down in the one comfortable chair. He began to consider his next move, confident that now the red king had found its place on the board, the game must end in checkmate.

At eleven o'clock – a proper hour to phone a peer of the realm – Max put a call through to Kennington Hall. When the butler transferred the call to Lord Kennington, his first words were, 'Did we get it?'

'Unfortunately not, my lord,' replied Max. 'We were outbid by an unknown party. I carried out your instructions to the letter, and stopped bidding at fifty thousand dollars.' He paused. 'The hammer price was fifty-five thousand.'

There was a long silence. 'Do you think the other bidder could have been my brother?'

'I've no way of knowing,' replied Max. 'All I can tell you is that they were bidding by phone, no doubt wishing to ensure their anonymity.'

'I'll find out soon enough,' responded Kennington, before hanging up.

'You certainly will,' agreed Max as he began to dial a number in Chelsea.

'Congratulations,' said Max the moment he heard the Hon. James's plummy voice. 'I've purchased the piece, so you're now in a position to claim your inheritance, under the terms of the will.'

'Well done, Glover,' said James Kennington.

'And the moment you deliver the rest of the set, my

lawyers have been instructed to hand over a cheque for four hundred and forty-five thousand dollars,' said Max.

'But we agreed on half a million,' snapped James.

'Minus the fifty-five thousand I had to pay for the red king.' Max paused. 'You'll find it's all spelled out in the contract.'

'But—' James began to protest.

'Would you prefer me to call your brother?' Max asked, as the front door bell rang. 'Because I'm still in possession of the piece.' James didn't immediately reply. 'Think about it,' added Max, 'while I answer the front door.' Max placed the receiver on the side table, and strolled out into the hall, almost rubbing his hands. He released the chain, undid the Yale lock, and pulled the door open a couple of inches. Two tall men wearing identical trench coats stood in front of him.

'Max Victor Glover?' enquired one of them.

'Who wants to know?' asked Max.

'I'm Detective Inspector Armitage of the Fraud Squad, and this is Detective Sergeant Willis.' They both produced warrant cards, with which Max was only too familiar. 'May we come in, sir?'

Once the police had taken down Max's statement, which consisted of little more than, 'I'll need to speak to my solicitor,' the two men departed. They then drove up to Yorkshire for a meeting with Lord Kennington. Having obtained a detailed statement from his lordship, they returned to London to interview his brother James. The police found him just as cooperative.

A week later Max was arrested for fraud. The judge took into account his past blemished record, and did not grant bail.

'But how did they find out that you'd stolen the red king?'
I asked.

'They didn't,' Max replied as he stubbed out his cigarette.

I put my pen down. 'I'm not sure I understand,' I
murmured from the upper bunk.

'And neither did I,' admitted Max, 'at least not until they
charged me.' I remained silent, as my pad mate began to roll
his next cigarette. 'When they read out the charge sheet,' he
continued, ' no one was more surprised than me.

'"Max Victor Glover, you are charged with attempting
to obtain money by false pretences. Namely that on October
seventeenth, two thousand, you bid fifty-five thousand
dollars for a red king, lot twenty-three at Phillips auctioneers in New York, while enticing other interested parties to
bid against you, without informing them that you were the
owner of the piece."'

A heavy key turned in the lock and our cell door cranked
open.

'Visits,' bellowed the wing officer.

'So you see,' said Max as he swung his legs off the bunk,
'I was charged with the wrong offence, and sentenced for
the wrong crime.'

'But why go through such an elaborate charade, when
you could have sold the red king to either of the brothers?'

'Because then I would have had to show them how I
got hold of the piece in the first place, and if I had been
caught . . .'

'But you were caught.'

'But not charged with theft,' Max reminded me.

'So what happened to the red king?' I demanded, as we
stepped out into the corridor and made our way across to
the visits centre.

'It was returned to my solicitor after the trial,' said Max, 'and locked up in his safe, where it will remain until I'm released.'

'But that means—' I began.

'Have you ever met Lord Kennington?' Max asked casually.

'No, I haven't,' I replied.

'Then I'll introduce you, old boy,' he mimicked, 'because he's coming to visit me this afternoon.' Max paused. 'I have a feeling that his lordship is about to make me an offer for the red king.'

'And will you accept his offer?' I asked.

'Steady on, Jeff,' Max replied as we entered the visits room. 'I won't be able to answer that question until next week, when I've had a visit from his brother James.'

The Wisdom Of Solomon

'MIND YOUR OWN business,' was Carol's advice.

'But it is my business,' I reminded my wife as I climbed into bed. 'Bob and I have been friends for over twenty years.'

'All the more reason to keep your own counsel,' she insisted.

'But I don't like her,' I replied tartly.

'You made that abundantly clear during dinner,' Carol reminded me as she switched off her bedside light.

'But surely you can see that it's going to end in tears.'

'Then you'll just have to buy a large box of Kleenex.'

'She's only after his money,' I muttered.

'He hasn't got any,' replied Carol. 'Bob's practice is quite successful, but hardly puts him in the Abramovich league.'

'That may well be the case, but it's still my duty, as a friend, to warn him not to marry her.'

'He doesn't want to hear that at the moment,' said Carol, 'so don't even think about it.'

'Explain to me, O wise one,' I said as I plumped up my pillow, 'why not.'

Carol ignored my sarcasm. 'If it should end up in the divorce courts, you'll just look smug. If the marriage turns out to be wedded bliss, he'll never forgive you – and neither will she.'

'I wasn't planning to tell her.'

'She already knows exactly how you feel about her,' said Carol. 'Believe me.'

'It won't last a year,' I predicted, just as the phone rang

on my side of the bed. I picked it up, praying it wasn't a patient.

'I've only got one question for you,' said a voice that needed no introduction.

'And what's that, Bob?' I asked.

'Will you be my best man?'

Bob Radford and I first met at St Thomas' Hospital when we were both house officers. To be more accurate, we had first come into contact with each other on the rugby field, when he tackled me just as I thought I was about to score the winning try. In those days we were on opposite sides.

After we were appointed senior house officers at Guy's, we started playing for the same rugby team and regularly had a mid-week game of squash – which he invariably won. In our final year we ended up sharing digs in Lambeth. We didn't need to look far for female companionship as St Thomas' had over three thousand nurses, most of whom wanted sex and for some unfathomable reason considered doctors a safe bet. Both of us looked forward to taking advantage of our new status. And then I fell in love.

Carol was also a house officer at Guy's, and on our first date made it abundantly clear that she wasn't looking for a long-term relationship. However, she underestimated my one talent, persistence. She finally gave in after I'd proposed for the ninth time. Carol and I were married a few months after she'd qualified.

Bob headed off in the opposite direction. Whenever we invited him to dinner, he would turn up escorted by a new companion. I sometimes got their names muddled up, a mistake Carol never made. However, as the years passed, even Bob's appetite to taste some new delicacy from the table d'hôte became less hearty than it had been during his student days; after all, we had both recently celebrated our fortieth birthdays. It didn't help when Bob was named in the student rag as the most eligible bachelor in the hospital, not least because he had built up one of the most successful private practices in London. He had a set of rooms in Harley Street, with none of the expenses associated with marital bliss. But now that finally seemed to be coming to an end.

When Bob invited Carol and me to join him for dinner so that he could introduce us to Fiona, whom he described as the woman he was going to spend the rest of his life with, we were both surprised and delighted. We were also a little perplexed as we couldn't recall the name of his last girlfriend. We were fairly confident it wasn't Fiona.

When we arrived at the restaurant, we saw the two of them seated in the far corner of the room, holding hands. Bob rose to greet us and immediately introduced Fiona as the most wonderful girl in the world. To be fair to the woman, no red-blooded male could have denied Fiona's physical attributes. She must have been about five foot nine, made up of thirty inches of leg, attached to a figure honed in the gym and no doubt perfected on a diet of lettuce leaves and water.

Our conversation during the meal was fairly limited, partly because Bob spent most of the time staring at Fiona in a way that should be reserved for one of Donatello's nudes. By the end of the meal, I had come to the conclusion that Fiona would end up costing about as much, and it wasn't just because she read the wine list from the bottom upwards, ordered caviar as a starter and asked, with a sweet smile, for her pasta to be covered in truffles.

Frankly, Fiona was the type of long-legged blonde whom you hope to bump into, while perched on a stool in a hotel bar, late at night and preferably on another continent. I am unable to tell you how old she was, but I did learn during dinner that she had been married three times before she met Bob. However, she assured us that, this time, she had found the right man.

I was only too happy to escape that night and, as you have already discovered, I didn't waste much time making my wife aware of my views on Fiona.

The marriage took place some three months later at the Chelsea Register Office in the King's Road. The ceremony was attended by several of Bob's friends from St Thomas' and Guy's – some of whom I hadn't set eyes on since our rugby days. I felt it unwise to point out to Carol that Fiona didn't seem to have any friends, or at least none who were willing to attend her latest nuptials.

I stood silently by Bob's side as the registrar intoned the words, 'If anyone can show lawful reason why these two should not be joined in matrimony, then they should declare that reason to me now.'

I wanted to offer an opinion, but Carol was too close at hand to risk it. I must confess that Fiona did look radiant on that occasion, not unlike a python about to devour a lamb – whole.

The reception was held at Lucio's on the Fulham Road. The best man's speech might have been more coherent if I hadn't consumed quite so much champagne, or if I'd believed a word I was uttering.

When I sat down to indulgent applause, Carol didn't lean across to congratulate me. I avoided her until we all joined the bride and groom on the pavement outside the restaurant. Bob and Fiona waved goodbye before stepping into a white stretch limousine that would take them to Heathrow. From there, they were to board a plane to Acapulco, where they would spend a three-week honeymoon. Neither the transport to Heathrow, which incidentally could have accommodated the entire wedding party, nor the final destination for the honeymoon, had been Bob's first choice. A piece of information I didn't pass on to Carol, as she would undoubtedly have accused me of being prejudiced – and she would have been right.

I can't pretend that I saw a lot of Fiona during their first year of marriage, although Bob called from time to time, but only from his practice in Harley Street. We even managed the occasional lunch, but he no longer seemed to be able to fit in a game of squash in the evening.

Over lunch Bob never failed to expound the virtues of his remarkable wife, as if only too aware of my attitude to his spouse – although I never at any time expressed my true feelings. I could only assume that this was the reason Carol and I were never invited to dinner at their home, and whenever we asked them to join us for supper, Bob made some unconvincing excuse about having to visit a patient, or being out of town on that particular evening.

The change was subtle to begin with, almost imperceptible. Our lunches became more regular, even the occasional game of squash was fitted in, and perhaps more relevant, there were fewer and fewer references to Fiona's pending sainthood.

It was soon after the death of Bob's aunt, a Miss Muriel Pembleton, that the change became far less subtle. To be honest, I didn't even realize that Bob had an aunt, let alone one who was the sole heir to Pembleton Electronics.

The Times revealed that Miss Pembleton had left a little over seven million pounds in shares and property, as well as a considerable art collection. With the exception of a few minor bequests to charitable organizations, her nephew turned out to be the sole beneficiary. God bless the man, because coming into an unexpected fortune didn't change Bob in any way; but the same couldn't be said of Fiona.

When I called Bob to congratulate him on his good fortune, he sounded very low. He asked if I could possibly join him for lunch, as he needed to seek my advice on a personal matter.

We met a couple of hours later, at a gastro pub just off Devonshire Place. Bob didn't talk about anything consequential until after the waiter had taken our order, but once the first course had been served, Fiona was the only other dish on the menu. He had received a letter that morning from Abbott Crombie & Co, Solicitors, stating, in unambiguous terms, that his wife was filing for divorce.

'Can't fault her timing,' I said tactlessly.

'And I didn't even spot it,' said Bob.

'Spot it?' I repeated. 'Spot what?'

'How Fiona's attitude to me changed not long after she'd met my aunt Muriel. In fact, that same night, she literally charmed the pants off me.'

I reminded Bob of what Woody Allen had said on the subject. Mr Allen could not understand why God had given man a penis and a brain, but not enough blood to connect the two. Bob laughed for the first time that day, but it was only moments before he lapsed back into a maudlin silence.

'Is there anything I can do to help?' I asked.

'Only if you know the name of a first-class divorce lawyer,' Bob replied, 'because I'm told that Mrs Abbott has a reputation for extracting the last drop of blood on behalf of her clients, especially following the latest law lords' ruling in favour of spouses.'

'Can't say I do,' I responded. 'Having been happily married for sixteen years, I fear I'm the wrong man to advise you. Why don't you have a word with Peter Mitchell? After all, with four ex-wives, he ought to be able to tell you who's the best advocate available.'

'I called Peter first thing this morning,' admitted Bob. 'He's always been represented by Mrs Abbott – told me that he keeps her on a permanent retainer.'

During the next few weeks, Bob and I returned to the squash court regularly, and I started beating him for the first time. He would then join Carol and me for dinner after-wards. We tried to steer clear of any talk about Fiona. However, he did let slip that she was refusing to leave the stage gracefully, even after he had offered her half of Aunt Muriel's bequest.

As the weeks turned into months, Bob began losing

weight and his golden locks were turning prematurely grey. Fiona, on the other hand, seemed to go from strength to strength, taking each new hurdle like a seasoned thorough-bred. When it came to tactics, Fiona clearly understood the long game, but then she had the advantage of having experienced three away victories, and was clearly looking forward to a fourth.

It must have been about a year later that Fiona finally agreed to a settlement. All of Bob's assets were to be divided equally between them, while he would also cover her legal costs. A date was set for a formal signing in chambers. I agreed to act as a witness and give Bob, as Carol described it, much-needed moral support.

I never even took the top off my pen because Fiona burst into tears long before Mrs Abbott had read out the terms, declaring that she was being cruelly treated and Bob was causing her to have a nervous breakdown. She then flounced out of the office without another word. I must confess that I had never seen Fiona looking less nervous. Even Mrs Abbott couldn't hide her exasperation.

Harry Dexter, whom Bob had selected as his solicitor, warned him that this was likely to end up in a lengthy and expensive courtroom battle if he couldn't agree to a settlement. Mr Dexter added, for good measure, that judges often instruct the defending party to shoulder the injured party's costs. Bob shrugged his shoulders, not even bothering to respond.

Once both sides had accepted that an out-of-court settle-ment could not be reached, a day was fixed in the judge's calendar for a hearing.

Mr Dexter was determined to counter Fiona's outrageous demands with equally fierce resistance, and to begin with Bob went along with all his recommendations. But with each new demand from the other side, Bob's resolve began to weaken until, like a punch-drunk boxer, he was ready to throw in the towel. He became more and more depressed as the day of the hearing drew nearer, and even began saying, 'Why don't I just give her everything because that's the only way she'll ever be satisfied?' Carol and I tried to lift his spirits, but with little success, and even Mr Dexter was finding it harder and harder to convince his client to hang in there.

We both assured Bob that we would be in court to support him on the day of the hearing.

Carol and I took our places in the gallery of court number three, matrimonial division, on the last Thursday in June, and waited for proceedings to begin. By ten to ten the court officials began to drift in and take their places. A few minutes later Mrs Abbott arrived, with Fiona by her side. I stared down at the plaintiff, who was wearing no jewellery and a black suit that would have been more appropriate for a funeral – Bob's.

A moment later Mr Dexter appeared with Bob in his wake. They took their places at a table on the other side of the courtroom.

As ten o'clock struck, my worst fears were realized. The judge entered the courtroom – a woman who immediately brought back memories of my old school matron – a martinet who didn't believe that the punishment should fit the crime. The judge took her place on the bench and smiled down at Mrs Abbott. They'd probably been at university together. Mrs Abbott rose from her place and returned the judge's smile. She then proceeded to do battle for every jot and tittle in Bob's possession, even arguing over who should end up with his college cufflinks, saying that it had been agreed that all Mr Radford's assets should be divided equally, so that if he had one cufflink, her client must be entitled to the other.

As each hour passed, Fiona's demands expanded. After all, Mrs Abbot explained, hadn't her client given up a rewarding and happy lifestyle in America, which included a thriving family business – something I'd never heard mentioned before – to devote herself to her husband? Only to discover that he rarely arrived home in the evening before eight, and then only after he'd been out with his friends to play squash, and when he eventually turned up – Mrs Abbott paused – drunk, he didn't want to eat the meal she had spent hours preparing for him – she paused again – and when they later went to bed, he quickly fell into a drunken slumber. I rose from my place in the gallery to protest, only to be told by an usher to sit down or I would be asked to leave the court. Carol tugged firmly on my jacket.

Finally, Mrs Abbot reached the end of her demands, with the suggestion that her client should be given their home in the country (Aunt Muriel's), while Bob would be allowed to keep his London apartment; she should have the villa in Cannes (Aunt Muriel's), while he kept his rooms at Harley Street (rented). Mrs Abbott finally turned her attention to Aunt Muriel's art collection, which she also felt should be divided equally; her client should have the Monet, while he kept the Manguin. She should have the Picasso, he the Pasmore, she the Bacon, etc. When Mrs Abbott finally sat down, Mrs Justice Butler suggested that perhaps they should take a break for lunch.

During a lunch, not eaten, Mr Dexter, Carol and I tried valiantly to convince Bob that he should fight back. But he wouldn't hear of it.

'If I can hold on to everything I had before my aunt died,' Bob insisted, 'that will be quite enough for me.'

Mr Dexter felt certain he could do far better than that, but Bob showed little interest in putting up a fight.

'Just get it over with,' he instructed. 'Try not to forget who's paying her costs.'

When we returned to the courtroom at two o'clock that afternoon, the judge turned her attention to Bob's solicitor.

'And what do you have to say about all this, Mr Dexter?' asked Mrs Justice Butler.

'We are happy to go along with the division of my client's assets as suggested by Mrs Abbott,' he replied with an exaggerated sigh.

'You're happy to go along with Mrs Abbott's recommendations, Mr Dexter?' repeated the judge in disbelief.

Once again Mr Dexter looked at Bob, who simply nodded, like a dog on the back shelf of a car.

'So be it,' said Mrs Justice Butler, unable to mask her surprise.

She was just about to pass judgement, when Fiona broke down and burst into tears. She leant across and whispered into Mrs Abbott's ear.

'Mrs Abbott,' said Mrs Justice Butler, ignoring the plaintiff's sobs, 'am I to sanction this agreement?'

'It seems not,' said Mrs Abbott, rising from her place and looking somewhat embarrassed. 'It appears that my client still feels that such a settlement favours the defendant.'

'Does she indeed?' said Mrs Justice Butler and turned to face Fiona. Mrs Abbott touched her client on the shoulder and whispered in her ear. Fiona immediately rose, and kept her head bowed while the judge spoke.

'Mrs Radford,' she began, looking down at Fiona, 'am I to understand that you are no longer happy with the settlement your solicitor has secured for you?'

Fiona nodded demurely.

'Then may I suggest a solution, that I hope will bring this case to a speedy conclusion.' Fiona looked up and smiled sweetly at the judge, while Bob sank lower into his seat.

'Perhaps it would be easier, Mrs Radford, if *you* were to draw up two lists for the court's consideration, that *you* believe to be a fair and equitable division of your husband's assets?'

'I'd be happy to do that, your honour,' said Fiona meekly.

'Does this meet with your approval, Mr Dexter?' asked Mrs Justice Butler, turning back to Bob's solicitor.

'Yes, m'lady,' said Mr Dexter, trying not to sound exasperated.

'Can I take it that those are your client's instructions?'

Mr Dexter glanced down at Bob, who didn't even bother to offer an opinion.

'And Mrs Abbott,' she said, turning her attention back to Fiona's solicitor, 'I want your word that your client will not back down from such a settlement.'

'I can assure you, m'lady, that she will comply with your ruling,' replied Fiona's solicitor.

'So be it,' said Mrs Justice Butler. 'We will adjourn until tomorrow morning at ten o'clock, when I will look forward to considering Mrs Radford's two lists.'

✷ ✷ ✷

Carol and I took Bob out for dinner that night – a pointless exercise. He rarely opened his mouth to either eat or speak.

'Let her have everything,' he finally ventured over coffee, 'because that's the only way I'm ever going to be rid of the woman.'

'But your aunt wouldn't have left you her fortune if she'd known this would have been the eventual outcome.'

'Neither Aunt Muriel nor I worked that one out,' Bob replied with resignation. 'And you can't fault Fiona's timing. She only needed another month after meeting my dear aunt before she accepted my proposal.' Bob turned and stared at me, an accusing look in his eyes. 'Why didn't you warn me not to marry her?' he demanded.

When the judge entered the courtroom the following morning all the officials were already in place. The two adversaries were seated next to their solicitors. All those in the well of the court rose and bowed as Mrs Justice Butler resumed her place, leaving only Mrs Abbott on her feet.

'Has your client had enough time to prepare her two lists?' enquired the judge, as she stared down at Fiona's counsel.

'She has indeed, m'lady,' said Mrs Abbott, 'and both are ready for your consideration.'

The judge nodded to the clerk of the court. He walked slowly across to Mrs Abbott, who handed over the two lists. The clerk then walked slowly back to the bench and passed them up to the judge for her consideration.

Mrs Justice Butler took her time studying the two inventories, occasionally nodding, even adding the odd 'Um', while Mrs Abbott remained on her feet. Once the judge had reached the last items on the lists, she turned her attention back to counsel's bench.

'Am I to understand,' enquired Mrs Justice Butler, 'that both parties consider this to be a fair and equitable distribution of all the assets in question?'

'Yes, m'lady,' said Mrs Abbott firmly, on behalf of her client.

'I see,' said the judge and, turning to Mr Dexter, asked, 'Does this also meet with your client's approval?'

Mr Dexter hesitated. 'Yes, m'lady,' he eventually managed, unable to mask the irony in his voice.

'So be it.' Fiona smiled for the first time since the case had opened. The judge returned her smile. 'However, before I pass judgement,' she continued, 'I still have one question for Mr Radford.' Bob glanced at his solicitor before rising nervously from his seat. He looked up at the judge.

What more can she want? was my only thought as I sat staring down from the gallery.

'Mr Radford,' began the judge, 'we have all heard your wife tell the court that she considers these two lists to be a fair and equitable division of all your assets.'

Bob bowed his head and remained silent.

'However, before I pass judgement, I need to be sure that you agree with that assessment.'

Bob raised his head. He seemed to hesitate a moment, but then said, 'I do, m'lady.'

'Then I am left with no choice in this matter,' declared Mrs Justice Butler. She paused, and stared directly down at Fiona, who was still smiling. 'As I allowed Mrs Radford the opportunity to prepare these two lists,' continued the judge, 'which in her judgement are an equitable and fair division of your assets –' Mrs Justice Butler was pleased to see Fiona

nodding her agreement – 'then it must also be fair and equitable,' the judge added, turning her attention back to Bob,
'to allow Mr Radford the opportunity to select which of the
two lists he would prefer.'

Know What I Mean

'IF YOU WANNA FIND out what's goin' on in this nick, I'm the man to 'ave a word with,' said Doug. 'Know what I mean?'

Every prison has one. At North Sea Camp his name was Doug Haslett. Doug was half an inch under six foot, with thick, black, wavy hair that was going grey at the temples, and a stomach that hung out over his trousers. Doug's idea of exercise was the walk from the library, where he was the prison orderly, to the canteen a hundred yards away, three times a day. I think he exercised his mind at about the same pace.

It didn't take me long to discover that he was bright, cunning, manipulative and lazy – traits that are common among recidivists. Within days of arriving at a new prison, Doug could be guaranteed to have procured fresh clothes, the best cell, the highest-paid job, and to have worked out which prisoners, and – more important – which officers he needed to get on the right side of.

As I spent a lot of my free time in the library – and it was rarely overcrowded, despite the prison accommodating over four hundred inmates – Doug quickly made me aware of his case history. Some prisoners, when they discover that you're a writer, clam up. Others can't stop talking. Despite the silence notices displayed all around the library, Doug fell into the latter category.

When Doug left school at the age of seventeen, the only exam he passed was his driving test – first time. Four years later he added a heavy goods licence to his qualifications, and at the same time landed his first job as a lorry driver.

Doug quickly became disillusioned with how little he could earn, traipsing backwards and forwards to the south of France with a load of Brussels sprouts and peas, often returning to Sleaford with an empty lorry and therefore no bonus. He regularly fouled up (his words) when it came to EU regulations, and took the view that somehow he was exempt from having to pay tax. He blamed the French for too much unnecessary red tape and a Labour government for punitive taxes. When the courts finally served a debt order on him, everyone was to blame except Doug.

The bailiff took away all his possessions – except the lorry, which Doug was still paying for on a hire-purchase agreement.

Doug was just about to pack in being a lorry driver and join the dole queue – almost as remunerative, and you don't have to get up in the morning – when he was approached by a man he'd never come across before, while on a stopover in Marseilles. Doug was having breakfast at a dockside cafe when the man slid on to the stool next to him. The stranger

didn't waste any time with introductions, he came straight to the point. Doug listened with interest; after all, he had already dumped his cargo of sprouts and peas on the dockside, and had been expecting to return home with an empty lorry. All Doug had to do, the stranger assured him, was to deliver a consignment of bananas to Lincolnshire once a week.

I feel I should point out that Doug did have some scruples. He made it clear to his new employer that he would never be willing to transport drugs, and wouldn't even discuss illegal immigrants. Doug, like so many of my fellow inmates, was very right wing.

When Doug arrived at the drop-off point, a derelict barn deep in the Lincolnshire countryside, he was handed a thick brown envelope containing £25,000 in cash. They didn't even expect him to help unload the produce.

Overnight, Doug's lifestyle changed.

After a couple of trips, Doug began to work part-time, making the single journey to Marseilles and back once a week. Despite this, he was now earning more in a week than he was declaring on his tax return for a year.

Doug decided that one of the things he'd do with his new-found wealth was to move out of his basement flat on the Hinton Road and invest in the property market.

Over the next month he was shown around several properties in Sleaford, accompanied by a young lady from one of the local estate agents. Sally McKenzie was puzzled how a lorry driver could possibly afford the type of properties she was offering him.

Doug eventually settled on a little cottage on the outskirts of Sleaford. Sally was even more surprised when he put down the deposit in cash, and shocked when he asked her out on a date.

Six months later Sally moved in with Doug, although it still worried her that she couldn't work out where all the money was coming from.

Doug's sudden wealth created other problems that he hadn't anticipated. What do you do with £25,000 in cash each week, when you can't open a bank account, or pay a

monthly cheque into a building society? The basement flat
on Hinton Road had been replaced with a cottage in the
country. The second-hand fork-lift truck had been traded
in for a sixteen-wheel Mercedes lorry. The annual holiday
at a bed and breakfast in Blackpool had been upgraded to
a rented villa in the Algarve. The Portuguese seemed quite
happy to accept cash, whatever the currency.

On their second visit to the Algarve a year later, Doug
fell on one knee, proposed to Sally and presented her with
a diamond engagement ring the size of an acorn: traditional sort of chap, Doug.

Several people, not least his young wife, remained
puzzled as to how Doug could possibly afford such a lifestyle while only earning £25,000 a year. 'Cash bonuses for
overtime,' was all he came up with whenever Sally asked.
This surprised Mrs Haslett because she knew that her
husband only worked a couple of days a week. And she might
never have found out the truth if someone else hadn't taken
an interest.

Mark Cainen, an ambitious young assistant officer with
HM Customs, decided the time had come to check exactly
what Doug was importing, after a nark tipped him off it
might not just be bananas.

When Doug was returning from one of his weekly trips
to Marseilles, Mr Cainen asked him to pull over and park
his lorry in the customs shed. Doug climbed down from the
cab and handed over his worksheet to the officer. Bananas
were the only entry on the manifest: fifty crates of them.
The young customs official set about opening the crates one
by one, and by the time he'd reached the thirty-sixth, was
beginning to wonder if he had been given a bum steer;
that opinion changed when he opened the forty-first crate,

which was packed tightly with cigarettes – Marlboro, Benson & Hedges, Silk Cut and Players. By the time Mr Cainen had opened the fiftieth crate, he had placed an estimated street value on the contraband of over £200,000.

'I had no idea what was in those crates,' Doug assured his wife, and she believed him. He repeated the same story to his defence team, who wanted to believe him, and for a third time, to the jury, who didn't. Doug's defence silk reminded his lordship that this was Mr Haslett's first offence and his wife was expecting a baby. The judge listened in stony silence, and sent Doug down for four years.

Doug spent his first week in Lincoln high-security prison, but once he'd completed an induction form and was able to place a tick in all the right boxes – no drugs, no violence, no previous offences – he was quickly transferred to an open prison.

At North Sea Camp, Doug, as I've already explained, opted to work in the library. The alternatives were the pig farm, the kitchen, the stores or cleaning out the lavatories. Doug quickly discovered that despite there being over four hundred residents in the prison, as librarian he was on to a cushy number. His income fell from £25,000 a week to £12.50, of which he spent £10 on phone cards so that he could keep in touch with his pregnant wife.

Doug rang Sally twice a week – you can only phone out when you're in prison, no one can call you – to promise his wife repeatedly that once he was released, he would never get into trouble with the law again. Sally was reassured by this news.

In Doug's absence, and despite being heavily pregnant, Sally was still holding down her job at the estate agent's, and had even managed to hire out Doug's lorry for the period of time he would be away. However, Doug wasn't telling his wife the whole story. While other prisoners were being sent in *Playboy, Readers' Wives* and the *Sun*, Doug was receiving *Haulage Weekly* and *Exchange & Mart* for his bedside reading.

He was browsing through *Haulage Weekly* when he found exactly what he was looking for: a second-hand, left-hand-drive, forty-ton, American Peterbilt lorry, which was being offered for sale at a knock-down price. Doug took a long time – but then he had a long time – considering the vehicle's added extras. While he sat alone in the library, he began to draw diagrams on the back of the magazine. He then used a ruler to measure the exact size of a box of Marlboro. He realized that the cash return might be smaller this time, but at least he wouldn't be caught.

Among the problems of earning £25,000 a week, and not having to pay tax, is that after being released from prison you are expected to settle for a job that only offers you £25,000 a year before tax; a common enough dilemma for most criminals, especially drug dealers.

With less than a month of his sentence to serve, Doug phoned his wife and asked her to sell his top-of-the-range Mercedes truck, in part exchange for the massive second-hand eighteen-wheel Peterbilt lorry that he'd seen advertised in *Haulage Weekly*.

When Sally first saw the truck, she couldn't understand why her husband wanted to exchange his magnificent vehicle for such a monstrosity. She accepted his explanation that he would be able to drive from Sleaford to Marseilles without having to stop for refuelling.

'But it's a left-hand drive.'

'Don't forget,' Doug reminded her, 'the longest section of the journey is from Calais to Marseilles.'

Doug turned out to be a model prisoner, so ended up serving only half of his four-year sentence.

On the day of his release, his wife and eighteen-month-old daughter Kelly were waiting for him at the prison gates. Sally drove them back to Sleaford in her old Vauxhall. On arrival, Doug was pleased to find the second-hand pantechnicon parked in the field next to their little cottage.

'But why haven't you sold my old Merc?' he asked.

'Haven't had a decent offer,' Sally admitted, 'so I hired it out for another year. At least that way it's showing us a small return.' Doug nodded. He was pleased to find that both vehicles were spotless, and after an inspection of the engines, discovered they were also in good nick.

Doug went back to work the following morning. He repeatedly assured Sally that he would never make the same mistake twice. He filled up his lorry with sprouts and peas from a local farmer, before setting out on his journey to Marseilles. He then returned to England with a full load of bananas. A suspicious, recently promoted Mark Cainen regularly pulled Doug over so that he could carry out a spot-check to find out what he was bringing back from Marseilles. But however many crates he prised open, they were always filled with bananas. The officer remained unconvinced, but couldn't work out what Doug was up to.

'Give me a break,' said Doug, when Mr Cainen pulled him over yet again in Dover. 'Can't you see that I've turned over a new leaf?' The customs officer didn't give him a break because he was convinced it was a tobacco leaf, even if he couldn't prove it.

Doug's new system was working like a dream, and although he was now only clearing £10,000 a week, at least this time he couldn't be caught. Sally kept all the books up to date for both lorries so that Doug's tax returns were always filled in correctly and paid on time, and any new EU regulations were complied with. However, Doug didn't brief his wife on the details of his new untaxed benefit scheme.

One Thursday afternoon, just after Doug had cleared customs in Dover, he drove into the nearest petrol station to refuel before continuing his journey north to Sleaford. An Audi followed him onto the forecourt, and the driver began to curse about how long he was going to have to wait before the massive pantechnicon would be filled up. To his surprise, the lorry driver only took a couple of minutes before he replaced the nozzle in its holder. As Doug drove out onto the road, the car behind moved up to take his place. When Mr Cainen saw the name on the side of the lorry, his curiosity was aroused. He checked the pump, to find that Doug had only spent £33. He stared at the massive eighteen-wheeler as it trundled off down the highway, aware that with that amount of petrol Doug could only hope to cover a few more miles before he would have to fill up again.

It took Mr Cainen only a few minutes to catch up with Doug's truck. He then followed the lorry at a safe distance for the next twenty miles before Doug pulled into another petrol station. Once Doug was back on the road a few minutes later, Mr Cainen checked the pump – £34 – only enough to cover another twenty miles. As Doug continued on his journey to Sleaford, the officer returned to Dover with a smile on his face.

When Doug was driving back from Marseilles the following week, he showed no concern when Mr Cainen asked him to pull over and park his lorry in the customs shed. He knew that every crate on board was, as the manifest stated, full of bananas. However, the customs officer didn't ask Doug to unlock the back door of the truck. He simply walked around the outside of the vehicle clutching a spanner as if it were a tuning fork while he tapped the massive fuel tanks. The officer was not surprised that the eighth tank rang out with a completely different timbre to the other seven. Doug sat around for hours while customs mechanics removed all eight fuel tanks from both sides of the lorry. Only one was half full of diesel, while the other seven contained over £100,000 worth of cigarettes.

On this occasion the judge was less lenient, and Doug was sent down for six years, even after his barrister pleaded that a second child was on the way.

Sally was horrified to discover that Doug had broken his word, and sceptical when he promised her never, ever, again. The moment her husband was locked up, she rented out the second vehicle and returned to her job as an estate agent.

A year later Sally was able to declare an increased income of just over £3,000, on top of her earnings as an estate agent.

Sally's accountant advised her to buy the field next door to the cottage, where the lorries were always parked at night, as she could claim it against tax. 'A carpark,' he explained, 'would be a legitimate business expense.'

As Doug had just begun a six-year sentence and was back to earning £12.50 a week as the prison librarian, he was hardly in a position to offer an opinion. However, even he was impressed when, the following year, Sally declared an income of £37,000, which included her added sales bonuses. This time, the accountant advised her to purchase a third lorry.

Doug was eventually released from prison having only served half his sentence (three years). Sally was parked outside the prison gates in her Vauxhall, waiting to drive her husband home. His nine-year-old daughter, Kelly, was strapped into the back, next to her three-year-old sister Sam. Sally had not allowed either of the children to visit their father in prison, so when Doug took the little girl in his arms for the first time, Sam burst into tears. Sally explained to her that the strange man was her father.

Over a welcome breakfast of bacon and eggs, Sally was able to report that she had been advised by her accountant to form a limited company. Haslett Haulage had declared a profit of £21,600 in its first year, and she had added two more lorries to their growing fleet. Sally told her husband that she was thinking of giving up her job at the estate agent's to become full-time chair of the new company.

'Chair?' said Doug. 'What's that?'

Doug was only too pleased to leave Sally to run the company, as long as he was allowed to take his place behind the wheel as one of her drivers. This state of affairs would have continued quite happily, if Doug had not once again been approached by the man from Marseilles – who never seemed to end up in jail – with what he confidently assured him was a fool-proof plan with no risks attached and, more important, this time his wife need never find out.

Doug resisted the Frenchman's advances for several months, but after losing a rather large sum in a poker game, finally succumbed. Just one trip, he promised himself. The man from Marseilles smiled, as he handed over an envelope containing £12,500 in cash.

Under Sally's chairmanship, the Haslett Haulage Company continued to grow, in both reputation and below the bottom line. Meanwhile, Doug once again became used to having cash in hand; money which did not rely on a balance sheet, and was not subject to a tax return.

Someone else was continuing to keep a close eye on the Haslett Haulage Company, and Doug in particular. Regular as clockwork, Doug could be seen driving his lorry through the Dover terminal, with a full load of sprouts and peas, destined for Marseilles. But Mark Cainen, now an anti-smuggling officer working as part of the Law Enforcement Unit, never once saw Doug make the return journey. This worried him.

The officer checked his records, to find that Haslett Haulage was now running nine lorries a week to different parts of Europe. Their chairman, Sally Haslett, had a spotless reputation – not unlike her vehicles – with everyone she dealt with, from customs to customers. But Mr Cainen was still curious to find out why Doug was no longer driving back through his port. He took it personally.

A few discreet enquiries revealed that Doug could still be seen in Marseilles unloading his sprouts and peas, and later loading up with crates of bananas. However, there was one slight variation. He was now driving back via Newhaven, which Cainen estimated must have added at least a couple of hours to Doug's journey.

All customs officers have the option of serving one month a year at another port of entry, to further their promotion prospects. The previous year Mr Cainen had selected Heathrow airport; that year he opted for a month in Newhaven.

Officer Cainen waited patiently for Doug's lorry to appear on the dockside, but it wasn't until the end of his second week that he spotted his old adversary waiting in line to disembark from an Olsen's ferry. The moment Doug's lorry drove onto the dock, Mr Cainen disappeared upstairs into the staffroom and poured himself a cup of coffee. He walked across to the window and watched Doug's vehicle came to a halt at the front of the line. He was waved quickly through by the two officers on duty. Mr Cainen made no attempt to intervene as Doug drove out onto the road to continue his journey back to Sleaford. He had to wait another ten days before Doug's lorry reappeared, and this time he noted that only one thing hadn't changed. Mr Cainen didn't think it was a coincidence.

When Doug returned via Newhaven five days later, the same two officers gave his vehicle no more than a cursory glance, before waving him through. The officer now knew that it wasn't a coincidence. Mr Cainen reported his observations to his boss in Newhaven and, as his month was up, made his way back to Dover.

Doug completed three more journeys from Marseilles via Newhaven before the two customs officers were arrested. When Doug saw five officers heading towards his truck, he knew that his new impossible-to-be-caught system had been sussed.

Doug didn't waste the court's time pleading not guilty, because one of the customs officers with whom he had been splitting the take had made a deal to have his sentence reduced if he named names. He named Douglas Arthur Haslett.

The judge sent Doug down for eight years, with no remission for good behaviour, unless he agreed to pay a fine of £750,000. Doug didn't have £750,000 and begged Sally to help out, as he couldn't face the thought of another eight years behind bars. Sally had to sell everything, including the cottage, the carpark, nine lorries and even her engagement ring, so that her husband could comply with the court order.

After serving a year at Wayland Category C prison in Norfolk, Doug was transferred back to North Sea Camp. Once again, he was appointed as librarian, which was where I first met him.

I was impressed that Sally and his two – now grown-up – daughters came to visit Doug every weekend. He told me that they didn't discuss business, even though he'd sworn on his mother's grave never, ever again.

'Don't even think about it,' Sally had warned him. 'I've already sent your lorry to the scrapyard.'

'Can't blame the woman, after all I've put her through,' said Doug when I next visited the library. 'But if they won't let me get behind a wheel once I'm released, what am I going to do for the rest of my life?'

I was released a couple of years before Doug, and if I hadn't been addressing a literary festival in Lincoln some years later, I might never have discovered what had become of the chief librarian.

As I stared down into the audience during questions, I thought I recognized three vaguely familiar faces looking up at me from the third row. I racked that part of my brain that is meant to store names, but it didn't respond. That was, until I had a question about the difficulties of writing while in prison. Then it all came flooding back. I had last seen Sally some three years before, when she was visiting Doug accompanied by her two daughters, Kelly and, and . . . Sam.

After I'd taken the final question, we broke for coffee, and the three of them came across to join me.

'Hi, Sally. How's Doug?' I asked even before they could introduce themselves. An old political ploy, and they looked suitably impressed.

'Retired,' said Sally without explanation.

'But he was younger than me,' I protested, 'and never stopped telling everyone what he planned to do once he was released.'

'No doubt,' said Sally, 'but I can assure you he's retired. Haslett Haulage is now run by me and my two daughters, with a backroom staff of twenty-one, not including the drivers.'

'So you're obviously doing well,' I said, fishing.

'You clearly don't read the financial pages,' she teased.

'I'm like the Japanese,' I countered, 'I always read my papers from back to front. So what have I missed?'

'We went public last year,' chipped in Kelly. 'Mum's chair, I'm in charge of new accounts and Sam is responsible for the drivers.'

'And if I remember correctly, you had about nine lorries?'

'We now have forty-one,' said Sally, 'and our turnover last year was just under five million.'

'And Doug doesn't play any role?'

'Doug plays golf,' said Sally, 'which doesn't require him to travel through Dover, or,' she added with a sigh, as her husband appeared in the doorway, 'back via Newhaven.'

Doug remained still, as his eyes searched the room for his family. I waved and caught his attention. Doug waved back and wandered slowly across to join us.

'We still allow him to drive us home from time to time,' whispered Sam with a grin, just as Doug appeared by my side.

I shook hands with my former inmate, and when Sally and the girls had finished their coffee, I accompanied them all back to their car, which gave me the chance to have a word with Doug.

'I'm delighted to hear that Haslett Haulage is doing so well,' I volunteered.

'Put it all down to experience,' said Doug. 'Don't forget I taught them everything they know.'

'And since we last met, Kelly tells me that the company's gone public.'

'All part of my long-term plan,' said Doug as his wife climbed into the back of the car. He turned and gave me a knowing look. 'A lot of people sniffing around at the moment, Jeff, so don't be surprised if there's a takeover bid in the near future.' Just as he reached the driver's side of the car, he added, 'Chance for you to make a few bob while the shares are still at their present price. Know what I mean?'

Charity Begins At Home

HENRY PRESTON, HARRY to his friends – and they didn't number many – wasn't the sort of person you'd bump into at the local pub, meet at a football match or invite home for a barbecue. Frankly, if there was a club for introverts, Henry would be elected chairman – reluctantly.

At school, the only subject in which he excelled was mathematics, and his mother, the one person who adored him, was determined that Henry would have a profession. His father had been a postman. With one A level in maths, the field was fairly limited – banking or accountancy. His mother chose accountancy.

Henry was articled to Pearson, Clutterbuck & Reynolds, and when he first joined the firm as a clerk he dreamt of the headed notepaper reading *Pearson, Clutterbuck, Reynolds & Preston*. But as the years went by, and younger and younger men found their names embossed on the left-hand side of the company notepaper, the dream faded.

Some men, aware of their limitations, find solace in another form – sex, drugs or a hectic social life. It's quite difficult to conduct a hectic social life on your own. Drugs? Henry didn't even smoke, although he allowed himself the occasional gin and tonic, but only on Saturday. And as for sex, he felt confident he wasn't gay, but his success rate with the opposite sex, 'hits' as some of his younger colleagues described them, hovered around zero. Henry didn't even have a hobby.

There comes a point in every man's life when he realizes *I'm going to live forever* is a fallacy. It came all too soon for Henry, as he progressed quickly through middle age and suddenly began to think about early retirement. When Mr Pearson, the senior partner, retired, a large party was held in his honour in a private room at a five-star hotel. Mr Pearson, after a long and distinguished career, told his colleagues that he would be retiring to a cottage in the Cotswolds to tend the roses and try to lower his golf handicap. Much laughter and applause followed. The only thing Henry recalled of that occasion was Atkins, the firm's latest recruit, saying to him as he left for the evening, 'I suppose it won't be that long, old chap, before we're doing the same sort of thing for you.'

Henry mulled over young Atkins's words as he walked towards the bus stop. He was fifty-four years old, so in six years' time, unless he made partner, in which case his tenure would be extended to sixty-five, they would be holding a farewell party for him. In truth, Henry had long ago given up any thought of becoming a partner, and he had already accepted that his party would not be held in the private room of a five-star hotel. He certainly wouldn't be retiring to a cottage in the Cotswolds to tend his roses, and he already had enough handicaps, without thinking about golf.

Henry was well aware that his colleagues considered him to be reliable, competent and thorough, which only added to his sense of failure. The highest praise he ever received was, 'You can always depend on Henry. He's a safe pair of hands.'

But all of that changed the day he met Angela.

Angela Forster's company, Events Unlimited, was neither large enough to be assigned to one of the partners, nor small enough to be handled by an articled clerk, which is how her file ended up on Henry's desk. He studied the details carefully.

Ms Forster was the sole proprietor of a small business that specialized in organizing events – anything from the local Conservative Association's annual dinner to a regional Hunt Ball. Angela was a born organizer and after her husband left her for a younger woman – when a man leaves his wife for a younger woman, it's a short story, when a woman leaves her husband for a younger man, it's a novel (I digress) – Angela made the decision not to sit at home and feel sorry for herself but, following our Lord's advice in the parable of the talents, opted to use her one gift, so that she could fully occupy her time while making a little pin money on the side. The problem was that Angela had become a little more successful than she'd anticipated, which is how she ended up having an appointment with Henry.

Before Henry finalized Ms Forster's accounts, he took her slowly through the figures, column by column, showing his new client how she was entitled to claim for certain items against tax, such as her car, travel and even her clothes. He pointed out that she ought to be dressed appropriately when she attended one of her functions. Henry managed to save Ms Forster a few hundred pounds on her tax bill; after all, he considered it a matter of professional pride that, having heeded his advice, all his clients left the office better off. That was even after they'd settled his company's fees, which, he pointed out, could also be claimed against tax.

Henry always ended every meeting with the words, 'I can assure you that your accounts are in apple-pie order, and the tax man will not be troubling you.' Henry was only too aware that very few of his clients were likely to interest the tax man, let alone be troubled by him. He would then accompany his client to the door with the words, 'See you next year.' When he opened the door for Ms Forster, she smiled, and said, 'Why don't you come along to one of my functions, Mr Preston? Then you can see what I get up to most evenings.'

Henry couldn't recall when he'd last been invited to anything. He hesitated, not quite sure how to respond. Angela filled the silence. 'I'm organizing a ball for African famine relief on Saturday evening. It's at the town hall. Why don't you join me?'

Henry heard himself saying, 'Yes, thank you, how nice. I'll look forward to it,' and regretted the decision the moment he had closed the door. After all, on Saturday nights he always watched film of the week on Sky, while enjoying a Chinese takeaway and a gin and tonic. In any case, he needed to be in bed by ten because on Sunday morning he was responsible for checking the church collection. He was also their accountant. Honorary, he assured his mother.

Henry spent most of Saturday morning trying to come up with an excuse: a headache, an emergency meeting, a previous engagement he'd forgotten about, so that he could ring Ms Forster and call the whole thing off. Then he realized that he didn't have her home number.

At six o'clock that evening Henry put on the dinner jacket his mother had given him on his twenty-first birthday, which didn't always have an annual outing. He looked at himself in the mirror, nervous that his attire must surely be out of date – wide lapels and flared trousers – unaware that this look was actually back in fashion. He was among the last to arrive at the town hall, and had already made up his mind that he would be among the first to leave.

Angela had placed Henry on the end of the top table, from where he was able to observe proceedings, while only occasionally having to respond to the lady seated on his left.

Once the speeches were over, and the band had struck up, Henry felt he could safely slip away. He looked around for Ms Forster. He had earlier spotted her dashing all over the place, organizing everything from the raffle and the heads-and-tails competition to the ten-pound-note draw and even the auction. When he looked at her more closely, dressed in her long red ball gown, her fair hair falling to her shoulders, he had to admit . . . Henry stood up and was about to leave, when Angela appeared by his side. 'Hope you've enjoyed yourself,' she said, touching his arm. Henry couldn't remember the last time a woman had touched him. He prayed she wasn't going to ask him to dance.

'I've had a wonderful time,' Henry assured her. 'How about you?'

'Run off my feet,' Angela replied, 'but I feel confident that we'll raise a record amount this year.'

'So how much do you expect to make?' asked Henry, relieved to find himself on safer ground.

Angela checked her little notebook. 'Twelve thousand, six hundred in pledges, thirty-nine thousand, four hundred and fifty in cheques, and just over twenty thousand in cash.' She handed over her notebook for Henry to inspect. He expertly ran a finger down the list of figures, relaxing for the first time that evening.

'What do you do with the cash?' Henry asked.

'I always drop it off on my way home at the nearest bank that has an overnight safe. If you'd like to accompany me, you'll have experienced the whole cycle from beginning to end.' Henry nodded. 'Just give me a few minutes,' she said. 'I have to pay the band, as well as my helpers – and they always insist on cash.'

That was probably when Henry first had the idea. Just a passing thought to begin with, which he quickly dismissed. He headed towards the exit and waited for Angela.

'If I remember correctly,' said Henry as they walked down the steps of the town hall together, 'your turnover last year was just under five million, of which over a million was in cash.'

'What a good memory you have, Mr Preston,' Angela said as they headed towards the High Street, 'but I'm hoping to raise over five million this year,' she added, 'and I'm already ahead of my target for March.'

'That may well be the case,' said Henry, 'but you still only paid yourself forty-two thousand last year,' he continued, 'which is less than one per cent of your turnover.'

'I'm sure you're right,' said Angela, 'but I enjoy the work, and it keeps me occupied.'

'But don't you consider you deserve a better return for your efforts?'

'Possibly, but I only charge my clients five per cent of the profits, and every time I suggest putting my fee up, they always remind me that they are a charity.'

'But you're not,' said Henry. 'You're a professional, and should be recompensed accordingly.'

'I know you're right,' said Angela as they stopped outside the Nat West bank and she dropped the cash into the night safe, 'but most of my clients have been with me for years.'

'And have taken advantage of you for years,' insisted Henry.

'That may well be so,' said Angela, 'but what can I do about it?'

The thought returned to Henry's mind, but he said nothing other than, 'Thank you for a most interesting evening, Ms Forster. I haven't enjoyed myself so much in years.' Henry thrust out his right hand, as he always did at the end of every meeting, and had to stop himself saying, 'See you next year.'

Angela laughed, leant forward and kissed him on the cheek. Henry certainly couldn't remember when that had last occurred. 'Goodnight, Henry,' she said as she turned and began to walk away.

'I don't suppose . . .' he hesitated.

'Yes, Henry?' she said, turning back to face him.

'That you'd consider having dinner with me some time?'

'I'd like that very much,' said Angela. 'When would suit you?'

'Tomorrow,' said Henry, suddenly emboldened.

Angela removed a diary from her handbag and began to flick through the pages. 'I know I can't do tomorrow,' she said. 'I have a feeling it's Greenpeace.'

'Monday?' said Henry, not having to check his diary.

'Sorry, it's the Blue Cross Ball,' said Angela, turning another page of her diary.

'Tuesday?' said Henry trying not to sound desperate.

'Amnesty International,' said Angela, flicking over another page.

'Wednesday,' said Henry, wondering if she had changed her mind.

'Looks good,' said Angela, staring at a blank page. 'Where would you like to meet?'

'How about La Bacha?' said Henry, remembering that it was the restaurant where the partners always took their most important clients to lunch. 'Eight o'clock suit you?'

'Suits me fine.'

Henry arrived at the restaurant twenty minutes early and read the menu from cover to cover – several times. During his lunch break, he'd purchased a new shirt and a silk tie. He was already regretting that he hadn't tried on the blazer that was displayed in the window.

Angela strolled into La Bacha just after eight. She was wearing a pale green floral dress that fell just below the knee. Henry liked the way she'd done her hair, but knew that he wouldn't have the courage to tell her. He also approved of the fact that she wore so little make-up and her only jewellery was a modest string of pearls. Henry rose from his place as she reached the table. Angela couldn't remember the last person who'd bothered to do that.

Henry had feared that they wouldn't be able to find anything to talk about – small talk had never been his forte – but Angela made it all so easy that he found himself ordering a second bottle of wine, long before the meal was over – another first.

Over coffee, Henry said, 'I think I've come up with a way of supplementing your income.'

'Oh, don't let's talk business,' said Angela, touching his hand.

'It's not business,' Henry assured her.

When Angela woke the following morning, she smiled as she remembered what a pleasant evening she'd spent with Henry. All she could recall him saying as they parted was, 'Don't forget that any winnings made from gambling are tax-free.' What was all that about?

Henry, on the other hand, could recall every detail of the advice he'd given Angela. He rose early on the following Sunday and began preparing an outline plan, which included opening several bank accounts, preparing spreadsheets and working on a long-term investment programme. He nearly missed matins.

The following evening Henry made his way to the Hilton Hotel on Park Lane, arriving a few minutes after midnight. He was carrying an empty Gladstone bag in one hand and an umbrella in the other. After all, he had to look the part.

The Westminster and City Conservative Association's annual ball was coming to an end. As Henry entered the ballroom, party-goers were beginning to burst balloons and drain the last drops of champagne from any remaining bottles. He spotted Angela seated at a table in the far corner, sorting out pledges, cheques and cash before placing them in three separate piles. She looked up and couldn't mask her surprise when she saw him. Angela had spent the day convincing herself that he didn't mean it and, if he did turn up, she wouldn't go through with it.

'How much cash?' he asked matter-of-factly, even before she could say hello.

'Twenty-two thousand three hundred and seventy pounds,' she heard herself saying.

Henry took his time. He double-checked the notes before placing the cash in his battered bag. Angela's calculation had proved to be accurate. He handed her a receipt for £19,400.

'See you later,' he said, just as the band struck up 'Jerusalem'. Henry left the ballroom as the words 'Bring me my bow of burning gold' were rendered lustily and out of tune. Angela remained transfixed as she watched Henry walk away. She knew that if she didn't chase after him and stop the man before he reached the bank, there could be no turning back.

'Congratulations on another well-organized event, Angela,' said Councillor Pickering, interrupting her thoughts. 'I don't know how we'd manage without you.'

'Thank you,' said Angela, turning to face the chairman of the ball committee.

Henry pushed his way through the hotel's swing doors and out onto the street, feeling for the first time that his anonymity was no longer a weakness but a strength. He could hear his heart beating as he headed towards the local branch of HSBC, the nearest bank with an overnight safe deposit. Henry dropped £19,400 into the safe, leaving £2,970 of the cash in his bag. He then hailed a taxi – another departure from his usual routine – and gave the cabby an address in the West End.

The taxi drew up outside an establishment that Henry had never entered before, although he had kept their accounts for over twenty years.

The night manager of the Black Ace Casino tried not to look surprised when Mr Preston walked onto the floor. Had he come to make a spot-check? It seemed unlikely, as the company accountant didn't acknowledge him but headed straight for the roulette table.

Henry knew the odds only too well because he signed off the casino's end-of-year balance sheet every April, and despite rent, rates, staff wages, security and even free meals and drinks for favoured customers, his client still managed to declare a handsome profit. But it wasn't Henry's intention to make a profit, or, for that matter, a loss.

Henry took a seat at the roulette table and saw red. He opened his Gladstone bag, extracted ten ten-pound notes and handed them across to the croupier, who in turn counted them slowly before he gave Henry ten little blue and white chips in return.

There were a number of gamblers already seated at the table, placing bets of different denominations, five, ten, twenty, fifty and even the occasional hundred-pound golden chip. Only one punter had a stack of golden chips in front of him, which he was spreading randomly around the different numbers. Henry was pleased to see that he held the attention of most of the onlookers standing round the table.

While the man on the far side of the table continued to litter the green baize with golden chips, Henry placed one of his ten-pound chips on red. The wheel spun and the little white ball revolved in the opposite direction until it finally settled in red 19. The croupier returned one ten-pound chip to Henry, while he raked in over a thousand pounds' worth of golden chips from the gambler on the other side of the table.

While the croupier prepared for the next spin of the wheel, Henry slipped his single chip in the left-hand pocket of his jacket, while leaving his original stake on red.

The croupier spun the wheel again and this time the little white ball came to a halt in black 4, and Henry's chip was raked in by the croupier. Two bets, and Henry had

broken even. He placed another ten-pound chip on red. Henry had already accepted that if he was to exchange all the cash for chips, it would be a long and arduous process. But then Henry, unlike most gamblers, was a patient man, whose only purpose was to break even. He placed another ten pounds on red.

Three hours later, by which time he had managed to exchange all £2,970 of cash for chips without anyone becoming suspicious, Henry left the table and headed for the bar. If any one had been following closely what Henry had been up to, they would have observed that he had just about broken even. But then that was his intention. He only ever meant to exchange all the surplus cash for chips before he could execute the second part of his plan.

When Henry reached the bar, his Gladstone bag empty and his pockets bulging with chips, he took a seat next to a woman who appeared to be on her own. He didn't speak to her and she showed no interest in him. When Angela ordered another drink, Henry bent down and deposited all of his chips into the open handbag she had left on the floor beside her. He was already walking towards the exit before the barman could take his order.

The manager pulled open the front door for him.

'I hope it won't be too long before we see you again, sir.'

Henry nodded, but didn't bother to explain that the whole exercise was about to become part of a nightly routine. Once Henry was back outside on the pavement, he walked towards the nearest tube station, but didn't start whistling until he'd turned the corner.

Angela bent down and closed her bag, but not before she'd finished her drink. Two men had propositioned her earlier in the evening and she'd felt quite flattered. She slipped off her stool and walked across to join a short queue of punters at the cashier's window. When she reached the front, Angela pushed the pile of ten-pound chips under the steel grille and waited.

'Cash or cheque, madam?' enquired the teller, once he'd counted her chips.

'A cheque please,' Angela replied.

'What name should the cheque be made out to?' was the teller's next question.

After a moment's hesitation, Angela said, 'Mrs Ruth Richards.'

The cashier wrote out the name Ruth Richards, and the figure, £2,930, before slipping the cheque under the grille. Angela checked the figure. Henry had lost £40. She smiled, remembering that he had assured her that over a year it would even out. After all, as he had explained often enough, he wasn't playing the odds, but simply exchanging any traceable cash for chips, so that she would end up with a cheque which no one would later be able to trace.

Angela slipped out of the casino when she saw the manager chatting to another customer who had clearly lost a large sum of money. Henry had warned her that the management keeps a much closer eye on winners than losers, and that as she was about to embark on a long and profitable run she shouldn't draw attention to herself.

One of Henry's stipulations was that there should not be any contact between the two of them, other than when he came to collect the takings, and then again for that brief moment when he deposited the chips into her open bag. He didn't want anyone to think that they might be an item. Angela reluctantly agreed with his reasoning. Henry's only other piece of advice was that she should not be seen collecting the cash herself during any function.

'Leave that to the volunteers,' he said, 'so that if anything goes wrong, no one will suspect you.'

There are one hundred and twelve casinos located across central London, so Henry and Angela didn't find it necessary to return to any particular establishment more than once a year.

For the next three years, Henry and Angela took their holidays at the same time, but never in the same place, and always in August. Angela explained that not many organizations hold their annual events in that particular month. During the season Henry had to make sure that he was never out of town because from September to December Sunday was the only night Angela could guarantee not to be working, and in the run-up to Christmas she often had a lunchtime event, followed by a couple more functions in the evening.

Although Henry had written the rulebook, Angela had insisted on adding a subclause. Nothing would be deducted from any organization which failed to reach the previous year's total. Despite this addendum, which incidentally Henry heartily agreed with, he rarely left a function with his Gladstone bag empty.

The two of them still met once a year at Mr Preston's office to go over Ms Forster's annual accounts, which was followed by a dinner a week later at La Bacha. Neither of them ever alluded to the fact that she had siphoned off £267,900, £311,150 and £364,610 during the past three years, and after each function deposited the latest cheque in different bank accounts right across London, always in the name of Mrs Ruth Richards. Henry's other responsibility was to ensure that their new-found wealth was invested shrewdly, remembering that he wasn't a gambler. However, one of the advantages of preparing other companies' accounts is that it isn't too difficult to predict who is likely to have a good year. As the cheques were never made out in his or her name, any subsequent profits couldn't be traced back to either of them.

After they had banked the first million, Henry felt that they could risk a celebration dinner. Angela wanted to go to Mosimann's in West Halkin Street, but Henry vetoed the idea. He booked a table for two at La Bacha. No need to draw attention to their new-found wealth, he reminded her.

Henry made two other suggestions during dinner. Angela was quite happy to go along with the first, but didn't want to talk about the second. Henry had advised her to transfer the first million to an offshore account in the Cook Islands, while he carried on with the same investment policy; he also recommended that in future whenever they cleared another hundred thousand, Angela would immediately transfer the sum to the same account.

Angela raised her glass. 'Agreed,' she said, 'but what is the second item on the agenda, Mr Chairman?' she asked, teasing him. Henry took her through the details of a contingency plan she didn't even want to think about.

Henry finally raised his glass. For the first time in his life, he was looking forward to retirement, and joining all his colleagues for a farewell party on his sixtieth birthday.

Six months later, the chairman of Pearson, Clutterbuck & Reynolds sent out invitations to all the firm's employees, asking them to join the partners for drinks at a local three-star hotel to celebrate the retirement of Henry Preston and to thank him for forty years of dedicated service to the company.

Henry was unable to attend his own farewell party, as he ended up celebrating his sixtieth birthday behind bars, and all for a mere £820.

＊───《O》───＊

Miss Florence Blenkinsopp double-checked the figures. She'd been right the first time. They were £820 short of the amount she had calculated before the uninvited guest dressed in a pinstriped suit had walked into the ballroom with his little bag and disappeared with all the cash. It couldn't be Angela who was responsible; after all, she had been one of her pupils at St Catherine's Convent. Miss Blenkinsopp dismissed the discrepancy as her mistake, especially as the takings were comfortably up on the previous year's total.

The following year would be the convent's one-hundredth anniversary, and Miss Blenkinsopp was already planning a centenary ball. She told her committee that she expected them to pull their socks up if they hoped to set records during the centenary year. Although Miss Blenkinsopp had retired as headmistress of St Catherine's some seven years before, she continued to treat her committee of old gals as if they were still adolescent pupils.

The centenary ball could not have been a greater success, and Miss Blenkinsopp was the first to single out Angela for particular praise. She made it clear that in her opinion, Ms Forster had certainly pulled her socks up.

493

However, Miss Blenkinsopp felt it necessary to triple-check the cash they had collected that night, before the little man turned up with his Gladstone bag and took it all away. When she went over the figures later in the week, although their previous record had been broken by a considerable amount, the cash entry was over two thousand short of the figure she had scribbled on the back of her place card.

Miss Blenkinsopp felt she had no choice but to point out the discrepancy (two years running) to her president, Lady Travington, who in turn sought the advice of her husband, who was chairman of the local watch committee. Sir David promised, before putting the light out that night, that he would have a word with the chief constable in the morning.

When the chief constable was informed of the misappropriation, he passed on the details to his chief superintendent. He sent it further down the line to a chief inspector, who would like to have told his boss that he was in the middle of a murder hunt and also staking out a shipment of heroin with a street value of over ten million. The fact that St Catherine's Convent had mislaid – he checked his notes – just over £2,000, wasn't likely to be placed at the top of his priority list. He stopped the next person walking down the corridor and passed her the file. 'See you have a full report on my desk, Sergeant, before the watch committee meet next month.'

Detective Sergeant Janet Seaton set about her task as if she was stalking Jack the Ripper.

First, she interviewed Miss Blenkinsopp, who was most cooperative, but insisted that none of her gals could possibly have been involved with such an unpleasant incident, and therefore they were not to be interviewed.

Ten days later, DS Seaton purchased a ticket for the Bebbington Hunt Ball, despite the fact that she had never mounted a horse in her life.

DS Seaton arrived at Bebbington Hall just before the gong was struck and the toastmaster bellowed out, 'Dinner is served.' She quickly identified Angela Forster, even before she had located her table. Although DS Seaton had to engage in polite conversation with the men on either side of her, she was still able to keep a roving eye on Ms Forster. By the time cheese and coffee were served, the detective had come to the conclusion that she was dealing with a consummate professional. Not only could Ms Forster handle the regular outbursts of Lady Bebbington, the Master of Hounds' wife, but she also found time to organize the band, the kitchen, the waiters, the cabaret and the voluntary staff without once breaking into a gallop. But, more interesting, she seemed to have nothing to do with the collecting of any money. That was carried out by a group of ladies, who performed the task without appearing to consult Angela.

When the band struck up its opening number, several young men asked the detective sergeant for a dance. She turned them all down, one somewhat reluctantly.

It was a few minutes before one, when the evening was drawing to a close, that the detective sergeant spotted the man she had been waiting for. Among the red and black jackets, he would have been easier to identify than a fox on the run. He also fitted the exact description Miss Blenkinsopp had provided: a short, rotund, bald-headed man of around sixty who would be more appropriately dressed for an accountant's office than a Hunt Ball. She never took her eyes off him as he progressed unobtrusively around the

THE NEW COLLECTED SHORT STORIES

outside of the dance floor to disappear behind the bandstand. The detective quickly left her table and walked to the other side of the ballroom, coming to a halt only when she had a perfect sighting of the two of them. The man was seated next to Angela counting the cash, unaware that an extra pair of eyes was watching him. The detective sergeant stared at Angela, as the man carefully placed the cheques, the pledges and the cash in separate piles. Not a word passed between them.

Once Henry had double-checked the amount of cash, he didn't even give Angela a second look. He placed the notes in his bag and handed her a receipt. With no more than a slight bow of the head, he retraced his steps round the outside of the dance floor and quickly left the ballroom. The whole operation had taken him less than seven minutes. Henry didn't notice that one of the revellers was only a few paces behind him, and, more important, her eyes never left him.

DS Seaton watched as the unidentified man made his way down the long drive, through the wrought-iron gates and on towards the village.

Since it was a clear night and the streets were empty, it was not difficult for DS Seaton to follow the progress of the man with the bag without being spotted. He must have been supremely confident because he never once looked back. She only had to slip into the shadows on one occasion, when her quarry came to a halt outside a local branch of the Nat West Bank. He opened his bag, removed a package and dropped it into the overnight safe. He then continued on his way, hardly breaking his stride. Where was he going?

The young detective had to make an instant decision. Should she follow the stranger, or return to Bebbington

Hall and see what Ms Forster was up to? Follow the money, she had always been instructed by her supervisor at Peel House. When Henry reached the station, the detective sergeant cursed. She had left her car in the grounds of the hall, and if she was to continue pursuing the bag man, she would have to abandon the vehicle and pick it up first thing in the morning.

The last train to Waterloo that night trundled into Bebbington Halt a few minutes later. It was becoming clear that the man with the bag had everything timed to the minute. The detective remained out of sight until her suspect had boarded the train. She then took a seat in the next carriage.

When they reached Waterloo, the man stepped off the train and made his way quickly across to the nearest taxi rank. The detective stood to one side and watched as he progressed to the front of the queue. The moment he climbed into a cab, the detective walked briskly to the top of the queue, produced her warrant card and apologized to the person who was about to step into a cab. She jumped in the taxi and instructed the driver to follow the one that had just moved off the rank.

When the driver pulled up outside the Black Ace Casino, the detective remained in the back of her cab until the man had disappeared inside.

She took her time paying the cab driver before she climbed out and followed her quarry into the casino. She filled in a temporary membership form, as she didn't want anyone to realize that she was on duty.

DS Seaton strolled onto the floor and glanced around the gaming tables. It only took her a few moments before she spotted her man seated next to one of the roulette wheels.

She took a step closer and joined a group of onlookers who formed a horseshoe around the table. The detective sergeant made sure that she remained some distance away from her quarry because, dressed in a long blue silk gown more appropriate for a ball, he might spot her and even wonder if she had followed him from Bebbington Hall.

For the next hour she watched the man remove wads of cash from his bag at regular intervals, then exchange them for chips. An hour later the bag was clearly empty because he left the table with a glum look on his face, and made his way towards the bar.

DS Seaton had cracked it. The anonymous man was siphoning off money from the evening events in order to finance his gambling habit, but she still couldn't be sure if Angela was involved.

The detective slipped behind a marble pillar as the man climbed onto a stool next to a lady in a blue suit with a short skirt.

Did he have enough money over to pay for a prostitute? The detective stepped out from behind the pillar to take a closer look, and nearly bumped into Henry as he began walking back towards the exit. Later, much later, DS Seaton thought it strange that he had left the bar without having a drink. Perhaps the woman on the stool had rejected him.

Henry stepped out onto the pavement and hailed a taxi. The detective grabbed the next one. She followed his cab as it made its way across Putney Bridge and continued its journey along the south side of the river. The taxi finally came to a halt outside a block of flats in Wandsworth. DS Seaton made a note of the address and decided that she had earned a taxi ride home.

The following morning, DS Seaton placed her report on the chief inspector's desk. He read it, smiled, left his office and walked down the corridor to brief the chief superintendent, who in turn phoned the chief constable. The chief decided not to mention it to the chairman of the watch committee until after an arrest had been made, as he wanted to present Sir David with an open-and-shut case, one that a jury could not fail to convict on.

Henry deposited the cash from the Butterfly Ball in the overnight vault of Lloyds TSB just a couple of hundred yards away from the hotel where the Masons were holding their annual dinner. He must have walked about another thirty yards before a police car drew up beside him. There wouldn't have been much point in making a dash for it, as Henry wasn't built for a change of gear. And in any case he had already planned for this moment, right down to the last detail. Henry was arrested and charged two days before the watch committee was due to meet.

Henry selected Mr Clifton-Smyth to represent him, a solicitor whose accounts he had handled for the past twenty years.

Mr Clifton-Smyth listened carefully to his client's defence, making copious notes, but when Henry finally came to the end of his tale, the lawyer only had one piece of advice to offer him: plead guilty.

'I will of course,' added the lawyer, 'brief counsel of any mitigating circumstances.'

Henry accepted his solicitor's advice; after all, Mr Clifton-Smyth had never once, in the past two decades, questioned *his* judgement.

Henry made no attempt to contact Angela during the run-up to the trial, and although the police felt fairly confident that she was playing Bonnie to his Clyde, they quickly worked out that they shouldn't have arrested him until he'd gone to the casino a second time. Who was the woman seated at the bar? Had she been waiting for him? The Special Crime Unit spent weeks collecting bank stubs from casinos right across London, but they couldn't find a single cheque made out to a Ms Angela Forster, and even more puzzling, they didn't come up with one for a Mr Henry Preston. Did he always lose?

When they checked Angela's events book, they discovered that Henry had always taken responsibility for counting the cash, and signed the receipt. Her bank account was then picked over by a bunch of treasury vultures, and found to be only £11,318 in credit, a sum that had showed very little movement either way for the past five years. When DS Seaton reported back to Miss Blenkinsopp, she seemed quite content to believe that the right man had been apprehended. After all, she told the detective, a St Catherine's gal couldn't possibly be involved in that sort of thing.

With the murder hunt still in progress, and the drugs stash not yet unearthed, the chief superintendent sent down an instruction to close the St Catherine's file. They'd made an arrest, and that was all that would matter when they reported their annual crime statistics.

Once the Treasury solicitors had accepted that they couldn't trace any of the missing money, Henry's solicitor managed to broker a deal with the CPS. If he pleaded guilty to the theft of £130,000, and was willing to return the full amount to the injured parties concerned, they would recommend a reduced sentence.

'And no doubt there are mitigating circumstances in this case that you wish to bring to my attention, Mr Cameron?' suggested the judge as he stared down from the bench at Henry's Silk.

'There most certainly are, m'lord,' replied Mr Alex Cameron QC as he rose slowly from his place. 'My client,' he began, 'makes no secret of his unfortunate addiction to gambling, which has been the cause of his tragic downfall. However,' Mr Cameron continued, 'I feel confident that your lordship will take into account that this is my client's first offence, and until this sad lapse of judgement he had been a pillar of the community with an unblemished reputation. Indeed, my client has given years of selfless service to his local church as its honorary treasurer, to which you will recall, m'lord, the vicar bore witness.'

Mr Cameron cleared his throat before continuing. 'M'lord, you see before you a broken and penniless man, who has nothing to look forward to except long lonely years of retirement. He has even,' added Mr Cameron, tugging at his lapels, 'had to sell his flat in Wandsworth in order to repay his creditors.' He paused. 'Perhaps you might feel, in the circumstances, m'lord, that my client has suffered quite enough and should therefore be treated leniently.' Mr Cameron smiled hopefully at the judge, and resumed his seat.

The judge looked down at Henry's advocate, and returned his smile. 'Not quite enough, Mr Cameron. Try not to forget that Mr Preston was a professional man who violated a position of trust. But first let me remind your client,' said the judge, turning his attention to Henry, 'that gambling is a sickness, and the defendant should seek some help for his malady the moment he is released from prison.' Henry braced himself as he waited to learn how long his sentence would be.

The judge paused for what seemed an eternity, as he continued to stare at Henry. 'I sentence you to three years,' he said, before adding, 'take the prisoner down.'

Henry was shipped off to Ford open prison. No one noticed him come and no one noticed him go. He led just as anonymous an existence on the inside as he had outside. He received no mail, made no phone calls and entertained no visitors. When they released him eighteen months later, having completed half his sentence, there was no one waiting at the barrier to greet him.

Henry Preston accepted his £45 discharge pay, and was last seen heading towards the local railway station, carrying a Gladstone bag containing only his personal belongings.

Mr and Mrs Graham Richards enjoy a pleasant, if somewhat uneventful retirement on the island of Majorca. They have a small, front-line villa overlooking the Bay of Palma, and both of them are proving to be popular with the local community.

The chairman of the Royal Overseas Club in Palma reported to the AGM that he considered he'd pulled off quite a coup, convincing the former finance director of the Nigerian National Oil Company to become the club's honorary treasurer. Nods, hear-hears and a sprinkling of applause followed. The chairman went on to suggest that the secretary should record a note in the minutes, that since Mr Richards had taken over the responsibility as treasurer, the club's accounts had been in apple-pie order.

'And by the way,' he added, 'his wife Ruth has kindly agreed to organize our annual ball.'

The Alibi

'HE GOT AWAY WITH murder, didn't he?' said Mick.

'How did he manage that?' I asked.

'Because if two screws say that's what happened, then that's what happened,' said Mick, 'and no con will be able to tell you any different. Understood?'

'No, I don't understand,' I admitted.

'Then I'll have to explain it to you, won't I?' said Mick. 'There's a golden rule among cons – never have sex with a mate's tart while he's banged up. It's all part of the code.'

'That might be a bit rough on a young girl whose boyfriend has just been given a lengthy sentence because then you'd be sentencing her to the same number of years without sex.'

'That's not the point,' said Mick, 'because Pete made it clear to Karen that he'd wait for her.'

'But he wasn't going anywhere for the next six years,' I suggested.

'You're missing the point, Jeff. It's the code and, to be fair to the tart, by all accounts Karen was as good as gold for the first six months and then she came off the rails. Truth is,' said Mick, 'Pete's best mate Brian had already had sex with Karen, but that was before she became Pete's girl, on account of the fact that they'd all been at secondary modern together. But that didn't count because Karen stopped whoring around once she'd moved in with Pete. Understood?'

'I think so,' I said.

'Mind you, the rule doesn't apply to Pete on account of the fact that he's a man. It's only logic, isn't it, because men are different. We're lions, they're lambs.' Lionesses would have seemed more appropriate. However, I confess I didn't voice my opinion at the time. 'Still,' Mick continued, 'the code is clear. You don't have sex with a mate's tart while he's banged up.'

I put my pen down and continued to listen to the Gospel according to St Mick – another burglar who was in and out of prison as if the building had revolving doors. I decided to abandon any attempt to write my daily diary. It was clear Mick was on a roll and nothing was going to stop him – certainly not me. And as the door was locked and I couldn't escape, I decided to take down his words. But first a little background.

Mick Boyle was my cell mate at Lincoln, and serving his ninth sentence during the past seventeen years, all for burglary. 'I may be a tea-leaf,' he proclaimed, 'but I can't be doing with violence. Don't approve,' he added, clearly attempting to capture the moral high ground. He told me that he had six children that he knew of, by five different women, but had had little or no contact with any of them since. I must have looked surprised, because he added, 'Don't worry yourself, Jeff, they're all taken care of by the Social.'

'If you want pussy,' Mick continued, 'there's quite enough going spare without having sex with your best mate's tart; after all, most of us are in and out, in and out,' he repeated, laughing at his own joke.

Mick's friend Pete Bailey – the hero or the villain in this tale, according to your viewpoint – had been charged with aggravated robbery, which covers a multitude of sins, especially if you ask the court – after you've been found guilty – to take into consideration one hundred and twelve similar offences.

'Result? Pete gets six years in the slammer.' Mick paused to draw breath. 'Mind you, he still killed his best mate while he was inside and got away with it, didn't he?'

'Did he?' I asked, showing a little more interest.

'Yeah, he sure did. Mind you, he knew he'd only have to serve three years on account of the fact that he was always on his best behaviour, whenever he was inside,' said Mick. 'Logic, isn't it? So after fifteen months in Wakefield – awful nick – they sent him off to Hollesley Bay open prison in Suffolk, didn't they, to finish off his sentence. Bloody holiday camp. See, the theory is,' continued Mick, 'an open prison is meant to prepare you for returning to society. Some hope. All Pete did was spend his time in the prison library reading through back copies of *Country Life*, supplied by some do-gooder, so he could work out in advance which houses he was going to rob the moment he got out. Now another rule in an open prison,' continued Mick, 'is that you're entitled to a visit once a week, not like the once a month you get in closed conditions; that is as long as you're enhanced, and not been put on report for at least a month.'

'Enhanced?' I ventured.

'That's when a con's been on good behaviour for at least three months. When he's enhanced he gets all sorts of privileges, like more time out of his cell, better job, even more pay in some nicks.'

'And how do you get put on report?'

'That's easy enough. Swear at a screw, turn up late for work, fail a drugs test. I was once put on report for nicking an orange from the kitchen. Diabolical liberty.'

'So was your friend Pete ever put on report?' I asked.

'Never,' Mick replied. 'Good as gold, wasn't he, because he wanted a visit from his tart. Well, he does his three months, works in the stores, keeps his nose clean, and Bob's your uncle, he's enhanced. Following Saturday his tart turns up at the nick to pay him a visit.

'In open prisons, visits are held in the biggest room available, usually the gym or the canteen. And you have to remember, security isn't like a closed nick, with sniffer dogs and CCTV cameras following your every move, so you can behave natural when you're with your tart.' He paused. 'Well, within limits. I mean you can't have sex like they do in Swedish prisons. You know – what do they call it?'

'Conjugal visits?'

'Well, whatever, it's sex, and we don't allow it. Mind you, a screw will turn a blind eye – when a con puts his hand up a tart's skirt, but then I remember in one prison—'

'Pete,' I reminded him.

'Oh, yeah, Pete. Well, Karen came to visit Pete the following Saturday. All's going well until Pete asks about his best mate, Brian. Karen clams up, doesn't say a word does she, then turns bright red. Pete susses straight away what she's been up to: tart, having it off with his best mate while he's inside. She lit his short fuse, didn't she? So Pete jumps up and puts one on her. Karen goes arse over tits, and lands up flat on the floor. The alarm goes off and screws come running through every door. They had to pull him off Karen and drag him away to segregation. Ever been to segregation, Jeff?'

'No, can't say I have.'

'Well, don't bother. Diabolical liberty. Bare cell, mattress on the floor, steel basin screwed into the wall and a steel bog what don't flush. Next day Pete's put on report, and comes up in front of the governor, who, you have to remember, is God Almighty. He don't need no judge or jury to help him decide if you're guilty – Home Office regulations are quite enough.'

'So what happened to Pete?'

'Sent back to closed conditions, wasn't he? Shipped off to Lincoln prison the same day, with another three months added to his sentence. Some cons, when they're sent back to a closed nick, lose their rag, start breaking the place up, taking drugs, setting their cell on fire, so they never get out. I was banged up with a muppet in Liverpool once. Started off with a three-year sentence and he's still there – eleven years later. Last time he came up in front of the governor for—'

'Pete,' I said, trying not to sound exasperated.

'Oh, yeah, Pete. Well, Pete goes the other way.'

'The other way?'

'Good as gold all the time he's banged up at Lincoln. Three months later he's back enhanced, with all his privileges restored. Gets a job in the kitchen, works like a slave, six months later he puts in a request for a visit and it's granted, with the exception of one Karen Slater. But he never wanted to see that whore again anyway. No, this time Pete applied for a visit from one of his old mates who was on the out at the time. Now this mate confirms that Brian is not only having it off with Karen, but now that Pete's safely banged up in Lincoln she's moved in with him. What a diabolical liberty,' said Mick. 'Pete's mate even asked if he wanted Brian done over. "No, don't go down that road," Pete told him. "I'll be taking care of him myself, all in good time." He never went into no detail of what he had in mind, on account of the fact that in the end someone always opens their mouth. Must be the same in politics, Jeff.'

'Pete.'

'Well, Pete goes on being as good as gold. Cleanest pad, working all hours, never swearing at no screws, never on report. Result? Twelve months later he's back at Hollesley Bay open prison, with only nine months left to serve.'

'And once he was back at Hollesley Bay, did he try to contact Karen?'

'No, didn't put in a request for a visit. In fact, never even mentioned her name.'

'So what was his game?' I asked, slipping into the prison jargon.

'He only had one game all along, Jeff: he wanted to get himself transferred to the enhancement block, on the other side of the prison, didn't he.'

'I've lost you,' I admitted.

'All part of his master plan, wasn't it? When you first arrive at Hollesley Bay, which, don't forget, is an open nick, you're allocated a room in one of the two main blocks.'

'Are you?'

'Yeah, north and south block. But if you get enhanced – another three more months of behaving like a saint – then they move you across to the enhancement block, which gives you even more privileges.'

'Like what?'

'You can have a visit from a mate every Saturday. Pete wasn't interested. You can go home once a month on a Sunday – he's still not interested. You can apply for a job outside of the prison during the week – still no interest, even though it would of given him a chance to pick up an extra bob or two before he's released.'

'Then why bother to earn all those privileges if you don't plan to take advantage of them?' I asked.

'Weren't part of Pete's master plan, was it? Trouble with you, Jeff, is that you don't think like a criminal.'

'So why was Pete so keen to get himself transferred to the enhancement block?'

'Good question at last, Jeff, but for that you'll need a little background. Pete 'ad already worked out that over on the enhancement block they 'ad five screws on duty during the day, but only two at night, on account of the fact that if a prisoner reaches enhanced status he can be trusted, not to mention how short-staffed the prison service is. And don't forget that, in an open nick, there are no cells, no bars, no keys and no perimeter walls, so anyone can abscond.'

'So why don't they?' I asked.

'Because not many cons who've made it to an open prison are that interested in escaping.'

'Why not?'

'Logic, isn't it? They're coming to the end of their sentence, and if they're caught, and nine out of ten of the morons are, you're sent straight back to a closed nick, with extra time added to your sentence. So forget it, it's just not worth it. I remember a con called Dale. What a muppet he was. He only had three weeks left to serve, when he—'

'Pete,' I tried again.

'You're such an impatient bastard, Jeff, and it's not as if you're going anywhere. So where was I?'

'Only two officers on duty in the enhancement block at night,' I said, checking my notes.

'Oh, yeah. But even on the enhancement block you have to report to the front office at seven in the morning, and then again at nine each night. Now Pete, as I told you, 'ad a job in the prison stores, handing out clothes to the new cons, and supplying laundry once a week for the regulars, so the screws always knew where he was, which was also part of Pete's plan. But if he hadn't reported to the front office at seven in the morning and then again at nine at night, he would have been put on report, which would have meant he'd be sent back to north block with all his privileges removed. So Pete never once misses a roll call, his cell was always spick and span, and his light is always out long before eleven.'

'All part of Pete's master plan?'

'You catch on fast,' said Mick. 'But then Pete came up against an obstacle – that the right word, Jeff?' I nodded, not wishing to interrupt his flow. 'During the night, one of the screws would walk round the block at one o'clock and then return again at four in the morning, to check that every con was in bed and asleep. All the screw has to do is pull back the curtain on the outside of the door, look through the glass panel and shine his torch on the bed to make sure the con is snoring away. Have I ever told you about the con who was caught in his room, with a—'

'Pete,' I said, not even looking up at Mick.

'Pete would lay awake at night until the first screw came round at one o'clock to make sure he was in his room. The screw lifts the curtain, shines the torch on his bed and then disappears. Pete would then go back to sleep, but he always set his alarm for ten to four when he'd carry out the same routine. A different screw always turns up at four to check you're still in bed. It took Pete just over a month to work out that there were two screws, Mr Chambers and Mr Davis, who didn't bother to make the nightly rounds and check everyone was in bed. Chambers used to fall asleep and Davis couldn't be dragged away from the TV. After that, all Pete had to do was wait until the two of them were on duty the same night.'

With only about six weeks to go before Pete was due to be released, he returned to the enhancement block after work to find that Chambers and Davis were the duty officers that night. When Pete signed the roll-call sheet at nine, Mr Chambers was already watching a football match on TV, and Mr Davis had his feet up on the table drinking a Coke and reading the sports pages of the *Sun*. Pete went up to his room, watched TV till just after ten, and then turned off his light. He got into bed and pulled the blanket over him, but kept on his tracksuit and trainers. He waited until a few minutes after one before he crept out into the corridor and checked to make sure no one was around – not a sign of Chambers or Davis. He then went to the end of the corridor, opened the fire-escape door, and disappeared down the back stairs, leaving a wedge of paper in the door, before he set off on an eight-mile run into Woodbridge.

No one can be sure when Pete got back that night, but he reported into the office as usual at seven the next morning. Mr Chambers ticked off his name. When Pete glanced down at the screw's clipboard, all four of his roll-call columns – nine, one, four and seven – had a tick in every box. Pete had breakfast in the canteen before reporting to the stores for work.

'So he got away with it?'

'Not quite,' said Mick. 'Later that morning the cops turn up in numbers and begin crawling all over the place, but they're only looking for one man. They end up in the stores, arrest Pete and haul him off to Woodbridge nick for questioning. They interrogate him for hours about the deaths of Brian Powell and Karen Slater, both found strangled in their bed. Rumour has it that they were having it off at the time. Pete stuck to the same line: "Can't have been me, guv. I was banged up in prison at the time. You only have to ask Mr Chambers and Mr Davis, the officers who were on duty that night." The copper in charge of the case visited the enhancement block and checked the roll-call sheet. Brian and the tart were strangled some time between three and five, according to the police doctor, so if Chambers saw Pete asleep in bed at four, he couldn't have been in Woodbridge at the same time, could he? Logic, isn't it?

'An independent inquiry was set up by the Home Office. Chambers and Davis both confirmed that they'd checked every prisoner at one o'clock and then again at four, and on both occasions Pete had been asleep in his room. Several of the other cons were only too happy to appear in front of the inquiry and confirm they'd been woken by the flashlight, when Chambers and Davis did their rounds. This only strengthened Pete's defence. So the inquiry concluded that Pete must have been in his bed at one o'clock and four o'clock on the night in question, so he couldn't have committed the murders.'

'So he got away with it,' I repeated.

'Depends on how you describe got away with it,' said Mick, 'because although the police never charged Pete, the copper in charge of the case later made a statement saying that they'd closed their inquiries, as there was no one else they wanted to interview – hint, hint. That wasn't what you call a good career move for Chambers and Davis, so they set about stitching Pete up.'

'But Pete only had six weeks to serve before he was due to be released,' I reminded Mick, 'and he was always as good as gold.'

'True, but another screw, a mate of Davis's, reported Pete for stealing a pair of jeans from the stores just a few days before he was due for release. Pete was carted off to segregation and the governor had him transported back to Lincoln nick even before they'd served up tea that night, with another three months added to his sentence.'

'So he ended up having to serve another three months?'

'That was six years ago,' said Mick. 'And Pete's still banged up in Lincoln.'

'So how do they manage that?'

'The screws just come up with a new charge every few weeks, so that whenever Pete comes up on report the governor adds another three months to his sentence. My bet is Pete's stuck in Lincoln for the rest of his life. What a liberty.'

'But how do they get away with it?' I asked.

'Haven't you been listening to anything I've been saying,

Jeff? If two screws say that's what happened, then that's what happened,' repeated Mick, 'and no con will be able to tell you any different. Understood?'

'Understood,' I replied.

On 12 September 2002 Prison Service Instruction No. 47/2002 stated that the judgement of the European Court of Human Rights in the case of Ezeh & Connors ruled that, where an offence was so extreme as to result in a punishment of additional days, the protections inherent in Article 6 of the European Convention of Human Rights applied. A hearing must be conducted by an independent and impartial tribunal, and prisoners are entitled to legal assistance at such hearings.

Pete Bailey was released from Lincoln prison on 19 October 2002.

A Greek Tragedy

GEORGE TSAKIRIS IS NOT ONE of those Greeks you need to beware of when he is bearing gifts.

George is fortunate enough to spend half his life in London and the other half in his native Athens. He and his two younger brothers, Nicholas and Andrew, run between them a highly successful salvage company, which they inherited from their father.

George and I first met many years ago during a charity function in aid of the Red Cross. His wife Christina was a member of the organizing committee, and she had invited me to be the auctioneer.

At almost every charity auction I have conducted over the years, there has been one item for which you just can't find a buyer, and that night was no exception. On this occasion, another member of the committee had donated a landscape painting that had been daubed by their daughter and would have been orphaned at a village fete. I felt, long before I climbed up onto the rostrum and searched around the room for an opening bid, that I was going to be left stranded once again.

However, I had not taken George's generosity into consideration.

'Do I have an opening bid of one thousand pounds?' I enquired hopefully, but no one came to my rescue. 'One thousand?' I repeated, trying not to sound desperate, and just as I was about to give up, out of a sea of black dinner jackets a hand was raised. It was George's.

'Two thousand,' I suggested, but no one was interested

in my suggestion. 'Three thousand,' I said looking directly at George. Once again his hand shot up. 'Four thousand,' I declared confidently, but my confidence was short-lived, so I returned my attention to George. 'Five thousand,' I demanded, and once again he obliged. Despite his wife being on the committee, I felt enough was enough. 'Sold for five thousand pounds, to Mr George Tsakiris,' I announced to loud applause, and a look of relief on Christina's face.

Since then poor George, or to be more accurate rich George, has regularly come to my rescue at such functions, often purchasing ridiculous items, for which I had no hope of arousing even an opening bid. Heaven knows how much I've prised out of the man over the years, all in the name of charity.

Last year, after I'd sold him a trip to Uzbekistan, plus two economy tickets courtesy of Aeroflot, I made my way across to his table to thank him for his generosity.

'No need to thank me,' George said as I sat down beside him. 'Not a day goes by without me realizing how fortunate I've been, even how lucky I am to be alive.'

'Lucky to be alive?' I said, smelling a story.

Let me say at this point that the tired old cliché, that there's a book in every one of us, is a fallacy. However, I have come to accept over the years that most people have experienced a single incident in their life that is unique to them, and well worthy of a short story. George was no exception.

'Lucky to be alive,' I repeated.

George and his two brothers divide their business responsibilities equally: George runs the London office, while Nicholas remains in Athens, which allows Andrew to roam around the globe whenever one of their sinking clients needs to be kept afloat.

Although George maintains establishments in London, New York and Saint-Paul-de-Vence, he still regularly returns to the home of the gods, so that he can keep in touch with his large family. Have you noticed how wealthy people always seem to have large families?

At a recent Red Cross Ball, held at the Dorchester, no one came to my rescue when I offered a British Lions' rugby shirt – following their tour of New Zealand – that had been signed by the entire losing team. George was nowhere to be seen, as he'd returned to his native land to attend the wedding of a favourite niece. If it hadn't been for an incident that took place at that wedding, I would never have seen George again. Incidentally, I failed to get even an opening bid for the British Lions' shirt.

George's niece, Isabella, was a native of Cephalonia, one of the most beautiful of the Greek islands, set like a magnificent jewel in the Ionian Sea. Isabella had fallen in love with the son of a local wine grower, and as her father was no longer alive, George had offered to host the wedding reception, which was to be held at the bride-groom's home.

In England it is the custom to invite family and friends to attend the wedding service, followed by a reception, which is often held in a marquee on the lawn of the home of the daughter's parents. When the lawn is not large enough, the festivities are moved to the village hall. After the formal speeches have been delivered, and a reasonable period of time has elapsed, the bride and groom depart for their honeymoon, and fairly soon afterwards the guests make their way home.

Leaving a party before midnight is not a tradition the Greeks have come to terms with. They assume that any festivities after a wedding will continue long into the early hours of the following morning, especially when the bride-groom owns a vineyard. Whenever two natives are married on a Greek island, an invitation is automatically extended to the locals so that they can share in a glass of wine and toast the bride's health. Wedding crasher is not an expression that the Greeks are familiar with. The bride's mother doesn't bother sending out gold-embossed cards with RSVP in the lower left-hand corner for one simple reason: no one would bother to reply, but everyone would still turn up.

Another difference between our two great nations is that it is quite unnecessary to hire a marquee or rent the village hall for the festivities, as the Greeks are unlikely to encounter the occasional downpour, especially in the middle of summer – about ten months. Anyone can be a weather forecaster in Greece.

The night before the wedding was due to take place, Christina suggested to her husband that, as host, it might be wise for him to remain sober. Someone, she added, should keep an eye on the proceedings, bearing in mind the bridegroom's occupation. George reluctantly agreed.

The marriage service was held in the island's small church, and the pews were packed with invited, and uninvited, guests long before vespers were chanted. George accepted with his usual grace that he was about to host a rather large gathering. He looked on with pride as his favourite niece and her lover were joined together in holy matrimony. Although Isabella was hidden behind a veil of white lace, her beauty had long been acknowledged by the young men of the island. Her fiancé, Alexis Kulukundis, was tall and slim, and his waistline did not yet bear testament to the fact that he was heir to a vineyard.

And so to the service. Here, for a moment, the English and the Greeks come together, but not for long. The ceremony was conducted by bearded priests attired in long golden surplices and tall black hats. The sweet smell of incense from swinging burners wafted throughout the church, as the priest in the most ornately embroidered gown, who also boasted the longest beard, presided over the marriage, to the accompaniment of murmured psalms and prayers.

George and Christina were among the first to leave the church once the service was over, as they wanted to be back at the house in good time to welcome their guests.

The bridegroom's rambling old farmhouse nestled on the slopes of a hill above the plains of the vineyard. The spacious garden, surrounded by terraced olive groves, was full of chattering well-wishers long before the bride and

bridegroom made their entrance. George must have shaken over two hundred hands, before the appearance of Mr and Mrs Kulukundis was announced by a large group of the bridegroom's rowdy friends who were firing pistols into the air in celebration; a Greek tradition which I suspect would not go down well on an English country lawn, and certainly not in the village hall.

With the exception of the immediate family and those guests selected to sit on the long top table by the side of the dance floor, there were, in fact, very few people George had ever set eyes on before.

George took his place at the centre of the top table, with Isabella on his right and Alexis on his left. Once they were all seated, course after course of overladen dishes was set before his guests, and the wine flowed as if it were a Bacchanalian orgy rather than a small island wedding. But then Bacchus – the god of wine – was a Greek.

When, in the distance, the cathedral clock chimed eleven times, George hinted to the best man that perhaps the time had come for him to make his speech. Unlike George, he *was* drunk, and certainly wouldn't be able to recall his words the following morning. The groom followed, and when he tried to express how fortunate he was to have married such a wonderful girl, once again his young friends leapt onto the dance floor and fired their pistols in the air.

George was the final speaker. Aware of the late hour, the pleading look in his guests' eyes, and the half-empty bottles littering the tables around him, he satisfied himself with wishing the bride and groom a blessed life, a euphemism for lots of children. He then invited those who still could to rise and toast the health of the bride and groom. Isabella and Alexis, they all cried, if not in unison.

Once the applause had died down, the band struck up. The groom immediately rose from his place, and, turning to his bride, asked her for the first dance. The newly married couple stepped onto the dance floor, accompanied by another volley of gunfire. The groom's parents followed next, and a few minutes later George and Christina joined them.

Once George had danced with his wife, the bride and the groom's mother, he made his way back to his place in the centre seat of the top table, shaking hands along the way with the many guests who wished to thank him.

George was pouring himself a glass of red wine – after all, he had performed all his official duties – when the old man appeared.

George leapt to his feet the moment he saw him standing alone at the entrance to the garden. He placed his glass back on the table and walked quickly across the lawn to welcome the unexpected guest.

Andreas Nikolaides leant heavily on his two walking sticks. George didn't like to think how long it must have taken the old man to climb up the path from his little cottage, halfway down the mountain. George bowed low and greeted a man who was a legend on the island of Cephalonia as well as in the streets of Athens, despite the fact that he had never once left his native soil. Whenever Andreas was asked why, he simply replied, 'Why would anyone leave Paradise?'

In 1942, when the island of Cephalonia had been over-run by the Germans, Andreas Nikolaides escaped to the hills

and, at the age of twenty-three, became the leader of the resistance movement. He never left those hills during the long occupation of his homeland and, despite a handsome bounty being placed on his head, did not return to his people until, like Alexander, he had driven the intruders back into the sea.

Once peace was declared in 1945, Andreas returned in triumph. He was elected mayor of Cephalonia, a position which he held, unopposed, for the next thirty years. Now that he was well into his eighties, there wasn't a family on

Cephalonia who did not feel in debt to him, and few who didn't claim to be a relative.

'Good evening, sir,' said George stepping forward to greet the old man. 'We are honoured by your presence at my niece's wedding.'

'It is I who should be honoured,' replied Andreas, returning the bow. 'Your niece's grandfather fought and died by my side. In any case,' he added with a wink, 'it's an old man's prerogative to kiss every new bride on the island.'

George guided his distinguished guest slowly round the outside of the dance floor and on towards the top table. Guests stopped dancing and applauded as the old man passed by. George insisted that Andreas take his place in the centre of the top table, so that he could be seated between the bride and groom. Andreas reluctantly took his host's place of honour. When Isabella turned to see who had been placed next to her, she burst into tears and threw her arms around the old man. 'Your presence has made the wedding complete,' she said.

Andreas smiled and, looking up at George, whispered, 'I only wish I'd had that effect on women when I was younger.'

George left Andreas seated in his place at the centre of the top table, chatting happily to the bride and groom. He picked up a plate and walked slowly down a table laden with food. George took his time selecting only the most delicate morsels that he felt the old man would find easy to digest. Finally he chose a bottle of vintage wine from a case that his own father had presented to him on the day of his wedding. George turned back to take the offering to his honoured guest just as the chimes on the cathedral clock struck twelve, hailing the dawn of a new day.

Once more, the young men of the island charged onto the dance floor and fired their pistols into the air, to the cheers of the assembled guests. George frowned, but then for a moment recalled his own youth. Carrying the plate in one hand and a bottle of wine in the other, he continued walking back towards his place in the centre of the table, now occupied by Andreas Nikolaides.

Suddenly, without warning, one of the young bandoliers, who'd had a little too much to drink, ran forward and tripped on the edge of the dance floor, just as he was discharging his last shot. George froze in horror when he saw the old man slump forward in his chair, his head falling onto the table. George dropped the bottle of wine and the plate of food onto the grass as the bride screamed. He ran quickly to the centre of the table, but it was too late. Andreas Nikolaides was already dead.

The large, exuberant gathering was suddenly in turmoil, some screaming, some weeping, while others fell to their knees, but the majority were hushed into a shocked, sombre silence, unable to grasp what had taken place.

George bent down over the body and lifted the old man into his arms. He carried him slowly across the lawn, the guests forming a corridor of bowed heads, as he walked towards the house.

George had just bid five thousand pounds for two seats at a West End musical that had already closed when he told me the story of Andreas Nikolaides.

'They say of Andreas that he saved the life of everyone on that island,' George remarked as he raised his glass in memory of the old man. He paused before adding, 'Mine included.'

The Commissioner

'WHY DOES HE WANT to see me?' asked the Commissioner.

'He says it's a personal matter.'

'How long has he been out of prison?'

The Commissioner's secretary glanced down at Raj Malik's file. 'He was released six weeks ago.'

Naresh Kumar stood up, pushed back his chair and began pacing around the room; something he always did whenever he needed to think a problem through. He had convinced himself – well, almost – that by regularly walking round the office he was carrying out some form of exercise. Long gone were the days when he could play a game of hockey in the afternoon, three games of squash the same evening and then jog back to police headquarters. With each new promotion, more silver braid had been sewn on his epaulet and more inches appeared around his waist.

'Once I've retired and have more time, I'll start training again,' he told his number two, Anil Khan. Neither of them believed it.

The Commissioner stopped to stare out of the window and look down on the teeming streets of Mumbai some fourteen floors below him: ten million inhabitants who ranged from some of the poorest to some of the wealthiest people on earth. From beggars to billionaires, and it was his responsibility to police all of them. His predecessor had left him with the words: 'At best, you can hope to keep the lid on the kettle.' In less than a year, when he passed on the responsibility to his deputy, he would be proffering the same advice.

Naresh Kumar had been a policeman all his life, like his

father before him, and what he most enjoyed about the job was its sheer unpredictability. Today was no different, although a great deal had changed since the time when you could clip a child across the ear if you caught him stealing a mango. If you tried that today, the parents would sue you for assault and the child would claim he needed counselling. But, fortunately, his deputy Anil Khan had come to accept that guns on the street, drug dealers and the war against terrorism were all part of a modern policeman's lot.

The Commissioner's thoughts returned to Raj Malik, a man he'd been responsible for sending to prison on three occasions in the past thirty years. Why did the old con want to see him? There was only one way he was going to find out. He turned to face his secretary. 'Make an appointment for me to see Malik, but only allocate him fifteen minutes.'

The Commissioner had forgotten that he'd agreed to see Malik until his secretary placed the file on his desk a few minutes before he was due to arrive.

'If he's one minute late,' said the Commissioner, 'cancel the appointment.'

'He's already waiting in the lobby, sir,' she replied.

Kumar frowned, and flicked open the file. He began to familiarize himself with Malik's criminal record, most of which he was able to recall because on two occasions – one when he had been a detective sergeant, and the second, a newly promoted inspector – he had been the arresting officer.

Malik was a white-collar criminal who was well capable of holding down a serious job. However, as a young man he had quickly discovered that he possessed enough charm and native cunning to con naive people, particularly old ladies, out of large sums of money, without having to exert a great deal of effort.

His first scam was not unique to Mumbai. All he required was a small printing press, some headed notepaper and a list of widows. Once he'd obtained the latter – on a daily basis from the obituary column of the *Mumbai Times* – he was in business. He specialized in selling shares in overseas companies that didn't exist. This provided him with a regular income, until he tried to sell some stock to the widow of another conman.

When Malik was charged, he admitted to having made over a million rupees, but the Commissioner suspected that it was a far larger sum; after all, how many widows were willing to admit they had been taken in by Malik's charms? Malik was sentenced to five years in Pune jail and Kumar lost touch with him for nearly a decade.

Malik was back inside again after he'd been arrested for selling flats in a high-rise apartment block on land that turned out to be a swamp. This time the judge sent him down for seven years. Another decade passed.

Malik's third offence was even more ingenious, and resulted in an even longer sentence. He appointed himself a life-assurance broker. Unfortunately the annuities never matured – except for Malik.

His barrister suggested to the presiding judge that his client had cleared around twelve million rupees, but as little of the money was available to be given back to those who were still living, the judge felt that twelve years would be a fair return on this particular policy.

By the time the Commissioner had turned the last page, he was still puzzled as to why Malik could possibly want to see him. He pressed a button under the desk to alert his secretary that he was ready for his next appointment.

Commissioner Kumar glanced up as the door opened. He stared at a man he barely recognized. Malik must have been ten years younger than he was, but they would have

passed for contemporaries. Although Malik's file stated that he was five foot nine and weighed a hundred and seventy pounds, the man who walked into his office did not fit that description.

The old con's skin was lined and parched, and his back was hunched, making him appear small and shrunken. Half a life spent in jail had taken its toll. He wore a white shirt that was frayed at the collar and cuffs, and a baggy suit that might at some time in the past have been tailored for him. This was not the self-confident man the Commissioner had first arrested over thirty years ago, a man who always had an answer for everything.

Malik gave the Commissioner a weak smile as he came to a halt in front of him.

'Thank you for agreeing to see me, sir,' he said quietly. Even his voice had shrunk.

The Commissioner nodded, waved him to the chair on the other side of his desk and said, 'I have a busy morning ahead of me, Malik, so perhaps you could get straight to the point.'

'Of course, sir,' Malik replied, even before he'd sat down. 'It's simply that I am looking for a job.'

The Commissioner had considered many reasons why Malik might want to see him, but seeking employment had not been among them.

'Before you laugh,' continued Malik, 'please allow me to put my case.'

The Commissioner leant back in his chair and placed the tips of his fingers together, as if in silent prayer.

'I have spent too much of my life in jail,' said Malik. He paused. 'I've recently reached the age of fifty, and can assure you that I have no desire to go back inside again.'

The Commissioner nodded, but didn't express an opinion.

'Last week, Commissioner,' continued Malik, 'you addressed the annual general meeting of the Mumbai Chamber of Commerce. I read your speech in the *Times* with great interest. You expressed the view to the leading businessmen of this city that they should consider employing people who had served a prison sentence – give them a second chance, you said, or they will simply take the easy option and return to a life of crime. A sentiment I was able to agree with.'

'But I also pointed out,' interrupted the Commissioner, 'that I was only referring to first offenders.'

'Exactly my point,' countered Malik. 'If you consider there is a problem for first offenders, just imagine what I come up against, when I apply for a job.' Malik paused and straightened his tie before he continued. 'If your speech was sincere and not just delivered for public consumption, then perhaps you should heed your own advice, and lead by example.'

'And what did you have in mind?' asked the Commissioner. 'Because you certainly do not possess the ideal qualifications for police work.'

Malik ignored the Commissioner's sarcasm and ploughed boldly on. 'In the same paper in which your speech was reported, there was an advertisement for a filing clerk in your records department. I began life as a clerk for the P & O Shipping Company, right here in this city. I think that you will find, were you to check the records, that I carried out that job with enthusiasm and efficiency, and on that occasion left with an unblemished record.'

'But that was over thirty years ago,' said the Commissioner, not needing to refer to the file in front of him.

'Then I will have to end my career as I began it,' replied Malik, 'as a filing clerk.'

The Commissioner didn't speak for some time while he considered Malik's proposition. He finally leant forward, placed his hands on the desk, and said, 'I will give some thought to your request, Malik. Does my secretary know how to get in touch with you?'

'Yes, she does, sir,' Malik replied as he rose from his place. 'Every night I can be found at the YMCA hostel on Victoria Street.' He paused. 'I have no plans to move in the near future.'

Over lunch in the officers' dining room, Commissioner Kumar briefed his deputy on the meeting with Malik.

Anil Khan burst out laughing. 'Hoist with your own petard, Chief,' he said with considerable feeling.

'True enough,' replied the Commissioner as he helped himself to another spoonful of rice, 'and when you take over from me next year, this little episode will serve to remind you of the consequences of your words, especially when they are delivered in public.'

'Does that mean that you are seriously considering employing the man?' asked Khan, as he stared across the table at his boss.

'Possibly,' replied Kumar. 'Why, are you against the idea?'

'You are in your last year as Commissioner,' Khan reminded him, 'with an enviable reputation for probity and competence. Why take a risk that might jeopardize such a fine record?'

'I feel that's a little over-dramatic,' said the Commissioner. 'Malik's a broken man, which you would have seen for yourself had you been present at the meeting.'

'Once a conman, always a conman,' replied Khan. 'So I repeat, why take the risk?'

'Perhaps because it's the correct course of action, given the circumstances,' replied the Commissioner. 'If I turn Malik down, why should anyone bother to listen to my opinion ever again?'

'But a filing clerk's job is particularly sensitive,' remonstrated Khan. 'Malik would have access to information that should only be seen by those whose discretion is not in question.'

'I've already considered that,' said the Commissioner. 'We have two filing departments: one in this building, which is, as you rightly point out, highly sensitive, and another based on the outskirts of the city that deals only with dead cases, which have either been solved or are no longer being followed up.'

'I still wouldn't risk it,' said Khan as he placed his knife and fork back on the plate.

'I've cut down the risk even more,' responded the Commissioner. 'I'm going to place Malik on a month's trial. A supervisor will keep a close eye on him, and then report directly back to me. Should Malik put so much as a toe over the line, he'll be back on the street the same day.'

'I still wouldn't risk it,' repeated Khan.

On the first of the month, Raj Malik reported for work at the police records department on 47 Mahatma Drive, on the outskirts of the city. His hours were eight a.m. to six p.m. six days a week, with a salary of nine hundred rupees a month. Malik's daily responsibility was to visit every police station in the outer district, on his bicycle, and collect any dead files. He would then pass them over to his supervisor, who would file them away in the basement, rarely to be referred to again.

At the end of his first month, Malik's supervisor reported back to the Commissioner as instructed. 'I wish I had a dozen Maliks,' he told the chief. 'Unlike today's young, he's always on time, doesn't take extended breaks, and never complains when you ask him to do something not covered by his job description. With your permission,' the supervisor added, 'I would like to put his pay up to one thousand rupees a month.'

The supervisor's second report was even more glowing. 'I lost a member of staff through illness last week, and Malik took over several of his responsibilities and somehow still managed to cover both jobs.'

The supervisor's report at the end of Malik's third month was so flattering that when the Commissioner addressed the annual dinner of the Mumbai Rotary Club, not only did he appeal to its members to reach out their hands to ex-offenders, but he went on to assure his audience that he had heeded his own advice and been able to prove one of his long-held theories. If you give former prisoners a real chance, they won't reoffend.

The following day, the *Mumbai Times* ran the headline: **COMMISSIONER LEADS BY EXAMPLE**

Kumar's sentiments were reported in great detail, alongside a photo of Raj Malik, with the caption, *a reformed character*. The Commissioner placed the article on his deputy's desk.

Malik waited until his supervisor had left for his lunch break. He always drove home just after twelve and spent an hour with his wife. Malik watched as his boss's car disappeared out of sight before he slipped back down to the basement. He placed a stack of papers that needed to be filed on the corner of the counter, just in case someone came in unannounced and asked what he was up to.

He then walked across to the old wooden cabinets that were stacked one on top of the other. He bent down and pulled open one of the files. After nine months he had reached the letter P and still hadn't come across the ideal candidate. He had already thumbed through dozens of Patels during the previous week, dismissing most of them as either irrelevant or inconsequential for what he had in mind. That was until he reached one with the first initials H.H.

Malik removed the thick file from the cabinet, placed it on the counter-top and slowly began to turn the pages. He didn't need to read the details a second time to know that he'd hit the jackpot.

He scribbled down the name, address and telephone numbers neatly on a slip of paper, and then returned the file to its place in the cabinet. He smiled. During his tea break, Malik would call and make an appointment to see Mr H.H. Patel.

With only a few weeks to go before his retirement, Commissioner Kumar had quite forgotten about his prodigy. That was until he received a call from Mr H.H. Patel, one of the city's leading bankers. Mr Patel was requesting an urgent meeting with the Commissioner – to discuss a personal matter.

Commissioner Kumar looked upon H.H. not only as a friend, but as a man of integrity, and certainly not someone who would use the word urgent without good reason.

Kumar rose from behind his desk as Mr Patel entered the room. He ushered his old friend to a comfortable chair in the corner of the room and pressed a button under his desk. Moments later his secretary appeared with a pot of tea and a plate of Bath Oliver biscuits. The Deputy Commissioner followed in her wake.

'I thought it might be wise to have Anil Khan present for this meeting, H.H., as he will be taking over from me in a few weeks' time.'

'I know of your reputation, of course,' said Mr Patel, shaking Khan warmly by the hand, 'and I am delighted that you are able to join us.'

Once the secretary had served the three men with tea, she left the room. The moment the door was closed, Commissioner Kumar dispensed with any more small talk. 'You asked to see me urgently, H.H., concerning a personal matter.'

'Yes,' replied Patel. 'I thought you ought to know that I had a visit yesterday from someone who claims to work for you.'

The Commissioner raised an eyebrow.

'A Mr Raj Malik.'

'He is a junior filing clerk in the—'

'In a private capacity, he was at pains to emphasize.'

The Commissioner began tapping the armrest of his chair with the palm of his right hand, as Patel continued. 'Malik said that you were in possession of a file that showed that I was under investigation for money laundering.'

'You were, H.H.,' said the Commissioner, with his usual candour. 'Following nine/eleven, the Minister of Internal Affairs instructed me to investigate any organization which dealt in large sums of cash. That included casinos, racetracks and, in your case, the Bank of Mumbai. A member of my team interviewed your chief teller and advised him about what he should be on the lookout for, and I personally signed the clearance certificate for your company.'

'I remember, you briefed me at the time,' said Patel, 'but your fellow, Malik –'

'He's not my fellow.'

'– said that he could arrange to have my file destroyed.' He paused. 'For a small consideration.'

'He said what?' said Kumar almost exploding out of his chair.

'How small?' asked Deputy Commissioner Khan calmly.

'Ten million rupees,' replied Patel.

'H.H., I don't know what to say,' said the Commissioner.

'You don't have to say anything,' said Patel, 'because it never crossed my mind, even for a moment, that you could be involved in anything quite so stupid, and I told Malik as much.'

'I am grateful,' said the Commissioner.

'No need to be,' said Patel, 'but I did think that perhaps others, less charitable . . .' He paused. 'Especially as Malik's visit came so close to your retirement . . .' He hesitated again. 'And were the press to get hold of the story, it might so easily be misunderstood.'

'I am grateful for your concern, and the speed with which you have acted,' said Kumar. 'I will remain eternally in your debt.'

'I want nothing more than to be sure that this city rightly remains eternally in your debt,' said Patel, 'so that when you leave office it will be in a blaze of glory, rather than with question marks hanging over your head, which, as we both know, would linger on long after your retirement.'

The Deputy Commissioner nodded his agreement as Patel rose from his place.

'You know, Naresh,' Patel said, turning to face the Commissioner, 'I would never have agreed to see the damn man, if you had not spoken so highly of him in your speech to the Rotary Club last month. He even produced the article in the *Mumbai Times*. I therefore assumed that the fellow had come with your blessing.' Mr Patel turned to face Khan. 'May I wish you luck when you take over as Commissioner,' he added, shaking hands with the deputy. 'I don't envy you having to follow such a fine man.' Kumar smiled for the first time that morning.

'I'll be back in a moment,' the Commissioner said to his deputy as he left his office to accompany Patel to the front door.

The Deputy Commissioner stared out of the window as he waited for the Chief to return. He munched on a biscuit as he mulled over several possible alternatives. By the time the Commissioner walked back into the room, Khan knew exactly what had to be done. But would he be able to convince his boss this time?

'I'll have Malik arrested and behind bars within the hour,' said the Commissioner as he picked up the phone on his desk.

'I wonder, sir,' said Deputy Khan quietly, 'if that's the best course of action – given the circumstances?'

'I don't have much choice,' said the Commissioner as he began dialling.

'You may be right,' said Khan, 'but before you make such an irrevocable decision, perhaps we should consider how this is all going to play –' he paused – 'with the press.'

'They'll have a field day,' said Kumar as he replaced the

phone and began pacing around the room. 'They won't be able to make up their minds if I should be hanged as a crook who's willing to accept bribes, or dismissed as the most naive fool ever to hold the office of Commissioner. Neither scenario bears thinking about.'

'But we have to think about it,' insisted Deputy Khan, 'because your enemies – and even good men have enemies – will happily settle for someone who's willing to take kickbacks, while your friends will not be able to deny the lesser charge of naivety.'

'But surely after forty years of service, people will believe . . .'

'People will believe whatever they want to believe,' said Khan, confirming the Commissioner's worst fears, 'and certainly you won't be able to send Malik back to prison until he's been given the chance to appear in a witness box and tell the world his side of the story.'

'But who would believe that old—'

'No smoke without fire, they'll be whispering in the corridors of the law courts, and that will be tame compared with the headlines in the morning papers once Malik has spent a couple of days in the witness box being questioned by a friendly barrister who sees you as nothing more than a stepping stone in his career.'

Kumar continued to pace around the room, but didn't respond.

'Let me try and second-guess the headlines that would follow such a cross-examination.' Khan paused before saying, '"Commissioner accepts bribes to destroy friends' files" might be the headline in the *Times*, while the tabloids will surely be a little more colourful – "Bung money left in Commissioner's office by delivery boy", or perhaps

"Commissioner Kumar employs ex-con to carry out his dirty work"?'

'I think I've got the picture,' said the Commissioner, as he sank back into the chair next to Khan. 'So what the hell am I supposed to do about it?'

'What you've always done in the past,' Khan replied. 'Play it by the book.'

The Commissioner looked across at his deputy quizzically. 'What do you have in mind?'

'Malik,' shouted the supervisor at the top of his voice, even before he'd put the phone down. 'Commissioner Kumar wants to see you, immediately.'

'Did he say why?' asked Malik nervously.

'No, he's not in the habit of confiding in me,' replied the supervisor, 'but don't hang about because he's not a man who likes to be kept waiting.'

'Yes, sir,' Malik replied. He closed the file he'd been working on and placed it back on the supervisor's desk. He walked across to his locker, removed his bicycle clips and left the building without another word. It wasn't until he was outside on the pavement that he began to shake. Had they caught on to his latest scam? Not that it had proved that successful. He unlocked the chain that was attached to the railings and began to consider his options. Should he make a run for it, or simply try to brazen it out? He hadn't been left with a lot of choice. After all, where would he run to? And even if he did decide to run, it would only be a matter of days, perhaps hours, before they caught up with him.

Malik slipped on his bicycle clips, mounted his third-hand Raleigh Lenton and began to pedal slowly towards the city centre. The dusty brown roads were teeming with other bicycles, cars and countless numbers of people, all heading in different directions. The incessant honking of horns, the multitude of different smells, the beating down of the sun and the bustle of everyday life ensured that Mumbai was like no other city on earth. Street traders thrust out their arms as Malik passed, trying to sell him their wares, while beggars with no arms ran by his side, not assisting his progress. Should he come clean and admit what he'd been up to?

He cycled for a few more yards. No, never admit to anything, a golden rule that he'd learnt after long years in prison. He swerved to avoid a cow and nearly fell off.

Assume they know nothing until you're cornered. Even then, deny everything. As he rounded the next corner, police headquarters loomed up in front of him. If he was going to make a dash for it, it would have to be now or never. He pedalled on, until he was only a few yards away from the steps leading up to the front entrance. He tugged firmly on the tired brake handles until his bike came to a slow, unsteady halt. He climbed off, and padlocked his one asset to the nearest railing. He walked slowly up the steps to police headquarters, pushed his way through the swing doors and headed nervously towards the reception desk. He told the duty officer his name. Perhaps there had been a mistake.

'I have an appointment with—'

'Ah, yes,' the duty officer replied ominously, without needing to consult his roster. 'The Commissioner is waiting to see you. You'll find his office is on the fourteenth floor.'

Malik turned and began walking towards the lifts, aware that the duty officer's eyes never left him. Malik glanced at the front door. This would be his last chance to escape, he thought, as the doors of one of the lifts slid open. He stepped into a crowded elevator, which made several stops on its slow interrupted journey to the fourteenth floor. By the time Malik reached the top floor, he was sweating profusely, and it wasn't just the crowded space and lack of air conditioning that caused his unease.

When the doors finally parted, he was on his own. Malik stepped out onto the only thickly carpeted corridor in the building. He looked around and then recalled his last visit. He began to walk slowly towards an office at the far end of the corridor. The word Commissioner was printed in bold stencilled letters on the door.

Malik knocked quietly – perhaps something more important had arisen, causing the Commissioner to leave the office without warning. He heard a female voice invite him to enter. He opened the door to find the Commissioner's secretary seated behind her desk, tapping away furiously. She stopped typing the moment she saw Malik.

'The Commissioner is expecting you,' was all she offered. She didn't smile and she didn't frown as she rose from her place. Perhaps she was unaware of his fate. The secretary disappeared through another door and returned almost immediately. 'The Commissioner will see you now, Mr Malik,' she said, and held the door open for him.

Malik walked into the Commissioner's office, to find him seated at his desk, eyes down, studying an open file. He raised his head, looked directly at him and said, 'Have a seat, Malik.' Not Raj, not Mr, just Malik.

Malik slipped into the chair opposite the Commissioner. He sat in silence, trying not to appear nervous as he watched the second hand of the clock on the wall behind the desk complete a full minute.

'Malik,' the Commissioner eventually said as he looked up from the papers on his desk, 'I've just been reading your supervisor's annual report.'

Malik remained silent, although he could feel a bead of sweat trickling down his nose.

The Commissioner looked back down again. 'He's very complimentary about your work,' said Kumar, 'full of praise. Far better than I could have hoped for when you sat in that chair just a year ago.' The Commissioner looked up and smiled. 'In fact, he's recommending that you should be promoted.'

'Promoted?' said Malik in disbelief.

'Yes, though it may not prove that easy, as there are not too many appropriate jobs available at the present time. However, I do believe I have come across a position that is ideally suited for your particular talents.'

'Oh, thank you, sir,' said Malik, relaxing for the first time.

'There is a vacancy –' the Commissioner opened another file and smiled – 'for an assistant in the city morgue.' He extracted a single sheet of paper and began reading from it.

'It would be your responsibility to scrub the blood off the slabs and clean the floor immediately after the bodies have been dissected and stored away. I'm told the stench is not all that pleasant, but a face mask is supplied, and I have no doubt that, in time, one gets used to it.' He continued to smile at Malik. 'The appointment comes with the rank of sub-supervisor, along with a corresponding rise in salary. It also has other perks, not least that you would have your own room directly above the morgue, so you wouldn't have to bed down any longer at the YMCA.' The Commissioner paused. 'And, should you continue to hold the post until your sixtieth birthday, you would also be entitled to a modest pension.' The Commissioner closed Malik's file and looked directly at him. 'Any questions?' he asked.

'Only one, sir,' said Malik. 'Is there any alternative?'

'Oh, yes,' replied the Commissioner. 'You can spend the rest of your life in jail.'

In The Eye Of The Beholder

OTHER THAN THE FACT that they had been to school together, the two of them had little in common.

Gian Lorenzo Venici had been a diligent child since his first roll call at the age of five, whereas Paolo Castelli somehow managed always to be late, even for his first roll call.

Gian Lorenzo felt at home in the classroom with books, essays and exams, where he outshone his contemporaries. Paolo achieved the same results on the football field, with a change of pace, a deceptive turn and a shot at goal which beguiled his own team as well as the opposition. Both young men progressed to St Cecilia's, the most prestigious high school in Rome, where they were able to display their talents to a wider audience.

When their school days were over, they both graduated to Roma: Gian Lorenzo to the nation's oldest university as a scholar, Paolo to the nation's oldest football club as a striker. Although they didn't mix in the same circles, they were both well aware of the other's achievements. While Gian Lorenzo collected honours in one field, Paolo won them on another, both achieving their goals.

After leaving university, Gian Lorenzo joined his father at the Venici Gallery. He immediately set about converting those years of study into something more practical, as he wished to emulate his father and become the most respected art dealer in Italy.

By the time Gian Lorenzo had began his apprenticeship, Paolo had been appointed captain of Roma. With the cheers and adulation of the fans ringing in his ears, he led them to championship and European glory. Gian Lorenzo only had to turn to the back pages of any newspaper, on an almost daily basis, to follow the exploits of his former classmate, and to the gossip columns to discover who was the latest beauty to be found dangling from his arm: another difference between them.

Gian Lorenzo quickly discovered that in his chosen profession long-term reputation would be built not on the occasional inspired goal, but on hours of dedicated research, combined with good judgement. He had inherited from his father the two most important gifts in any art dealer's armoury – a good eye and a good nose. Antonio Venici also taught his son not only how to look, but *where* to look, when searching for a masterpiece. The old man only dealt in the finest examples of Renaissance painting and sculpture, which would never appear on the open market. Unless a piece was exclusive, Antonio didn't venture out of his gallery. His son followed in his footsteps. The gallery bought and sold only three, perhaps four, paintings a year, but those masters changed hands at around the same price as one of Roma's strikers. After forty years in the business, Gian Lorenzo's father knew not only who possessed the great collections, but more important, who might be willing or, better still, needed to part with the occasional masterpiece.

Gian Lorenzo became so engrossed in his work that he missed the injury Paolo Castelli sustained while playing for Italy against Spain in the European Cup. This personal setback placed Paolo on the sidelines of the football field, as well as the newspapers, especially when it became clear that he had reached his sell-by date.

Paolo left the world stage just as Gian Lorenzo strode onto it. He began to travel around Europe representing the gallery in an endless quest to seek out only the rarest examples of genius, and, having acquired a masterpiece, to find someone who could afford to purchase it.

Gian Lorenzo often wondered what had become of Paolo since he'd stopped playing football and the press no longer reported his every move. He was to discover overnight when Paolo announced his engagement.

Paolo's choice of marriage partner ensured that his exploits were transferred from the back pages to the front.

Angelina Porcelli was the only daughter of Massimo Porcelli, president of Roma Football Club and chairman

of Ulitox, the largest pharmaceutical company in Italy. *A marriage of two heavyweights*, declared the banner headline in one of the tabloids.

Gian Lorenzo turned to page three to discover what merited such a comment. Paolo's bride-to-be was six foot two – an advantage for a model, I hear you say – but there the comparison ended, because the other vital statistic the reporters latched on to was Angelina's weight. This seemed to vary between three hundred and three hundred and fifty pounds, according to whether it was reported by a broadsheet or a tabloid.

A picture is worth a thousand words. Gian Lorenzo studied several photographs of Angelina, and concluded that only Rubens would have considered her as a model. In every picture of Paolo's future bride, no amount of skill displayed by the couturiers of Milan, the stylists of Paris, the jewellers of London, not to mention the legions of personal trainers, dietitians and masseurs, was able to transform her image from sugar plum fairy to prima ballerina. Whichever angle the photographers took, however considerate they tried to be, and some didn't, they only emphasized the transparent difference between her and her fiancé, especially when she stood alongside Roma's former hero. The Italian press, clearly obsessed by Angelina's size, reported nothing else about her of any interest.

Gian Lorenzo turned to the arts pages, and had quite forgotten about Paolo and his future bride when he strode into the gallery later that morning. As he opened the door to his office, he was greeted by his secretary, who thrust a large, gold-embossed card into his hand. Gian Lorenzo glanced down at the invitation.

Signor Massimo Porcelli
has pleasure in inviting

Gian Lorenzo Venici

to the marriage of his daughter,
Angelina,
to Signor Paolo Castelli
at the Villa Borghese.

Six weeks later Gian Lorenzo joined a thousand guests in the grounds of the Villa Borghese. It soon became clear that Signor Porcelli was determined his only child would enjoy a wedding that not only she, but everyone else present, would never forget.

The setting in the Borghese Gardens, perched on one of the seven hills overlooking Rome, with its imposing terracotta and cream villa in the background, was the stuff of fairytales. Gian Lorenzo strolled around the grounds, admiring the sculptures and fountains while catching up with old friends and contemporaries, some of whom he had not seen since his school days. Some twenty minutes before the ceremony was due to take place, a dozen liveried ushers, in long blue coats trimmed with gold braid and wearing white wigs, moved among the throng. They invited the guests to take their seats in the rose garden as the wedding ceremony was about to commence.

Gian Lorenzo joined a large crowd as they made their way towards a recently constructed stand with an elevated semi-circle of seats surrounding a raised stage with an altar as its centrepiece; not unlike a football ground where a different form of worship takes place on a Saturday afternoon. His connoisseur's eye took in the magnificent view over Rome, a scene made even more dazzling by the number of beautiful women, dressed in clothes that he suspected had never been worn before, and in some cases would never be worn again. They were complemented by elegantly dressed men in tailcoats and white shirts, with only different coloured ties and cravats to suggest the peacock in them. Gian Lorenzo looked around to find that he was surrounded by leading politicians, captains of industry, actors, socialites, as well as many of Paolo's old team-mates.

The next actor to take his place on the stage was Paolo himself, accompanied by his best man. Gian Lorenzo knew he was a well-known footballer, but couldn't recall his name. As Paolo strode down the grass path and onto the pitch, Gian Lorenzo understood only too well why women could not take their eyes off the man. Paolo walked up onto the stage, took his place on the right of the altar and waited to be joined by his bride.

A forty-piece string orchestra, almost hidden among the trees behind the altar, struck up the opening chords of Mendelssohn's Wedding March. A thousand guests rose from their seats and turned to see the bride as she progressed slowly up the thick grass carpet on the arm of her proud father.

'What a beautiful dress,' said the lady standing in front of Gian Lorenzo. He nodded his agreement and, staring at the yards of Persian silk that formed a magnificent train behind Angelina, didn't express the one thought that must have been on everyone's mind. Nevertheless, the look on

Angelina's face was that of a bride displaying total content-ment with her lot. She was walking towards the man she adored, aware that many of the women present would have been only too happy to take her place.

As Angelina climbed the steps up onto the stage, the boards creaked. Her future husband smiled as he took a pace forward to join his bride. They both turned to face Cardinal Montagni, the Archbishop of Naples. One or two guests failed to stifle a smile when the cardinal turned to Paolo and enquired, 'Do you take this woman to be your lawful wedded wife, for better for worse, for richer for poorer . . .'

Once bride and groom had been joined together in holy matrimony, Gian Lorenzo made his way to the Long Garden, to join a thousand other guests for dinner. A feast followed that began with champagne and truffle risotto, and ended with chocolate soufflé and a Chateau d'Yquem. Gian Lorenzo could barely move by the time Paolo rose to reply to his best man's speech.

'I am the happiest man on earth,' he declared, as he turned to face his beaming bride. 'I have found the ideal woman for me, and I am only too aware that I must be the envy of every bachelor present.' A sentiment which Gian Lorenzo could not quite agree with, but he quickly banished the ungracious thought from his mind. Paolo continued, 'You know, I was the first suitor to win Angelina's heart. No longer will I have to search for the perfect woman because I have found her. Please rise and join me in a toast to Angelina, my little angel.' The gathering rose as one and toasted, 'Angelina.' One or two even managed 'his little angel'.

After the speeches were over, the dancing began to yet another band – this time one that had been flown in from

New Orleans. Gian Lorenzo overheard that Angelina had once mentioned to Papa that she liked jazz.

As the band struck up and the champagne continued to flow, the newlyweds moved among their guests, which gave Gian Lorenzo a fleeting moment to thank Paolo and his bride for including him in such an unforgettable occasion. 'Medici would have swooned,' he told her, as he kissed her hand. She gave him a warm, gentle smile, but didn't respond.

'Let's keep in touch,' suggested Paolo as the two of them drifted away. 'Angelina is fascinated by art, you know, and is thinking of starting her own collection,' were the last words Gian Lorenzo heard, before Paolo moved on to another guest.

Just before the sun rose and breakfast was about to be served, Signor and Signora Castelli set off for the airport, with a thousand hands waving their farewells. They drove out of the grounds of the Borghese with Paolo at the wheel of his latest Ferrari – not the ideal car for his bride. When they reached the airport, Paolo drove out onto a private airstrip and brought the car to a halt by the side of a Lear jet that was waiting for two passengers. The newlyweds left the Ferrari parked on the runway, climbed the steps and disappeared inside Papa's aircraft. Within minutes of fastening their seatbelts, the jet took off for Acapulco, the first stop on their three-month honeymoon.

Despite Paolo's parting words, when the Castellis returned from their honeymoon they made no attempt to keep in touch with Gian Lorenzo. However, he was able to follow their exploits on an almost daily basis in the gossip columns of the national press.

A year later he read that they would be moving to Venice, where they had purchased the type of villa that makes the covers, not the inside pages, of glossy magazines. Gian Lorenzo assumed that he and his old friend were unlikely to bump into each other again.

When Antonio Venici retired, he happily handed over the responsibility for the family business to his son. As the new owner of the Venici Gallery, Gian Lorenzo spent half his time travelling around Europe in search of that elusive painting which makes collectors gasp, while not insulting the dealer with any suggestion of bargaining.

One such journey was to Venice, to view a Canaletto owned by the Contessa di Palma – a lady who, having divorced her third husband and sadly no longer possessing the looks to guarantee a fourth, had decided she would have to part with one or two of her treasures. The Contessa's only stipulation was that no one must discover that she was facing temporary financial difficulties. Every leading dealer in Italy knew of her mounting debts and unpaid creditors. Gian Lorenzo was only thankful that the Contessa had chosen him to share her confidences with.

Gian Lorenzo took some time to study the Contessa's considerable collection and concluded that she had an eye not only for rich men. After he had agreed a price for the Canaletto, he expressed the hope that this might be the beginning of a long and fruitful relationship.

'Let's start with dinner at Harry's Bar, my darling,' said the Contessa, once she had Gian Lorenzo's cheque in her hand.

Gian Lorenzo was making up his mind between an affogato or an espresso when Paolo and Angelina strolled into Harry's Bar. Everyone in the room followed their progress, as the maître d' ushered them unctuously to a corner table.

'Now there's someone who can afford to buy my *entire* collection,' whispered the Contessa.

'Without a doubt,' agreed Gian Lorenzo, 'but unfortunately Paolo only collects rare cars.'

'And even rarer women,' interjected the Contessa.

'And I'm not altogether sure what Angelina collects.'

'A few extra pounds each year,' suggested the Contessa. 'She once came to tea with my second husband and literally ate us out of house and home. By the time she left we were down to the water biscuits.'

'Well, let's try and make up for that tonight,' said Gian Lorenzo. 'I'm told the zabaglione is their signature dish?'

The Contessa showed no interest in the zabaglione, but simply sailed on, ignoring her companion's unsubtle hint. 'Can you imagine what those two get up to, when they're in bed?'

Gian Lorenzo was surprised that the Contessa was willing to voice a question he had often thought about but never felt able to express. And there was worse to come as the Contessa went on to describe things that hadn't, until then, even crossed Gian Lorenzo's mind.

'Do you think he climbs on top of her?' Gian Lorenzo didn't offer an opinion. 'A feat in itself,' she continued, 'because if they did it the other way round, surely she'd suffocate him.'

Gian Lorenzo didn't care to think about the image, so he tried once again to change the subject. 'We went to the same school, you know – one hell of an athlete.'

'You'd have to be, to satisfy her.'

'I even attended their wedding,' he added. 'A truly memorable occasion, though I doubt after all this time that he would even remember I was among the guests.'

'Would you really be willing to spend the rest of your life with such a creature, however much money she had to offer?' asked the Contessa, not paying attention to her host's words.

'He claims to adore her,' said Gian Lorenzo, 'calls her his little angel.'

'In that case, I wouldn't want to meet up with his idea of a big angel.'

'But if he felt otherwise,' suggested Gian Lorenzo, 'he could always divorce her.'

'Not a chance,' said the Contessa. 'You clearly haven't been told about their pre-nuptial agreement.'

'No, I haven't,' admitted Gian Lorenzo, trying not to sound interested.

'Her father had much the same opinion of that clapped-out footballer as I do. Old man Porcelli made him sign an agreement which spelt out that if Paolo ever divorced his daughter he would end up with nothing. Paolo was also forced to sign a second document stating that he would never reveal the contents of the pre-nuptial to anyone, including Angelina.'

'Then how do you know about it?' prompted Gian Lorenzo.

'When you've signed as many pre-nuptials as I have, darling, you hear things.'

Gian Lorenzo laughed and called for the bill.

The maître d' smiled. 'It's already been taken care of, signor,' he said, nodding in the direction of Paolo, 'by your old school friend.'

'How kind of him,' said Gian Lorenzo.

'No, her,' the Contessa reminded him.

'Please excuse me for a moment,' said Gian Lorenzo.

'I must just thank them before we leave.' He rose from his place, and made his way slowly across the crowded room.

'How are you?' said Paolo, who was on his feet long before Gian Lorenzo had reached their table. 'You know my little angel, of course,' he said, turning to smile at his wife, 'but then how could you ever forget?'

Gian Lorenzo took Angelina's hand and kissed it gently. 'And I will also never forget your magnificent wedding.'

'Medici would have swooned,' said Angelina.

Gian Lorenzo gave a slight bow in acknowledgement.

'Is that the Contessa di Palma you are dining with?' asked Paolo. 'Because if it is, she has something my little angel desires.' Gian Lorenzo made no comment. 'I do hope, Gian Lorenzo, that she's a client, not a friend, because if my little angel wants something, then I will stop at nothing to ensure she gets it.' Gian Lorenzo still considered it wise to remain silent. Never forget, his father had once told him, only restaurateurs close deals in restaurants – when they hand you the bill. 'And as it's a field I know little about,' continued Paolo, 'and you are acknowledged as one of the nation's leading authorities, perhaps you would be kind enough to represent Angelina on this occasion?'

'I would be delighted to do so,' said Gian Lorenzo, as the head waiter placed a chocolate trifle in front of Paolo's wife, with a bowl of crème fraîche on the side.

'Excellent,' said Paolo, 'let's keep in touch.'

Gian Lorenzo smiled and shook his old friend by the hand. He well remembered the last occasion Paolo had made such an offer. But then some people consider such suggestions nothing more than polite conversation. Gian Lorenzo turned to Angelina and bowed low before walking back across the restaurant to rejoin the Contessa.

'Time for us to leave, I fear,' said Gian Lorenzo, glancing at his watch, 'especially if I'm to catch the first plane to Rome in the morning.'

'Did you manage to sell my Canaletto to your friend?' asked the Contessa, as she rose from her place.

'No,' replied Gian Lorenzo, as he waved in the direction of Paolo's table, 'but he did suggest that we keep in touch.'

'And will you?'

'That might be quite difficult,' admitted Gian Lorenzo, 'as he didn't give me his number, and I have a feeling Signor and Signora Castelli may not be listed.'

Gian Lorenzo took the first flight back to Rome the following morning. The Canaletto was to follow him at a more leisurely pace. No sooner had he set foot in the gallery than his secretary rushed out of the office, spilling out the words, 'Paolo Castelli has already called twice this morning. He apologized for not giving you his number,' she added, 'and wondered if you would be kind enough to phone him, just as soon as you get in.'

Gian Lorenzo walked calmly into his office, sat down at his desk and composed himself. He then tapped out the number his secretary had placed in front of him. The call was first answered by a butler, who transferred him to a secretary, before he was finally connected to Paolo.

'After you left last night, my little angel spoke of nothing else,' began Paolo. 'She has never forgotten her visit to the Contessa's home, where she first saw her magnificent art collection. She wondered if the reason you were meeting with the Contessa was—'

'I don't think it would be wise to discuss this matter over the phone,' said Gian Lorenzo, whose father had also taught him that deals are rarely made on the telephone, but almost always face to face. One needs the client to view the picture, and then you allow them to hang it on a wall in their home for several days. There is a crucial moment when the buyer considers the painting already belongs to them. Not until then do you start to negotiate the price.

'Then you'll have to return to Venice,' said Paolo matter-of-factly. 'I'll send the private jet.'

Gian Lorenzo flew to Venice the following Friday. A Rolls-Royce was parked on the runway, waiting to take him to the Villa Rosa.

A butler greeted Gian Lorenzo at the front door before escorting him up a large marble staircase to a suite of private rooms that exhibited barren walls – an art dealer's fantasy. Gian Lorenzo was reminded of the collection that his father had put together for Agnelli over a period of thirty years, now considered to be one of the finest in private hands.

Gian Lorenzo spent most of the Saturday – between meals – being escorted round the one hundred and forty-two rooms of the Villa Rosa by Angelina. He quickly discovered that there was far more to his hostess than he had anticipated.

Angelina showed a genuine interest in wanting to start her own art collection, and had clearly visited all the great galleries round the world. Gian Lorenzo concluded that she only lacked the courage of her own convictions – a not uncommon problem for the only child of a self-made man – although she didn't lack knowledge or, to Gian Lorenzo's surprise, taste. He felt guilty for making assumptions based only on comments he had read in the press. Gian Lorenzo found himself enjoying Angelina's company, and even began to wonder what this shy, thoughtful young woman could possibly see in Paolo.

Over dinner that night, Gian Lorenzo could not miss the adoration in her eyes whenever Angelina looked at her husband, even though she rarely interrupted him.

Over breakfast the following morning, Angelina hardly uttered a word. It was not until Paolo suggested that his wife show their guest round the grounds that his little angel once again came alive.

Angelina escorted Gian Lorenzo round a sixty-acre garden that possessed no immovable objects, or even havens where they might rest to cool their brows. Whenever Gian Lorenzo made a suggestion, she responded with enthusiasm, clearly willing to be led, if only he would take her by the hand.

Over dinner that night, it was Paolo who confirmed that it was his little angel's desire to build a great collection in memory of her late father.

'But where to begin?' asked Paolo, stretching a hand across the table to take his wife's hand.

'Canaletto, perhaps?' suggested Gian Lorenzo.

Gian Lorenzo spent the next five years commuting between Rome and Venice as he continued to coax pictures out of the Contessa, before rehanging them in the Villa Rosa. But as each new gem appeared, Angelina's appetite only became more voracious. Gian Lorenzo found himself having to travel as far afield as America, Russia and even Colombia, so that he could keep Paolo's 'little angel' satisfied. She seemed determined to outdo Catherine the Great.

Angelina became more and more captivated by each new masterpiece Gian Lorenzo put before her – Canaletto, Caravaggio, Tintoretto, Bellini and Da Vinci were among the natives. Not only did Gian Lorenzo begin to fill up the few remaining places on the walls of the villa, but he also had statues crated and sent from every quarter of the globe to be sited alongside other immigrants on the vast lawn – Moore, Brancusi, Epstein, Miró, Giacometti and, Angelina's favourite, Botero.

With every new purchase she made, Gian Lorenzo presented her with a book about the artist. Angelina would devour them in one sitting and immediately demand more. Gian Lorenzo had to acknowledge that she had become not only the gallery's most important client but also his most ardent student – what had begun as a flirtation with Canaletto was fast turning into a promiscuous affair with almost all the great masters of Europe. And it was

Gian Lorenzo who was expected to continually supply new lovers. Something else Angelina had in common with Catherine the Great.

Gian Lorenzo was visiting a client in Barcelona, who for tax reasons had to dispose of a Murillo, *The Birth of Christ*, when he heard the news. He considered that the asking price for the painting was too high, even though he knew that Angelina would be willing to pay it. He was in the middle of haggling when his secretary called. Gian Lorenzo took the next available flight back to Rome.

Every paper reported, some in great detail, the death of Angelina Castelli. A massive heart attack while she was in her garden trying to move one of the statues.

The tabloids, unwilling to mourn the lady for a single day, went on to inform their readers in the second paragraph that she had left her entire fortune to her husband. A photograph of a smiling Paolo – taken long before her death – ran alongside the story.

Four days later Gian Lorenzo flew to Venice to attend the funeral.

The little chapel in the grounds of the Villa Rosa was packed with Angelina's family and friends, some of whom Gian Lorenzo hadn't seen since the wedding celebration, a generation before.

When the six pallbearers carried the coffin into the chapel, and lowered it gently on a bier in front of the altar, Paolo broke down and sobbed. After the service was over, Gian Lorenzo offered his condolences, and Paolo assured him that he had enriched Angelina's life beyond recompense. He went on to say that he intended to continue building the collection in her memory. 'It is no more than my little angel would have wanted,' he explained, 'so it must be done.'

Paolo didn't get in touch with him again.

Gian Lorenzo was about to dip a spoon into a pot of Oxford marmalade – another habit he had acquired from his father – when he saw the headline. The spoon remained lodged in the marmalade while he read the words a second time. He wanted to be sure that he hadn't misunderstood the headline. Paolo was back on the front page, declaring it was 'love at first sight – turn to page 22 for details'.

Gian Lorenzo quickly flicked through the pages to a column he rarely troubled himself with. 'Gossip Roma, we give you the truth behind the stories.' Paolo Castelli, former captain of Roma, and the ninth richest man in Italy, is to marry again, only four years after the death of his little angel. 'There's more to her than meets the eye,' declared the headline. The paper went on to assure its readers that there couldn't be a bigger contrast between his first wife, Angelina, a billionairess, and Gina, a twenty-four-year-old waitress from Naples, and the daughter of a tax inspector.

Gian Lorenzo chuckled when he saw Gina's photograph, aware that many of Paolo's friends wouldn't be able to resist teasing him.

Every morning Gian Lorenzo found himself turning to *Gossip Roma*, in the hope of learning some new titbit about the forthcoming marriage. The wedding, it seemed, would be held in the chapel of the Villa Rosa, which only had enough space to seat a mere two hundred, so the guests would be restricted to close family and friends. The bride could no longer leave her little home without being pursued by a legion of paparazzi. The groom, they informed their readers, had returned to the gym, in the hope of losing a few pounds before the ceremony took place. But the biggest surprise for Gian Lorenzo came when *Gossip Roma* claimed – in an exclusive – that Signor Gian Lorenzo Venici, Roma's leading art dealer, and old school chum of Paolo, would be among the fortunate guests.

An invitation arrived in the morning post the following day.

Gian Lorenzo flew into Venice on the evening before the ceremony and checked into the Hotel Cipriani. He decided a light meal and an early night might perhaps be wise when he thought about the previous wedding.

Gian Lorenzo rose early the following morning and took some time dressing for the occasion. Despite this, he still arrived at the Villa Rosa long before the service was due to commence. He wished to stroll among the statues that littered the lawn and become reacquainted with some old friends. Donatello smiled down on him. Moore looked regal. Miró made him laugh, and Giacometti stood tall and thin, but his favourite remained the fountain which graced the centre of the lawn. Ten years before he had removed each piece of the fountain, stone by stone, statue by statue, from a courtyard in Milan. Bellini's *The Escaping Hunter* looked even more magnificent in its new surroundings. It gave Gian Lorenzo particular pleasure to see how many other guests had also arrived early, clearly with the same thought in mind.

A single usher in a smart dark suit walked among the guests suggesting that they might like to make their way to the chapel as the ceremony was about to begin. Gian Lorenzo was one of the first to heed his advice, as he wanted to be well placed to watch the bride make her entrance.

Gian Lorenzo found a vacant seat on the aisle about halfway back that would allow him an uninterrupted view of the proceedings. He could see the little choir in their stalls, already singing vespers accompanied by a string quartet.

At five minutes to three Paolo and his best man entered the chapel and walked slowly down the aisle. Gian Lorenzo knew he'd been a well-known footballer, but he still couldn't remember his name. They both took their places by the side of the altar, while Paolo waited for his young bride to appear. Paolo looked fit, tanned and trim, and Gian Lorenzo noted that women still stared at him with adoring eyes. Paolo didn't notice them and a grin that would have excited comment from Lewis Carroll never left the bridegroom's face.

There was a buzz of expectation as the string quartet

struck up the opening chords of the Wedding March, to herald the entrance of the bride. The young woman walked slowly down the aisle on the arm of her father, and drew intakes of breath as she passed each new row.

Gian Lorenzo could hear her approaching, so he turned to look at Gina for the first time. How would he respond, when asked to describe the bride, to someone who hadn't been invited to the ceremony? Should he emphasize her beautiful long, thick, raven hair, or possibly comment on the smooth olive texture of her skin, or even add some remark about the magnificent wedding dress that he remembered so well? Or would Gian Lorenzo simply tell all those who enquired that it had become immediately clear to him why Paolo had declared that it was love at first sight. The same shy smile as Angelina, the same bright enthusiastic twinkle in her eyes, the same gentleness that was clear for all to see, or was it, as Gian Lorenzo suspected, that the journalists would only report that she fitted snugly into Angelina's old wedding dress – the yards and yards of silk forming a magnificent train behind the bride as she walked slowly towards her lover.

The End

AND THEREBY
HANGS A TALE

For Simon Bainbridge

Acknowledgements

I would like to thank the following people for their valuable advice and assistance:

Simon Bainbridge, Rosie de Courcy, Alison Prince, Billy Little, David Russell, Nisha and Jamwal Singh, Jerome Kerr-Jarrett, Mari Roberts, Jonathan Ticehurst, Mark Boyce and Brian Wead.

GRUMIO
First, know my horse is tired, my master and mistress fallen out.

CURTIS
How?

GRUMIO
Out of their saddles into the dirt, and thereby hangs a tale.

CURTIS
Let's ha't, good Grumio.

The Taming of the Shrew
IV, i, ll. 47–52.

FOREWORD

During the past six years I have gathered together several of these stories while on my travels around the world. Ten of them are based on known incidents and are marked as in my past collections with an asterisk, while the remaining five are the result of my imagination.

I would like to thank all those people who have inspired me with their tales, and while there may not be a book in every one of us, there is so often a damned good short story.

JEFFREY ARCHER
May 2010

STUCK ON YOU*

1

JEREMY LOOKED ACROSS the table at Arabella and still couldn't believe she had agreed to be his wife. He was the luckiest man in the world.

She was giving him the shy smile that had so entranced him the first time they met, when a waiter appeared by his side. 'I'll have an espresso,' said Jeremy, 'and my fiancée' – it still sounded strange to him – 'will have a mint tea.'

'Very good, sir.'

Jeremy tried to stop himself looking around the room full of 'at home' people who knew exactly where they were and what was expected of them, whereas he had never visited the Ritz before. It became clear from the waves and blown kisses from customers who flitted in and out of the morning room that Arabella knew everyone, from the maître d' to several of 'the set', as she often referred to them. Jeremy sat back and tried to relax.

They'd first met at Ascot. Arabella was inside the royal enclosure looking out, while Jeremy was on the outside, looking in; that was how he'd assumed it would always be, until she gave him that beguiling smile as she strolled out of the enclosure and whispered as she passed him, 'Put your shirt on Trumpeter.' She then disappeared off in the direction of the private boxes.

Jeremy took her advice, and placed twenty pounds on Trumpeter – double his usual wager – before returning to the stands to see the horse romp home at 5–1. He hurried back to the royal enclosure to thank her, at the same time hoping she might give him another tip for the next race, but she was nowhere to be seen. He was disappointed, but still placed fifty pounds of his winnings on a horse the *Daily Express* tipster fancied. It turned out to be a nag that would be described in tomorrow's paper as an 'also-ran'.

Jeremy returned to the royal enclosure for a third time in the hope of seeing her again. He searched the paddock full of elegant men dressed in morning suits with little enclosure badges hanging from their lapels, all looking exactly like each other. They were accompanied by wives and girlfriends adorned in designer dresses and outrageous hats, desperately trying not to look like anyone else. Then he spotted her, standing next to a tall, aristocratic-looking man who was bending down and listening intently to a jockey dressed in red-and-yellow hooped silks. She didn't appear to be interested in their conversation and began to look around. Her eyes settled on Jeremy and he received that same friendly smile once again. She whispered something to the tall man, then walked across the enclosure to join him at the railing.

'I hope you took my advice,' she said.

'Sure did,' said Jeremy. 'But how could you be so confident?'

'It's my father's horse.'

'Should I back your father's horse in the next race?'

'Certainly not. You should never bet on anything unless you're sure it's a certainty. I hope you won enough to take me to dinner tonight?'

If Jeremy didn't reply immediately, it was only because he couldn't believe he'd heard her correctly. He eventually stammered out, 'Where would you like to go?'

'The Ivy, eight o'clock. By the way, my name's Arabella

Warwick.' Without another word she turned on her heel and went back to join her set.

Jeremy was surprised Arabella had given him a second look, let alone suggested they should dine together that evening. He expected that nothing would come of it, but as she'd already paid for dinner, he had nothing to lose.

Arabella arrived a few minutes after the appointed hour, and when she entered the restaurant, several pairs of male eyes followed her progress as she made her way to Jeremy's table. He had been told they were fully booked until he mentioned her name. Jeremy rose from his place long before she joined him. She took the seat opposite him as a waiter appeared by her side.

'The usual, madam?'

She nodded, but didn't take her eyes off Jeremy.

By the time her Bellini had arrived, Jeremy had begun to relax a little. She listened intently to everything he had to say, laughed at his jokes, and even seemed to be interested in his work at the bank. Well, he had slightly exaggerated his position and the size of the deals he was working on.

After dinner, which was a little more expensive than he'd anticipated, he drove her back to her home in Pavilion Road, and was surprised when she invited him in for coffee, and even more surprised when they ended up in bed.

Jeremy had never slept with a woman on a first date before. He could only assume that it was what 'the set' did, and when he left the next morning, he certainly didn't expect ever to hear from her again. But she called that afternoon and invited him over for supper at her place. From that moment, they hardly spent a day apart during the next month.

What pleased Jeremy most was that Arabella didn't seem to mind that he couldn't afford to take her to her usual haunts, and appeared quite happy to share a Chinese or Indian meal when they went out for dinner, often insisting that they split the bill. But he didn't believe it could last, until one night she said, 'You do realize I'm in love with you, don't you, Jeremy?'

Jeremy had never expressed his true feelings for Arabella. He'd assumed their relationship was nothing more than what her set would describe as a fling. Not that she'd ever introduced him to anyone from her set. When he fell on one knee and proposed to her on the dance floor at Annabel's, he couldn't believe it when she said yes.

'I'll buy a ring tomorrow,' he said, trying not to think about the parlous state of his bank account, which had turned a deeper shade of red since he'd met Arabella.

'Why bother to buy one, when you can steal the best there is?' she said.

Jeremy burst out laughing, but it quickly became clear Arabella wasn't joking. That was the moment he should have walked away, but he realized he couldn't if it meant losing her. He knew he wanted to spend the rest of his life with this beautiful and intoxicating woman, and if stealing a ring was what it took, it seemed a small price to pay.

'What type shall I steal?' he asked, still not altogether sure that she was serious.

'The expensive type,' she replied. 'In fact, I've already chosen the one I want.' She passed him a De Beers catalogue. 'Page forty-three,' she said. 'It's called the Kandice Diamond.'

'But have you worked out how I'm going to steal it?' asked Jeremy, studying a photograph of the faultless yellow diamond.

'Oh, that's the easy part, darling,' she said. 'All you'll have to do is follow my instructions.'

Jeremy didn't say a word until she'd finished outlining her plan.

That's how he had ended up in the Ritz that morning, wearing his only tailored suit, a pair of Links cufflinks, a Cartier Tank watch and an old Etonian tie, all of which belonged to Arabella's father.

'I'll have to return everything by tonight,' she said, 'otherwise Pa might miss them and start asking questions.'

'Of course,' said Jeremy, who was enjoying becoming acquainted with the trappings of the rich, even if it was only a fleeting acquaintance.

The waiter returned, carrying a silver tray. Neither of them spoke as he placed a cup of mint tea in front of Arabella and a pot of coffee on Jeremy's side of the table.

'Will there be anything else, sir?'

'No, thank you,' said Jeremy with an assurance he'd acquired during the past month.

'Do you think you're ready?' asked Arabella, her knee brushing against the inside of his leg while she once again gave him the smile that had so captivated him at Ascot.

'I'm ready,' said Jeremy, trying to sound convincing.

'Good. I'll wait here until you return, darling.' That same smile. 'You know how much this means to me.'

Jeremy nodded, rose from his place and, without another word, walked out of the morning room, across the corridor, through the swing doors and out on to Piccadilly. He placed a stick of chewing gum in his mouth, hoping it would help him to relax. Normally Arabella would have disapproved, but on this occasion she had recommended it. He stood nervously on the pavement and waited for a gap to appear in the traffic, then nipped across the road, coming to a halt outside De Beers, the largest diamond merchant in the world. This was his last chance to walk away. He knew he should take it, but just the thought of her made it impossible.

He rang the doorbell, which made him aware that his palms were sweating. Arabella had warned him that you couldn't just stroll into De Beers as if it was a supermarket, and that if they didn't like the look of you, they would not even open the door. That was why he had been measured for his first hand-tailored suit and acquired a new silk shirt, and was wearing Arabella's father's watch, cufflinks and old Etonian tie. 'The tie will ensure that the door is opened immediately,' Arabella had told him, 'and once they spot the watch and the cufflinks, you'll be invited into the private salon, because by then they'll be convinced you're one of the rare people who can afford their wares.'

Arabella turned out to be correct, because when the doorman appeared, he took one look at Jeremy and immediately unlocked the door.

'Good morning, sir. How may I help you?'

'I was hoping to buy an engagement ring.'

'Of course, sir. Please step inside.'

Jeremy followed him down a long corridor, glancing at photographs on the walls that depicted the history of the company since its foundation in 1888. Once they had reached the end of the corridor, the doorman melted away, to be replaced by a tall, middle-aged man wearing a well-cut dark suit, a white silk shirt and a black tie.

'Good morning, sir,' he said, giving a slight bow. 'My name is Crombie,' he added, before ushering Jeremy into his private lair. Jeremy walked into a small, well-lit room. In the centre was an oval table covered in a black velvet cloth, with comfortable-looking leather chairs on either side. The assistant waited until Jeremy had sat down before he took the seat opposite him.

'Would you care for some coffee, sir?' Crombie enquired solicitously.

'No, thank you,' said Jeremy, who had no desire to hold up proceedings any longer than necessary, for fear he might lose his nerve.

'And how may I help you today, sir?' Crombie asked, as if Jeremy were a regular customer.

'I've just become engaged . . .'

'Many congratulations, sir.'

'Thank you,' said Jeremy, beginning to feel a little more relaxed. 'I'm looking for a ring, something a bit special,' he added, still sticking to the script.

'You've certainly come to the right place, sir,' said Crombie, and pressed a button under the table.

The door opened immediately, and a man in an identical dark suit, white shirt and dark tie entered the room.

'The gentleman would like to see some engagement rings, Partridge.'

'Yes, of course, Mr Crombie,' replied the porter, and disappeared as quickly as he had arrived.

'Good weather for this time of year,' said Crombie as he waited for the porter to reappear.

'Not bad,' said Jeremy.

'No doubt you'll be going to Wimbledon, sir.'

'Yes, we've got tickets for the women's semi-finals,' said Jeremy, feeling rather pleased with himself, remembering that he'd strayed off script.

A moment later, the door opened and the porter reappeared carrying a large oak box which he placed reverentially in the centre of the table, before leaving without uttering a word. Crombie waited until the door had closed before selecting a small key from a chain that hung from the waistband of his trousers, unlocking the box and opening the lid slowly to reveal three rows of assorted gems that took Jeremy's breath away. Definitely not the sort of thing he was used to seeing in the window of his local H. Samuel.

It was a few moments before he fully recovered, and then he remembered Arabella telling him he would be presented with a wide choice of stones so the salesman could estimate his price range without having to ask him directly.

Jeremy studied the box's contents intently, and after some thought selected a ring from the bottom row with three perfectly cut small emeralds set proud on a gold band.

'Quite beautiful,' said Jeremy as he studied the stones more carefully. 'What is the price of this ring?'

'One hundred and twenty-four thousand, sir,' said Crombie, as if the amount was of little consequence.

Jeremy placed the ring back in the box, and turned his attention to the row above. This time he selected a ring with a circle of sapphires on a white-gold band. He removed it from the box and pretended to study it more closely before asking the price.

'Two hundred and sixty-nine thousand pounds,' replied the same unctuous voice, accompanied by a smile that suggested the customer was heading in the right direction.

Jeremy replaced the ring and turned his attention to a large single diamond that lodged alone in the top row, leaving no doubt of its superiority. He removed it and, as with the others, studied it closely. 'And this magnificent stone,' he said, raising an eyebrow. 'Can you tell me a little about its provenance?'

'I can indeed, sir,' said Crombie. 'It's a flawless, eighteen-point-four carat cushion-cut yellow diamond that was recently extracted from our Rhodes mine. It has been certified by the Gemmological Institute of America as a Fancy Intense Yellow, and was cut from the original stone by one of our master craftsmen in Amsterdam. The stone has been set on a platinum band. I can assure sir that it is quite unique, and therefore worthy of a unique lady.'

Jeremy had a feeling that Mr Crombie might just have delivered that line before. 'No doubt there's a quite unique price to go with it.' He handed the ring to Crombie, who placed it back in the box.

'Eight hundred and fifty-four thousand pounds,' he said in a hushed voice.

'Do you have a loupe?' asked Jeremy. 'I'd like to study the stone more closely.' Arabella had taught him the word diamond merchants use when referring to a small magnifying glass, assuring him that it would make him sound as if he regularly frequented such establishments.

'Yes, of course, sir,' said Crombie, pulling open a drawer on his side of the table and extracting a small tortoiseshell loupe. When he looked back up, there was no sign of the Kandice Diamond, just a gaping space in the top row of the box.

'Do you still have the ring?' he asked, trying not to sound concerned.

'No,' said Jeremy. 'I handed it back to you a moment ago.'

Without another word, the assistant snapped the box closed and pressed the button below his side of the table. This time he didn't indulge in any small talk while he waited. A moment later, two burly, flat-nosed men who looked as if they'd be more at home in a boxing ring than De Beers entered the room. One remained by the door while the other stood a few inches behind Jeremy.

'Perhaps you'd be kind enough to return the ring,' said Crombie in a firm, flat, unemotional voice.

'I've never been so insulted,' said Jeremy, trying to sound insulted.

'I'm going to say this only once, sir. If you return the ring, we will not press charges, but if you do not—'

'And I'm going to say this only once,' said Jeremy, rising from his seat. 'The last time I saw the ring was when I handed it back to you.'

Jeremy turned to leave, but the man behind him placed a hand firmly on his shoulder and pushed him back down into the chair. Arabella had promised him there would be no rough stuff as long as he cooperated and did exactly what they told him. Jeremy remained seated, not moving a muscle. Crombie rose from his place and said, 'Please follow me.'

One of the heavyweights opened the door and led Jeremy out of the room, while the other remained a pace behind him. At the end of the corridor they stopped outside a door marked

'Private'. The first guard opened the door and they entered another room which once again contained only one table, but this time it wasn't covered in a velvet cloth. Behind it sat a man who looked as if he'd been waiting for them. He didn't invite Jeremy to sit, as there wasn't another chair in the room.

'My name is Granger,' the man said without expression. 'I've been the head of security at De Beers for the past fourteen years, having previously served as a detective inspector with the Metropolitan Police. I can tell you there's nothing I haven't seen, and no story I haven't heard before. So do not imagine even for one moment that you're going to get away with this, young man.'

How quickly the fawning *sir* had been replaced by the demeaning *young man*, thought Jeremy.

Granger paused to allow the full weight of his words to sink in. 'First, I am obliged to ask if you are willing to assist me with my inquiries, or whether you would prefer us to call in the police, in which case you will be entitled to have a solicitor present.'

'I have nothing to hide,' said Jeremy haughtily, 'so naturally I'm happy to cooperate.' Back on script.

'In that case,' said Granger, 'perhaps you'd be kind enough to take off your shoes, jacket and trousers.'

Jeremy kicked off his loafers, which Granger picked up and placed on the table. He then removed his jacket and handed it to Granger as if he was his valet. After taking off his trousers he stood there, trying to look appalled at the treatment he was being subjected to.

Granger spent some considerable time pulling out every pocket of Jeremy's suit, then checking the lining and the seams. Having failed to come up with anything other than a handker-chief – there was no wallet, no credit card, nothing that could identify the suspect, which made him even more suspicious –

Granger placed the suit back on the table. 'Your tie?' he said, still sounding calm.

Jeremy undid the knot, pulled off the old Etonian tie and put it on the table. Granger ran the palm of his right hand across the blue stripes, but again, nothing. 'Your shirt.' Jeremy undid the buttons slowly, then handed his shirt over. He stood there shivering in just his pants and socks.

As Granger checked the shirt, for the first time the hint of a smile appeared on his lined face when he touched the collar. He pulled out two silver Tiffany collar stiffeners. Nice touch, Arabella, thought Jeremy as Granger placed them on the table, unable to mask his disappointment. He handed the shirt back to Jeremy, who replaced the collar stiffeners before putting his shirt and tie back on.

'Your underpants, please.'

Jeremy pulled down his pants and passed them across. Another inspection which he knew would reveal nothing. Granger handed them back and waited for him to pull them up before saying, 'And finally your socks.'

Jeremy pulled off his socks and laid them out on the table. Granger was now looking a little less sure of himself, but he still checked them carefully before turning his attention to Jeremy's loafers. He spent some time tapping, pushing and even trying to pull them apart, but there was nothing to be found. To Jeremy's surprise, he once again asked him to remove his shirt and tie. When he'd done so, Granger came around from behind the table and stood directly in front of him. He raised both his hands, and for a moment Jeremy thought the man was going to hit him. Instead, he pressed his fingers into Jeremy's scalp and ruffled his hair the way his father used to do when he was a child, but all he ended up with was greasy nails and a few stray hairs for his trouble.

'Raise your arms,' he barked. Jeremy held his arms high in

the air, but Granger found nothing under his armpits. He then stood behind Jeremy. 'Raise one leg,' he ordered. Jeremy raised his right leg. There was nothing taped underneath the heel, and nothing between the toes. 'The other leg,' said Granger, but he ended up with the same result. He walked round to face him once again. 'Open your mouth.' Jeremy opened wide as if he was in the dentist's chair. Granger shone a pen-torch around his cavities, but didn't find so much as a gold tooth. He could not hide his discomfort as he asked Jeremy to accompany him to the room next door.

'May I put my clothes back on?'

'No, you may not,' came back the immediate reply.

Jeremy followed him into the next room, feeling apprehensive about what torture they had in store for him. A man in a long white coat stood waiting next to what looked like a sun bed. 'Would you be kind enough to lie down so that I can take an X-ray?' he asked.

'Happily,' said Jeremy, and climbed on to the machine. Moments later there was a click and the two men studied the results on a screen. Jeremy knew it would reveal nothing. Swallowing the Kandice Diamond had never been part of their plan.

'Thank you,' said the man in the white coat courteously, and Granger added reluctantly, 'You can get dressed now.'

Once Jeremy had his new school tie on, he followed Granger back into the interrogation room, where Crombie and the two guards were waiting for them.

'I'd like to leave now,' Jeremy said firmly.

Granger nodded, clearly unwilling to let him go, but he no longer had any excuse to hold him. Jeremy turned to face Crombie, looked him straight in the eye and said, 'You'll be hearing from my solicitor.' He thought he saw him grimace. Arabella's script had been flawless.

The two flat-nosed guards escorted him off the premises,

looking disappointed that he hadn't tried to escape. As Jeremy stepped back out on to the crowded Piccadilly pavement, he took a deep breath and waited for his heartbeat to return to something like normal before crossing the road. He then strolled confidently back into the Ritz and took his seat opposite Arabella.

'Your coffee's gone cold, darling,' she said, as if he'd just been to the loo. 'Perhaps you should order another.'

'Same again,' said Jeremy when the waiter appeared by his side.

'Any problems?' whispered Arabella once the waiter was out of earshot.

'No,' said Jeremy, suddenly feeling guilty, but at the same time exhilarated. 'It all went to plan.'

'Good,' said Arabella. 'So now it's my turn.' She rose from her seat and said, 'Better give me the watch and the cufflinks. I'll need to put them back in Daddy's room before we meet up this evening.'

Jeremy reluctantly unstrapped the watch, took out the cufflinks and handed them to Arabella. 'What about the tie?' he whispered.

'Better not take it off in the Ritz,' she said. She leaned over and kissed him gently on the lips. 'I'll come to your place around eight, and you can give it back to me then.' She gave him that smile one last time before walking out of the morning room.

A few moments later, Arabella was standing outside De Beers. The door was opened immediately: the Van Cleef & Arpels necklace, the Balenciaga bag and the Chanel watch all suggested that this lady was not in the habit of being kept waiting.

'I want to look at some engagement rings,' she said shyly before stepping inside.

'Of course, madam,' said the doorman, and led her down the corridor.

During the next hour, Arabella carried out almost the same routine as Jeremy, and after much prevarication she told Mr Crombie, 'It's hopeless, quite hopeless. I'll have to bring Archie in. After all, he's the one who's going to foot the bill.'

'Of course, madam.'

'I'm joining him for lunch at Le Caprice,' she added, 'so we'll pop back this afternoon.'

'We'll look forward to seeing you both then,' said the sales associate as he closed the jewel box.

'Thank you, Mr Crombie,' said Arabella as she rose to leave.

Arabella was escorted to the front door by the sales associate without any suggestion that she should take her clothes off. Once she was back on Piccadilly, she hailed a taxi and gave the driver an address in Lowndes Square. She checked her watch, confident that she would be back at the flat long before her father, who would never find out that his watch and cufflinks had been borrowed for a few hours, and who certainly wouldn't miss one of his old school ties.

As she sat in the back of the taxi, Arabella admired the flawless yellow diamond. Jeremy had carried out her instructions to the letter. She would of course have to explain to her friends why she'd broken off the engagement. Frankly, he just wasn't one of our set, never really fitted in. But she had to admit she would quite miss him. She'd grown rather fond of Jeremy, and he was very enthusiastic between the sheets. And to think that all he'd get out of it was a pair of silver collar stiffeners and an old Etonian tie. Arabella hoped he still had enough money to cover the bill at the Ritz.

She dismissed Jeremy from her thoughts and turned her attention to the man she'd chosen to join her at Wimbledon, whom she had already lined up to assist her in obtaining a matching pair of earrings.

◄○►

When Mr Crombie left De Beers that night, he was still trying to work out how the man had managed it. After all, he'd had no more than a few seconds while his head was bowed.

'Goodnight, Doris,' he said as he passed a cleaner who was vacuuming in the corridor.

'Goodnight, sir,' said Doris, opening the door to the viewing room so she could continue to vacuum. This was where the customers selected the finest gems on earth, Mr Crombie had once told her, so it had to be spotless. She turned off the machine, removed the black velvet cloth from the table and began to polish the surface; first the top, then the rim. That's when she felt it.

Doris bent down to take a closer look. She stared in disbelief at the large piece of chewing gum stuck under the rim of the table. She began to scrape it off, not stopping until there wasn't the slightest trace of it left, then dropped it into the rubbish bag attached to her cleaning cart before placing the velvet cloth back on the table.

'Such a disgusting habit,' she muttered as she closed the viewing-room door and continued to vacuum the carpet in the corridor.

THE QUEEN'S
BIRTHDAY TELEGRAM*

2

Her Majesty the Queen sends her congratulations
to Albert Webber on the occasion of his 100th birthday,
and wishes him many more years of good health and happiness.

ALBERT WAS STILL SMILING after he'd read the message
for the twentieth time.

'You'll be next, ducks,' he said as he passed the royal missive
across to his wife. Betty only had to read the telegram once for
a broad smile to appear on her face too.

The festivities had begun a week earlier, culminating in a
celebration party at the town hall. Albert's photograph had
appeared on the front page of the *Somerset Gazette* that
morning, and he had been interviewed on *BBC Points West*,
his wife seated proudly by his side.

His Worship the Mayor of Street, Councillor Ted Harding,
and the leader of the local council, Councillor Brocklebank,
were waiting on the town hall steps to greet the centenarian.
Albert was escorted to the mayor's parlour where he was
introduced to Mr David Heathcote-Amory, the local Member
of Parliament, as well as the local MEP, although when asked
later he couldn't remember her name.

After several more photographs had been taken, Albert
was ushered through to a large reception room where over a

hundred invited guests were waiting to greet him. As he entered the room he was welcomed by a spontaneous burst of applause, and people he'd never met before began shaking hands with him.

At 3.27 p.m., the precise minute Albert had been born in 1907, the old man, surrounded by his five children, eleven grandchildren and nineteen great-grandchildren, thrust a silver-handled knife into a three-tier cake. This simple act was greeted by another burst of applause, followed by cries of *speech, speech, speech!*

Albert had prepared a few words, but as quiet fell in the room, they went straight out of his head.

'Say something,' said Betty, giving her husband a gentle nudge in the ribs.

He blinked, looked around at the expectant crowd, paused and said, 'Thank you very much.'

Once the assembled gathering realized that was all he was going to say, someone began to sing 'Happy Birthday', and within moments everyone was joining in. Albert managed to blow out seven of the hundred candles before the younger members of the family came to his rescue, which was greeted by even more laughter and clapping.

Once the applause had died down, the mayor rose to his feet, tugged at the lapels of his black and gold braided gown and cleared his throat, before delivering a far longer speech.

'My fellow citizens,' he began, 'we are gathered together today to celebrate the birthday, the one hundredth birthday, of Albert Webber, a much-loved member of our community. Albert was born in Street on the fifteenth of April 1907. He married his wife Betty at Holy Trinity Church in 1931, and spent his working life at C. and J. Clark's, our local shoe factory. In fact,' he continued, 'Albert has spent his entire life in Street, with the notable exception of four years when he served as a private soldier in the Somerset Light Infantry. When the war

ended in 1945, Albert was discharged from the army and
returned to Street to take up his old job as a leather cutter at
Clark's. At the age of sixty, he retired as Deputy Floor Manager.
But you can't get rid of Albert that easily, because he then took
on part-time work as a night watchman, a responsibility he
carried out until his seventieth birthday.'

The mayor waited for the laughter to fade before he
continued. 'From his early days, Albert has always been a loyal
supporter of Street Football Club, rarely missing a Cobblers'
home game, and indeed the club has recently made him an
honorary life member. Albert also played darts for the Crown
and Anchor, and was a member of that team when they were
runners-up in the town's pub championship.

'I'm sure you will all agree,' concluded the mayor, 'that
Albert has led a colourful and interesting life, which we all
hope will continue for many years to come, not least because
in three years' time we will be celebrating the same landmark
for his dear wife Betty. It's hard to believe, looking at her,' said
the mayor, turning towards Mrs Webber, 'that in 2010 she will
also be one hundred.'

'Hear, hear,' said several voices, and Betty shyly bowed her
head as Albert leaned across and took her hand.

After several other dignitaries had said a few words, and
many more had had their photograph taken with Albert, the
mayor accompanied his two guests out of the town hall to a
waiting Rolls-Royce, and instructed the chauffeur to drive Mr
and Mrs Webber home.

Albert and Betty sat in the back of the car holding hands.
Neither of them had ever been in a Rolls-Royce before, and
certainly not in one driven by a chauffeur.

By the time the car drew up outside their council house in
Marne Terrace, they were both so exhausted and so full of
salmon sandwiches and birthday cake that it wasn't long before
they retired to bed.

The last thing Albert murmured before turning out his bedside light was, 'Well, it will be your turn next, ducks, and I'm determined to live another three years so we can celebrate your hundredth together.'

'I don't want all that fuss made over me when my time comes,' she said. But Albert had already fallen asleep.

—◦—

Not a lot happened in Albert and Betty Webber's life during the next three years: a few minor ailments, but nothing life-threatening, and the birth of their first great-great-grandchild, Jude.

When the historic day approached for the second Webber to celebrate a hundredth birthday, Albert had become so frail that Betty insisted the party be held at their home and only include the family. Albert reluctantly agreed, and didn't tell his wife how much he'd been looking forward to returning to the town hall and once again being driven home in the mayor's Rolls-Royce.

The new mayor was equally disappointed, as he'd antici-pated that the occasion would guarantee his photograph appearing on the front page of the local paper.

When the great day dawned, Betty received over a hundred cards, letters and messages from well-wishers, but to Albert's profound dismay, there was no telegram from the Queen. He assumed the Post Office was to blame and that it would surely be delivered the following day. It wasn't.

'Don't fuss, Albert,' Betty insisted. 'Her Majesty is a very busy lady and she must have far more important things on her mind.'

But Albert did fuss, and when no telegram arrived the next day, or the following week, he felt a pang of disappointment for his wife who seemed to be taking the whole affair in such good spirit. However, after another week, and still no sign of a telegram, Albert decided the time had come to take the matter into his own hands.

Every Thursday morning, Eileen, their youngest daughter, aged seventy-three, would come to pick up Betty and drive her into town to go shopping. In reality this usually turned out to be just window shopping, as Betty couldn't believe the prices the shops had the nerve to charge. She could remember when a loaf of bread cost a penny, and a pound a week was a working wage.

That Thursday Albert waited for them to leave the house, then he stood by the window until the car had disappeared around the corner. Once they were out of sight, he shuffled off to his little den, where he sat by the phone, going over the exact words he would say if he was put through.

After a little while, and once he felt he was word perfect, he looked up at the framed telegram on the wall above him. It gave him enough confidence to pick up the phone and dial a six-digit number.

'Directory Enquiries. What number do you require?'

'Buckingham Palace,' said Albert, hoping his voice sounded authoritative.

There was a slight hesitation, but the operator finally said, 'One moment please.'

Albert waited patiently, although he quite expected to be told that the number was either unlisted or ex-directory. A moment later the operator was back on the line and read out the number.

'Can you please repeat that?' asked a surprised Albert as he took the top off his biro. 'Zero two zero, seven seven six six, seven three zero zero. 'Thank you,' he said, before putting the phone down. Several minutes passed before he gathered enough courage to pick it up again. Albert dialled the number with a shaky hand. He listened to the familiar ringing tone and was just about to put the phone back down when a woman's voice said, 'Buckingham Palace, how may I help you?'

'I'd like to speak to someone about a one hundredth birthday,' said Albert, repeating the exact words he had memorized.

'Who shall I say is calling?'

'Mr Albert Webber.'

'Hold the line please, Mr Webber.'

This was Albert's last chance of escape, but before he could put the phone down, another voice came on the line.

'Humphrey Cranshaw speaking.'

The last time Albert had heard a voice like that was when he was serving in the army. 'Good morning, sir,' he said nervously. 'I was hoping you might be able to help me.'

'I certainly will if I can, Mr Webber,' replied the courtier.

'Three years ago I celebrated my hundredth birthday,' said Albert, returning to his well-rehearsed script.

'Many congratulations,' said Cranshaw.

'Thank you, sir,' said Albert, 'but that isn't the reason why I'm calling. You see, on that occasion Her Majesty the Queen was kind enough to send me a telegram, which is now framed on the wall in front of me, and which I will treasure for the rest of my life.'

'How kind of you to say so, Mr Webber.'

'But I wondered,' said Albert, gaining in confidence, 'if Her Majesty still sends telegrams when people reach their hundredth birthday?'

'She most certainly does,' replied Cranshaw. 'I know that it gives Her Majesty great pleasure to continue the tradition, despite the fact that so many more people now attain that magnificent milestone.'

'Oh, that is most gratifying to hear, Mr Cranshaw,' said Albert, 'because my dear wife celebrated her hundredth birthday some two weeks ago, but sadly has not yet received a telegram from the Queen.'

'I am sorry to hear that, Mr Webber,' said the courtier. 'It must be an administrative oversight on our part. Please allow me to check. What is your wife's full name?'

'Elizabeth Violet Webber, née Braithwaite,' said Albert with pride.

'Just give me a moment, Mr Webber,' said Cranshaw, 'while I check our records.'

This time Albert had to wait a little longer before Mr Cranshaw came back on the line. 'I am sorry to have kept you waiting, Mr Webber, but you'll be pleased to learn that we have traced your wife's telegram.'

'Oh, I'm so glad,' said Albert. 'May I ask when she can expect to receive it?'

There was a moment's hesitation before the courtier said, 'Her Majesty sent a telegram to your wife to congratulate her on reaching her hundredth birthday some five years ago.'

Albert heard a car door slam, and moments later a key turned in the lock. He quickly put the phone down, and smiled.

HIGH HEELS★

3

I was at Lord's for the first day of the Second Test against Australia when Alan Penfold sat down beside me and introduced himself.

'How many people tell you they've got a story in them?' he asked.

I gave him a closer look before I replied. He must have been around fifty years old, slim and tanned. He looked fit, the kind of man who goes on playing his chosen sport long after he's past his peak, and as I write this story, I recall that his handshake was remarkably firm.

'Two, sometimes three a week,' I told him.

'And how many of those stories make it into one of your books?'

'If I'm lucky, one in twenty, but more likely one in thirty.'

'Well, let's see if I can beat the odds,' said Penfold as the players left the field for tea. 'In my profession,' he began, 'you never forget your first case.'

‑‑◦‑‑

Alan Penfold put the phone gently back on the hook, hoping he hadn't woken his wife. She stirred when he slipped stealthily out of bed and began to dress in yesterday's clothes, as he didn't want to put the light on.

'And where do you think you're going at this time in the morning?' she demanded.

'Romford,' he replied.

Anne tried to focus on the digital clock on her side of the bed.

'At ten past eight on a Sunday morning?' she said with a groan.

Alan leaned over and kissed her on the forehead. 'Go back to sleep, I'll tell you all about it over lunch.' He quickly left the room before she could question him any further.

Even though it was a Sunday morning, he calculated that it would take him about an hour to get to Romford. At least he could use the time to think about the phone conversation he'd just had with the duty reports officer.

Alan had joined Redfern & Ticehurst as a trainee actuary soon after he'd qualified as a loss adjuster. Although he'd been with the firm for over two years, the partners were such a conservative bunch that this was the first time they'd allowed him to cover a case without his supervisor, Colin Crofts.

Colin had taught him a lot during the past two years, and it was one of his comments, oft repeated, that sprang to Alan's mind as he headed along the A12 towards Romford: 'You never forget your first case.'

All the reports officer had told him over the phone were the basic facts. A warehouse in Romford had caught fire during the night and by the time the local brigade had arrived, there wasn't a lot that could be done other than to dampen down the embers. Old buildings like that often go up like a tinderbox, the reports officer said matter-of-factly.

The policy holders, Lomax Shoes (Import and Export) Ltd, had two insurance policies, one for the building, and the other for its contents, each of them for approximately two million pounds. The reports officer didn't consider it to be a complicated assignment, which was probably why he allowed Alan to cover the case without his supervisor.

Even before he reached Romford, Alan could see where the site must be. A plume of black smoke was hovering above what was left of the hundred-year-old company. He parked in a side street, exchanged his shoes for a pair of Wellington boots and headed towards the smouldering remains of Lomax Shoes (Import and Export) Ltd. The smoke was beginning to disperse, the wind blowing it in the direction of the east coast. Alan walked slowly, because Colin had taught him that it was important to take in first impressions.

When he reached the site, there was no sign of any activity other than a fire crew who were packing up and preparing to return to brigade headquarters. Alan tried to avoid the puddles of sooty water as he made his way across to the engine. He introduced himself to the duty officer.

'So where's Colin?' the man asked.

'He's on holiday,' Alan replied.

'That figures. I can't remember when I last saw him on a Sunday morning. And he usually waits for my report before he visits the site.'

'I know,' said Alan. 'But this is my first case, and I was hoping to have it wrapped up before Colin comes back from his holiday.'

'You never forget your first case,' said the fire officer as he climbed up into the cab. 'Mind you, this one's unlikely to make any headlines, other than in the *Romford Recorder*. I certainly won't be recommending a police inquiry.'

'So there's no suggestion of arson?' said Alan.

'No, none of the usual tell-tale signs to indicate that,' said the officer. 'I'm betting the cause of the fire will turn out to be faulty wiring. Frankly, the whole electrical system should have been replaced years ago.' He paused and looked back at what remained of the site. 'It was just fortunate for us that it was an isolated building and the fire broke out in the middle of the night.'

'Was there anyone on the premises at the time?'

'No, Lomax sacked the night watchman about a year ago. Just another victim of the recession. It will all be in my report.'

'Thanks,' said Alan. 'I don't suppose you've seen any sign of the rep from the insurance company?' he asked as the fire chief slammed his door closed.

'If I know Bill Hadman, he'll be setting up his office in the nearest pub. Try the King's Arms on Napier Road.'

Alan spent the next hour walking around the waterlogged site searching for any clue that might prove the fire chief wrong. He wasn't able to find anything, but he couldn't help feeling that something wasn't right. To start with, where was Mr Lomax, the owner, whose business had just gone up in smoke? And why wasn't the insurance agent anywhere to be seen, when he was going to have to pay out four million pounds of his company's money? Whenever things didn't add up, Colin always used to say, 'It's often not what you *do* see that matters, but what you *don't* see.'

After another half-hour of not being able to work out what it was he couldn't see, Alan decided to take the fire chief's advice and headed for the nearest pub.

When he walked into the King's Arms just before eleven, there were only two customers seated at the bar, and one of them was clearly holding court.

'Good morning, young man,' said Bill Hadman. 'Come and join us. By the way, this is Des Lomax. I'm trying to help him drown his sorrows.'

'It's a bit early for me,' said Alan after shaking hands with both men, 'but as I didn't have any breakfast this morning, I'll settle for an orange juice.'

'It's unusual to see someone from your office on site this early.'

'Colin's on holiday and it's my first case.'

'You never forget your first case,' sighed Hadman, 'but I fear this one won't be something to excite your grandchildren with. My company has insured the Lomax family from the day they first opened shop in 1892, and the few claims they've made over the years have never raised an eyebrow at head office, which is more than I can say for some of my other clients.'

'Mr Lomax,' said Alan, 'can I say how sorry I am that we have to meet in such distressing circumstances?' That was always Colin's opening line, and Alan added, 'It must be heartbreaking to lose your family business after so many years.' He watched Lomax carefully to see how he would react.

'I'll just have to learn to live with it, won't I?' said Lomax, who didn't look at all heartbroken. In fact, he appeared remarkably relaxed for someone who'd just lost his livelihood but had still found the time to shave that morning.

'No need for you to hang around, old fellow,' said Hadman. 'I'll have my report on your desk by Wednesday, Thursday at the latest, and then the bargaining can begin.'

'Can't see why there should be any need for bargaining,' snapped Lomax. 'My policy is fully paid up, and as the world can see, I've lost everything.'

'Except for the tiny matter of insurance policies totalling around four million pounds,' said Alan after he'd drained his orange juice. Neither Lomax nor Hadman commented as he placed his empty glass on the bar. He shook hands with them both again and left without another word.

'Something isn't right,' Alan said out loud as he walked slowly back to the site. What made it worse was that he had a feeling Colin would have spotted it by now. He briefly considered paying a visit to the local police station, but if the fire officer and the insurance representative weren't showing any concern, there wasn't much chance of the police opening an inquiry. Alan could hear the chief inspector saying, 'I've got enough real crimes to solve without having to follow up one of your "something doesn't feel right" hunches.'

As Alan climbed behind the wheel of his car, he repeated, 'Something isn't right.'

◄◦►

Alan arrived back in Fulham just in time for lunch. Anne didn't seem particularly interested in how he'd spent his Sunday morning, until he mentioned the word shoes. She then began to ask him lots of questions, one of which gave him an idea.

At nine o'clock the following morning, Alan was standing outside the claim manager's office. 'No, I haven't read your report,' Roy Kerslake said, even before Alan had sat down.

'That might be because I haven't written it yet,' said Alan with a grin. 'But then, I'm not expecting to get a copy of the fire report or the insurance evaluation before the end of the week.'

'Then why are you wasting my time?' asked Kerslake, not looking up from behind a foot-high pile of files.

'I'm not convinced the Lomax case is quite as straight-forward as everyone on the ground seems to think it is.'

'Have you got anything more substantial to go on other than a gut feeling?'

'Don't let's forget my vast experience,' said Alan.

'So what do you expect me to do about it?' asked Kerslake, ignoring the sarcasm.

'There isn't a great deal I can do before the written reports land on my desk, but I was thinking of carrying out a little research of my own.'

'I smell a request for expenses,' said Kerslake, looking up for the first time. 'You'll need to justify them before I'll consider parting with a penny.'

Alan told him in great detail what he had in mind, which resulted in the claims manager putting his pen down.

'I will not advance you a penny until you come up with something more than a gut feeling by the next time I see you. Now go away and let me get on with my job . . . By the way,' he said as Alan opened the door, 'if I remember correctly, this is your first time flying solo?'

'That's right,' said Alan, but he'd closed the door before he could hear Kerslake's response.

'Well, that explains everything.'

◄o►

Alan drove back to Romford later that morning, hoping that a second visit to the site might lift the scales from his eyes, but still all he could see were the charred remains of a once-proud company. He walked slowly across the deserted site, searching for the slightest clue, and was pleased to find nothing.

At one o'clock he returned to the King's Arms, hoping that Des Lomax and Bill Hadman wouldn't be propping up the bar as he wanted to chat to one or two locals in the hope of picking up any gossip that was doing the rounds.

He plonked himself down on a stool in the middle of the bar and ordered a pint and a ploughman's lunch. It didn't take him long to work out who were the regulars and who, like him, were passing trade. He noticed that one of the regulars was reading about the fire in the local paper.

'That must have been quite a sight,' said Alan, pointing to the photograph of a warehouse in flames which took up most of the front page of the *Romford Recorder*.

'I wouldn't know,' said the man after draining his glass. 'I was tucked up in bed at the time, minding my own business.'

'Sad, though,' said Alan, 'an old family company like that going up in flames.'

'Not so sad for Des Lomax,' said the man, glancing at his

empty glass. 'He pockets a cool four million and then swans off on holiday with his latest girlfriend. Bet we never see him around these parts again.'

'I'm sure you're right,' said Alan and, tapping his glass, he said to the barman, 'Another pint, please.' He turned to the regular and asked, 'Would you care to join me?'

'That's very civil of you,' said the man, smiling for the first time.

An hour later, Alan left the King's Arms with not a great deal more to go on, despite a second pint for his new-found friend and one for the barman.

Lomax, it seemed, had flown off to Corfu with his new Ukrainian girlfriend, leaving his wife behind in Romford. Alan had no doubt that Mrs Lomax would be able to tell him much more than the stranger at the bar, but he knew he'd never get away with it. If the company were to find out that he'd been to visit the policy-holder's wife, it would be his last job as well as his first. He dismissed the idea, although it worried him that Lomax could be found in a pub on the morning after the fire and then fly off to Corfu with his girlfriend while the embers were still smouldering.

When Alan arrived back at the office he decided to give Bill Hadman a call and see if he had anything that might be worth following up.

'Tribunal Insurance,' announced a switchboard voice.

'It's Alan Penfold from Redfern and Ticehurst. Could you put me through to Mr Hadman, please?'

'Mr Hadman's on holiday. We're expecting him back next Monday.'

'Somewhere nice, I hope,' said Alan, flying a kite.

'I think he said he was going to Corfu.'

◄○►

Alan leaned across and stroked his wife's back, wondering if she was awake.

'If you're hoping for sex, you can forget it,' Anne said without turning over.

'No, I was hoping to talk to you about shoes.'

Anne turned over. 'Shoes?' she mumbled.

'Yes, I want you to tell me everything you know about Manolo Blahnik, Prada and Roger Vivier.'

Anne sat up, suddenly wide awake.

'Why do you want to know?' she asked hopefully.

'What size are you, for a start?'

'Thirty-eight.'

'Is that inches, centimetres or—'

'Don't be silly, Alan. It's the recognized European measure-ment, universally accepted by all the major shoe companies.'

'But is there anything distinctive about . . .' Alan went on to ask his wife a series of questions, all of which she seemed to know the answers to.

◄○►

Alan spent the following morning strolling around the first floor of Harrods, a store he usually only visited during the sales. He tried to remember everything Anne had told him, and spent a considerable amount of time studying the vast department devoted to shoes, or to be more accurate, to women.

He checked through all the brand names that had been on Lomax's manifest, and by the end of the morning he had narrowed down his search to Manolo Blahnik and Roger Vivier. Alan left the store a couple of hours later with nothing more than some brochures, aware that he couldn't progress his theory without asking Kerslake for money.

When Alan returned to the office that afternoon, he took his time double-checking Lomax's stock list. Among the shoes lost in the fire were two thousand three hundred pairs of Manolo Blahnik and over four thousand pairs of Roger Vivier.

'How much do you want?' asked Roy Kerslake, two stacks of files now piled up in front of him.

'A thousand,' said Alan, placing yet another file on the desk.

'I'll let you know my decision once I've read your report,' Kerslake said.

'How do I get my report to the top of the pile?' asked Alan.

'You have to prove to me that the company will benefit from any further expenditure.'

'Would saving a client two million pounds be considered a benefit?' asked Alan innocently.

Kerslake pulled the file back out from the bottom of the pile, opened it and began to read. 'I'll let you know my decision within the hour.'

◄○►

Alan returned to Harrods the next day, after he'd had another nocturnal chat with his wife. He took the escalator to the first floor and didn't stop walking until he reached the Roger Vivier display. He selected a pair of shoes, took them to the counter and asked the sales assistant how much they were. She studied the coded label.

'They're part of a limited edition, sir, and this is the last pair.'

'And the price?' said Alan.

'Two hundred and twenty pounds.'

Alan tried not to look horrified. At that price, he realized he wouldn't be able to buy enough pairs to carry out his experiment.

'Do you have any seconds?' he asked hopefully.

'Roger Vivier doesn't deal in seconds, sir,' the assistant replied with a sweet smile.

'Well, if that's the case, what's the cheapest pair of shoes you have?'

'We have some pairs of ballerinas at one hundred and twenty pounds, and a few penny loafers at ninety.'

'I'll take them,' said Alan.

'What size?'

'It doesn't matter,' said Alan.

It was the assistant's turn to look surprised. She leaned across the counter and whispered, 'We have five pairs of size thirty-eight in store, which I could let you have at a reduced price, but I'm afraid they're last season's.'

'I'm not interested in the season,' said Alan, and happily paid for five pairs of Roger Vivier shoes, size thirty-eight, before moving across the aisle to Manolo Blahnik.

The first question he asked the sales assistant was, 'Do you have any of last season's, size thirty-eight?'

'I'll just check, sir,' said the girl, and headed off in the direction of the stockroom. 'No, sir, we've sold out of all the thirty-eights,' she said when she returned. 'The only two pairs left over from last year are a thirty-seven and a thirty-five.'

'How much would you charge me if I take both pairs?'

'Without even looking at them?'

'All I care about is that they're Manolo Blahnik,' said Alan, to another surprised assistant.

Alan left Harrods carrying two bulky green carrier bags containing seven pairs of shoes. Once he was back in the office, he handed the receipts to Roy Kerslake, who looked up from behind his pile of files when he saw how much Alan had spent.

'I hope your wife's not a size thirty-eight,' he said with a grin. The thought hadn't even crossed Alan's mind.

—◦—

While Anne was out shopping on Saturday morning, Alan built a small bonfire at the bottom of the garden. He then disappeared into the garage and removed the two carrier bags of shoes and the spare petrol can from the boot of his car.

He had completed his little experiment long before Anne returned from her shopping trip. He decided not to tell her that Manolo Blahnik had been eliminated from his findings, because, although he had a spare pair left over, sadly they were not her size. He locked the boot of his car, just in case she discovered the four remaining pairs of Roger Vivier, size thirty-eight.

◀◇▶

On Monday morning, Alan rang Des Lomax's secretary to arrange an appointment with him once he'd returned from his holiday. 'I just want to wrap things up,' he explained.

'Of course, Mr Penfold,' said the secretary. 'We're expecting him back in the office on Wednesday. What time would suit you?'

'Would eleven o'clock be convenient?'

'I'm sure that will be just fine,' she replied. 'Shall we say the King's Arms?'

'No, I'd prefer to see him on site.'

◀◇▶

Alan woke early on Wednesday morning and dressed without waking his wife. She'd already supplied him with all the information he required. He set off for Romford soon after breakfast, allowing far more time for the journey than was necessary. He made one stop on the way, dropping into his local garage to refill the spare petrol can.

When Alan drove into Romford he went straight to the site and parked on the only available meter. He decided that an hour would be more than enough. He opened the boot, took out the Harrods bag and the can of petrol, and walked on to the middle of site where he waited patiently for the chairman of Lomax Shoes (Import and Export) Ltd to appear.

Des Lomax drove up twenty minutes later and parked his brand-new red Mercedes E-Class Saloon on a double yellow line. When he stepped out of the car, Alan's first impression was that he looked remarkably pale for someone who'd just spent ten days in Corfu.

Lomax walked slowly across to join him, and didn't apologize for being late. Alan refused his outstretched hand and simply said, 'Good morning, Mr Lomax. I think the time has come for us to discuss your claim.'

'There's nothing to discuss,' said Lomax. 'My policy was for four million, and as I've never missed a payment, I'm looking forward to my claim being paid in full, and sharpish.'

'Subject to my recommendation.'

'I don't give a damn about your recommendation, sunshine,' said Lomax, lighting a cigarette. 'Four million is what I'm entitled to, and four million is what I'm going to get. And if you don't pay up pretty damn quick, you can look forward to our next meeting being in court, which might not be a good career move, remembering that this is your first case.'

'You may well prove to be right, Mr Lomax,' said Alan. 'But I shall be recommending to your insurance broker that they settle for two million.'

'Two million?' said Lomax. 'And when did you come up with that Mickey Mouse figure?'

'When I discovered that you hadn't spent the last ten days in Corfu.'

'You'd better be able to prove that, sunshine,' snapped Lomax, 'because I've got hotel receipts, plane tickets, even the hire car agreement. So I wouldn't go down that road if I were you, unless you want to add a writ for libel to the one you'll be getting for non-payment of a legally binding contract.'

'Actually, I admit that I don't have any proof you weren't in Corfu,' said Alan. 'But I'd still advise you to settle for two million.'

'If you don't have any proof,' said Lomax, his voice rising, 'what's your game?'

'What we're discussing, Mr Lomax, is your game, not mine,' said Alan calmly. 'I may not be able to prove you've spent the last ten days disposing of over six thousand pairs of shoes, but what I *can* prove is that those shoes weren't in your warehouse when you set fire to it.'

'Don't threaten me, sunshine. You have absolutely no idea who you're dealing with.'

'I know only too well who I'm dealing with,' said Alan as he bent down and removed four boxes of Roger Vivier shoes from the Harrods bag and lined them up at Lomax's feet.

Lomax stared down at the neat little row of boxes. 'Been out buying presents, have we?'

'No. Gathering proof of your nocturnal habits.'

Lomax clenched his fist. 'Are you trying to get yourself thumped?'

'I wouldn't go down that road, if I were you,' said Alan, 'unless you want to add a charge of assault to the one you'll be getting for arson.'

Lomax unclenched his fist, and Alan unscrewed the cap on the petrol can and poured the contents over the boxes. 'You've already had the fire officer's report, which confirms there was no suggestion of arson,' said Lomax, 'so what do you think this little fireworks display is going to prove?'

'You're about to find out,' said Alan, suddenly cursing himself for having forgotten to bring a box of matches.

'Might I add,' said Lomax, defiantly tossing his cigarette stub on to the boxes, 'that the insurance company has already accepted the fire chief's opinion.'

'Yes, I'm well aware of that,' said Alan. 'I've read both reports.'

'Just as I thought,' said Lomax, 'you're bluffing.'

Alan said nothing as flames began to leap into the air, causing both men to take a pace back. Within minutes, the tissue paper, the cardboard boxes and finally the shoes had been burnt to a cinder, leaving a small cloud of black smoke spiralling into the air. When it had cleared, the two men stared down at all that was left of the funeral pyre – eight large metal buckles.

'It's often not what you do see, but what you don't see,' said Alan without explanation. He looked up at Lomax. 'It was my wife,' continued Alan, 'who told me that Catherine Deneuve made Roger Vivier buckles famous when she played a courtesan in the film *Belle de Jour*. That was when I first realized you'd set fire to your own warehouse, Mr Lomax, because if you hadn't, according to your manifest, there should have been several thousand buckles scattered all over the site.'

Lomax remained silent for some time before he said, 'I reckon you've still only got a fifty-fifty chance of proving it.'

'You may well be right, Mr Lomax,' said Alan. 'But then, I reckon you've still only got a fifty-fifty chance of not being paid a penny in compensation and, even worse, ending up behind bars for a very long time. So as I said, I will be recommending that my client settles for two million, but then it will be up to you to make the final decision, sunshine.'

◄◊►

'So what do you think?' asked Penfold as a bell sounded and the players began to stroll back out on to the field.

'You've undoubtedly beaten the odds,' I replied, 'even if I was expecting a slightly different ending.'

'So how would you have ended the story?' he asked.

'I would have held on to one pair of Roger Vivier shoes,' I told him.

'What for?'

'To give to my wife. After all, it was her first case as well.'

BLIND DATE

4

THE SCENT OF JASMINE was the first clue: a woman.

I was sitting alone at my usual table when she came and sat down at the next table. I knew she was alone, because the chair on the other side of her table hadn't scraped across the floor, and no one had spoken to her after she'd sat down.

I sipped my coffee. On a good day, I can pick up the cup, take a sip and return it to the saucer, and if you were sitting at the next table, you'd never know I was blind. The challenge is to see how long I can carry out the deception before the person sitting next to me realizes the truth. And believe me, the moment they do, they give themselves away. Some begin to whisper, and, I suspect, nod or point; some become attentive; while a few are so embarrassed they don't speak again. Yes, I can even sense that.

I hoped someone would be joining her, so I could hear her speak. I can tell a great deal from a voice. When you can't see someone, the accent and the tone are enhanced, and these can give so much away. Pause for a moment, imagine listening to someone on the other end of a phone line, and you'll get the idea.

Charlie was heading towards us. 'Are you ready to order, madam?' asked the waiter, his slight Cornish burr leaving no doubt that he was a local. Charlie is tall, strong and gentle.

How do I know? Because when he guides me back to the pavement after my morning coffee, his voice comes from several inches above me, and I'm five foot ten. And if I should accidentally bump against him, there's no surplus weight, just firm muscle. But then, on Saturday afternoons he plays rugby for the Cornish Pirates. He's been in the first team for the past seven years, so he must be in his late twenties, possibly early thirties. Charlie has recently split up with his girlfriend and he still misses her. Some things you pick up from asking questions, others are volunteered.

The next challenge is to see how much I can work out about the person sitting at the next table before they realize I cannot see them. Once they've gone on their way, Charlie tells me how much I got right. I usually manage about seven out of ten.

'I'd like a lemon tea,' she replied, softly.

'Certainly, madam,' said Charlie. 'And will there be anything else?'

'No, thank you.'

Thirty to thirty-five would be my guess. Polite, and not from these parts. Now I'm desperate to know more, but I'll need to hear her speak again if I'm to pick up any further clues.

I turned to face her as if I could see her clearly. 'Can you tell me the time?' I asked, just as the clock on the church tower opposite began to chime.

She laughed, but didn't reply until the chimes had stopped. 'If that clock is to be believed,' she said, 'it's exactly ten o'clock.' The same gentle laugh followed.

'It's usually a couple of minutes fast,' I said, staring blankly up at the clock face. 'Although the church's perpendicular architecture is considered as fine an example of its kind as any in the West Country, it's not the building itself that people flock to see, but the *Madonna and Child* by Barbara Hepworth in the Lady Chapel,' I added, casually leaning back in my chair.

'How interesting,' she volunteered, as Charlie returned and

placed a teapot and a small jug of milk on her table, followed by a cup and saucer. 'I was thinking of attending the morning service,' she said as she poured herself a cup of tea.

'Then you're in for a treat. Old Sam, our vicar, gives an excellent sermon, especially if you've never heard it before.'

She laughed again before saying, 'I read somewhere that the *Madonna and Child* is not at all like Hepworth's usual work.'

'That's correct,' I replied. 'Barbara would take a break from her studio most mornings and join me for a coffee,' I said proudly, 'and the great lady once told me that she created the piece in memory of her eldest son, who was killed in a plane crash at the age of twenty-four while serving in the RAF.'

'How sad,' said the woman, but added no further comment.

'Some critics say,' I continued, 'that it's her finest work, and that you can see Barbara's devotion for her son in the tears in the Virgin's eyes.'

The woman picked up her cup and sipped her tea before she spoke again. 'How wonderful to have actually known her,' she said. 'I once attended a talk on the St Ives School at the Tate, and the lecturer made no mention of the *Madonna and Child*.'

'Well, you'll find it tucked away in the Lady Chapel. I'm sure you won't be disappointed.'

As she took another sip of tea, I wondered how many out of ten I'd got so far. Clearly interested in art, probably lives in London, and certainly hasn't come to St Ives to sit on the beach and sunbathe.

'So, are you a visitor to these parts?' I ventured, searching for further clues.

'Yes. But my aunt is from St Mawes, and she's hoping to join me for the morning service.'

I felt a right chump. She must have already seen the *Madonna and Child*, and probably knew more about Barbara

Hepworth than I did, but was too polite to embarrass me. Did she also realize I was blind? If so, those same good manners didn't even hint at it.

I heard her drain her cup. I can even tell that. When Charlie returned, she asked him for the bill. He tore off a slip from his pad and handed it to her. She passed him a banknote, and he gave her back some coins.

'Thank you, madam,' said Charlie effusively. It must have been a generous tip.

'Goodbye,' she said, her voice directed towards me. 'It was nice to talk to you.'

I rose from my place, gave her a slight bow and said, 'I do hope you enjoy the service.'

'Thank you,' she replied. As she walked away I heard her say to Charlie, 'What a charming man.' But then, she had no way of knowing how acute my hearing is.

And then she was gone.

I sat waiting impatiently for Charlie to return. I had so many questions for him. How many of my guesses would turn out to be correct this time? From the buzz of cheerful chatter in the café, I guessed there were a lot of customers in that morning, so it was some time before Charlie was once again standing by my side.

'Will there be anything else, Mr Trevathan?' he teased.

'There most certainly will be, Charlie,' I replied. 'For a start, I want to know all about the woman who was sitting next to me. Was she tall or short? Fair or dark? Was she slim? Good-looking? Was she—'

Charlie burst out laughing.

'What's so funny?' I demanded.

'She asked me exactly the same questions about you.'

WHERE THERE'S A WILL*

5

Now, you've all heard the story about the beautiful young nurse who takes care of a bedridden old man, convinces him to change his will in her favour, and ends up with a fortune, having deprived his children of their rightful inheritance. I confess that I thought I'd heard every variation on this theme; at least that was until I came across Miss Evelyn Beattie Moore, and even that wasn't her real name.

Miss Evelyn Mertzberger hailed from Milwaukee. She was born on the day Marilyn Monroe died, and that wasn't the only thing they had in common: Evelyn was blonde, she had the kind of figure that makes men turn and take a second look, and she had legs you rarely come across other than in an ad campaign for stockings.

So many of her friends from Milwaukee commented on how like Marilyn Monroe she looked that it wasn't surprising when as soon as Evelyn left school she bought a one-way ticket to Hollywood. On arrival in the City of Angels, she changed her name to Evelyn Beattie Moore (half Mary Tyler Moore and half Warren Beatty), but quickly discovered that, unlike Marilyn, she didn't have any talent as an actress, and no number of directors' couches was going to remedy that.

Once Evelyn had accepted this – not an easy thing for any

aspiring young actress to come to terms with – she began to look for alternative employment – which was difficult in the city of a thousand blondes.

She had spent almost all of her savings renting a small apartment in Glendale and buying a suitable wardrobe for auditions, agency photographs and the endless parties young hopefuls had to be seen at.

It was after she'd checked her latest bank statement that Evelyn realized a decision had to be made if she was to avoid returning to Milwaukee and admitting she wasn't quite as like Marilyn as her friends had thought. But what else could she do?

The idea never would have occurred to Evelyn if she hadn't come across the entry while she was flicking through the Yellow Pages looking for an electrician. It was some time before she was willing to make the necessary phone call, and then only after a final demand for the last three months' rent dropped through her mailbox.

The Happy Hunting agency assured Evelyn that their escorts were under no obligation to do anything other than have dinner with the client. They were a professional agency that supplied charming young ladies as companions for discreet gentlemen. However, it was none of their business if those young ladies chose to come to a private arrangement with the client. As the agency took 50 per cent of the booking fee, Evelyn got the message.

She decided at first that she would only sleep with a client if she felt there was a chance of their developing a long-term relationship. However, she quickly discovered that most men's idea of a long-term relationship was about an hour, and in some cases half an hour. But at least her new job made it possible for her to pay off the landlord, and even to open a savings account.

When Evelyn celebrated – or, to be more accurate, remained silent about – her thirtieth birthday, she decided the time had come to take revenge on the male species.

While not quite as many men were turning to give her a second look, Evelyn had accumulated enough money to enjoy a comfortable lifestyle. But not enough to ensure that that lifestyle would continue once she reached her fortieth birthday, and could no longer be sure of a first look.

Evelyn disappeared, and once again she changed her name. Three months later, Lynn Beattie turned up in Florida, where she registered for a diploma course at the Miami College of Nursing.

You may well ask why Lynn selected the Sunshine State for her new enterprise. I think it can be explained by some statistics she came across while carrying out her research. An article she read in *Playboy* magazine revealed that Florida was the state with the greatest number of millionaires per capita, and that the majority of them had retired and had a life expectancy of less than ten years. However, she quickly realized that she would need to carry out much more research if she hoped to graduate top of that particular class, as she was likely to come up against some pretty formidable rivals who had the same thing in mind as she did.

In the course of a long weekend spent with a middle-aged married doctor, Lynn discovered, without once having to refer to a textbook, not only that Jackson Memorial Hospital was the most expensive rest home in the state, but also that it didn't offer special rates for deserving cases.

Once Lynn had graduated with a nursing diploma, and a grade which came as a surprise to her fellow students but not to her professor, she applied for a job at Jackson Memorial.

She was interviewed by a panel of three, two of whom, including the Medical Director, were not convinced that Ms Beattie came from the right sort of background to be a Jackson nurse. The third bumped into her in the car park on his way home, and the following morning he was able to convince his colleagues to change their minds.

Lynn Beattie began work as a probationary nurse on the first day of the following month. She did not rush the next part of her plan, aware that if the Medical Director found out what she was up to, he would dismiss her without a second thought.

From the first day, Lynn went quietly and conscientiously about her work, melting into the background while keeping her eyes wide open. She quickly discovered that a hospital, just like any other workplace, has its gossip-mongers, who enjoy nothing more than to pass on the latest snippet of information to anyone willing to listen. Lynn was willing to listen. After a few weeks Lynn had discovered the one thing she needed to know about the doctors, and, later, a great deal more about their patients.

There were twenty-three doctors who ministered to the needs of seventy-one residents. Lynn had no interest in how many nurses there were, because she had no plans for them, provided she didn't come across a rival.

The gossip-monger told her that three of the doctors assumed that every nurse wanted to sleep with them, which made it far easier for Lynn to continue her research. After another few weeks, which included several 'stopovers', she found out, without ever being able to make a note, that sixty-eight of the residents were married, senile or, worse, received regular visits from their devoted relatives. Lynn had to accept the fact that 90 per cent of women either outlive their husbands or end up divorcing them. It's all part of the American dream. However, Lynn still managed to come up with a shortlist of three candidates who suffered from none of these deficiencies: Frank Cunningham Jr, Larry Schumacher III and Arthur J. Sommerfield.

Frank Cunningham was eliminated when Lynn discovered that he had two mistresses, one of whom was pregnant and had recently served a paternity suit on him, demanding that a DNA test be carried out.

Larry Schumacher III also had to be crossed off the list when Lynn found out he was visited every day by his close friend Gregory, who didn't look a day over fifty. Come to think of it, not many people in Florida do.

However, the third candidate ticked all her boxes.

Arthur J. Sommerfield was a retired banker whose worth according to *Forbes* magazine – a publication which had replaced *Playboy* as Lynn's postgraduate reading – was estimated at around a hundred million dollars: a fortune that had grown steadily through the assiduous husbandry of three generations of Sommerfields. Arthur was a widower who had only been married once (another rarity in Florida), to Arlene, who had died of breast cancer some seven years earlier. He had two children, Chester and Joni, both of whom lived abroad. Chester worked for an engineering company in Brazil, and was married with three children, while his sister Joni had recently become engaged to a landscape gardener in Montreal. Although they both wrote to their father regularly, and phoned most Sundays, visits were less frequent.

Six weeks later, after a slower than usual courtship, Lynn was transferred to the private wing of Dr William Grove, who was the personal physician of her would-be victim.

Dr Grove was under the illusion that the only reason Lynn had sought the transfer was so she could be near him. He was impressed by how seriously the young nurse took her responsibilities. She was always willing to work unsociable hours, and never once complained about having to do overtime, especially after he'd informed her that poor Mr Sommerfield didn't have much longer to live.

Lynn quickly settled into a daily routine that ensured her patient's every need was attended to. Mr Sommerfield's preferred morning paper, the *International Herald Tribune*, and his favourite beverage, a mug of hot chocolate, were to be found on his bedside table moments after he woke. At ten, she would help Arthur – he insisted she call him Arthur – to get dressed. At eleven, they would venture out for their morning constitutional around the grounds, during which he would always cling on to her. She never once complained about which part of her anatomy he clung on to.

After lunch she would read to the old man until he fell asleep, occasionally Steinbeck, but more often Chandler. At five, Lynn would wake him so that he could watch repeats of his favourite television sitcom, *The Phil Silvers Show*, before enjoying a light supper.

At eight, she allowed him a single glass of malt whisky – it didn't take her long to discover that only Glenmorangie was acceptable – accompanied by a Cuban cigar. Both were frowned upon by Dr Grove, but encouraged by Lynn.

'We just won't tell him,' Lynn would say before turning out the light. She would then slip a hand under the sheet, where it would remain until Arthur had fallen into a deep, contented sleep. Something else she didn't tell the doctor about.

◄○►

One of the tenets of the Jackson Memorial Hospital was to make sure that patients were sent home when it became obvious they had only a few weeks to live.

'Much more pleasant to spend your final days in familiar surroundings,' Dr Grove explained to Lynn. 'And besides,' he added in a quieter voice, 'it doesn't look good if everyone who comes to Jackson Memorial dies here.'

On hearing the news of his imminent discharge – which, loosely translated, meant demise – Arthur refused to budge

unless Lynn was allowed to accompany him. He had no intention of employing an agency nurse who didn't understand his
daily routine.

'So, how would you feel about leaving us for a few weeks?'
Dr Grove asked her in the privacy of his office.

'I don't want to leave you, William,' she said, taking his
hand, 'but if it's what you want me to do . . .'

'We wouldn't be apart for too long, honey,' Dr Grove said,
taking her in his arms. 'And in any case, as his physician, I'd
have to visit the old man at least twice a week.'

'But he could live for months, possibly years,' said Lynn,
clinging to him.

'No, darling, that's not possible. I can assure you it will be a
few weeks at the most.' Dr Grove was not able to see the smile
on Lynn's face.

◄○►

Ten days later, Arthur J. Sommerfield was discharged from
Jackson Memorial and driven to his home in Bel Air.

He sat silently in the back seat, holding Lynn's hand. He
didn't speak until the chauffeur had driven through a pair of
crested wrought-iron gates and up a long driveway, and brought
the car to a halt outside a vast redbrick mansion.

'This is the family home,' said Arthur proudly.

And it's where I'll be spending the rest of my life, thought
Lynn as she gazed in admiration at the magnificent house
situated in several acres of manicured lawns, bordered by flower
beds and surrounded by hundreds of trees, the likes of which
Lynn had only ever seen in a public park.

She soon settled into the room next door to Arthur's master
suite and continued to carry out her routine, always completing
the day with a happy-ending massage, as they used to call it at
the agency.

It was on a Thursday evening, after his second whisky (only

allowed when Lynn was certain Dr Grove wouldn't be visiting his patient that day), that Arthur said, 'I know I don't have much longer to live, my dear.' Lynn began to protest, but the old man waved a dismissive hand before adding, 'And I'd like to leave you a little something in my will.'

A little something wasn't exactly what Lynn had in mind. 'How considerate of you,' she replied. 'But I don't want anything, Arthur . . .' She hesitated. 'Except perhaps . . .'

'Yes, my dear?'

'Perhaps you could make a donation to some worthy cause? Or a bequest to your favourite charity in my name?'

'How typically thoughtful of you, my dear. But wouldn't you also like some personal memento?'

Lynn pretended to consider the offer for some time before she said, 'Well, I've grown rather attached to your cane with the silver handle, the one you used to take on our afternoon walks at Jackson Memorial. And if your children wouldn't object, I'd also like the photo of you that's on your desk in the study – the one taken when you were a freshman at Princeton. You were so handsome, Arthur.'

The old man smiled. 'You shall have both of them, my dear. I'll speak to my lawyer tomorrow.'

◄○►

Mr Haskins, the senior partner of Haskins, Haskins & Purbright, was not the kind of man who would easily have succumbed to Miss Beattie's charms. However, he wholeheartedly approved when his client expressed the desire to add several large donations to selected charities and other institutions to his will – after all, he was a Princeton man himself. And he certainly didn't object when Arthur told him that he wanted to leave his cane with the silver handle, and a photo of himself when he was at Princeton, to his devoted nurse, Miss Lynn Beattie.

'Just a keepsake, you understand,' Lynn murmured as the lawyer wrote down Arthur's words.

'I'll send the documents to you within a week,' Mr Haskins said as he rose to leave, 'in case there are any further revisions you might wish to consider.'

'Thank you, Haskins,' Arthur replied, but he had fallen asleep even before they'd had a chance to shake hands.

◄○►

Mr Haskins was as good as his word, and a large legal envelope, marked Private & Confidential, arrived by courier five days later. Lynn took it straight to her room, and once Arthur had fallen asleep she studied every syllable of the forty-seven-page document carefully. After she had turned the last page, she felt that only one paragraph needed to be amended before the old man put his signature to it.

When Lynn brought in Arthur's breakfast tray the following morning, she handed him his newspaper and said, 'I don't think Mr Haskins likes me.'

'What makes you say that, my dear?' asked Arthur as he unfolded the *Herald Tribune*.

She placed a copy of the will on his bedside table and said, 'There's no mention of your cane with the silver handle, or of my favourite photo of you. I'm afraid I won't have anything to remember you by.'

'Damn the man,' said Arthur, spilling his hot chocolate. 'Get him on the phone immediately.'

'That won't be necessary,' said Lynn. 'I'll be passing by his office later this afternoon. I'll drop the will off and remind him of your generous offer. Perhaps he simply forgot.'

'Yes, why don't you do that, my dear. But be sure you're back in time for Phil Silvers.'

Lynn did indeed pass by the Haskins, Haskins & Purbright building that afternoon, on her way to the office of a Mr

Kullick, whom she had rung earlier to arrange an appointment. She had chosen Mr Kullick for two reasons. The first was that he had left Haskins, Haskins & Purbright some years before, having been passed over as a partner. There were several other lawyers in the town who had suffered the same fate, but what tipped the balance in Mr Kullick's favour was the fact that he was the vice-president of the local branch of the National Rifle Association.

Lynn took the lift to the fourth floor. As she entered the lawyer's office, Mr Kullick rose to greet her, ushering his potential client into a chair. 'How can I help you, Miss Beattie?' he asked even before he'd sat down.

'You can't help me,' said Lynn, 'but my employer is in need of your services. He's unable to attend in person because, sadly, he's bedridden.'

'I'm sorry to hear that,' said Mr Kullick. 'However, I'll need to know who it is that I'd be representing.' When he heard the name, he sat bolt upright in his chair and straightened his tie.

'Mr Sommerfield has recently executed a new will,' said Lynn, 'and he wishes one paragraph on page thirty-two to be amended.' She passed over the will that had been prepared by Mr Haskins, and the reworded paragraph she had neatly typed on Arthur's headed notepaper above a signature he had scrawled after a third whisky.

Once Mr Kullick had read the emendation, he remained silent for some time. 'I will happily draw up a new will for Mr Sommerfield, but of course I'll need to be present when he signs the document.' He paused. 'It will also have to be countersigned by an independent witness.'

'Of course,' said Lynn, who had not anticipated this problem and realized she would need a little time to find a way round it. 'Shall we say next Thursday afternoon at five o'clock, Mr Kullick?'

The lawyer checked his diary, crossed something out and

entered the name Sommerfield in its place. Lynn rose from her chair.

'I see that this will was originally drawn up by Haskins, Haskins & Purbright,' said Kullick.

'That is correct, Mr Kullick,' Lynn said just before she reached the door. She turned back and smiled sweetly. 'Mr Sommerfield felt that Mr Haskins's charges had become . . . exorbitant, I think was the word he used.' She opened the door. 'I do hope you don't make the same mistake, Mr Kullick, as we may be in need of your services at some time in the future.' She closed the door quietly behind her.

—◦—

By four o'clock the following Thursday, Lynn felt confident that she had addressed all the problems posed by Mr Kullick's demands and that everything was in place. She knew if she made the slightest mistake she would have wasted almost a year of her life, and all she would have to show for it would be a cane with a silver handle and a photograph of a young man at Princeton whom she didn't particularly like.

As she and Arthur sat and watched yet another episode in the life of Sergeant Bilko, Lynn went over the timing in her mind, trying to think of anything that might crop up at the last moment and derail her. Mr Kullick would need to be on time if her plan was to work. She checked her watch every few minutes.

When the show finally came to an end, with Bilko somehow managing to outsmart Colonel John T. Hall once again, Lynn turned off the television, poured Arthur a generous measure of whisky and handed him a Havana cigar.

'What have I done to deserve this?' he asked, patting her on the bottom.

'Someone's coming to see you, Arthur, so you mustn't fall asleep.'

'Who?' demanded Arthur, but not before he'd taken a sip of his whisky.

'A Mr Kullick. He's one of Mr Haskins's associates.'

'What does he want?' he asked as Lynn lit a match and held it up to the cigar.

'He's bringing over the latest version of your will, so you can sign it. Then you won't have to bother about it again.'

'Has he included my bequests to you this time?'

'He assured me that your wishes would be carried out to the letter, but he needed them confirmed in person,' said Lynn as the doorbell rang.

'Good,' said Arthur, taking another swig of whisky before Lynn plumped up his pillows and helped him to sit up.

Moments later there was a gentle knock on the bedroom door and a maid entered, accompanied by Mr Kullick. Arthur peered intently at the intruder through a cloud of smoke.

'Good afternoon, Mr Sommerfield,' said the lawyer as he walked towards the bed. He had intended to shake hands with the old man, but when he saw the look of disdain on his face, he decided against it. 'My name is Kullick, sir,' he said, remaining at the foot of the bed.

'I know,' said Arthur. 'And you've come about my will.'

'Yes, sir, I have, and—'

'And have you remembered to include the bequests for my nurse this time?'

'Yes, he has, Arthur,' interrupted Lynn. 'I told you all about it after I'd returned from visiting Mr Kullick last week.'

'Ah, yes, I remember,' said Arthur, draining his glass.

'You've given me everything – ' she paused ' – that I asked for.'

'Everything?' said Arthur.

'Yes,' she said, 'which is so much more than I deserve. But if you want to change your mind . . .' she added as she refilled his glass.

'No, no, you've more than earned it.'

'Thank you, Arthur,' she said, taking him by the hand.

'Let's get on with it,' said the old man wearily, turning his attention back to Kullick.

'Would you like me to take you through the will clause by clause, sir?'

'Certainly not. Haskins took long enough doing that last time.'

'As you wish, sir. Then all that remains to be done is for you to sign the document. But, as I explained to Ms Beattie, that will require a witness.'

'I'm sure Mr Sommerfield's personal maid will be happy to act as witness,' said Lynn as the front doorbell rang again.

'I'm afraid that won't be possible,' said Kullick.

'But why not?' demanded Lynn, who had already given Paula twenty dollars to carry out the task.

'Because she's a beneficiary of the will,' said Kullick, 'and therefore ineligible to be a witness.'

'She is indeed,' said Arthur. Turning to Lynn he explained, 'I've left her the silver-plated dinner service.' He leaned across and whispered, 'But I can assure you, my dear, that the silver cane is, like you, sterling.'

Lynn smiled as she desperately tried to think who could take Paula's place. Her first thought was the chauffeur, but then she remembered that he was also a beneficiary – Arthur's ancient car. She didn't want to risk going through the whole process again, but she couldn't think of anyone suitable to take the maid's place at such short notice.

'Could you come back this time tomorrow?' she asked, trying to remain calm. 'By then I'm sure—' She was interrupted by a knock on the door and Dr Grove strode into the room.

'How are you, Arthur?' he asked.

'Not too bad,' said Arthur. 'I'd be even better if you felt able to witness my signature. Or is Grove also a beneficiary of my will?' he asked Kullick.

'Certainly not,' said Dr Grove before the lawyer could speak. 'It's against company policy for any employee of Jackson Memorial to benefit from a bequest left by a patient.'

'Good, then you can earn your fee for a change, Grove. That is, assuming Kullick agrees you're acceptable.'

'Eminently so, Mr Sommerfield,' said Kullick as he opened his briefcase and extracted three thick documents. He slowly turned the pages, pointing to the small pencil crosses at the bottom of each page indicating where both signatures should be placed.

Although Lynn had taken a step back so as not to appear too involved in the process, her heartbeat didn't return to normal until the last page of all three copies had been signed and witnessed.

Once the ceremony had been completed, Kullick gathered up the documents, placed one copy in his briefcase and handed the other two to Mr Sommerfield, who waved them away, so Lynn placed them in the drawer by his bed.

'I'll take my leave, sir,' said Kullick, still not confident enough to shake hands with his latest client.

'Give Haskins my best wishes,' said Arthur as he screwed the top back on his fountain pen.

'But I no longer work for—'

'Just be sure to tell Mr Haskins when you next see him,' Lynn said quickly, 'that he obviously didn't fully appreciate Mr Sommerfield's wishes when it came to the very generous bequest he had in mind for me. But at the same time, do assure him I am not someone who bears grudges.'

Dr Grove frowned, but said nothing.

'Very magnanimous of you in the circumstances, my dear,' said Arthur.

'When I next see him,' Kullick repeated. Then he added, 'I feel it's my duty to point out to you, Mr Sommerfield, that your children may feel they are entitled to—'

'Not you as well, Kullick. When will you all accept that I've made my decision, and nothing you can say will change my mind? Now please leave us.'

'As you wish, sir,' said Kullick, stepping back as Dr Grove stuck a thermometer into his patient's mouth.

Lynn accompanied the lawyer to the door. 'Thank you, Mr Kullick, the maid will show you out.'

Kullick left without another word and after Lynn had closed the door behind him she returned to Arthur's bedside where Dr Grove was studying the thermometer.

'Your temperature is up a little, Arthur, but that's hardly surprising, considering all the excitement you've just been put through.' Turning to Lynn, he added, 'Perhaps we should leave him to have a little rest before supper.' Lynn nodded. 'Goodbye, Arthur,' he said in a louder voice. 'See you in a few days' time.'

'Good day, Grove,' said Arthur, switching the television back on.

'He's looking very frail,' said Dr Grove as Lynn accompanied him down the stairs. 'I'm going to advise his children to fly home in the next few days. I can't believe it will be much longer.'

'I'll make sure their rooms are ready,' said Lynn, 'and that Mr Sommerfield's driver picks them up at the airport.'

'That's very thoughtful of you,' said Dr Grove as they walked across the hall. 'I want you to know, Lynn, how much I appreciate all you're doing for Arthur. When you come back to Jackson Memorial, I'm going to recommend to the medical director that you're given a promotion and a rise in salary to go with it.'

'Only if you think I'm worth it,' said Lynn coyly.

'You're more than worth it,' Grove said. 'But you do realize,' he added, lowering his voice when he spotted the maid coming out of the kitchen, 'that if Arthur left you anything in his will, however small, you would lose your job?'

'I would lose so much more than that,' said Lynn, squeezing his hand.

Grove smiled as the maid opened the door for him. 'Goodbye, honey,' he whispered.

'Goodbye, Dr Grove,' Lynn said, for the last time.

She ran back up the stairs and into the bedroom to find Arthur, cigar in one hand and an empty glass in the other, watching *The Johnny Carson Show*. Once she'd poured him a second whisky, Lynn sat down by his side. Arthur had almost fallen asleep when Carson bade goodnight to his thirty million viewers with the familiar words, 'See you all at the same time tomorrow.' Lynn turned off the TV, deftly removed the half-smoked cigar from Arthur's fingers and placed it in an ashtray on the side table, then switched off the light by his bed.

'I'm still awake,' said Arthur.

'I know you are,' said Lynn. She bent down and kissed him on the forehead before slipping an arm under the sheet. She didn't comment when a stray hand moved slowly up the inside of her leg. She stopped when she heard the familiar sigh, that moments later was followed by steady breathing. She removed her hand from under the sheet and strolled into the bathroom, wondering how many more times she would have to . . .

Sadly, the children arrived home just a few hours after Arthur passed away peacefully in his sleep.

◄◦►

Mr Haskins removed the half-moon spectacles from the end of his nose, put down the will and looked across his desk at his two clients.

'So all I get,' said Chester Sommerfield, not attempting to hide his anger, 'is a silver-handled cane, while Joni ends up with just a picture of Dad taken when he was a freshman at Princeton?'

'While all his other worldly goods,' confirmed Mr Haskins, 'are bequeathed to a Miss Lynn Beattie.'

'And what the hell has she done to deserve that?' demanded Joni.

'To quote the will,' said Haskins, looking back down at it, 'she has acted as "my devoted nurse and close companion".'

'Are there no loopholes for us to exploit?' asked Chester.

'That's most unlikely,' said Haskins, 'because, with the exception of one paragraph, I drew up the will myself.'

'But that one paragraph changes the whole outcome of the will,' said Joni. 'Surely we should take this woman to court. Any jury will see that she is nothing more than a fraudster who tricked my father into signing a new will only days after you had amended the old one for him.'

'You may well be right,' said Haskins, 'but, given the circumstances, I couldn't advise you to contest the validity of the will.'

'But your firm's investigators have come up with irrefutable evidence that Ms Beattie was nothing more than a common prostitute,' said Chester, 'and her nursing qualifications were almost certainly exaggerated. Once the court learns the truth, surely our claim will be upheld.'

'In normal circumstances I would agree with you, Chester, but these are not normal circumstances. As I have said, I could not advise you to take her on.'

'But why not?' came back Joni. 'At the very least we could show that my father wasn't in his right mind when he signed the will.'

'I'm afraid we'd be laughed out of court,' said Haskins, 'when the other side points out that the will was witnessed by a highly respected doctor who was at your father's bedside right up until the day he died.'

'I'd still be willing to risk it,' said Chester. 'Just look at it from her perspective. She's a penniless whore who has recently been dismissed from her job without a reference, and she sure won't want her past activities aired in court and then reported on the early evening news followed by the front page of every morning paper.'

'You may well be right,' said Haskins. 'But it's still my duty as a lawyer to inform my clients when I believe their case cannot be won.'

'But you can't be worried about taking on Kullick in court,' said Chester. 'After all, you didn't even think he was good enough to be a partner in your firm.'

Haskins raised an eyebrow. 'That may well be the case, but it wouldn't be Mr Kullick I would be up against.' He replaced his half-moon spectacles on the end of his nose and once again picked up the will, then turned over several pages before identifying the relevant clause. He looked solemnly at his clients before he began to read.

'"I also bequeath ten million dollars to my alma mater, Princeton University; five million dollars to the Veterans Association of America; five million dollars to the Conference of Presidents, to assist their work in Israel; five million dollars to the Republican Party, which I have supported all my life; and finally five million dollars to the National Rifle Association, the aims of which I approve, and which I have always supported."'

The old lawyer looked up. 'I should point out to you both that none of these bequests was in your father's original will,' he said, before adding, 'and although I am in no doubt that we could beat Mr Kullick if he was our only opponent, I can assure you that we would have little chance of defeating five of the largest and most prestigious law firms in the land. Between them they would have bled you dry long before the case came to court. I fear I can only recommend that you settle for a cane with a silver handle and a photograph of your father at Princeton.'

'While she walks away with a cool seventy million dollars,' said Joni.

'Having sacrificed thirty million to ensure she would never have to appear in court,' said Haskins as he placed the will back on his desk. 'Clever woman, Ms Lynn Beattie, and that wasn't even her real name.'

DOUBLE-CROSS★

6

THE JUDGE LOOKED DOWN at the defendant and frowned.

'Kevin Bryant, you have been found guilty of armed robbery. A crime you clearly planned with considerable skill and ingenuity. During your trial it has become clear that you knew exactly when to carry out the attack upon your chosen victim, Mr Neville Abbott, a respected diamond merchant from Hatton Garden. You held up the security guard at his workshop with a shotgun, and forced him to open the strongroom where Mr Abbott was showing a dealer from Holland a consignment of uncut diamonds he had recently purchased from South Africa for just over ten million pounds.

'Thanks to outstanding police work, you were arrested within days, although the diamonds have never been found. During the seven months you have spent in custody you have been given every opportunity to reveal the whereabouts of the diamonds, but you have chosen not to do so.

'Taking that fact, as well as your past record, into consideration, I am left with no choice but to sentence you to twelve years in prison. However, Mr Bryant, I would consider a reduction to your sentence if at any time you should change your mind and decide to inform the police where the diamonds are. Take the prisoner down.'

Detective Inspector Matthews frowned as he watched Bryant

being led down to the cells before being shipped off to Belmarsh prison. As a policeman, you're meant to feel a certain professional pride, almost pleasure, when you've been responsible for banging up a career criminal, but this time Matthews felt no such pride, and wouldn't until he got his hands on those diamonds. He was convinced Bryant hadn't had enough time to sell them on and must have hidden them somewhere.

Detective Inspector Matthews had attempted to make a deal with Bryant on more than one occasion. He even offered to downgrade his charge to aggravated burglary, which carries a far shorter sentence, but only if he pleaded guilty and told him where the diamonds were. But Bryant always gave the same reply: 'I'll do my bird, guv.'

If Bryant wasn't willing to make a deal with him, Matthews knew someone doing time in the same prison who was.

—◇—

Benny Friedman, known to his fellow inmates as Benny the Fence, was serving a six-year sentence for handling stolen goods. A burglar would bring him the gear and Benny would pay him 20 per cent of its value in cash, then sell it on to a middle man for about 50 per cent, walking away with a handsome profit.

From time to time Benny got caught and had to spend some time in the nick. But as he didn't pay a penny in tax, was rarely out of work and had no fears of being made redundant, he considered the occasional spell in prison no more than part of the job description. But if the police ever offered him an alternative to going back inside, Benny was always willing to listen. After all, why would you want to spend more time behind bars than was necessary?

'Drugs check,' bellowed the wing officer as he pulled open the heavy door of Benny's cell.

'I don't do drugs, Mr Chapman,' said Benny, not stirring from his bunk.

'Get your arse upstairs, Friedman, and sharpish. Once they've checked your piss you can come back down and enjoy a well-earned rest. Now move it.'

Benny folded his copy of the *Sun*, lowered himself slowly off the bottom bunk, strolled out of his cell into the corridor and made his way up to the medical wing. No officer ever bothered to accompany him while he was out of his cell, as he never caused any trouble. You can have a reputation, even in prison.

When Benny arrived at the medical wing, he was surprised to find that none of the usual reprobates was waiting in line to be checked for drugs. In fact, he seemed to be the only inmate in sight.

'This way, Friedman,' said an officer he didn't recognize. Moments after he had entered the hospital, he heard a key being turned in the lock behind him. He looked around and saw his old friend Detective Inspector Matthews, who had arrested him many times in the past, sitting on the end of one of the beds.

'To what do I owe this honour, Mr Matthews?' Benny asked without missing a beat.

'I need your help, Benny,' said the detective inspector, not suggesting that the old lag should sit down.

'That's a relief, Mr Matthews. For a minute I thought you were being tested for drugs.'

'Don't get lippy with me, Benny,' said Matthews sharply. 'Not when I've come to offer you a deal.'

'And what are you proposing this time, Mr Matthews? A packet of fags in exchange for a serial killer?'

Matthews ignored the question. 'You're coming up for appeal in a few months' time,' he said, lighting a cigarette but not offering Benny one. 'I might be able to arrange for a couple of years to be knocked off your sentence.' He took a deep drag and blew out a cloud of smoke before adding, 'Which would mean you could be out of this hell hole in six months' time.'

'How very thoughtful of you, Mr Matthews,' said Benny. 'What are you expecting me to do in return for such munificence?'

'There's a con on his way to Belmarsh from the Old Bailey. He should be checking in any moment now. His name's Bryant, Kevin Bryant, and I've arranged for him to be your new cellmate.'

—<o>—

When the cell door was pulled open, Benny looked up from his copy of the *Sun* and watched as Bryant swaggered into the cell. The man didn't say a word, just flung his kit bag on the top bunk. New prisoners always start off on the top bunk.

Benny went back to his paper while Bryant placed a thin bar of white soap, a green flannel, a rough green towel and a Bic razor on the ledge above the washbasin. Benny put his paper down and studied the new arrival more closely. Bryant was every inch the armed robber. He was about five foot five, stockily built, with a shaved head. He unbuttoned his blue-and-white striped prison shirt to reveal a massive tattoo of a red devil. Not much doubt which football team Bryant supported. On the fingers of one hand were tattooed the letters HATE, and on the other, LOVE.

Bryant finally glanced across at Benny. 'My name's Kev.'

'Mine's Benny. Welcome to Belmarsh.'

'It's not my first time in the slammer,' said Bryant. 'I've been here before.' He chuckled. 'Several times, actually. And you?' he asked once he'd climbed up on to the top bunk and settled down.

'Fourth time,' said Benny. 'But then, I don't like to hang around for too long.'

Bryant laughed for the first time. 'So what are you in for?' he asked.

Benny was surprised that Bryant had broken one of prison's golden rules: never ask a fellow con what he's in for. Wait for him to volunteer the information. 'I'm a fence,' he replied.

'What do you fence?'

'Almost anything. But I draw the line at drugs, and that includes marijuana, and I won't handle porn, hard or soft. You've got to have some standards.'

Bryant was silent for some time. Benny wondered if he'd fallen asleep, which would be unusual on your first day inside, even for a regular. 'You haven't asked me what I'm in for,' said Bryant eventually.

'No need to, is there?' said Benny. 'Your mugshot's been on the front page of the tabloids every day for the past week. Everyone at Belmarsh knows what you're in for.'

Bryant didn't speak again that night, but Benny was in no hurry. The one thing you've got plenty of in prison is time. As long as you're patient, everything will eventually come out, however secretive an inmate imagines he is.

─◄○►─

Benny didn't much like being in jail, but most of all he dreaded the weekends, when you could be banged up for eighteen hours at a stretch, with only a short break to collect an oily meal of spam fritters and chips from the hotplate.

The screws allowed the prisoners out for a forty-five-minute break in the afternoon. Benny could choose between watching football on television or taking a stroll around the yard, whatever the weather. He had no interest in football, but as Bryant always went straight to the yard, he settled for watching television. He was grateful for any break he could get in this hastily arranged marriage, and if Bryant was ever going to say anything about where the diamonds were, it was more likely to

THE NEW COLLECTED SHORT STORIES

be in the privacy of their cell than in the bustling, noisy, over-crowded yard where other prisoners could eavesdrop.

Benny was reading an article about how the Italian Prime Minister spent his weekends when Bryant broke into his thoughts. 'Why don't you ever ask me about the diamonds?'

'None of my business,' said Benny, not looking up from his paper.

'But you must be curious about what I've done with them?'

'According to the *Sun*'s crime correspondent,' said Benny, 'you sold them to a middle man for half a million.'

'Half a million?' said Bryant. 'Do I look that fuckin' stupid?'

'So how much did you sell 'em for?'

'Nothin'.'

'Nothin'?' repeated Benny.

'Because I've still got 'em, haven't I?'

'Have you?'

'Yeah. And I can tell you one thing. The fuzz ain't never gonna find out where I stashed 'em, however hard they look.'

Benny pretended to go on reading his paper. He'd reached the sports pages by the time Bryant spoke again.

'It's all part of my retirement plan, innit? Most of the muppets in this place will walk out with nothin', while I've got myself a guaranteed income for life, haven't I?'

Benny waited patiently, but Bryant didn't utter another word before lights out, four hours later. Benny would have liked to ask Bryant just one more question, but he knew he couldn't risk it.

'What do you think about this guy Berlusconi?' he asked finally.

'What's he in for?' asked Bryant.

◄○►

Benny always attended the Sunday morning service held in the prison chapel, not because he believed in God, but because it

666

got him out of his cell for a whole hour. The long walk to the chapel on the other side of the prison, the body search for drugs – by a female officer if you got lucky – the chance for a gossip with some old lags, a sing-song, followed by a saunter back to your cell in time for lunch, were a welcome break from the endless hours of being banged up.

Benny settled down in his usual place in the third row, opened his hymn sheet and, when the organ struck up, joined in lustily with 'Fight the good fight'.

Once the prison chaplain had delivered his regular sermon on repentance and forgiveness, followed by the final blessing, the cons began to make their way slowly out of the chapel and back to their cells.

'Can you spare me a moment, Friedman?' asked the chaplain after Benny had handed in his hymn sheet.

'Of course, Father,' said Benny, feeling a moment of apprehension that the chaplain might ask him to sign up for his confirmation class. If he did, Benny would have to come clean and admit he was Jewish. The only reason he'd ticked the little box marked C of E was so he could escape from his cell for an hour every Sunday morning. If he'd admitted he was a Jew, a Rabbi would have visited him in his cell once a month, because not enough Jews end up in prison to hold a service for them.

The chaplain asked Benny to join him in the vestry. 'A friend has asked to see you, Benny. I'll leave you alone for a few minutes.' He closed the vestry door and returned to those repenting souls who did want to sign up for his confirmation class.

'Good morning, Mr Matthews,' said Benny, taking an unoffered seat opposite the detective inspector. 'I had no idea you'd taken up holy orders.'

'Cut the crap, Friedman, or I may have to let your wing officer know that you're really a Jew.'

'If you did, Inspector, I'd have to explain to him how I'd seen the light on the way to Belmarsh.'

'And you'll see my boot up your backside if you waste any more of my time.'

'So, to what do I owe this pleasure?' asked Benny innocently.

'Has he sold the diamonds?' asked Matthews, not wasting another word.

'No, Inspector, he hasn't. In fact, he claims they're still in his possession. The story about selling them for half a million was just a smokescreen.'

'I knew it,' said Matthews. 'He would never have sold them for so little. Not after all the trouble he went to.' Benny didn't comment. 'Have you managed to find out where he's stashed them?'

'Not yet,' said Benny. 'I've got a feeling that might take a little longer, unless you want me to—'

'Don't press him,' interrupted Matthews. 'It'll only make him suspicious. Bide your time and wait for him to tell you himself.'

'And when I've elicited this vital piece of evidence, Inspector, I'll get two years knocked off my sentence, as you promised?' Benny reminded him.

'Don't push your luck, Friedman. I accept that you've earned a year off, but you won't get the other year until you find out where those diamonds are. So get back to your cell, and keep your ears open and your mouth shut.'

―◦―

It was on a Saturday morning that Bryant asked Benny, 'Have you ever fenced any diamonds?'

Benny had waited weeks for Bryant to ask that question. 'From time to time,' he said. 'I've got a reliable dealer in Amsterdam, but I'd need to know a lot more before I'd be willing to contact him. What sort of numbers are we talkin' about?'

'Is ten mill out of your league?' asked Bryant.

'No, I wouldn't say that,' said Benny, trying not to rise, 'but it might take a little longer than usual.'

'All I've got is time,' said Bryant, slipping back into one of his long, contemplative silences. Benny prayed that it wasn't going to be another six weeks before he asked the next question.

'What percentage would you pay me if I let you fence the diamonds?' asked Bryant.

'My usual terms are twenty per cent of the face value, strictly cash.'

'And how much do you sell them on for?'

'Usually around fifty per cent of face value.'

'And how much will your contact make?'

'I've got no idea,' said Benny. 'He doesn't ask me where it comes from, and I don't ask him how much he makes out of it. As long as we all make a profit, the less anyone knows the better.'

'Does it matter what kind of stones they are?'

'The smaller the better,' said Benny. 'Always avoid the big stuff. If you brought me the Crown Jewels, I'd tell you to fuck off, because I'd never find a buyer. Small stones aren't easy to trace, you can lose them on the open market.'

'So you'd cough up a couple of mill, if I deliver?'

'If they're worth ten million, yes, but I'd need to see them first.'

'Why wouldn't they be?' asked Bryant, looking Benny straight in the eye.

'Because figures reported in the press aren't always reliable. Crime reporters like numbers with lots of noughts, and they only ever round them up.'

'But they were insured for ten million,' said Bryant, 'and don't forget the insurance company paid up in full.'

'I won't make an offer until I've seen the goods,' said Benny.

Bryant fell silent again.

'So where are they?' asked Benny, trying to make the words sound unrehearsed.

'It doesn't matter where they are,' said Bryant.

'It matters if you expect me to give you a valuation,' snapped Benny.

'What if I could show you half a dozen of them right now?'

'Stop pissing me about, Kev. If you're serious about doin' a deal, tell me where they are. If not, fuck off.' Not tactics Inspector Matthews would have approved of, but with his appeal coming up in a few days' time, Benny couldn't afford to wait another six weeks before Bryant spoke again.

'I'm serious,' said Bryant quietly. 'So shut up and listen for a minute, unless you're doing a bigger deal this week?' Benny thought about another year being knocked off his sentence and remained silent. 'While I was banged up on remand, one of the cons was arrested for possession. Heroin, class A.'

'So what?' said Benny. 'People get arrested for possession every day.'

'Not while they're in prison, they don't.'

'But how did he get the gear in?' asked Benny, suddenly taking an interest.

'This con picks up the stuff from a mate while he's on trial at the Old Bailey. Durin' one of the breaks he asks to go to the toilet, knowing that the guard has to stay outside while he's in the cubicle. While he's on the john, he stuffs the gear into a condom, ties a knot in it and swallows it.'

'But if the condom split open in his stomach,' said Benny, 'he'd be history.'

'Yeah, but if he gets it into prison, he can make a grand. Five times what he'd pick up on the out.'

'Tell me something I don't know,' said Benny.

'Once he's banged up in here, he waits till the middle of the night, sits on the toilet, where the screws can't see him through the spy hole, and—'

'Spare me the details.'

After another long pause, Bryant said, 'On the day I was sentenced I did the same thing.'

'You swallowed two ounces of heroin?' asked Benny in disbelief.

'No, you stupid bugger, you've not been payin' attention.' Benny remained silent while Bryant rolled a cigarette then kept him waiting until he'd lit it and inhaled several times. 'I swallowed six of the diamonds, didn't I?'

'Why in Gawd's name would you do that?'

'Prison currency, in case I ever found myself dealin' with a bent screw, or in need of a favour from an old lag.'

'So where are they now?' asked Benny, pushing his luck.

'They've been in this cell for the past three months, and you haven't even set eyes on them.'

Benny said nothing as Bryant climbed down from the top bunk and took a plastic fork from the table. He slowly began to unstitch the centre strip that ran down the side of his Adidas tracksuit bottoms. It was some time before he was able to extract one small diamond. Benny's eyes lit up when he saw it sparkle under the naked light bulb.

'Six stripes means six diamonds,' Bryant said in triumph. 'If any screw checked my tracksuit, he would have found more stashed in there than he earns in a year.'

Bryant handed the diamond over to Benny, who took it across to the tiny barred window and studied it closely while he tried to think.

'So, what do you think?' asked Bryant.

'Can't be sure yet, but there's one way to find out. Let me see your watch.'

'Why?' asked Bryant, holding out his arm.

Benny didn't reply, but ran the edge of the stone across the glass, leaving a thin scratch on the surface.

'Hey, what's your game?' said Bryant, pulling his arm away. 'I paid good money for that watch.'

'And I won't be wasting good money on this piece of shit,' said Benny, handing the stone back to Bryant before returning to the bottom bunk and pretending to read his newspaper.

'Why the fuck not?' asked Bryant.

'Because it's not a diamond,' said Benny. 'If it was, it would have shattered the glass on your watch, not just left a scratch on the surface. You've been robbed, my friend,' said Benny, 'and by a very clever man who's palmed you off with paste.'

Bryant stared at his watch. It was some time before he stammered out, 'But I saw Abbott fill the bag with diamonds from his safe.'

'I've no doubt you saw him fill the bag with something, Kevin, but whatever it was, it wasn't diamonds.'

Bryant collapsed on to the only chair in the cell. Eventually he managed to ask, 'So how much are they worth?'

'Depends how many you've got.'

'A sugar bag full. It weighed about two pounds.'

Benny wrote down some numbers on the back of his newspaper before offering his considered opinion. 'Two grand perhaps, three at the most. I'm sorry to say, Kev, that Mr Abbott saw you coming.'

Bryant began picking at the remaining stripes on his track-suit bottoms with the plastic fork. Each time a new stone fell out, he rubbed it across his watch. The result was always the same: a faint scratch, but the glass remained firmly intact.

'Twelve years for a few fuckin' grand,' Bryant shouted as he paced up and down the tiny cell like a caged animal. 'If I ever get my hands on that bastard Abbott, I'll tear him apart limb from limb.'

'Not for another twelve years you won't,' said Benny helpfully.

Bryant began thumping the cell door with his bare fists, but he knew that no one could hear him except Benny.

Benny didn't say another word until lights out at ten o'clock, by which time Bryant had calmed down a little, and had even stopped banging his head against the wall.

Benny had spent the time working out exactly what he was going to say next. But not before he was convinced that Bryant was at his most vulnerable, which was usually about an hour after lights out. 'I think I know how you could get revenge on your friend Mr Abbott,' whispered Benny, not sure if Bryant was still awake.

Bryant leapt off the top bunk and, towering over Benny, their noses almost touching, shouted, 'Tell me. Tell me. I'll do anything to get even with that bastard!'

'Well, if you don't want to wait twelve years before you next bump into him, you've got it in your power to make him come to you.'

'Stop talking in fuckin' riddles,' said Bryant. 'How can I get Abbott to come to Belmarsh? He's hardly likely to apply for a visiting order.'

'I was thinking of something more permanent than a visit,' said Benny. It was Bryant's turn to wait impatiently for his cellmate to continue. 'You told me the judge offered to reduce your sentence if you told where you stashed the diamonds.'

'That's right. But have you forgotten they ain't diamonds no more?' shouted Bryant, inching even closer towards him.

'Exactly my point,' said Benny, not flinching, 'so it shouldn't take the police long to work out that they've been taken for a ride, while Abbott has ended up with ten million of insurance money in exchange for two pounds of paste.'

'You're fuckin' right,' said Bryant, clenching his fist.

'As soon as the police realize the diamonds aren't kosher, they're gonna throw the book at Abbott: fraud, theft, criminal deception, not to mention perverting the course of justice. I wouldn't be surprised if he was sent down for at least ten years.' Benny lit a cigarette and slowly inhaled before he added, 'And there's only one place he's heading once he leaves the Old Bailey.'

'Belmarsh!' said Bryant, punching his fist in the air as if Manchester United had just won the Cup.

—◇—

The physical instruction officer at Belmarsh had never seen this particular con in the gym before, despite the fact that he clearly needed some exercise, nor, for that matter, the police officer he was deep in conversation with, who clearly didn't. The governor had told him to lock the gym door and make sure that no one, screw or con, entered while the two men were together.

'Bryant has made a full confession,' said Detective Inspector Matthews, 'including where we'd find the diamonds. Half a dozen of them were missing, of course. I presume there's no chance of retrieving them.'

'None,' said Benny with a sigh. 'It broke my heart to watch him flushing them down the toilet. But, Inspector Matthews, I was thinking of the bigger picture.'

'The one where you leave this place in a few weeks' time?' suggested the detective inspector.

'I admit it had crossed my mind,' said Benny. 'But I'm still curious to know what happened to the rest of the diamonds?'

'The insurance company sold them back to Mr Abbott at a

slightly reduced price, on the understanding that neither side would refer to the matter again.'

'That's a relief,' said Benny, 'because I've got a favour to ask you, Inspector Matthews.'

'Isn't two years off your sentence enough to be going on with?'

'It certainly is, Inspector Matthews, and don't think I'm not grateful, but it won't be long before Bryant works out the reason you haven't arrested Abbott is because the diamonds *are* kosher, and I double-crossed him.'

'Go on,' said the detective inspector.

'I just wondered if you could find it in your heart, Mr Matthews, if I was ever foolish enough to be found wanting again, to make sure that I'm never sent back to Belmarsh.'

Matthews rose from the bench at the far end of the gym and looked down at the old con. 'Not a hope, Benny,' he said with a grin. 'I can't think of a better way of ensuring that you finally get yourself a proper job and stay on the straight and narrow. And by the way, there may even come a time when you want to come back to Belmarsh.'

'You must be joking, Mr Matthews. Why would I ever want to come back to this shit hole?'

'Because the judge was as good as his word,' said Matthews. 'He's cut Bryant's sentence in half. So, with good behaviour, he should be out in a couple of years' time. And when he is, Benny, I have a feeling it won't be Mr Abbott he comes looking for.'

'I WILL SURVIVE'*

7

WHEN THE DOORBELL RANG, Julian Farnsdale looked up.

The first decision he always had to make was whether to engage a potential customer in conversation, or simply leave them to browse. There were several golden rules that you adopted after so many years in the trade. If the customer looked as if he needed some assistance, Julian would rise from behind his desk and say either, 'Can I help you?' or, 'Would you prefer just to browse?' If they only wanted to browse, he would sit back down, and although he would keep an eye on them, he wouldn't speak again until they began a conversation.

Julian wasn't in any doubt that this customer was a browser, so he remained seated and said nothing. Browsers fall into three categories: those simply passing the time of day who stroll around for a few minutes before leaving without saying anything; dealers who know exactly what they are looking for but don't want you to know they're in the trade; and, finally, genuine enthusiasts hoping to come across something a little special to add to their collections.

This particular customer unquestionably fell into the third category.

Julian studied him out of the corner of one eye, an art he had perfected over the years. He decided he was probably an American – the tailored blazer, neatly pressed chinos and striped preppy tie. The man may have been a browser but he was a browser with real knowledge and taste because he only stopped to consider the finest pieces: the Adam fireplace, the Chippendale rocking chair and the Delft plate. Julian wondered if he would spot the one real treasure in his shop.

A few moments later, the customer came to a halt in front of the egg. He studied the piece for some time before looking across at Julian. 'Has it been signed by the master?'

Julian rose slowly from his chair. Another golden rule: don't appear to be in a hurry when you're hoping to sell something very expensive.

'Yes, sir,' said Julian as he walked towards him. 'You'll find Carl Fabergé's signature on the base. And of course the piece is listed in the catalogue raisonné.'

'Date and description?' enquired the customer, continuing to study the egg.

'1910,' said Julian. 'It was made to celebrate the Tsarina's thirty-eighth birthday, and is one of a series of Easter eggs commissioned by Tsar Nicholas the Second.'

'It's magnificent,' said the customer. 'Quite magnificent. But probably out of my price range.'

Julian immediately recognized the bargaining ploy, so he mentally added 20 per cent to the asking price to allow a little room for manoeuvre.

'Six hundred and eighty thousand,' he said calmly.

'Pounds?' asked the man, raising an eyebrow.

'Yes,' said Julian without further comment.

'So, about a million dollars,' said the customer, confirming that he was American.

Julian didn't reply. He was distracted by a screeching sound outside, as if a car was trying to avoid a collision. Both men glanced out of the window to see a black stretch limousine that had come to a halt on the double yellow line outside the shop.

A woman dressed in a stylish red coat and wearing a diamond necklace, matching earrings and dark glasses stepped out of the back of the car.

'Is that who I think it is?' asked Julian.

'Looks like it is,' said the customer, as the woman stopped to sign an autograph.

'Gloria Gaynor.' Julian sighed as she disappeared into the jewellery shop next door. 'Lucky Millie,' he added without explanation.

'I think she's doing a gig in town this week,' said the customer.

'She's performing at the Albert Hall on Saturday,' said Julian. 'I tried to get a ticket but it's completely sold out.'

The customer was clearly more interested in the jewel-encrusted egg than the jewel-covered pop star so Julian snapped back into antique-dealer mode.

'What's the lowest price you'd consider?' asked the American.

'I suppose I could come down to six hundred and fifty thousand.'

'My bet is that you'd come down to five hundred thousand,' said the American.

'Six hundred and twenty-five thousand,' said Julian. 'I couldn't consider a penny less.'

The American nodded. 'That's a fair price. But my partner will need to see it before I can make a final decision.' Julian tried not to look disappointed. 'Would it be possible to reserve the piece at six twenty-five?'

'Yes, of course, sir.' Julian pulled open a drawer in his desk, removed a small green sticker and placed it on the little description card fixed to the wall. 'And when might we expect to see you again, sir?'

'My partner flies in from the States on Friday, so possibly

Friday afternoon. But as he suffers badly from jetlag it's more likely to be Saturday afternoon. What time do you close on Saturdays?'

'Around five, sir,' said Julian.

'I'll make sure we're with you before then,' said the American.

Julian opened the door to allow his customer to leave just as Miss Gaynor walked out of the jewellery shop. Once again she stopped to sign autographs for a little group that had gathered on the pavement outside. The chauffeur ran to open the door of the limousine and she disappeared inside. As the car slipped out into the traffic, Julian found himself waving, which was silly because he couldn't see a thing through the smoked-glass windows.

Julian was about to return to his shop when he noticed that his next-door neighbour was also waving. 'What was she like, Millie?' he asked, trying not to sound too much like an adoring fan.

'Charming. And so natural,' Millie replied, 'considering all that she's been through. A real star.'

'Did you learn anything interesting?' asked Julian.

'She's staying at the Park Lane Hotel, and she's off to Paris on Sunday for the next leg of her tour.'

'I already knew that,' said Julian. 'Read it in Londoner's Diary last night. Tell me something I don't know.'

'On the day of a concert she never leaves her room and won't speak to anyone, even her manager. She likes to rest her voice before going on stage.'

'Fascinating,' said Julian. 'Anything else?'

'The air conditioning in her room has to be turned off, because she's paranoid about catching a cold and not being able to perform. She once missed a concert in Dallas when she came off the street at a hundred degrees straight into an air-conditioned room, and ended up coughing and sneezing for a week.'

'Why's she staying at the Park Lane,' asked Julian, 'and not Claridges or the Ritz where all the big stars stay?'

'It's only a five-minute drive from the Albert Hall and she has a dread of being held up in a traffic jam and being late for a concert.'

'You're beginning to sound like an old friend,' said Julian.

'Well, she was very chatty,' said Millie.

'But did she buy anything?' asked Julian, ignoring a man carrying a large package who strolled past him and through the open door of his antique shop.

'No, but she did put a deposit down on a pair of earrings and a watch. She said she'd be back tomorrow.' Millie gave her next-door neighbour a warm smile. 'And if you buy me a coffee, I'll tell her about your Fabergé egg.'

'I think I may already have a buyer for that,' said Julian. 'But I'll still get you a coffee, just as soon as I've got rid of Lenny.' He smiled and stepped back into his shop, not bothering to close the door.

'I thought you might be interested in this, Mr Farnsdale,' said a scruffily dressed man, handing him a heavy helmet. 'It's Civil War, circa 1645. I could let you have it for a reasonable price.'

Julian studied the helmet for a few moments.

'Circa 1645 be damned,' he pronounced. 'More like circa 1995. And if you picked it up in the Old Kent Road, I can even tell you who made it. I've been around far too long to be taken in by something like that.'

Lenny left the shop, head bowed, still clutching the helmet. Julian closed the door behind him.

Julian was bargaining with a lady over a small ceramic figure of the Duke of Wellington in the shape of a boot (circa 1817). He wanted £350 for the piece but she was refusing to pay more than £320, when the black stretch limousine drew up outside. Julian left his customer and hurried over to the window just in time to see Miss Gaynor step out on to the pavement and walk into the jewellery shop without glancing in his direction. He sighed and turned to find that his customer had gone, and so had the Duke of Wellington.

Julian spent the next hour standing by the door so he wouldn't miss his idol when she left the jewellery shop. He was well aware that he was breaking one of his golden rules: you should never stand by the door. It frightens off the customers and, worse, it makes you look desperate. Julian was desperate.

Miss Gaynor finally strolled out of the jewellery shop clutching a small red bag which she handed to her chauffeur. She stopped to sign an autograph, then walked straight past the antique shop and into Art Pimlico, on the other side of Julian's shop. She was in there for such a long time that Julian began to wonder if he'd missed her. But she couldn't have left the gallery because the limousine was still parked on the double yellow lines, the chauffeur seated behind the wheel.

When Miss Gaynor finally emerged she was followed by the gallery owner, who was carrying a large Warhol silk-screen print of Chairman Mao. Lucky Susan, thought Julian, to have had a whole hour with Gloria. The chauffeur leapt out, took the print from Susan and placed it in the boot of the limousine. Miss Gaynor paused to sign a few more autographs before taking the opportunity to escape. Julian stared out of the window and didn't move until she'd climbed into the back of the car and had been whisked away.

Once the car was out of sight, Julian joined Millie and Susan on the pavement. 'I see you sold the great lady a Warhol,' he said to Susan, trying not to sound envious.

'No, she only took it on appro,' said Susan. 'She wants to live with it for a couple of days before she makes up her mind.'

'Isn't that a bit of a risk?' asked Julian.

'Hardly,' said Susan. 'I can just see the headline in the *Sun*: Gloria Gaynor steals Warhol from London gallery. I don't think that's the kind of publicity she'll be hoping for on the first leg of her European tour.'

'Did you manage to sell her anything, Millie?' asked Julian, trying to deflect the barb.

'The earrings and the watch,' said Millie, 'but far more important, she gave me a couple of tickets for her concert on Saturday night.'

'Me too,' said Susan, waving her tickets in triumph.

'I'll give you two hundred pounds for them,' said Julian.

'Not a chance,' said Millie. 'Even if you offered double, I wouldn't part with them.'

'How about you, Susan?' Julian asked desperately.

'You must be joking.'

'You may change your mind when she doesn't return your Chairman Mao,' said Julian, before flouncing back into his shop.

◄○►

The following morning, Julian hovered by the door of his shop, but there was no sign of the stretch limousine. He didn't join Millie and Susan in Starbucks for coffee at eleven, claiming he had a lot of paperwork to do.

He didn't have a single customer all day, just three browsers and a visit from the VAT inspector. When he locked up for the night, he had to admit to himself that it hadn't been a good week so far. But all that could change if the American returned on Saturday with his partner.

On Thursday morning the stretch limousine drove up and parked outside Susan's gallery. The chauffeur stepped out,

685

removed Chairman Mao from the boot and carried the Chinese leader inside. A few minutes later he ran back on to the street, slammed the boot shut, jumped behind the steering wheel and drove off, but not before a parking ticket had been placed on his windscreen. Julian laughed.

—<o>—

The next morning, while Julian was discussing the Adam fireplace with an old customer who was showing some interest in the piece, the doorbell rang and a woman entered the shop.

'Don't worry about me,' she said in a gravelly voice. 'I just want to look around. I'm not in any hurry.'

'Where did you say you found it, Julian?'

'Buckley Manor in Hertfordshire, Sir Peter,' said Julian without adding the usual details of its provenance.

'And you're asking eighty thousand?'

'Yes,' said Julian, not looking at him.

'Well, I'll think about it over the weekend,' said the customer, 'and let you know on Monday.'

'Whatever suits you, Sir Peter,' said Julian, and without another word he strode off towards the front of the shop, opened the door and remained standing by it until the customer had stepped back out on to the pavement, a puzzled look on his face. If Sir Peter had looked round, he would have seen Julian close the door and switch the OPEN sign to CLOSED.

'Stay cool, Julian, stay cool,' he murmured to himself as he walked slowly towards the lady he'd been hoping to serve all week.

'I was in the area a couple of days ago,' she said, her voice husky and unmistakable.

I know you were, Gloria, Julian wanted to say. 'Indeed, madam,' was all he managed.

'Millie told me all about your wonderful shop, but I just didn't have enough time.'

'I understand, madam.'

'Actually, I haven't come across anything I really like this week. I was hoping I might be luckier today.'

'Let's hope so, madam.'

'You see, I try to take home some little memento from every city I perform in. It always brings back so many happy memories.'

'What a charming idea,' said Julian, beginning to relax.

'Of course, I could hardly fail to admire the Adam fireplace,' she said, running a hand over the marble nymphs, 'but I can't see it fitting in to my New York condo.'

'I'm sure you're right, madam,' said Julian.

'The Chippendale rocking chair is unquestionably a master-piece, but sadly it would look somewhat out of place in a Beverly Hills mansion. And Delft isn't to my taste.' She continued to look around the room, until her eyes came to rest on the egg. 'But I do love your Fabergé egg.' Julian smiled ingratiatingly. 'What does the green dot mean?' she asked innocently.

'That it's reserved for another customer, madam; an American gentleman I'm expecting tomorrow.'

'What a pity,' she said, staring lovingly at the egg. 'I'm working tomorrow, and flying to Paris the following day.' She smiled sweetly at Julian and said, 'It clearly wasn't meant to be. Thank you.' She began walking slowly towards the door.

Julian hurried after her. 'It's possible, of course, that the customer won't come back. They often don't, you know.'

She paused by the door. 'And how much did he agree to pay for the egg?' she asked.

'Six hundred and twenty-five thousand,' said Julian.

'Pounds?'

'Yes, madam.'

She walked back and took an even longer look at the egg. 'Would six hundred and fifty thousand convince you that he won't be returning?' she asked, giving him that same sweet smile.

Julian beamed as she sat down at his desk and took a chequebook out of her bag. 'Whom shall I make it out to?' she asked.

'Julian Farnsdale Fine Arts Ltd,' he said, placing one of his cards in front of her.

She wrote out the name and the amount slowly, and double-checked them before signing 'Gloria Gaynor' with a flourish. She handed the cheque to Julian who tried to stop his hand from shaking.

'If you're not doing anything special tomorrow night,' she said as she rose from her chair, 'perhaps you'd like to come to my concert?'

'How kind of you,' said Julian.

She took two tickets out of her bag and passed them across to him. 'And perhaps you'd care to join me backstage for a drink after the show?'

Julian was speechless.

'Good,' she said. 'I'll leave your name at the stage door. Please don't tell Millie or Susan. There just isn't enough room for everyone. I'm sure you understand.'

'Of course, Miss Gaynor. You can rely on me. I won't say a word.'

'And if I could ask you for one small favour?' she said as she closed her bag.

'Anything,' said Julian. 'Anything.'

'I wonder if you'd be kind enough to deliver the egg to the Park Lane Hotel, and ask a porter to send it up to my room.'

'You could take it with you now if you wish, Miss Gaynor.'

'How kind of you,' she said, 'but I'm lunching with Mick . . .' She hesitated. 'I'd prefer if it could be delivered to the hotel.'

'Of course,' said Julian. He accompanied her out of the

shop to the waiting car, where the chauffeur was holding open the back door.

'How silly of me to forget,' she said just before stepping into the car. She turned back to Julian and whispered into his ear, 'For security reasons, my room is booked in the name of Miss Hampton.' She smiled flirtatiously. 'Otherwise I'd never get a moment's peace.'

'I quite understand,' said Julian. He couldn't believe it when she bent down and kissed him on the cheek.

'Thank you, Julian,' she said. 'I look forward to seeing you after the show,' she added as she climbed into the back seat.

Julian stood there shaking as Millie and Susan joined him on the pavement.

'Did she give you any tickets for her show?' asked Millie as the car drove away.

'I'm not at liberty to say,' said Julian, then walked back into his shop and closed the door.

◄◦►

The smartly dressed young man writing down some figures in a little black book reminded her of the rent collector from her youth. 'How much did it cost us this time?' she asked quietly.

'Five days at the Park Lane came to three thousand three hundred, including tips, the stretch limo was two hundred pounds an hour, sixteen hundred in all.' His forefinger continued down the handwritten inventory. 'The two items you purchased from the jewellery shop came to fifteen hundred.' She touched a pearl earring and smiled. 'Meals along with other expenses, including five extras from the casting agency, five autograph books and a parking fine, came to another nine hundred and twenty-two pounds. Six tickets for tonight's concert purchased from a tout, a further nine hundred pounds, making eight thousand, two hundred and twenty-two pounds in all, which, at today's exchange rate, comes to about thirteen thousand three hundred and sixty-nine dollars. Not a bad return,' he concluded as he smiled across at her.

She glanced at her watch. 'Dear sweet Julian should be arriving at the Albert Hall about now,' she said. 'Let's at least hope he enjoys the show.'

'I would have liked to go with him.'

'Behave yourself, Gregory,' she teased.

'When do you think he'll find out?'

'When he turns up at the stage door after the show and finds his name isn't on the guest list, would be my guess.'

Neither of them spoke while Gregory went over the figures a second time, then finally closed his little book and placed it in an inside pocket.

'I must congratulate you on your research this time,' she said. 'I must admit I'd never heard of Robert Adam, Delft or Chippendale before you briefed me.'

Gregory smiled. 'Napoleon once said that time spent on reconnaissance is rarely wasted.'

'So where does Napoleon stay when he's in Paris?'

'The Ritz Carlton,' Gregory replied matter-of-factly.

'That sounds expensive.'

'We don't have much choice,' he replied. 'Miss Gaynor has booked a suite at the Ritz because it's convenient for the Pleyel concert hall. In any case, it gives the right image for someone who's planning to steal a Modigliani.'

'This is your captain speaking,' said a voice over the inter-com. 'We've been cleared for landing at Charles de Gaulle airport, and should be on the ground in around twenty minutes. All of us at British Airways hope you've had a pleasant flight and that you enjoy your stay in Paris, whether it be for business or pleasure.'

A flight attendant leaned over and said, 'Would you be kind enough to fasten your seat belt, madam? We'll be beginning our descent very shortly.'

'Yes, of course,' she said smiling up at the flight attendant.

The attendant took a second look at the passenger and said, 'Has anyone ever told you that you look just like Gloria Gaynor?'

A GOOD EYE

8

THERE HAVE BEEN Grebenars living in the small town of
Hertzendorf, nestled in the Bavarian hills, for more than three
hundred years.

The first Grebenar of any note was Hans Julius, born in
1641, the youngest son of a miller. Hans worked diligently as a
pupil at the town's only school, and became the first member
of the family to attend university. After four years of conscien-
tious study, the young man left Heidelberg with a law degree.
Despite this achievement, Hans did not hanker after the cos-
mopolitan life of Munich or even the more gentle charm of
Friedrichsville. Rather, he returned to the place of his birth,
where he rented a set of rooms in the centre of the town and
opened his own law practice.

As the years went by, Hans Julius was elected to the local
council, later becoming a freeman of the town as well as an
elder of the parish church. Towards the end of his days he was
responsible for establishing the town's first municipal museum.
If that had been all Herr Grebenar achieved, commendable
though it was, he would have gone to his grave unworthy of
even a short story. However, there is more to be said about this
man because God had given him a rare gift: a good eye.

Young Grebenar began to take an interest in paintings and
sculptures while he was at university, and once he'd seen

everything Heidelberg had to offer (several times), he took every opportunity to travel to other cities in order to view their treasures.

During his bachelor years he put together a small but worthy collection, his limited means not allowing him to acquire anything of real significance. That changed the day he prosecuted Friedrich Bloch, who appeared before the court on a charge of being drunk and disorderly.

Herr Grebenar wouldn't have given the uncouth ruffian a second thought had Bloch not described himself on the court sheet as a painter. Curiosity got the better of the prosecutor, and after Bloch had been fined ten marks, an amount he was ordered to pay within seven days or face a three-month jail sentence, Grebenar decided to follow him back to his home in the hope of finding out if he painted walls or canvases.

Over the years, Grebenar had come to admire the works of Caravaggio, Rubens and Bruegel, and on one occasion he had even travelled to Amsterdam to view the works of Rembrandt at his studio, but the moment he set eyes on his first Bloch, *Child Pushing a Wheelbarrow*, he realized that he was in the presence of a remarkable talent.

An hour later, the lawyer left Bloch's studio with an empty purse but in possession of two self-portraits in oil, as well as *Child Pushing a Wheelbarrow*. He then went straight to the guild house, where he withdrew a large enough sum of money to cause the clerk to raise an eyebrow.

After a light lunch he returned to court, where he discharged the artist's fine, which caused several more raised eyebrows, because he had successfully prosecuted the miscreant only that morning.

When the court rose later that afternoon, Grebenar, still wearing his long black gown and wing collar, took a carriage back to the artist's home. Bloch was surprised to see the prosecutor for a third time that day, and was even more surprised when he handed over the largest number of coins the artist had ever seen, in return for every painting, drawing and notebook that bore Bloch's signature.

—◦—

Herr Grebenar did not come across Friedrich Bloch again until the artist was arrested a year later, on the far more serious charge of attempted murder.

Grebenar visited the artist in prison where he languished while awaiting trial. He informed an incredulous Bloch that he was willing to defend him against the charge of attempted murder, but should he get him off, he would require a rather unusual recompense. Bloch, having gone through all his money, agreed to the lawyer's terms without question.

On the morning of the trial Herr Grebenar was inspired; he had rarely experienced a better day in court. He argued that as at least twelve men had been involved in the drunken brawl, how could the constable, who had arrived some time after the victim had been stabbed, possibly know which one of them had been responsible for the crime?

The jury agreed, and Bloch was acquitted on the charge of attempted murder, although he was found guilty of the lesser offence of drunken affray and sentenced to six months in prison.

When Bloch was released, Herr Grebenar was waiting for him in his carriage outside the prison gates. Grebenar outlined his terms during the journey to the artist's home and Bloch listened intently, nodding from time to time. He made only one request of his patron. Grebenar readily agreed to supply him with a large canvas, several new brushes and any pigments and powders he required. He also paid Bloch a weekly stipend to ensure that he could live comfortably, but not excessively, while carrying out his commission.

It took Bloch almost a year to complete the work and

Grebenar accepted it was the weekly stipend that had caused him to take his time. However, when the lawyer saw the oil painting *Christ's Sermon on the Mount* he did not begrudge the artist one mark, as even an untutored eye would have been left in no doubt of its genius.

Grebenar was so moved by the work that he immediately offered the young maestro a further commission, even though he realized it might take him several years to execute. 'I want you to paint twelve full-length portraits of Our Lord's disciples,' he told the artist with a collector's enthusiasm.

Bloch happily agreed, as the commission would ensure a regular supply of money for years to come.

He began his commission with a portrait of St Peter standing at the gates of Jerusalem holding crossed keys. The sadness in the eyes of the saint revealed how ashamed he was for betraying Our Lord.

Grebenar visited the artist's home from time to time, not to study any unfinished canvases, but to check that Bloch was in his studio, working. If he discovered the artist was not at his easel, the weekly stipend was suspended until the lawyer was convinced Bloch had returned to work.

The portrait of St Peter was presented to Herr Grebenar a year later, and the prosecutor made no complaint about its cost, or the amount of time it had taken. He simply rejoiced in his good fortune.

St Peter was followed by Matthew sitting at the seat of Custom, extracting Roman coins from the Jews; another year. John followed, a painting that some critics consider Bloch's finest work: indeed, three centuries later Sir Kenneth Clark has compared the brushwork to Luini's. However, no scholar at the time was able to offer an opinion, as Bloch's works were only seen by one man, so the artist grew neither in fame nor reputation – a problem Matisse was to face two hundred years later.

This lack of recognition didn't seem to worry Bloch so long as he continued to receive a weekly income, which allowed him to spend his evenings in the ale house surrounded by his friends. In turn, Grebenar never complained about Bloch's nocturnal activities, as long as the artist was sober enough to work the next day.

Ten months later, James followed his brother John, and Grebenar thanked God that he had been chosen to be the artist's patron. Doubting Thomas staring in disbelief as he placed a finger in Christ's wound took the maestro only seven months. Grebenar was puzzled by the artist's sudden industry, until he discovered that Bloch had fallen for a steatopygous barmaid from a local tavern and had asked her to marry him.

James the son of Alphaeus appeared just weeks before their first child was born, and Andrew, the fisher of men, followed soon after their second.

After Bloch, his wife and their two children moved into a small house on the outskirts of Hertzendorf, Philip of Galilee and Simon the Zealot followed within months, as the rent collector needed to be paid. What pleased Grebenar most was that the quality of each new canvas remained consistent, whatever travails or joys its creator was going through at the time.

There was then an interval of nearly two years when no work was forthcoming. Then, without warning, Thaddaeus and Bartholomew followed in quick succession. Some critics have suggested that each new canvas coincided with the appearance of the latest mistress in Bloch's life, although there is little or no historical evidence to back up their claims.

Herr Grebenar was well aware that Bloch had deserted his wife, returned to his old lodgings and was once again frequenting the ale houses at night. He feared that the next time he came across his protégé it would be in court.

Grebenar only needed one more disciple to complete the twelve, but when no new canvas had appeared for over a year and Bloch was never to be found in his studio during the day, the lawyer decided the time had come to withhold his weekly allowance. But it was not until every ale house in Hertzendorf had refused to serve him before his slate had been cleared that Bloch reluctantly returned to work.

Five months later he produced a dark, forbidding image of Judas Iscariot, thirty pieces of silver scattered on the floor around his feet. Historians have suggested the portrait mirrored the artist's own mood at the time, as the face is thought to be in the image of his patron. Grebenar was amused by Bloch's final effort, and bequeathed the twelve portraits of Christ's disciples to the town's recently built museum, so that they could be enjoyed by the local citizens long after both the artist and his patron had departed this world.

◄○►

It was over a game of chess with his friend Dr Müller that Grebenar learned his protégé had contracted syphilis and had only months to live – a year at the most.

'Such a waste of a truly remarkable talent,' said Dr Müller.

'Not if I have anything to do with it,' retorted Grebenar, as he removed the doctor's queen from the board.

The following morning Herr Grebenar visited Bloch in his rooms and was horrified to discover the state the artist was in. He was lying flat on his back, fully clothed, stinking of ale, his arms and legs covered in raw, pustulous scabs.

The lawyer perched on the end of the bed. 'It's Herr Grebenar,' he said softly. 'I'm distressed to find you in this sorry state, old friend,' he added to a man who was only thirty-four. 'Is there anything I can do to help?'

Bloch turned to face the wall, like an animal who knows death approaches.

'Dr Müller tells me you're unable to pay his bills, and it's

700

no secret you've been running up debts all over town and no one will grant you any more credit.'

Not even the usual cursory grunt followed this observation. Grebenar began to wonder if Bloch could hear him. The lawyer leaned over and whispered in his ear, 'If you paint one last picture for me, I'll clear all your debts and make sure the doctor supplies you with any drugs you need.'

Bloch still didn't move.

Grebenar saved his trump card until last, and when he'd played it, the artist turned over and smiled for the first time in weeks.

◄○►

It took Bloch nearly a month to recover enough strength to pick up a paintbrush, but when he finally managed it, he was like a man possessed. No drink, no women, no debts. Just hour after hour spent working on the canvas that he knew would be his final work.

He completed the painting on 17 March, 1679, a few days before he died, drunk, in a whore's bed.

When Grebenar first set eyes on *The Last Supper* he recalled the final words he had spoken to the artist: 'If you achieve what you are capable of, Friedrich, unlike me you will be guaranteed immortality.'

Grebenar couldn't take his eyes off the haunting image. The twelve disciples were seated around a table, with Christ at the centre breaking the communion bread. Although each one of the Apostles sat in different poses and leaned at different angles, they were unmistakably the same twelve men whose portraits Bloch had painted during the past decade. Grebenar marvelled at how Bloch had achieved such a feat since once they had left his studio, the artist had never set eyes on them again. Grebenar decided there was only one place worthy of such a masterpiece.

Herr Grebenar fulfilled the Maker's contract of three score years and ten. As he approached death, he had only one interest left in life: to ensure that his protégé's works would remain on permanent display in the town museum, so that in time everyone would acknowledge Friedrich Bloch's genius, and he himself would at least be guaranteed a footnote in history.

—◦—

Two hundred and ninety-eight years later . . .

It all began when a drop of rain fell on the chief sidesman's forehead during Monsignor Grebenar's Sunday morning sermon. Several members of the congregation looked up at the roof and one of the choirboys pointed to a small crack.

Once Monsignor Grebenar had delivered his final blessing and the congregation began to depart, he approached an elder of the church to seek his advice. The master builder promised the priest he would climb up on to the roof and inspect the timbers the following morning.

A preliminary opinion and a rough estimate as to the costs of repair were delivered to the Grebenars' family home on the Wednesday afternoon, along with a warning that if the church council did not act quickly, the roof might well collapse. Monsignor Grebenar received confirmation of the master builder's opinion from above when, during Vespers on the following Sunday, a steady trickle of rain began to fall on the front row of the choir as they chanted the 'Nunc Dimittis'.

Monsignor Grebenar fell on his knees in front of the altar, looked up at Friedrich Bloch's *Last Supper* and prayed for guidance.

The collection that followed raised the princely sum of 412 euros, which wasn't going to make much of an impression on the master builder's estimate of the 700,000 euros needed to repair the roof.

If Monsignor Grebenar had been a more worldly man, he might not have considered what happened next to be divine intervention. When he had finished praying, he crossed himself, rose from his knees, bowed to the altar and turned to find someone he had never seen before seated in the front pew.

'I understand you have a problem, Father,' the man said, looking up at the roof. 'And I think I may be able to help you solve it.'

Monsignor Grebenar looked more closely at the stranger. 'What did you have in mind, my son?' he asked.

'I would be willing to pay you seven hundred thousand euros for that painting,' he said, glancing up at *The Last Supper*.

'But it's been in my family for over three hundred years,' replied Monsignor Grebenar, turning to look at the painting.

'I'll leave you to think it over,' said the stranger. When the priest turned round, he was gone.

Monsignor Grebenar once again fell to his knees and sought God's guidance, but his prayer had not been answered by the time he rose to his feet an hour later. In fact, if anything, he was in even more of a dilemma. Had the stranger really existed, or had he imagined the whole thing?

During the following week Monsignor Grebenar canvassed opinion among his parishioners, some of whom attended the following Sunday's service with umbrellas. Once the service was over, he sought advice from a lawyer, another elder of the church.

'Your father left the painting to you in his will, as did his father before him,' said the lawyer. 'Therefore it is yours to dispose of as you wish. But if I may offer you one piece of advice,' he added.

'Yes, of course, my son,' said the priest hopefully.

'Whatever you decide, Father, you should place the painting in the town's museum before it's damaged by water leaking from the roof.'

'Do you consider seven hundred thousand a fair price?' asked the priest.

'I have no idea, Father. I'm a lawyer, not an art dealer. You should seek advice from an expert.'

As Monsignor Grebenar did not have an art dealer among his flock, he phoned the leading auction house in Frankfurt the following day. The head of the Renaissance department did not assist matters when he told him there was no way of accurately estimating the true value of Bloch's masterpiece, since none of his works had ever come on the market. Every known example was hanging in one museum, with the notable exception of *The Last Supper*. The priest was about to thank him and put down the phone when the man added, 'There is, of course, one way you could find out its true value.'

'And what might that be?'

'Allow the painting to come under the hammer in our next Renaissance sale.'

'When is that?'

'Next October, in New York. We're preparing the catalogue at the moment, and I can assure you your painting would attract considerable interest.'

'But that's not for another six months,' said the priest. 'By then I may not have a roof, just a swimming pool.'

When the service the following Sunday had to be moved to a church on the other side of town, Grebenar felt that Our Lord was giving him a sign, and most of his parishioners agreed with him. However, like the lawyer, when it came to selling the painting they felt it had to be his decision.

Once again, the Monsignor prostrated himself before the masterpiece, wondering what his great-great-great-great-great-great-great-great-great-great-grandfather would have done if faced with the same dilemma. His eyes settled on the thirty pieces of silver scattered around Judas's feet. When he finally rose and crossed himself, he was still undecided. He was about to leave the church, when he found the stranger once again sitting in the front pew. The stranger smiled, but did not speak. He extracted a cheque for seven hundred thousand euros from an inside pocket, handed it over to the priest, then left without a word.

When they were told about the chance meeting, several of Monsignor Grebenar's parishioners described it as a miracle. How else could the man have known the exact sum that was needed to repair the roof? Others looked upon the stranger as their Good Samaritan. When a part of the roof caved in the following day, the priest handed the cheque to the master builder.

The stranger returned within the hour and took away the painting.

◄○►

This tale might well have ended here, but for a further twist that Monsignor Grebenar surely would have described as divine intervention, but would have caused Herr Grebenar to become suspicious.

On the day the new roof was finally completed, Monsignor Grebenar held a service of thanksgiving. The church was packed to hear his sermon. The words 'miracle', 'Good Samaritan' and 'divine intervention' could be heard on the lips of several members of the congregation.

When Monsignor Grebenar had given the final blessing and his flock had departed, he once again thanked God for guiding him in his hour of need. He looked briefly at the blank, newly painted white wall behind the altar and sighed. He then turned his eyes to the brand new roof and smiled, thanking the Almighty a second time.

After returning home for a simple lunch prepared by his housekeeper, the priest settled down by the fire to enjoy the *Hertzendorfer Gazette*, an indulgence he allowed himself once a week. He read the headline several times before he fell to his knees and thanked God once again.

Grebenar Museum burnt to the ground
Police suspect arson

The London *Times* described the loss of Friedrich Bloch's work as devastating, and far more significant than the destruction of the museum itself. After all, the arts correspondent pointed out, Hertzendorf could always build another museum, while the portraits of Christ and his twelve disciples were works of true genius, and quite irreplaceable.

During his closing prayers the following Sunday, Monsignor Grebenar thanked God that he had not taken the lawyer's advice and transferred *The Last Supper* to the museum for safe-keeping; another miracle, he suggested.

'Another miracle,' murmured the congregation in unison.

—◦—

Six months later, *The Last Supper* by Friedrich Bloch (1643–1679) came under the hammer at one of the leading auction houses in New York. In the catalogue were Bloch's *Christ's Sermon on the Mount* (1662), while the portraits of the twelve disciples were displayed on separate pages. The cover of the catalogue carried an image of *The Last Supper*, and its unique provenance reminded potential buyers of the tragic loss of the rest of Bloch's work in a fire earlier that year. The foreword to the catalogue suggested this tragedy had greatly increased the historic significance, and value, of Bloch's only surviving work.

The following day a headline in the arts pages of the *New York Times* read:

Bloch's masterpiece, *The Last Supper*, sells for $42,000,000.

MEMBERS ONLY*

9

'PINK FORTY-THREE.'

'You've won first prize,' said Sybil excitedly as she looked down at the little strip of pink raffle tickets on the table in front of her husband.

Sidney frowned. He'd wanted to win the second prize – a set of gardening implements which included a wheelbarrow, a rake, a spade, a trowel, a fork and a pair of shears. Far more useful than the first prize, he thought, especially when you've spent a pound on the tickets.

'Go and collect your prize, Sidney,' said Sybil sharply. 'You mustn't keep the chairman waiting.'

Sidney rose reluctantly from his place. A smattering of applause accompanied him as he made his way through the crowded tables and up to the front of the hall.

Shouts of 'Well done, Sidney', 'I never win anything' and 'You're a lucky bastard' greeted him as he climbed up on to the stage.

'Good show, Sidney,' said the chairman of Southend Rotary Club, handing over a brand new set of golf clubs to the winner.

'Blue one hundred and seven,' the chairman announced as Sidney left the stage and headed back to his table, the golf clubs slung over his right shoulder. He slumped down in his chair and managed a smile when his friends, including the member who had won the gardening implements, came over to congratulate him on drawing first prize in the annual raffle.

Once midnight struck and the band had played the last waltz, everyone stood and joined in a lusty rendering of 'God Save the King'.

As Mr and Mrs Chapman made their way home, Sidney received some strange looks from passers-by who had rarely seen a man carrying a set of golf clubs along the seafront, and certainly not at twenty to one on a Sunday morning.

'Well, Sidney,' said Sybil as she took the front door key out of her handbag, 'who would have thought you'd win first prize?'

'What use is a set of golf clubs when you don't play golf?' Sidney moaned as he followed his wife into the house.

'Perhaps you should take up the game,' suggested Sybil. 'After all, it's not long before you retire.'

Sidney didn't bother to respond as he climbed the stairs. When he reached the landing he pushed open the hatch in the ceiling, pulled down the folding ladder, climbed the steps and dumped the golf clubs in the loft. He didn't give them another thought until the family sat down for Christmas dinner six months later.

◄○►

Christmas dinner at the Chapman household wouldn't have differed greatly from that in a thousand other homes in Southend in 1921.

Once grace had been said, Sidney rose from his place at the top of the table to carve the turkey. Sybil sat proudly at the other end of the table while their two sons, Robin and Malcolm, waited impatiently for their plates to be laden with turkey, Brussels sprouts, roast potatoes and sage and onion stuffing. Once Sidney had finished carving the bird, he drowned his plate with thick Bisto gravy until the meat was almost floating.

'Superb, quite superb,' declared Sidney, digging into a leg.

After a second mouthful he added, 'But then, Sybil, everyone knows you're the finest cook in Southend.'

Sybil beamed with satisfaction, even though her husband had paid her the same compliment every Christmas Day for the past eighteen years.

Only snippets of conversation passed between the Chapman family as they dug contentedly into their well-filled plates. It wasn't until second helpings had been served that Sidney addressed them again.

'It's been another capital year for Chapman's Cleaning Services,' he declared as he emptied the gravy boat over the second leg, 'even if I do say so myself.' The rest of the family didn't comment, as they were well aware that the chairman had only just begun his annual speech to the shareholders.

'The company enjoyed a record turnover, and declared slightly higher profits than last year,' said Sidney, placing his knife and fork on his plate, 'despite the Chancellor of the Exchequer, in his wisdom, raising taxes to fifteen per cent,' he added solemnly. Sidney didn't like Mr Lloyd George's coalition government. He wanted the Conservatives to return to power and bring stability back to the country. 'And what's more,' Sidney continued, nodding in the direction of his older son, 'Robin is to be congratulated on passing his Higher Certificate. Southend Grammar School has done him proud,' he added, raising a glass of sherry that the boy wouldn't be allowed to sample for another year. 'We can only hope that young Malcolm' – he turned his attention to the other side of the table – 'will, in time, follow in his brother's footsteps. And talking of following in another's footsteps, when the school year is over I look forward to welcoming Robin into the firm where he will begin work as an apprentice, just as I did thirty-six years ago.' Sidney raised his glass a second time. 'Let us never forget the company's motto: "Cleanliness is next to Godliness."'

This was the signal that the annual speech had come to an

end, which was always followed by Sidney rolling a cigar lovingly between his fingers. He was just about to light up when Sybil said firmly, 'Not until after you've had your Christmas pudding, dear.'

Sidney reluctantly placed the cigar back on the table as Sybil disappeared into the kitchen.

She reappeared a few moments later, carrying a large Christmas pudding which she placed in the centre of the table. Once again, Sidney rose to conduct the annual ceremony. He slowly uncorked a bottle of brandy that had not been touched since the previous year, poured a liberal amount over the burnt offering, then lit a match and set light to the pudding as if he were a high priest performing a pagan sacrifice. Little blue flames spluttered into the air and were greeted by a round of applause.

Once second helpings had been devoured and Sidney had lit his cigar, the boys became impatient to pull their crackers and discover what treasures awaited them.

The four of them stood up, crossed hands and held firmly on to the ends of the crackers. An almighty tug was followed by four tiny explosions, which, as always, caused a ripple of laughter before each member of the family sat back down to discover what awaited them.

Sybil was rewarded with a sewing kit. 'Always useful,' she remarked.

For Sidney, a bottle opener. 'Very satisfactory,' he declared.

Malcolm didn't look at all pleased with his India rubber, the same offering two years in a row.

The rest of the family turned their attention to Robin, who was shaking his cracker furiously, but nothing was forthcoming, until a golf ball fell out and rolled across the table.

None of them could have known that this simple gift would change the young man's whole life. But then, as you are about to discover, this tale is about Robin Chapman, not his father, mother or younger brother.

—◦—

Although Robin Chapman was not a natural games player, his sports master often described him as a good team man.

Robin regularly turned out as the goalkeeper for the school's Second XI hockey team during the winter, while in the summer he managed to secure a place in the cricket First XI as a bit of an all-rounder. However, none of those seated around that Christmas dinner table in 1921 could have predicted what was about to take place.

Robin waited until Tuesday morning before he made his first move, and then only after his father had left for work.

'Always a lot of dry-cleaning to be done following the Christmas holiday,' Mr Chapman declared before kissing his wife on the cheek and disappearing off down the driveway.

Once his father was safely out of sight, Robin climbed the stairs, pushed open the ceiling hatch and dragged the dust-covered golf bag out of the loft. He carried the clubs back to his room and set about removing the dust and grime that had accumulated over the past six months with a zeal he'd never displayed in the kitchen; first the leather bag followed by the nine clubs, each one of which bore the signature of someone called Harry Vardon. Once he had completed the task, he slung the bag over his shoulder, crept down the stairs, slipped out of the house and headed towards the seafront.

When he reached the beach, Robin dropped the bag on the ground and placed the little white ball on the sand by his feet. He then studied the array of shining clubs, not sure which one to select. He finally chose one with the word 'mashie' stamped on its head. He focused on the ball and took a swing at it, causing a shower of sand to fly into the air, while the ball remained resolutely in place. After several more attempts he finally made contact with the ball, but it only advanced a few feet to his left.

Robin chased after it and repeated the exercise again and again, until the ball finally launched into the air and landed with a plop a hundred yards in front of him. By the time he'd returned home for lunch, late, he considered himself to be the next Harry Vardon. Not that he had any idea who Harry Vardon was.

Robin didn't go back to the beach that afternoon, but instead paid a visit to the local library, where he went straight to the sports section. As he could only take out two books on his library card, he needed to be selective. After much deliberation, he removed from the shelf, *Golf for Beginners* and *The Genius of Harry Vardon*.

Back at home, he locked himself in his bedroom and didn't reappear until he heard his mother calling up the stairs, 'Supper, boys', by which time he knew the difference between a putter, a cleek, a niblick and a brassie. After supper he leafed through the pages of the other book, and discovered that Harry Vardon hailed from Jersey in the Channel Islands, which Robin hadn't even realized was part of the British Empire. He also found out that Mr Vardon had won the Open Championship on six separate occasions, a record that had never been equalled and, in the author's opinion, never would be.

The following morning, Robin returned to the beach. He placed the book on the ground, open at a photograph of Harry Vardon in mid-swing. He dropped the ball at his feet and managed to hit it over a hundred yards on several occasions, if not always in a straight line. Once again he steadied himself, checked the photograph, raised his club and addressed the ball, an expression regularly repeated in *Golf for Beginners*.

He was about to take another swing when he heard a voice behind him say, 'Keep your eye on the ball, my boy, and don't raise your head until you've completed the shot. That way you'll find the ball goes a lot further.'

Robin obeyed the instruction without question, and was indeed rewarded with the promised result, although the ball disappeared into the sea, never to be seen again.

He turned to see his instructor smiling.

'Young man,' he said, 'even Harry Vardon occasionally needed more than one ball. You have potential. If you present yourself at the Southend Golf Club at nine o'clock on Saturday morning, the club's professional will try to turn that potential into something a little more worthwhile.' Without another word the gentleman strode off down the beach.

Robin had no idea where the Southend Golf Club was, but he did know that the local library had always managed to answer all his questions in the past.

On Saturday morning he took the number eleven bus to the outskirts of town and was waiting outside the clubhouse a few minutes before the appointed hour.

Thus began a hobby which turned into a passion, and finally became an obsession.

◄○►

Robin joined his father as an apprentice at Chapman's Cleaning Services a few days after he left school and, despite working long hours, he could still be found on the beach at six o'clock every morning practising his swing, or putting at a target on his bedroom carpet late into the night.

His progress at Chapman's Cleaning Services and at the town's golf club went hand in hand. On his twenty-first birthday Robin was appointed as a trainee manager with the firm, and a few weeks later he was invited to play for Southend in the annual fixture against Brighton. When he stood on the first tee the following Saturday, he was so nervous he hit his opening shot into the nearest flower bed, and he didn't fare much better for the next nine holes. By the turn, he'd left it far too late to recover and was well beaten by his opponent from Brighton.

Robin was surprised to be selected the following week for the fixture against Eastbourne. Although still nervous, he put up a far better performance and managed to halve his match. After that, he rarely missed a first-team fixture.

Although Robin began to take over many of his father's responsibilities at work, he never allowed business to interfere with his first love. On Mondays he would practise his driving, Wednesdays his bunker shots and on Fridays his putting. On Saturdays his brother Malcolm, who had recently completed his apprenticeship with the firm, kept a watchful eye on the shop while Robin kept his eye on the ball, until it had finally sunk into the eighteenth hole.

On Sundays, after attending church – his mother still wielded some influence over him – Robin would head for the club and play nine holes before lunch.

He wasn't sure which gave him more satisfaction: his father asking him to take over the business on his retirement, or Southend Golf Club inviting him to be the youngest captain in the club's history.

The following Christmas, his father sat at the head of the table as usual, puffing away on his cigar, but it was Robin who presented the annual report. He didn't rub in the fact that the profits had almost doubled during his first year as manager, and nor did he mention that at the same time he'd become a scratch player. This happy state of affairs might have continued without interruption, and indeed this story would never have been written, had it not been for an unexpected invitation landing on the club captain's desk.

◄○►

When the Royal Jersey Golf Club wrote to enquire if Southend would care for a fixture, Robin jumped at the opportunity to visit the birthplace of Harry Vardon and play on the course that had made him so famous.

Six weeks later Robin and his team took a train to Weymouth before boarding the ferry for St Helier. Robin had planned that they should arrive in Jersey the day before the match so they would have enough time to become acquainted with a course none of them had played before. Unfortunately, he hadn't planned for a storm breaking out during the crossing. The ancient vessel somehow managed to sway from side to side while at the same time bobbing up and down as it made its slow progress to Jersey. During the crossing, most of the team were to be found, a pale shade of green, leaning over the side being violently sick, while Robin, oblivious to their malady, strolled up and down the deck, enjoying the sea air. One or two of his fellow passengers looked at him with envy, while others just stared in disbelief.

When the ferry finally docked at St Helier, the rest of the team, several pounds lighter, made their way straight to their hotel where they quickly checked into their rooms and were not to be seen again before breakfast the following morning. Robin took a taxi in the opposite direction, and instructed the driver to take him to the Jersey Royal Golf Club.

'Royal Jersey,' corrected the cabbie politely. 'Jersey Royal is a potato,' he explained with a chuckle.

When the taxi came to a halt outside the main entrance of the magnificent clubhouse, Robin didn't budge. He stared at the Members Only sign, and if the driver hadn't said, 'That'll be two shillings, guv', he might not have moved. He settled the fare, got out of the cab and walked hesitantly across the gravel towards the clubhouse. He tentatively opened the large double door and stepped into an imposing marble entrance hall to be greeted by two full-length oil portraits facing each other on opposite walls. Robin immediately recognized Harry Vardon, dressed in plus fours and a Fair Isle cardigan, and carrying a niblick in his left hand. He gave him a slight bow before turning his attention to the other picture, but he did not recognize the elderly, chisel-faced gentleman wearing a long black frock-coat and grey pinstriped trousers.

Robin suddenly became aware of a young man looking at him quizzically. 'My name's Robin Chapman,' he said uncertainly, 'I'm—'

' – the captain of the Southend Golf Club,' the young man said. 'And I'm Nigel Forsyth, captain of the Royal Jersey. Care to join me for a drink, old fellow?'

'Thank you,' said Robin. He and his opposite number strolled through the hall to a thickly carpeted room furnished with comfortable leather chairs. Nigel pointed to a seat in a bay window overlooking the eighteenth hole, and went over to the bar. Robin wanted to look out of the window and study the course, but forced himself not to.

Nigel returned carrying two half-pints of shandy and placed one on the table in front of his guest. As he sat down he raised his own glass. 'Are you a one-man team, by any chance?' he asked.

Robin laughed. 'No, the rest of my lot are probably tucked up in bed,' he said, 'their rooms still tossing around.'

'Ah, you must have come over on the Weymouth Packet.'

'Yes,' said Robin, 'but we'll get our revenge on the return fixture.'

'Not a hope,' said Nigel. 'Whenever we travel to the mainland we always go via Southampton. That route has modern vessels fitted with stabilizers. Perhaps I should have mentioned that in my letter,' he added with a grin. 'Care for a round before it gets dark?'

Once they were out on the course, it soon became clear to Robin why so many old timers were always recalling rounds they had played at the Royal Jersey. The course was the finest he'd ever played, and the thought that he was walking in Harry Vardon's footsteps only added to his enjoyment.

When Robin's ball landed on the eighteenth green some five feet from the hole, Nigel volunteered, 'If the rest of your team are as good as you, Robin, we'll have one hell of a game on our hands tomorrow.'

'They're far better,' said Robin, not missing a beat as they walked off the green and made their way back to the clubhouse.

'Same again?' asked Nigel as they headed towards the bar.

'No, this one's on me,' insisted Robin.

'Sorry, old fellow, guests are not allowed to pay for a drink. Strict rule of the club.'

Robin came to a halt once again in front of the large portrait of the elderly gentleman. Nigel answered his unasked question. 'That's our president, Lord Trent. He's not half as frightening as he looks, as you'll discover tomorrow evening when he joins us for dinner. Have a seat while I go and fetch those drinks.'

Nigel was standing at the bar when a young woman came in. She walked briskly across and whispered something in his ear. He nodded, and she left as quickly as she'd arrived.

From the moment she entered the room to the moment she left, Robin had been unable to take his eyes off her. 'You didn't tell me you had a goddess on the island,' he said when Nigel handed him another half-pint of shandy.

'Ah, you must be referring to Diana,' he said as the young lady disappeared.

'An appropriate name for a goddess,' said Robin. 'And how enlightened of you to allow women members.'

'Certainly not,' said Nigel, grinning. 'She's Lord Trent's secretary.' He took a sip of his drink before adding, 'But I think she's attending the dinner tomorrow night, so you'll have a chance to meet your goddess.'

When Robin returned to the hotel later that evening, only

one other member of the team felt able to join him for dinner. Robin wondered whether the rest would have recovered sufficiently to be standing on the first tee by ten o'clock the following morning. Though in truth, he was already thinking more about tomorrow evening.

—◁◦▷—

Southend somehow managed a full turnout by the time the chief steward asked the two captains to tee up at the first hole.

As the visiting captain, Robin struck the first ball. Five hours later the score board showed that the Royal Jersey had beaten Southend Golf Club by four and a half matches to three and a half. Not a bad result, Robin considered, given the circumstances, but then he'd never played a better round in his life, which may have been because Diana seemed to be following Nigel around the course. Another home advantage.

After a few drinks in the clubhouse, with no sign of Diana, the Southend team returned to their hotel to change for dinner. Robin was the first one waiting in the foyer. Nervously he touched his bow tie after he'd checked with the receptionist that three taxis had been ordered for seven o'clock.

Robin didn't speak on the journey back to the Royal Jersey, and when he led his team into the dining room, Nigel was waiting to greet him. Diana was standing by his side. Lucky man, thought Robin.

'Good to see you again, old fellow,' Nigel said, and turning to Diana, he added, 'I don't believe you've met my sister.'

—◁◦▷—

'You're going to do what?' said his father.

'I'm going to move to Jersey, where I intend to open a branch of Chapman's Cleaning Services.'

'But I always thought you planned to open a second branch

720

in Southend, while I took over the main shop,' said Malcolm, sounding equally bemused by his brother's news.

'You'll still be taking over the main shop, Malcolm, while I open our first overseas branch.'

Robin's father seemed to be momentarily struck dumb, so his mother took advantage of this rare occurrence. 'What's the real reason you want to go back to Jersey?' she asked, looking her son in the eye.

'I've found the finest golf course on earth, Mother, and if they'll have me, I intend to become a member and play on it for the rest of my life.'

'No,' said his mother quietly, 'I asked for the real reason.' The rest of the family remained silent as they waited for Robin's reply.

'I've found the most beautiful woman on earth, and if she'll have me, I'd like her to become my wife.'

—‹o›—

Robin boarded the boat back to Jersey the following Friday, despite having failed to answer his mother's third question: 'Has this young lady agreed to be your wife?'

The only thing Diana had agreed to was to join him on the dance floor for a quickstep, but during those three minutes Robin knew he wanted to hold on to this woman for the rest of his life. 'I'll be coming back next weekend,' he told her.

'But the team are playing away at Wentworth next Saturday,' she remarked innocently.

—‹o›—

Robin was surprised to find Diana standing on the quayside when the ferry sailed into the harbour the following Saturday. Whom had she come to meet, he wondered, and only hoped it wasn't another man.

When he stepped off the gangway, Diana gave him the same warm smile that had remained in his mind for the past week.

'I wasn't sure you believed me when I said I'd be coming back,' he said shyly as they shook hands.

'I wasn't sure you would,' admitted Diana, 'but then I thought, if the poor man is willing to give up a weekend's golf just to spend some time with me, the least I can do is meet him off the boat.'

Robin smiled at the thought that he couldn't even remember who Southend were playing that day, and took Diana's hand as they walked along the causeway.

If you had asked him how they spent the weekend, all he could remember was reluctantly climbing back on the ferry on Sunday evening, after kissing her for the first time.

'See you same time next Saturday, Diana,' he shouted down as he leaned over the railings, but the boat's foghorn drowned his words.

Diana was standing on the quayside the following Saturday, and every Saturday until Robin stopped taking the ferry back to Weymouth.

During the week, Robin would book a trunk call so they could speak to each other every evening. Diana spent her spare time looking at properties in St Helier that might meet his requirements. She finally found a shop on the high street whose lease was about to expire, with a hotel across the road that needed to change its bed linen and towels every day, and several restaurants that believed in spotless napkins and fresh tablecloths. Robin agreed that it was the ideal location to open a branch of Chapman's Cleaning Services.

The following Saturday he signed a three-year renewable lease, and immediately moved into the flat above the shop. If he hadn't won Diana's hand by the end of the lease, and also become a member of the Royal Jersey Golf Club, he would have to admit defeat, return to the mainland and open a second branch of Chapman's in Southend.

Although he was confident that, given time, both challenges would be surmounted, becoming a member of the RJGC turned out to be a far more difficult proposition than getting Diana to agree to be his wife.

It didn't take long for Robin to qualify as a playing member of the Royal Jersey, and he was delighted when Nigel invited him to represent the club in the hotly contested local derby against Guernsey. Robin won his match, and proposed to Diana that night.

'What if you hadn't been picked for the team?' she asked, unable to take her eyes off the small, sparkling diamond on the third finger of her left hand.

'I'd have whisked you off to England and sunk the Weymouth ferry,' said Robin without hesitation.

Diana laughed. 'So, what are my champion's plans for conquering the old guard who make up the committee of the Royal Jersey?'

'They've granted me an interview next month,' he told her, 'so we'll soon find out if we're going to spend the rest of our lives in St Helier or Southend-on-Sea.'

'Don't forget that only one in three people who apply for full membership even get on to the waiting list,' Diana reminded him.

Robin smiled. 'Possibly so, but with Lord Trent as my proposer, and your brother as my seconder, I must have a better than one-in-three chance.'

'So that's why you asked me to marry you,' Diana said, still staring at her ring.

◄○►

When the appointed hour came for Robin to appear before the committee, he admitted to Diana that he had never been so nervous, even though everyone seated on the other side of the table seemed to smile whenever he answered their undemanding questions, and nods of approval greeted the Englishman's detailed knowledge of the life of Harry Vardon.

Ten days later, Robin received a letter from the club secretary to say that his application had been successful and his name would be placed on the waiting list.

'The waiting list?' said Robin in frustration. 'How long do they expect me to hang about before I become a member?'

'My brother warned me,' said Diana, 'that if you weren't born on the island, it usually takes ten to fifteen years.'

'Ten to fifteen years?' repeated Robin in disgust, before adding, 'Lord Trent wasn't born on the island.'

'True,' said Diana, 'but at the time the committee was looking for a new president, preferably with a title, so they made him an honorary life member.'

'And are there any other honorary life members?'

'Only Harry Vardon,' replied Diana.

'Well, I'm no Harry Vardon,' said Robin.

'There's one other way you could automatically become a life member,' said Diana.

'And what's that?' said Robin eagerly.

'Win the President's Cup.'

'But I was knocked out in the second round last year,' Robin reminded her. 'In any case, your brother's in a different class to me.'

'Just make sure you get to the final this year,' said Diana. 'I'll fix my brother.'

◄○►

Robin and Diana were married at the local parish church later that summer. The vicar agreed to conduct the ceremony on a Sunday, but only because the Royal Jersey had a crucial match against Rye on the Saturday.

Robin's father, mother and brother had travelled over on the ferry from Southampton earlier in the week, and they spent a happy few days getting to know Diana. Long before the day of the wedding, Sybil fully understood why her son had wanted to return to Jersey after one dance. When the bride walked down the aisle, she found that the ceremony was so well attended that extra chairs had been placed at the back of the church.

Mr and Mrs Chapman left the parish church of St Helier as man and wife, to be greeted with a shower of confetti thrown by Diana's friends, while two rows of young men in RJGC blazers held up golf clubs to form an arch all the way to their waiting car.

The reception was held at the Royal Jersey, where Malcolm delivered such an accomplished best-man's speech that it came as no surprise to Robin that Chapman's of Southend continued to flourish in his absence.

Lord Trent rose to reply on behalf of the guests. He let slip the worst-kept secret on the island when he told everyone that the newly-weds would be sailing around the French coast on his yacht for their honeymoon, but only for ten days, because Robin needed to be back in time for the first round of the President's Cup. Diana couldn't be sure if he was joking.

When Mr and Mrs Chapman sailed into St Helier ten days later, the skipper informed Lord Trent that Robin had turned out to be such a good sailor that he had allowed him to take the wheel whenever he needed a break.

The following day, Robin was knocked out in the first round of the President's Cup.

◄○►

Robin and Diana quickly settled into their new home on the seafront, and for the first time since he'd arrived in Jersey, Robin had to walk to work. Eleven months later, Diana gave birth to a boy whom they christened Harry.

'Will you do anything to become a member of that damned club?' Diana asked her husband as she sat in the hospital bed surrounded by flowers and cards from well-wishers.

'Anything,' replied Robin, picking up the sleeping baby.

'Well, I have one piece of information that might speed up the process,' said Diana, smiling.

'And what's that?' asked Robin, handing the suddenly screaming infant back to its mother.

'My brother tells me that the St Helier lifeboat is looking for a new crew member, and as you spent more time at the helm of Lord Trent's yacht than you did in our cabin, you must be an obvious candidate.'

'And how will that help me get elected to the Royal Jersey?' enquired Robin.

'Guess who's president of the RNLI?' said Diana coyly.

The day after Robin failed to make the third round of that year's President's Cup, he filled in an application form to join the crew of the lifeboat.

◄○►

Robin's interview for a place in the lifeboat turned out to be not so much a meeting as an endurance test. John Poynton, the coxswain, put all the applicants through a series of rigorous trials to make sure only the most resilient would want to return a week later.

Robin couldn't wait to get home and tell Diana how much he'd enjoyed the whole experience, the camaraderie of the crew, the chance to learn new skills and, most important, the opportunity to do something worthwhile. He only hoped the coxswain would take his application seriously, despite his lack of experience.

When the time came for Mr Poynton to select his new crew member, he unhesitatingly placed a tick by one name, telling his bosun that young Chapman was such a natural he wouldn't be surprised if the man could walk on water.

As the weeks passed, Robin found himself enjoying being tested by the rigorous drills the crew were put through on the high seas. Whenever the klaxon sounded, the crew were expected to drop everything and report to the boathouse within ten minutes. Robin could never be sure if it would be just another dry run, or if this time they would be going to the aid of someone who was genuinely in distress. The coxswain regularly reminded his crew that all the hours of hard work would prove worthwhile when someone called for their assistance, and only then would they discover which of them could handle the pressure.

—◦—

It was the middle of the night when the klaxon sounded, waking everyone within a mile of the boathouse. Robin leapt out of bed in the middle of a dream, just as he was taking a putt to win the President's Cup. He switched on the light and quickly got dressed.

'Off to see your other girlfriend?' enquired Diana, turning over.

'All eight of them,' Robin replied. 'But let's hope I'll be back in time for breakfast.'

'You'll be back,' said Diana. 'After all, it's the final of the President's Cup on Saturday, and as you're playing my brother, you may never have a better chance of winning.'

'I beat him in my dream,' said Robin as he picked up his bicycle clips.

'In your dreams,' said Diana, smiling.

Robin was pedalling frantically through the empty streets when the klaxon sounded a second time. He pedalled even harder.

He was among the first to arrive at the boathouse, and the

look on the coxswain's face left him in no doubt that he was about to experience his first distress call.

'We've had an SOS from a small sailing boat that's capsized just off the Arden Rock,' the coxswain told his crew as they pulled on their oilskins and sea boots. 'It seems a young couple thought it would be fun to sail around the bay after midnight,' he grunted. 'I'll be launching in a couple of minutes.' None of the crew spoke as they climbed on board and carefully checked their stations.

'Knock her out!' the coxswain called to the head launcher once the last crew member had given a thumbs-up.

Robin felt a rush of adrenaline pump through his body as the lifeboat made its way across the lapping waves inside the harbour. Once they had passed the breakwater, the boat reared up and down in the open sea. None of the crew showed any sign of fear, which gave Robin confidence. They had only one thing on their minds as they each carried out their separate duties.

The lookout was the first to spot the capsized yacht. He pointed and bellowed against the high wind, 'Nor' nor'west, skipper, about three hundred yards.'

Robin felt exhilarated as they edged slowly towards the capsized vessel. All the drills they had practised during the past months were about to be put to the test. As they came alongside, Robin stared into the eyes of a terrified young couple, who couldn't believe there were eight people on that little island who were willing to risk their lives to rescue them. But however much the coxswain shouted at them to catch hold of one of the grab lines, they kept clinging to the keel of their sinking yacht. Robin began to feel that nothing would make either of them let go, and, if anything, the boy looked even more terrified than his girlfriend. The waves refused to let up, making Robin wonder how long it would be before the coxswain decided his own crew was in just as much danger as the yacht.

They tried one more time to manoeuvre the lifeboat alongside the stricken vessel.

When the boat was at its highest point in the water, Robin wondered if he dare risk it. It was not something to spend much time thinking about. When the bow of the boat plunged into the next wave, he leapt into the sea and with all the strength he could muster managed to grab on to the side of the yacht. He waited for the wave to rise again before he pulled himself up on to what was left of the floating wreck. With the help of the next wave he hauled himself up on to the keel and somehow managed to smile at the two disbelieving faces.

'Take my hand!' he hollered to the girl. After a moment's hesitation, she released her grip on the keel and clung on to Robin's outstretched arm. For a moment he feared she might panic and push him back into the sea.

'You'll have to jump when I give you the signal,' screamed Robin above the noise of the wind. The girl didn't look convinced. 'Are you ready?' he cried as the next wave headed towards them. As the lifeboat reared into the air like a startled horse, Robin shouted, 'Now!' and pushed her off the yacht with all the strength left in his body.

Two arms grabbed her as she landed in the water by the side of the lifeboat and hauled her unceremoniously on board. Robin waited for the next wave before the young man obeyed the same instruction. He was not as lucky as his companion, and cracked his head on the gunnel before he was finally dragged on to the boat. Robin could see blood pouring from his forehead. He knew there was a first-aid kit in the cockpit but no one would be able to open it, let alone administer any succour, during such a storm.

Robin felt the yacht sinking beneath him and his thoughts switched from the young man's problems to his own survival. He would only have one chance before the boat disappeared below the waves.

He hunched up in a ball as he waited for the lifeboat to arch on the peak of the wave, then propelled himself towards it like an athlete bursting out of the blocks. But it turned out to be a false start because he missed the grab line by several feet and found himself floundering in the sea. His last thoughts as he sank below the unforgiving waves were of Diana and his son Harry, but then he bobbed up in a trough and a hand grabbed his hair while another clung to a shoulder and dragged him inch by inch, wave by wave, towards the boat. But the sea still refused to give him up, and when the next wave hurled him against the side of the lifeboat, he felt his arm snap. As he was dragged on to the deck he screamed, but no one heard him above the storm. He would have thanked the coxswain, but all he could manage was to unload a stomach full of sea-water all over him. At least Poynton had the grace to laugh.

Robin couldn't recall much of the journey back to port, except for the excruciating pain in his right arm and the looks of relief on the faces of the young couple he'd rescued.

'We'll be back in time for breakfast,' said the coxswain as they passed the lighthouse and sailed into the relative calm of the harbour. When the crew finally disembarked, they were greeted by a cheering crowd.

Diana was standing on the quay, her eyes frantically searching for her husband. Robin smiled and waved at her with the arm that wasn't broken.

It wasn't until she read a full report in the *Jersey Echo* the following day that she realized just how close she'd been to becoming a widow. John Poynton described Robin's decision to leave the boat to rescue the stranded couple, who undoubtedly owed their lives to him, as an act of selfless courage in the face of overwhelming odds. He had told Robin privately that he thought he was mad, and then shook him by the hand. It was the wrong hand, and Robin screamed again.

All Robin had to say while he sat propped up in a hospital bed, one arm in plaster, the other attempting to handle a spoon and a bowl of cornflakes, was, 'I won't be able to play in the final of the President's Cup.'

A year later, Diana gave birth to a girl whom they christened Kate, and Robin fell in love for a second time.

Chapman's Cleaning Services continued to flourish, not least because Robin had become such a popular member of the community, with some of the residents now treating him as if he were a local and not a newcomer.

The following year, he was elected a vice-president of the local rotary club, and when the head launcher stepped down, the RNLI committee voted unanimously to invite Robin to take his place. Despite these minor honours being bestowed upon him, he reminded his wife that he was no nearer to becoming a full member of the Royal Jersey, and as his handicap had begun to move in the wrong direction, he'd probably missed his one chance to win the President's Cup and automatically become a life member.

'You could always join another club,' Diana suggested innocently. 'After all, the Royal Jersey's not the only golf club on the island.'

'If I were to join another club, the committee would strike me off the waiting list without a second thought. No, I'm just going to have to be patient. After all, it should only be about another eight years before they get round to me,' he said, not attempting to hide the sarcasm in his voice.

Diana would have laughed if the klaxon hadn't sounded for the ninth time that year. Robin dropped his paper and leapt up from the table without a second thought. Diana wondered if her husband had any idea of the anxiety she experienced every time he was away at sea. It hadn't helped when a few weeks earlier one of the crew had been swept overboard during an abortive rescue attempt.

Robin kissed his wife before leaving her with the familiar parting words, 'See you when I see you, my darling.'

When he returned, four hours later, he crept quietly into bed, not wanting to wake Diana. She wasn't asleep.

◄◦►

Robin smiled after he'd read the letter a second time. It was just a short note from the club secretary, nothing official, of course, but he was confident that it wouldn't be too much longer before the committee was able to ratify his membership of the RJGC. What did 'too much longer' mean? Robin wondered. In theory he still had another four years to wait, and he was well aware that there were several other names ahead of his on the waiting list. However, Diana had told him that several members felt he should have been elected after he'd broken his arm and been forced to withdraw from the final of the President's Cup.

Robin's spell as head launcher on the lifeboat was coming to an end, as the job required a younger man. Diana couldn't wait for the day when her husband would become more preoccupied with propelling a little white ball towards a distant hole than with rescuing helpless bodies from a merciless sea.

The following year, Robin opened a second shop in St Brêlade, and was considering a third, on Guernsey. He felt a little guilty because his brother Malcolm was now running four establishments on the mainland, and contributing far more to the company's bottom line, while at the same time keeping an eye on his two children, who were at prep school on the mainland.

Robin was a contented man, and on his thirty-sixth birthday he promised Diana that he would serve only one more year as head launcher, even if he wasn't elected to the Royal Jersey. He raised his glass. 'To the future,' he said.

Diana raised her glass and smiled. 'To the future,' she repeated, unaware that another man on the far side of Europe had other plans for Robin Chapman's future.

◂◦▸

When Britain declared war on Germany on 3 September 1939, Robin's first instinct was to return to England and sign up, especially as several younger members of his crew had already found their way to Portsmouth and joined the Royal Navy. Diana talked him out of the idea, convincing him that he was too old, and in any case his expertise would be needed on Jersey.

They decided to leave the children at school in England, and Malcolm and his wife unhesitatingly agreed to look after them during the holidays.

When the German army goose-stepped down the Champs-Élysées nine months later, Robin knew it could only be a matter of weeks before Hitler decided to invade the Channel Islands. Thirty thousand islanders had been evacuated to Britain, including his own children, and German bombs had fallen on St Helier and St Peter Port on Guernsey.

'I'll have to stay on as head launcher,' Robin told Diana. 'With so few young men available, they'll never find a replacement before the war is over.'

Diana reluctantly agreed to what she imagined to be the lesser of two evils.

◂◦▸

When Lord Trent phoned Robin at home and asked if they could have a private meeting at the club, he assumed the old man was at last going to confirm his membership of the Royal Jersey.

Robin arrived a few minutes early and the club steward ushered him straight into Lord Trent's study. The look on the President's face was not one that suggested glad tidings. Lord Trent rose from behind his desk, indicated that they should sit in the more comfortable leather chairs by the fire, and poured two large brandies.

'I need to ask you a special favour, Robin,' he said once he'd settled in his chair.

'Of course, sir,' said Robin. 'How can I help?'

'As you know, the ferries from Weymouth and Southampton have been requisitioned by the Government as part of the war effort, and although I thoroughly approve this decision, it presents me with something of a problem, as the Prime Minister has asked me to return to England at the first possible opportunity.'

Before Robin could ask why, Trent took a telegram from an inside pocket and handed it to him. Robin's heart missed a beat when he saw the address: 'No.10 Downing Street, London, SW1'. Trent waited until he had finished reading the telegram from Winston Churchill.

'The Prime Minister may well wish to see me urgently,' said Trent, 'but he seems to have forgotten that I have no way of getting off this island.' He took another sip of his brandy. 'I rather hoped you might feel able to take Mary and me across to the mainland in the lifeboat.'

Robin knew that the lifeboat was never meant to leave the harbour unless it was answering a distress call, but a direct request from the Prime Minister surely allowed him to tear up the rule book. Robin considered the request for some time before he responded. 'We'd have to slip out after nightfall, then I could be back before sunrise and no one need be any the wiser.'

'Whatever you say,' said Trent, command changing hands.

'Would tomorrow night suit you, sir?'

The old man nodded. 'Thank you, Robin.'

Robin rose from his place. 'Then I'll see you and Lady

Trent on the quayside at nine tomorrow night, sir.' He left without another word, his brandy untouched.

—◦—

Robin was assisted by two young crew members who also wanted to reach the mainland, as they wished to join up. He was surprised by how uneventful the Channel crossing turned out to be. It was a full moon that night and the sea was remarkably calm for October, although Lady Trent proved to be a far better sailor than his lordship, who never opened his mouth during the entire voyage except when he leaned over the side.

When the lifeboat entered Weymouth harbour, a patrol boat escorted them to the dockside, where a Rolls-Royce was waiting to whisk the Trents off to London. Robin shook hands with the old man for the last time.

After a bacon sandwich and half a pint of Courage in a dockside pub, he wished his two crew members good luck before they boarded a train for Portsmouth, and he set off on the return voyage to Jersey. Robin checked his watch and reckoned he should be back in time to join Diana for breakfast.

Robin slipped back into St Helier before first light. He had just stepped on to the dock when the fist landed in his stomach, causing him to double up in pain and collapse on to his knees. He was about to protest when he realized that the two uniformed men who were now pinning him to the ground were not speaking English.

He didn't waste any time protesting as they marched him down the High Street and into the nearest police station. There was no friendly desk sergeant on duty to greet him. He was pushed roughly down a flight of stone steps before being flung into a cell. He felt sick when he saw Diana seated on a bench against the wall. She jumped up and ran to him as the cell door slammed behind them.

'Are they safe?' she whispered as he held her in his arms.

'Yes,' he replied. 'But a spell in prison isn't going to help my membership application for the Royal Jersey,' he remarked, trying to lighten the mood. Diana didn't laugh.

They didn't have long to wait before the heavy iron door was pulled open once again. Two young soldiers marched in, grabbed Robin by the elbows and dragged him back out. They led him up the stairs and out on to an empty street. There were no locals to be seen in any direction as a curfew had been imposed. Robin assumed that he was about to be shot, but they continued to march him up the high street, and didn't stop until they reached the Bailiff's Chambers.

Robin had visited the seat of local government many times in the past, as each new bailiff required his dress robes to be spotless on inauguration day, a ceremony he and Diana always attended. But on this occasion Robin was led into the front office, where he found a German officer seated in the Bailiff's chair. One look at his crisp uniform suggested that he wasn't going to enquire about Chapman's services.

'Mr Chapman,' the officer said with no trace of an accent, 'my name is Colonel Kruger, I am the new commandant for the Channel Islands. Perhaps you could start by telling me why you took Lord Trent back to England?'

Robin didn't reply.

'No doubt Lord and Lady Trent are enjoying breakfast at the Ritz Hotel while you languish in jail for your troubles.' The officer rose and walked across the room, coming to a halt when the two men were standing face to face. 'If you feel unable to assist me, Mr Chapman, you and your wife will remain in jail until there is space on a ship to transport you to the Fatherland.'

'But my wife was not involved,' Robin protested.

'In normal circumstances, I would be willing to accept your word, Mr Chapman, but as your wife was Lord Trent's sec-retary . . .' Robin said nothing. 'You will be sent to one of our less well-appointed camps, unless, of course, one of you decides to enlighten me on the reason Lord Trent needed to rush back to England.'

-◄◊►-

Robin and Diana remained in their tiny cell for nineteen days. They were fed on bread and water, which until then Robin had always assumed was a Dickensian myth. He began to wonder if the authorities had forgotten about them.

He managed to pick up snippets of information from those islanders who had been forced to work at the police station, but the only thing of any consequence he was able to find out was that German ships were docking at St Helier regularly to unload more soldiers, arms and ammunition.

On the twentieth morning, one of their informants told them that a ship would be arriving from Hamburg the following day, and that he had seen their names on the embarkation log for its return journey. Diana wept. Robin never slept while his wife was awake.

In the middle of the night, when they were both sleeping fitfully, the cell door was pulled open without warning. Two German soldiers stood in the doorway. One of them asked politely if Mr Chapman would join them. Robin was puzzled by the officer's courteous manner, and wondered if this was how German soldiers behaved just before they shot you.

He accompanied the soldiers up the stairs. Was he being escorted to the ship? Surely not, or they would have taken Diana as well. Once again he was taken down the street in the direction of the Bailiff's Chambers, but this time the soldiers walked by his side, making no attempt to hold on to him.

When he entered the Bailiff's office, Colonel Kruger looked up from behind his desk, an anxious look on his face. He didn't waste his words. 'The ship that was meant to transport prisoners to Hamburg has struck a rock just outside the harbour.' Robin wondered which brave islander had managed to remove the warning lights. 'It's sinking fast,' continued the colonel. 'The lives of all those on board will be lost, including several civilians, unless the lifeboat is sent out to rescue them.' He avoided saying 'my countrymen'.

'Why are you telling me this, Colonel?' asked Robin.

'The lifeboat crew is refusing to cast off without their head launcher, so I am asking you – ' he paused – 'begging you, to join them before it's too late.'

Strange, the things that pass through one's mind when faced with a moral dilemma, Robin thought. He knew the directive by heart. It is the duty of every member of the RNLI to go to the aid of anyone in distress on the high seas, irrespective of their nationality, colour or creed, even if they are at war with Britain. He nodded curtly at the colonel.

Out on the street a car was waiting, its door open, to take him to the harbour. Fifteen minutes later they cast off.

Robin and the rest of the crew returned to Arden Rock several times that night. In all, they rescued 73 passengers, including 11 German officers and 37 crew members. The remainder were civilians who had been selected to assist in the administration of the island. A cargo of arms, ammunition and transport vehicles was resting on the bottom of the ocean.

When Robin carried the last of the survivors back to the safety of the island, two German officers were waiting for him as he stepped off the lifeboat. They handcuffed him and escorted him back to the police station. As he walked into the cell, Diana smiled for the first time in days.

◄○►

When the cell door was opened the following morning, two plates of bacon and eggs, along with cups of hot tea, were laid before them by a young German corporal.

'Last breakfast before they execute us,' suggested Robin as the guard slammed the cell door behind him.

'It wouldn't be hard to guess what your final request will be,' said Diana, smiling.

A few minutes after they'd devoured their unexpected feast, another soldier appeared and told them he was taking them to the commandant's headquarters.

'I shall be happy to accompany you to the Bailiff's Chambers,' said Robin defiantly.

'We're not going to the Connétable,' said the soldier. 'The commandant has requisitioned the golf club as his new headquarters.'

'Your final wish has been granted,' said Diana as she and Robin settled into the back seat of a staff car, which brought a puzzled expression to the young German's face.

When they arrived at the club, they were taken to Lord Trent's office. Colonel Kruger stood up and offered them both a seat. Diana sat down, but Robin remained standing.

'This morning,' the colonel said, 'I rescinded the order that you were to be shipped to prison in Germany, and issued a new directive, releasing you immediately. You will therefore be allowed to return to your home. Should you be foolish enough to break the law a second time, Mr Chapman, you will both be aboard the next ship that sails for Germany. Think of it as what's called, in your country, a suspended sentence.'

The commandant once again rose from behind his desk. 'You are a remarkable man, Mr Chapman. If your fellow countrymen are forged from the same steel, your nation may not prove quite as easy to defeat.'

'Perhaps you should read *Henry V*,' suggested Robin.

'I have,' replied the commandant. He paused and looked out of the window towards the weed-covered eighteenth green before adding, 'But I'm not sure the Führer has.'

◄◦►

The remainder of Robin's war turned out to be something of an anticlimax, except for those occasions when the klaxon sounded and he had to pedal furiously along the seafront to join his crew at the boathouse. He stayed on as the lifeboat's head launcher while the Germans remained on the island.

During the occupation, members of the Royal Jersey were not permitted to enter the clubhouse, let alone play a round of golf. As the years passed, the finely tended course became so overgrown with weeds and nettles you couldn't tell where the rough ended and the fairways began. Clubs rusted in the storeroom, and there were only tattered flags fluttering on the ends of their poles to show where the greens had been.

◄○►

On 9 May 1945, the day after VE day, an advance party of English troops landed on Jersey and the German commandant on the Channel Islands surrendered.

Once the thirty-six thousand intruders had finally departed, the locals quickly did everything in their power to restore the old order. This didn't prove easy, as the Germans had destroyed many of the island's records, including applications for membership of the Royal Jersey Golf Club.

Other forms of life did return to normal. Robin and Diana were standing on the dockside waiting to welcome the first ferry from Weymouth when she sailed into St Helier on 12 July.

'Oh my goodness!' cried Diana the moment she saw her children. 'How they've grown.'

'It's been more than five years since we last saw them, darling,' Robin was reminding her as a young man accompanied by his teenage sister stepped on to the quayside.

The Chapman family spent six happy weeks together before Harry reluctantly returned to the mainland to take up his place at Durham University, and Kate went back to Weybridge to

740

begin her final year at St Mary's; both were looking forward to returning to Jersey at Christmas.

◄○►

Robin was reading the morning paper when he heard a knock on the door.

'I have a recorded delivery for you, Mr Chapman,' said the postman. 'I'll need a signature.'

Robin signed on the dotted line, recognizing the crest of the Royal Jersey Golf Club stamped in the top left-hand corner of the envelope. He ripped it open and read the letter as he returned to the kitchen, and read it a second time before he handed it across to Diana.

THE ROYAL JERSEY GOLF CLUB
St Helier, Jersey

9 September 1946

Dear Sir,

We have reason to believe that at some time in the past you applied to become a member of the Royal Jersey Golf Club, but unfortunately all our records were destroyed during the German occupation.

If you still wish to be considered for membership of the club, it will be necessary for you to go through the application process once again and we will be happy to arrange an interview.

Should your application prove successful, your name will be placed on the waiting list.

Yours sincerely,

J. L. Tindall
(Secretary)

Robin swore for the first time since the Germans had left the island.

Diana could do nothing to console him, despite the fact that his brother was coming across from the mainland to spend his first weekend with them since the end of the war.

Robin was standing on the dockside when Malcolm stepped off the Southampton ferry. Malcolm was able to lift his older brother's spirits when he told him and Diana all the news about the company's expansion plans, as well as delivering several messages from their children.

'Kate has a boyfriend,' he told them, 'and—'

'Oh, God,' said Robin. 'Am I that old?'

'Yes,' said Diana, smiling.

'I'm thinking of opening a fourth branch of Chapman's in Brighton,' Malcolm announced over dinner that night. 'With so many factories springing up in the area, they're sure to be in need of our services.'

'Not looking for a manager are you, by any chance?' asked Robin.

'Why, are you available?' replied Malcolm, looking genuinely surprised.

'No, he isn't,' said Diana firmly.

◄○►

By the time Malcolm took the boat back home to Southend the following Monday, Robin had perked up considerably. He even felt able to joke about attending the interview at the Royal Jersey. However, when the day came for him to face the committee, Diana had to escort him to the car, drive him to the club and deposit him at the entrance to the clubhouse.

'Good luck,' she said, kissing him on the cheek. Robin grunted. 'And don't even hint at how angry you are. It's not their fault that the Germans destroyed all the club's records.'

'I shall tell them they can stick my application form up their jumpers,' said Robin. They both burst out laughing at the latest expression they'd picked up from the mainland. 'Do they have any idea how old I'll be in fifteen years' time?' he added as he stepped out of the car.

Robin checked his watch. He was five minutes early. He straightened his tie before walking slowly across the gravel to the clubhouse. So many memories came flooding back: the first time he had seen Diana, when she had walked into the bar to speak to her brother; the day he was appointed captain of the club – the first Englishman to be so honoured; that missed putt on the eighteenth that would have won him the President's Cup; not being able to play in the final the following year because he'd broken his arm; the evening Lord Trent had asked him to sail him to the mainland because the Prime Minister needed his services; the day a German officer had shown him respect and compassion after he had saved the lives of his countrymen. And now, today . . . he opened the newly painted door and stepped inside.

He looked up at the portrait of Harry Vardon and gave him a respectful bow, then turned his attention to Lord Trent, who had died the previous year, having served his country during the war as the Minister for Food.

'The committee will see you now, Mr Chapman,' said the club steward, interrupting his thoughts.

Diana had decided to wait in the car, as she assumed the interview wouldn't take long. After all, every member of the committee had known Robin for over twenty years. But after half an hour she began to glance at her watch every few minutes, and couldn't believe that Robin still hadn't appeared an hour later. She had just decided to go in and ask the steward what was holding her husband up when the clubhouse door swung open and Robin marched out, a grim look on his face. She jumped out of the car and ran towards him.

'Anyone who wishes to reapply for membership cannot

hope to be elected for at least another fifteen years,' he said, walking straight past her.

'Are there no exceptions?' asked Diana, chasing after him.

'Only for the new president,' said Robin, 'who will be made an honorary life member. The rules don't seem to apply to him.'

'But that really is so unfair,' said Diana, bursting into tears. 'I shall personally complain to the new president.'

'I'm sure you will, my dear,' said Robin, taking his wife in his arms. 'But that doesn't mean I'll take any notice.'

THE UNDIPLOMATIC
DIPLOMAT★

10

PERCIVAL ARTHUR Clarence Forsdyke – his mother called
him Percival, while the few friends he had called him Percy –
was born into a family which had played its part in ensuring
that the sun never set on the British Empire.

Percy's grandfather, Lord Clarence Forsdyke, had been
Governor General of the Sudan, while his father, Sir Arthur
Forsdyke KCMG, had been our man in Mesopotamia. So,
naturally, great things were expected of young Percy.

Within hours of entering this world, he had been put down
for the Dragon prep school, Winchester College and Trinity,
Cambridge, establishments at which four generations of Fors-
dykes had been educated.

After Cambridge, it was assumed that Percy would follow
his illustrious forebears into the Foreign Office, where he would
be expected at least to equal and possibly even to surpass their
achievements. All might have gone to plan had it not been for
one small problem: Percy was far too clever for his own good.
He won a scholarship to the Dragon at the age of eight, an
election to Winchester College before his eleventh birthday,
and the Anderson Classics Prize to Trinity while he was still
in short trousers. After leaving Cambridge with a double first in
Classics, he sat the Civil Service exam, and frankly no one was
surprised when he came top in his year.

Percy was welcomed into the Foreign and Commonwealth Office with open arms, but that was when his problems began. Or, to be more accurate, when the Foreign Office's problems began.

The mandarins at the FCO, who are expected to identify high flyers worthy of being fast-tracked, came to the reluctant conclusion that, despite Forsdyke's academic achievements, the young man lacked common sense, possessed few social skills and cared little for the diplomatic niceties required when representing your country abroad – something of a disadvantage if you wish to pursue a career in the Foreign Office.

During his first posting, to Nigeria, Percy told the Minister of Finance that he had no grasp of economics. The problem was that the minister *didn't* have any grasp of economics, so Percy had to be dispatched back to England on the first available boat.

After a couple of years in administration, Percy was given a second chance, and sent to Paris as an assistant secretary. He might have survived this posting had he not told the French President's wife at a government reception that the world was overpopulated, and she wasn't helping matters by producing so many children. Percy had a point, as the lady in question had seven offspring and was pregnant at the time, but he was still to be found packing his bags before lunch the following day. A further spell in admin followed before he was given his third, and final, chance.

On this occasion he was dispatched to one of Her Majesty's smaller colonies in Central Africa as a deputy consul. Within six months he had managed to cause an altercation between two tribes who had lived in harmony for over a century. The following morning Percy was escorted on to a British Airways plane clutching a one-way ticket to London, and was never offered a foreign posting again.

On returning to London, Percy was appointed as an archives clerk (no one gets the sack at the FCO), and allocated a small office in the basement.

As few people at the FCO ever found any reason to visit the basement, Percy flourished. Within weeks he had instigated a new procedure for cataloguing statements, speeches, memoranda and treaties, and within months he could locate any document, however obscure, required by even the most demanding minister. By the end of the year he could offer an opinion on any FCO demand, based on historic precedent, often without having to refer to a file.

No one was surprised when Percy was appointed Senior Archivist after his boss unexpectedly took early retirement. However, Percy still yearned to follow in his father's footsteps and become our man in some foreign field, to be addressed by all and sundry as 'Your Excellency'. Sadly, it was not to be, because Percy was not allowed out of the basement for the next thirty years, and only then when he retired at the age of sixty.

At Percy's leaving party, held in the India Room of the FCO, the Foreign Secretary described him in his tribute speech as a man with an unrivalled encyclopaedic memory who could probably recite every agreement and treaty Britain had ever entered into. This was followed by laughter and loud applause. No one heard Percy mutter under his breath, 'Not every one, Minister.'

Six months after his retirement, the name of Percival Arthur Clarence Forsdyke appeared on the New Year's Honours List. Percy had been awarded the CBE for services to the Foreign and Commonwealth Office.

He read the citation without any satisfaction. In fact, he felt he was a failure and had let the family down. After all, his grandfather had been a peer of the realm, his father a Knight Commander of St Michael and St George, whereas he ended up a mere Commander of a lower order.

However, Percy had a plan to rectify the situation, and to rectify it quickly.

-◄◦►-

Once he had left the FCO, Percy did not head straight for the British Library to begin work on his memoirs, as he felt he had achieved nothing worthy of historic record, nor did he retire to his country home to tend his roses, possibly because he didn't have a country home, or any roses. However, he did heed the Foreign Secretary's words, and decided to make use of his unrivalled encyclopaedic memory.

Deep in the recesses of his remarkable mind, Percy recalled an ancient British law which had been passed by an Act of Parliament in 1762, during the reign of King George III. It took Percy some considerable time to double-check, in fact, triple-check, that the Act had not been repealed at any time in the past two hundred years. He was delighted to discover that, far from being repealed, it had been enshrined in the Treaty of Versailles in 1919, and again in the Charter of the United Nations in 1945. Clearly neither organization had someone of Percy's calibre tucked away in its basement. Having read the Act several times, Percy decided to visit the Royal Geographical Society on Kensington Gore, where he spent hours poring over charts that detailed the coastal waters surrounding the British Isles.

After completing his research at the RGS, Percy was satisfied that everything was in place for him to comply with clause 7, addendum 3, of the Territories Settlement Act of 1762.

He returned to his home in Pimlico and locked himself away in his study for three weeks – with only Horatio, his three-legged, one-eyed cat, for company – while he put the final touches to a detailed memorandum that would reveal the real significance of the Territories Settlement Act of 1762, and its relevance for Great Britain in the year 2009.

Once he'd completed his task, he placed the nineteen-page

handwritten document, along with a copy of the 1762 Act showing one particular clause highlighted, in a large white envelope
which he addressed to Sir Nigel Henderson KCMG, Permanent Secretary to the Foreign and Commonwealth Office, King
Charles Street, Whitehall, London SW1A 2AH. He then put the
unsealed envelope in the top drawer of his desk, where it would
remain for the next three months while he disappeared off the
face of the earth. Horatio purred.

-<o>-

On 22 June 2009, Percy took a taxi to Euston station, where he
boarded the overnight sleeper for Inverness. His luggage consisted of an overnight bag and his old school trunk, while inside
his jacket pocket was a wallet containing two thousand pounds
in cash.

On arrival in Inverness, Percy changed platforms and, an
hour later, boarded a train that would take him even further
north. The five-carriage shuttle stopped at every station on its
long and relentless journey up the north-east coast of Scotland,
until it finally came to a halt at the remote harbour town of
Wick.

When Percy left the station, he commandeered the only
taxi, which took him to the only hotel, where he booked into
the only available room. After a one-course meal – the menu
being fairly limited, and the kitchen staff having all left at nine
o'clock – Percy retired to his room and read *Robinson Crusoe*
before falling asleep.

The following morning he rose before the sun, as do most
of the natives of the outer reaches of Scotland. He feasted on a
large bowl of porridge oats and a pair of kippers that would
have graced the Savoy, but rejected an offer of the *Scotsman* in
favour of studying a long list of the items that would have to be
acquired before the sun had set that afternoon.

Percy spent the first hour after breakfast walking up and

down the high street, trying to identify the shops he would have to patronize if his trunk was to be filled by the time he left the following morning.

The first establishment he entered was MacPherson's Camping Store. 'Everything a hiker needs when trekking in the Highlands' was stencilled boldly on the window. After much bending over, lying down and crawling in and out, Percy purchased an easy-to-erect, all-weather tent that the proprietor assured him would still be standing after a desert storm or a mountain gale.

By the time Percy had left the store he had filled four large brown carrier bags with his tent, a primus stove, a kettle, a goose-down sleeping bag with an inflatable pillow, a Swiss army knife (he had checked that it had a tin opener), a pair of Wellington boots, a fishing rod, a camera, a compass and a portable telescope.

Mr MacPherson directed Percy towards the MacPherson General Store on the other side of the road, assuring him that his brother Sandy would be happy to fulfil any other requirements he might still have.

The second Mr MacPherson supplied Percy with a shovel, a plastic mug, plate, knife, fork and spoon, a dozen boxes of matches (Swan Vesta), a Roberts radio, three dozen Eveready batteries, four dozen candles and a first-aid kit, which filled three more carrier bags. Once Percy had established that there wasn't a third MacPherson brother to assist him, he settled for Menzies, where he was able to place several more ticks against items on his long list – a copy of the *Radio Times*, the *Complete Works of Shakespeare* (paperback), a day-to-day 2009 diary (half price) and an Ordnance Survey map showing the outlying islands in the North Sea.

Percy took a taxi back to his hotel, accompanied by nine carrier bags, which he dragged in relays up to his room on the second floor. After a light lunch of fish pie and peas, he set off once again for the high street.

He spent most of the afternoon pushing a trolley up and down the aisles of the local supermarket, stocking up with enough provisions to ensure he could survive for ninety days. Once he was back in his hotel room, he sat on the end of the bed and checked his list once again. He still required one essential item; in fact, he couldn't leave Wick without it.

Although Percy had failed to find what he wanted in any of the shops in town, he had spotted a perfect second-hand example on the roof of the hotel. He approached the proprietor, who was surprised by the guest's request but, noticing his desperation, drove a hard bargain, insisting on seventy pounds for the family heirloom.

'But it's old, battered and torn,' said Percy.

'If it's nae guid enough fur ye, sur,' said the owner loftily, 'ah feel sure y'll bi able tae find a superior wan in Inverness.' Percy gave in, having discovered the true meaning of the word *canny*, and handed over seven ten-pound notes. The proprietor promised that he would have it taken down from the roof before Percy left the following morning.

After such an exhausting day, Percy felt he had earned a rest, but he still had one more task to fulfil before he could retire to bed.

At supper in the three-table dining room, the head waiter (the only waiter) told Percy the name of the man who could solve his final problem, and exactly where he would be located at that time of night. After cleaning his teeth (he always cleaned his teeth after a meal), Percy made his way down to the harbour in search of the Fisherman's Arms. He tapped his jacket pocket to check he hadn't forgotten his wallet and the all-important map.

When Percy entered the pub he received some curious

stares from the locals, who didn't approve of stray Englishmen invading their territory. He spotted the man he was looking for seated in a far corner, playing dominoes with three younger men, and made his way slowly across the room, every eye following him, until he came to a halt in front of a squat, bearded man dressed in a thick blue sweater and salt-encrusted jeans.

The man looked up and gave the stranger who had dared to interrupt his game an unwelcoming gaze.

'Are you Captain Campbell?' Percy enquired.

'Who wants tae ken?' asked the bearded man suspiciously.

'My name is Forsdyke,' said Percy, and then, to the astonishment of everyone in the pub, delivered a short, well-rehearsed speech at the top of his voice.

When Percy came to the end, the bearded man placed his double four reluctantly back on the table and, in a brogue that Percy could just about decipher, asked, 'An wur exactly dae ye expect mi tae tak' ye?'

Percy opened his map and spread it out on the table, propelling dominoes in every direction. He then placed a finger in the middle of the North Sea. Four pairs of eyes looked down in disbelief. The captain shook his head, repeating the words 'Nae possible' several times, until Percy mentioned the figure of five hundred pounds. All four of the men seated around the table suddenly took a far greater interest in the Englishman's preposterous proposal. Captain Campbell then began a conversation with his colleagues that no one south of Inverness would have been able to follow without a translator. He finally looked up and said, 'Ah want a hundred pound up front, noo, an' the ether four hundred afore ah let ye oan ma boat.'

Percy extracted five twenty-pound notes from his wallet and handed them across to the captain, who smiled for the first time since they'd met. 'Bi stannin' on the dockside ae *Bonnie Belle* at five tamorra moarnin',' said Campbell as he distributed the cash among his mates. 'Once I have the ether four hundred, I'll tak' ye to your island.'

―◦―

Percy was standing on the quayside long before five the following morning, an overnight bag, his battered old school trunk and a ten-foot pole at his feet. He was dressed in a three-piece suit, white shirt, his old school tie, and was carrying a rolled umbrella. Standard FCO kit when one is posted to some foreign field. He braced himself against the biting wind as he waited for the captain to appear. He felt both exhilarated and terrified at the same time.

He turned his attention to the little fishing vessel he'd chartered for this expedition, and wondered if it had ever ventured outside territorial waters, let alone into the middle of the North Sea. For a moment he considered returning to his hotel and abandoning the whole exercise, but the vision of his father and grandfather standing on the dock beside him strengthened his resolve.

The captain and his three mates appeared out of the early morning mist at one minute to five. All four of them were dressed in exactly the same clothes they had been wearing the night before, making Percy wonder if they'd come straight from the Fisherman's Arms. Was it a seafarer's gait they displayed as they strolled towards him, or had they spent his hundred pounds on what the Scots are most celebrated for?

The captain gave Percy a mock salute, and thrust out his hand. Percy was about to shake it, when he realized that it was being held palm upwards. He handed over four hundred pounds, and Captain Campbell ordered his crew to carry Percy's luggage on board. Two of the young men were clearly surprised by how heavy the trunk was. Percy followed them up the gangway, clinging on to the pole which never left his side, even when he joined the captain on the bridge.

The captain studied several oceanographic charts before confirming the exact location at which Percy had asked to be abandoned and then gave the order to cast off. 'Ah think it'll tak' us at least a day an' a night afore wi reach oor destination,' said the captain, 'so perhaps, laddie, it might bi wise fur ye tae lay doon. The waves cin bi a wee bit choppy wance wi leave the shelter ae the harbour.'

They had only just passed Wick lighthouse when Percy began to appreciate the true meaning of Captain Campbell's words, and to regret having had a second helping of porridge that morning. He spent most of the day leaning over the railing, depositing what he'd eaten the previous day into the waves. It wasn't much different during the night, except that it was dark and the crew couldn't see him. He declined the captain's offer to join them for a supper of fish stew.

After thirty hours of Percy wishing the ship would sink, or someone would throw him overboard, the first mate pointed through the mist and hollered, 'Land ahoy!' But it was some time before the blurred dot on the horizon finally turned into a piece of land that might just have been described by an assiduous cartographer as an island.

Percy wanted to cheer, but his voice became muffled as the little vessel continued to circle the island in a valiant attempt to find a landing place. All they could see ahead of them were treacherous rocks and unassailable cliffs that didn't require a 'no entry' sign to warn them off. Percy sank down on to the deck, feeling that the whole exercise simply mirrored his career and would end in failure. He bowed his head in despair, so didn't see the captain pointing to a cove that boasted a small beach.

The crew were experienced at landing far more slippery objects than Percy, and an hour later they left him on the beach along with all his worldly goods. His parting words to the skipper as he climbed back into his small dinghy were, 'If you return in ninety-one days and take me back to the mainland, I'll pay you a further thousand pounds.'

He had anticipated the captain's response, and without waiting to be asked handed over two hundred pounds in cash; but not before he had confirmed the exact date on which the *Bonnie Belle* was to return.

'If you turn up even one hour before the ninety-first day,' he said without explanation, 'you will not be paid another penny.'

Captain Campbell shrugged his shoulders, as he was past trying to understand the eccentric Englishman, but he did manage another salute once he'd pocketed the cash. The crew then rowed him back to his little fishing vessel so they could go about their normal business on the high seas, though not until they were back within the 150-mile legal limit.

Percy placed his feet wide apart and tried to steady himself, but after thirty hours on the *Bonnie Belle* it felt as if the whole island was swaying from side to side. He didn't move until his former companions were out of sight.

He then dragged his belongings up the beach on to higher ground before he went in search of a suitable piece of land on which to pitch his tent. The relentless wind and squalls of rain did not assist his progress.

The flattest piece of land Percy came across during his initial recce turned out to be the highest point on the island, while the most sheltered spot was a large cave nestled in a cliff on the west side. It took him the rest of the day to move all his belongings from the beach to his new home.

After devouring a can of baked beans and a carton of long-life milk, he climbed into his sleeping bag and spent his first night on Forsdyke Island. He missed Horatio.

◅○▻

Most people would find trying to survive for three months on a small, uninhabited island in the North Sea somewhat daunting, but having spent thirty years in the basement of the Foreign and Commonwealth Office, Percy Forsdyke was equal to the task. Moreover, he knew that his father and grandfather would regard it as nothing more than character building.

Percy spent his first full day on the island unpacking his trunk and making his new home as comfortable as possible. He stacked all the food at the coldest end of the cave and placed his equipment neatly along the sides.

For some weeks Percy had been planning the routine he'd follow on the island. He would begin the day with a bowl of cornflakes, a boiled egg (until he could bear them no more) and a mug of tea while listening to the *Today Programme* on Radio Four. This would be followed by a session of digging on the highest point of the island, weather permitting. Lunch, usually spam and baked beans, would be followed by a siesta. Not that Percy was avoiding the heat of the sun, you understand; he was just tired. When he woke, Percy would spend the rest of the afternoon exploring the island until he was familiar with every nook and cranny of his kingdom. Once the sun had set, which was very late at that time of year, he would prepare his dinner: more spam and baked beans. It didn't take long for Percy to regret his lack of culinary imagination.

After listening to the ten o'clock news and reading some Shakespeare by candlelight, he would climb into his sleeping bag and carry out the last ritual of the day, bringing his diary up to date. He would detail everything he'd done that day, as it would be part of the evidence he would eventually present to the Foreign Office.

Percy had selected his ninety days of isolation carefully. He was able to follow the ball-by-ball commentary of all five Test matches against Australia, as well as the seven One Day Internationals. He also enjoyed thirteen plays of the week, and sixty-four episodes of *The Archers*, but he stopped listening to *Gardeners' Question Time* when he realized it didn't provide many useful tips for someone living on a small island in the North Sea.

If Percy had one regret, it was that he hadn't been able to bring his ginger cat with him. Not that Horatio would have appreciated exchanging his warm kitchen for a cold cave. He had left clear instructions with his housekeeper that she should feed him every morning, and before she left at night.

Percy had more than enough food and drink to survive for ninety days, and was determined to revisit the *Complete Works of Shakespeare*, all 37 plays and 154 sonnets, by the time he returned to the mainland.

By the end of the first month, Percy felt he was well qualified to appear on *Desert Island Discs*, even though that nice Mr Plomley was no longer in charge.

On a more practical level, Percy learned to catch a fish with a sharpened stick. To be accurate, he speared his first fish on the thirty-ninth day, by which time he considered himself a fully domiciled resident.

On the sixty-third day, he completed digging a five-foot hole at the highest point of the island. One of the problems Percy hadn't anticipated was that whenever he visited his hole each morning, it would be full of water, as hardly a day went by when it didn't rain. It took Percy about an hour to scoop out yesterday's water with his plastic mug before he could start digging again, sometimes longer, if it was still raining. He then roamed the island searching for large stones which he lugged back and deposited by the side of the hole.

On the morning of the eighty-ninth day, Percy dragged his pole slowly up to the summit of the island, some 227 feet above sea level, and dumped it unceremoniously by the hole. He then returned to the cave and listened to *Woman's Hour* on Radio Four before having lunch. He'd learned a great deal about women during the past three months. He spent the afternoon shining his shoes, washing his shirt and rehearsing the speech he would deliver on behalf of Her Majesty.

He retired to bed early, aware that he needed to be at his best for the ceremony he would be performing the following day.

-◆-

Percy rose with the sun on 23 September 2009, and ate a light breakfast consisting of a bowl of cornflakes and an apple while he listened to Jim Naughtie discuss with Mr Cameron whether the three party leaders should take part in a television debate before the election. Percy didn't care for the idea: not at all British.

At nine o'clock he shaved, cutting himself in several places, then put on a white shirt, now not quite so white, his three-piece suit, old school tie and shining black shoes, none of which he'd worn for the past three months.

When Percy emerged from the cave carrying his radio, he had a pleasant surprise awaiting him on this, the most important day of his life. The sun was shining brightly in a clear blue sky, and what a blue. When he reached the top of his hill, there was not a drop of water in the hole. God clearly was an Englishman.

He checked his watch: ten twenty-six. Too early to begin proceedings if he intended to keep to the letter of the law. He sat on the ground and recited his favourite speeches from *Henry V*, while checking his watch every few minutes.

At eleven o'clock, Percy lifted the flagpole on to his shoulder and lowered one end into the hole. He then spent forty minutes selecting the stones that would secure it firmly in place. Having completed the task he sat down on the ground, exhausted. Once he'd got his breath back he turned on the radio and still had to wait for some time before Big Ben struck twelve times and the sun reached its highest point. At one minute past twelve, Percy stood to attention, slowly raised the Union Jack up the flagpole and delivered the exact words required by the Territories Settlement Act of 1762: 'I claim this sovereign territory in the name of Her Majesty Queen Elizabeth II, to whom I swear my allegiance.' He then sang the 'National Anthem', and ended with three rousing cheers.

The ceremony completed, Percy fell to his knees and thanked God, and all his ancestors, that like them he had been able to serve the British Empire.

He then picked up his telescope and began to search the high seas for a bobbing fishing vessel. As each hour passed, he became more and more anxious as to where the *Bonnie Belle*, Captain Campbell and his three shipmates might be. He feared they were in the Fisherman's Arms, spending his money.

Once the sun had set on this part of the British Empire, Percy restricted himself to half-rations before spending a sleepless night wondering if he was destined to spend the rest of his days on Forsdyke Island, having fulfilled his mission, but without anyone realizing what he had achieved.

He rose early the following morning, skipped breakfast, missed the *Today Programme* and climbed back up to the highest point on the island, where he was delighted to see the Union Jack still fluttering in the breeze.

He picked up his telescope, swung it slowly through 180 degrees, and there she was, ploughing determinedly, if slowly, through the waves. Not usually a demonstrative man, Percy leapt up and down, shouting with joy. He ran back to his cave, packed his overnight bag with all the evidence he needed to support his claim, then made his way down to the beach. He left everything else in the cave, including his trunk, in case anyone should require more proof that he really had been a resident for ninety days.

Percy waited patiently on the beach, but it was another three hours before the little dinghy came ashore to collect the unappointed ambassador who wished to be transported back to the mainland, having served his tour of duty.

Captain Campbell showed no interest in why Mr Forsdyke had wished to spend ninety-one days on a deserted island, and left him in his cabin to rest. Although Percy was just as sick on the voyage back to Wick as he had been on the way to Forsdyke Island, his heart was full of joy.

Once the captain, the three crew members and their passenger had disembarked from the *Bonnie Belle* they all went to the nearest bank, where Percy withdrew eight hundred pounds. But he didn't hand over the cash until Captain Campbell and his first mate had signed a one-page document confirming that they had taken him to Forsdyke Island on 25 June 2009, and hadn't picked him up again until 24 September 2009, when they had accompanied him back to the mainland. The local bank manager witnessed both signatures.

A taxi took Percy to Wick station, from where he began the slow journey back along the coast to Inverness before boarding the overnight train to London. He found his first-class bunk bed uncomfortable, while the clattering wheels kept him awake most of the night, and the fish served for breakfast had unquestionably left the North Sea some days before he had. He arrived at Euston more tired and hungry than he'd been for the past three months, and then had to hang about in a long taxi queue before he was driven back to his home in Pimlico.

Once he'd let himself in he went straight to his study, unlocked the centre drawer of his desk and retrieved the unsealed envelope containing his detailed memorandum and the copy of the 1762 Territories Settlement Act. He placed Captain Campbell's sworn affidavit in the envelope along with two maps and a diary, then sealed the envelope and wrote on the front, in capital letters, FOR YOUR EYES ONLY.

Despite his impatience to fulfil his dream, Percy didn't leave the house until he'd checked that his one-eyed, three-legged cat was sound asleep on the kitchen boiler. 'I did it, Horatio, I did it,' whispered Percy as he left the kitchen. Once he'd locked the front door, he hailed a passing taxi.

'The Foreign Office,' said Percy as he climbed into the back seat.

When the taxi drew up outside the King Charles Street entrance, Percy said, 'Please wait, cabbie, I'll only be a minute.'

The security guard at the FCO was about to prevent the dishevelled tramp from entering the building when he realized it was Mr Forsdyke.

'Please deliver this to Sir Nigel Henderson immediately,' said Percy, handing over the bulky envelope.

'Yes, Mr Forsdyke,' said the duty clerk, giving him a salute.

Percy sat in the cab on the way back home chanting the 'Nunc Dimittis'.

The first thing Percy did on returning to Pimlico was to feed the cat. He then fed himself and watched the early evening news on television. It was too early for any announcement about his triumph, although he did wonder if it would be the Foreign Secretary or perhaps even the Prime Minister who would be standing at the dispatch box in the House of Commons to deliver an unscheduled announcement. He climbed into bed at ten, and quickly fell into a deep sleep.

◂◦▸

Percy wasn't surprised to receive a call from Sir Nigel the following afternoon, but he was surprised by the Permanent Secretary's request. 'Good afternoon, Percy,' said Sir Nigel. 'The Foreign Secretary wonders if you could spare the time to drop in and have a chat with him at your earliest convenience.'

'Of course,' said Percy.

'Good,' said Sir Nigel. 'Would eleven tomorrow morning suit you?'

'Of course,' repeated Percy.

'Excellent. I'll send a car. And Percy, can I just check that no one else has seen any of the documents you sent me?'

'That is correct, Sir Nigel. You'll note that everything is handwritten, so you are in possession of the only copies.'

'I'm glad to hear that,' said Sir Nigel without explanation, and the phone went dead.

—◁○▷—

A staff car picked up Percy at ten-thirty the following morning, and drove him to the Foreign Office in Whitehall. He was dressed in his only other Savile Row suit, a fresh white shirt and a new, old school tie, in anticipation of his triumph.

Percy always enjoyed entering the FCO, but even he was flattered to find a clerk waiting to escort him to the Foreign Secretary's office. He savoured every moment as they walked slowly up the broad marble staircase, past the full-length portraits of Castlereagh, Canning, Palmerston, Salisbury and Curzon, before continuing down a long, wide corridor where photographs of Stewart, Douglas-Home, Callaghan, Carrington, Hurd and Cook adorned the walls.

When they reached the Foreign Secretary's office, the clerk tapped lightly on the door before opening it. Percy was ushered into a room large enough to hold a ball, to find the Foreign Secretary and the head of the Foreign Service awaiting him at the far end.

'Welcome back, Percy,' said the Foreign Secretary as if he were greeting an old chum, although he had only met him once before, at his retirement party. 'Come and join myself and Sir Nigel by the fire. There are one or two things I think we need to have a chat about. Didn't we do well to win the Ashes?' he added as he sat down. 'Although I suppose you missed the entire series, remembering that—'

'I was able to follow the ball-by-ball commentary on Radio Four,' Percy assured the Foreign Secretary, 'and it was indeed a magnificent series.' Percy relaxed back in his chair, and was served with a coffee.

'That must have helped kill the time,' said Sir Nigel, who waited until the coffee lady had left the room before he addressed the subject that was on all their minds.

'I read your report yesterday morning, Percy. Quite brilliant,' said Sir Nigel. 'And I must congratulate you on identifying an anomaly in the 1762 Act that we'd all previously overlooked.'

'For well over two hundred years,' chipped in the Foreign Secretary. 'After Sir Nigel had read your memorandum, he phoned me at home and briefed me. I went straight to Number Ten and had a private meeting with the PM, at which I was able to tell him what you've been up to since leaving the FCO. He was most impressed. Most impressed,' repeated the Foreign Secretary. Percy beamed with delight. 'He asked me to send you his congratulations, and best wishes.'

'Thank you,' said Percy, and only just stopped himself from saying, 'And please return mine.'

'The PM also asked me to let him know,' continued the Foreign Secretary, 'what decision you'd come to.'

'What decision I'd come to?' repeated Percy, no longer sounding quite so relaxed.

'Yes,' said Sir Nigel. 'You see, a problem has arisen that we felt we ought to share with you.'

Percy was prepared to answer any queries relating to treaty rights, sovereign status or the relevance of the Territories Settlement Act of 1762.

'Percy,' continued Sir Nigel, giving his former colleague a

warm smile, 'you'll be pleased to know that the Lord Chancellor has confirmed that your claim on behalf of the Sovereign is valid, and would stand up in any international court.' Percy began to relax again. 'And indeed, should you press your suit, Forsdyke Island would become part of Her Majesty's Overseas Territories. You were quite correct in your assessment that if you occupied the island for ninety days, without any other person or government making a claim on it, it would become the sole possession of the occupier, and would be governed by the laws of whichever country the occupier is a citizen of, as long as that claim is ratified within six months – if I remember the words of the 1762 Act correctly?'

Almost word perfect, thought Percy. 'Which means,' he said, turning to the Foreign Secretary, 'that we can lay claim not only to the fishing rights, but also to the oil reserves within a radius of one hundred and fifty miles, not to mention the obvious strategic advantage its location gives to our defence forces.'

'And thereby hangs a tale,' said the Permanent Secretary.

Percy wondered which of four possible Shakespeare plays Sir Nigel was quoting from, but decided this wasn't the time to enquire. 'I am also confident,' continued Percy, 'that should you present our case to a plenary session of the United Nations, it would have no choice but to ratify my claim on behalf of the British Government.'

'I'm sure you're right, Percy,' said Sir Nigel, 'but it is the responsibility of the Foreign Office to look at the wider picture and consider all the implications.' As if on cue, both men rose from their places. Percy followed them to the centre of the room, where they halted before a vast globe.

Sir Nigel gave the globe a spin. When it stopped, he pointed to a tiny speck in the Pacific Ocean. 'If the Russians were to lay claim to that island, it could turn out to be a bigger problem for the Americans than Cuba.'

He spun the globe again and when it stopped he pointed to another apparently unnamed island, this time in the middle of the South China Sea. 'If either country laid claim to this, you could end up with a war between Japan and China.'

He spun the globe a third time and, when it stopped, he placed a finger on the Dead Sea. 'Let us pray that the Israelis never get to hear about the Territories Settlement Act of 1762, because that would be the end of any Middle East peace process.'

Percy was speechless. All he had wanted was to prove himself worthy of his father and grandfather, and emulate the contribution they had made to the Foreign Office but, once again, all he'd achieved was to bring embarrassment to the family name and to the country he loved more than life itself.

The Foreign Secretary placed his arm round Percy's shoulder. 'If you felt able to allow us to file your submission in the archives, and to leave this meeting unrecorded, I know that the PM, and I suspect Her Majesty, would be eternally grateful.'

'Of course, Foreign Secretary,' said Percy, his head bowed.

He slipped out of the Foreign Office a few minutes later, and never mentioned the subject of Forsdyke Island again to anyone other than Horatio. But should anyone ever find themselves lost in the North Sea and come across a fluttering Union Jack . . .

—<o>—

On 1 January 2010, among the knighthoods listed in the New Year's Honours, was that of Sir Percival Arthur Clarence Forsdyke, awarded the KCMG for further services to the Foreign and Commonwealth Office.

THE LUCK OF THE IRISH ★

11

No one would believe this tale unless they were told that an Irishman was involved.

Liam Casey was born in Cork, the son of a tinker. One of many things he learned from his shrewd father was that while a wise man can spend all day making a few bob, a foolish one can lose them in a few minutes.

During Liam's lifetime, he made over a hundred million 'few bobs', but despite his father's advice, he still managed to lose them all in a few minutes.

After Liam left school, he didn't consider going to university, explaining to his friends that he wanted to join the real world. Liam quickly discovered that you also had to graduate from the University of Life before you could place your foot on the first rung of the ladder to fortune. After a few false starts, as a petrol pump attendant, bus conductor and door-to-door *Encyclopaedia Britannica* salesman, Liam ended up as a trainee with Hamptons, an established English estate agent that had branches all over Ireland.

He spent the next three years learning about the value of property, commercial and residential, the setting and collecting of rents, and how to close a deal on terms that ensured you made a profit but didn't lose a customer. The average person will move house five times during their lifetime, the

English manager informed Liam, so you need to retain their confidence.

'I wish I'd been James Joyce's estate agent,' was all Liam had to say on the subject.

'Why?' asked the Englishman, sounding puzzled.

'He moved house over a hundred times during his lifetime.' It was about the only thing Liam could remember about James Joyce.

Working for an English company, Liam quickly discovered that if you have a gentle Irish brogue and are graced with enough charm, the invaders have a tendency to underestimate you – a mistake the English have made for over a thousand years.

Another important lesson he learned, and one they certainly don't teach you at any university, was that the only difference between a tinker and a merchant banker is the sum of money that changes hands. However, Liam couldn't work out how to take advantage of this knowledge until he met Maggie McBride.

Maggie didn't consider the tinker's son from Cork to be much of a catch, even if he was good-looking and fun to be with, but when he invited her to join him for a holiday in Majorca, she began to show a little more interest.

Liam's current account at the Allied Irish Bank was just enough in credit for him to be able to afford a package holiday to Magaluf, a resort on the south-west coast of the island, which for three months of every year is taken over by the British.

Maggie was not impressed when they booked into a one-star hotel and were shown to a room with a double bed. She made it absolutely clear that she might have agreed to come on holiday with Liam, but that didn't mean they would be sleeping together. Liam booked himself into a separate room, which he knew would stretch his budget to the limit. Another lesson learned. Before you sign a contract, check the small print.

The next day Liam was lying next to Maggie on an overcrowded beach in a pair of tight-fitting swimming trunks, becoming redder and redder by the minute. His mother had once told him that the Irish have the greenest grass and the whitest skins on earth, but he had not, until then, realized the significance of the second part of her statement.

On the second day, Liam, still having failed to make any progress with Maggie, was beginning to wonder why he'd bothered to take her on holiday in the first place. But then he discovered that the thousand Englishwomen walking up and down the beach had only one thing on their minds – and a handsome young Irishman who would be disappearing back to Cork in two weeks' time ticked most of their boxes.

Liam was telling a girl from Doncaster how he'd discovered Riverdance when she said, 'You're getting very red.' So red that he had to lie on his stomach all night, quite unable to move, which was not at all what the girl from Doncaster had planned.

The next morning Liam smothered himself with factor thirty suncream, put on a long-sleeved shirt and long trousers, ignored the signs to the beach and took a bus into Palma, wondering if it would turn out to be just another Magaluf.

The medieval capital took him by surprise, with its wide streets lined with palm trees and flower baskets, and the narrow alleys with picturesque pavement restaurants and stylish boutiques. He could have been in a different country.

As he strolled down the Paseo Maritimo, Liam found himself stopping to look in the estate agents' windows. He was surprised how cheap the houses were compared to Cork, and even more surprised to discover that the banks were offering 80, sometimes even 90 per cent mortgages.

He considered entering one of the estate agents' offices, as he had a hundred questions he wanted answering, but as he couldn't speak a word of Spanish, he satisfied himself with looking in the windows and admiring the large colour photographs of properties described as *deseable, asequible, sensational.* He was thinking of returning to Magaluf when he spotted a familiar green, white and orange flag flapping in the wind outside a shopfront with a sign which announced, 'Patrick O'Donovan, International Real Estate Co.'

Liam pushed open the front door without bothering to look in the window. As he stepped into the office, a smartly dressed woman looked up, and an older man, unshaven and wearing soiled jeans and a T-shirt, swung his feet off a desk and smiled.

'I was just wondering—' began Liam.

'A fellow Irishman!' exclaimed the man, leaping up. 'Allow me to introduce myself. I'm Patrick O'Donovan.'

'Liam Casey,' said Liam, shaking him by the hand.

'Is it to be business or pleasure, Liam?' asked O'Donovan.

'I'm not quite sure,' Liam replied, 'but as I'm here on holiday—'

'Then it's pleasure,' said O'Donovan. 'So let's begin our relationship as any self-respecting Irishmen should. Maria, if anyone calls, my friend and I can be found at the Flanagan Arms.'

Without another word, O'Donovan led Liam out of the office, across the road and into a side alley where they entered a pub few tourists would ever come across. The next words O'Donovan uttered were, 'Two pints of Guinness', without asking his new-found friend what he would like.

Liam was able to get through most of his questions while O'Donovan was still sober. He learned that Patrick had been living on the island for over thirty years, and was convinced that Majorca was about to take off like California at the time of the gold rush. O'Donovan went on to tell Liam that the island was attracting a record number of tourists but, more important, it had recently become the most popular destination for Brits who wanted to spend their retirement years abroad.

'When I set up my agency,' he told Liam between gulps of

his third Guinness, 'it was long before Majorca became fashionable. In those days there were only a dozen of us in the business; now, everybody on the island thinks they're an estate agent. I've done well, can't complain, but I only wish I was your age.'

'Why?' asked Liam innocently.

'We're about to enter a boom period,' said O'Donovan. 'An ageing population with disposable incomes and an awareness of their own mortality are migrating here like a flock of starlings searching for warmer climes.'

By the fifth Guinness, Liam had only one or two more questions left to ask. Not that it mattered, as O'Donovan was no longer capable of answering them.

◄○►

The next morning, and every morning for the following week, Liam did not join Maggie on the overcrowded beaches but took the bus that was heading into Palma. He had some serious research to carry out before he met up with Patrick O'Donovan again.

During the day, he made appointments with several estate agents to view apartments and other properties. What he was shown confirmed O'Donovan's opinion – Majorca was about to enter a period of rapid growth.

On the final morning of his holiday, having not once returned to the beach in the past ten days, even though his red Majorca skin had faded back to Irish white, Liam boarded the bus to Palma for the last time.

Once he'd been dropped off in the city centre, he headed straight for the Paseo Maritimo and didn't stop walking until he reached the offices of Patrick O'Donovan, International Real Estate Co. He had only one more question to ask his fellow countryman. 'Would you consider taking me on as a junior partner?'

'Certainly not,' said O'Donovan. 'But I would consider taking you on as a partner.'

Maggie McBride flew back to Ireland, *virgo intacta*, while the tinker from Cork remained in Majorca.

◄o►

Liam's first year in Majorca didn't turn out to be quite the bonanza his new partner had promised, despite his working night and day and making full use of the skills he'd honed in Cork. While he spent most of his days in the office or showing clients around properties, O'Donovan spent more and more of his time in the Flanagan Arms, drinking away the company's dwindling profits.

By the end of his second year, Liam was considering returning to Ireland, which was experiencing its own economic boom, fuelled by massive grants from the European Union. And then, without warning, the decision was taken out of his hands. O'Donovan failed to return to work after the pub had closed for the afternoon siesta. He'd dropped dead in the street a hundred yards from the office.

Liam organized Patrick's funeral, held a wake at the Flanagan Arms and was the last to leave the pub that night. By the time he crawled into bed at three in the morning, he'd made a decision.

The first person he called after arriving at the office the next day was a sign-writer he'd found in the Yellow Pages. By twelve o'clock, the name above the door read 'Casey & Co, International Estate Agents'.

The second phone call Liam made was to Pepe Miro, a young man who worked for a rival company and had beaten him to several deals in the past two years. They agreed to meet in a tapas bar that evening, and after another late night, during which a José Ferrer L. Rosado replaced Guinness, Liam was able to convince Pepe they would both be better off working together as partners.

A month later, a Spanish flag was raised beside the Irish one, and the sign-writer returned. When he left, the name above the door read, 'Casey, Miro & Co.' While Pepe handled the natives, Liam took care of any foreign intruders; a genuine partnership.

The new company's profits grew slowly to begin with, but at least the graph was now heading in the right direction. But it wasn't until Pepe told his new partner about an old local custom that their fortunes began to change.

Majorca is a small island with a large, fertile, central plain where vineyards, almond and olive trees thrive. Traditionally, when a Majorcan farmer dies, he leaves any property in the fertile heartland to his eldest son, while any daughters end up with small pieces of craggy coastline. Liam's Irish charm and good looks did no harm when he advised these daughters how they could benefit from this chauvinistic injustice.

He purchased his first plot of land in 1991, from a middle-aged lady who was short of cash and boyfriends: a tiny strip of infertile coastline with uninterrupted views of the Mediterranean. A bulldozer levelled the ground, and within a few weeks, after a bunch of itinerant workers had cleaned up the site, a developer purchased the plot for almost double Liam's original outlay.

Liam bought his second piece of land from a grieving widow. It had splendid panoramic views all the way to Barcelona. Once again he flattened the plot, and this time he built a path wide enough to allow a car to reach it from the main road. On this occasion he made an even larger return, which he used to build a small house on a piece of land Pepe had purchased from a lady who spoke only Spanish. A year later they sold the property for triple their original investment.

By the time Liam had purchased their fourth piece of coastal land, which was large enough to divide into three plots, he realized he was no longer an estate agent but had unwittingly become a property developer. While Pepe continued to woo an endless stream of Spanish daughters and widows, Liam converted their scraggy inheritances into saleable properties. As time went by and the company's profits increased, it became clear to Liam that the only obstacle preventing him from progressing at an even more rapid pace was a lack of capital. He decided to make one of his rare trips back to Ireland.

The property manager of the Allied Irish Bank in Dublin – Liam avoided Cork – listened with interest to the proposals put forward by his fellow countryman, and eventually agreed to advance him a hundred thousand pounds with which to purchase two new sites. When Liam delivered a profit of over 40 per cent the following year, the bank agreed to double its investment.

Liam closed his first million-pound deal in 1997, and his success might have continued unabated, if only he'd recalled his father's sound advice. *While a wise man can spend all day making a few bob, a foolish one can lose them in a few minutes.*

–◦–

On the evening of 31 December 1999, Liam and Pepe held a party for their friends and clients at the Palace Hotel in Palma to celebrate their good fortune. As they were now both millionaires, they had every reason to look forward to the new millennium with confidence, especially as Pepe announced, just before the sun rose on 1 January 2000, that he had come across the deal of a lifetime. Liam had to wait two more days before Pepe had recovered sufficiently to tell him the details.

A Majorcan from one of the oldest families on the island had recently died intestate. After some considerable legal wrangling, the court had decided that his wife was entitled to inherit his entire estate – an area of land in Valldemossa that stretched for several kilometres, from the slopes of the Sierra de Tramuntana all the way down to the coast.

Liam spent a week in Dublin trying to convince the Allied Irish that it should put up the largest property loan in its history. Once the bank had agreed terms, which included personal guarantees from both Liam and Pepe, something Liam's tinker father would never have advised, he returned to Majorca and began to conduct negotiations with the widow. She finally agreed to sell her two-thousand-hectare site for twenty-three million euros.

Within days, Liam had hired a leading architect from Barcelona, a highly respected surveyor from Madrid and a well-connected lawyer in Palma, and began to prepare the necessary documents to ensure that outline planning per- mission would be granted by the local council. They divided the land into 360 individual plots that included roads with broad pavements, street lighting, electricity, drainage and sew- erage, an eighteen-hole golf course, a shopping centre, a cinema, eleven restaurants and a sports complex. Every home would have its own swimming pool, while some of the larger plots would even have their own tennis courts. But the feature that made the development unique was that whichever house a customer purchased, from the top of the mountain all the way down to the coast, they were guaranteed an uninterrupted view of the ocean.

Liam and Pepe both accepted that because of the huge amount of work involved with the project, it would be years before they could consider taking on any other commitments.

Liam had a large-scale model of the site built, and com- missioned a documentary film maker to produce a twenty- minute promotional video entitled *Valldemossa Vision*. The

Allied Irish Bank clearly bought into this vision, and released an initial two point three million euros to Liam as a deposit on the land.

It was another year before Liam was ready to present his outline planning application to the Consell Insular de Mallorca. When Liam rose to make his speech to the Valldemossa council, every elected member was seated in his place. He took them slowly through his master plan, and when his presentation came to an end, he called for questions.

If only to persuade people they haven't fallen asleep, politicians always have well-prepared questions to hand. However, Liam's experts had spent hours anticipating each and every question they were asked, and others that hadn't even been thought of. When Liam finally sat down, he was greeted by warm applause from both main political parties.

The governor of the Balearics rose to congratulate Liam and his team on a splendid and imaginative scheme, while the Mayor of Valldemossa enthusiastically assured his colleagues that the project would undoubtedly attract wealthy residents, ensuring increased revenue for the council's coffers for many years to come.

No one was surprised when, six weeks later, the Consell Insular de Mallorca granted outline planning permission to Casey, Miro & Co. for its Valldemossa project, which the mayor described to the press as bold, imaginative and of civic importance. But Pepe had already warned Liam there was one more hurdle that had to be negotiated before they could return to the bank and ask for the remaining twenty point seven million euros of their advance. It was still necessary for the Supreme Court in Madrid to rubber-stamp the whole project before the first bulldozer would be allowed on the site, and the court was well known for rejecting projects at the last moment.

Three different sets of lawyers worked night and day in

Madrid, Barcelona and Palma, and nine months later to every-one's relief the Supreme Court gave its imprimatur.

The following day Liam flew to Dublin, where even more lawyers were working on the documentation that would allow him to be able to draw on a rolling fifty-million-euro loan. Building costs only ever go in one direction.

Within minutes of the ink drying on the paper, four of the leading construction companies in Europe were driving their vehicles on to the site, followed by over a thousand workers who were looking forward to being employed for the next ten years.

—◦—

Liam had never taken a great deal of interest in Majorcan politics, and he made a point of not supporting either main party when it came to the local elections. He made it a policy to donate exactly the same amount to the campaign funds of both the major parties so he could continue to deal with whichever one was in power.

Over the years, it had always been a close-run thing between the Partido Socialista Obrero Español and the Partido Popular, with power changing hands every few years. But to everyone's surprise, when the election result was announced from the town hall steps later that year, the Green Party had captured three seats and, more important, held the balance of power, as the other two parties were evenly split with twenty-one seats each. Liam didn't give the result a great deal of thought, even when the *Mallorca Daily Bulletin* informed its readers that the Greens would join a coalition with which-ever party was willing to support their ideological aims. The most important of which, as had been stated in their mani-festo, was not to grant any future planning permission in Valldemossa.

This suited Liam as it would cut out any further rivals, making his the last project to be approved by the Supreme Court in Madrid. But once the resolution had been passed in council, with the backing of both main parties, the Greens, encouraged by their success, immediately announced that any projects currently underway should have their planning permission rescinded. This time Liam was concerned, because his lawyers warned him that even if the Supreme Court eventually overruled the council's decision, his project could be held up for years.

'Every day we're not working will cost us money,' Liam warned Pepe. He realized that if the Greens were able to get either of the two main parties to support their proposal, he and Pepe would be bankrupt within weeks.

When the council met to take a vote on the Greens' resolution, Liam and his team sat nervously in the public gallery waiting to learn their fate. Passionate speeches were made from all sides of the chamber, and even after the last councillor had offered his opinion, no one could be sure how the numbers would fall.

The chief clerk called for the vote, and for the first time that evening the chamber fell silent. A few minutes later the Mayor solemnly announced that the Greens' proposal to rescind all current planning permissions had been carried by twenty-three votes to twenty-two.

Liam had lost all his few bobs in a few minutes.

Every one of his workers immediately deserted the site. Unfinished houses were left without doors or windows, cranes stood unmanned and expensive equipment and materials were left to rust. By the time Liam recalled his late father's wise advice, it was too late to turn the clock back.

The company's lawyers recommended an appeal. Liam reluctantly agreed, although, as they had pointed out to him, even if they were eventually able to overturn the council's decision, by then years would have passed and any possible profit would have been swallowed up by interest payments alone, not to mention lawyers' fees.

◄○►

The Allied Irish Bank quickly responded to the news from Valldemossa by placing an immediate stop order on all Liam's accounts. They also issued a directive instructing Casey, Miro & Co, and any of its associates, to repay the outstanding thirty-seven-million-euro loan at the first possible opportunity, although it must have known that neither Liam nor Pepe could any longer afford the airfare to Dublin.

Liam informed the bank that he intended to appeal against the council's decision, but *he* knew, and so did they, that even if he won, they still would have lost everything by the time the Supreme Court reached its verdict.

An appeal date was set for the Supreme Court of Madrid to sit in judgement on the Valldemossa project, but before then Liam and Pepe had been forced to sell their homes, as well as what was left of the company's assets, to pay lawyers' bills on both sides of the Irish Sea.

Liam returned to the Flanagan Arms for the first time in twenty-three years.

◄○►

When Liam and Pepe appeared before the Supreme Court two years later, the senior panel judge expressed considerable sympathy for Mr Casey and Mr Miro, as they had invested ten years of hard work, as well as their personal fortunes, in a project that both the Valldemossa council and the Supreme Court had considered to be bold, imaginative and of civic importance. However, the court did not have the authority to overturn the decision of an elected council, even when it was retrospective. Liam bowed his head.

783

THE NEW COLLECTED SHORT STORIES

'Nevertheless,' the judge continued, 'this court does have the authority to award compensation in full to the appellants, who carried out their business in good faith, and fulfilled every obligation required of them by the Valldemossa council. With that in mind, this court will appoint an independent arbitrator to assess the costs Mr Casey and Mr Miro have incurred, which will include any projected losses.'

As Spaniards were involved, it was another year before the arbitrator presented his findings to the Supreme Court, which necessitated a further six months of making some minor adjustments to the costs so that no one would be in any doubt about how seriously the court had taken their responsibilities.

The day after the senior judge announced the court's findings, *El Pais* suggested in its leader that the size of the award was a warning to all politicians not to consider making retrospective legislation in the future.

The Valldemossa Council was ordered to pay 121 million euros in compensation to Mr Liam Casey, Mr Pepe Miro and their associates.

At the local council election held six months later, the Green Party lost all three of its seats by overwhelming majorities.

Pepe took over the business in Majorca, while Liam retired to Cork, where he purchased a castle with a hundred acres of land. He tells me he has no intention of seeking planning permission, even for an outhouse.

POSTSCRIPT

Observant readers who have followed the timescale during which this story took place might feel that even if the Green Party had failed to overturn Liam and Pepe's planning permission, they would have gone bankrupt anyway following the sudden downturn in the world's economy, and without being paid any compensation. But, as I said at the outset, no one would believe this tale unless they were told that an Irishman was involved.

POLITICALLY CORRECT

12

'NEVER JUDGE A BOOK by its cover,' Arnold's mother always used to tell him.

Despite this piece of sage advice, Arnold took against the man the moment he set eyes on him. The bank had taught him to be cautious when it came to dealing with potential customers. You can have nine successes out of ten and then one failure can ruin your balance sheet, as Arnold had found to his cost soon after he had joined the bank; he was still convinced that was why his promotion had been held up for so long.

Arnold Pennyworthy – he was fed up with being told by all and sundry, *That's an appropriate name for a banker* – had been deputy manager of the Vauxhall branch of the bank for the past ten years, but had recently been offered the chance to move to Bury St Edmunds as branch manager. Bury St Edmunds might have been one of the bank's smaller branches, but Arnold felt that if he could make a fist of it, he still had one more promotion left in him. In any case, he couldn't wait to get out of London, which seemed to him to have been over-run by foreigners who had changed the whole character of the city.

When Arnold's wife had left him without giving a reason – at least, that's what he told his mother – he had moved into Arcadia Mansions, a large block of flats which he liked to refer to as apartments. The rent was extortionate, but at least there was a hall porter. 'It gives the right impression whenever anyone visits me,' Arnold told his mother. Not that he had many visitors since his wife had walked out on him. Arcadia Mansions also had the advantage of being within walking distance of the bank, so the extra money he paid out on rent he clawed back on bus and train fares. The only real disadvantage was that the Victoria line ran directly below the building, so the only time you could be guaranteed any peace was between twelve-thirty and five-thirty in the morning.

The first time Arnold caught sight of his new neighbour was when they found themselves sharing a lift down to the ground floor. Arnold waited for him to speak, but he didn't even say good morning. Arnold wondered if the man even spoke English. He stood back to take a closer look at the most recent arrival. The man was a little shorter than Arnold, around five feet seven inches, solidly built but not overweight, with a square jaw and what Arnold later described to his mother as soulless eyes. His skin was dark, but not black, so Arnold couldn't be sure where he was from. The unkempt beard reminded him of another of his mother's homilies: 'Never trust a man with a beard. He's probably hiding something.'

Arnold decided to have a word with the porter. Dennis was the fount of all knowledge when it came to what took place in Arcadia Mansions and was certain to know all about the man. When the lift doors opened, Arnold stood back to allow the new resident to get out first. He waited until the man had left the building before strolling across to join Dennis at the reception desk.

'What do we know about him?' asked Arnold, nodding at the man as he disappeared into a black cab.

'Not a lot,' admitted Dennis. 'He's taken a short-term lease and says he won't be with us for long. But he did warn me that he'd be having visitors from time to time.'

'I don't like the sound of that,' said Arnold. 'Any idea where he comes from, or what he does for a living?'

'Not a clue,' said Dennis. 'But he certainly didn't get that tan holidaying in the South of France.'

'That's for sure,' said Arnold, laughing. 'Don't misunderstand me, Dennis, I'm not prejudiced. I've always liked Mr Zebari from the other end of my corridor. Keeps himself to himself, always respectful.'

'That's true,' said Dennis. 'But then you must remember that Mr Zebari is a radiologist.' Not that he was altogether sure what a radiologist was.

'Well, I must get a move on,' said Arnold. 'Can't afford to be late for work. Now that I'm going to be manager, I have to set an example to the junior staff. Keep your ear to the ground, Dennis,' he added, touching the side of his nose with a forefinger. 'Although our masters have decided it's not politically correct, I have to tell you I don't like the look of him.'

The porter gave a slight nod as Arnold pushed through the swing doors and headed off in the direction of the bank.

The next time Arnold came across the new resident was a few days later; he was returning from work when he saw him chatting to a young man dressed from head to toe in leather and sitting astride a motorbike. The moment the two of them spotted Arnold, the young man pulled down his visor, revved up and shot away. Arnold hurried into the building, relieved to find Dennis sitting behind the reception desk.

'Those two look a bit dodgy to me,' said Arnold.

'Not half as dodgy as some of the other young men who've been visiting him at all hours of the night and day. There are times when I can't be sure if this is Albert Embankment or the Khyber Pass.'

'I know what you mean,' said Arnold as the lift door opened and Mr Zebari stepped out.

'Good evening, Mr Zebari,' said Dennis with a smile. 'On night duty again?'

'Afraid so, Dennis. No rest for the wicked when you work for the NHS,' he added as he left the building.

'A real gentleman, that Mr Zebari,' said Dennis. 'Sent my wife a bunch of flowers on her birthday.'

―◁○▷―

It was a couple of weeks later, after arriving home late from work, that Arnold spotted the motorbike again. It was parked up against the railing but there was no sign of its owner. Arnold walked into the building, to find a couple of young men chatting loudly in a tongue he didn't recognize. They headed towards the lift, so he held back, as he had no desire to join them.

Dennis waited until the lift door had closed before saying, 'No prizes for guessing who they're visiting. God knows what they get up to behind closed doors.'

'I have my suspicions,' said Arnold, 'but I'm not going to say anything until I've got proof.'

When he got out of the lift at the fourth floor, Arnold could hear raised voices coming from the apartment opposite his. Noticing that the door was slightly ajar, he slowed down and casually glanced inside.

A man was lying flat on his back on the floor, his arms and legs pinned down by the two men he'd seen getting into the lift, while the youth he'd spotted on the motorbike was holding a kitchen knife above the man's head. All around the room were large blown-up photographs of the devastation caused by the 7/7 bus and tube bombings that had recently appeared on the front pages of every national newspaper. The moment the youth spotted Arnold staring at him, he walked quickly across the room and closed the door.

For a moment, Arnold just stood there shaking, unsure what to do next. Should he run downstairs and tell Dennis what he'd witnessed, or make a dash for the relative safety of his apartment and call the police?

Hearing what sounded like a roar of laughter coming from inside the apartment, Arnold ran across to his front door, fumbled for his keys and attempted to push his office Yale into the lock, while continually looking over his shoulder. When he eventually found the right key, he was so nervous he tried to force it in upside down and ended up dropping it on the floor. He picked it up and managed to open the door with his third attempt.

Once Arnold was inside he quickly double-bolted the door and put the safety chain in place, although he still didn't feel safe. When he'd caught his breath, he dragged the largest chair in the room across the floor and rammed it up against the door, then collapsed into it, trembling, as he tried to think what he should do next.

He thought again about phoning the police, but then became fearful that the man would discover who had reported him and the kitchen knife would end up hovering above his head. And when the police raided the building, a fight might break out in the corridor. How many innocent people would become involved? Mr Zebari would surely open his door to find out what was going on and come face to face with the terrorists. It was a risk Arnold wasn't willing to take.

Several minutes passed, and as he could hear nothing happening outside, Arnold nipped across to the sideboard and shakily poured himself a large whisky. He drank it down in two gulps, then poured himself another before slumping back into the chair, clinging on to the bottle. He took another gulp of whisky, more than he usually drank in a week, but his heart was still pounding. He sat there, his shirt saturated with sweat, terrified to move, until the sun had disappeared behind the highest building. He took another swig, and then another, until he finally passed out.

Arnold couldn't be sure how many hours he'd slept, but he woke with a start when the clickety-clack of the first tube could be heard rumbling below him. He saw the empty bottle of whisky lying on the floor by his feet and tried to sober up. In the cold, clear light of morning, he knew exactly what his mother would expect him to do.

When the time came for him to leave for work, he tentatively pulled the heavy chair back a few inches, then placed an ear against the door. Were the men standing outside in the corridor waiting for him to come out? He unlocked the door without making the slightest sound and slowly removed the safety chain. He waited for some time before gingerly opening the door an inch, and then another inch, before peeping into the corridor. He was greeted by silence and no sign of anyone.

Arnold took off his shoes, stepped out into the corridor, closed the door quietly behind him and tiptoed slowly towards the lift, never once taking his eyes off the door on the other side of the corridor. There was no sound coming from inside, and he wondered if they'd panicked and made a run for it. He jabbed at the lift button several times, and it seemed to take forever before the doors finally slid open. He jumped inside and pressed G, but even when the doors had closed, he didn't feel safe. By the time the lift reached the ground floor he'd put his shoes back on and tied the laces. When the doors slid open he ran out of the building, not even looking in Dennis's direction when he said, 'Good morning.' He didn't stop running until he had reached the bank. Arnold opened the front door with the correct key and quickly stepped inside, setting off the alarm. It was the first time he'd had to turn it off.

Arnold went straight to the lavatory, and when he looked at himself in the mirror two bleary red eyes in an unshaven face stared back at him. He tidied himself up as best he could before creeping into his office. He hoped that when the staff arrived, not too many of them would notice that he hadn't shaved and was wearing the same clothes as he had worn the day before.

He sat at his desk and began to write down everything he'd witnessed during the past month, going into particular detail when it came to what had taken place the night before. Once he'd finished, he sat staring into space for some time before he picked up the phone on his desk and dialled 999.

'Emergency services, which service do you require?' said a cool voice.

'Police please,' said Arnold, trying not to sound nervous. He heard a click, then another voice came on the line and said, 'Police service. What is the nature of your emergency?'

Arnold looked down at the pad in front of him, and read out the statement he had just prepared. 'My name is Arnold Pennyworthy. I need to speak to a senior police officer, as I have some important information concerning the possibility of a serious crime having been committed, in which terrorists may be involved.'

Another click, another voice, this time with a name. 'Control room. Inspector Newhouse.'

Arnold read his statement a second time, word for word.

'Could you be a little more specific, sir?' the inspector asked. Once Arnold had told him the details, the officer said, 'Hold on, please, sir. I'm going to put you through to a colleague at Scotland Yard.'

Another line, another voice, another name. 'Sergeant Roberts speaking. How can I help?'

Arnold repeated his prepared statement a third time.

'I think it may be wise, sir, if you didn't say too much more over the phone,' suggested Roberts. 'I'd prefer to come and see you so we can discuss it in person.'

Arnold didn't realize that this suggestion was used to get rid of crank callers and those who simply wanted to waste police time.

'That's fine by me,' he said, 'but I'd prefer it if you visited me at the bank rather than my apartment.'

'I quite understand, sir. I'll be with you as soon as I can.'

'But you don't know the address.'

'We know your address, sir,' said Sergeant Roberts without explanation.

Arnold didn't leave his office that morning, even to carry out his usual check on the tellers. Instead, he busied himself opening the post and checking his emails. There were several phone messages he should have responded to, but they could wait until the man from Scotland Yard had come and gone.

Arnold was pacing up and down in his office when there was a tap on the door.

'There's a Sergeant Roberts to see you,' said his surprised-looking secretary. 'Says he has an appointment.'

'Show him in, Diane,' said Arnold, 'and make sure that we're not disturbed.'

Arnold's secretary stood aside to allow a tall, smartly dressed young man to enter the office. She closed the door behind him.

The sergeant introduced himself and the two men shook hands before he produced his warrant card.

'Would you like a tea or coffee, Sergeant Roberts?' Arnold asked after he had carefully checked the card.

'No, thank you, sir,' the sergeant replied, sitting down opposite Arnold and opening a notebook.

'Where shall I start?' said Arnold.

'Why don't you take me through exactly what you saw taking place, Mr Pennyworthy. Don't spare me any details, however irrelevant you may consider they are.'

Arnold checked through his notes once again. He began by describing in great detail everything he'd seen during the past month, ending with a full account of what he'd witnessed in the flat opposite the previous night. When he finally came to the end, he poured himself a glass of water.

'What's your neighbour's name?' was the sergeant's first question.

'Good heavens,' said Arnold, 'I have no idea. But I can tell you that he's recently moved into the block, and has taken a short lease.'

'Which floor are you on, Mr Pennyworthy?'

'The fourth.'

'Thank you. That will be more than enough to be going on with,' said the sergeant, closing his notebook.

'So what happens next?' asked Arnold.

'We'll put a surveillance team on the building immediately, keep an eye on the suspect for a few days and try to find out what he's up to. It could all be completely innocent, of course, but should we come up with anything, Mr Pennyworthy, be assured we'll keep you informed.'

'I hope it won't turn out to be a waste of your time,' said Arnold, suddenly feeling a little foolish.

'We'll find out soon enough,' said the young detective with a smile. 'Let me assure you, Mr Pennyworthy, I only wish there were more members of the public who were as vigilant. It would make my job much easier. Good luck with your new job,' he added as he stood to leave.

As soon as the policeman had left, Arnold picked up the phone on his desk and called his mother. 'Can I come and stay with you for a few days, Mother, before I move to Bury St Edmunds?'

'Yes, of course, dear,' she replied. 'Nothing wrong, I hope?'

'Nothing for you to worry about, Mother.'

⦿

Once Arnold had moved to Bury St Edmunds, running the branch took up most of his time, and as the weeks passed and he heard nothing from Sergeant Roberts, the incident at Arcadia Mansions began to fade in his memory.

From time to time he read reports in the *Daily Telegraph* about police raids on terrorist cells in Leeds, Birmingham and Bradford. He always studied the photos of the suspects being led away by the police, and on one occasion he could have sworn that. . .

Arnold had just finished interviewing a customer about a mortgage application when the phone on his desk rang.

'There's a Sergeant Roberts on the line,' said his secretary.

'Just give me a moment,' said Arnold. He could feel his heart racing as he bustled the customer out of his office and closed the door behind him.

'Good morning, Sergeant.'

'Good morning, sir,' came back a voice he recognized. 'I was wondering if you were planning to be in London during the next few days. It's just that I'd like to bring you up to date on what our surveillance team has come up with.' Arnold began to thumb through his diary. 'If that's not convenient,' the sergeant continued, 'I'd be happy to visit you in Bury St Edmunds.'

'No, no,' said Arnold, 'I'll be coming up to London on Friday evening. It's my sister's birthday, and I'm taking her to see *The Sound of Music* at the London Palladium.'

'Good, then I wonder if you could spare the time to pop in to Scotland Yard, say around five o'clock, because I know that Commander Harrison is very keen to have a word with you.'

'That will be fine,' said Arnold, looking down at the blank page. He made a note in his diary, not that he was likely to forget.

'Good,' said the sergeant. 'I'll meet you in reception at five o'clock on Friday.'

As the week went by, Arnold couldn't help thinking that he was looking forward to meeting Commander Harrison more than he was to seeing *The Sound of Music*.

―◇―

Arnold left the office just after lunch on Friday, explaining to his secretary that he had an important appointment in London. When he arrived at Liverpool Street station he went straight to the taxi rank, as he didn't want to be late for the meeting.

The taxi swung into the forecourt of Scotland Yard a few minutes before five, and Arnold was pleased to see Sergeant Roberts standing by the reception desk waiting for him.

'Good to see you again, Mr Pennyworthy,' said Roberts. They shook hands, and the sergeant guided Arnold towards a bank of lifts. He chatted about *The Sound of Music*, which he'd taken his wife to see at Christmas, while they waited for the lift, and about the parlous state of English rugby while they were in the lift. He hadn't even hinted why Commander Harrison wanted to see Arnold by the time the lift doors opened on the sixth floor.

Roberts led Arnold to a door at the far end of the corridor, which displayed the name Commander Mark Harrison OBE. He gave a gentle tap, waited for a moment, then opened the door and walked in.

The commander immediately rose from behind his desk and gave Arnold a warm smile before shaking hands with him. 'Good to meet you at last,' he said. 'Can I offer you a drink?'

'No, thank you,' said Arnold, now even more desperate to discover why such a senior officer wanted to see him.

'I know you're going to the theatre this evening, Mr Penny-worthy, so I'll get straight to the point,' said the commander, waving Arnold to a seat. 'I must explain from the outset,' he continued, 'that the case I'm going to discuss with you is due to begin at the Old Bailey next week, so there will be some details I'm not at liberty to disclose, although I feel sure I can rely on your complete discretion, Mr Pennyworthy.'

'I fully understand,' said Arnold.

'Let me begin by saying how grateful we all are at the Yard for the information you supplied. I think I can say without exaggeration that you have been responsible for uncovering one of the most active terrorist cells in this country. In fact, it's hard to quantify just how many lives you may have been responsible for saving.'

'I did no more than what I considered to be my duty,' said Arnold.

'You did far more, believe me,' said the commander. 'Because of the information you supplied, Mr Pennyworthy, we've been able to arrest fifteen terrorist suspects, one of whom, the man who rented the flat on your corridor, was undoubtedly the cell chief. At a house in Birmingham which he led us to, we discovered explosive devices, bomb-making equipment and detailed plans of buildings, along with the names of high-profile individuals the group planned to target, including a member of the royal family. Frankly, Mr Pennyworthy, you contacted us just in time.'

Arnold beamed as the commander continued, 'I only wish we could make your contribution public, but you will understand the restrictions we're under in such cases, not least when it comes to your own safety.'

'Yes, of course,' said Arnold, trying not to sound disappointed.

'But when you read the press reports of the case next week, you can take some satisfaction from knowing the role you played in bringing this group of violent criminals to justice.'

'Couldn't agree more, sir,' chipped in the sergeant.

Arnold didn't know what to say.

'I won't keep you any longer, Mr Pennyworthy,' said the commander. 'I wouldn't want you to be late for the theatre. But be assured that the Yard will remain in your debt, and my door will always be open.'

Arnold bowed his head and tried to look suitably humble.

The commander shook hands with Arnold and thanked him once again, before Sergeant Roberts escorted him out of the room. 'And may I add my personal thanks, Mr Pennyworthy,' Roberts said as they walked down the corridor, 'because on the first of the month, I'm to be promoted to Inspector.'

'Many congratulations,' said Arnold. 'Well deserved, I feel sure.'

Arnold walked out of the building and made his way down Whitehall. He held his head high as he strolled past Downing Street, wondering how much he could tell his sister about the meeting that had just taken place. He checked his watch and decided to hail another taxi. After all, it was a special day.

'Where to, guv?' asked the taxi driver.

'The Palladium,' said Arnold as he climbed into the back seat.

Arnold thought about his meeting with the commander as the taxi made its slow progress into the West End. He played the conversation over and over again in his mind as if he was pressing the repeat button on a tape recorder. The cab came to a halt on Great Marlborough Street, a police cordon preventing them from going any further.

'What's the problem?' Arnold asked the driver.

'There must be a member of the royal family or some foreign head of state going to the show tonight. I'm afraid you'll have to walk the last hundred yards.'

'Not a problem,' said Arnold, handing over a ten-pound note and not waiting for any change.

He made his way past the large crowd of people pressing against the safety barriers hoping to discover who was causing so much interest. When he reached the theatre entrance, his ticket was carefully checked before he was allowed to enter the foyer. He walked up the wide red-carpeted steps and looked around for his sister. A few moments later he spotted a programme being waved energetically. Janet was never late for anything.

Arnold gave his sister a kiss on both cheeks, wished her a happy birthday and asked her if she'd like a glass of champagne before the curtain went up.

'Certainly not,' said Janet. 'Let's go and find our seats. A member of the royal family is expected in tonight, and I want to see who it is.'

'Please take your seats,' said a voice over the tannoy. 'The performance will begin in five minutes.'

'I've been looking forward to this for weeks,' said Janet as an usher tore their tickets in half and said, 'Halfway down on the left-hand side.'

'What wonderful seats, Arnold,' said Janet when they reached row G.

'Well, you're not forty every day,' said Arnold, giving her arm a squeeze.

'I wish,' she said as they made their way to the centre of the row, trying not to tread on anyone's toes but causing several people to have to stand.

'I thought we'd go to Cipriani afterwards,' said Arnold once they'd settled down.

'Isn't that a bit extravagant?' said Janet.

'Not on my sister's birthday, it isn't. In any case, it's turned out to be a rather special day for me as well.'

'And why's that?' asked Janet as she handed him a programme. 'Not another promotion?'

'No, more important than that—' began Arnold as people around him began to rise and start clapping as the Princess Royal entered the royal box. She gave the audience a wave before taking her seat. Janet waved back.

'She's always been one of my favourites,' Janet said as the audience sat back down. 'But do tell me, Arnold, why it's such a special day for you?'

'Well, it all began when he moved into our block—'

'Who are you talking about?' interrupted Janet as the lights went down.

'I must confess, I had my doubts about him from the start . . .' Arnold whispered as the conductor raised his baton. 'I'll tell you all about it over dinner,' he added as the orchestra began to play a melody most of the audience knew off by heart.

Arnold enjoyed the first half of the musical, and when the curtain fell for the interval, it was clear from the rapturous applause that he was not alone.

Several members of the audience rose and peered up at the royal box, where Princess Anne was chatting to her husband. Suddenly the door at the back of the box opened, and a man whose face Arnold could never forget walked in, dressed in a scruffy dinner jacket, one hand in his pocket.

'Oh my God,' said Arnold, 'it's him!'

'It's who?' said Janet, her eyes not straying from the royal box.

'The man I was telling you about,' said Arnold. 'He's a terrorist, and somehow he's managed to escape and get into the royal box.' Arnold didn't wait to hear his sister's next question. He knew his duty, and quickly squeezed past the people in his row, not caring whose toes he trod on while ignoring a barrage of angry protests. When he reached the aisle he began to run towards the exit, pushing aside anyone who got in his way. Once he was in the foyer he quickly looked around then charged up the sweeping staircase that led to the dress circle, while the majority of theatregoers were making their way slowly down to the crush bar on the ground floor. Several people stopped and stared at the ill-mannered man going so rudely against the tide. Arnold ignored them, as well as several caustic comments addressed directly at him. At the top of the stairs he set off in the direction of the royal box, but when he came to a red rope barrier, two burly police officers stepped forward and blocked his path.

'Can I help you, sir?' one of them asked politely.

'There's a dangerous terrorist in the royal box,' shouted Arnold. 'The princess's life is in danger.'

'Please calm down, sir,' said the officer. 'The only guest in the royal box this evening is Professor Naresh Khan, the distinguished American orthopaedic surgeon who is over here to give a series of lectures on the problems he encountered following 9/11.'

'Yes, that's him,' said Arnold. 'He may be posing as a famous surgeon, but I assure you, he's an escaped terrorist.'

'Why don't you show this gentleman back to his seat,' said the officer, turning to his colleague.

'And why don't you call Commander Harrison at Scotland Yard,' said Arnold. 'He'll confirm my story. My name is Arnold Pennyworthy.'

The two officers looked at each other for a moment, and then more closely at Arnold. The senior officer dialled a number on his mobile phone.

'Put me through to the Yard.' A few moments passed, too long for Arnold, who was becoming more frantic by the second.

'I need to speak to Commander Harrison, urgently,' the officer said.

After what seemed an eternity to Arnold, the commander came on the line.

'Good evening, sir, my name is Bolton, Royal Protection team, currently on duty at the London Palladium. A member of the public – a Mr Pennyworthy – is convinced there's a terrorist in the royal box, and he says you'll confirm his story.' Arnold hoped they would still be in time to save her life. 'I'll put him on, sir.' The officer handed the phone to Arnold, who tried to remain calm.

'That man we discussed this afternoon, Commander, he must have escaped, because I've just seen him in the royal box.'

'I can assure you, Mr Pennyworthy,' said the commander calmly, 'that's not possible. The man we spoke about this afternoon is locked up in a high-security prison from which he's unlikely to be released in your lifetime.'

'But I've just seen him in the royal box!' shouted Arnold desperately. 'You must tell your men to arrest him before it's too late.'

'I don't know whom you've just seen in the royal box, sir,' said the commander, 'but I can assure you that it isn't Mr Zebari.'

BETTER THE DEVIL
YOU KNOW

13

THE CHAIRMAN CLIMBED OUT of the back of his car and strode into the bank.

'Good morning, Chairman,' said Rod, the young man standing behind the reception desk.

The chairman walked straight past without acknowledging him and headed towards a lift that had just opened. A group of people who'd been expecting to take it stood aside. None of them would have considered sharing a lift with the chairman, not if they wanted to keep their jobs.

The lift whisked him up to the top floor and he marched into his office. Four separate piles of market reports, telephone messages, press clippings and emails had been placed neatly on his desk by his secretary, but today they could wait. He checked his diary, although he knew he didn't have any appointments before his check-up with the company's doctor at twelve o'clock.

He walked across to the window and looked out over the City. The Bank of England, the Guildhall, the Tower, Lloyd's of London and St Paul's dominated the skyline. But his bank, the bank he'd built up to such prominence over the past thirty years, looked down on all of them, and now they wanted to take it away from him.

There had been rumours circulating in the City for some time. Not everyone approved of his methods, or some of the tactics he resorted to just before closing a deal. 'Brings the very reputation of the City into question,' one of his directors had dared to suggest at a recent board meeting. The chairman had made sure the man was replaced a few weeks later, but his departure had caused even more unease not only amongst the rest of the board but also as far as the inner reaches of Threadneedle Street.

Perhaps he'd bent the rules a little over the years, possibly a few people had suffered on the way, but the bank had thrived and those who'd remained loyal to him had benefited, while he had built one of the largest personal fortunes in the City.

The chairman was well aware that some of his colleagues hoped he would retire on his sixtieth birthday, but they didn't have the guts to put the knife in and hasten his departure. At least, not until a story appeared in one of the gossip columns hinting that he'd been seen paying regular visits to a clinic in Harley Street. They still didn't make a move until the same story appeared on the front page of the *Financial Times*.

When the chairman was asked at the next board meeting to confirm or deny the reports, he procrastinated, but one of his colleagues, someone he should have got rid of years ago, called his bluff and insisted on an independent medical report so that the rumours could be scotched. The chairman called for a vote and didn't get the result he'd anticipated. The board decided by eleven votes to nine that the company's doctor, not the chairman's personal physician, should carry out a full medical examination and make his findings known to the board. The chairman knew it would be pointless to protest. It was exactly the same procedure he insisted on for all his staff when they had their annual check-ups. In fact, over the years, he'd found it a convenient way to rid himself of any incompetent or overzealous executives who'd dared to question his judgement. Now they intended to use the same tactic to get rid of him.

The company's doctor was not a man who could be bought,

so the board would find out the truth. He had cancer, and although his personal physician said he could live for another two years, possibly three, he knew that once the medical report was made public, the bank's shares would collapse, with no hope of recovering until he'd resigned and a new chairman had been appointed in his place.

He'd known for some time that he was dying, but he'd always beaten the odds in the past, often at the last moment, and he believed he could do it once again. He'd have given anything, anything for a second chance . . .

'Anything?' said a voice from behind him.

The chairman continued to stare out of the window, as no one was allowed to enter his office without an appointment, even the deputy chairman. Then he heard the voice again. 'Anything?' it repeated.

He swung round to see a man dressed in a smartly tailored dark suit, white silk shirt and thin black tie.

'Who the hell are you?'

'My name is Mr De Ath,' the man said, 'and I represent a lower authority.'

'How did you get into my office?'

'Your secretary can't see or hear me.'

'Get out, before I call security,' said the chairman, pressing a button under his desk several times.

A moment later the door opened and his secretary came rushing in. 'You called, Chairman?' she said, a notepad open in her hand, a pen poised.

'I want to know how this man got into my office without an appointment,' he said, pointing at the intruder.

'You don't have any appointments this morning, Chairman,' said his secretary, looking uncertainly around the room, 'other than with the company doctor at twelve o'clock.'

'As I told you,' said Mr De Ath, 'she can't see or hear me. I can only be seen by those approaching death.'

THE NEW COLLECTED SHORT STORIES

The chairman looked at his secretary and said sharply, 'I don't want to be disturbed again unless I call.'

'Of course, Chairman,' she said and quickly left the room.

'Now that we've established my credentials,' said Mr De Ath, 'allow me to ask you again. When you said you'd do anything to be given a second chance, did you mean anything?'

'Even if I did say it, we both know that's impossible.'

'For me, anything is possible. After all, that's how I knew what you were thinking at the time, and at this very moment I know you're asking yourself, "Is he for real? And if he is, have I found a way out?"'

'How do you know that?'

'It's my job. I visit those who'll do anything to be given a second chance. In Hell, we take the long view.'

'So what's the deal?' asked the chairman, folding his arms and looking at Mr De Ath defiantly.

'I have the authority to allow you to change places with anyone you choose. For example, the young man working on the front desk in reception. Even though you're scarcely aware of his existence and probably don't even know his name.'

'And what does he get, if I agree to change places with him?' asked the chairman.

'He becomes you.'

'That's not a very good deal for him.'

'You've closed many deals like that in the past and it's never concerned you before. But if it will ease what passes for your conscience, when he dies, he will go up,' said De Ath, pointing towards the ceiling. 'Whereas if you agree to my terms, you will eventually be coming down, to join me.'

'But he's just a clerk on the front desk.'

'Just as you were forty years ago, although you rarely admit as much to anyone nowadays.'

'But he doesn't have my brain—'

'Or your character.'

'And I know nothing about his life, or his background,' said the chairman.

'Once the change has taken place, he'll be supplied with your memory, and you with his.'

'But will I keep my brain, or be saddled with his?'

'You'll still have your own brain, and he'll keep his.'

'And when he dies, he goes to Heaven.'

'And when you die, you'll join me in Hell. That is, if you sign the contract.'

Mr De Ath took the chairman by the elbow and led him across to the window, where they looked down on the City of London. 'If you sign up with me, all this could be yours.'

'Where do I sign?' asked the chairman, taking the top off his pen.

'Before you even consider signing,' said Mr De Ath, 'my inferiors have insisted that because of your past record when it comes to honouring the words "legal and binding", I'm obliged to point out all the finer points should you decide to accept our terms. It's part of the lower authority's new regulations to make sure you can't escape the final judgement.' The chairman put his pen down. 'Under the terms of this agreement, you will exchange your life for the clerk at the reception desk. When he dies, he'll go to Heaven. When you die, you'll join me in Hell.'

'You've already explained all that,' said the chairman.

'Yes, but I have to warn you that there are no break clauses. You don't even get a period in Purgatory with a chance to redeem yourself. There are no buy-back options, no due diligence to enable you to get off the hook at the last moment, as you've done so often in the past. You must understand that if you sign the contract, it's for eternity.'

'But if I sign, I get the boy's life, and he gets mine?'

'Yes, but my inferiors have also decreed that before you put pen to paper, I must honestly answer any questions you might wish to put to me.'

'What's the boy's name?' asked the chairman.

'Rod.'

'And how old is he?'

'Twenty-five next March.'

'Then I only have one more question. What's his life expectancy?'

'He's just been put through one of those rigorous medical examinations all your staff are required to undertake, and he came out with a triple A rating. He plays football for his local club, goes to the gym twice a week and plans to run the London Marathon for charity next April. He doesn't smoke, and drinks only in moderation. He's what life assurance companies call an actuary's dream.'

'It's a no-brainer,' said the chairman. 'Where do I sign?'

Mr De Ath produced several sheets of thick parchment. He turned them over until he had reached the last page of the contract, where his name was written in what looked a lot like blood. The chairman didn't bother to read the small print – he usually left that to his team of lawyers and in-house advisors, none of whom was available on this occasion.

He signed the document with a flourish and handed the pen to Mr De Ath, who topped and tailed it on behalf of a lower authority.

'What happens now?' asked the chairman.

◄○►

'You can get dressed,' said the doctor.

The chairman put on his shirt as the doctor examined the X-rays. 'For the moment the cancer seems to be in remission,' he said. 'So, with a bit of luck, you could live for another five, even ten years.'

'That's the best news I've heard in months,' said the chairman. 'When do you think you'll need to see me again?'

'I think it would be wise for you to continue with your usual six-monthly check-ups, if for no other reason than to keep your colleagues happy. I'll write up my report and have it biked over to your office later today, and I shall make it clear that I can't see any reason why you shouldn't continue as chairman for a couple more years.'

'Thank you, Doctor, that's a great relief.'

'Mind you, I do think a holiday might be in order,' said the doctor as he accompanied his patient to the door.

'I certainly can't remember when I last had one,' said the chairman, 'so I may well take your advice.' He shook the doctor warmly by the hand. 'Thank you. Thank you very much.'

Later that afternoon a large brown box was delivered to the surgery.

'What's this?' the doctor asked his assistant.

'A gift from the chairman.'

'Two surprises in one day,' said the doctor, examining the label on the box. 'A dozen bottles of a 1994 Côtes du Rhône. How very generous of him.' He didn't add until his assistant had closed the door, 'And how out of character.'

The chairman sat in the front seat of his car and chatted to his chauffeur as he was driven back to the bank. He hadn't realized that, like him, Fred was an Arsenal supporter.

When the car drew up outside the bank, he leapt out. The doorman saluted and held the door open for him.

'Good morning, Sam,' said the chairman, then walked across reception to the lift which a young man was holding open for him.

'Good morning, Chairman,' said the young man. 'Would it be possible to have a word with you?'

'Yes, of course. By the way, what's your name?'

'Rod, sir,' said the young man.

'Well, Rod, what can I do for you?'

'There's a vacancy coming up on the Commodities floor, and I wondered if I might be considered for it.'

'Of course, Rod. Why not?'

'Well, sir, I don't have any formal qualifications.'

'Neither did I when I was your age,' said the chairman. 'So why don't you go for it?'

'I hope you know what you're up to,' said the senior clerk when Rod returned to his place behind the reception desk.

'I sure do. I can tell you I don't intend to spend the rest of my life on the ground floor like you.'

The chairman held open the lift doors to allow two women to join him. 'Which floor?' he asked as the doors closed.

'The fifth please, sir,' one of them said nervously.

He pressed the button, then asked, 'Which department do you work in?'

'We're cleaners,' said one of the girls.

'Well, I've wanted to have a word with you for some time,' said the chairman.

The girls looked anxiously at each other.

'Yours must be a thankless task at times, but I can tell you, these are the cleanest offices in the City. You should be very proud of yourselves.'

The lift came to a halt at the fifth floor.

'Thank you, Chairman,' the girls both said as they stepped out. They could only wonder if their colleagues would believe them when they told them what had just happened.

When the lift reached the top floor, the chairman strolled into his secretary's office. 'Good morning, Sally,' he said, and sat down in the seat next to her desk. She leapt up. He waved her back down with a smile.

'How did the medical go?' she asked nervously.

'Far better than I'd expected,' said the chairman. 'It seems the cancer is in remission, and I could be around for another ten years.'

'That is good news,' said Sally. 'So there's no longer any reason for you to resign?'

'That's what the doctor said, but perhaps the time has come for me to accept the fact that I'm not immortal. So there are going to be a few changes around here.'

'What exactly did you have in mind?' the secretary asked anxiously.

'To start with, I'm going to accept the board's generous retirement package and stay on as non-executive director, but not before I've taken a proper holiday.'

'But will that be enough for you, Chairman?' asked his secretary, not certain she was hearing him correctly.

'More than enough, Sally. Perhaps the time has come for me to do some voluntary work. I could start by helping my local football club. They need some new changing rooms. You know, when I was a youngster, that club was the only thing that kept me off the streets, and who knows, maybe they even need a new chairman?'

His secretary couldn't think what to say.

'And there's something else I must do before I go, Sally.'

She picked up her notepad as the chairman removed a chequebook from an inside pocket.

'How many years have you been working for me?'

'It will be twenty-seven at the end of this month, Chairman.'

He wrote out a cheque for twenty-seven thousand pounds and passed it across to her. 'Perhaps you should take a holiday as well. Heaven knows, I can't have been the easiest of bosses.'

Sally fainted.

◄◦►

'Well, I'm off for lunch,' said Rod, checking his watch.

'Where have you got in mind?' asked Sam. 'The Savoy Grill?'

'All in good time,' said Rod. 'But for now I'll have to be satisfied with the Garter Arms because the time has come for me to get to know my future colleagues in Commodities.'

'Aren't you getting a bit above yourself, lad?'

'No, Sam, just keep your eyes open. It won't be long before I'm their boss, because this is just the first step on my way to becoming chairman.'

'Not in my lifetime,' said Sam as he unwrapped his sandwiches.

'Don't be so sure about that, Sam,' said Rod, taking off his long blue porter's coat and replacing it with a smart sports jacket. He strolled across the foyer, pushed his way through the swing doors and out on to the pavement. He glanced across the road at the Garter Arms, looking forward to taking his first step on the corporate ladder.

Rod checked to his right as a double-decker bus came to a halt and disgorged several passengers. He spotted a gap in the traffic and stepped out into the road just as a motorcycle courier overtook the bus. The biker threw on his brakes the moment he saw Rod, swerved and tried to avoid him, but he was a fraction of a second too late. The bike hit Rod side-on, dragging him along the road until it finally came to a halt on top of him.

Rod opened his eyes and stared at a package marked URGENT, which had landed in the road by his side: *The Chairman's Medical Report*. He looked up to see a man dressed in a smartly tailored dark suit, white silk shirt and thin black tie looking down at him.

'If only you'd asked me how long the young man had to live, and not what his life expectancy was,' were the last words Rod heard before departing from this world.

NO ROOM AT THE INN

14

RICHARD EDMISTON climbed off the bus feeling tired and hungry. It had been a long day, and he was looking forward to a meal and a bath, although he wasn't sure if he could afford both.

He was coming to the end of his holiday, which was a good thing because he was also coming to the end of his money. In fact, he had less than a hundred euros left in his wallet, along with a return train ticket to London.

But he wasn't complaining. He'd spent an idyllic month in Tuscany, even though Melanie had dropped out at the last minute without offering any explanation. He would have cancelled the whole trip but he'd already bought his ticket and put a deposit down at several small *pensioni* dotted around the Italian countryside. In any case, he'd been looking forward to exploring northern Italy for the past year, ever since he'd read an article in *Time* magazine by Robert Hughes which said that half the world's treasures were to be found in one country. He was finally persuaded to go after he and Melanie had attended a lecture given by John Julius Norwich at the Courtauld, at which the celebrated historian ended with the words, 'If you were given two lives, you'd spend one of them in Italy.'

Richard may well be ending his holiday penniless, tired and hungry, but he'd quickly discovered just how accurate Hughes and Norwich were after he'd visited Florence, San Gimignano, Cortona, Arezzo, Siena and Lucca, each of which contained masterpieces that in any other country would have been worthy of several pages in the national tourist guides, whereas in Italy were often no more than a footnote.

Richard needed to leave for England the following day because he would start his first job on Monday, as an English teacher at a large comprehensive in the East End of London. His old headmaster at Marlborough had offered him the chance to return and teach English to the lower fifth, but what could he hope to learn by going back to his old school and simply repeating his experiences as a child, even if he did exchange his blazer for a graduates gown?

He adjusted his rucksack and began to trudge slowly up the winding path that led to the ancient village of Monterchi, perched on top of the hill. He'd saved Monterchi until last because it possessed the Madonna del Parto, a fresco of the pregnant Virgin Mary and two angels by Piero della Francesca. It was considered by scholars to be one of the artist's finest works, which was why many pilgrims and lovers of the Renaissance period came from all parts of the world to admire it.

Richard's rucksack felt heavier with each step he took, while the view of the valley below became more spectacular, dominated by the River Arno winding its way through vineyards, olive groves and green-sculpted hills. But even this paled into insignificance when he reached the top of the hill and saw Monterchi in all its glory for the first time.

The fourteenth-century village had been stranded in a backwater of history and clearly did not approve of anything modern. There were no traffic lights, no signposts, no double yellow lines and not a McDonald's in sight. As Richard strolled into the market square, the town hall clock struck nine times. Despite the hour, the evening was warm enough to allow the natives and an occasional interloper to dine al fresco. Richard spotted a restaurant shaded by ancient olive trees and walked across to study the menu. He reluctantly accepted that it might have suited his palate, but sadly not his purse, unless he was willing to sleep in a field that night before walking the ninety kilometres back to Florence.

He noticed a smaller establishment tucked away on the far side of the square, where the tables didn't have spotless white cloths and the waiters weren't wearing smart linen jackets. He took a seat in the corner and thought about Melanie, who should have been sitting opposite him. He'd planned to spend a month with her so they could finally decide if they should move in together once they'd both settled in London, she as a barrister, he as a teacher. Melanie clearly hadn't felt she needed another month to make up her mind.

For the past couple of weeks, whenever Richard had studied a menu, he'd always checked the prices rather than the dishes before he came to a decision. He selected the one dish he could afford before rummaging around in his rucksack and pulling out the book of short stories that had been recommended to him by his tutor. He'd advised Richard to ignore the sacred cows of Indian literature and instead enjoy the genius of R. K. Narayan. Richard soon became so engrossed by the problems of a tax collector living in a small village on the other side of the world that he didn't notice when a waitress appeared with a pitcher of water in one hand, and a basket of freshly baked bread and a small bowl of olives in the other. She placed them on the table and asked if he was ready to order.

'*Spaghetti all' Amatriciana,*' he said, looking up, '*e un bicchiere di vino rosso.*' He wondered how many kilos he'd put on since crossing the Channel; not that it mattered, because once he began the new job he would return to his old routine of running five miles a day, which he'd managed even when he was taking his exams.

He'd only read a few more pages of *Malgudi Days* when the waitress reappeared and placed a large bowl of spaghetti and a glass of red wine in front of him.

'*Grazie*,' he said, looking up briefly from his book.

He became so involved in the story that he continued to read as he forked up his food until he suddenly realized his plate was empty. He put the book down and mopped up the remains of the thick tomato sauce with his last piece of bread, before devouring what remained of the olives. The waitress returned and removed his empty plate before handing him the menu.

'Would you like anything else?' she asked in English.

'I can't afford anything else,' he admitted without guile, not even opening the menu for fear it might tempt him. '*Il conto, per favore*,' he added, giving her a warm smile.

He was preparing to leave when the waitress reappeared carrying a large portion of tiramisu and an espresso. 'But I didn't order—' he began, but she put a finger to her lips and hurried away before he could thank her. Melanie had once told him it was his boyish charm which made women want to mother him – a charm which clearly no longer worked on Melanie.

The tiramisu was delicious, and Richard even put his book down so he could fully appreciate the delicate flavours. As he sipped his coffee, he began to think about where he would spend the night. His thoughts were interrupted when the waitress returned with the bill. As he checked it, he realized she hadn't charged him for the glass of house red. Should he draw her attention to the omission? Her smile suggested he shouldn't.

He handed her a ten-euro note and asked if she could recommend somewhere he might spend the night.

'There are only two hotels in the village,' she told him. 'And La Contessina – ' she hesitated – 'might be . . .'

'Out of my price range?' suggested Richard.

'But the other one is not expensive, if a little basic.'

'Sounds like my kind of place,' said Richard. 'Is it far?'

'Nothing is far in Monterchi,' she said. 'Walk to the end of the via dei Medici, turn right and you'll find the Albergo Piero on your left.'

Richard stood up, leaned over and kissed her on the cheek. She blushed and hurried away, bringing to his mind Harry Chapin's sad lyrics in the ballad, 'A Better Place to Be'. He threw his rucksack over his shoulder and began to walk down via dei Medici. At the end he turned right and, as the waitress had promised, the hotel was on his left.

He stood outside, uncertain if he could still afford a room now he was down to his last eighty-six euros. Through the glass door he could see a receptionist, head down, checking the register. She looked up, handed a waiting couple a large key, and a porter picked up their bags and led them to the lift.

When he saw her for the first time, he didn't dare take his eyes off her, for fear the mirage might disappear. She had flawless olive skin, long dark hair that curled up as it touched her slim, graceful shoulders and large brown eyes that lit up when she smiled. Her dark tailored suit and white blouse had an elegance that Italian men take for granted and English women spend a fortune trying to emulate. She must have been around thirty, perhaps thirty-five, but she was graced with the kind of ageless beauty that made Richard wish he hadn't only just graduated.

Even if he couldn't afford a room, nothing was going to stop him speaking to her. He pushed open the door, walked up to the counter and smiled. She returned the compliment, which made her look even more radiant.

'*Vorrei una camera per la notte*,' he said.

She looked down at the register. 'I'm sorry,' she replied in English, revealing only the slightest accent, 'but we're fully booked. In fact, the last room was taken just a few moments ago.'

Richard glanced across at a row of keys dangling on hooks behind her. 'Are you sure you don't have anything?' he asked. 'I don't care how small the room is,' he added as he peered over the counter at a short list of upside-down names.

Once again, she glanced down at the guest register. 'No, I'm sorry,' she repeated. 'One or two guests haven't checked in yet, but I can't release their rooms because they've paid in advance. Have you tried La Contessina? They may still have a room.'

'Not one that I can afford,' said Richard.

She nodded understandingly. 'There's an old lady who runs a guest house at the bottom of the hill, but you'll have to hurry because she locks her door at eleven.'

'Would you be kind enough to call her and ask if she has a room?'

'She doesn't have a phone.'

'Perhaps I could spend the night in the lounge?' said Richard hopefully. 'Would anyone notice?' He tried out the boyish grin Melanie had once assured him was irresistible.

The receptionist frowned for the first time. 'If the manageress were to discover you were sleeping in the lounge, not only would she throw you out, but I'd probably lose my job.'

'So it will have to be the nearest field,' he said.

She looked at Richard more closely, leaned across the counter and whispered, 'Take the lift to the top floor and wait there. If any of the bookings don't show up before midnight, you can have their room.'

'Thank you,' said Richard, wanting to give her a hug.

'You'd better leave your bag in reception,' she added without explanation.

He took off his rucksack and she quickly placed it under the counter. 'Thank you,' he repeated, before making his way across to the lift. When the door opened, the porter stepped out and stood to one side, giving Richard a warm smile as he entered it.

The little lift whirred its way slowly up to the top floor and when he stepped out into a dark corridor that was lit by a single, uncovered bulb, Richard couldn't believe he was still in the same hotel. As there wasn't a chair to be seen, he hunched down on the well-trodden carpet, his back against the wall, already regretting that he hadn't taken the book out of his rucksack. For a moment he considered returning to the lobby to retrieve it, but the thought of coming face to face with the manageress and being thrown out onto the street was enough to convince him to stay put.

After a few minutes he stood up and began to pace restlessly up and down the corridor, frequently checking his watch.

When midnight struck on the town hall clock, he decided he'd rather sleep in the open air than hang around in that corridor a moment longer. He walked across to the lift, pressed the button and waited. When the doors finally opened, she was standing there, looking even more seductive in the half-light. She stepped out of the lift, took him by the hand and led him along the corridor until they reached a door with no number. She placed a key in the lock, opened the door and pulled him inside.

Richard looked around a room that wasn't much larger than his college study, and was almost completely taken up by a bed that was neither a single nor quite a double. The family photographs dotted around the walls suggested that this was where she lived. As there was only one small chair, he wondered where she expected him to sleep.

'I won't be a moment,' she said, and gave him that disarming smile again before disappearing into the bathroom. Richard sat down on the wooden chair and waited for her to reappear, not certain what he should do next. When he heard a shower being turned on, a hundred thoughts began to race through his head. He was thinking about Melanie, his first real girlfriend, when the bathroom door swung open. He hadn't looked at another woman for the past two years. She stepped out, dressed in a bathrobe, the cord undone.

'You look as if you need a shower,' she said, leaving the door open as she brushed past him.

'Thank you,' he replied, and disappeared inside, closing the door behind him. Richard enjoyed the feeling of the warm water cascading down on him, and with the assistance of a bar of soap he slowly removed the dirt and grime of a long, hot, sweaty day. After he'd dried himself, he once again regretted leaving his rucksack downstairs, as he didn't want to put his dirty clothes back on. He looked around the room and spotted another hotel bathrobe hanging on the back of the door. He was surprised how well it fitted.

Richard turned out the bathroom light and tentatively opened the door. The room was dark, but he could see the outline of her lithe body under a single sheet. As he stood there, a hand pulled the sheet back. He tiptoed across the room and sat upright on the edge of the bed. She pulled the sheet further back, but didn't speak. He lay down on the bed, his back to her.

A moment later, he felt a hand undo the cord of his bathrobe, while the other hand tried to take it off. He was thinking about Melanie when the receptionist finally pulled off his robe, threw it on the floor and slid her naked body up against his back. When she began to kiss the nape of his neck, Melanie evaporated. Richard didn't move a muscle as she began to explore his body, first his neck, then his back, with one hand, while the other moved slowly up the inside of his thigh. He turned over and took her in his arms. She felt so enticing that he wanted to switch the light back on and enjoy the sight of her naked body. When he kissed her, he felt a desire he'd never experienced with any other woman, and when they made love, it was as if it were the first time. As she lay back, Richard still held her in his arms, not wanting to fall asleep.

He woke when he felt her hand moving gently up the inside of his leg. This time he made love slowly and with more confidence, and she made no attempt to disguise her feelings. He couldn't be sure how many times they made love before the morning sun came streaming into the room, and he saw, for the first time, just how beautiful she was.

When the town hall clock struck eight, she whispered, 'You'll have to leave, *amore mio*. I'm expected back on duty at nine.'

Richard kissed her gently on the lips, slipped out of bed and went into the bathroom. After a quick shower, he put on his old clothes. When he returned to the bedroom she was standing by the window. He walked across, took her in his arms and looked hopefully down at the bed.

'Time for you to go,' she whispered after giving him one last kiss.

'I'll never forget you,' he told her. She smiled wistfully.

She pushed the window up and pointed silently to the fire escape. Richard climbed out and began to tiptoe down the iron staircase, trying not to make too much noise. When his feet touched the ground, he looked up and caught a final glimpse of her naked body. She blew him a kiss, making him wish it was the first day of his holiday and not the last.

He crept stealthily around some flower pots and down a gravel pathway that led to a trellised gate. He opened the gate and found himself back on the street. He made his way to the front of the hotel, and once again looked through the glass door. The beautiful vision of last night had been replaced by an overweight middle-aged woman, who could only have been the manager.

Richard checked his watch. He needed to collect his rucksack and be on his way if he hoped to see the fresco of the Madonna del Parto and still leave himself enough time to catch the train for Florence.

He walked into the hotel more confidently this time, and strolled up to the counter. The manager raised her head, but didn't smile. 'Buongiorno,' said Richard.

'Buongiorno,' she replied, taking a closer look at him. 'How can I help you?'

'I left my rucksack here last night and I've come back to collect it.'

'Do you know anything about this, Demetrio?' she asked, not taking her eyes off Richard.

'Si, signora,' the porter replied, removing the rucksack from behind his desk and placing it on the counter. 'This one, if I remember, sir,' he said, giving Richard a wink.

'Thank you,' said Richard, who would have liked to give him a tip, but . . . he pulled the rucksack over his shoulder and turned to leave.

'Did you stay with us last night?' asked the manager just as he reached the door.

'No I didn't,' said Richard, turning round. 'Unfortunately, I arrived a little too late, and you didn't have a room.'

The manager glanced down at the register and frowned. 'You say you tried to get a room last night?'

'Yes, but you were fully booked.'

'That's strange,' she said, 'because there were several rooms available last night.'

Richard couldn't think of a suitable reply.

'Demetrio,' she said, turning to the porter, 'who was on duty last night?'

'Carlotta, signora.'

Richard smiled. Such a pretty name.

'Carlotta,' the manager repeated, shaking her head. 'I'll need to have a word with the girl. When is she back on?'

Nine o'clock, Richard almost blurted out.

'Nine o'clock, *signora*,' said the porter.

The manager turned back towards Richard. 'I must apologize, *signor*. I hope you were not inconvenienced.'

'Not at all,' said Richard as he opened the door, but he didn't look back for fear that she might see the smile on his face.

The manager waited until the door was closed before she turned to the porter and said, 'You know, Demetrio, it's not the first time she's done that.'

CASTE-OFF★

15

THE DRIVER OF the open-top red Porsche touched his brakes, slipped the gear lever into neutral and brought the car to a halt at the lights before checking his watch. He was running a few minutes late for his lunch appointment. As he waited for the light to turn green, he noticed several men admiring his car, while the women smiled at him.

Jamwal gently touched the accelerator. The engine purred like a tiger and the smiles became even broader. Far more men than usual seemed to be looking in his direction. As the light turned green, he heard an engine revving up to his left. He glanced across to see a Ferrari accelerate away before dodging in and out of the morning traffic. He put his foot down and chased after the man who had dared to steal his thunder.

The Ferrari screeched to a halt at the next set of lights, only just avoiding a cow that was sitting in the middle of the road like a traffic bollard. Jamwal drew up by the side of his challenger, and couldn't believe his eyes. The young woman seated behind the wheel didn't give him so much as a glance, although he couldn't take his eyes off her.

When the light turned green, she accelerated away and left him standing again. Jamwal threw the gear lever into first and chased after her, searching for even the hint of a gap in the traffic that might allow him to overtake her. For the next minute, he kept one hand on the steering wheel and the other on the horn as he swerved from lane to lane, narrowly missing bicycles, rickshaws, taxis, buses and trucks that had no intention of moving aside for him. She matched him yard for yard, and he only just managed to catch her up by the time she came to a reluctant halt at the next traffic lights.

Jamwal drew up by her side and took a closer look. She was wearing an elegant cream silk dress that, like her car, could only have been designed by an Italian, although his mother certainly wouldn't have approved of the way the hemline rose high enough for him to admire her shapely legs. His eyes returned to her face as she once again accelerated away, leaving him in her slipstream. When he caught up with her at the next intersection, she turned and graced him with a smile that lit up her whole face.

When the lights changed this time, Jamwal was ready to pounce, and they took off together, matching each other cyclist for cyclist, cow for cow, rickshaw for rickshaw, until they both had to throw on their brakes and screech to a halt when a traffic cop held up an insistent arm.

When the policeman waved them on, Jamwal took off like a greyhound out of the slips and shot into the lead for the first time. But his smile of triumph turned to a frown when he glanced in his rear-view mirror to see her slowing down and driving into the entrance of the Taj Mahal Hotel. He cursed, threw on his brakes and executed a U-turn that resulted in a cacophony of horns, shaking fists and crude expletives as he tried not to lose sight of her.

He glided up to the front of the hotel, where he watched as she stepped out of her car and handed the keys to a valet. Jamwal leapt out of his Porsche without bothering to open the door, threw his keys to the valet, ran up the steps and followed her into the hotel. As he entered the lobby, she was disappearing into a lift. He waited to see which floor she would get out on. First stop was the mezzanine: fashionable shops, a hair salon and a French bistro. Would it be minutes or hours before she reappeared? Jamwal walked over to the reception desk. 'Did you see that girl?' he asked the clerk.

'I think every man in the lobby saw her, sahib.'

Jamwal grinned. 'Do you know who she is?'

'Yes, sir, she is Miss Chowdhury.'

'The daughter of Shyam Chowdhury?'

'I believe so.'

Jamwal smiled again. A few phone calls and he would know everything he needed to about Shyam Chowdhury's daughter. By the time they next met, he would already be in first gear. The only thing that surprised him was that he hadn't come across her before. He picked up the guest phone and dialled a local number.

'Hi, Sunita. I've been held up at the office, someone needed to see me urgently. Let's try and catch up this evening. Yes, of course I remembered,' he said, keeping a watchful eye on the bank of lifts. 'Yes, yes. We're having dinner tonight. I'll be with you around eight,' he promised.

The lift door opened and she stepped out carrying a Ferragamo bag. 'Got to rush,' he said. 'Can't keep my next appointment waiting.' He put the phone down, just as she walked past him, and quickly caught up with her.

'I didn't want to bother you . . .' he began.

She turned and smiled sweetly, but did not stop walking. 'It's no bother, but I'm not looking for a chauffeur at the moment.'

'How about a boyfriend?' he said, not missing a beat.

'Thank you but no. I don't think you could handle the pace.'

'Well, why don't we try and find out over dinner tonight?'

'How kind of you to ask,' she said, still not slackening her pace, 'but I already have a dinner date tonight.'

'Then how about tomorrow?'

'Not tomorrow, and tomorrow, and tomorrow.'

'Creeps in this petty pace from day to day,' he quoted back at her.

'Sorry,' she said, as an attendant opened the door for her, 'but I don't have a day free before the last syllable of recorded time.'

'How about a coffee?' said Jamwal. 'I'm free right now.'

'I feel sure you are,' she said, finally coming to a halt and looking at him more closely. 'You've clearly forgotten, Jamwal, what happened the last time we met.'

'The last time we met?' said Jamwal, unusually lost for words.

'Yes. You tied my pigtails together.'

'That bad?'

'Worse. You tied them round a lamp post.'

'Is there no end to my infamy?'

'No, there isn't, because not satisfied with tying me up, you then left me.'

'I don't remember that. Are you sure it was me?' he added, refusing to give up.

'I can assure you, Jamwal, it's not something I'd be likely to forget.'

'I'm flattered that you still remember my name.'

'And I'm equally touched,' she said, giving him the same sweet smile, 'that you clearly don't remember mine.'

'But how long ago was that?' he protested as she stepped into her car.

'Certainly long enough for you to have forgotten me.'

'But perhaps I've changed since—'

'You know, Jamwal,' she said as she switched on the ignition, 'I was beginning to wonder if you could possibly have grown up after all these years.' Jamwal looked hopeful. 'And had you bothered to open the car door for me, I might have been persuaded. But you are so clearly the same arrogant, self-satisfied child who imagines every girl is available, simply because you're the son of a maharaja.' She put the car into first gear and accelerated away.

Jamwal stood and watched as she eased her Ferrari into the afternoon traffic. What he couldn't see was how often she checked in her rear-view mirror to make sure he didn't move until she was out of sight.

Jamwal drove slowly back to his office on Bay Street. Within an hour he'd found out all he needed to know about Nisha Chowdhury. His secretary had carried out similar tasks for him on several occasions in the past. Nisha was the daughter of Shyam Chowdhury, one of the nation's leading industrialists. She had been educated in Paris, before going on to Stanford University to study fashion design. She would graduate in the summer and was hoping to join one of the leading couture houses when she returned to Delhi.

Such gaps as Jamwal's secretary hadn't been able to fill in, the gossip columns supplied. Nisha was currently to be seen on the arm of a well-known racing driver, which answered two more of his questions. She had also been offered several modelling assignments in the past, and even a part in a Bollywood film, but had turned them all down as she was determined to complete her course at Stanford.

Jamwal had already accepted that Nisha Chowdhury was going to be more of a challenge than some of the girls he'd been dating recently. Sunita Desai, who he was meant to be having lunch with, was the latest in a long line of escorts who had already survived far longer than he'd expected, but that would rapidly change now that he'd identified her successor.

Jamwal wasn't all that concerned who he slept with. He didn't care what race, colour or creed his girlfriends were. Such matters were of little importance once the light was switched off. The only thing he would not consider was sleeping with a girl from his own Rajput caste, for fear that she might think there was a chance, however slim, of ending up as his wife. That decision would ultimately be made by his parents, and the one thing they would insist on was that Jamwal married a virgin.

As for those who had ideas above their station, Jamwal had a well-prepared exit line when he felt the time had come to move on: 'You do realize that there's absolutely no possibility of us having a long-term relationship, because you simply wouldn't be acceptable to my parents.'

This line was delivered with devastating effect, often when he was dressing to leave in the morning. Nine out of ten girls never spoke to him again. One in ten remained in his phone book, with an asterisk by their names which indicated 'available at any time'.

Jamwal intended to continue this very satisfactory way of life until his parents decided the time had come for him to settle down with the bride they had chosen for him. He would then start a family, which must include at least two boys, so he could fulfil the traditional requirement of siring an heir and a spare.

As Jamwal was only months away from his thirtieth birthday, he suspected his mother had already drawn up a list of families whose daughters would be interviewed to see if they would make suitable brides for the second son of a maharaja.

Once a shortlist had been agreed upon, Jamwal would be introduced to the candidates, and if his parents were not of one mind, he might even be allowed to offer an opinion. If by chance one of the contenders was endowed with intelligence or beauty, that would be considered a bonus, but not one of real significance. As for love, that could always follow some time later, and if it didn't, Jamwal could return to his old way of life, albeit a little more discreetly. He had never fallen in love, and he assumed he never would.

Jamwal picked up the phone on his desk, dialled a number he didn't need to look up, and ordered a bunch of red roses to be sent to Nisha the following morning – hello flowers; and a bunch of lilies to be sent to Sunita at the same time – farewell flowers.

—◁◦▷—

Jamwal arrived a few minutes late for his date with Sunita that evening, something no one complains about in Delhi, where the traffic has a mind of its own.

The door was opened by a servant even before Jamwal had reached the top step, and as he walked into the house, Sunita came out of the drawing room to greet him.

'What a beautiful dress,' said Jamwal, who had taken it off several times.

'Thank you,' said Sunita as he kissed her on both cheeks. 'A couple of friends are joining us for dinner,' she continued as they linked arms and began walking towards the drawing room. 'I think you'll find them amusing.'

'I was sorry to have to cancel our lunch date at the last moment,' he said, 'but I became embroiled in a takeover bid.'

'And were you successful?'

'I'm still working on it,' Jamwal replied as they entered the drawing room together.

She turned to face him, and the second impression was just as devastating as the first.

'Do you know my old school friend, Nisha Chowdhury?' asked Sunita.

'We bumped into each other quite recently,' said Jamwal, 'but were not properly introduced.' He tried not to stare into her eyes as they shook hands.

'And Sanjay Promit.'

'Only by reputation,' said Jamwal, turning to the other guest. 'But of course I'm a great admirer.'

Sunita handed Jamwal a glass of champagne, but didn't let go of his arm.

'Where are we dining?' Nisha asked.

'I've booked a table at the Silk Orchid,' said Sunita. 'So I hope you all like Thai food.'

Jamwal could never remember the details of their first date, as Nisha so often described it, except that during dinner he couldn't take his eyes off her. The moment the band struck up, he asked her if she would like to dance. To the undisguised annoyance of both their partners, they didn't return to the table again until the band took a break. When the evening came to an end, Jamwal and Nisha reluctantly parted.

As Jamwal drove Sunita home, neither of them spoke. There was nothing to say. When she stepped out of the car, she didn't bother to kiss him goodbye. All she said was, 'You're a shit, Jamwal,' which meant that at least he could cancel the farewell flowers.

The following morning Jamwal sent a handwritten note with Nisha's red roses, inviting her to lunch. Every time the phone on his desk rang, he picked it up hoping to hear her voice saying, 'Thank you for the beautiful flowers, where shall we meet for lunch?' But it was never Nisha on the end of the line.

At twelve o'clock he decided to call her at home, just to make sure the flowers had been delivered.

'Oh, yes,' said the houseman who answered the phone, 'but Miss Chowdhury was already on her way to the airport by the time they arrived, so I'm afraid she never saw them.'

'The airport?' said Jamwal.

'She took the early morning flight to Los Angeles. Miss Chowdhury begins her final term at Stanford on Monday,' the houseman explained.

Jamwal thanked him, put the phone down and pressed a button on his intercom. 'Get me on the next plane to Los Angeles,' he said to his secretary. He then called home and asked his manservant to pack a suitcase, as he would be going away.

'For how long, sahib?'

'I've no idea,' Jamwal replied.

-◆◇◆-

Jamwal had visited San Francisco many times over the years, but had never been to Stanford. After Oxford he had completed his education on the Eastern seaboard, finishing up at Harvard Business School.

Although the gossip columns regularly described Jamwal Rameshwar Singh as a millionaire playboy, the implied suggestion was far from the mark. Jamwal was indeed a prince, the second son of a maharaja, but the family wealth had been steadily eroding over the years, which was the reason the palace had become the Palace Hotel. And when he had left Harvard to return to Delhi, the only extra baggage he carried with him was the Parker Medal for Mathematics, along with a citation recording the fact that he had been in the top ten students of his year, which now hung proudly on the wall of the guest toilet. However, Jamwal did nothing to dispel the gossip columnists' raffish image of him, as it helped to attract exactly the type of girl he liked to spend his evenings with, and often the rest of the night.

On returning to his homeland, Jamwal had applied for a position as a management trainee with the Raj Group, where he was quickly identified as a rising star. Despite rumours to the contrary, he was often the first to arrive in the office in the morning, and he could still be found at his desk long after most of his colleagues had returned home.

But once he had left the office, Jamwal entered another world, to which he devoted the same energy and enthusiasm that he applied to his work.

The phone on his desk rang. 'There's a car waiting for you at the front door, sir.'

◄○►

Jamwal had rarely been known to cross the dance floor for a woman, let alone an ocean.

When the 747 touched down at San Francisco International Airport at five forty-five the following morning, Jamwal took the first available cab and headed for the Palo Alto Hotel.

Some discreet enquiries at the concierge's desk, accompanied by a ten-dollar bill, produced the information he required. After a quick shower, shave and change of clothes, another cab drove him across to the university campus.

When the smartly dressed young man wearing a Harvard tie walked into the registrar's office and asked where he might find Miss Nisha Chowdhury, the woman behind the counter smiled and directed him to the north block, room forty-three.

As Jamwal strolled across the campus, few students were to be seen, other than early morning joggers or those returning from very late-night parties. It brought back memories of Harvard.

When he reached the north block, he made no attempt to enter the building, fearing he might find her with another man. He took a seat on a bench facing the front door and waited. He checked his watch every few minutes, and began to wonder if she had already gone to breakfast. A dozen thoughts flashed through his mind while he waited. What would he do if she appeared on Sanjay Promit's arm? He'd slink back to Delhi on the next flight, lick his wounds and move on to the next girl. But what if she was away for the weekend and didn't plan to return until Monday morning, when term began? He had several pressing appointments on Monday, none of whom would be impressed to learn that Jamwal was on the other side of the world chasing a girl he'd only met twice – well, three times if you counted the pigtail incident.

When she came through the swing doors, he immediately knew why he'd circled half the globe to sit on a wooden bench at eight o'clock in the morning.

Nisha walked straight past him. She wasn't ignoring Jamwal this time, but simply hadn't registered who it was sitting on the bench. Even when he rose to greet her, she didn't immediately recognize him, perhaps because he was the last person on earth she expected to see. Suddenly her whole face lit up, and it seemed only natural that he should take her in his arms.

'What brings you to Stanford, Jamwal?' she asked once he'd released her.

'You,' he replied simply.

'But why—' she began.

'I'm just trying to make up for tying you to a lamp post.'

'I could still be there for all you cared,' she said, grinning. 'So tell me, Jamwal, have you already had breakfast with another woman?'

'I wouldn't be here if there was another woman,' he said.

'I was only teasing,' she said softly, surprised that he had risen so easily to her bait. Not at all his reputation. She took his hand as they walked across the lawn together.

Jamwal could always recall exactly how they had spent the rest of that day. They ate breakfast in the refectory with five hundred chattering students; walked hand-in-hand around the lake – several times; lunched at Benny's diner in a corner booth, and only left when they became aware that they were the last customers. They talked about going to the theatre, a film, perhaps a concert, and even checked what was playing at the Globe, but in the end they just walked and talked.

When he took Nisha back to the north block just after midnight, he kissed her for the first time, but made no attempt to cross the threshold. The gossip columnists had got that wrong as well, at least that was something his mother would approve of. His final words before they parted were, 'You do realize that we're going to spend the rest of our lives together?'

◄○►

Jamwal couldn't sleep on the long flight back to Delhi as he thought about how he would break the news to his parents that he had fallen in love. Within moments of landing, he was on the phone to Nisha to let her know what he'd decided to do.

'I'm going to fly up to Jaipur during the week and tell my parents that I've found the woman I want to spend the rest of my life with, and ask for their blessing.'

'No, my darling,' she pleaded. 'I don't think it would be wise to do that while I'm stuck here on the other side of the world. Perhaps we should wait until I return.'

'Does that mean you're having second thoughts?' he asked in a subdued voice.

'No, I'm not,' she replied calmly, 'but I also have to think about how I break the news to *my* parents, and I'd prefer not to do it over the phone. After all, my father may be just as opposed to the marriage as yours.'

Jamwal reluctantly agreed that they should do nothing until Nisha had graduated and returned to Delhi. He thought about visiting his brother in Chennai and asking him to act as an intermediary, but just as quickly dismissed the idea, only too aware that in time he would have to face up to his father. He would have discussed the problem with his sister Shilpa, but however much she might have wanted to keep his secret, within days she would have shared it with their mother.

In the end Jamwal didn't even tell his closest friends why he boarded a flight to San Francisco every Friday afternoon, and why his phone bill had recently tripled.

As each week went by, he became more certain that he'd

found the only woman he would ever love. He also accepted that he couldn't put off telling his parents for much longer.

Every Saturday morning Nisha would be standing by the arrivals gate at San Francisco International airport waiting for him to appear. On Sunday evening, he would be among the last passengers to have their passports checked before boarding the overnight flight to Delhi.

─◇─

When Nisha walked up on to the stage to be awarded her degree by the President of Stanford, two proud parents were sitting in the fifth row warmly applauding their daughter.

A young man was standing at the back of the hall, applauding just as enthusiastically. But when Nisha stepped down from the stage to join her parents for the reception, Jamwal decided the time had come to slip away. When he arrived back at his hotel, the concierge handed him a message:

> *Jamwal,*
> *Why don't you join us for dinner at the Bel Air?*
> *Shyam Chowdhury*

It became clear to Jamwal within moments of meeting Nisha's parents that they had known about the relationship for some time, and they left him in no doubt that they were delighted to have a double cause for celebration: their daughter's graduation from Stanford, and meeting the man there she'd fallen in love with.

The dinner lasted long into the night, and Jamwal found it easy to relax in the company of Nisha's parents. He only wished . . .

'A toast to my daughter on her graduation day,' said Shyam Chowdhury, raising his glass.

'Daddy, you've already proposed that toast at least six times,' said Nisha.

'Is that right?' he said, raising his glass a seventh time. 'Then let's toast Jamwal's graduation day.'

'I'm afraid that was several years ago, sir,' said Jamwal.

Nisha's father laughed, and turning to his prospective son-in-law, said, 'If you plan to marry my daughter, young man, then the time has come for me to ask you about your future.'

'That may well depend, sir, on whether my father decides to cut me off, or simply sacrifice me to the gods,' he replied. Nobody laughed.

'You have to remember, Jamwal,' said Nisha's father, placing his glass back on the table, 'that you are the son of a maharaja, a Rajput, whereas Nisha is the daughter of a—'

'I don't give a damn about that,' said Jamwal.

'I feel sure you don't,' said Shyam Chowdhury. 'But I have no doubt that your father does, and that he always will. He is a proud man, steeped in the Hindi tradition. So if you decide to go ahead and marry my daughter against his wishes, you must be prepared to face the consequences.'

'I appreciate what you are saying, sir,' said Jamwal, now calmer. 'I love my parents, and will always respect their traditions. But I have made my choice and I will stand by it.'

'It is not only you who will have to stand by it, Jamwal,' said Mr Chowdhury. 'If you decide to defy the wishes of your father, Nisha will have to spend the rest of her life proving that she is worthy of you.'

'Your daughter has nothing to prove to me, sir,' said Jamwal.

'It isn't you I am worried about.'

◄○►

Nisha returned to Delhi a few days later and moved back into her parents' home in Chanakyapuri. Jamwal wanted them to be married as soon as possible, but Nisha was more cautious, only because she wanted him to be certain before he took such an irrevocable step.

Jamwal had never been more certain about anything in his life. He worked harder than ever by day, buoyed up by the knowledge that he would be spending the evening with the woman he adored. He no longer had any desire to visit the flesh-pots of the young. The fashionable clubs and fast cars had been replaced by visits to the theatre and cinema, followed by quiet dinners in restaurants that cared more about their cuisine than about which Bollywood star was sitting next to which model at which table. Each night after he'd driven her home he always left her with the same words: 'How much longer do I have to wait before you will agree to be my wife?'

Nisha was about to tell him that she could see no reason why they should wait any longer, when the decision was taken out of her hands.

—◦—

One evening, just as Jamwal had finished work and was leaving to join Nisha for dinner, the phone on his desk rang.

'Jamwal, it's your mother. I'm so glad to catch you.' He could feel his heart beating faster as he anticipated her next sentence. 'I was hoping you might be able to come up to Jaipur for the weekend. There's a young lady your father and I are keen for you to meet.'

After he had put the phone down, Jamwal didn't call Nisha. He knew that he would have to explain to her face to face why there had been a change of plan. Jamwal drove slowly over to her home in Chanakyapuri, relieved that her parents were away for the weekend visiting relatives in Hyderabad.

When Nisha opened the front door, she only had to look into his eyes to realize what must have happened. She was about to speak, when he said, 'I'll be flying up to Jaipur this weekend to visit my parents, but before I leave, there's some-thing I have to ask you.'

Nisha had prepared herself for this moment, and if they

were to part, as she had always feared they might, she was determined not to break down in front of him. That could come later, but not until he'd left. She dug her fingernails into the palms of her hands – something she'd always done as a child when she didn't want her parents to realize she was trembling – before looking up at the man she loved.

'I want you to try to understand why I'm flying to Jaipur,' he said. Nisha dug her nails deeper into the palms of her hands, but it was Jamwal who was trembling. 'Before I see my father, I need to know if you still want to be my wife, because if you do not, I have nothing to live for.'

◄○►

'Jamwal, welcome home,' said his mother as she greeted her son with a kiss. 'I'm so glad you were able to join us for the weekend.'

'It's wonderful to be back,' said Jamwal, giving her a warm hug.

'Now, there's no time to waste,' she said as they walked into the hall. 'You must go and change for dinner. Your father and I have something very important to discuss with you before our guests arrive.'

Jamwal remained at the bottom of the sweeping marble staircase while a servant took his bags up to his room. 'And I have something very important to discuss with you,' he said quietly.

'Nothing that can't wait, I'm sure,' said his mother smiling up at her son, 'because among our guests tonight is someone who I know is very much looking forward to meeting you.'

How Jamwal wished it was he who was saying those same words because he was about to introduce his mother to Nisha. But he doubted if petals would ever be strewn at the entrance of this home to welcome his bride on their wedding day.

'Mother, what I have to tell you can't wait,' he said. 'It's something that has to be discussed before we sit down for dinner.' His mother was about to respond when Jamwal's father came out of his study, a broad smile on his face.

'How are you, my boy?' he asked, shaking hands with his son as if he'd just returned from prep school.

'I'm well, thank you, Father,' Jamwal replied, giving him a traditional bow, 'as I hope you are.'

'Never better. And I hear great things about your progress at work. Most impressive.'

'Thank you, Father.'

'No doubt your mother has already warned you that we have a little surprise for you this evening.'

'And I have one for you, Father,' he said quietly.

'Another promotion in the pipeline?'

'No, Father. Something far more important than that.'

'That sounds ominous, my boy. Shall we retire to my study for a few moments while your mother changes for dinner?'

'I would like Mother to be present when I tell you my news.'

The Maharaja looked apprehensive, but stood aside to allow his wife and son to enter the study. Both men remained standing until the Maharani had taken her seat.

Once the Maharani had sat down, Jamwal turned to his mother and said in a gentle voice, 'Mother, I have fallen in love with the most wonderful young woman, and I want you to know that I have asked her to be my wife.'

The Maharani bowed her head.

Jamwal turned to face his father, who was gripping the arms of his chair, ashen-faced, but before Jamwal could continue, the Maharaja said, 'I have never concerned myself with the way you conduct your life in Delhi, even when those activities have been reported in the gutter press. Heaven knows, I was young myself once. But I have always assumed that you were aware of your duties to this family, and that in time would marry a young woman not only from your own background, but who also met with the approval of your mother and myself.'

'Nisha and I are from the same background, Father, so let's be frank, it's not her background we're discussing, but my caste.'

'No,' said his father, 'what we are discussing is your responsibility to the family that raised you, and bestowed on you all the privileges you have taken for granted since the day you were born.'

'Father,' said Jamwal quietly, 'I didn't fall in love simply to annoy you. What has happened between Nisha and me is something rare and beautiful, and a cause for celebration, not anger. That is why I returned home in the hope of receiving your blessing.'

'You will never have my blessing,' said his father. 'And if you are foolish enough to go ahead with this unacceptable union, you will not be welcome in this house again.'

Jamwal looked towards his mother, but her head remained bowed and she didn't speak.

'Father,' Jamwal said, turning back to face him, 'won't you even meet Nisha before you make your decision?'

'Not only will I never meet this young woman, but also no member of this family will ever be permitted to come into contact with her. Your grandmother must go to her grave unaware of this misalliance, and your brother, who married wisely, will now become not only my successor, but also my sole heir, while your sister will enjoy all the privileges that were once to be bestowed on you.'

'If it was a lack of wisdom that caused me to fall in love, Father, so be it, because the woman I have asked to be my wife and the mother of my children is a beautiful, intelligent and remarkable human being, with whom I intend to spend the rest of my life.'

'But she is not a Rajput,' said his father defiantly.

'That was not her choice,' replied Jamwal, 'as it was not mine.'

'It is clear to me,' said his father, 'that there is no point in continuing with this conversation. You have obviously made up your mind, and chosen to bring dishonour on this house and humiliation to the family we have invited to share our name.'

'And if I were not to marry Nisha, having given her my word, Father, I would bring dishonour on the woman I love and humiliation to the family whose name she bears.'

The Maharaja rose slowly from his chair and glowered defiantly at his youngest child. Jamwal had never seen such anger in those eyes. He stood to face his wrath, but his father didn't speak for some time, as if he needed to measure his words.

'As it appears to me that you are determined to marry this young woman against the wishes of your family, and that nothing I can say will prevent this inappropriate and distasteful union, I now tell you, in the presence of your mother, that you are no longer my son.'

-◦-

Nisha had been standing by the barrier for over an hour before Jamwal's plane was due to land, painfully aware that as he was returning on the same day, it could not be good news. She did not want him to see that she'd been crying. While he was away she had resolved that if his father demanded he must choose between her and his family, she would release him from any obligation he felt to her.

When Jamwal strode into the arrivals hall, he looked grim-faced but resolute. He took Nisha firmly by the hand and, without saying a word, led her out on to the concourse, clearly unwilling to tell her what had happened in front of strangers. She feared the worst, but said nothing.

At the taxi rank, Jamwal opened the door for Nisha before climbing in beside her.

'Where to, sahib?' asked the driver cheerfully.

'The District Court,' Jamwal said without emotion.

'Why are we going to the District Court?' asked Nisha.

'To get married,' Jamwal replied.

—◦—

Nisha's mother and father held a more formal ceremony on the lawn of their home in Chanakyapuri a few days later to celebrate their daughter's marriage. The festivities had gone on for several days, and culminated in a large party that was attended by over a thousand guests, although not a single member of Jamwal's family attended the ceremony.

After completing the seven pheras of the sacred flame, the final confirmation of their wedding vows, the newly married couple strolled around the grounds, speaking to as many of their guests as possible.

'So where are you spending your honeymoon, dare I ask?' said Noel Kumar.

'We're flying to Goa, to spend a few days at the Raj,' said Jamwal.

'I can't think of a more beautiful place to spend your first few days as man and wife,' said Noel.

'A wedding gift from your uncle,' said Nisha. 'So generous of him.'

'Just be sure you have him back in time for the board meeting on Monday week, young lady, because one of the items under discussion is a new project that I know the chairman wants Jamwal to mastermind.'

'Any clues?' asked Jamwal.

'Certainly not,' said Noel. 'You just go away and enjoy your honeymoon. Nothing's so important that it can't wait until you're back.'

'And if we hang around here any longer,' said Nisha, taking her husband by the hand, 'we might miss our plane.'

A large crowd gathered by the entrance to the house and threw marigold petals in their path and waved as the couple were driven away.

When Mr and Mrs Rameshwar Singh drove on to the airport's private runway forty minutes later, the company's Gulfstream jet awaited them, door open, steps down.

'I do wish someone from your family had attended the wedding,' said Nisha as she fastened her seat belt. 'I was hoping that perhaps your brother or sister might have turned up unannounced.'

'If either of them had,' said Jamwal, 'they would have suffered the same fate as me.' Nisha felt the first moment of sadness that day.

Two and a half hours later the plane touched down at Goa's Dabolim airport, where another car was waiting to whisk them off to their hotel. They had planned to have a quiet supper in the hotel dining room, but that was before they were shown around the bridal suite, where they immediately started undressing each other. The bellboy left hurriedly and placed a 'Do not disturb' sign on the door. In fact, they missed dinner, and breakfast, only surfacing in time for lunch the following day.

'Let's have a swim before breakfast,' said Jamwal as he placed his feet on the thick carpet.

'I think you mean lunch, my darling,' said Nisha as she slipped out of bed and disappeared into the bathroom.

Jamwal pulled on a pair of swimming trunks and sat on the end of the bed waiting for Nisha to return. She emerged from the bathroom a few minutes later wearing a turquoise swimsuit that made Jamwal think about skipping lunch.

'Come on, Jamwal, it's a perfect day,' Nisha said as she drew the curtains and opened the French windows that led on to a freshly cut lawn surrounded by a luxuriant tropical garden of deep red frangipani, orange dahlias and fragrant hibiscus.

They were walking hand in hand towards the beach when Jamwal spotted the large swimming pool at the far end of the lawn. 'Did I ever tell you, my darling, that when I was at school I won a gold medal for diving?'

'No, you didn't,' Nisha replied. 'It must have been some other woman you were showing off to,' she added with a grin.

'You'll live to regret those words,' he said, releasing her hand and beginning to run towards the pool. When he reached the edge of the pool he took off and leapt high into the air before executing a perfect dive, entering the water so smoothly he hardly left a ripple on the surface.

Nisha ran towards the pool laughing. 'Not bad,' she called out. 'I bet the other girl was impressed.'

She stood at the edge of the pool for a moment before falling to her knees and peering down into the shallow water. When she saw the blood slowly rising to the surface, she screamed.

◄○►

I have a passion, almost an obsession, about not being late, and it's always severely tested whenever I visit India. And however much I cajoled, remonstrated with and simply shouted at my poor driver, I was still several minutes late that night for a dinner being held in my honour.

I ran into the dining room of the Raj and apologized profusely to my host, who wasn't at all put out, although the rest of the party were already seated. He introduced me to some old friends, some recent acquaintances and a couple I'd never met before.

What followed was one of those evenings you just don't want to end: that rare combination of good food, vintage wine and sparkling conversation which was emphasized by the fact that we were the last people to leave the dining room, long after midnight.

One of the guests I hadn't met before was seated opposite me. He was a handsome man, with the type of build that left you in no doubt he must have been a fine athlete in his youth. His conversation was witty and well informed, and he had an opinion on most things, from Sachin Tendulkar (who was certain to be the first cricketer to reach fifty test centuries) to Rahul Gandhi (undoubtedly a future prime minister, if that's the road he chooses to travel down). His wife, who was sitting on my right, possessed that rare middle-aged beauty that the callow young can only look forward to, and rarely achieve.

I decided to flirt with her outrageously in the hope of getting a rise out of her self-possessed husband, but he simply flicked me away as if I were some irritating fly that had interrupted his afternoon snooze. I gave up the losing battle and began a serious conversation with his wife instead.

I discovered that Mrs Rameshwar Singh worked for one of India's leading fashion houses. She told me how much she always enjoyed visiting England whenever she could get away. It was not always easy to drag her husband from his work, she explained, adding, 'He's still quite a handful.'

'Do you have any children?' I asked.

'Sadly not,' she replied wistfully.

'And what does your husband do?' I asked, quickly changing the subject.

'Jamwal is on the board of the Raj Group. He's headed up their hotel operation for the past fifteen years.'

'I've stayed at six Raj hotels in the last nine days,' I told her, 'and I've rarely come across their equal.'

'Oh, do tell him that,' she whispered. 'He'll be so touched, especially as the two of you have spent most of the evening trying to prove how macho you are.' Both of us put nicely in our place, I felt.

When the evening finally came to an end, everyone stood except the man seated opposite me. Nisha moved swiftly round to the other side of the table to join her husband, and it was not until that moment that I realized Jamwal was in a wheelchair.

I watched sympathetically as she wheeled him slowly out of the room. No one who saw the way she touched his shoulder and gave him a smile the rest of us had not been graced with, could have had any doubt of their affection for each other.

He teased her unmercifully. 'You never stopped flirting with the damn author all evening, you hussy,' he said, loud enough to be sure that I could hear.

'So he did get a rise out of you after all, my darling,' she responded.

I laughed, and whispered to my host, 'Such an interesting couple. How did they ever get together?'

He smiled. 'She claims that he tied her to a lamp post and then left her.'

'And what's his version?' I asked.

'That they first met at a traffic light in Delhi . . . and she left him.'

And thereby hangs a tale.